"Judith Michael has struck again . . . a ride through the fast lane, where greed is the passion that rules all else . . . *PRIVATE AFFAIRS* has plenty to please the fans."

—*Richmond Times-Dispatch*

"The strength of *PRIVATE AFFAIRS* is the . . . emphasis on unity and hope, a beautifully creative vision of what it takes for a man and a woman to find each other again and again . . ."

—*United Press International*

"*PRIVATE AFFAIRS* is charmed lives, repressed passion, and fantasies come true . . ."

—ALA *Booklist*

"Absorbing . . . first-rate . . . an enjoyable read. Take it along on your next vacation."

—*Mansfield* (Ohio) *Journal*

"A story of romance and ambition . . . *PRIVATE AFFAIRS* offers large doses of entertainment."

—*The Chattanooga Times*

"*PRIVATE AFFAIRS* is a gripping novel . . . I liked it enough to read it well into the wee hours . . . entertaining and easy to read."

—(Providence) *Sunday Journal*

Books by Judith Michael

Deceptions
Possessions
Private Affairs
Inheritance
A Ruling Passion
Sleeping Beauty
Pot of Gold

Published by POCKET BOOKS

For orders other than by individual consumers, Pocket Books grants a discount on the purchase of **10 or more** copies of single titles for special markets or premium use. For further details, please write to the Vice-President of Special Markets, Pocket Books, 1230 Avenue of the Americas, New York, NY 10020.

For information on how individual consumers can place orders, please write to Mail Order Department, Paramount Publishing, 200 Old Tappan Road, Old Tappan, NJ 07675.

JUDITH MICHAEL

○

PRIVATE AFFAIRS

POCKET BOOKS

New York London Toronto Sydney Tokyo Singapore

This book is a work of fiction. Names, characters, places and incidents are products of the author's imagination or are used fictitiously. Any resemblance to actual events or locales or persons, living or dead, is entirely coincidental.

POCKET BOOKS, a division of Simon & Schuster Inc.
1230 Avenue of the Americas, New York, NY 10020

ISBN: 0-671-89957-0

First Pocket Books printing March 1987

20 19 18 17 16 15 14

POCKET and colophon are registered trademarks of
Simon & Schuster Inc.

Cover art by Brian Bailey

Printed in the U.S.A.

For
Ann Patty
Jane Berkey
Andrea Cirillo, Don Cleary, and Meg Ruley
who help make dreams come true

Part

I

CHAPTER 1

Elizabeth and Matthew Lovell," the minister announced, as if he were introducing them to each other instead of making them husband and wife. "You may kiss," he said benignly, but they were ahead of him: their hands clasped, fingers twined, as they turned to each other and their lips touched lightly—a promise for later, when they were alone. Then, shading their eyes against the bright June sun, they turned to greet their guests.

Elizabeth's mother hugged her. "I've never seen you look so happy. Both of you." She reached up to kiss Matt. "As if there's not a cloud in the world."

"Not one," Elizabeth said. She looked at Matt, tall and lean, his dark hair unruly in the afternoon breeze, his deep-set blue eyes cool and private until they met her gray ones and then became warm, as if in an embrace. "How could there be clouds? Everything is perfect."

Her father was there, holding his cheek against hers. "Where did the years go?" he murmured. "Just the other day you were the most beautiful baby in the world; suddenly you're the most beautiful bride." He held her at arm's length. "At least you're staying in Los Angeles; we won't lose you entirely."

"Say it softly," said Matt. "My father isn't very happy

2

about—" He stopped as his father appeared. "Dad, I'm so glad you got here!" They hugged each other, Matt a head taller, his dark hair contrasting with the iron gray of his father's as he bent to kiss him. "I was afraid you wouldn't be here at all."

"Couldn't get away yesterday." His father's voice, like Matt's, was deep and easy, with a faint western drawl. He put his hands on Matt's shoulders and kissed him on both cheeks. "Made me mad as hell to miss your graduation. Were you impressive?"

"He was the class star," Elizabeth said, her eyes shining. "They kept calling his name for every prize—"

"Except all those Elizabeth won," said Matt. Gently he adjusted the ruffled neckline of her dress, folded over from all the hugging. "The real star was my bride; everyone predicted she'd be the first of all of us to be famous. Oh, Dad, I'm sorry, you haven't met Elizabeth's parents, Spencer and Lydia Evans . . ."

"Zachary Lovell," Matt's father said, shaking hands. He gazed at Lydia, his grizzled eyebrows raised in admiration. "I see where Elizabeth gets her beauty. Except—you can't be her mother. Her sister, maybe . . ."

Lydia smiled, pleased, but accustomed to it, knowing it was more than gallantry: she and Elizabeth did look alike. Both of them were as slender and graceful as dancers; both looked at the world with a direct gaze through wide-spaced gray eyes beneath dark brows; both were fair, though Elizabeth's hair was ash blond while Lydia's had darkened over the years to a golden bronze.

The five of them greeted the guests in the center of Lydia's garden. Tall delphiniums were a lacy blue backdrop to spikes of bright red Chinese ginger flowers, and, in front of them, a riot of orange and pink snapdragons, white phlox, and golden daylilies. Farther away, bordering the yard, were kumquat plants and dwarf nectarines, and spilling over the high fence behind them, a bright curtain of burnt-orange pyracantha.

Amid that brilliance, Elizabeth was a slender white flower, her long moiré dress, full-skirted, swirling as she moved; a white orchid in her white-gold hair. She, and Matt, in a pale gray summer suit, a white rose in his lapel, drew everyone's

3

eyes, their happiness reaching out to all those congratulating them: friends, favorite professors from the university, a few of the Evanses' neighbors, friends and co-workers from their offices.

"The best and the brightest," said a voice at Spencer's elbow, and he turned to see one of the professors who had voted Elizabeth and Matt the Harper award, given each year by the *Los Angeles World*. It was the first time in the history of the journalism school that the award had been given jointly. "But we couldn't decide between them," the professor told Spencer. "Every story they were assigned this past year they wrote together. And, do you know, we waited for those stories like kids waiting for Christmas, because any story signed Elizabeth Evans and Matt Lovell would be the best we'd get. They made it exciting to be a teacher."

The professor gazed at them almost wistfully. "They have a bright future; they'll do us proud. Matt will be a publisher and Elizabeth will write that column she's been dreaming of, and someday they'll own their own paper and we'll all nod and say it's just what we expected. They're quite a team, you know."

Waiters put up round tables, swiftly set them with china, silver, and crystal, and, when everyone was seated, served dinner. A flute and guitar duo played show tunes and ballads, and voices and laughter mingled with the music as the breeze quickened, curling Elizabeth's skirt around her long legs and lifting the ends of her long hair.

Spencer stood beside his chair, lifting his glass of champagne. "To Elizabeth and Matt, our dearest daughter and son: a long and wonderful life, filled with love and dreams, fulfillment and success. We wish you good fortune in your new jobs and everything else you do, not only for yourselves, but also for your professors who are counting on you to bring them the prestige of their top students' winning a Pulitzer Prize." As the guests laughed and applauded, he added, "May you have everything you dream of. Nothing stands in your way; the world waits for you to conquer it."

He drank from his glass, Lydia drank from hers, Elizabeth

and Matt drank to each other; and Anthony Rourke snapped their picture.

"Thank you, Tony," Elizabeth said. "We didn't want a professional photographer; it was sweet of you to offer."

"Dear Elizabeth, I like being needed," he said. "Especially by you. After all these years of friendship, I mean. Have you met my wife? Ginger, this is the Elizabeth Evans I talk about all the time. No, no . . . it's Elizabeth Lovell, now. That is it, isn't it, Elizabeth? With the emphasis on *love?*"

"That's it," she said, smiling because he was being dramatic as usual, pretending to be frivolous and slightly foolish instead of intense and driven to prove himself, as he'd been ever since she could remember. "I'm glad to meet you," she said to Ginger Rourke, and then, a little nervously, she turned back to Tony. "I saw you and Matt talking before dinner, so of course you've met."

"Matt and I found a great deal in common," Tony said promptly. "Past histories, for one." Elizabeth glanced swiftly from Matt's noncommittal face to Tony's smiling one. Tony paused, timing it like an actor. "Fathers," he said. "We have the same kind of fathers."

Tony's father, Keegan Rourke, arrived at the table in time to hear the last words. "Weddings are not occasions for complaining about fathers," he said, pulling out his chair to sit down. Tony's face darkened; he shifted his chair away from his father, but no one noticed except Elizabeth—and Rourke, who missed nothing, even when he was talking. "Lydia. Spencer. Wonderful to see you again; it's been far too long. And Elizabeth. We've missed you. All these years of separation after we'd been so close."

"Who was the one who moved away?" demanded Lydia. "We're still here; you moved to Houston."

"And bought an apartment big enough to welcome all of you for visits." Rourke paused, and Elizabeth contemplated him, wondering why it never occurred to him that others wouldn't follow or seek him out just because he was Keegan Rourke. He was strikingly handsome: she had to admit he was the most impressive man she'd ever met. Black-haired, with heavy brows

5

and a square chin with a cleft, he was as tall as Tony and Matt—in fact, the three of them were the tallest men at the wedding—but heavier, though his bulk and powerful shoulders were slimmed by an impeccably-cut suit. He was an older, more polished version of Tony, whose slender handsomeness seemed young, even at thirty, beside his father's dominance. "Sometimes," Rourke was saying, "I'm almost sorry I moved away."

Not sorry enough, Elizabeth thought. Moving made you a millionaire—how many times over?—and that was the most important thing in your life. Maybe it still is.

"Is this your father-in-law?" Rourke asked Elizabeth. He held out his hand to Zachary. "Keegan Rourke. Houston. Old friend of Spencer and Lydia and Elizabeth."

Zachary's eyes gleamed. "Zachary Lovell. Santa Fe. Father of Matthew. Old friend of Luke and John."

Instantly, Rourke came back. "You win. There's not a single Keegan in the Bible."

They grinned at each other. "Rewrite it," suggested Zachary.

Rourke shook his head. "Couldn't get away with it. No matter how much money I make, some things resist my touch."

Zachary appraised him. "Not many, I'd guess."

"Not many. I make sure of that. Were you born in Santa Fe?"

"Nuevo." Zachary dipped an oyster into hot sauce and slipped it into his mouth. "You never heard of it. A small town tucked away in the mountains, only an hour east of Santa Fe, but another world." He looked up, his eyes on a distant point. "There's a long valley, twenty miles or more, and part of it, maybe four miles long, is so narrow at each end it's almost cut off from the rest. That's where Nuevo is, with a stream meandering through it and the town nestled in the center, isolated, quiet, so beautiful . . ."

Rourke was concentrating on his oysters. "Who lives there now?" he asked.

"Hispanics, a few Anglos—only about thirty families left. The Indians settled the place but moved on in the early 1600s. Later, when the Spanish were kicked out of Santa Fe in the

6

Indian revolt, some of them fled to the mountains and settled there; they named it Nuevo, Spanish for *new*: a new beginning. Later some Anglos came: ranchers, a couple of blacksmiths, maybe some escapees from jail—nobody asked. They all lived together, still do, no fights, no crime—not much money, either, but it's a good place. My grandfather was one of the ranchers; he bought some land, built a house; my father and uncle were born there. Matt and I are the last of the family; a friend works the land for us and watches the house. I'm planning to retire there someday. Long way off, of course, but—"

"I'd like to see it," Rourke said. "I'll come to Santa Fe one of these days and you can take me there." He turned to Elizabeth. "And you and Matt will visit me. You will, won't you?" He dropped his voice. "I really have missed you, my dear. I always wished you'd been my daughter. Did you know I even had plans once for you and Tony?"

A startled look, confused and embarrassed, swept across Elizabeth's face. "Forgive me," Rourke said smoothly. "It's bad form to revive old romantic schemes at a wedding. Have you and Matt found a place to live?"

"A wonderful apartment," Elizabeth said, her face clearing. "Only three rooms, but they're huge. We have space to work at home if we need to, and there's a deck off the living room with a perfect view of the mountains. A friend at the paper told us about the ad when it was phoned in, before anyone else had a chance at it."

"You're having lots of luck, aren't you?" Tony's wife, Ginger, said abruptly, her first words all afternoon. "I mean, an apartment and prizes and getting that award . . . didn't you win some kind of award?"

Zachary stabbed an oyster. "To work in Los Angeles."

"Dad," said Matt quietly.

"Well, I know it's a good job," Zachary said gruffly. "Did I ever say it wasn't? And your professors tell me how much you deserve it; how talented you are. *I* know you're talented; I knew it before they did. But am I allowed to say I'm not dancing for joy because after I spent years building a company for my son, he's not interested? And I won't have you with me now that I'm getting old and gray and feeble—?"

"Dad." Matt laughed, but his eyes were somber. "You're fifty-six and feeble is hardly the word for you. And you know you built that printing company for yourself; it's been your whole life."

"I wanted to have something to leave to you."

"That's years in the future . . ." Matt began with a trace of impatience.

"But we all think about the future," Lydia said. "Especially at our age. Spencer and I are already planning our retirement . . ."

"Weddings and retirements," Matt said. "Quite a combination." He was smiling, but his voice was firm as he led them to other subjects, and the talk around the table turned to Los Angeles, and Santa Fe, and then Houston.

"A rampaging city, crude, no class." Tony's criticism was bitter.

"A lot of anger there," Matt murmured to Elizabeth.

"I'm not sure it's Houston he hates," she said, her voice low. "It's probably working for his father instead of being an actor. He's dreamed of acting all his life; I don't know why he ended up in an oil company in Houston."

"I'll bet morale is terrific in his part of the company," Matt said dryly.

The wedding cake was cut, a dozen toasts proposed, the champagne dwindled, and the talk turned back to the jobs Elizabeth and Matt would begin after a honeymoon trip to British Columbia. Even Zachary joined in, his unhappiness eclipsed by his son's excitement and Elizabeth's radiance. And later, as Spencer and Lydia said goodbye to the guests, he kissed Elizabeth. "You're all right; you're sweet to an old man and you're pretty and it looks like you appreciate Matt the way you should. You go ahead and write your column and publish your own newspaper; I promise I'll read it. If my eyesight holds up."

The echo of his father's voice, wistful and pugnacious at the same time, stayed with Matt through dinner and into the eve-

8

ning. "He won't forgive us," he said to Elizabeth as they sat on the deck of their new apartment beneath fading streaks of sunset. "He feels abandoned, and he'll remind us of it every chance he gets."

"I feel sorry for him," Elizabeth said. "He's been waiting all these years for you to come back."

"He has friends; we'll visit him; he'll visit us. That's the best we can do." He stood, bringing Elizabeth to her feet with him. "And it's time we stopped worrying about him. We have some personal matters to take care of."

Elizabeth put her arms around him. "Do you know, I haven't called you my husband yet."

"'Husband,'" Matt repeated, his lips coming down to hers. "I like the sound of that. What about 'wife'?"

"Give me fifty or sixty years to get used to it," Elizabeth murmured, and they kissed, Matt's hands finding the zipper on the back of her dress and sliding it down as she unbuttoned his shirt, and then her breasts were against his bare chest and they stood that way, their mouths together, tongues slowly exploring, discovering, after living together for the last year, that somehow there was a difference now in making love. "I don't know what it is," Elizabeth said. "Just because of a ceremony . . . what is it that makes me feel different?"

"The oysters," Matt said, and as they laughed together, he slipped her dress off her shoulders and let it fall. Elizabeth put her hands behind his head and brought him down with her to the chaise, just wide enough for the two of them, and in the faint lamplight from the living room, and the cool white of a full moon, they slipped off each other's remaining clothes, slowly, as if for the first time, as if they were just beginning because that afternoon they had vowed their love in a formal ceremony: permanent, part of the community, part of past and future.

"My dear love," Matt said, his lips on her breast. "Dearest Elizabeth." He murmured it against one nipple and then the other, and his voice, speaking her name, seemed to slide inside her, stirring and rippling through her body as his lips moved along her skin and he repeated it—"Elizabeth, my wife, my

9

love"—again and again until she heard nothing else, felt nothing else, dissolving beneath his mouth and hands into ripples that spread wider and deeper, and at last pulled him down to lie on her, and they were no longer separate, but one, as the last streaks of sunset were swallowed by the black, star-studded sky.

Looking at the stars, feeling her husband's weight upon her, Elizabeth's lips curved in a smile. Matt turned his head to kiss them. "You are a remarkably seductive lady."

She put her hand along his face, loving him, thinking she never wanted anything but this: the two of them, loving each other, weaving their lives together. "You make me feel seductive. And wanted. And loved."

Her orchid had fallen to the deck and Matt reached down to pick it up. One of the petals was bent and he gently brushed it back as he held it to Elizabeth's hair. "And extraordinarily beautiful. And adored." He felt the coolness of her skin and sat up. "Too chilly to stay out here. What do you say to bed? Too ordinary, perhaps, for a wedding night, but warmer than—"

They heard the telephone ring in the living room. Matt's eyebrows drew together. "Ignore it. Whoever has the bad taste to call at such a—"

"I can't," said Elizabeth. "I'm sorry, Matt, but I never could ignore a telephone." He watched her slender form disappear through the sliding glass doors.

"Mrs. Lovell?" a voice asked when she picked up the telephone. "This is the emergency room at Johnston Hospital. Mr. Zachary Lovell was just brought in; it looks like he's had a stroke; the doctor is with him now—"

"Is he alive?" Elizabeth cried.

"Who?" Matt said. "Elizabeth, who—?"

"Yes," said the voice from the hospital. "But until the doctor finishes examining him we won't know—"

"Your father," Elizabeth said to Matt, holding out the telephone. "He's had a stroke—he's alive—"

Matt grabbed it. "Is he conscious?" he demanded.

"Is this Mr. Lovell's son?"

"Damn it, of course it is. *Is he conscious? Can he talk? How is he?*"

"We don't know yet, Mr. Lovell; the doctor is with him. If you could be here—"

"As soon as we can. Tell him—if he asks for us—tell him we're on our way."

In bed in the Intensive Care Unit, Zachary was as white as the uniform of the nurse who came to check green waves moving across a monitor's screen. His lips worked, and Matt and Elizabeth bent to hear him. ". . . need you . . . don't go . . ." The words were slurred. "Just for a while . . . just till . . . myself again." He closed his eyes. "Hold me together . . . company, I mean . . . hold printing company together . . . all I have now, keep it safe . . . Matt, don't leave me. Please, Matt . . . worked all my life . . . *I can't lose it.* Elizabeth? Talk to him . . . *I beg you* . . . tell him I need him . . . need you both . . . *please* . . ."

The last word was a fading sigh. The doctor beckoned to Matt and Elizabeth and numbly they followed her into the hall.

"Not as bad as it might have been," she said. "There may be some lasting paralysis of the left side—we won't be sure for a day or two—and temporary confusion, but, in time, he should recover without crippling damage. It will be slow, however; you should be prepared for that. Is there a history of stroke in your family?"

"I don't think so." Matt frowned. "I can't even remember Dad's being sick. My grandparents, either. They ranched all their lives, bred horses in Nuevo; they only died a couple of years ago, in their eighties. I don't know," he repeated helplessly.

"I'll need a family history," the doctor said. "My office is down the hall." She turned to Elizabeth. "You could wait upstairs if you'd like, in the solarium. It's more pleasant there."

"All right." Elizabeth put her hand on Matt's arm and he gave her a brief kiss. "Wait for me," he said, and followed the doctor down the hall.

Pacing about the solarium, barely aware of lush trees and

hanging plants, Elizabeth felt tears rise in her throat. After a while, when Matt had not arrived, she called her mother. "I just need to talk," she told Lydia. "Just to hear you tell me I'm wrong to be afraid."

"I'm coming over," Lydia said. "Give me five minutes to put some clothes on."

When she arrived, she found Elizabeth huddled on a wicker couch. "How is he?"

"I don't know. Matt hasn't come back; I haven't heard. Mother, we're going to have to stay with him."

"Stay with Zachary? You mean have him live with you. Well, that's a problem, but if you find a bigger apartment—"

"No. Stay with him in Santa Fe. He wants Matt to run his company until he can run it by himself again."

"But you can't do that!" They looked at each other in silence, then Lydia sat beside Elizabeth and put her arms around her.

Like a young girl, Elizabeth put her head on her mother's shoulder and began to cry. "I'm sorry, I know it sounds mean and selfish, but I don't want to give everything up . . ."

"You're not mean, or selfish," Lydia said. "But can't you wait before you decide to give anything up? Even if he needs a month or two, we can figure something out . . . if necessary we'll pay for a manager to run his company until he's back on his feet . . ."

"I won't let you spend your retirement money. Anyway, I don't think it would help. The doctor said . . ." Elizabeth took a deep breath, pushing back her tears. "It will be a slow recovery; I don't think a month or two or even twice that would be enough."

"Then he could close the company for a while. And go to a convalescent home."

"That isn't what he wants."

"What he wants, Elizabeth, and what you can do, are two different things."

"Are they? Oh, mother—" Her tears welled up. "I love him and I want to help him—"

"Zachary? Or Matt?"

"Oh . . . both of them. But Matt's feeling about his father

12

is so special . . . I told you about his mother, how she walked out and left them, and all the years of Matt's growing up they were more like brothers than father and son . . . they were everything to each other. Mother, is there any way in the world I can ask Matt to stay here with me if his father asks him to take care of him in Santa Fe and run his company?"

"Not . . . easily," Lydia said. "It could come back to haunt you, years later."

Slowly, Elizabeth shook her head. "Whatever we do is going to come back to haunt us."

When Matt came in a while later, he found Lydia with her arm around Elizabeth, the two of them talking in low voices. He kissed Lydia. "I'm glad you're here." Sitting beside Elizabeth, he kicked off his shoes. "Fuck it," he said tiredly.

"You're going back," Elizabeth said.

"We'll decide together." In a moment he sprang up and strode away from her and then back. "What the hell can I do, Elizabeth? I'm all he's got. He never left me when I depended on him."

"I know." She was crying again, the tears streaking her face. "I know. There isn't anything else we can do."

"Christ, all our plans, everything we wanted . . . But what can I do? What am I supposed to tell him? 'We've got these neat jobs, Dad, so you're on your own.' Can I tell him that?"

"No."

" 'We've got an apartment, Dad.' Can I say that? 'And we plan to buy our own newspaper someday, so you'll have to handle your life yourself because we have our own to live.' *Can I say that?*"

"No." Elizabeth wiped her face on her shirt sleeve. "Matt, sit with me."

He sat down. "It's his printing company, not mine. It's his life, not mine. I don't want them. But I don't see a way out."

"Not for a while." Elizabeth swallowed the last of her tears and steadied her voice. "It isn't forever, you know; only until he's himself again. Didn't the doctor say there wouldn't be crippling damage? He'll only need us for a while, until he can take care of himself again and run his company. And he will:

13

he's only fifty-six; he'll *want* to feel useful and active as soon as he can, don't you think?"

In the silence, Lydia stood up. "I'm very proud of you," she said softly to Elizabeth. "I'm going to find a cafeteria and have a cup of coffee. Will you and Matt join me when you're ready?"

"Thank you, Mother." Elizabeth was looking at Matt as Lydia quietly left them. "What did you tell Zachary?"

"Nothing. I wanted to talk to you first." He clenched his fist, opened it, clenched it again. "Elizabeth, I promise it will only be for a while. As soon as he recovers, or we find someone to help him at home, and in the company, we'll come back here. Or we'll go somewhere else. We won't have trouble finding jobs; newspapers are always looking for brilliant prize-winning journalists."

She nodded and smiled, knowing he was trying to convince himself as well as her. "I promise," Matt repeated. "We'll pick up where we left off; we're young, there's plenty of time. This is a detour, that's all. I promise."

Elizabeth circled his neck with her arms, as she had earlier that night, when their dreams were as bright as the sunset. "It's all right, Matt. There isn't anything else we can do."

"All the dreams," he murmured, holding her. As if, Elizabeth thought, they were propping each other up. "Everything we want. We'll have it all, we'll do it all. It will just take a little longer than we'd planned."

She put her cheek to his, then kissed him. "It's all right, Matt," she repeated, whispering against his lips. "Don't worry. We'll be fine." Her tears had dried, but she still felt them, flowing inside her. *Don't be selfish. Think of Zachary. Think of Matt. Don't be mean. You're young. You have everything ahead of you.* "It's all right," she said one more time. "We have each other. That's all that matters. Now—shall we get some coffee? And maybe we should make a list. We have so many things to do."

Undo, she thought, but she kept it to herself, with the tears still flowing inside her, as she and Matt walked down the stairs, leaving the moonlight behind.

14

CHAPTER 2

The bride and groom stood on the brick patio within the *placita* of the great house as the guests moved past, murmuring greetings in Spanish and English. Nearby, beneath the arching branches of an olive tree heavy with silver leaves and clusters of tiny, unripened olives, long tables were laden with food and drink, silver goblets, and decorations symbolizing long life, joy, and many children.

The groom's father slipped away from the reception line. Mopping his forehead with an oversize handkerchief, he stopped to ask the barman for two glasses of champagne punch, then made his way across the garden and handed a glass to Elizabeth. "To drink our health. And to sustain us in our hour of need."

"What do you need?" she asked, laughing.

"Patience, since I dislike parties; a look of gratitude for my son's advantageous marriage; and stamina, since soon I must dance with women I have no desire to hold in my arms. I wouldn't mind if it were you: you are extraordinarily beautiful; more so every year. To our health." They touched glasses. "And what makes you so quiet?" he went on when Elizabeth did not speak.

"I've been remembering my own wedding," she said meditatively. "It was in a garden, almost as beautiful as this, on a

15

June afternoon just like this one. And everyone had the same look of expectation. Predicting a marvelous future for the happy couple."

"And how many years ago was that?"

"Sixteen," she said.

"And were they right—about the marvelous future?"

"Of course," she replied automatically. The groom's father looked closely at her but they were interrupted by guests politely jostling for a chance to talk to Elizabeth, and, with a sigh, he returned to his place in the reception line. Elizabeth listened to the guests, occasionally making notes on a pad of paper, her eyes still on the bride and groom, looking so young, smiling and smiling even as they wilted beneath the white-hot Santa Fe sun. Everyone else sought the shade; bright dresses and dark suits blended into the carefully tended gardens, smooth lawns, and a quietly flowing stream with a wooden bridge leading to the swimming pool and bathhouses.

Elizabeth breathed in the mingled fragrances and admired the lavish *placita*. No one ever saw it but invited guests, since it was shielded on three sides by the sprawling adobe house; and the house itself, with its driveway and gravel parking area, was completely enclosed by a high adobe wall with heavy wooden gates. A year ago, she and Matt had enlarged their own house and built an adobe wall around their garden, but they had nothing as sprawling and magnificent as this. Not enough land, she thought, and added ruefully, not enough money.

The shadows lengthened; the reception line came to an end. Musicians tuned their guitars; servants lit wrought-iron lanterns and swung open tall doors leading to the long salon; and the bridal couple danced, sweeping the length of the room, their fatigue gone, their faces bright, seeing only each other. In a few minutes their parents joined them, and then the guests, filling the high-ceilinged room with the gay confetti of festive gowns. The groom's father returned to Elizabeth. "You will dance with me?"

"One dance," she said. "And then I have work to do."

He put his hand correctly at her waist. "A woman of your loveliness should be cared for and spoiled, not forced to work."

He was very serious and Elizabeth was careful not to laugh. He was an Anglo whose father had come to Santa Fe from Detroit only forty years earlier, but he was a member of the New Mexico legislature and had adopted many of the attitudes of the city's oldest Spanish families, who, like the bride's, could trace their genealogy through twelve or more generations. So Elizabeth said only, "My work is important to me," and when the dance ended she excused herself with a formality that matched his, to find a quiet place to sit. She chose a bench between the *placita* and the salon, where she was inconspicuous as she wrote a description of the wedding for the society page of the *Santa Fe Examiner*.

"Ivory satin with seed pearls," she scrawled, glancing at the bride. "Triple-tiered lace veil, an heirloom handed down from mother to daughter since 1730 when the family, members of Spanish royalty, came to Mexico and then Santa Fe."

She wrote swiftly: the bride's genealogy, the groom's newly-established law practice, his father's influential committee chairmanship in the state legislature, a list of the guests, including the positions and family background of the most prominent, and colorful descriptions of clothes and food. But she had been a part-time reporter for the *Examiner* long enough to let her mind wander while she scribbled notes, and so she thought about her family: Holly and Peter, who should be home now from summer classes at the College of Santa Fe; Matt, who had advertised that week for a new assistant at the printing plant so he could spend more time at home; and Zachary— who had died three months ago but still seemed part of their lives, since everything they had done for sixteen years had revolved around him.

His death had hit Matt terribly hard, but Elizabeth, too, was shaken by it, as if it had left them at loose ends, without a reason for their life. *"Carne Adovada,"* she wrote, describing the dinner. "Green Chile Soufflé, *Tocina del Cielo* . . ." while she thought: We need a vacation, to get away from the house and reminders of Zachary. The four of us could go hiking, or drive to Denver . . .

But who would manage the printing plant? They'd never

been able to afford a full-time manager. And what about her job? There wasn't much security for a part-time reporter, and a lot of aspiring journalists wanted to work for the *Examiner*, since its opposition, the *Chieftain*, was a small failing weekly. And Holly and Peter were involved in their own projects; they might not want to go anywhere right now. Probably they should wait for a better time . . .

We've always said, Not now, not yet, later.

She bent again to her notes and when she had finished, went to the parents of the bride and groom to say good-bye. Guests reached out to her as she walked through the crowded room; everyone knew her, knew she was writing the story for the *Examiner*, and wanted to make sure they were in it and properly identified. But when they asked about her story, Elizabeth simply smiled and shook her head. Everything she wrote was her secret until it was printed.

Matt was the only one who saw her stories before she delivered them to her editor, but even he hadn't looked at most of them for a long time. So many things they didn't share anymore, she mused as she drove home. Mostly they talked about their daily affairs: the house, the children, Zachary— no, not Zachary anymore. What was wrong with her? Why couldn't she get used to it that Zachary was gone? And why did she think so much about changes in her marriage that bothered her, instead of the things that were good?

It was only a short distance from the wedding party to her home on Camino Rancheros, through narrow streets lined with adobe walls with carved wooden gates, and treetops towering above them from gardens on the other side. Adobe and trees, Elizabeth reflected. Someday, if she ever had her own column, she would write a description of Santa Fe. The words were already there, in her mind.

. . . a small town like a painting in two colors: dusty pink adobe and dark green trees, block after block, serene, soothing, almost hypnotic. Color comes from the people: bright Spanish and Indian clothing, jewelry, furniture, and art. But when the streets are empty, at the dinner hour and

18

at dawn, the unbroken dusty pink and dark green are dreamlike, a tapestry washed clean of colors, then flung upon the desert to dry, blending in with pale, sage-dotted sand—

Stop it. She drove through open gates to park beside her house. Why did she pretend? She didn't have a column because editors gave space to full-time writers, and she couldn't be a full-time writer—not when she also had to help Matt at the printing company and take care of a house and two children.

"Mom!" Peter was waving to her from the door. "Telephone!" He leaned against the doorway, crushing morning glories beneath his shoulder as he watched her cross the gravel. He was going to be as tall as Matt, Elizabeth thought, and as handsome, beneath his tangle of red hair, once he got through the agonies of adolescence. Each day, in fits and starts, he went from a round-faced, sweet-tempered little boy to a gangly fourteen-year-old, grumbling one minute, sharing family jokes the next, lurching into furniture at home but riding a horse with grace and balance, shying away from his mother's kisses but then, without warning, putting his arms around her and whirling her about the room with an infectious laugh that reminded Elizabeth of Matt—and made her realize how long it had been since he had laughed that way.

"It's you-know-who," Peter said. "Your glamorous television star."

"Tony Rourke," Elizabeth said. "You know his name perfectly well." Kissing him on the cheek, she walked with him into the cool house and picked up the telephone in the kitchen. Instantly, Tony's smooth voice flowed around her, like an embrace.

"Dear Elizabeth, I'm at the airport—"

"Which airport?" she asked, alarmed.

"Los Angeles. I've been trying to reach you to tell you I'm on my way to New York and stopping off in Santa Fe to see you. It's been much too long. Can you meet my plane in three hours? We'll have a late dinner and then you can drive me to

La Posada—I've reserved a room—and tomorrow I'll go on to New York. My plane arrives at—"

"Tony, stop. I can't have dinner with you tonight."

"Why not? Do you know how difficult it is for me to create these opportunities? My manager guards me like a dragon, my secretaries arrange schedules that are like prisons . . . Elizabeth, Marjorie left me."

"Oh." Marjorie. Tony had mentioned her a few times in the past year, but Elizabeth knew no more about her than she did about any of his wives. Vaguely she remembered Ginger, who had been at her wedding, but since then she hadn't followed his marriages and divorces. "I'm sorry," she said.

"So am I. I liked her. She said she found me impossible to live with. True, perhaps, but perhaps I just haven't married the right woman. Why can't you have dinner with me tonight?"

"Because it's our anniversary and we're going out."

"To celebrate. How many years?"

"Sixteen."

"With the same person. Incredible. Do you still look at each other the way you did at your wedding? I keep waiting for that to happen to me. But I lost my chance—didn't I?—a long time ago."

"Tony, stop being dramatic."

"It's my nature to be dramatic. But I mustn't keep you; you want to dress up in your finery and go out on the town with your husband. And you don't want—or your husband doesn't want—Anthony Rourke, television host adored by millions, waiting in the wings. Of course I won't come tonight. But may I stop off on my way home? Next Wednesday; is that all right? You do want to see me, don't you? At least half as much as I want to see you?"

His careful voice, warm as velvet, slipped now and then into self-mockery: he never could let anyone know whether he was truly serious. Perhaps he didn't know himself. Ten years earlier, he'd left his father's company with nothing but the few dollars he'd managed to save from his extravagant life in Houston, called Elizabeth to tell her he was going to Los Angeles to become the top television personality in America—and had done exactly that. Now he was famous and rich; he lived in a mansion in Malibu; and for the past year he had been calling Elizabeth two or three times a month, saying she was the only one he could talk to, the only one who understood him, the only one who'd known him when he was young, before he got involved in the crazy play-acting of television stardom.

"Dear Elizabeth, please let me come," he said. "I need to see you. I have no one to talk to but my refrigerator, which hums back at me in some exotic language I don't understand. And I have so much to tell you: I've just finished taping some shows in Spain and on the way home I stopped off in Italy and bought a small cottage—twenty rooms, I think—in Amalfi, *and I need to tell someone my news*. Elizabeth, are you listening?"

"Maybe in a week or two," Elizabeth said, piqued and disturbed, as always, by the way he could make her feel desirable and at the same time like a dull housewife in a little house in the middle of the New Mexican desert, waiting for Anthony Rourke to float down to her from the heights of his glamorous world.

"By then I have to be back in Europe. How about four weeks from today? I'll force myself to wait that long."

"All right," Elizabeth said. "But for lunch, not dinner. Let me know what time; I'll meet your plane."

"Does he want to interview you or what?" Peter asked as she hung up the telephone.

"We're not famous or notorious enough for Tony's show," Elizabeth said lightly. "Would you like it if we were?"

He reflected. "I guess not. I'm not like Holly; I can't do things in public. I'd rather nobody noticed me at all." He caught Elizabeth's quick glance and added, "On that guy's show anyway. You've seen him, Mom: his favorite thing is to make somebody look like an ass . . . with a hundred million people watching."

"Thirty million," Elizabeth said absently, thinking she and Matt ought to talk about Peter's shyness and aloneness. They'd thought he would find friends in high school, but instead he'd become even more withdrawn, seeming younger than others

21

his age, spending his spare time with the Indians of nearby pueblos and letting his sister be the talented center of attention. "Isn't Holly home?" Elizabeth asked.

"She was; she went back for some kind of audition. If he doesn't want to interview you, what *does* he want?"

"A friend."

"Anybody with thirty million people watching him has lots of friends."

"Is that so?"

"Why wouldn't he? People stop *you* on the street, and you only write for one paper. Somebody like him—people probably call him all the time, invite him to parties, hang around, tell him how wonderful he is . . . Stars have plenty of friends. You know that, Mom."

"I know they have hangers-on," said Elizabeth. "People who hope to get on television or have some glamour rub off on them. But I wouldn't call them friends. Anyway, not the kind you'll have when you find people who like you just because you're Peter Lovell and fun to be with and interested in lots of things and *very* lovable."

"Oh, *Mom.*" Peter met Elizabeth's smiling eyes and, almost reluctantly, grinned. Then they were both laughing and he gave his mother a quick hug. "Thanks."

Elizabeth kissed his cheek. "Give it time, Peter," she said gently. "You'll have friends. And girls, too."

"Yeh, well . . ." He shrugged. "I suppose. Is he coming here?"

"You mean Tony?"

"Right."

"He might, in a few weeks."

"I don't know why you like him."

"There are lots of reasons for friendship, Peter. And it isn't necessary to explain them."

He shrugged again and wandered around the kitchen, nibbling pine nuts while Elizabeth took meat and chiles from the refrigerator. Why do I like Tony? she asked herself. He makes me feel dull and backward—but he also brings me the excitement of the outside world and sometimes I need that. And he

22

makes me laugh and feel young, and there are lots of times when I need that, too.

But Matt is the one who should do that. Cutting the meat into cubes, she frowned, wondering again what was the matter with her. Why, all of a sudden, did she keep thinking of things that were wrong? Well, maybe not all of a sudden; maybe those thoughts had been cropping up for months. But they seemed to come in a deluge since Zachary died.

And then there was the wedding that afternoon, reminding her of all the passion and excitement and hope that had been in her parents' garden sixteen years ago. Where were they now? Somewhere along the way, they'd just . . . faded. And what did she and Matt have left? A pleasant, friendly marriage, calm and stable, that hadn't changed or given them any surprises in years.

But we're happy, she said. *We have a good life, a wonderful family, a home, our own business . . .*

She slid the meat into hot oil in an iron skillet, stirring the cubes as they browned. *Maybe we have the perfect marriage. Sixteen years of passion would have left us a pair of frazzled wrecks.*

Ruefully, she smiled. *It might be nice to be a frazzled wreck once in a while.* And then the front door was flung open and Holly rushed in.

"Hello, hello, hello, isn't it the most beautiful, wonderful, marvelous, *perfect* evening?"

"You got a part," Peter said.

"Two parts." She danced about the room. "You are looking at the first high school freshman in history—and I won't even *be* a freshman till September, but it doesn't matter—the first one to get *two* solo parts in the College of Santa Fe summer choral concert. You are looking at a future star!"

They were looking, Elizabeth thought, at a lovely young girl, almost a woman, flushed with excitement as she took another step in growing up, away from childhood, away from home. *Both my children,* she reflected, *only a few years from going off to make their own lives. How had it happened so quickly?*

"Mother?" Holly asked. "Aren't you happy?"

"Of course I am," Elizabeth said. "And proud." She hugged Holly and, as she felt her daughter's arms tighten around her, it struck her how much she loved her children, and how busy and rich and fun they had kept her life, masking a fading marriage. As if she stood apart, she saw herself with Holly, their blond heads close together. Hers had darkened over the years, like Lydia's, to a golden bronze so that Holly was the ash blond now, with Matt's deep blue eyes, Elizabeth's high cheekbones and slender face, and a pure soprano voice all her own—the only singer in either the Evans or Lovell family. "But I must say," she told Holly, "I'm not surprised. I've always known you're wonderful and I've always been proud of you."

"Today the chorus," Peter intoned. "Tomorrow the Broadway stage. You'll be as famous as Mom's television star who's coming here in a few weeks to be friendly."

"Tony?" Holly cried. "When is he coming? Maybe he'll interview me; he said he would, someday."

"He was making fun of you," Peter scoffed. "Nobody in this family is famous or notorious enough for his show."

"How do you know? I'm going to be famous and maybe he'll want me because of that."

"I doubt it, Holly," Elizabeth said. "Tony only wants celebrities. He doesn't make people famous; he interviews them when they're already famous."

"But he *said* it!"

"He may have thought he meant it at the time. But you shouldn't take him seriously." She paused, thinking how difficult it was to explain Tony to anyone who didn't know what he was like beneath the actor's pose. "He doesn't want people to understand him. He thinks he's more interesting if he's dramatic and mysterious."

"I think so, too," Holly said.

"Maybe so," Elizabeth said dismissively. "Now tell us more about the auditions—"

The telephone rang and Peter picked it up. "Dad," he said to Elizabeth. "Still at work."

"Matt?" Elizabeth said into the telephone. "Did something happen? You said you'd be home early."

"I got waylaid." His voice was tight and Elizabeth knew he was holding his temper. *He gets angry more often than he used to; something else that's changed since Zachary died.* "Simon got drunk last night. Staggered in at noon and created havoc for half an hour before I sent him home. That left two of us to get out the brochures for the Crownpoint Rug Auction. I'm sorry, Elizabeth; I'll be there within an hour. Can you change the reservation?"

"If not, we'll go somewhere else. Rancho de Chimayo isn't the only restaurant around."

"But it was the one you wanted." The first place we went, Matt thought, when we moved here and needed a special place to splurge and pretend everything was fine. Now we're pretending again. "See what you can do; I'll get out of here as soon as I can. Would you rather I called them?"

"No, I'll do it."

"See you soon, then." Matt hung up slowly and stood at his desk, absently watching his pressman stack brochures for the post office. Anger and frustration knotted his stomach and he breathed deeply, trying to loosen up so he could finish and get the hell out of there. Too much was happening at once, one crisis after another; there was no chance to sort things out. Ever since Zachary died, time had speeded up, the days whirling around him and then away, like dust in a windstorm. Men should be prepared to lose their fathers, and he'd known for sixteen years, through three strokes that left Zachary progressively weaker, that he would lose his. But Zachary had insisted on working until almost the end, so in a way Matt was unprepared, and when he woke one day to the full realization that he would never see his father again, talk to him and laugh at his tall tales, the pain had struck him with a fierceness he had not expected.

"Matt?" His pressman was pulling on his jacket. "All done. I'll drop them off at the post office on my way home. Unless you have something else you want me to do . . . ?"

"No, you've gone way beyond the call of duty. Thanks for staying."

"You sure there's nothing else I can do? Buy you a drink? Buy you two?"

"Frank," Matt said, "are you doing what you want to do?"

"At the moment or generally?"

"Both."

"At the moment, I'm going home, which is what I want to do. Generally . . . I guess so. I don't think about it much."

"Why not? Did you always want to be a pressman or did you ever want something else? Don't you wonder what might have happened if you'd gone a different direction when you were starting out?"

Frank looked him up and down. "This your birthday or something, Matt? Is that why you're thinking deep thoughts?"

Matt hesitated, then chuckled. "Okay, Frank. Sorry I asked. The end of a very long day is no time for philosophy. Go on home; I'll close up. I'll take you up on that drink some other time."

"Hey, look, I wasn't poking fun. I just didn't know what to say. I really don't think about it much. You know, you get busy, you have good days and bad days, the kids are a pain in the ass or they do good in school and then you feel proud, like you're a good parent . . . Shit, Matt, I don't think about it." There was a long pause. "I wanted to be a baseball player. Outfield. I liked looking up at the sky, you know, and watching those long fly balls float right down into my glove, and if it was the third out I'd hear the cheers and run across the field to the dugout like I was king of the world." He turned to go. "I never found out if I was good enough. My girl was pregnant, so we got married and I got this job with your dad and that was that. I still like her, though, the wife, that is; that's one good thing. Be a real crock if we split after I gave up the outfield for her. Good night, Matt; see you tomorrow. I hope you feel better."

Frowning slightly, Matt washed his hands, put on his tie, locked the front door, set the burglar alarm, and left through the back. It was after the rush hour and traffic on Cerrillos

26

Road was light; he could be home in ten minutes. Speeding up, he thought of Frank, and the past three months since Zachary's death, and Elizabeth, who seemed to be having her own problems dealing with it, though they hadn't talked about it—actually, they weren't talking about very much these days; he couldn't remember when they'd last had a conversation about anything but the kids or the house or the printing company—and then he thought again about Frank, who'd wanted to play outfield, and that brought him back to Zachary.

My father died and left me. It was almost a joke. Sixteen years ago Zachary had begged Matt not to leave him, and Matt hadn't, and now Zachary had left *him*.

Sixteen years of guarding my father's dream, instead of my own.

And that's what was running around in his head. He loved his father, he missed him—but every time he thought of him, it was as if those sixteen years were a dead weight around his neck. *Sixteen years.* Where the hell had they gone? What had they left him with?

He thought of his wedding: all those predictions of a great future for Elizabeth and Matthew Lovell. Wrong. Instead, they'd put off their dreams—until Zachary was well enough to run the company again; until they had the money for a full-time manager to replace Matt; until Holly and Peter were older; until Holly and Peter were through college. And the years passed.

You have good days and you have bad days and you don't think about it much.

Sixteen years.

But they were good years, he thought. Don't forget that.

He didn't forget it. He had a wife he loved, two children, a home, his own business, friends, vacations . . . didn't he have everything he could want?

Turning onto the Paseo de Peralta, his tires squealed; he was going too fast. No, damn it. He didn't have the life he'd given up when he was twenty-three. Instead, he was here, driving the route his father had taken for twenty-five years and he himself had taken for sixteen, going to the house on Camino

Rancheros his father had bought in 1962 and they had enlarged to make room for all of them.

Matthew Lovell was left without a father, but stuck in his father's dream.

How did I end up almost forty—and nowhere?

He barely slowed at the stop sign and turned onto Cordova Road, remembering again those predictions of success. He and Elizabeth had even won a prize. What was the name of it? He couldn't remember. And everyone said they could do anything they wanted.

And they'd done a lot. But inside him was all this anger, boiling up after Zachary died. He remembered when it started: he was watching a plasterer repair a crumbling wall and he'd wondered how long the house would last and how they could afford another one . . . and suddenly he'd seen himself sitting in that chair for the rest of his life and then dying, just like his father—

A horn blasted through his thoughts and he saw a car bearing down on his left in the instant he knew he'd run a stop sign. *Goddamn it!* A turmoil of shouts clanged through his head as his hands swung the wheel hard to the right. *Turn! Get over! Get away—!* The car passed, narrowly missing him, but he couldn't turn back fast enough; his car hit the curb and rode over it. He stood on his brake, but he was traveling too fast to stop; the car skidded along the sidewalk, then crashed into a light pole and bounced off into an adobe wall. Matt heard the explosion of steel against stucco and the shattering of glass; he felt a sudden excruciating pain, like a battering ram in his stomach. Then everything stopped. There was only the dark. And silence.

CHAPTER 3

"Last time we were here," said Holly, her voice small and wavering, "Grandpa died."

Awkwardly, Peter put his arm around her. In the waiting room of St. Vincent Hospital, eerily empty at four-thirty in the morning, he sat tense and rigid, with his arm around his sister, holding himself together, because he felt like he was going to burst. Everything inside him was screaming and yelling and scared; bitter stuff kept coming up in his throat and he swallowed hard to keep it down. Don't let me throw up, he pleaded silently; don't let me throw up all over the floor and make a mess and everybody would think I'm a baby and—*DAD, DON'T DIE, PLEASE, PLEASE DAD, DON'T DIE*—

"What are you thinking?" Holly whispered.

Peter tightened his muscles until they hurt. "Dad," he said, forcing the word through clenched teeth.

"Why doesn't Mother come back?" Holly wailed.

Peter tried to clear his throat but that made him feel like vomiting again, and he was silent.

"Peter? Do you think—if she's not here—?"

"She's with Dad!" Peter blurted, and suddenly he was shaking all over. "In the"—he was almost gasping—"Intensive . . . Care . . . Unit."

29

At the sound of his strangled voice, Holly seemed to crumple. "You think Daddy's dead."

"He's not! People have car accidents all the time and they don't . . . die!"

"I hate this place," Holly said. "I feel sick." She burst into tears. "I don't want Daddy to die!"

At that, Peter let go too, sobs tearing through his body. He held Holly with both arms and felt hers around his back, and the two of them gripped each other, crying in the empty room.

Elizabeth found them that way a few minutes later when she came in, carrying three Styrofoam cups. "Oh, my God . . . Holly . . . Peter . . ." She put the cups down and knelt beside the couch, her arms around the little huddle they made. "He's going to be all right. Don't cry; he's going to be all right. I should have come back earlier, I'm so sorry, I just wanted to be sure—"

"He really is?" Peter demanded. He lifted his face from Holly's shoulder and glared through red eyes at his mother. "We're old enough—you can tell us the truth—"

"He's going to be all right!" Elizabeth stood up from her crouching position and handed them two of the cups. Her face was pale and drawn. "Cocoa. Drink it right away; it's not very hot. Now listen: I'm telling the truth. Daddy had a ruptured spleen and internal bleeding and he was in shock, but those things happen a lot after automobile accidents and doctors know what to do about them. I'll explain it later, but the main thing is, the operation went fine. He'll be in the hospital a couple of weeks and then we'll bring him home. And in another six or eight weeks he can go back to work."

"The same as ever?" Holly asked. She and Peter were sitting straight now, watching their mother for signs of evasiveness.

"The same as ever," Elizabeth repeated firmly. "It's not as if his brain was damaged. He won't be any different."

"Can we see him?" Peter asked, and just then broke into a huge yawn. "Sorry."

"You can't see him because he's sound asleep," Elizabeth said. "And you should be, too. There's nothing to do here until this afternoon; you can see him then for a little while. Right

30

now I want you to go home; we'll get you a cab." She opened her purse and handed Peter a ten dollar bill. "You've been up all night and you're in no shape to go to school; get some sleep, then come back here and we'll have a bedside reunion."

"What about you?" Holly asked.

"They're putting a cot in Daddy's room; I'll lie down there. Then when he wakes up he won't be alone. Come on, now, finish your cocoa so we can get you a cab."

Holly shook her head. "Somebody has to take care of you. I'll stay here."

"There's no place for you in Daddy's room," Elizabeth said, becoming impatient. "Please, Holly, I want you to go home. Get a good sleep and come back this afternoon."

Stifling another yawn, Peter took his sister by the hand. "We'll go if you promise you're telling the truth."

"Peter, I *told* you—!"

"Okay, okay, I just had to make sure. And you'll call us if anything, uh, happens?"

"Yes. Now *please*—"

"We're going. Right now. Where do we get a cab?"

"I'll go with you."

When she had seen them off, Elizabeth went back to the waiting room and crumpled in a heap on the couch, no longer pretending to be calm and strong. She was shaking with fear and exhaustion, and a kind of superstitious refrain kept running through her head: *You weren't satisfied with your marriage; it wasn't exciting enough for you. And you almost lost it. You almost lost Matt. Almost lost—*

"Mrs. Lovell?" The doctor stood in the doorway and Elizabeth shot up from the couch, forcing open her heavy eyes. "Mr. Lovell is asking for you; you can see him in the ICU for a few minutes. He's very restless," the doctor added as they walked down the corridor. "Talking about his father. Perhaps you can calm him down."

Matt's face was ashen, the skin pulled tight over his bones. His deep-set blue eyes looked even deeper, so dark they were almost black. "Competing with Dad," he whispered with grim

31

humor when Elizabeth bent over him. "Couldn't let him be the only one to die."

Elizabeth kissed him and smoothed back his hair. She put her cheek to his, her lips close to his ear. "It's not a contest. He's gone, Matt; we're here. And we don't want to lose you."

He grunted. "Close call."

"Yes, but it's all right now," she said. "Really all right, Matt. The doctor—"

"Just like Dad. Funny, isn't it? Strokes . . . they were close calls, too . . . and then he died."

"Matt, you're going to be fine!" She held his hand between both of hers. "Try to believe me; you are not going to die!" He turned his head away. "Matt!" she cried.

The nurse intervened. "Mrs. Lovell, we hoped you'd calm your husband down."

"I'm sorry," Elizabeth said, and repeated it to Matt. "I'm sorry. We'll talk about it when you're stronger." She kissed him on his forehead and his lips. "We want you home. We love you."

It wasn't enough, Matt thought later when he woke in his hospital room and saw Elizabeth asleep on a nearby cot. You're going to be fine, he recalled her saying through the anesthesia still fogging his mind. It's all right now. You're going to be fine.

But it wasn't that simple. Because even when he was out of the hospital and home again, he knew something was wrong with him that lay beyond the reach of any surgeon. He felt trapped, smothered beneath a kind of cloud that had settled over him.

My father is dead.

I came damn near dying myself.

I'm running out of time.

"Leave it alone," he said to Elizabeth as she adjusted a pillow behind him. He was sitting in an armchair beside the doors to the garden; it was a warm June morning, almost hot, two weeks after he'd come home. "It's fine."

"A minute ago you said you were uncomfortable."

"It doesn't matter."

32

"It matters to me."

"Elizabeth, will you please not *hover*." She took a quick step back and he threw out his hands. "I'm sorry. I'm a lousy patient. You shouldn't have to suffer my moods. Aren't you going to the printing plant? Or, no, you were going to write up that Woman's Club thing today."

"Frank can handle the plant for one day without me, and the Woman's Club story isn't important."

"It's part of your newspaper job, and you've always said your job was important to you."

"I'd rather not leave you alone today."

"But you know what I want most is to be left alone."

"Matt," Elizabeth said after a moment, "what can I do?"

"Nothing. Elizabeth, stop worrying about me. Go to work."

"*You're* my work right now!" she said bluntly. "Either I find a way to cheer you up or I ship you somewhere else for a while. It's been like a graveyard around here ever since you got home; you're so bitter and . . . *angry*. What are you angry about? Your accident? Zachary's death? Something about your work?"

"All of the above," he said with a flash of humor. "I'm sorry," he added, and it occurred to Elizabeth that what they did most of the time lately was apologize to each other for one thing or another. "It's just that . . . I'm running out of time!" he blurted. "Don't you see that? In two months I'll be forty years old—"

"So will I," she said quietly, but he did not hear her.

"The years are going so damned fast I can't keep track of them, and I'm standing still. A failure. What the hell have I got to show for forty years?"

"A family," Elizabeth said, repeating the things she'd told herself only a few days before. "A home, your own business—"

"I know all that. *It's not enough!*"

Elizabeth tested the coffee pot with her hand, found it still hot, and poured each of them a cup. She carried hers to the chair opposite Matt's and sat down. "Go on," she said. "You've been bottling it up; why don't you tell me all of it?"

He smiled at her, a quick, loving smile, and Elizabeth felt the pain of what had slipped away from them over the years. She wanted to put her arms around him and get back the rest of it, all the love and passion that she remembered, but she stayed where she was, carefully holding her cup so the coffee would not spill, and said again, "Tell me about it."

He gazed out the window. "Do you know what happens when I sit here? I listen to Holly singing in her room: voice exercises, scales, those wonderful songs . . . and I imagine Peter in his room, writing down those legends his pueblo friends tell . . . and I say to myself: they're the lucky ones, doing what they love best. And then I think, at thirteen and fourteen, with no other demands pinning them down, why the hell shouldn't they do what they love? It's crazy for me to resent my children's good fortune just because I'm a loser."

"You're not a loser," Elizabeth said. "You're depressed over Zachary's death and your accident, but you are not a loser."

He smiled faintly and looked at the table beside him, cluttered with a telephone and piles of notes, memos, and bills Elizabeth brought home each night from the office for him to act on. "I can't do these, you know," he said almost casually. "I can't concentrate on them or care about them. Because I keep coming back to that minute when I knew I couldn't stop the car—and the things I was thinking about just before it happened—and that's all that matters. If I'd been killed, that would have been the end of all those plans I had once upon a time. And I go around and around, trying to sort out what's important to me, what's necessary, what's right. I'm not getting any younger, as the saying goes, and *when the hell am I going to break out and do the things I really want?*"

Elizabeth held his eyes with hers. "I feel slightly invisible," she said. "Where do I fit in all those questions?" Stunned surprise swept across his face; he opened his mouth to answer, but before he could, the doorbell rang.

Matt grimaced. "More good Samaritans bearing food, drink, and half the books in Santa Fe. When will I read them all? Do they think I'm going to be an invalid for ten years?"

"I'll be right back," Elizabeth said, escaping his ill humor.

34

She went through the arched entry hall to open the front door, and found Tony, leaning casually against the garden wall, arms folded, waiting for her.

"If I'd called first," he said calmly, "you would have found some reason to tell me not to come."

"Tony, you should have called; this is a terrible time—"

"But we had a date. Four weeks ago you gave me permission to come for lunch. You may have forgotten, but I didn't." He walked past her through the shadowed entry hall to the brightness of the living room. He paused so his eyes could adjust to the clear desert light pouring through a wall of paned windows and a paned double door leading to the courtyard. The room came into focus, with its white walls, dark *vigas*, or beams, half embedded in the low stucco ceiling, and vivid Indian rugs in red, blue, and black scattered on the cream-colored, tiled floor. "Always takes me by surprise," he mused aloud. "The air . . . the light . . . after the smog of my beloved Los An—"

He stopped abruptly as he became aware of Matt, unmoving in his armchair, wearing a bathrobe. "Matt! What's wrong? Ailing? Wounded? Hangover?" Smoothly shifting from Elizabeth's private visitor to a warm friend of the family, he pulled a chair close to Matt's and sat down. "Don't glower at me; I don't stand on ceremony with long-time friends. Did someone beat you up? I'll avenge you as soon as I can assemble an army; I myself am a man of peace." He waited, but Matt, his face expressionless, said nothing. "You and your horse disagreed on which direction to go? One of your printing machines ran amok? Or another Indian uprising, though I rather thought those had ended a century ago. Elizabeth, won't you sit down and join us?"

Taken aback by his sudden, overwhelming presence, Elizabeth stood still, gazing at him. Fame had made him sleek and breezy, and his tall, handsome confidence, especially beside Matt's depression, made him even more attractive and dominating than she remembered. The air around him was electric, as if he were a messenger from a world filled with excitement and success, buzzing, bustling, bursting with energy, while she

35

and Matt sat in their static little house in their quiet little town, waiting for the Tonys of that world to bring them news of all they were missing.

Matt must feel it, too, she thought, seeing his scowl, and she took a step forward, phrasing a graceful way to get Tony out of the house. But he had settled back in his chair, listening attentively to Matt's brief description of his accident, then, in turn, regaling him with the antics of the producer of his television show, called "Anthony." And when Matt chuckled at something he said—the first time in weeks Matt had come close to a laugh—it occurred to Elizabeth that maybe it was good that Tony was there. Matt needed amusement, something to think about other than himself and Zachary.

And maybe Tony's forceful presence could break down the wall of Matt's self-absorption. Sometimes it took someone from outside to get a husband and wife talking to each other again.

"You'll stay for lunch?" she asked, ignoring Matt's deeper scowl at her invitation.

"Of course," Tony said, smiling easily. "It's been too long since I've seen . . . the two of you. Nothing fancy, though; if you spend hours in the kitchen I won't have a chance to talk to you before my plane leaves."

"We'll talk in the kitchen," Elizabeth responded. "All of us. Matt? Please? Tony can tell us all the gossip from Los Angeles."

"And you can fill me in on the scandals that shake Santa Fe," said Tony, offering Matt a hand.

Matt stood up by himself. "Few scandals shake Santa Fe. We natives are cautious, ingrown, and very protective of our little backwater."

"Do I hear a note of dissatisfaction?" Tony asked. "Why don't you leave?" He kept pace with Matt's slow steps as they walked into the kitchen and sat in wicker chairs in an alcove opening onto the courtyard. "I've often wondered why you haven't."

"My father was here," Matt replied briefly.

"My father was in Houston," said Tony. "Still is. I'm not." He leaned back in his chair, stretched out his legs in their perfectly pressed white duck pants, and accepted the glass of

36

Mexican beer Elizabeth offered him. "I left Houston; I left my father. Left his business and his shadow and the reach of his long arm. Made my own fortune that has nothing to do with Keegan Rourke and owes nothing to him. I had to get out, you know, to survive. After eleven interminable years, I had to get out or be his little boy forever. And as Elizabeth knows, I am not the little boy type."

After a moment, Matt said evenly, "You were telling me about your producer. And your interview with Sophia Loren."

"So I was," said Tony, smoothly changing subjects. "A remarkable woman, magnificently beautiful, warm, earthy, honest . . ." He broke off as Elizabeth brought to the table a platter of *sopapilla rellenos*, stuffed with meat, beans, and chile, and covered with cheese. "Elizabeth, I'm ashamed; you did make something special. You work too hard; I should have taken you to a restaurant."

Matt's mouth tightened and Elizabeth said quickly, "I didn't want to go to a restaurant; I wanted to eat right here. And I would love to hear about your producer and Sophia Loren."

"In a minute." Tony dug into the *rellenos*. "Incredible. What a marvelous cook you are, Elizabeth." Between bites he told them anecdotes about his producer, and some of his guests, bringing reluctant chuckles from Matt and laughter from Elizabeth. "Could I have another one of these?" he asked after a while. "Or even two? I don't want to be greedy—"

"No one could accuse you of that," said Matt blandly.

Tony smiled. "I pride myself on never going after anything that truly belongs to someone else."

"An interesting rule," Matt observed with an edge in his voice. "People who talk about priding themselves on it are usually the ones who pride themselves on violating it."

Tony gave him a sharp look. "I've noticed that people with injuries tend to be bad-tempered. It's good to see you've avoided that, Matt."

"Oh, why don't both of you just eat?" Elizabeth said in exasperation. She handed Tony the platter. "Help yourself. As much as you want."

"Thank you," he said meekly. "Well, you wanted to hear

37

about Sophia. My producer wanted me to zero in on her fantasies, get her to describe them; you know producers are voyeurs, all of them. But I'll tell you something, if you won't laugh at me." He gave a small smile, like a little boy afraid to give himself away, but at the same time wanting to share a secret. In spite of himself, Matt was drawn to him, and impressed. No wonder the guy was a success. How the hell did he get all that into one smile—and almost fool Matt Lovell, who couldn't stand having him around, who kept hearing echoes of that smooth voice saying *I left my father. Left his business. Had to get out to survive.*

"No, you wouldn't laugh," Tony went on, almost to himself. "I'll tell you: I was so awed by Sophia—how beautiful and generous she was, helping make my show better—that I could barely ask her anything, much less about her fantasies. In fact, I was having a few of my own." He gave a small laugh, asking Matt and Elizabeth to share a joke on himself. "Of course, it's no secret that I'm interested in women: their sexual fantasies, longings, dreams, and the way they act them out"—Matt shot an involuntary look at Elizabeth; he knew Tony saw it, but Tony went on without a pause—"and my audience wants to know about them, too, but they're dying to know all of it: what weaknesses celebrities have, what they're faking or hiding, the skeletons in their closets, the tender touches that make them human and frail when they want to seem untouchable, above all of us . . ."

He's forty-six, Matt thought, and doing exactly what he was dreaming of when Elizabeth knew him in Los Angeles. He's got it all: money, fame, success—and he's had them for ten years.

"That's what I expose on my show," Tony was saying. "A whole person. Sometimes that makes glamorous people more glamorous, knowing their secrets, because you assume they're keeping back something even worse. Others become less glamorous: their warts show. Either way, audiences eat it up. Why *are* you still living here?"

"We're not glamorous people," said Matt shortly, and then they ate Elizabeth's caramel flan, and drank coffee flavored

38

with cinnamon, and Tony talked about other interviews, in Russia, Afghanistan, Hong Kong, India, Brazil, the Netherlands—"and even in Amalfi, where I have my new villa; I do want you to see it; we'll have to get you over there. Both of you, of course."

How civilized this is, Elizabeth thought; but she wanted Tony gone, and when dessert and coffee were finished he did leave, citing plane schedules, meetings and interviews in New York, and a hectic week ahead. He thanked them for lunch and good company, and when Elizabeth saw him to the door he did not even say, as he usually did, that he would telephone as soon as he could, and stop off to see her again whenever he could. He simply lifted her hand in his, kissed it gently, and then was gone, leaving Elizabeth wondering how he had managed to control his arrival and departure and almost all the conversation in between.

"Holly and Peter will be home soon," she said to Matt when she returned to the kitchen. "I want to talk to you before they get here."

He was standing at the counter making another pot of coffee. "How often does he show up?"

Stacking dishes at the table, Elizabeth glanced at him. "I've told you every time he's been here. About five times in the past year."

He nodded. "So you did. You did tell me. And he calls more often than that."

"I've told you that, too."

"And he didn't think I'd be home today."

"I'm not sleeping with him, Matt."

"You brought it up; I didn't."

"But that's what you meant," she said angrily.

"That's what he wants. That's what he expects. Does he think I'm blind? Do you?"

"Yes, if you think I'd go to bed with him. Why would you accuse—?" She caught herself.

"Past history. Isn't that enough?"

"Matt! It was more than twenty years ago! And it ended long

39

before I met you, and I told you about it before we were married. We agreed we wouldn't talk about it again."

"We didn't know he'd be lounging in our kitchen sixteen years later, gorging himself, lording it over us with his fame and fortune."

"You're jealous!" Elizabeth said hotly.

"Is that what you call it? Because I'm not an adoring fan of my wife's former lover? You let him call; you let him come for long lunches, 'between planes' as they say. Who the hell believes that? *Between planes*. Now there's an idea for a new airline bonus plan: Los Angeles to New York, with a stopover for screwing—"

"Matt, stop it!" Elizabeth perched on the edge of the table. "You're looking for reasons to be angry. You're not jealous because Tony and I were lovers one crazy summer when I was seventeen; you're jealous because he's made it very big and he has a lot of the things you want, or seems to have." She went to him where he stood leaning against the counter. "Please let's not quarrel. When you were in the hospital I was thinking I'd almost lost you and I couldn't bear it; it was so terrible. We mustn't fight, especially over Tony, of all people; he doesn't mean a thing to me."

"Doesn't he? Didn't someone say first loves never die?"

"That's the most idiotic— Who was yours?" she asked abruptly.

"You," he said, and smiled—in memory, Elizabeth thought, not to end their quarrel.

She threw back her head. "Why can't we be grown up and laugh together? I told you, it took me a long time to get over Tony after he dropped me, but I did, and then a couple of years later I met you and you were so much more wonderful—more honest, more real—I was crazy about you from the minute you put your arms around me and made me feel I belonged . . . Oh, damn it, Matt, there hasn't been anyone else since then. You *know* that."

"I know your friend is on our doorstep. After all these years, showing up *between planes*, droning on about his superiority."

"Matt, let it go!" She began stacking dishes again, banging

40

them recklessly. "Why do you keep bringing him up? He's not a serious person!"

"He's a very serious person. In his own dramatic way he's as serious as they come. He's decided he loves you. From afar, of course. It's safer that way, as long as you're married, and it adds to the drama: unattainable love, at least for now, like a shining star, remote, unreachable—what is it?"

Elizabeth was staring at him. "I didn't think you understood—"

"My God, you don't give me much credit. If you'd asked me what I thought about him, I would have told you."

"You could have brought it up without being asked. Whenever I told you he'd been here you didn't say anything. We never talked about him."

"Or anything else. I'd better sit down; I'm feeling shaky."

"Let me help you."

"No thanks." He made his way to the living room and Elizabeth followed, biting her lip. The truth was, she hadn't wanted to talk to Matt about Tony, about those phone calls and long lunches where he pretended she'd been his one true love for more than twenty years, that he should have stayed with her instead of marrying someone else, that he'd longed for her ever since. Matt would have asked why she listened to it, and how could she tell him she listened because even though she knew it was play-acting it made her feel young?

And I don't, Matt would say.

We never talk about that.

"No, we never talked about him," Matt said as if there had been no break in the conversation. He was in his chair again, gazing through the window, his face hard. "But, at the very least, isn't it a bit curious—and worth a discussion between husband and wife? Old lover comes calling. Between planes."

"*Matt.*" She sat on a hassock beside his chair, her chin on her clasped hands. "We have more important things to talk about."

"Such as?"

"Your lousy mood. Your depression. What you'll do when you're recovered. What I'll do. What this family will do."

Matt looked at her curiously. "Why should anything change?"

"It already has. You know that. It's been changing for years, but I didn't really think about it until Zachary died. Now I think about it all the time."

"Think about what?"

"What's happened to us. What we've lost. It's not only Tony we don't talk about; we don't talk about anything except the house and the children, the printing company, sometimes my job at the *Examiner* . . . Everyday things; *surface* things."

Matt nodded. He was looking at the garden again, thinking it had never looked so lovely. Flowers bordered the patio, vegetables flourished in the corner, irrigated by a system Peter had invented when he was ten. A beautiful courtyard in a beautiful home, filled with life. Maybe that's why it looked especially lovely. Another few inches in the car, and he'd never have seen it again.

How short is a man's life?

Once I might have asked how long it was. No more.

He glanced at Elizabeth, and suddenly, thinking of Tony, he realized how beautiful she was. Other men and women frequently told him so and he always agreed, but when had he last looked at her through the eyes of someone else? When had he last thought of his wife as a stunning woman, instead of thinking that Holly was growing up to be as lovely as her mother? When had he last *thought* of Elizabeth?

In two months they'd both be forty. Did she think time was slipping away from her, leaving so much undone? Did she think she was a failure? Did she ask herself how short was a woman's life?

"Matt." Elizabeth was studying him, her chin still resting on her hands. "How much have we lost? We had so much love and excitement about each other; we talked about everything. And you never would have thought I was sleeping with another man."

He pondered it. "We let other things fill our time, use up our energy, wear us down . . ."

"I'd like to be a frazzled wreck," Elizabeth murmured.

"What?"

"Oh, just something silly that occurred to me, weeks ago, when I was thinking about us: that we'd gotten . . . stale. Static. And then, after Zachary died, and you were always so angry, so dissatisfied with what we have—"

"Aren't you?" he demanded, and then it all burst from him. "Christ, Elizabeth, aren't you angry and upset over what's happened to us? You asked me what we've lost. I'll tell you: we've lost the idea that we could be anything we want! Doesn't that scare you? It scares the hell out of me. Once upon a time you won prizes, everyone predicted a wonderful future—"

"You won the same prizes—"

"God damn it, that's the whole point! Did we ever imagine we'd be—what was it you said? Stale. Static. If anyone had predicted that for us we'd have said he was crazy. We knew what we wanted, remember? You couldn't wait to have your own column; I was going to be a publisher; we were going to buy a newspaper. Maybe two. *Do* you remember? What the hell happened to us, Elizabeth? We're almost forty and where are we? How did we get to be such different people? Doesn't that bother you? Am I the only one with this *rage* eating me up inside?"

Elizabeth had straightened her back and was watching him, her eyes bright with anger. "I don't rage. I've thought we were pretty lucky in what we had. But you're right: I don't always like writing for other people. And it's nice to know you haven't forgotten that I had my own dreams; that you aren't the only one who gave up a lot when we came here—"

"I never forgot that."

"Maybe I heard you wrong. Just before Tony arrived I thought I heard you say you weren't getting any younger. And I thought I heard, *When the hell am I going to break out and do the things I really want?*"

Slowly, Matt nodded. "And you said you felt invisible. You're right; I was feeling sorry for myself."

"You were wallowing in it. You still are." Elizabeth began to walk about the room. "That's all you've done since Zachary died: feel sorry for yourself." She turned on him. "Damn it, if you're so frustrated and unhappy, why don't you do some-

43

thing about it instead of moping around making the rest of us miserable? If the printing company is a millstone, get rid of it! Who's forcing you to keep it? If you want a newspaper, buy one! What's stopping you?"

"I'm not an irresponsible infant, that's what's stopping me! For Christ's sake, I have a family, a home, a father who . . . no, scratch that; I don't have a father. But I have people dependent on me and I don't go running off in all directions satisfying my deepest desires until I know my family is taken care of."

"Did you ask your family how they felt about it? Did you try to find out which they'd rather have—an unhappy grouch or someone going after his dreams?"

"Dreams don't buy groceries."

"*Did you ask us!*"

"No." Matt shifted in his chair. "What if I had? What would you have said if I'd told you I was selling the company?"

"I'd ask how much you could get for it."

Surprise flashed across his face. "And if I said I was buying a newspaper?"

"I'd ask if it was the *Chieftain*."

His eyebrows shot up. "Why?"

"Because it's in trouble and it's been for sale for six months and if you were buying a paper, that's the kind you'd look for."

Smiling slightly, he said, "And if I'd looked, I'd have learned they want two million for it."

"So you *have* looked. Then you know they're desperate and would probably take half that."

His smile broadened. "Only half? Only one measly million?"

Elizabeth stopped pacing. "Only one," she said lightly. "We might have to hock a few things to raise it—"

"Small things. The house—"

"And the cars—"

"Only one of them. We'd need the other to get to work."

And suddenly they were laughing together, the first time in months. Elizabeth came back to the hassock and sat down. Matt touched her hair. "We need shelter, too."

"We'll rent a place," she said.

"In the tourist season? Few places; high prices."

44

"Then we'll camp in the mountains until Labor Day. When we sell everything, we'll keep our camping gear."

"Back to nature for the pioneering Lovells. Of course, if we fail, we'd be left with nothing, but I suppose we could always—"

"How could we fail?" She smiled gaily. "You were just telling me how everyone predicted our success. And we're not youngsters just starting out; maybe it's not so bad, being forty. It means we're mature, experienced, and sensible."

Matt laughed shortly. "Mature and sensible." And Elizabeth knew he meant, *That's why this is only a game.*

But what if it weren't? What if they were really planning to start fresh, make a new life, fall in love all over again, believe in endless possibilities as they had, long ago?

She closed her eyes. The idea was a tantalizing flame. But then she thought, two children close to college, our home, our security, maybe other accidents, or illness: we're not getting any younger, so many things can happen . . .

Wait a minute! We're not *old!* Though we will be if Matt doesn't pull out of his depression, get rid of his rage, stop feeling like a failure . . .

And what about me? Elizabeth remembered how restless and impatient she'd been lately, pushing aside thoughts of things that were wrong. Was it because she was a woman that she pushed them aside while Matt raged? Was she too easily satisfied? What had happened to *her* ambitions?

We're a cautious bunch, Matt had told Tony. In our little backwater.

Does Matt think I'm too cautious, tying him down in a backwater?

"If we're really mature," she said, "we'd know when it's time to change. Do sensible people stand still if they have a choice?"

"The choice is to risk everything we have."

Panic flared inside her; she fought it down. They'd just been laughing together, for the first time in months. And she'd seen the brightness in Matt's eyes. "How mature and sensible of us to recognize that. Because when people try to pick up where

45

they left off and go after something they've wanted as long as they can remember, they ought to start out with their eyes wide open. Don't you think so?" Then the fear came back and she added, "Unless there's too much risk. We don't have to decide now; this is a game we can play around with for a while . . ."

But Matt's head was tilted in the way he had when he was weighing choices and coming to a conclusion. He reached out his hand and took hers. "Thank you, my love." His voice was husky. "You're a remarkable woman. You know we're not playing a game. You've known we weren't from the beginning. We've been shaping a life."

For a while they kept it to themselves, a secret they hugged close until they were alone at night and then endlessly discussed. For two weeks it was all they talked about. They read back issues of the *Chieftain* and then the *Examiner*, studying it as if it were their competition; they looked at circulation figures and advertising rates and scribbled numbers: a million to purchase the paper, a quarter of a million a year for the staff of fifteen people, costs of supplies, maintenance on equipment and the building, financing new equipment when they needed it, the cost of typesetting computers as soon as they could afford them, revenue from subscriptions and advertising.

"Money," Matt kept muttering. "I feel like a banker, not a publisher." *Publisher*. They looked at each other. "Are we really doing this?" he asked. "Or am I still in the hospital, drunk on anesthesia and raving mad?"

"You are at home," Elizabeth said. "Sober on coffee, quite sane, and soon to be a publisher."

He leaned over and kissed her, and their excitement made the kiss seem as new as their plans. "Starting again," Matt said. Everything was starting again.

Each night the handwritten columns grew longer, the total expenses larger, the income less certain. But each day the difficulties seemed to shrink. Because Matt was getting well, Elizabeth thought, and because they were doing everything together: working at the printing company, making plans, plotting as they drove around Santa Fe, seeing its people as subscribers, its businesses as advertisers, each other as partners.

"What's with you two?" Peter asked. "You look like you won a prize or something. I mean, you told us not to bug Dad because he's depressed and then all of a sudden everybody's got these grins on their faces . . . Did we inherit a million dollars or what?"

"We're working on an idea that we're excited about," Elizabeth replied. "We'll tell you about it pretty soon."

"Why not now?"

"Because it isn't all worked out yet."

Talking, planning, sharing, they fed each other's excitement. They looked forward to the evenings, as they had long ago when they were dating and pushing the hours away until they could be together. Now they waited for the quiet time when they could sit at the kitchen table with notebooks and folders and sharpened pencils, talking about their secret, making it more possible, more real. They waited for the time when they would go to bed, kissing and holding each other with the same sense of beginning that was part of everything they did these days. They were changing their life. They were starting again.

It was all risk, it was all discovery, it was bolstering each other up when their fears returned. "We can't sell the house," Matt said. "We have to live somewhere . . ."

"Which is cheaper?" Elizabeth asked, turning to a clean piece of paper. "Renting or taking a mortgage on this place?"

They wrote down numbers, percentage points, tax deductions. "Keep the house," Matt said finally. "It makes more sense. I hate to mortgage it to the hilt after Dad had it paid off, but—"

"It's better than camping in the mountains," Elizabeth finished, and kissed him. "I hated the idea of giving it up." Then she looked again at the number he had written. "It's a large payment, isn't it? Month after month . . . And there's the personal loan, too . . ."

He put his arms around her. "If we buy the paper, we'll make so much money you'll never notice it."

She nodded. "Of course."

47

Neither of them quite believed it, but neither of them said so. And at last, one night as they lay together in bed, talking in the last drowsy minutes before sleep, both of them said, at the same time, "When we buy the paper . . ." and they knew they'd leaped the final hurdle. No longer were they saying "If." The next day they would begin to sign the papers that would make it irrevocable. In the darkness they held each other tightly. "I believe in you," said Elizabeth almost fiercely. And, still clasped in each other's arms, they fell asleep.

Elizabeth's parents had retired from their jobs in Los Angeles eight years earlier and moved to Santa Fe, converting one of the narrow, deep adobe buildings on Canyon Road to the Evans Bookshop and Art Gallery, and buying a house in the nearby mountain town of Tesuque. They had their own friends, but the most important people in their lives were Matt and Elizabeth and the children, so, on a warm, starry night in August, Elizabeth asked them to dinner, because there was something they wanted to talk about. And when they were all at the table on the brick patio—Holly and Peter uneasy because they figured something really big was coming; Lydia and Spencer curious— Matt made the announcement of their plans.

Peter broke the stunned silence. "You promised Grandpa Zachary you wouldn't sell the company."

"He's gone," said Matt gently. "We kept it for him as long as he was alive."

"Do we have to sell everything?" Holly asked. "Like the house and the cars?"

Elizabeth shook her head. "We can manage—"

"Hold on a minute!" Spencer commanded. His white hair flew out as he swung his head from Elizabeth to Matt. "This is pretty sudden! You can't spring things like this on your family!"

"Can't?" Matt asked.

"Can't, damn it! You have responsibilities; you can't decide to change jobs like a teenager who gets tired of—"

"Now *you* wait a minute—" Matt began, but Spencer tore

48

ahead. "What's the asking price for this paper you think you're buying?"

"The price of the paper we're going to buy is a little over a million," Matt said deliberately.

"The owners are very anxious—" Elizabeth started to say.

"A million *dollars?*" Peter yelled.

"A million dollars," Holly whispered.

Spencer shook his head. "Insane! Do you think you have rich parents? You know we haven't anything to spare; we've told you so. We thought we were doing you a favor by scrimping and saving so we could take care of ourselves and not be a burden to you: we did that for you—!"

"You did it because you were afraid," Matt said coldly. "Too afraid to do what we're doing."

"You damn fool, we were being sensible; not afraid! You will not have us to fall back on! Have you thought about that?"

"Of course we thought about it," Matt retorted, but Elizabeth cut in quietly. "We know you'd help if you could. We want to make it on our own."

"How?" Lydia asked curiously. "You're so young; we never could have done it at your age."

"A second mortgage on the house; a loan from the bank. It will be close, but—"

"We'll owe money all over town," said Peter.

"But we'll own a newspaper," said Matt.

Holly looked from her father to her mother. "You're excited. Your faces look all shiny."

Matt's eyebrows rose. "Shiny?"

"Like you said mine was when I got those two parts in the concert."

"It's called burning your bridges," Peter observed.

Holly swung on him. "Why are you so stuffy?" she demanded. "You're just like Grandpa, and you're not nearly as old as he is. Or are you just thinking about yourself? College and all that." Her voice wavered on the last words.

"See!" Peter shouted triumphantly. "You're worried about it, too!"

"We've taken care of that," Elizabeth said. "We're setting up a trust for each of you; you won't lose college, we promise."

"Just a minute!" Spencer demanded again. "We keep getting off the subject! What the hell do you know about running a newspaper?"

"Not a lot," Matt said. "But I've run a printing company for sixteen years, so I know the business end; we studied journalism, both of us were editor of our college paper; and Elizabeth's been writing for the *Examiner* for years."

"That's it?" Spencer asked. His face was red; his palms made slapping sounds as he clasped and unclasped his hands.

"Not quite. We've researched the paper and its competition. We're not going in blind; we know the problems and we have ideas for solving them. And the *Chieftain* has a good managing editor; he'll keep it going in the beginning, until we know what we're doing."

Spencer slammed both hands on the table. "Putting the welfare of your children in the hands of someone you don't even know. You can't even be sure he'll stick around to help you."

"Don't talk to me as if I'm a child!" Matt roared. Elizabeth put a hand on his arm and he lowered his voice. "Did I ever tell you my father wanted to be an artist?"

"Zachary?" said Spencer, surprised. "No."

"It wasn't something he talked about a lot. But when he was young he studied every art form he could think of: painting, sculpture, woodcuts, silkscreen, even linoleum cuts. And he was good. He just wasn't great. So he stopped; he didn't want to be a second-rate artist. Instead he bought into the printing company that later became his, and did lithography for the artists who lived here, and in Taos. An invisible assistant, he called himself. Except, he hated it. He told me he hated every minute of it and the more he hated it the more he put everything he had into it, not only for artists, but for himself, designing brochures and posters and maps for tourists: his only way of being an artist. Then, one day, the hating stopped and he was proud of what he made. That's why he was so terrified of losing it. Though I think he dreamed that someday, when he retired to Nuevo, he'd try again, to see if he'd do better than when he was young. Or just to have fun with what he called his small talent."

"But he died before he could try," said Elizabeth.

"Right. He died."

Spencer grimaced at the lanterns hanging above the table. "I hear what you're saying, but it doesn't wash. Nobody knows what's going to happen; nobody has a guarantee of living long enough to do everything. That's no excuse for risking your security, throwing away a thriving business—"

"We've weighed the risks," Matt said flatly. "And you have no right to tell us—"

"Daddy," Elizabeth said softly, "don't you understand? We need this."

"You mean your marriage is in trouble, is that it? And you think buying a newspaper will make it better?"

"We're not talking about our marriage," Matt said.

Elizabeth heard the ominous note in his voice. "Our marriage probably has as many ups and downs as yours," she told her father lightly. "What I meant was, we think we have to do this now. If we don't, we might never do it. We might keep putting it off—"

"We put it off!" Spencer's voice rose. "We put off indulging ourselves; we were responsible adults! Why can't you keep the printing company—a guaranteed income!—and buy into a paper? Be partners with someone! Do a little bit at a time—"

"No." Matt pushed aside his plate and leaned his arms on the table. "We believe in ourselves. We have to try with everything we have, because if we hold back, and then fail, we'll never know if we might have succeeded if only we'd had enough courage."

"I understand that," Lydia said very quietly. Spencer's face darkened. "Now listen—!" he began.

"My dear, it's my turn to talk," Lydia said. "And I want to say that I'm very impressed with Elizabeth and Matt, and I envy them."

"Mother!" Elizabeth exclaimed.

"Your father was miserable the last five years he was working," Lydia said. "He may sputter at you about waiting, but

51

he knows he was counting the days until he could get out. You're quite right; he was afraid to do it before he had his full pension, and I admit I was worried, too, and didn't encourage him. But I was counting the days, too, until we could leave. Not because I didn't like my job—I loved it—but who could live with an angry, frustrated man?"

"Elizabeth knows something about that," Matt said.

"But what if it doesn't work?" Peter demanded. "I mean, what if you . . . what if . . ." He stopped. How could he say he was afraid his parents would be failures?

"What if we fail?" Matt asked, for him. "Then we go job hunting. Are you afraid, Peter?"

"I guess so. Shouldn't I be?"

"Sure. We all should be. We've been comfortable and secure for years; now we're talking about taking some big chances. And we're asking you to take them with us."

"Peter." Elizabeth leaned forward. "We've thought about this a lot; it's something we want and need very much. You and Holly have your lives ahead of you, but when you get older the years slip away so fast . . . I wish I could make you understand how it feels to turn around and find it's another spring or summer or Christmas and another year of your life is gone. And you can't get it back; you can't make up for what you haven't done in those twelve months. What we're afraid of is waking up one day and finding out it's too late to do the things we dreamed about and gave up and started thinking about again after Grandpa Zachary died. If we don't try now, when we have our health and enough energy to begin something new, we're afraid we may never try. Then we'd look back someday and know we missed our chance, maybe our only chance. And we don't want to live with that regret."

"I didn't think we had such an awful life," Peter mumbled.

Holly turned on her brother. "Can't you have some imagination? You and I could get jobs, you know! If you don't shape up you'll be a stodgy old man before you're fifteen."

"Somebody has to be careful around here!" Peter shouted, and on the last word his voice cracked, ending on a high note.

52

He flushed in embarrassment. "I can't help it if nobody feels like me."

"We do feel like you," Elizabeth said. "But we also feel we have to make a choice. Can't you understand that? Isn't there anything you want to do *now* without waiting?"

"Be an anthropologist and study Indians," Peter said promptly. "But you always say I have to go to college first, that I have to do things in the right order. Isn't that what Grandpa said he and Grandma did? Wait till the right time to buy their shop?"

Elizabeth and Matt exchanged a glance, amused and exasperated, wondering why parents' good advice often came back in a way they never expected. "It's close," Elizabeth admitted. "But not the same. A bookshop doesn't take the same time and energy as a newspaper; some jobs can't be started after a certain age. And I keep trying to tell you, Peter: the years are running away from us. We've waited sixteen years for this dream to come true. What if you had to wait sixteen years to be an anthropologist, or Holly had to wait that long to get a part in a Broadway musical?"

"I'd die," Holly said simply.

"Or learn to wait," Elizabeth said, smiling. "But then one day you'd say, 'Okay, it's now or never.' And you'd go after it."

"Peter," Lydia said, "there's no such thing as absolute security. Maybe everybody should take a big chance at least once. Maybe everybody should be greedy for more, at least once."

Elizabeth put her hand on Lydia's, feeling that from now on, they would be friends in a new way. "Thank you," she said, and kissed Lydia's cheek. "That means so much to me."

"How about me?" Holly demanded. "I thought it was a good idea, too! I think you're as wonderful as Grandma does!"

"And we thank you," said Matt. "We need you behind us."

"Well, if it works, of course it would be . . . fine," rumbled Spencer, not wanting to be left out of what was clearly building to a vote of confidence. "And of course I'm behind you as much as Lydia; and we'll help with something, if things get really tight . . ."

"Well, I can help too!" Peter exclaimed. "If you need money

I'll sell my pottery collection—and get a job," he added with a dark look at his sister.

Matt took Elizabeth's hand, feeling her slender fingers link with his. "We won't ask you to sell anything, Peter, or go to work just yet. All we want is your faith in us. That's all we want from all of you. Because we have faith in ourselves. We know we're going to make it." He looked at Elizabeth with love and anticipation, and put his arm around her shoulders. "When something is now or never," he told all of them, "and when you're working with someone you love, you don't hold back. You put everything you've got into it."

Holly drew in her breath at the look on her parents' faces. A sharp pain went through her: envy, hope—and a fear that maybe no one would ever look at her like that. "When do we start?" she asked, trying to share in their intimacy.

"In a couple of months," Elizabeth said. "When we close on buying the paper. October, probably. We start in October."

As Matt's arm tightened around her, she looked around the table at her family. A warm breeze lifted a corner of the tablecloth; the lantern lights flickered. "We're so happy," she said. "We know what we're getting into, and we know that everything is going to be so wonderful, from now on."

"Happily ever after," Holly said in a small voice.

"Yes," Elizabeth said. "I guess it sounds silly, but that's exactly right. The two of us. Happily ever after."

CHAPTER 4

It was the beginning of the best time they had ever known: our golden time, Elizabeth called it, but softly, almost as if she were crossing her fingers, as she had in childhood, wondering how long it could last.

Because it was also a time when they felt as if they had launched a small boat on a stormy sea, one minute riding high and confident, the next plunged into worries about the crazy chances they were taking. They signed large documents filled with small print—each time cutting off a piece of themselves, Elizabeth thought—until it was all done: Lovell Printing sold, their house mortgaged; money borrowed from the bank. The only thing untouched was Zachary's house and land at Nuevo; at the last minute, Matt hadn't been able to bring himself to sell them. Then they signed the last documents, wrote a terrifyingly large check—and the Santa Fe *Chieftain* was theirs.

That night they took the family to see it. With Spencer and Lydia, and Holly and Peter behind them, Matt turned the key in the front door of the *Chieftain* building. But then, while the others went ahead, he and Elizabeth held back, gazing at the dark building that hulked unusually large in the light of the street lamp. Elizabeth shivered slightly in the cool October air, and Matt took her hand. "Forward," he murmured, and they followed the others inside.

A newspaper office is never really silent; even when empty it echoes with the day's frenetic activity: people rummaging through papers, photographs, and books, piling them on desks and the floor, tacking cartoons and notes helter-skelter on walls and partitions, leaving cold coffee in the bottom of Styrofoam cups, typing stories for new editions to join yellowing old ones piled haphazardly in corners and under desks.

As Holly and Peter dashed ahead with Spencer and Lydia following, their footsteps rang on the hard floor, but Elizabeth and Matt heard instead the familiar echoes that made them feel they'd gone back in time: to the university, and the daily campus newspaper; to the *Los Angeles Times* where they'd had summer jobs as intern reporters; to the years when they grabbed every chance to be together—in the classroom, in parks and city streets, in bed—falling in love, planning their future.

"And it's here," Elizabeth whispered in the large room. She gestured toward a glass-walled corner office. "Yours," she said, her voice shaking with the enormity of what they had done. "It's yours, Matt. Publisher and editor-in-chief. Try it out."

Still holding hands, they walked into the office and Matt twirled the high-backed leather chair at the desk. From there he could see the entire newsroom crammed with file cabinets and desks, those in the center for four reporters, two photographers, and two secretaries; others along one wall, separated by low partitions, for the managing editor, features editor, and advertising and circulation managers.

"Our empire," Matt mused.

"We snap our fingers," Elizabeth said whimsically, "and a staff leaps to obey."

"Creating hordes of new readers . . ."

"Luring advertisers . . ."

"Moving mountains at our command . . ."

"Or at least moving the furniture," Elizabeth said as their laughter filled the small office. "Matt, I feel like a little girl with my first real toy."

He kissed the tip of her nose. "I keep wanting to giggle. Except that that's for kids."

"I like feeling like a kid once in a while."

He grinned. "Your father thinks we should be worrying."

They smiled at each other. "I love you," Elizabeth said.

"Now that is the best part of all. How many publishers and features editors are crazy about each other? Which reminds me. We're running this show together, but I have all this grandeur"—he looked at the cramped space and shabby furniture—"and all you have is one of those cubicles out there. We'll build you a real office, next to this one."

Elizabeth shook her head. "I should be with the others. They expect it, and we don't want to make them more suspicious of new owners than they probably are." She took a deep breath. "Matt—I'm beginning to believe it."

He grinned again. "So am I. Elizabeth, my love, this is *ours* and it's going to be all right."

They put their arms around each other, excited, scared, eager, exhilarated. "Free," Matt murmured, his lips against Elizabeth's hair. "Beginning again: my own way, my own dream." He caught himself as he felt the surprised tensing of Elizabeth's body. *"Our* way. We'll do everything we dreamed of. We waited so long, now we'll do it all. My God, we're going to be the greatest Mom and Pop business in America!"

Elizabeth laughed and they kissed, holding each other, their bodies fitting together.

"Excuse *us,*" said Peter, lounging in the doorway. "We thought we were here for a guided tour from the boss. Bosses."

"I didn't want to interrupt you," Holly said. "I thought it was crude."

"So I'm crude." Peter shrugged, attempting nonchalance. "I just thought it'd be sorta nice to see what we bought."

"Yes it would be," said Elizabeth, still in Matt's arms. "I just thought that first it would be sorta nice to kiss your father."

Peter reddened. "Sorry," he mumbled.

"No problem," Matt said casually. "We'll make time for everything. And right now," he added as Lydia and Spencer came up, "the tour is about to begin."

Elizabeth watched Matt lead the others through the long, low building, organizing the tour so that when they reached the back loading ramp, he'd given them a complete explanation of how a newspaper is planned, written, printed, and distributed through the city and nearby towns. But she was only half listening, letting her mind wander. *We'll make time for everything.* Nothing was ordinary anymore; everything was new. She thought about what she would be doing tomorrow and in the days to come. Making assignments instead of having them made for her. Writing the way she wanted instead of the way she was told. Working with Matt. Owning their paper. *Ours.*

The glow began to fade the next morning, when sunlight showed the *Chieftain* to be simply another of Santa Fe's brownish-pink adobe buildings where there was work to be done, and Elizabeth and Matt tried to build up courage for their first meeting with the staff.

"Friday morning," Matt said. "Next issue of the paper due out next Thursday. All we have to do is get to know a bunch of people who have their own ways of doing things, convince them we're not going to change everything at once, make them feel needed, and at the same time sell ourselves as new owners who deserve respect and loyalty because we know what we're doing . . ."

"Nothing to it," Elizabeth smiled. "Just be our usual charming selves." She picked up an envelope on Matt's desk. "Someone's already writing us letters."

"Maybe they have a welcome wagon." Matt saw her face change as she read. "What is it?"

"Ned Engle. He's quit. As of today."

"Quit—?"

Matt skimmed the letter, his face darkening. "The son of a bitch. He gave me his word he'd stay on as managing editor. At least six months, he said; that lying son of a bitch—"

"Matt, he knew this paper inside out; what are we going to do without him?"

Matt paced the small office. "Bastard. Didn't even wait to

see how we run the place—*if* we run it. Six days to get the paper out. You'd think he wants us to fall on our face . . ."

"Of course he does!" Elizabeth exclaimed. "That's exactly what he wants! He's waiting for us to call and beg him to come back."

Matt stopped pacing. "Right. And he can wait until he grows roots. We're not going to be at the mercy of any son of a bitch who thinks he holds all the cards."

Elizabeth's throat was dry. Her father had warned them, but they'd brushed it aside, so sure Engle would be there, his competence making their inexperience less obvious, giving them time to learn and take charge. "The reporters," she said, casting about. "They know the paper. Couldn't one of them take over, just for a while?"

"I am not going to start out the first day by asking reporters to run our paper for us. God damn it!" Matt kicked his chair, making it spin a full revolution. "That bastard managed the whole operation; obviously he wasn't the greatest, since the paper was going downhill, but he did run it." And we've never run a newspaper, he thought. Not off the protected turf of a university.

Elizabeth lined up a row of pencils on Matt's desk, very carefully, very neatly, trying to keep down the fear spreading through her. "What do you think we should do?"

He shrugged and began pacing again. In a minute he stopped beside her where she perched on the corner of his desk. "Hold on," he said, and took her face between his hands. "This is both of us, remember? The whiz kids who are going to do everything together. So let me ask you: can two smart, talented, mature, ambitious people replace one crude, thoughtless, probably inept bastard?"

Elizabeth gave a small laugh and she brought Matt's face to hers and kissed him. "If you're willing to be half a managing editor, I'm willing to be the other half."

"Top or bottom?" he grinned, sitting beside her.

"Anything you say." She became thoughtful. "But if I'm features editor and half a managing editor—"

"Not much time for eating and sleeping. About the same as my being the other half, plus editor-in-chief."

"And publisher," Elizabeth added. "But I was thinking about my column. I was going to start it in a couple of weeks."

There was a pause. "It's going to have to wait," Matt said.

She was silent. It had waited sixteen years. "Not for long," he went on, with more assurance than he felt. "As soon as we know what we're doing around here, we'll hire a new managing editor. I'll tell you what," he went on when she still said nothing. "We'll set a deadline. Two months. You'll be writing your column in two months, if I have to raid the New York and Chicago newspapers to find someone."

Elizabeth smiled faintly. "More likely the University of New Mexico Journalism School; that's all we can afford. It's all right, Matt, I can wait." Through the glass wall, they saw the staff coming in, moving restlessly about the large room, making coffee, perching on the edges of chairs, glancing covertly or openly at Matthew and Elizabeth Lovell: their new bosses.

"They're nervous," Elizabeth said. "I wonder if they know we are too."

Matt stood. "As long as we're calm, confident, knowledge-able, and in control, everything will be fine."

She laughed. "You take control; I'll sit back and admire you. I think that's what they expect of a woman. Forward," she added, echoing Matt from the night before, and they went out to greet their staff.

Since the *Chieftain* had been sold, its fifteen staff members had been speculating about Matt, whom none of them knew, and Elizabeth, whose byline they'd seen for years in their rival newspaper. "And she's good," they said. "Good writer. But what she's like to work for . . . and what *he's* like . . . what the hell does a *printer* know about running a newspaper?"

The previous management had been a disaster, but that didn't mean they were ready to welcome new owners with open arms, and when they took a look at the young couple walking out of Matt's office, the older ones looked at each other and shook their heads. She was a stunner; nobody that gorgeous was serious about hard work. And he had a long stride and confident

60

air that meant he probably was stubborn. So they were cool and watchful when Matt introduced himself and Elizabeth, and they listened in silence as he described their backgrounds and their determination to make the *Chieftain* as big as its rival, the *Examiner,* and then bigger.

"I want to hear your problems and suggestions," he said. "But first you ought to know that Ned Engle has resigned as managing editor" —he waited for the flurry of comments to die down—"and until we hire a new one, Elizabeth and I will handle that job."

"*Handle* it?" asked Herb Kirkpatrick, gray-bearded with fierce eyebrows to match. "When you've never worked on a real paper before? Do you have a step-by-step manual?"

"Shut up, Herb." The lines in Barney Kell's face deepened in a scowl. "It isn't their fault; they didn't fire him. Did you?" he asked Matt, suddenly anxious.

"No. We asked him to stay. He said he would. And then quit. By letter."

"Son of a bitch," Barney said sourly. "Leaving you in the lurch. So how *will* you do his job?"

"We'll write a manual," Matt said shortly.

"We'll ask your help," Elizabeth cut in quietly. "All of you. You know the paper; we don't. But you'll be surprised at how fast we learn."

"Bravo," said Wally McLain under his breath.

Matt, cooler now, ignored Kirkpatrick's disdainful look and asked the rest of them for their comments. And as if floodgates had been opened, complaints poured out: major ones, minor ones, gripes they'd been making for years and new ones they thought of as they went along: wages, hours, vacation time, medical benefits, the lousy coffee machine, the obsolete darkroom enlarger, the former owner's crackpot decision not to buy computers.

"The computers are being ordered," said Matt, who had been taking notes. He looked up to see smiles on the faces before him.

"Well done," murmured Barney. In forty years he'd seen five different owners tackle the *Chieftain,* none of them off to

61

this fast a start. "Maybe this old dog can learn some new tricks with it."

"We'll all be learning new tricks," said Matt, grateful for some support. "Anything else?"

"More sensation," said Cal Artner, long-chinned and narrow-nosed, his black eyes magnified by thick glasses. "Only way to sell papers. Dig up lots of dirt, sex, secrets—"

"No!" burst out Wally McLain, young and handsome in the starched shirt his girlfriend had ironed for his first meeting with his paper's new owners. "Serious investigations. People in this town don't always get along, but if you read the *Chieftain* you think we're paradise. We should write about problems between Anglos and Spanish, and how we're getting ripped off by developers who build for the rich, ignoring local people who can't afford—"

"We're not here to knock Santa Fe," Herb Kirkpatrick interrupted. "How many tourists would we have if word got around that the town is full of troubles?"

"I didn't say troubles; I said problems."

"Just as bad."

"Bullshit."

Mildly, Matt said, "I've always liked investigative journalism; we'll do a lot of it. Not to tear Santa Fe down," he added to Kirkpatrick. "To make it better. And to increase circulation. People like to know somebody's peering behind doors and over politicians' shoulders, reporting what's really going on in their town." He paused. "Other comments before I make mine?"

"Increase circulation how much?" asked Barney Kell.

"Double it within a year," Matt said calmly.

They stared at him. Elizabeth's pencil skidded on her notepad, though she kept her face still so no one would see her surprise. Matt had never told her that; they'd always talked about struggling to keep circulation at its current ten thousand, since it had been going down for the past two years.

"Double it," mused Barney, his seamed face showing more approval by the minute. "How would you do that?"

Matt started talking, going through the plans he and Elizabeth had worked on together. They would change the layout of the

62

pages: wider columns, larger, easier-to-read type, more pictures, bolder headlines. They would increase investigative stories, buy a food section from a newspaper in Denver, a fashion section from a paper in Los Angeles, and run a new column by Elizabeth Lovell, "Private Affairs," about people in the area. They'd cut expenses to the bone, which meant no new equipment except for the computers already ordered. When circulation began to go up, they'd look at equipment, salaries, hours, benefits, and vacation time. "Until circulation shows a steady climb, you can expect to work longer and harder than ever before," he said flatly. "Elizabeth and I want your suggestions and criticism, but we make the rules and that's the first one: if you turn out a paper so good another ten thousand people want to buy it, we'll all get rewarded. Otherwise, we won't."

"But the enlarger . . ." began the photographer, Bill Dunphy.

"I'll take a look at it. That may be an exception."

"And the coffeemaker," said Herb Kirkpatrick. "Coffee is essential to my health and productivity. Without coffee I am weak in the morning, helpless by noon, and barely conscious by three o'clock."

Amid the friendly laughter, Matt began to relax. Kirkpatrick, the potential troublemaker, had chosen humor over confrontation. A good beginning, he reflected as he gave Kirkpatrick the job of pricing coffeemakers, but he still had to face Elizabeth.

"You've been thinking about speeding up our plans for a long time," she said when they were back in his office. She sat on the edge of a chair beside his desk. "You didn't get that idea on the spur of the moment. But you never mentioned it."

"You'd have said I was being unrealistic."

"Aren't you?"

"I don't know, and neither do you. What can that crew turn out if they're really pushed? What will readers buy? We don't know. I'm guessing." His stubborn jaw reminded Elizabeth of Zachary—obstinate but anxious for approval. "We won't get anywhere if you're too timid—"

"Just a minute." She was tense from the meeting—after all,

63

she'd let him do all the talking, to make those men more comfortable; she hadn't challenged him in front of them; and now he accused her of timidity! Feeling her anger build, she lowered her voice. "We came out on this limb together, we worked out a schedule together, and I don't expect you to accuse me of being timid if I want to stick to it."

"I'm sorry; I didn't mean that." Matt leaned forward. "I know we had a schedule, Elizabeth, but it's too slow! You heard them: they're still not convinced we know what we're doing. But if we can get them excited, shake them up, give them a goal they think has a chance, even if it sounds crazy, don't you think we could speed everything up? Didn't you feel it? It went so much better than I'd hoped—you haven't said a word about how well it went—"

"I meant to. I was going to tell you you're wonderful, but then I was thinking about—"

"You should never think about anything else when you're about to tell your husband he's wonderful."

She smiled. "Probably not."

"I love you," Matt said. "And I know you're not timid." Through the glass wall, he saw Cal Artner hesitate before knocking. "I want to kiss you but I think we'd better wait." He motioned Artner in.

"I've got a terrific idea," Artner said to Matt. "Been working on it for a long time, waiting for somebody who'll go all out to get more readers. There's a Feast Day Dance coming up at Nambé Pueblo—you may not know about it . . ."

Amused, Matt said, "We go to it every year."

"Oh. Do you. Well then, you probably know they don't like to have the dance photographed—"

"Don't like?" said Elizabeth. "They don't allow it. They don't even allow anyone to make sketches."

Artner glanced at her, then spoke to Matt. "A friend of mine has a helicopter and he can fly me in low enough to get some shots. It's dynamite; nobody's ever done it and those ceremonies are a big mystery to people who've never gone out to the pueblos. We'd blow the mystery wide open; the tourists would eat it up. And we could sell the pictures to other papers

64

around the country . . . shit, it can't miss; we'd put the *Chieftain* on the map."

"Cal, don't you understand?" Elizabeth said. *"It's not allowed."*

"Look," Artner said with exaggerated patience, "I'm making a suggestion to Matt."

A heavy silence fell. Looking at Matt's face, Artner got the clear message that he'd made a mistake. "To both of you," he backtracked hastily. "It's just that I'd like to be taken seriously."

"We do take you seriously; that's what bothers us," Matt said evenly. "It's the Nambés' reservation, it's their pueblo, it's their ceremony. And they say photos aren't allowed."

"I know what they say! But they couldn't stop a helicopter; you don't suppose they'd shoot us down, do you? Are you saying you don't want these photos?"

"I'm saying we are not going to be known as a newspaper that violates the holiness of Indian religious ceremonies or flouts pueblo laws. Which means you aren't going to photograph them."

"Of all the sanctimonious shit—! You don't know a fucking thing about the newspaper business! I've been in it for twenty years and I know a scoop when I see one; Christ, we could beat the shit out of the *Examiner*—isn't that what we're in business for?"

"We're in the business of running a paper," Matt said tightly. "And you work for us. You'll accept that or you'll get the hell out."

"I don't take that," Artner began, but his words had lost their steam; he was trying to figure Matt out.

Elizabeth stood up beside Matt. It had suddenly occurred to her that Artner might quit and they'd have two people to replace instead of one. "Our son Peter has friends in the pueblos, Cal. We know how they feel; if we publish photographs of them, they might close the ceremonies to visitors."

"They can't afford it. They need the money."

"They need their religion, too."

Again Artner spoke to Matt. "I thought you'd understand how important this is to us."

65

"*We* understand it's important to you," Matt snapped. "But *we* have already told you we won't be a party to it."

"You mean it? You won't okay it?"

"We won't okay it. Photos are out. You're a writer; do a story on the dance with good writing and plenty of adjectives and adverbs. The tools of a good reporter."

"Someone said a picture is worth a thousand words."

"Sometimes it's true. If you can get the picture. We can't." Matt took a deep breath. "Look, Cal, I appreciate the thought you've put into this, but this is final. No pictures. Save the helicopter, though; we'll find a use for it. And thanks for coming in; I look forward to reading your story."

"Well done," Elizabeth said quietly when they were alone.

"You mean I mostly kept my temper. Aside from his half-assed idea, why couldn't the son of a bitch talk to both of us?"

"I don't suppose he's the only man who doesn't like working for a woman," Elizabeth said dryly. "Maybe he'll get used to it."

"He's going to be trouble."

"Yes, but we'll handle him. I don't think he'll endanger his job." She gathered up a stack of papers. "Do you need me for anything else? I have work to do if I'm going to leave at six."

"I thought we were setting an example by working late."

"You can do that. I have to make dinner for my family."

"Maybe that's why there are no women on the staff."

"There is one now," Elizabeth said serenely. "And if she doesn't finish her work by six, she'll take it home with her. See you later, my love."

And as she closed the glass door behind her, they both felt the same glow of pleasure and fulfillment: that after years of drifting apart, they were together again in every way—working, sharing, and loving, without a wrinkle in their harmony.

In the next two weeks a secretary was out with the flu; a sudden rainstorm revealed a dozen leaks in the roof; the production manager pasted the last half of a story on page one and the first half on page twenty, so the two pages had to be redone at the last minute; and when a *Chieftain* delivery truck broke down in the middle of the Paseo de Peralta, the repairman said it was in such bad shape the only sensible thing to do was buy another one.

Holding the telephone, Matt stared unseeing through the glass wall before him. Elizabeth, looking up from her typewriter, smiled at him, then her smile faded and she came to his office. When she closed the door behind her, he told her what had happened. "So we have to buy a truck, and even a used one will run us about five thousand dollars, which we don't have."

"And we have to patch the roof," Elizabeth said. "We really ought to redo the whole thing. We didn't check it, or the trucks—"

"We were in too much of a hurry. A couple of innocents, buying a new toy."

Elizabeth heard his anger—at himself, no one else. "Well, we're stuck with it now," she said, purposely casual. "I think it's time to take up my father's offer of help, don't you?"

"Take money from Spencer and Lydia? No."

"Not take, Matt. Borrow. They know we'll pay them back. With interest."

Matt wrote $5000 on a scrap of paper. *We'll owe everybody in town,* Peter had said. And it was true; they were at the limit of their credit; there was no one else but Elizabeth's parents. "I'll call them," he said at last. "Your father will tell me I should have listened to him in the first place."

"He likes being right," Elizabeth said.

Matt glanced up and saw the small frown between her eyes. For the first time since she came into his office, he really looked at her. Had she lost weight? She seemed thin and pale, though it could have been the simple, almost severe, black suit she wore, or the way she'd pulled her hair back, holding it with two silver and turquoise combs—but Matt wasn't sure. They'd been working so hard, at the office and at home, eating erratically, sleeping restlessly, with no time for relaxation, no social life, barely a chance to spend an hour or two with Peter and Holly—probably both of them looked worn down.

"But he wasn't right," Elizabeth said suddenly. "We did

67

exactly what we should have done and I love doing it. I love working with you, even in a place that sounds like an African jungle with the drumbeat of water dripping into buckets . . ."

He laughed. "That's what *I* love; having a wife who can joke in a downpour and look beautiful talking about trucks."

"If you keep that up I'll kiss you," Elizabeth said. "And Cal will photograph us from a helicopter and put it on the front page."

They smiled at each other. "You are very special," Matt said. "Thank you. It's the first time all day I've felt good about the world."

Elizabeth went to the coffee pot in the corner of the office and filled two Styrofoam cups. She sniffed the coffee. "How long has this been sitting here?"

"About four hours, I suppose. I've been too busy to notice."

"I'll make some fresh." She left and brought back a pitcher of water she had filled at the water fountain. "Matt, can we talk about some other things? I've put together samples of special pull-out sections for you to look at; we should start them as soon as possible. And we have to do something about our political coverage—Herb Kirkpatrick needs more direction; he isn't as good as he thinks he is—and there's my column; I'd like to—"

"This isn't the time to discuss it," Matt said absently.

She turned, the coffee pot in her hand. "Why not?"

"We've just added another debt to our little empire; is that a time to talk about expanding? Just staying alive is more important than new projects and your col—" He caught himself. "Hell, I'm sorry, sweetheart. I know how important that column is to you. But I'm trying to keep a newspaper together."

"*You're* trying? What am I doing?"

"Talking about spending money. I'm not criticizing you, but one of us has to think about the future—"

"And that's you, is that right?" Elizabeth's voice was cool. "What about my ideas to make the paper more exciting to attract new readers and advertisers—"

"Your ideas cost money."

68

"Of course they do. But you were the one who wanted to double circulation in less than a year—"

"Damn it, don't throw that back at me now! I'm out one truck, I need a new roof on this place—"

"You're out one truck? *You* need a new roof?"

"We. We need a new roof. You know that's what I meant."

Elizabeth was silent. A few minutes earlier they were luxuriating in being together. But there was another side to that. *Maybe we're together too much; working, eating, living together . . . maybe we're getting on each other's nerves.*

"Just let me take care of the truck," said Matt. "And the roof. And I have to balance the books for the month, and the IRS quarterly reports—someday we'll be able to afford a business manager—and I promised Dunphy I'd look at that enlarger . . . then we'll talk about your column. And any other problems you have."

"I don't have any other problems I can't handle," Elizabeth said, almost distantly. "That is, if I get to work on them. I'll be at my desk if you need me."

They stayed apart for the rest of the day. Matt called Spencer and that afternoon, together, they picked out a used truck. Spencer waved aside Matt's typewritten IOU. "Personal loan, Matt. Of course if you'd listened to me in the first place . . . well damn it, there I go! Promised Lydia I wouldn't bring it up. You'll keep it to yourself, right? And don't be in a hurry to pay this back; we think the two of you are a good bet."

A good bet, Matt thought later that afternoon when his secretary had arranged for a roof repairman and he finally was able to tackle the pile of stories on his desk. Elizabeth had edited most of them and before he turned to the rest he scanned hers, reading her penciled changes. Incredible how good she was—too good to be editing others; she ought to be doing her own writing. *Writing,* he thought. We were going to talk about her column.

But as he was getting up from his desk Herb Kirkpatrick stormed in. Elizabeth had assigned him the story on the Taos crafts show because Artner wasn't around, but why the hell should he do it? He had his own story to write on a political race for sheriff in——

"Hold on," Matt said. He didn't want to argue with Kirkpatrick; he wanted to smooth things over with his wife. And why the hell was this dumped on his desk anyway? "Herb, Elizabeth and I are sharing the job of managing editor, and she's also features editor. If she gives you an assignment, you damn well do it."

"I'm a political expert," Kirkpatrick declared. "I don't give a shit about arts and crafts."

"So we'll turn to you only in an emergency." When Kirkpatrick started to object again, Matt stood up. "Herb, it's an assignment. You're a reporter. Write the story." Their eyes met; Kirkpatrick was the one to look away. "By the way," Matt added, "did Cal tell anyone he was taking the afternoon off?"

"No," Kirkpatrick said shortly, and turned on his heel and left.

By eight o'clock, Matt was able to leave the office. Elizabeth had left at seven, and when he got home he found her eating dinner with Holly and Peter. "Can a partner apologize?" he asked. "Can a husband join his family for dinner?"

"Yes to both," Elizabeth said, smiling, and they kissed briefly before he sat down. But the air about them was still tense and there was no time to make everything right: they spent the evening talking about the day's crises and the schedule for the next day and when they got to work in the morning they worked separately on last-minute stories and changes that had to go to Axel Chase before four-thirty, when he printed the paper. Only when the finished papers were bundled and tied and being trucked to hundreds of points in Santa Fe and surrounding towns did they finally sit together in Matt's office, drinking coffee, with a newly printed, unopened newspaper in front of each of them.

Matt held out his hand and Elizabeth put hers in it. "Crazy week," he sighed. "But you've been wonderful. You're the best editor, the best partner, anyone could dream of. I'm sorry for my bad tempers; you have a lot to put up with."

70

"Love conquers tempers," Elizabeth said lightly. "I think we're pretty good together."

"I think so too. Now let's talk about your column."

"As soon as we unwind." Sipping her coffee, Elizabeth opened the newspaper in front of her. Her face froze. "Matt."

"What?" Following her gaze, he saw the paper, upside down, and flung open his own. Together they stared at the pictures across the bottom of the front page: two large photographs looking down on Indian dancers, with the headline: EXCLUSIVE INSIDE LOOK AT A SACRED DANCE, and the story beneath them, datelined Nambé Pueblo, written by Cal Artner.

Elizabeth had never seen Matt so enraged. Her own anger was a hard knot inside her, tempered by the need to be a sounding board for Matt. At first he'd been ready to fire everyone on the paper; later, when he was cooling, the Nambés' lawyer had called them at home, threatening to sue the paper, and that set him off again. Elizabeth wanted to smash something, shout at someone, vent her own frustration over the sidetracking of their plans, but she couldn't do any of those wonderfully violent things: she had to make coffee, sit at the kitchen table, and talk calmly to Matt. "We have to fire Cal."

Matt nodded, his mood swinging from rage to suspicion. "No question about it; Cal goes. But who else goes too? Someone did a new paste-up after you'd approved the front page, and sent it to the pressroom, and Axel Chase made a new plate from it . . . Of course if you'd followed through—"

"What was that?" Elizabeth sat straight in her chair. "Am I one of those you're going to fire?"

"I said you didn't follow through. Did you?"

"I checked and initialed each page and when the plates were made I checked and initialed them. When the paper went to press, I assumed—"

"Incorrectly."

She took a long breath. "What about Matthew Lovell, editor-in-chief? Why didn't he follow through and check each page of the paper as it came out of the pressroom?"

"That's the managing editor's job."

71

"Which we supposedly share. I did my half. Are you saying I should do it all so you have someone to blame if we're sued?"

"It's not a question of blame; it's whether we're behaving like professionals or amateurs."

"We're learning to be professionals. And *we* made a mistake. We knew Cal was going to be trouble. I suppose when he didn't show up yesterday we should have paid more attention—"

"He works for you. Did you try to find him?"

"He works for us. And, no, I didn't. I was very busy yesterday, putting a newspaper together, and I had to spend time on an idiotic argument with Herb Kirkpatrick over whether a woman has the right to assign him to a story he doesn't want to do."

"I backed you up on that."

"Did you? Did you tell him I was the features editor and he was to follow my orders?"

"Yes."

"Or did you—" Elizabeth stopped short. "You did?"

"In almost those words."

She frowned. "That isn't what he said."

"What did he say?"

"That you told him no one else could take on an assignment at the last minute, and you promised him twice the space next week for his sheriff story."

Matt began to laugh. "The self-serving son of a bitch! I told him one thing: that he was a reporter and he'd been assigned a story and he'd damn well better write it."

After a moment, Elizabeth sat back in her chair. "I wish you'd told me yesterday."

"I had other things on my mind. You're taking things too seriously, my love."

"Am I? How would you describe a man who talks as if he might fire his wife who is also his partner?"

Matt cleared his throat. "I'd say he's lost his mind. In the first place, I couldn't fire you; you own half the joint. In the second place—my God, Elizabeth, I couldn't run this place without you. I need your steady hand . . . a partner to talk to . . ." He frowned. "Which brings me back to the angry Nambés. What the hell are we going to do about them?"

"Apologize in print."

"They want more."

"Then we'll have to give it to them. We can't win this one, Matt; we're so clearly in the wrong."

"It's too bad you aren't writing your column yet: you could do a spectacular profile of one of their top people and that plus a front-page apology might make them feel so kindly they'd call off their lawyer. We can't afford a court case: we don't have the money and we need good publicity, not bad."

Elizabeth ran her finger around the edge of her coffee cup. "Who says I'm not writing my column?"

"You did. You said you were waiting to talk about it."

"But I could be writing it now. That's why I brought it up the other day. When we vetoed Cal's helicopter idea, I thought the next best thing would be a portrait of a Nambé leader."

"That's what you wanted to talk about? I thought you were just impatient even though you'd agreed to wait two months—"

"We weren't communicating very well," Elizabeth said quietly.

"No." Matt scowled at his coffee cup. "We're quarreling too much. This was supposed to be such a wonderful time . . . why do you suppose it isn't?"

"Isn't it?"

"Not all the time. Not often enough."

We're together too much. "Maybe because we don't have any place to escape. Other people get away from the office by going home, or they get away from home by going to the office, but we can't do that. We just dump all our problems on each other."

"I'm the one who does most of the dumping," Matt said. "You deserve better."

"A better partner? But I love the one I've got."

"Amazing. So do I." He stood, bringing her with him. "I'm sorry for hurting you, I'm sorry I make your life harder—"

"You make my life wonderful."

73

"Not always, and I know it; things pile up and I lose sight of what's most important . . . but it's always you, my love, even if sometimes it doesn't seem that way." Their lips touched, lightly, then with growing intensity. "Bed," Matt murmured. "There isn't much of the night left."

"A good idea. Would you turn out the lights?" And as he nodded, she slipped away.

Her muscles ached with fatigue, but the warmth of their talk still flowed through her. In bed, she stretched out, eyes closed, listening to Matt move about the room, opening windows, winding his watch, undressing. He slid beneath the covers. "You're not asleep," he said. "Your mind is spinning."

Eyes still closed, she asked, "How do you know?"

"Eyelids flickering, beautiful mouth smiling, nose twitching."

Her eyes flew open. "My nose does not twitch."

He kissed the tip of it. "I know. I wanted to see if you were listening."

"I always listen when my husband is about to make love to me."

"How do you know he is?"

"He kept the light on."

Matt chuckled. "No mysteries anymore. You're not tired?"

"I'm always tired these days. I'm ignoring it. What about you?"

"Tired and ignoring it. I wish we could get away for a while, just the two of us."

"We will. When things quiet down, and we find a managing editor, and my column is started, and we have money for vaca—"

"Stop. I'm sorry I brought it up." Raising himself on his elbow, Matt pulled back the covers and looked at his wife's slender body, her delicate bones barely outlined in the muted light of the bed lamp. In the midst of the hectic days of buying the *Chieftain*, they'd both celebrated their fortieth birthdays, but Elizabeth was as slim as a girl, firm and lithe from tennis and skiing—though who had time for sports anymore? Matt thought wryly—her loveliness stronger, more individual than

74

the softer beauty of the girl he married. Extraordinary woman, he said to himself, and leaned down to kiss her breasts, smiling as the nipples puckered beneath his tongue. "Not too tired at all," he murmured.

"What do you think my mind was spinning about?" Elizabeth retorted, and then she closed her eyes again and let herself sink into the sensations of his mouth and hand tracing the curves of her body and the feel of him beneath her own hand as she slid it slowly down the length of his back and around his narrow hips. And as their bodies came together, so familiar but somehow so new, Matt kissed Elizabeth and said, as if for the first time, "I love you."

At seven-thirty the next morning they were at the newspaper, waiting for the staff. In his office Matt plucked dead leaves off a sad ficus tree left by the previous publisher. "Do you remember what time the Nambés' lawyer said he'd call?"

"About eleven. I'll talk to him if you want, and tell him about my column: he may suggest someone for me to interview."

"I think we both should talk to him, but you can go first."

"And you'll take care of firing Cal?"

He chuckled. "Since we're learning how to be partners, we should do it together. There he is."

Artner was talking nonstop to Barney Kell as he walked in, looking everywhere but at Matt and Elizabeth. Barney's face was heavy, and when Herb Kirkpatrick came in, Barney and Wally joined him at the coffeemaker, leaving Artner alone. The pressman, Axel Chase, walked in, followed by the advertising manager, the production manager, and the two photographers. No one went near Artner, who stood at his desk, rolling a pencil between his palms.

Matt went to the door. "Come on in, Cal," he said, his voice carrying through the newsroom. But they all came in and stood in what looked like a protective semicircle behind Artner.

Matt's shoulders stiffened. As he stood, with Elizabeth beside him, the room was divided into two groups facing each other across his desk. Matt gazed at the uninvited staff, thinking of asking them to leave. Then, mentally, he shrugged. What the hell; it was a small paper; they were all involved. "Since this has become a staff meeting," he said evenly, "we'll discuss the first item now, then continue with the regular Friday meeting in the newsroom, where there are chairs for everyone."

No one spoke. "Cal, I assume you know you're fired. I'm damned if I can figure out why you pulled that half-assed trick after I'd expressly forbidden it, and I'm sorry, because you're a good reporter, but you can't work for me—for us—and do your own thing as if we don't exist. This staff takes orders or it doesn't work here. Clean out your desk; I want you gone by ten."

"Matt." Barney Kell looked like a worried father. "Would you take a few minutes to think this over? We don't want—"

"I've thought it over," Matt said curtly. "Elizabeth and I have talked about nothing else since we saw yesterday's paper."

"God damn it," Herb Kirkpatrick sputtered, "can't you see that we're standing with Cal? We won't allow an arbitrary firing—"

"Not that way," Barney warned Kirkpatrick. "Matt, of course Cal shouldn't have done it; he knows it and he's ready to apologize and promise it won't happen again. But we don't want anyone fired."

"It worries us," added Bill Dunphy earnestly. "If you fire one of us, who's safe? We work better, you know, when we feel secure."

Axel Chase chimed in, "Everybody should get a second chance, right? Shouldn't penalize somebody for one slip—"

"It was more than a slip," Barney objected.

"Whatever," Kirkpatrick said. He challenged Matt. "We all go if Cal goes."

"I don't . . . " Barney began, but then he stopped, uncomfortable, but standing with the others. Artner gave Matt a triumphant look and Elizabeth saw Matt's rigid back begin to give way: not a slump, but close. She put her hand on his arm, noticing that her fingers were trembling—*Well why not? We could lose everything*—and said to him, as if they were alone,

76

"We're going to be busy, putting out the *Chieftain* by ourselves until we hire a new staff."

Artner's eyes slid from Matt's face to hers. She looked at him contemptuously. "You disobey an order, you violate a sacred ceremony, and then you encourage others to destroy a newspaper. You get a tin star, Cal. I hope it makes you feel proud and grown up."

"Good job," said Wally McLain under his breath.

"Bullshit," Artner spat. "You couldn't turn out a one-page flyer without us. Who's kept this rag going all these weeks while you two've been playing editor?"

"Cal, stop it," Barney ordered.

"Good advice," said Elizabeth. "Don't you talk to us like—"

"Fuck it, lady, you fired me, right? I'll talk any way I goddam please. You two babes in the woods had a chance to make this the best paper in New Mexico and you blew it. If you'd made me managing editor when Engle left, this place would be running like a fucking steam engine. That was *my* job! I waited five years for it and then those bastards sold out to a couple of spoiled, rich ignoramuses—married, for Christ's sake! Lovey-dovey, necking in the office, taking the whole show for themselves—and when they get bored, bring in somebody from the outside. Right? Not somebody who's waited five fucking years—"

"*Shut up,* Cal." Kirkpatrick looked at Elizabeth. "He's saying we don't like the idea of outsiders taking jobs we've worked up to."

"I heard him," Elizabeth replied curtly. "The paper was dying; we decided it needs a managing editor who has nothing vested in the past, who can change *everything* if necessary." Matt was watching her and she took a deep breath. "We're not rich, we're not taking the whole show. We've dreamed of owning a newspaper for a long time and we're trying to build this one up without much money or experience—you're right; we have a lot to learn; we told you that when we first got here. But we're not ignorant or stupid; we know what we want to do and we're pretty sure how we're going to do it. *And nobody here*

77

is going to stop us or destroy what we've started." Her breath came faster. "Every one of you can walk out of here this minute, but it won't shut us down. We'll put out a two-page newsletter if that's all we can manage—it doesn't matter as long as it's called the *Chieftain*—and we'll keep publishing every week until we hire another staff and go back to full size, because you may be willing to let this paper die, but we're not."

"Terrific!" exclaimed Wally. "By God—!"

"Terrific?" echoed Kirkpatrick sarcastically. "For firing the entire staff of a newspaper?"

"We're not firing anyone but Cal," said Elizabeth. "If the rest of you leave, you'll do it on your own. And the two of us will—"

"Three!" Wally burst out. "I'm staying!"

Behind the desk, Matt's hand found Elizabeth's and they stood close together, their hands gripped for support. He smiled at her, then turned to Wally. "We're glad to have you with us. The rest of you have until ten to clear out."

"Matt, don't be a fool!" Barney growled.

"The fools are the ones who quit because of Cal." Matt scanned their faces. "You don't like worrying about the future? I don't either. We put everything we have into this paper—we sold a good company and mortgaged our house, we're in debt up to our ears, and we work twenty hours a day to keep from going under. But *you* don't like worrying about the future. Well there's a way to take care of that. You can work your asses off *the way we do*, and protect your jobs by making the paper a success. If you can't handle that, we don't want you." He looked at his watch. "It's close to ten. Get going. Elizabeth and Wally and I have work to do."

No one moved. Bill Dunphy cleared his throat. "If you don't mind, I'd like to stay. Even a newsletter needs photos."

Matt nodded. "Who shot the photo of the Nambé dance?"

"I don't know, Matt. Nobody told me about it."

"Okay, I'll believe that. I'm glad you're staying."

"Well." Barney shuffled his feet. "I don't want to leave, either. Where would I go, at my age? Anyway, I like your style, Matt. You and Elizabeth. The thing was—you know—

solidarity. But of course on any paper someone has to be in charge . . ."

"You shit," muttered Artner.

Barney's shuffling had carried him across the office. "I'd like to stay, if you'll have me."

"That would please us," Matt said quietly.

"Mmmm," Kirkpatrick hummed awkwardly. "Perhaps I'll—"

"Herb, God damn it!" Artner burst out.

"You'll need top political coverage," Kirkpatrick went on. "I wouldn't deny you my skills, since you do need them."

Matt and Elizabeth kept straight faces, squeezing each other's hands. "Good of you," Matt said.

One by one the others followed. Only Axel Chase was silent. His agonized face told Elizabeth he'd been in on it; as pressman, he'd be the likely one to help Cal paste up the new page. But they had no proof, and they needed him.

But Chase didn't wait to be fired. "I'm with Cal," he said defiantly. "You can print your paper without me. I don't like people kicked out after years of service—"

"Save your breath," Artner snorted. He looked at Matt. "You fucking bastard, I'll get you some day." Matt returned his look in silence. "I don't forget what people do to me," Artner flung at him, then strode from the office. Chase followed, disappearing into the pressroom. The others, shocked by Artner's venom, watched him yank open his desk drawers and throw into a carton papers, pencils, photographs, a coffee mug, a battered pair of shoes—until Elizabeth, feeling she was prying, turned away. "We should have our staff meeting now," she said to Matt. "If everyone can find a place to perch . . ."

They found places on the frayed couch and leather chair, the two folding chairs, and the deep window ledges in the adobe walls. From a corner of Matt's desk, Elizabeth looked about. They were terribly short-handed; no managing editor, no pressman, only three reporters. But at the moment, none of it mattered. Because, she thought, for the first time this newspaper is truly ours.

* * *

Their long days became longer. Peter and Holly divided their time between their grandparents' home and their own, while their parents were at the newspaper office until midnight or later, doing their own jobs, sharing the managing editor's job, filling in for Artner's reporting and Chase's management of the pressroom: Elizabeth helping with production and Matt printing the paper.

"Thought I'd gotten out of this business," he said ruefully to Elizabeth the first Thursday after Chase's departure. His hands and shirt were smeared with ink, his eyes, like hers, were red-rimmed from exhaustion, and the paper was two hours late, keeping the drivers waiting impatiently in their delivery trucks at the loading dock in back. "At least I know how to do it. I guess I should be grateful. This is one time Dad would be proud of me."

"He'd be proud of you for everything you're doing," Elizabeth said. "And so is everyone else. Look at them."

He did, and saw what she meant. The newsroom looked as if someone had speeded up a film, with everyone trying to do everything at once. By plunging in themselves, instead of waiting for others to do it, Elizabeth and Matt had galvanized the staff. Elizabeth had left her features desk to stand for hours at a counter pasting up the paper, learning as she went along how to visualize a full page before she began to paste stories, headlines, and photographs, and at the same time plan ahead to the inside pages where the stories would be continued and had to fit neatly together with more headlines, more photographs, and display advertisements. Matt had left his glass office to run the press, even making mechanical repairs that were second nature to him, after sixteen years with the Lovell Printing Company, but unfathomable to the rest of the staff.

And from the receptionist to Herb Kirkpatrick, they were won over by their new bosses; with no more reservations, they drew together, cooperated more generously, became a community.

"Axel did it, bless his heart," said Matt after the first wild week. "We're almost a family."

"You did it," Elizabeth said, but Matt countered, "No, you

did," and it became a private joke. And even when they hired a new pressman and Matt went back to his office and Elizabeth to her desk, no one forgot the picture they had made: Matt Lovell, their ink-covered editor-in-chief, and Elizabeth Lovell, features editor, standing at a counter, pasting up stories while the rest of them went home.

"They came through," they all said whenever anyone brought it up. "They did fine. They really came through. Like pros."

The Nambés and their lawyer had consulted and found acceptable the Lovells' offer of a front-page apology plus a story by Elizabeth on one of their leaders. In fact, they found the idea fascinating and it took only half a day of discussion to withdraw the threat of a court case and arrange an interview with Edward Ortega, whose Indian name was Soe Khuwa Pin, "Fog Mountain."

Ortega was a friend of Peter's—one of the Indians who drove him to and from the pueblos after school and on weekends when they had business in Santa Fe—and so Peter went along when Elizabeth interviewed him in his home. He listened, squirming, as his mother probed and persisted in her questions to uncover the private Ortega behind the public one. "Those were *personal* questions," he told her as she drove home.

Elizabeth nodded. "Did you notice how he skirted the ones he didn't want to answer? But he told me enough. Sometimes, you see, a picture *isn't* worth a thousand words. Sometimes only the best words, put together in the best way, can show readers what a person is really like."

But later, when she sat at the kitchen table where she had set up her typewriter, no words came. For years she'd written smoothly and easily for others; now, writing for herself, she tightened up, head pounding as her thoughts darted back and forth, searching for something to say, trying out phrases, discarding them, trying others, before she even touched the typewriter keys.

It was late; everyone had gone to bed. Earlier, Peter and Holly had tiptoed into the kitchen to wish their mother good luck with her first column, then disappeared down the hallway to their bedrooms. Matt finished the work he had brought home, read the day's New York, Denver, and Albuquerque newspapers, asked Elizabeth if she wanted to talk, and, when she thanked him and said no, he too went to bed.

Elizabeth sat alone at the scrubbed pine table and ordered herself to relax. Pine cabinets and countertops of buff-colored Mexican tiles reflected the light from the wrought-iron chandelier; in the deep window seats Holly's collection of Kachina dolls sat in rows, round black eyes watching her critically. In the typewriter, a blank sheet of paper waited to be filled.

At three in the morning, Matt came in, tying his bathrobe, and found her frowning as she Xed out a sentence. He filled the teakettle and put it on the stove. "Stagefright?" he asked.

Elizabeth gave a small laugh. "Something like it. All these years I've complained about not being able to do my own writing in my own way. And now I'm terrified."

He kissed the top of her head. "That's why you're better than most writers. You respect writing; you don't dash it off."

"That makes it harder," she commented ruefully. "I never realized how comforting it was—I can't believe I'm saying this—to work for someone else who was responsible for deciding whether my work was good enough to print."

"Something like my discovery that it was comforting to have the security of the Lovell Printing Company, and my father, behind me."

They exchanged a look in the circle of light around the table. Elizabeth's frown disappeared, and in a minute they were laughing. "Both of us," said Matt, pouring boiling water into the teapot. "Scared of having to prove ourselves in the big world." He touched Elizabeth's cheek. "I wouldn't even have tried, without you."

She held his hand against her face. "Neither would I. We keep propping each other up when we get scared. But, Matt, this time I'm alone: just me and a typewriter and words tumbling in my head. And I can't seem to do anything with them."

"Listen to me." He poured their tea and sat opposite her. "I'm telling you, as your editor, not your husband, that you are one hell of a writer. You can make words dance and sing;

82

you can make people and places seem so real I swear I can touch and hear them. There isn't anything you can't do with words, as long as you trust yourself. Now stop worrying about whether you can do it or not; let the words come from whatever mysterious place inside yourself they're born, and just start writing. If you want to be scared, wait until tomorrow, when you show me your story and I tell you what I think of it."

Elizabeth burst out laughing. "After that, how can you say it's no good?"

"The best writers have bad days," he said with a grin. "And bad nights. But I'm not worried; you'll be fine." He stood behind her chair, kissing the back of her neck, sliding his hands over her breasts. "I love you and I want you, but I'm going to leave you alone so you can write." And taking his cup of tea, he left the kitchen.

Leaning her head on her hand, Elizabeth gazed at the typewriter, thinking of Matt. He'd found a way to prop her up, so why wasn't she writing in a fury of creativity? Because she could feel his hands on her breasts and she wanted him. And it was still so special, this renewed passion, that she let it grow within her, treasuring it, loving the fact that she loved her husband. I could go to him, she thought. By now he's back in bed, and as long as we're awake . . .

But then her glance took in a sentence on the page in the typewriter, and as she read it the words rearranged themselves in her head. She rolled the paper back to retype them, and along the way she came across another sentence that hadn't seemed right all evening. But it's simple, she thought; why didn't I see how to do it before? And then a phrase came to her—*Edward Ortega hangs onto his dreams the way a rock climber clings to a ledge*—and she knew she had her opening sentence. She pulled her chair closer to the table. Dearest Matt, thank you, she said silently. And she began to type.

"Private Affairs" appeared the following Thursday, spread across the bottom third of the *Chieftain's* front page. Since it was her first column, Elizabeth began with an explanation. "These will be portraits of people who aren't in the spotlight," she wrote. "People in rural towns and back roads, sparsely-settled valleys and crowded city neighborhoods. Some are poor, others are comfortable; some are beautiful, others plain; some are angry, others content. All have stories to tell, with as much drama as any book or movie—but almost always private, unseen by the world. When their stories are told here, if they wish to remain private, they'll be given a different name. But with their own name or a pseudonym, in 'Private Affairs' they will share their stories with all of us. 'Private Affairs' *is* all of us."

Then the story began.

Edward Ortega hangs onto his dreams the way a rock climber clings to a ledge. He's held on to them all his forty-eight years. Black-haired, black-browed, with eyes that puncture pretense, he creates a whirlwind of rapid speech, joyful laughter, roaring anger at injustice, and a dreamy storytelling that sounds like a chant as he describes his vision for the future of his people.

As the article went on, in Elizabeth's words and his own, Edward Ortega grew as real and vivid as if he strode across the page. His home seemed real, too: a cluster of small houses almost lost in the vastness of the pink-gray-brown desert dotted with green; the curve of a highway between irregular fields of grazing and farm land, watered, in good years, by a twisting stream that came from the blue-gray mountains on the horizon. Elizabeth wove together Ortega's stories of the Indians' past and present, loves and legends, wars and feasts, and the Anglos and Spanish who surrounded the pueblo, attracting young people, making it harder for the older ones to keep a separate language and sacred ways.

The next morning Elizabeth found on her desk a rare cactus plant with a spray of white flowers, and a card. "For the best writer and the best story the *Chieftain* ever had. Are we going to be famous!" And everyone had signed it.

But it was only the beginning. That day three people called, one scolding Elizabeth for making an Indian some kind of hero, the others thanking her. "I never knew how they felt," one caller said. "You made me think maybe I ought to help them," said the other. And the next day the mail brought ten letters of praise and three saying if she loved Indians so much why didn't she go live with them?

Matt was jubilant. "Thirteen letters!" he said at the Friday morning staff meeting. "From one column!"

Jack Jarvis, the advertising and circulation manager, tapped his pencil on the desk. "And for every reader who takes the trouble to write, hundreds more have an opinion but don't write—and how many hundreds of others read the story, talk about it to their friends, begin to look for Elizabeth's column, maybe even buy the paper to find out what she writes next? Thirteen letters. Very impressive."

"Print them," Wally said. "We've never had Letters to the Editor."

"We'll run an ad for the column in the Features section," Jarvis went on.

"Send copies to school teachers," Barney said. "They could use them in social studies. Learning about pueblos. Or learning how to write."

Jarvis made a note. "Good idea; sell a few hundred more each week."

Kirkpatrick inspected his cigar. "You have your work cut out for you," he told Elizabeth. "You won't always find controversial subjects that get so much attention."

"You sour son of a bitch," Barney rumbled.

Kirkpatrick barely glanced at him. "We all carry our weight around here. However, I congratulate you, Elizabeth. It was a well-done story. I hope you can keep it up."

Elizabeth broke into laughter. "Thank you, Herb. I'll try not to get a swelled head from such lavish praise."

"Don't pay any attention to him," Wally said heatedly. "He's jealous. So am I. Elizabeth, I wish I could write like you."

"And I," Barney said quickly. It was the highest praise writers could give each other and Elizabeth felt again the flush of triumph that had come when she found the plant on her desk.

"All right," said Matt. "We have the rest of the paper to do; let's go over the main stories for the week."

They settled down, but there was a new excitement in the discussion. Because they had all been in the business long enough to know what it meant when readers began talking back to a newspaper. They were on their way.

Peter and Holly were washing and drying dishes, comparing problems. "He criticized everything I sang," Holly said mournfully. "It was the worst lesson I ever had."

"He was in a lousy mood," Peter suggested. "His wife's cooking gave him food poisoning. His mistress found somebody with a bigger, longer—"

"Peter!"

"Well, something was wrong with him and it wasn't your singing. He usually tells you what a brilliant future you have. You'll see: next time he'll be back to normal. Or dead of food poisoning."

She laughed. "Thanks. What did you do after school?"

"Went to Nuevo."

"Nuevo! We haven't been there for ages. How did you get there?"

"Hitched a ride with Maya's father."

"Maya?"

Peter got very red and scrubbed a pot so vigorously that soapy water splashed on his shirt. "I've been going there. She's studying pottery-making with Isabel—you know, Mom's friend, or she *was* Mom's friend; she says she never sees Mom anymore . . ."

"I've talked to her on the phone, when I've called Luz. If I'd known you went there I'd have gone along. Tell me about Maya; I hardly remember her."

"She's little and beautiful and . . . fragile. And she listens a lot. And laughs at my jokes."

"Smart," Holly said. "Well, I'm glad you finally got a girl. Too bad you couldn't find one at school, closer to home."

Peter shook his head. "I like Nuevo. It makes me remember Grandpa."

"I like it too. Could I go with you next time? I haven't seen Luz forever and I miss her. We were so close all those years

86

when Grandpa was alive . . . I wish Mother and Daddy weren't so busy."

"It's their goddamn precious paper."

"I know." Holly sighed. "I guess it makes them happy, though. Like when I'm singing, that's when I'm really happy."

"If you had kids, you'd be happy spending time with them."

"I know, but right now they really love the paper—"

"They ought to love us! That's what I meant!"

"They do love us! We just don't need taking care of like the paper. That's their baby; we're grown up."

"That's a dumb thing to say."

"It's not dumb. It's the truth."

"Hah!"

"They're at home now," Holly said.

"Working," Peter retorted.

"Well . . ." She sighed again. "I guess I should be, too; I have homework."

"Me too. Holly?"

"What?"

"Do you think we're normal?"

"Who? Our family?"

"I guess. Or . . . I don't know . . . do you ever feel *alone?* Like you don't belong anywhere? See . . . I do. Except with Maya, and this one guy I met who's okay . . . But nobody else is like that; they all have friends and . . . *groups.* And I don't. That's not normal, is it?"

"I don't know. I feel like that a lot, too, except when I'm singing."

"But the rest of the time—?"

Holly shrugged. "I don't think teenagers are supposed to be happy."

"Well, I want to be."

"We're too young," said Holly sadly.

"For what?"

"Almost everything." She spread the damp towel on a rack. "I guess I'd better go do my homework."

"Me too. *Homework.* I wish the next ten years would just disappear."

"Well, maybe just the next five . . ." Holly said, drifting off to her room.

Elizabeth saw her pass the living room arch and wondered what she and Peter had talked about to make her look so mournful. "Isn't this supposed to be the best time of their lives?" she asked Matt.

He looked up. "Was high school the best time for you?"

"No; that's true, it wasn't. I was never sure what I was supposed to be or how I was supposed to act."

He smiled at her. "You've learned. Tell Holly there's hope."

"I'll try. She may not believe me."

"Tell her if she's like her mother she'll be the best there is."

Elizabeth laughed, an intimate laugh that embraced the two of them as they sat in deep armchairs on either side of the round corner fireplace. Then Matt turned back to the stack of applications that had poured in when he advertised for a managing editor and Elizabeth picked up her pencil and the story she was writing. A family at home, she mused. Only Zachary was missing. Everything else was perfect. *How long can it last?* She shook her head, annoyed at herself. *Forever. Why not?* And she bent to her work.

Crossing out lines, changing words, she felt herself knotting up inside. There is nothing to worry about, she said silently, repeating everything Matt had said the night she wrote her first column. But still she worried. Six "Private Affairs" columns had been printed after that first, magical day, but only two letters had come in. It was as if her stories were stuffed into bottles and tossed into the ocean—and sank immediately to the bottom: unseen and unread.

Controversial subjects that get attention, Herb Kirkpatrick had said. Elizabeth kept trying to find others, and waited for the mail. Barney told her to relax; most columns get no response until they're established, he said; the one on Ortega was a fluke. But she didn't want flukes; she wanted success. "You're trying too hard," Matt said. "Write about someone who reminds people of their sons or daughters or neighbors; isn't that the real idea of 'Private Affairs'?"

And soon after that she found Heather Farrell, who had just

begun working for Spencer and Lydia at their shop on Canyon Road. The daughter of wealthy, indulgent parents in St. Paul, Heather had lived a sheltered life until she decided to marry a man her parents called a fortune hunter. When she argued, they cut off her weekly allowance. So, for the first time Heather defied them. She left Minnesota and followed her lover to Santa Fe—and found him happily ensconced with an oil heiress amid all the comforts he had not found in St. Paul.

Alone in a strange town, Heather sat on a bench in the Plaza, watching families and lovers parade by. She couldn't go home and admit she'd been wrong, but she couldn't stay, either, unless she found a job. Which was why, the next day, she stood tentatively in the Evans Bookshop and said to Lydia, all in a rush, "I can't do very much of anything, but I love books and paintings and I love your shop—it looks like somebody's living room—and I'll do anything you say if you'll let me work for you."

Lydia offered her coffee and at that small touch of mothering, Heather broke down in a torrent of confidences: her lover, her rejection, her dwindling money, and her awful aloneness—the first in her twenty-two protected years.

Lydia hired her on the spot, though, as she told Elizabeth on the telephone, she wasn't sure what they would do with her since November was hardly a tourist month.

"Can you keep her for a while?" Elizabeth asked. "We'll be hiring another secretary as soon as we can afford one. Can she type?"

"I have no idea. I doubt it. She wraps packages beautifully."

Elizabeth smiled. "That's not in the job description for a secretary. But I'd like to meet her. I'll be over this afternoon."

When Lydia introduced them, Heather sighed. "I thought maybe Lydia was exaggerating, like all mothers, but she wasn't. You're as beautiful as she said. Did she tell you anything about me?"

Elizabeth studied her. Small, fine-boned, with heavy-lidded green eyes and wildly frizzled brown hair, she stood there hoping for approval. Elizabeth smiled, liking her lively face, her openness, and the stubborn set of her chin. "She didn't tell me why you don't go home to your family and let them take care of you."

The stubborn chin thrust forward. "I don't want anybody to take care of me but me."

That was when Elizabeth knew she wanted Heather in her next column. Matt would approve: Heather Farrell was like so many daughters and sons, struggling for independence and self-esteem and discovering that life was a lot more complicated and difficult than they'd thought.

She interviewed her for a whole evening, then wrote and rewrote her story a dozen times, trying to bring Heather to life in a way that both parents and their children would understand. Then they might call or write to tell her so; just a few, she thought; so I'll know someone is out there, reading what I write.

She heard the telephone ring; then Holly came dancing down the hall. "Tony Rourke is on the telephone; he wants to visit us tomorrow. I told him it sounded fine. It is, isn't it?"

Matt had looked up, then quickly down again, but Elizabeth knew he was listening. She hesitated. Only a few months ago she'd enjoyed the excitement Tony brought; now she had no time for him.

"He's your friend," Holly declared. "And mine, too, and he hasn't been here for ages and he wants to hear about my sing-ing—my career, he called it!—and he'll only have a few hours between planes, so can't he come? Mother, he's *waiting* on the *telephone!*"

"I'd better say hello, then." Elizabeth stood up. "But we can't invite him here, Holly. Tomorrow is Thursday and we won't have a minute until the paper goes to press. And then we like to have the evening with you and Peter. Maybe he can come some other time . . . we'll see." Still holding her clip-board, she went down the hall to their bedroom and picked up the telephone.

"Dear Elizabeth, it's been five months," Tony said, his voice deep and close. "Much too long. I'm on my way to New York tomorrow and I can be with you . . . or did Holly tell you all this?"

90

"Yes. I'm sorry, Tony . . ." She told him about the newspaper. "Everything has changed," she said. "We're doing all of it together. I even have my own column; remember I told you I wanted one?"

"You told me that when you were seventeen."

While we lay in your bed. And you don't want me to forget. But that was so long ago; I'm a different person now.

Knowing he'd made a mistake, he said warmly, "Tell me about the column. How wonderful you must feel—and scared? At least a little bit?"

"Yes." She was surprised he knew that. "More than a little bit. But sometimes I begin to think I'm really a writer."

"I never doubted it; I've always believed in you. Will you read me something you wrote? If you won't let me see you, at least let me hear what you're doing."

Elizabeth found herself liking him; his voice was honest, and he seemed more interested in her than in himself. "I was just finishing a piece for tomorrow's paper," she said, looking at her clipboard. "Do you really want to hear it?"

"Very much."

"It's about a young woman who works for my parents. It ends this way:

Not long ago, Heather Farrell dreamed of romance; now she's been awakened by a bucket of cold reality. "The world isn't as neat as I thought; as a matter of fact, it's kind of messy, when you think about it." But as she says that, Heather Farrell's stubborn chin lifts and she gives a small, shivery smile of pleasure. She's discovering that *kind of messy* means life has more possibilities than she ever dreamed of, and she can't wait to go after them, messiness and all.

Tony was silent. "No comment?" Elizabeth asked nervously.

"It's damned good," he said. "More sophisticated than I expected. You always surprise me. You know, I can *see* your Heather: she probably used to follow like a nice little girl; now I'll bet she walks ahead of everybody."

"How do you know that?"

"I told you: I can see her. You got her, Elizabeth: pinned like a butterfly to a board. You're terrific. You want a job?"

"I've got a job."

"Not a very big one. How would you like a national audience? I need a new writer for my show. Five grand a week and an audience of millions. It's yours if you want it."

The words rang in her head. Forcibly, she silenced them. *It's a fairy tale. It has nothing to do with me. With us.* "Tony, Matt and I own a newspaper together. We work together. I'm very flattered, but—"

"You won't take it. I didn't think you would. The offer stands, though, dear Elizabeth; keep it in mind. Is it all right if I call you now and then, even though *everything* is changed?"

"If you'd like."

"Obviously not as much as seeing you . . . but we mustn't talk about that. Will you send me a copy of your Heather story?"

"Of course."

"Will you send me all your columns? Better yet, I'll subscribe to the—what's it called? The *Warrior?*"

"Chieftain, and you know it. But you don't have to subscribe, Tony; I'll be glad to send you my columns."

"No, I want to see the whole paper, every week. Of course I'm always traveling, but when I get home I'll find them waiting, and that way I'll know what you and Matt are up to. And I'll call again soon. Be well, dear Elizabeth. Oh, and give my love to your family."

She hung up and sat unmoving on the edge of the bed. In spite of everything, he still could make her world seem small and slow. He'd been so pleasant, and then he dangled before her an audience of millions and a salary that made anything she could earn sound like pocket money, no matter how big the *Chieftain* ever got.

Stop it. She looked about the small bedroom, its corners and low ceiling in shadow. She and Matt had bought the blue and black Indian rug at the Crownpoint auction; they'd found the early American wedding ring quilt at an antique shop up the Hudson on a trip to New York state; they'd chosen the Spanish bed on a visit to Mexico City. Everything in the bedroom, everything in the house, they'd chosen together.

And we've chosen our life together now. They worked for no one but themselves and they loved it. And they loved each other. And Tony, with his grandiose offers, had no part in any of that.

Turning out the lamp, Elizabeth decided she wouldn't talk to him again, after all. Even at his nicest, there was something destructive about him. She didn't like the way Holly was beginning to idolize him, either. *Next time I'll tell him not to call any more,* she thought. *I suppose I'll have the Chieftain sent to him; there's no harm in that. But nothing else. We're better off without his play-acting; he can find another audience. He already has millions; he told me so himself.*

An audience of millions. But he didn't really mean it, she told herself. He wasn't serious. And even if he meant every word, it would be impossible. *I'm doing what I want, and I'm doing it with Matt. And I believe in us.*

And she walked back through the shadowed hallway to the lights of the living room, where Matt was waiting.

CHAPTER 5

S aul Milgrim was lanky and loose-limbed, with a melancholy face that was transformed when it crinkled into laughter. A street-wise New Yorker and prize-winning investigative reporter, he had been offered jobs by every major newspaper in the country, but all he wanted now, he told Matt and Elizabeth as he lounged in Matt's office, was to work on a small paper in a small town. "I am your perfect managing editor," he told them seriously. "I know everything there is to know about newspapers, but I've had enough of the big time. I want to get back to basics—poke my nose into every part of the operation. Like quitting Macy's to run a small-town general store."

"What happens when you start missing the big time?" asked Matt.

"Won't happen. I've had enough of it for a lifetime: too many of my peers trying to beat me out, too many women, too much booze . . . Good Lord, it's time I slowed down, even settled down." (*Heather*, Elizabeth thought involuntarily.) "I'm almost thirty-five, getting old—" He saw Matt and Elizabeth exchange a smile. "Did I say something funny?"

"We're forty," Elizabeth smiled. "So thirty-five hardly seems 'old' to us."

Saul contemplated her. "Nobody'd guess." He leaned forward and his voice lost its casual drawl. "Look, I've been on a fast track since I was thirteen: odd jobs after school until I was old enough to be copy boy on a newspaper; worked my way through college driving a cab and bartending and was editor of the school paper at the same time; worked for six major papers since I graduated, racing after the big stories to beat out everybody else and see my name on the front page; won a few prizes, too. You know all this from my application. Well, I'm tired of racing around. I was married, by the way, for a few months; it fell apart because my fast track had room for sex and chit-chat but not for tender care and a future. What I want now is to relax, think about the world and what I want to do with the rest of my life. And do it on a newspaper in a town that's small but sophisticated enough to get international visitors." He leaned back again. "I like you two; I like your ideas for the paper; I like Santa Fe. It's quiet; it doesn't shout the way New York does. I drove around before coming here; know what I liked best? Narrow streets, laid-back shopkeepers, people who keep their affairs private behind adobe walls instead of flaunting their wealth. And dust."

"Dust?" echoed Elizabeth.

"Good clean desert dust. Has a nice feel when you've been breathing city grit all your life. I figure it'll take ten years for my lungs to clean out and by then I'll know what I want to do with myself. My guess is I'll be so content I'll stay put, rocking on my porch and publishing the Santa Fe *Chieftain*."

Matt's eyebrows went up. "After you've knocked off the current publisher?"

"Won't be necessary. You'll be long gone; you want bigger and better things than a small town weekly. I recognize the signs." Once again he saw Elizabeth and Matt exchange a look. "None of my business, however; all I want right now is to be managing editor of your paper. Shall I remove myself so you can discuss me in private?"

Elizabeth smiled, liking him so much she was afraid she might wake up and find she'd dreamed him. "Matt pretty much decided from your application, and he was right. So were you when you said you were our perfect managing editor." She stood up and held out her hand. "Welcome to the *Chieftain.*"

Saul stood, his face lighting in a broad smile as he took her hand. "We're going to be friends. What luck. It doesn't always work that way. Must be rough for the two of you—working together and being married."

"Occasionally," Matt said briefly. "But it's what we want." He stood with them and shook Saul's hand. "We're glad to have you with us. Elizabeth will introduce you to everyone and then we'll have lunch. I'll see you at one. We'll introduce you to blue corn tortillas at The Shed."

"Blue—" Saul shook his head dubiously. "Sounds like an initiation. If I pass, will you give me some ideas about places to rent? And maybe some congenial female friends—?"

"I've already thought of that," Elizabeth said, and led the way to the newsroom.

With Saul's arrival, everything seemed to fall into place. Because he relieved them of so many little details, Elizabeth and Matt could spend more time together, working and relaxing. One Thursday, after the paper went to press, they went for a leisurely drive out the old Taos Highway to browse in ancient churches and have dinner at Rancho de Chimayo, at long last having the anniversary dinner they'd planned the night of Matt's accident. In February they took Holly and Peter skiing at Taos for a weekend, and on other weekends drove into the mountains to Nuevo as they had done so often before, to visit Cesar Aragon and his daughter Isabel and Isabel's daughter Luz.

"I never see you enough!" Luz bubbled to Holly. "Tell me about Santa Fe High and your singing and *everything* about the boys you're dating!" They sat crosslegged on the floor near the fireplace, carving X's in chestnuts, Luz's dark red curls close to Holly's straight ash blond hair as they both talked at once.

Isabel, tall and large-boned, with black eyes above high cheekbones, put her hands on Elizabeth's shoulders and searched her face. "You look good. A little pale maybe, but it's been so long I'm not sure."

"Isabel," Elizabeth said reproachfully. "We've talked on the telephone; you know how busy we've been."

"Four months without a visit."

Elizabeth put her arms around her. "I'm sorry."

"Well so am I," Isabel said, suddenly brisk. She returned Elizabeth's hug. "Mainly for whining. I'm just jealous because I sit in my little ghost of a valley and make pottery while you're out there having all that excitement. And of course I missed you. There aren't so many good friends around that I can afford to lose one."

"You haven't lost me; the time just got away from me. It won't happen again. I need you; the only friend I've had lately has been my husband."

Isabel laughed. "Not enough, is it? What's going on? You together too much? No place to let off steam?"

Elizabeth glanced at Matt as he stacked firewood with Cesar. "Saul helps," she said. "But I've missed you more than I realized."

Isabel looked at the two young girls beside the fireplace. "Luz missed Holly, too. Pecos High makes her feel out of things. Funny how all of a sudden we feel so far from that big world of yours."

That big world of yours. Once Elizabeth had felt that way after Tony's visits and telephone calls. It doesn't take much, she thought, to make the world seem bigger. But she and Isabel had been friends for sixteen years and she didn't want to lose that any more than Isabel did. "We'll always have room for Nuevo," she said. "It's our peaceful place to unwind. And who else understands me as well as you do?" They exchanged a smile. "We'll make time," Elizabeth said. "I promise."

Between weekend trips and Saul's increased authority, Elizabeth and Matt settled into a schedule. They worked nearly regular hours; Elizabeth had more time to write her columns; Matt had time to read them before they went to press; and once or twice a week they went out for late dinners alone, sitting in a booth at the Pink Adobe or a candlelit corner of the Com-

97

pound, where other diners recognized them and often stopped by to say they liked the new look of the *Chieftain*. Once in a while a local businessman told them he was planning to advertise in both Santa Fe papers for a change, and see how it went.

The other nights the family ate dinner together, and lingered, talking, at the table as they had before the *Chieftain* was theirs. There was time, too, for Matt and Elizabeth to sit in their courtyard at night, until the chill air drove them indoors, to slip between cold sheets and warm themselves against each other, inside each other, so much a part of each other they could not imagine ever being separate again.

Tony did not call. For a time, Elizabeth waited, ready to tell him she was busy and happy and had no time to talk. But after a while she stopped waiting, and then she stopped thinking about Tony altogether. He was part of the life she and Matt had left behind. They had another life now.

And as they thrived together, their newspaper thrived. The first real sign was the success of "Private Affairs." A few letters and calls had come in after the story on Heather, and other columns brought a trickle of response, but, though no one at the paper realized it, word was getting around. Then one Friday afternoon in March, Lydia called. "Elizabeth, people are talking about your column. My customers . . . and then in the grocery store . . . *people are talking about it!* And telling others to read it! Can you imagine—!"

"No," Elizabeth said truthfully, because she hadn't realized it was happening—that phenomenon called "word of mouth" that makes books, movies, and newspaper columns become a success. It had taken months, but to Elizabeth it seemed to happen overnight. The letters and telephone calls increased, and one day shoppers began asking for her autograph as she pushed her grocery cart through the Safeway aisles.

"Maybe it's just a fad," she told Saul and Matt at lunch. But she didn't really believe it; she didn't want to. She wanted to believe she was becoming famous. At least in Santa Fe.

Fame wasn't something she'd thought about. She and Matt were known as the couple who ran the *Chieftain*, but it was

Matt Lovell, publisher, who was gaining prominence among local businessmen as the real force behind the paper's growth. Now, suddenly, Elizabeth realized that if she couldn't be prominent as co-owner of the *Chieftain*, she'd make it as Elizabeth Lovell, author of "Private Affairs."

Letters from readers came to her desk, ten or twelve a day, often more. Some scolded her because they didn't agree with her; others praised her because they did; but most wrote to suggest a special person for her to write about. Some telephoned to say "Private Affairs" was the best part of the paper. And one day a carver of Indian pipes, who owned his own shop, called to say his business had doubled after she wrote about him, and now for the first time he could advertise—and where else but in the *Chieftain*?

And since advertising is a newspaper's road to profit, it was new advertising that galvanized the staff a second time. Matt offered a bonus for every line of classified ads that ran each week; that spurred Jack Jarvis and his assistant to go after them, calling employers who had "Help Wanted" signs outside their businesses, helping people write ads for house sales, lost dogs, piano tuning, landscaping, even baby-sitting. And their sales pitch was that all the people who read "Private Affairs" would also read the advertisements in the same paper.

Everyone knew that classified ads were moneymakers because so many lines of tiny print could be squeezed onto a page. And it was when their classified ads went from one full page to two, and then close to three, that Herb Kirkpatrick was heard to mutter, "I'll be damned. This paper may have a future."

Saul was walking past, and heard him. "Say it out loud," he ordered, startling him, and as everyone laughed Kirkpatrick laughed with them, knowing that he wasn't the butt of a joke: they were laughing from relief because even that gloomy son of a bitch Herb Kirkpatrick thought things were going to be all right.

Display advertising followed. Shops, art galleries, movie theaters, and realtors bought space for boxed, illustrated ads: evidence that the Santa Fe business community was finally taking the *Chieftain* seriously.

"Time for something new," said Saul at dinner with Elizabeth and Matt one hot night in July. Stretching out his long legs on their patio, he drained his third glass of lemonade. "We're overdue for a critic for opera, theater, chamber music—the whole culture bit; and we can afford another reporter so we can start those special sections Elizabeth planned months ago."

"Good idea," Matt said lazily. He was watching Elizabeth, in a long peasant skirt and white camisole, her skin luminous, her hair like dark honey in the lantern light. She turned and met his eyes and smiled, a private, promising smile, and they heard Saul draw in his breath. "Something wrong?" Matt asked.

"Nothing serious. Just murderous jealousy. Isn't it time I stopped being a monk and found some female companionship?"

"I was going to introduce you to someone six months ago," Elizabeth protested. "But you changed your mind and said no matchmaking until you were settled at the paper."

"So I did. I'm settled."

"Then I'll invite Heather next time we have dinner," said Elizabeth promptly.

Saul cocked an eyebrow. "Heather. A pleasant name. Not Spanish, not Indian, not Jewish. What is she?"

"Lovable," said Matt. "Elizabeth's parents have almost adopted her. She lives in their guest house and insists on paying rent. She wraps packages beautifully. She's learning to type because she wants to work at the paper. You can read more about her in one of Elizabeth's first columns. Is there anything else you need to know?"

"Yes, when is 'next time'?"

"Tomorrow night," said Elizabeth, already planning a menu, but the next night, from the moment they met, neither Saul nor Heather noticed anything but each other. It had been eight months since Heather came to the Evans Bookshop; since then, Lydia's mothering had given her more confidence but hadn't made a dent in her stubbornness. Saul saw in her green eyes and determined chin the same kind of obstinacy that had led him to leave home at fifteen and become a reporter instead of the lawyer his family dreamed of. Did they have anything else in common? Probably not: a New York Jew who'd scrabbled for a living since he was a boy, and a wealthy Minnesota Methodist . . . but it was worth a try, Saul thought, and besides, he already loved that strong chin.

"The trouble with my family," Heather said at dinner when he asked about them, "is that they were always right. They made me feel I had to be wrong or I wasn't me."

"So you were frequently wrong," he said.

"Not frequently." Her voice was regretful. "Most of the time I did whatever made my parents love me. Then one day I did one very large wrong thing. You'd think I'd been saving up for it all my life."

"Hijacked a shipment of mink coats," Saul suggested. "Forged a Rembrandt."

"You're making fun of me."

"Yes, I am, and I apologize. I just can't see you doing anything terrible."

"It *was* terrible. I got taken in by a man."

He contemplated her. "Why was that a terrible thing?"

"Why! Because if you're taken in by someone, you're a victim."

"Instead of a conqueror?"

"No . . ."

"Well, what's between a victim and a conqueror?"

"The sheriff," said Matt, seeing Heather's confusion. "Is this a quiz, Saul?"

"I apologize again," Saul said to Heather. "But I don't understand what's so awful about believing someone. Even if you're wrong, isn't it trust that keeps us human?"

"I'll tell you what keeps us human," said Heather. "It's what stands between a victim and a conqueror. Partnership. Equality. Trust that's rewarded, not stomped on. And I was a fool not to make sure I had that."

"Trust means you're not sure," Saul responded. "It means you allow for some unknowns."

They faced each other as if they knew already this was only the first of a long line of disagreements. Elizabeth and Matt exchanged a look. "Thank God we don't have to go through that anymore," Matt murmured. "Dancing around, comparing

101

notes, getting acquainted . . ." Elizabeth nodded, warm and content. "Much better this way."

Saul gazed at Heather. She was a foot shorter than he, and thirteen years younger, but she had a half-fearful, half-fierce quality that reminded him of himself before he learned to be cynical. He knew Elizabeth was watching with pleased eyes and wondered whether he was attracted because Heather had so much to learn, or because she was Elizabeth's friend, or because he needed a woman, or simply because she was interesting to look at and presented a challenge. What the hell, he thought. Why analyze? And he invited her to the opera for the next night.

After that, Lydia knew more about them than Elizabeth, since Saul's car was frequently in front of the guest house, and Elizabeth was too busy to keep track of them. On top of her other work, she had begun producing pull-out sections, like individual magazines built around themes such as winter sports, restaurants, fashions, travel, home entertaining, arts and crafts, and the Fiesta de Santa Fe. Readers began saving them, and advertisers, sniffing out another popular item, suddenly were calling Jack Jarvis about buying space, instead of his having to cajole them to buy, as he had for years.

There were other reasons the *Chieftain* was talked about: Saul was demanding livelier stories and photographs covering more of the life of Santa Fe than ever before, and Matt was writing thundering editorials that no one could ignore. People argued over them, readers wrote furious or applauding letters, politicians sent them to voters, and at community meetings Matt was called names he couldn't print in the *Chieftain*, or praised so extravagantly he was embarrassed. But he reveled in it. "This town needs controversy," he said. "Besides, it sells papers."

It also brought in new advertisers. And as new ads took up more space, the *Chieftain* needed more stories to follow the newspaper industry's guidelines of roughly sixty percent ads to forty percent articles. So Elizabeth, Matt, and Saul thought up more stories and made more assignments, and the reporters and photographers leaped to it, overworked (and underpaid, they muttered, because salaries were still frozen), but loving every minute of it, because the newsroom was alive and adrenaline was flowing. Everyone worked at top speed to meet Saul's impossible deadlines, clutter and chaos were greater than ever before, voices were raised in passionate debate over which story would get the front page headline and which photographs would appear across the bottom: the prize location where Cal Artner once slipped in photos of Nambé dancers.

And when so many letters poured in, responding to "Private Affairs" and Matt's editorials, that Saul finally inaugurated a Letters to the Editor section, Barney Kell danced a jig beside his desk and roared, "By God, there are people out there—real flesh and blood human beings—*and they are reading our paper!*"

"Bonuses by Christmas," Matt told the staff at a Friday meeting. "That is, if circulation keeps going up. I'd say keep your fingers crossed, but then you couldn't type. Try prayer."

They laughed, because prayer never printed a newspaper, as Saul said when he made each week's assignments. But work did, and at Christmas the bonus checks were there, tucked inside everyone's pay envelope. "Small but mighty," Saul murmured. "The first of many: bigger and better each year. Who could ask for a better Christmas present? Or Chanukah, for that matter?"

"Or anniversary," Elizabeth said. "One year with the *Chieftain*. Come for dinner; we have so much to celebrate."

Heather was helping Spencer and Lydia clean up from the Christmas rush, so it was just the three of them who toasted their first year together, and especially Saul's ferocious work, as he pulled the whole newspaper into his orbit. Lazily, they went over the whole year, recalling crises and triumphs, Elizabeth's growing confidence with "Private Affairs," and Matt's handling of the paper's finances, and meetings with local people about making the *Chieftain* a bigger part of the life of Santa Fe. They shared anecdotes and reminiscences through dessert and another pot of coffee, while the candles burned down, sputtering in their pools of ivory wax.

"I'm sorry to do this," Matt said at last. "But it really is getting late." And in the near darkness of the room he turned on the overhead chandelier. They blinked in the sudden light.

"Nice evening," Saul commented. "Home cooking, kids in the background doing homework . . . Every time I'm here I realize how much I like it."

Elizabeth waited for a mention of Heather, but none came. She might have asked Saul, but a glance from Matt—*not our business*—warned her not to. "We can do this as often as you like," she told Saul. "As long as it isn't Wednesday, just before the paper comes out. Do you know how all our entertaining revolves around the paper? I have no idea what I'd do if we published every day."

"Maybe we should think about that," Matt said casually.

The lazy atmosphere froze. Saul gazed at Matt, frowning. "What's wrong with a weekly?"

"You know damn well what's wrong: it comes out once a week. We'll always be smaller than the *Examiner* because we miss the breaking stories. Of all people, you know that, Saul."

"No question. I left a daily to come here. But you're talking apples and oranges. A weekly does some things better than a daily."

"Right. But it won't ever be as big."

Saul sighed. "There's that ambition I saw when I got here."

"And you knew then you'd help us grow. And eventually sit on your porch—remember?—being publisher of the *Chieftain*."

"After you left. Are you leaving?"

"No. But we have to grow or the paper will get stale and go downhill. The way it was going when we bought it."

"Then buy another weekly."

"That's another possibility I'm considering."

Elizabeth shoved back her chair, its legs scraping on the tile floor. "Since when is this a one-man operation?"

"I'm sorry, Elizabeth; I got sidetracked. I hadn't expected Saul to be so goddamn negative—"

"What did you expect from *me?*" she asked coldly. "A wifely kiss on your ambitious brow? A meek cheer from the sidelines? Did you ask me what I thought about a daily? Or another weekly? When was your partner consulted about expanding our little empire?"

"Damn it, I said I'm sorry!" Matt strode around the table, his hands deep in his pants pockets. "You've told me often enough you want to go a step at a time; I want to skip a few steps, that's all. With Saul here, I don't see why—"

"That isn't what we're talking about." Elizabeth's voice was still cold. "We are talking about *talking*. We don't take one step or two or five without discussing it first. Or isn't that your idea of a partnership?"

Saul cleared his throat. "Am I witnessing a dispute between officers of a corporation, or a marital tiff? If it's the first, I might legitimately participate. If it's the second, I want to go home."

After a moment, Elizabeth gave a small laugh. "I'm not sure what it is, Saul. This is the first time we've had a witness."

"Well, then, I'm defining it as a corporate dispute and I'm going to mediate. Matt, would you sit down? You look like you're about to lunge at something. Or someone." He waited while Matt came around the table and took his seat. "Is there more coffee?"

"It's cold," Elizabeth said. "I can make another pot."

"Cold coffee is the lifeblood of newspapermen. Newspaper people," he amended. "Now listen. We are not ready to be a daily, Matt. *And you know it.* You're a hotshot publisher and you know it as well as I do. So why bring it up?"

"Because we can't stand still." Matt spread his hands, wishing they were larger, swifter, capable of miracles. He'd felt this way on and off through the years, as far back as his wedding night when he and Elizabeth had no choice but to rearrange their life around Zachary. Each time, he'd felt frustrated, stifled, wanting to lunge—just as he was now. Saul had seen that.

He stared at his hands. Christ, he'd thought finally he could take charge of his life and work for himself with no one holding him back; he thought his wife was with him, he felt *in control*. And so his dreams got bigger. Because if a man didn't try to beat the odds, how would he ever know how much he could force them to go his way?

I've got to know how far I can go.

But he wasn't ready to fight with either Saul or Elizabeth. "Of course I know we can't go to a daily yet. I know we can't afford twenty new people and we wouldn't have room for them anyway unless we had a new building—and I'd like one but we can't do that yet, either. I know our printing press is senile and we ought to have a new one and a second as backup. I know we'd have to subscribe to a wire service, buy syndicated columns and articles, revamp our distribution system—"

"Matt," Elizabeth said, "how long have you been thinking about this?"

"Six months or so. Any publisher worth his salt thinks about expanding; Saul knows that. I've got to have goals, Elizabeth. Not piddling ones; major ones. And I'd like to think my partner and my managing editor share them, even if they can't share my enthusiasm. I've never kept it secret that I want to expand, increase our influence . . . My God!" he burst out. "Do you really expect me to be satisfied to stay where I am for the rest of my life?"

The room was silent. Matt went to the carved cabinet beside the corner fireplace and took out a bottle of cognac. "Elizabeth? Saul?" When they nodded, he brought snifters to the table and poured from the bottle. Swirling his glass, he said, "We've owned the paper almost eighteen months; we doubled the circulation in a little over a year. That was a goal we set in the beginning"—Elizabeth started to say something, then caught herself—"and we have to go on from there. Double it again, expand into new towns, force the legislature to pay more attention to us . . . find out how influential we can be. How else do we keep the staff working at a high pitch, turning out terrific stuff? Damn it, they're excited and involved; we have to keep them that way."

"And you, too," said Saul. He breathed deeply of his cognac, sipped it, smiled seraphically. "I don't suppose this magical brew would do it."

"I don't suppose." Matt smiled in return. "But you're right,

I'm restless and not always patient." Bending down, he kissed the top of Elizabeth's head. "But I'm in love with my partner and I have gone along with our timetable."

Elizabeth could feel the frustration churning within Matt. Her love for him was so strong, especially after the last few golden months, it washed away her anger when his imagination flew ahead without her. She knew that every time she talked about waiting it reminded Matt of sixteen years when he could have been buying newspapers instead of running a printing company. It reminded him that he was forty-one years old. And she knew it wouldn't work to use arguments about timetables and salaries and debt. She could hear him say: We're in debt already; what difference if we increase it? We're surviving. Didn't we decide we'd go for broke?

And how did she know he wasn't right? Maybe there was something wrong with her that she preferred a more certain pace and the leisure they'd had the last few months to enjoy each other and their family. But leisure didn't build an empire— or a larger audience for "Private Affairs." What had happened to *her* ambition, and her desire to have the kind of fame Matt was making for himself? If I'm too cautious, she thought, Matt will go higher and farther and I'll be left behind. And he'll think I was a stumbling block.

"All right," she said abruptly. "Let's buy another weekly. How much money do we need?"

Saul turned admiring eyes on her, wondering if Heather, or anyone, would ever put aside her own wishes for his.

"A hundred thousand," Matt said. "The Alameda *Sun* is about to fold and we can get it for three hundred thousand— a hundred down."

"My, my, the answer is right at hand," Saul observed. "I'd almost guess this is how you planned the conversation to go."

"Is it?" Elizabeth demanded of Matt. "Have I been manipulated?"

"I couldn't manipulate you," he said. "I wouldn't want to. If you hadn't suggested buying another paper, I would have asked you about buying the *Sun*. And I'd have hoped you'd agree."

Elizabeth stopped herself from asking what would have happened if she hadn't agreed. What difference did it make? They were committed, and they were doing it together. "Can we borrow another hundred thousand?" she asked.

"Not all of it." He pulled out his pencil. "But if we sell Dad's property at Nuevo—"

"Matt!"

"We knew we'd have to do it some time," he said flatly. "I don't like it any better than you do, but I've had a good offer for it and if the money buys us a paper it will do more for us than land and a house." He paused. "I don't like it, Elizabeth. But we can't get the money any other way."

She nodded, realizing again the strength of Matt's ambitions. Forward, she thought wryly, remembering the moment when they had held hands and walked into the *Chieftain* building as its new owners. Forward. There was no other way to go.

They celebrated the signing of the agreement to purchase the Alameda *Sun* by taking a ski trip to Aspen, their first vacation in two years. Everyone conspired to make it possible. "Of course you should go," Lydia said when Matt brought it up at dinner. "We'll move into your house for a week so Holly and Peter won't feel abandoned"—catching the indignant look they exchanged she went serenely on—"not because I think they're children, but because it will make me feel loved and useful." Unable to argue with that, they were silent.

The plane tickets were a present from Lydia and Spencer. "Because you've worked so hard and you're succeeding," Lydia said. "It's good to know that one generation can do what its elders couldn't." And Saul found them a condominium by calling an old friend in New York. "It's all theirs, and no charge," his friend said. "Let the newlyweds have a ball." Saul did not correct him. Elizabeth and Matt might have been married close to eighteen years, but right now, planning their vacation, they could have passed for newlyweds.

No one in Aspen noticed. They were anonymous: two more tourists in a town consumed by skiing, especially since it was the end of March and the season was almost over. Alone and private, Elizabeth and Matt flew from the desert plateau of Santa Fe to the Roaring Fork valley of Colorado and then drove through town to a complex of buildings on the lower slopes of Aspen Mountain.

Their apartment was cozy, brightly furnished, looking onto the Little Nell ski slope. "So lucky," Elizabeth sighed as she stood with Matt on the deck, breathing the crisp air. "To find such a perfect place . . ."

Arms around each other's waist, they looked up the slope before them, bordered by dark pines. Below, the town of Aspen lay nestled in its valley, brown, gray, green. The snow was gone; only the mountain was white. Across the valley, houses covered the lower half of Red Mountain, their windows mirroring the late afternoon sun. To the west, the mountains faded into blue and violet.

Shadows slipped over the valley; the air chilled. Shutting the glass doors behind them, they unpacked in the bedroom. "Too early for dinner," Matt said. "A drink in front of the fire?"

It was like a story she might have written, Elizabeth thought. The flames leaped and swayed; beyond the window the mountain grew pale and ghostly in the darkness. They drank a velvety Cabernet and nibbled on crackers and Stilton cheese found in the refrigerator. Silence wrapped itself around them: absolute silence, with no chatter of teenage children, not even their sleeping presence, no street sounds, no telephone or neighbor's dog, no doorbell. They lay propped against woven pillows before the fire. "Santa Fe, families, newspapers—all wiped out," Matt said. "There's only this room, and us. It makes me want to seduce you."

Elizabeth smiled and put down her glass. With one hand she brought his face down to hers and with the other she began unbuttoning his shirt. "Partners," Matt murmured. "Not seducers. I like that."

They kissed, their mouths slow and searching. Together they unbuttoned each other's shirts, unbuckled each other's belts, slid off each other's corduroy jeans. "Floor or bed?" Matt asked. His hands were on Elizabeth's breasts, his lips in her hair.

"Here," she said, the word barely a whisper. She sank back, pulling Matt with her. "Here. Now."

They lay together on the heaped pillows, the Egyptian cotton as soft a caress as their hands and the touch of skin on skin. Matt's fingers traced the inside of Elizabeth's thighs, then slipped inside her, and Elizabeth kissed him, her breathing quick, small sounds murmuring against his cheek, his mouth, the dark hair on his chest, the beating of his heart beneath her lips.

They lay wrapped in their small circle of silence. The room danced in the flickering light to its own heartbeat and the sound of their breathing, their murmurs and half-spoken words, and the desire that grew steadily, like a rising lake.

Matt turned, bringing Elizabeth beneath him and she clasped him with her thighs, her hands pressing against the long line of his back and the muscles at his narrow waist. "Dear love . . ." he said, lingering on the words, and Elizabeth felt the warmth of them as she felt the heat of the fire and the heat inside her, spreading from Matt's weight upon her to the tips of her fingers and the soles of her feet. All of her was burning, open, longing, and she opened her legs and pulled him inside her, deep into the wet passage waiting for him. He filled her; the muscles of the passage tightened, clinging to him, fitting the two of them to each other.

He held himself above her, and as he found a rhythm that matched hers, the two of them looked down and watched his hard shaft rise and then plunge, disappearing inside Elizabeth, part of her, held by her and, in turn, holding her with sensations so powerful they swept away everything but the ripples of desire and passion that still grew like the rising lake that nothing could stop. It caught them in its whirlpools, lifting and spinning them in smaller and smaller eddies, dizzily, faster and faster, to the center, one small point where the spinning stopped and they were motionless for a piercing second. Then, slowly, the room came back, the firelight, the shadows, the pillows, and they lay quietly, smiling into each other's eyes.

"I keep rediscovering you," Matt said at last. "Each time you seem so new . . . my new love . . ."

Elizabeth ran her finger along his dark, tousled hairline, and

110

down his face. "How handsome you are. Sometimes I forget . . ."

He caught her finger between his teeth. "You're mesmerized by pillows and firelight."

"Only by my husband. I love you, Matt."

His arm tightened around her shoulders and he moved above her, his mouth just touching hers. "My lovely, magnificent wife. Partner. Friend. I love you." They kissed, and the kiss seemed to Elizabeth even more of a pledge—*We will never lose this*—than the passion they had just shared.

The days were gold and white, green and blue. A blazing sun in a vaulting, deep blue sky sparkled on newfallen snow that blanketed the mountains. In the crystal silence, sprays of snow fell with a soft whoosh from the spreading branches of dark green firs outlined in white. Skiers flew down the slopes in vibrant reds, yellows, blues, greens, brighter still against the blinding snow, faces glowing in the sun, dark glasses reflecting mountains, trees, the cloudless sky, the rainbows of other skiers sweeping past.

As Matt and Elizabeth took the chairlifts up the mountain, they saw farther the higher they rode: range after range of snow-covered peaks with craggy rock jutting through the snow, and lower slopes clad in feathery groves of leafless aspens woven through green-black forests of Douglas fir. Memories came back of their first years in Santa Fe, when ski trips to Aspen had been the treat they gave themselves every winter.

"Why did we stop coming here?" Matt asked.

Elizabeth zipped up her jacket. "I don't know. Different habits, different patterns . . . I don't know. We lost so much."

"Misplaced," he said. "Not lost." They were nearing the top. "We've found it again. Ready?"

"For anything."

He grinned and they skied off the chair as it reached the top. Near a wooden signboard with a ski trail map, they stopped to tighten their boots, breathing deeply in the thin air. "Years at a desk," Matt muttered. "Muscles out of condition, technique rusty. I think I'm getting old."

111

She laughed. "You could have fooled me yesterday, on the floor in front of the fire. Come on, show me how old you are. I'll race you to the number three lift." And without waiting for an answer, she pushed off. She felt the strain in her thighs and the small jolts in her arms as she placed her poles in the snow. Working too hard, she thought. Relax. She made wider turns, swooping across the slope, and then Matt caught up with her, shouting a promise to wait for her at the lift. "Oh no you won't," she said under her breath, but he was a more aggressive skier and as she reached the level stretch near the lift, she saw snow spray out from his skidding stop seconds before she stopped beside him.

"A fine partner you are," he said. "Nothing like a crazy run first thing in the morning to knock the stuffing out of an old man. I thought we shared decisions around here. Want another one?"

"No. Please. I'm sorry for the first one." He laughed and led the way to the lift, where they sat down with a sigh as the attendant steadied the moving chair behind them.

"Not bad, though," he commented. "For a couple of old newspaper folk who haven't had much playtime lately. We make quite a team."

Quite a team. Elizabeth repeated it all day, as they made more easygoing descents, turning, gliding, exulting in weight-lessness, side by side or one following the other through the moguls built up by skiers carving turns on the steeper slopes. They grew warm and unzipped their jackets; they rubbed suntan cream on their noses when they rode the chair; at an overlook on Copper Trail they stopped to admire Aspen and its valley, like a pastel painting far below, and in the sunlit, pine-scented air, they stood together in a long, slow kiss before going on. Some time after noon they ate outside at the Sundeck, removing their jackets, loosening their ski boots, stretching their legs, gazing in silence at the view.

"It's so perfect," Elizabeth said. "Why did we wait so long?"

"We were putting out a newspaper." Matt scraped the last bit of chicken gumbo from his bowl. "I could eat three more.

112

But then how would I get down the mountain? How would I have the energy to make love to my wife?"

"How would you have room for dinner?"

He took her hand. "A practical woman. I love you. I want to ski some more; are you ready to go?"

They crammed years of delayed vacations into one week. In the mornings they woke early, spent the sun-filled days on the mountain, coming down in afternoon shadows to the warmth of their house, where they took steaming showers and drank cold white wine while drying each other with fluffy towels, until they could no longer hold up their heads and slipped into bed to sleep for an hour before dinner.

One night they took a taxi up Castle Creek to the ghost town of Ashcroft, where the plowed road ended and they switched to cross country skis. Beneath a three-quarter moon, they glided on a trail through mounded, unmarked snow, in and out of fantastic shadows, to the Pine Creek Cookhouse, where they were greeted by the warmth of a fat black stove, candles on checkered tableclothes, and an open kitchen with the smells of their dinner making them so ravenous they could barely wait for the hors d'oeuvres and Hungarian red wine. And though the tiny room was full, with strangers sharing the long tables, they might have been alone, sitting across from each other beside the window, talking in low voices.

"I'm afraid to say this because I'm feeling superstitious," Matt said. "Of course I'm never superstitious, but—can I say I've never been so content, and not have it disappear in a puff of smoke?"

"It won't disappear." Elizabeth looked through the window at the rustic porch. "I won't let it."

"We won't let it," Matt said. "Because everything is exactly the way it should be."

She smiled at him, loving the way he looked, his face tanned from sun and snow, his plaid shirt collar showing above the white cableknit sweater she'd made for his birthday the year before they bought the *Chieftain*—the last year she'd had time to knit. She loved his smile, the warmth of his deep-set blue eyes, the memory of his hands waking her body that morning.

"I feel so lazy," she said. "All I can think about is love and eating and skiing."

"What else does anyone think about in Aspen? Except, perhaps, how beautiful one's wife is." She looked so much better, he thought: relaxed and rested, instead of pale and nervous as she was at the end of every hectic week. He gazed at the delicate lines of her face, her skin glowing with color, her gray eyes flecked with green reflected from her jade angora sweater, her honey-colored hair loosely curled and falling to her shoulders, instead of tied back to be out of her way as she worked. "Beautiful and desirable," he said. "I can't get enough of you."

She nodded dreamily, remembering their day on the mountain.

"But there was a time," Matt said, "when you told me our problem was that we had no way to escape from each other."

"Oh. But that was a long time ago. We were having trouble running the paper, learning to work together . . ."

"Then you don't think about that now."

"How could I? Everything is so good now."

"I wanted to hear you say it. Crazy, isn't it? After all these years to feel as if I'm just discovering you, how much I love you and need you, and what we can be together. What did we do for the first sixteen years?"

A small shiver went through Elizabeth. "Matt, we aren't wiping out those years. We've just made some changes—"

"We've changed everything. And we've just begun. Wait until I tell you what I have in mind for next year."

"You have. The *Sun*."

"That's only the beginning." He saw a shadow cross her face. "But this isn't the time to talk about it. Love and eating and skiing, this week. Remember?"

He lifted her hand and kissed the palm, feeling the muscles relax beneath his lips, knowing she was willing herself to let it go, think of it later. In a moment the shadow was gone from her face, and, holding hands, they drank their hot coffee and talked of other things.

Skiing back from the restaurant, they felt the softness of falling snow on their faces and the next morning found unbroken powder on mountain trails where their long, deep S's were the only marks on the slope as they flew down, with plumes of snow thrown up behind them like great angel wings. At noon, when the mountain grew crowded, they skied down to spend the afternoon browsing through designer boutiques, art galleries, a sculpture courtyard, a charming bookshop in a restored Victorian house that reminded Elizabeth of her parents' shop on Canyon Road, and shops along the cobblestoned mall. "Holly," Elizabeth murmured, choosing an embroidered sweater at Pitkin County Dry Goods. "Peter, Heather, Saul, my parents . . . I can't believe how far away they all seem. I can't even imagine going back."

"We have three more days," said Matt. "It's too early to think about going back. Anyway, my love, this is only the beginning. We'll have other vacations. Bigger and better."

"I like this one." Elizabeth put her arm through his, tucking her hand in his pocket, and they turned to stroll back to their apartment. Looking up, they saw skiers making their last run of the day: tiny, swaying figures coming down the huge mountain. They left the shops behind, walking along the base of the mountain, then heard the high-pitched chatter of voices as the door of the Tippler swung open and shut.

"A drink?" Matt asked, and they plunged into the din of conversations in half a dozen languages. Squeezed together at a small table, they looked at the crowd. "Let's go back to Chestnut Run," Matt suggested. "I'll buy you that eight hundred dollar sweater you liked." "You're not serious," Elizabeth said. "Probably not," he said gravely. "But if anyone notices we're wearing the only fifty dollar sweaters in the place, they might ask us to leave, and I don't want you to feel deprived."

Elizabeth burst out laughing. "I can't feel deprived; I have you. And the women here couldn't care less about my sweater; they're all wondering where they can find a husband like mine, and of course they can't, at any price, so they're the ones feeling deprived. Drink your wine and stop worrying. Nothing can touch us."

The most serious topic in Aspen, once the day's skiing has been exhaustively discussed, is dinner. "Three more nights,"

115

Matt said as they walked back from the Tippler. "Three more restaurants. The last two are your choice; I've already arranged for tonight."

"Arranged what?"

He unlocked their door. "Your husband is treating you to dinner and a show at—" The telephone was ringing and they started; they hadn't heard a telephone for four days. Elizabeth leaped for it. "No one would call unless something was wrong at home . . ."

But the call was not from Santa Fe; it was from Houston. "Elizabeth? Keegan Rourke. It seems a lifetime since I saw you, but you do remember—?"

"Yes, of course, but . . ." *Keegan Rourke?* Why would Keegan Rourke, whom she had last seen at her wedding, almost eighteen years ago, be calling her, and in Aspen, of all places? Unless— "Has something happened to Tony?"

Matt was watching her with a puzzled frown. "Keegan Rourke," she said with her hand over the mouthpiece.

"Who?"

"Tony's father."

"No, my dear," Rourke was saying. "Tony is his usual self. I talked to him yesterday, in Alaska." Rourke's voice, like Tony's, was smooth and deep, hinting at sexual desire and mysterious surprises. "I'm sorry to break in on your vacation," he said. "I called Matt's office and they gave me your number. I'm coming up tomorrow for some skiing and I'd like to see you—ski together, perhaps? Definitely have dinner."

Elizabeth was silent. *What is this all about?*

"Elizabeth?"

"Of course we can ski together, Keegan, if you'd like. But I don't think dinner—"

"Please. As my guest. It would give me great pleasure. I've never really had a chance to talk to Matt, you know."

"What does he want?" Matt asked.

"Keegan, please wait a minute." Elizabeth covered the mouthpiece again. "He's coming to Aspen; he wants to ski with us and take us to dinner and get to know you."

116

Matt's eyebrows went up. "He's been struck by a sudden desire to get to know me?"

"It doesn't make sense to me, either. Shall I tell him we can't see him? I already told him we couldn't have dinner."

"That's all he said? He wants to get to know me?"

"He's not a direct person. At least he wasn't when I knew him in Los Angeles. There's no reason for us to spend an evening with him, is there?"

"Curious," Matt said thoughtfully. "How did he find us?"

"He called your office."

"My office? Not our house? Elizabeth, let's do it. Would you really mind? I'd like to know what he's up to. You wouldn't mind one dinner, would you?"

Yes, Elizabeth thought. But into the telephone she said, "Thank you, Keegan, we'll be glad to have dinner with you."

"Very good." She heard the satisfaction in his voice. "I'll call you when I get in; I may not make it early enough for skiing. In fact, let's have dinner Thursday, instead of tomorrow, in case I'm delayed. I thought we'd go to Krabloonik, if you like it."

"We've never been there."

"Then I'll help you discover it. Will you make reservations?"

"If you like. Three of us at—eight o'clock?"

"Eight o'clock is fine. But make it for four; I'm bringing a friend. I'm greatly looking forward to seeing you, my dear. My regards to your husband."

Elizabeth turned from the telephone. "I don't understand it."

"Tell me about him," said Matt. "All I know is your parents gave him a kind of second home when his wife died."

She nodded. "Tony was three; it was before I was born. I have trouble talking about Keegan; I'm embarrassed by how much I idolized him while I was growing up. He was like a king to me, rich and powerful, or at least sure of himself, especially next to my father, who seemed so helpless: hating his job, hating the smog . . ."

"What did Keegan hate?"

"We never knew. He never let on that anything bothered him. I know Mother stopped liking him after a while; probably

117

because she never liked devious people, and Keegan was. He did things in roundabout ways; people had to guess what he was up to; he always kept them at a distance. And I guess it bothered Mother that my father seemed . . . stuck, while Keegan was making it very big."

"Big in what?"

"Oil. Tony told me he made a fortune when he moved to Houston. I think he's worth about half a billion dollars—"

"Billion?"

"That's what Tony said. He went into real estate and, I think, television stations. Tony stopped talking about him a long time ago; I didn't know they were even in touch . . ." Her voice trailed away.

Matt put his arm around her. "What's wrong, my love?"

"Oh . . . that roundabout way of his—making us guess why he wants to see you. And I don't like anybody poking into our vacation."

"He won't take much of it. Where does he want to eat?"

"Krabloonik."

"Wonderful; I've been wanting to try it. We'll allow him one dinner, and that's all. And speaking of dinner—what's wrong?"

"I just realized—we're meeting him Thursday, not tomorrow. Matt, that's our last night in Aspen; I don't want to spend it with Keegan Rourke and some woman I've never met."

"He's bringing a woman? Then he'll want to be with her as much as we want to be with each other. We'll find out what he wants, eat our dinner, and still have the night to ourselves. Now can we forget millionaire Rourke and think about the hungry Lovells? I was telling you, when we were interrupted, that we have reservations for the late seating at the Crystal Palace. And if we don't hurry, we're going to miss it."

They hurried, and arrived as the last of the waiting crowd was being seated. Their table was on the balcony of the restaurant, beside the brass railing, where they could look across the room at the tiny stage and piano below a massive tear-drop chandelier. On all sides, illuminated stained glass windows covered the walls; the large room was full and bright, the noise level high, and gradually, between their roast duck, a bottle of burgundy, and chocolate mousse, Elizabeth and Matt felt the outside world slide away. By the second song in the musical revue performed by the restaurant's waiters and waitresses— young, talented, and awesomely energetic—millionaire Rourke was forgotten.

Until the next evening, when he called from his home on Red Mountain. "Delayed by business and repairs on my plane," he told Matt, who answered the telephone. "Nicole wants to ski at Snowmass tomorrow, so we won't be together unless you want to join us."

"No," said Matt. "We'll ski here."

"Dinner, then. Elizabeth made reservations?"

"For eight o'clock."

"Excellent. I'll send my car for you at seven-thirty. It will be a pleasure to talk to you, Matt."

About what? Matt wondered, but didn't mention it to Elizabeth. Neither of them talked about Rourke; it was their last full day of skiing and they took advantage of it, weaving in and out of the trails on Bell Mountain until the lifts closed. They pulled off their clothes, showered, and stretched out on the cushions in front of the fire where their vacation had begun. "I think I've melted," Elizabeth sighed. "No more bones or muscles, just jelly."

Matt put his arms around her, holding her close, and they lay quietly, lulled to drowsiness on the soft pillows. "I don't want to move," he said. "Ever. I just want to hold you and love you and feel you against me, half of me, part of me."

"We can stay home." Elizabeth's lips barely moved against his chest. "Make an omelet, eat in front of the fire, pretend there's nobody else in the world."

"Sounds wonderful."

But after they dozed and woke to darkness, with only a few glowing coals in the fireplace, Matt rubbed his chin. "I'll have to shave before dinner. Do you have any idea what time it is?"

So much for the omelet, Elizabeth thought. She looked at her watch. "Six-thirty."

"Better get moving."

"How are we getting there?" she asked.

"He's sending a car."

"He's what?"

"He says he has a limousine picking us up at seven-thirty."

"You didn't tell me."

"It didn't seem important. He also mentioned a private plane. Limousine, plane, house on Red Mountain. Someday we'll have them, too."

"Fine," Elizabeth said absently, thinking about what she would wear.

"Are you wearing your white sweater?" Matt asked.

"I don't know. Why?"

"Because I bought you something. Wait here." He put a log on the fire and went into the bedroom, returning with a small white box. Elizabeth watched his nude body in the dancing light of the flames. Tall, lean, muscular, he moved with grace and a kind of coiled energy, as if he were holding himself back. *Where would he leap if he had the chance?* "To celebrate our week," he said, sitting beside her. "And to tell you I love you."

It was a Zuni necklace: ten ovals of silver filigree suspended in a V, each framing a polished sphere of deep red coral. "It's so beautiful . . ." Elizabeth said softly.

He fastened it about her neck. "Nude with Necklace," he murmured, as if she were an oil painting. He kissed her mouth, her throat, her breasts. "My lovely and most loved Elizabeth. And now I'm going to get dressed."

Elizabeth stayed by the fire. She didn't want to go; she had no interest in Rourke or his friend. Her hand touched the necklace. *I could go as I am. Nude with Necklace. I'd certainly be noticed. And remembered.* She smiled, then sighed. *Get it over with. So we can be alone again.*

As tall as Matt, and as lean, though twenty-eight years older, Keegan Rourke was silver-haired, with a thin, patrician nose, pale eyes, and the casual confidence of an impressively handsome man of wealth and power. At Krabloonik, he was the one who attracted attention. The restaurant, high in the mountains at Snowmass, was decorated in a style that managed to be both rustic and elegant, from its dark wood walls to the

120

intimacy of its few tables and booths and the antique gas lamps hanging from the low ceiling. In the corner booth, Rourke sat across from Elizabeth, meeting her puzzled eyes with an admiring scrutiny. "You're as lovely as Tony said; far lovelier than the young woman I last saw on her wedding day . . . how long ago?"

"Seventeen years," Elizabeth replied. "Almost eighteen."

"My God, the years fly." Rourke shook his head. "I did visit Zachary once; he took me to Nuevo. You and Matt were away, probably skiing, now that I think about it. And I meant to stop by again to see you two, and Spencer and Lydia when they moved there, but it never worked out. Of course Tony kept me informed. Ah, Nicole," he said as a woman was led to their table. "May I present my friends. Elizabeth and Matthew Lovell: Nicole Renard. Nicole found acquaintances at the bar and stopped to talk with them. Wine, my dear? Or something else?"

With a swift glance at the others' wine glasses, Nicole adapted. "Wine, thank you." And as Rourke filled her glass she openly studied Matt and Elizabeth, her gaze moving slowly from the honey-dark hair framing Elizabeth's face to her white cashmere sweater and Zuni necklace, and then on to Matt.

She was the most strikingly beautiful woman Elizabeth had ever seen. Wearing black velvet pants and a black sweater beaded with jet, her black hair swept back from her face, she wore no makeup, letting her smooth features and heavy-lidded amber eyes impress with their own pale perfection. Elizabeth guessed she was about thirty; young, polished, aloof, she made Elizabeth suddenly aware of her age. But when Nicole turned back to her after an inspection of Matt, Elizabeth, returning look for look, saw the flaw in what had seemed perfect beauty: a small curve at the corners of her mouth, hinting at greed and calculation. But it was not easy to spot; only women whose husbands had received a long, measured look from those amber eyes would see it.

"How was Aspen Mountain?" Rourke asked, making conversation as they studied the menu. "Good skiing over here. No crowds at Campground and we found a little devil of a run, Garret Gulch . . ."

"It's been a quiet week," Matt said absently. He didn't want the obligatory discussion of skiing, or a lengthy debate over dinner. He always selected quickly and decisively at restaurants, impatient with those who wavered, and he was ready for Rourke to come to the point. He had been struck by Nicole's beauty and briefly curious—she was, he guessed, nearly forty years younger than Rourke—but it was not unusual in Aspen to find stunning young women in the company of wealthy men, and Matt was more interested in Rourke. "I wondered why you called my office—" he began, but the waitress interrupted, reciting the evening's specials.

When they had made their choices, Rourke ordered two bottles of Zinfandel and talked casually about skiing in St. Moritz, Gstaad, and Aspen. "Which do you prefer?" he asked Elizabeth.

"I have no idea," she said, "since we've never been to Europe."

"Never been—! I would have thought, surely you would have . . ."

Too polite to ask if it was money, Elizabeth thought. "We never found the time," she said simply.

"But you must find the time." Rourke was emphatic. "You and Matt are perfect for Europe because you'd get more from it than most people." He nodded to himself. "Certainly you must find a way to go."

It was as if he were dangling Europe before them, like bait, Elizabeth thought. "We plan to," she said briefly, uncomfortable and annoyed and wishing she could just ask him what he wanted. But they were all being very polite, so she said nothing else, turning to look out the window at the terrace, while Rourke talked about music festivals in Aspen, Salzburg, and the cathedral towns of England. Like Tony he controlled the conversation with a smooth voice and perfect timing. This was the father Tony had escaped, Elizabeth remembered: *His shadow, the reach of his long arm.* I'd like to escape, too, she thought. And as soon as we've eaten, we will, whether he's revealed his mysteries or not. I don't even care what they are.

Rourke was talking about ski lodges in Switzerland when

the waitress brought their wild mushroom soup. He picked up his spoon. "Of course you should have a local agent check out any lodge for you before you make reservations. That's as true of Aspen as it is of St. Moritz. What changes are you and Milgrim planning for the *Sun?*"

It took a moment to sink in; then Matt said sharply, "That sale hasn't gone through."

"And it hasn't been made public," Elizabeth added. "And how do you know Saul? He's never worked in Houston."

Rourke chuckled. "I read the *Chieftain*; his name is on the masthead. And because my interests require accurate information, I have various sources reporting to me. Nothing mysterious about it."

Drama, Elizabeth thought. Just like Tony. Again.

"I like what you've done with the *Chieftain*," Rourke said to Matt. "Though I think you could have knocked out the Taos and Española papers if you'd staffed offices in those towns instead of hiring local reporters. Was Milgrim the cautious one? Or Elizabeth? I wouldn't say caution is one of your traits." Matt had put aside his soup and was watching Rourke, angry, baffled, reluctantly admiring. "And you're buying the *Sun,*" Rourke went on, "because all you could afford in Albuquerque was a suburban paper. You asked a couple of bankers about the *Daily News*, but it wasn't for sale and you probably knew you couldn't afford it anyway, but you were storing information for the future. The *Sun* isn't big enough for you, of course, but you had to start somewhere. We really should pay attention to the soup; it's the best I've ever tasted."

He was right about everything, including the soup, Elizabeth thought. Rourke had switched subjects and was talking knowledgeably about picking chanterelle and giant boletus mushrooms around Lincoln Creek and Cobey Park. "Aspen has always been a favorite of mine, winter and summer. And I like the top of Red Mountain—superb views of town and the valley. You might want to use the house sometime."

"When I'm no longer starting out on papers too small for me," Matt said evenly.

Rourke laughed. "You'll always be starting, Matt; there'll

123

be another challenge for you around every corner." He held Matt's dark eyes with his pale ones. "I've been looking around corners all my life, going after whatever I discovered there. I don't find that in many other men." He refilled their glasses, slowly, deliberately, letting the silence stretch out.

"Go on," Matt said, knowing he'd lost a small battle of wills by letting Rourke force him to break the silence.

Rourke nodded. "I own two newspapers, the Albuquerque *Daily News* and the *Houston Record*. You would have found Rourke Enterprises as the owner of the *Daily News* if you'd checked in Ayer, but since it wasn't for sale, you didn't bother. I need a publisher for both papers. And to buy others."

After a moment, Matt asked, "How many others?"

"Who knows?" Rourke spread his hands, large-knuckled, with manicured nails. "Must there be a limit at the outset?"

"No." It was so husky it was almost lost. *Must there be a limit?* The vagueness was more seductive than a specific number. "Where would you start?"

Rourke listed a string of cities, suburbs, and small towns between Houston and Los Angeles. Elizabeth was stunned; if he meant what he said, he was planning one of the largest newspaper chains in the country. He described the towns and their areas, familiar with the history and rough demographics of every one. And the descriptions, played out like a film narrated in his smooth voice, brought to life images and ideas Matt had been storing up for years. He heard Rourke through the churning of a hunger that the purchase of the *Chieftain* had only whetted. *If I had all those to work with . . .* He took a deep breath. "Why those?" he asked.

"Because they're the future of the sun belt. High-tech industries will move into some of them as living costs in California get too high; others are future retirement cities; others will be major resorts. Populations will grow, businesses and shopping malls will follow, transportation will boom. As a whole, it will be a nice power base for someone who gets in early and gives all those people and businesses modern, savvy newspapers." Elizabeth caught the odd word, sticking out like a small thorn in Rourke's suave speech, as if he wanted to make sure he had their attention.

Well, he has mine, she thought. The enormity of his dream—and he made it sound so simple!—had caught her imagination, and she knew from the pitch of Matt's body, leaning forward as if to follow wherever Rourke led, it had caught his, too. She thought of their little empire. It had been swallowed up in Rourke's dream. *And if we're here, doesn't that mean he wants us as part of it?*

The waitress put Matt's dinner before him and he stared at it. "What did I order?" he asked Elizabeth.

"Venison," she said quietly, loving him, knowing he probably had leaped ahead and was already planning how they would run the whole—

The thought came to an abrupt stop. How *they* would run it? Who had said anything about *they?*

She thought back over the past hour. Rourke had talked to her twice: about traveling to Europe and about how lovely she looked. *As lovely as Tony said.* He and Tony had been talking about her. And about Matt. And he'd been reading the *Chieftain.* And he'd called Santa Fe looking for Matt.

He wanted Matt, but what about her? He was dangling the bait of a newspaper chain in front of Matt, but where did Matt's wife come into it?

This is our dream he's playing with. Our life.

No; he'd gone beyond that. Keegan Rourke was talking not about their shared plans, but about Matt's ambition.

"Power base for what?" Matt asked Rourke.

"There are always uses for power." Rourke sliced into his buffalo steak. "Must it be limited with specifics at the outset?"

That seductive vagueness, again, Elizabeth thought. "What's wrong with being specific?" she asked.

Rourke smiled at her. "Nothing—at the proper time."

"It seems to me," she said, "that it's always good to be specific about information, unless you're hiding something."

"Ah." He nodded. "That may be. But the easiest way to hide something is to give the wrong information." He waited for Elizabeth to respond, but she was silent.

Rourke took a deliberate bite of buffalo, sipped his wine, then with a small smile in Elizabeth's direction, turned again to Matt. "Let's play a little game. I'm interested in buying newspapers. I have in my wallet two hundred million dollars. I want to spend it and increase it through profits. I ask your advice. What would you suggest?"

Get a bigger wallet, thought Elizabeth wildly, and a small laugh broke from her. But no one laughed with her. Nicole slid her glance briefly to Elizabeth, then back to the men. Rourke smiled once again, courteously. Matt gave her a quick glance, too preoccupied to ask why she laughed, then answered Rourke.

"I'd buy newspapers and television stations in key cities, and tie them together. Special sections and programs each week on local events—put fifty people on those alone, move them to different cities as I needed them. I'd run contests that could be entered only by families—no individuals. I'd run a weekly full page of cartoons on local and national issues and do an animated version of them on television one night a week, for adults, not kids, combined with some kind of no-holds-barred debate on the cartoons plus editorials and features from that week's papers. I'd organize town meetings, televise them, and print excerpts to give to schools for classes in government and politics . . ."

He talked and Rourke listened. Nicole watched, her amber eyes never leaving Matt's face. Elizabeth sat unmoving and incredulous. Matt had never mentioned most of these ideas to her, yet they were clear in his mind: expensive, fanciful, many of them impractical, but *thought out*.

Matt had stopped talking. The waitress appeared and asked about dessert. "Coffee," said Rourke. "Then we'll decide."

Finally, giving in again, Matt spoke first. "I've emptied your wallet. We've played your game. What would you like to do now?"

"Bring you in as my publisher." Rourke divided the last of the wine among their glasses. "I watched you make up your mind on dinner the instant you read the menu; I make up my mind the same way. You're the man I want. I'd about decided before I came here; your pipe dreams just settled it." Once more he turned a smile in Elizabeth's direction, ignoring the growing anger in her eyes. "About a year ago, Tony sent me some of Elizabeth's columns—brilliant pieces; I'd want them in all our papers. Since then I've subscribed to the *Chieftain* and watched it change. Saul Milgrim is the best there is; if he's working for you, he believes in you. You're intelligent and aggressive, you know publishing, you get along with businessmen, you have enough ideas to fuel a newspaper chain for years. And ambition is eating you up inside. Which, as you have guessed by now, is exactly what I'm looking for."

Something overwhelming was happening to Matt. He and Rourke were talking to each other, understanding each other, almost as if they were father and son. But this was not a father pleading with Matt to take care of him; this was a father offering him the world. Exhilaration swept through Matt: he understood this man; this man understood him. They wanted the same thing and they would go after it. A power base. With no limitations. An open-ended dream.

He became aware of a hand on his, beneath the table. "Hey, partner," Elizabeth said softly. "Are we still in business?"

Slowly her words got through to him. Fighting against the tendrils of Rourke's web, Matt took her hand and said, "You've been talking about me. Elizabeth and I are partners."

"We'll want Elizabeth's columns," Rourke responded. "I meant what I said: they're brilliant, with enormous appeal. And if you want to be features editor of the chain, you can try it," he said to Elizabeth. "Though I should think you'd rather write than spread yourself thin on jobs that less talented people can handle. However, we'll leave that up to you; it's separate from my other offer." He looked at Matt. "I am not in the market for a husband and wife team. I'm looking for a publisher. One voice. One spokesman. One authority."

In the silence, he gestured to the waitress. "Courvoisier. And more coffee." He drained his cup. "The wallet is full," he said to Matt. "Two hundred million is what I'm prepared to invest as a start. Of course, as we said, you and I are always starting; we'll find something new around every corner. But that's your wallet at the beginning. You'll take over as editor-in-chief of the Albuquerque *Daily News*, at eighty thousand a year; if Elizabeth wants features editor, it pays thirty thousand. In a year, or as soon as the paper stops losing money and begins to show a profit, you'll move up to publisher of Rourke Enterprises at double or triple your salary depending on how well you've done, plus shares in the corporation. You and I will decide which papers to buy, in what order, on what schedule, but you're the one who will run them. It will be your show. Of course, I expect you to make a significant profit."

Numbly, Matt put his hands on the table and stared at them. *Once I was frustrated because there was so much I couldn't do.* With a start, he realized he'd left Elizabeth's hand empty. He turned to look at her. But he didn't really see her: his eyes were shining as if he had emerged suddenly from shadows into brilliant sunlight and was momentarily blinded.

Without waiting, he turned back to Rourke. "When do we start?" he asked.

Part

II

CHAPTER 6

Elizabeth slipped away from the meeting and went to her office to call Isabel. "We can't make dinner after all; I'm sorry, I wanted so much to come, but we're running late."

"Come late. I'll keep dinner warm."

"Isabel, it's such a long drive from Albuquerque, we couldn't get there until after ten. I'm sorry," she repeated. "I don't know what I expected when we took over a newspaper five times as big as the *Chieftain*, but whatever I thought, I underestimated it. There's just too much to do and not enough time. At least, not this weekend. I wish we could make it, but we just can't."

"I wish you could, too. Your kids are already here."

"In Nuevo? They were supposed to be with my parents. How did they get there?"

"Saul and Heather brought them. Then they went mooning off to discover nature together. Or something."

"Who went off?"

"Well, actually, Saul and Heather in one direction and Peter and Maya in another. Lots of sweet nothings being whispered in the valley this evening."

"And Holly?"

"With Luz, as usual. Two sixteen-year-olds bemoaning the lack of sensitive men in the world. She's getting to be a real

130

beauty, Elizabeth. Looks like you. And to hear her sing! She'll make you prouder than your star-struck husband."

"Star-struck," Elizabeth repeated. "What an extraordinary thing to say."

"Good? Bad? I didn't mean to be insulting."

"You weren't; you just described him better than I could."

"But I got it from you, when you told me he was hung up on this macho Texan with all the money. He still is, I suppose; it's only been four months. Less."

"The stakes are high," Elizabeth said briefly, suddenly reluctant to talk about Matt, even with Isabel. "Let's make a new dinner date." She looked at her calendar. "A week from today? Next Saturday? We have a meeting in the morning, but we can be in Nuevo by five."

"If you're sure."

Elizabeth heard the plea in her voice. "What's wrong, Isabel?"

"I don't know; maybe nothing. But something's going on in the valley and I'd like to talk to you and Matt about it."

"I promise we'll be there."

The meeting had ended by the time Elizabeth returned to Matt's office. "Long phone call," he said, writing a note on his calendar.

"I thought we'd finished with my part. Did you need me?"

"I don't like people leaving a meeting in the middle."

"Oh. I'm sorry. It won't happen again. Sir."

He looked up and saw the hurt in her gray eyes. "I'm the one who should apologize. I'm sorry, my sweet. There was a problem after you left and I needed you to back me up and help me keep my temper."

"A problem?"

"Nothing serious; I handled it."

"But what happened?"

"Chet showed up. Whenever he comes in from Houston he sits in a corner like an innocent schoolboy and stares at me. Trying to make me believe Keegan sent him to check up on me."

131

"Like an owl."

"What?"

"His round eyes and round glasses and round cheeks. He looks like an owl, puffed up to convince others how important he is."

Matt laughed. "That helps. I told you I need you. I think I'll send him packing."

"Are you sure he'll go?"

"He'll do what I tell him."

"Even if Keegan did send him?"

"He didn't. He wouldn't do that; he trusts me. I know you don't believe it, but I do and I don't want to argue about him."

"Chet or Keegan?"

"Either one. Now let's talk about 'Private Affairs.' Do you have a list of the people you're going to be writing about?"

She looked at him in surprise. "No."

"How far ahead are you working?"

"Two weeks. Three if I have time."

"I need the names of people you'll write about through October."

"Why?"

"For long-range planning."

"I thought we do that together."

"We do. But I'm going to Houston next weekend and I want to be able to talk to Keegan about our plans."

After a moment, Elizabeth said, "You didn't tell me you were going to Houston."

"He called just before the meeting; we decided then."

"You're going alone."

"I've gone twice; it's not different from the other times."

"The other times we talked about it and decided together that I should stay home with Peter and Holly."

"And since we'd talked about it twice I didn't think we needed to talk about it again."

"I see." There was a pause. "I made a date with Isabel for dinner next Saturday."

"Well, you can go, with Peter and Holly. You don't need me."

"But you need me, when you want me, to back you up and help you hold your temper . . ."

"Oh, for Christ's sake——!"

Stop whining like a neglected wife. "Matt, we decided to run this paper together. A new town, a daily instead of a weekly, a staff of ninety-five instead of the *Chieftain*'s fifteen, six months to show a profit, which didn't give us much time: only until October—" She stopped. *A list of people through October.* "You're going to Houston to plan what happens after October. You and Keegan."

"Since we're halfway through August, we'd better be talking about it, don't you think?"

"Yes. I wondered why we hadn't."

"We've been busy turning this paper around. And we're doing it, Elizabeth; the figures for July came in last night; I've been going over them. Listen to this . . ." He took a computer printout from a drawer and began to read totals for circulation, classified and display advertising, and advertising rates. "And something else: more than half our advertisers say they want their ad on the same page as 'Private Affairs.'" When Elizabeth made no response, he said, "I thought that would please you."

"It does. It's going to be a crowded page."

He flung his pencil on the desk. "I can't force him to ask both of us to come to Houston."

"I understand that. But he knows we run the paper together."

"That wasn't the way he intended it."

"I know that, too. But he didn't object when we told him what we'd decided. He could invite me to Houston as a courtesy."

Matt shrugged. "Whatever he does, you don't like him. I thought you'd gotten over that; you don't talk about him as much as you did when we got back from Aspen."

"I've been holding my tongue. It isn't that I don't like him, Matt; I don't know what he's after."

"He's told you. You don't believe him?"

"Not as easily as you do."

"On what grounds?"

"None. Instinct."

133

"Not good enough."

"Reporters have gotten scoops because they listened to their instincts."

"And followed up with research, interviews, digging for facts, and hours of writing to make sure everything fits together."

"I know. That's why I haven't talked about it. But, Matt, remember, on our way home from Aspen I asked you, *Why us?* Why us, Matt? I love you and I think you're wonderful, but Keegan doesn't love you and all he knew about us when he came to Aspen was that we were two small-town editors with practically no experience. There are cities all over the country with editors who have credentials a mile long. *Why us?*"

"He told us. He liked the way we turned the *Chieftain* around, and he liked the ideas I had when we talked in Aspen."

"He liked your ambition."

"There is nothing wrong with ambition. You have it, too."

"Yes, but not enough to keep me from asking questions when somebody hands me the pot of gold at the end of a rainbow."

"All right," Matt said after a moment. "Why did he choose us?"

"I don't know. But instinct says maybe he was looking for small-town, inexperienced people because those are the kind he can manipulate."

"For what purpose?"

"I don't know. If I did, I wouldn't be worried. I'd either be going along with him or quitting."

Thoughtfully, Matt rolled a pencil along his desk. Finally, he said, "I think you should stop worrying. We may be small town, but we're not inexperienced, not after the past year and a half; and we're not stupid. If Keegan Rourke thinks he can use us, he'll find he can't. I don't believe that's what he's after, though; there's been no sign of it in the past four months. I think he wants someone he can count on——"

"He has a staff. And he has Chet Colfax. You said yourself you thought he might have been sent here——"

"I also said I didn't believe it. Rourke knew your family; he read the *Chieftain* for a year before calling me; he likes what he knows about me so far. We talk on the telephone three or four times a week and he's comfortable with me. That's enough for me. And I wish to hell it was enough for you, because I'm tired of this endless speculating about a man I like and trust."

The small office was silent. Elizabeth opened one of the folders she was holding. "I'd like to talk about my proposals for new weekly columns. One on new books for the Book-mobiles, one on flower arranging, which the Ikebana Club has agreed to write, and one written by members of the Leads Club on organizing women's networks."

"I'd like an answer. Is that enough for you or do you still think he's some kind of devil in disguise?"

"It isn't important. I work for him and I'll do the best I can. Matt, I have a lot to do, including the list of names you wanted for 'Private Affairs.' Can we get started?"

He hesitated, then gave a short nod. Elizabeth spread some sample pages on his desk and they bent over them. But the atmosphere that had been so warm when he laughed at her comparison of Chet Colfax to an owl had become chilly; they were brisk and business-like, and within half an hour Elizabeth was back at her desk and Matt had left to have lunch with a group of local businessmen.

You can go with Peter and Holly. You don't need me.
Who says?

The trouble was, she couldn't fight him, at least not now. All Matt could see at the moment was the vision of the newspaper empire Rourke had dangled before him, and Elizabeth couldn't stand in his way. Everything we've built together, she thought, depends on my staying with him, helping him, *backing him up.*

And maybe our marriage depends on it, too.

"Well, I don't believe that for a minute," Lydia said the next evening when Elizabeth came to pick up Peter and Holly, who had spent Sunday with their grandparents. "Matt wouldn't let your marriage suffer over a few newspapers. Come sit in the courtyard for a few minutes. Have some iced tea and relax; you look exhausted. Have you had dinner?"

"We grabbed a bite," Elizabeth said. "I *am* tired; a day of rest now and then would be nice." She followed Lydia through the house to the *placita*, where roses climbed on trellises and chrysanthemums grew against the surrounding adobe walls. "Wherever you live, you make the most beautiful garden I ever saw." She took the cold glass Lydia handed her and sat back with a sigh on a cushioned chaise. The house was in the hills of Tesuque and the air was cooling as the sun set. "Better than Albuquerque; it's so hot there, even at night. Where are Peter and Holly?"

"In the garage with Spencer. He's been cleaning it out for weeks; I have no idea why. Your children are worried about you."

"About me?"

"About their family. They say they haven't much of one."

"I told them we'd have a rough six months and then get back to normal. Do they think I didn't mean it?"

"They think you won't be able to control it."

"Oh. Well, assuming my husband and I stay friends, I can."

"Friends! You'll be lovers and partners and everything else you've been since you bought your paper; that doesn't disappear just because a man has a new job dangled in front of him. Matt's going through a stage; it won't be long before he stops chasing moonbeams and comes back to the *Chieftain*."

Elizabeth shook her head. "He won't come back to the *Chieftain;* he wants the moonbeams. And the point is, Mother, I can't tell him not to go after them, because I want some of my own."

"What does that mean?"

Elizabeth finished her iced tea, set the glass on the table beside her, and put back her head, looking at the darkening sky and the first planets blinking above the mountains, as bright as tiny spotlights. "It means Matt isn't the only one who's dazzled. I don't know why Keegan chose us, or what he really wants, but that doesn't mean I'm not excited about the possibility of a newspaper chain that stretches from Los Angeles to Houston. Do you know how many hundreds of thousands of readers I'd have for 'Private Affairs'? And space! I could write twice a week, three times . . . . When I think about it, I'm like Matt, itching to get started and see what I can do; I can almost hear the applause. Can I turn my back on that?"

Lydia's face was blank. "I never knew you were ambitious."

There is nothing wrong with ambition. "It's not a weakness to want applause, Mother."

"But if it hurts your marriage? You were worried about staying friends with Matt."

"I didn't mean that. We're worn out, we have too much to do, and sometimes we snap at each other." Elizabeth stood and slipped her shoulder bag over her arm. "Time to go; Peter and Holly want to come to Albuquerque tomorrow, and Matt and Saul are working on fall plans for the *Chieftain* and I want to be in on the features part. Saul's so good he really doesn't need us, but we like to keep in touch." She bent and kissed Lydia. "Don't worry about us. I can't be an obstacle in Matt's path; I have to be with him all the way. But the closer I stay, the more we can talk and understand each other and want the same things."

They walked together into the house. "Are you sure you know what you want?" Lydia asked.

Elizabeth gave a small laugh. "I want all of it. My husband, my children, our partnership, and applause just for me. Maybe it's too much, but why shouldn't I try? I'm almost forty-two and I've never felt younger or more full of energy. When would I try, if not now?" She kissed Lydia good-bye, called Peter and Holly, and met them at the car. And it was as she was driving home, listening to them tell her about their day, that she thought over what she had said to her mother and realized how many times she had said "I."

For all my brave talk, how much do I still believe in "We"?

"We're looking for an assistant editor at the paper," said Saul casually as he started the car.

"Which department?" Heather asked, settling beside him.

"Those special sections Elizabeth started."

She nodded, keeping her face calm. She and Saul had talked dozens of times about the possibility of her working at the

137

paper when the budget allowed it, but now she refused to ask for it.

Saul knew that stubborn silence, and knew she would not risk being accused of taking advantage of their affair. "You could handle it," he said.

She nodded again. "Probably."

"You've helped us plan them; you used to help Elizabeth when she needed it . . ."

"I know."

"You wanted to be an assistant so you could learn the newspaper business. And you learn faster than anyone I know."

"But you've told me I'm foolish for turning down your generous offer of marriage. If I am so foolish, how can I handle the job of assistant editor at the *Chieftain?*"

"You're being childish."

She sighed. "That is one of your favorite lines."

"The two have nothing to do with each other. You'd make a superb assistant editor. But if the idea is painful, don't take the job."

"I don't know if it would be painful. How much would we be working together?"

"Some days intimately; others not at all."

She nodded. "I might enjoy that."

Which? Saul wondered, his face longer and more melancholy than usual. Remember, he told himself, you were thirteen when this young woman was born; you're supposed to be a wise and mature man of the world. Act like it. He turned onto Camino Rancheros, slowing to avoid sending up clouds of dust from the road. "I don't think of you as a child," he said. "If I did, I wouldn't want to marry you."

"Yes, so you've said before."

"I've said that before?"

"Something like it." She looked at him. "I do not want to marry you. I do not want to marry anyone. I like being in bed with you and you like it, too; I like going places with you and you like it, too; that should satisfy you."

"It doesn't satisfy me."

138

"It satisfied you with other women for thirty-eight years—"

"Thirty-seven, God damn it! I'm only thirty-seven!"

A smile curved the corners of her full mouth and her green eyes danced. "I'm sorry; I forget."

"You do not forget. You remember everything."

She nodded, suddenly somber. "Yes. I do."

Saul put his hand on hers. "Heather. Darling Heather. All men are not like that son of a bitch you followed to Santa Fe. I don't resemble him in the slightest. You can't live your entire life in fear of being hurt because you trusted someone."

"But I can go slowly. I'm only twenty-four."

"Yes, so you've told me before."

"We're repeating ourselves," she said. "Like an old married couple. What time will Holly and Peter be ready?"

Saul gave a resigned shrug. "At three. Or have I said that before?"

"You're behaving like a child."

He burst out laughing. "You win," he said, and as he pulled to a stop at the Lovells' house he leaned over and gave her a quick kiss.

"Nice," Peter said, getting into the back seat. "Nice to see you two getting along for a change."

"Peter," Heather said mildly, "that is very personal."

"Just a comment. I'm interested in people who get along with each other."

"Why?" Saul asked.

"Because my parents don't seem to these days."

Holly appeared and got in the car next to Peter. "Don't seem to what?"

"Get along," answered Peter.

"You don't know anything about it," Holly protested. "We don't see enough of them to know whether they do or not."

"Now that is a true statement," Peter said moodily.

"We are sitting in a car on a lovely Saturday afternoon," Saul pointed out. "Your parents enjoy knowing the four of us are together. I'd like to enjoy it, too. Does anyone have a suggestion on how to do that?"

"We go to Nuevo," Peter said.

Saul turned in his seat. "Peter, you may have a standing invitation but we don't, and I'm not about to make that trip twice in one day to take you and bring you back."

"We're invited," Holly said. "Isabel made dinner because she was expecting Mother and when I called she said we should come."

"She was expecting Mother because Mother promised to come," Peter added. "Another one of Mother's promises."

"That's not fair!" Holly said angrily. "Why are you so down on her? She keeps as many as she can. And she really meant to see Isabel today; she just decided at the last minute she ought to go to Houston with Daddy instead."

"Right." Peter slumped in his seat. "The big man always comes first, and after him the goddam newspaper, and somewhere along the line the rest of us. Are we going to Nuevo or not?" he asked Saul.

Saul looked at Heather. "What would you like?"

"Let's take Peter to Nuevo. Holly, what about you?"

"I want to go there, too. Luz is expecting me."

"Well, then, we'll go. And we'll eat with Isabel so her dinner won't be unappreciated."

Saul started the car and the conversation divided, Saul and Heather talking in low voices in the front seat, Peter and Holly in the back, their murmurs unintelligible beneath the rush of cooled air that kept the dusty August heat from the car. But as Saul made the turn into Nuevo, Peter leaned forward, looking out the window, then suddenly commanded, "Stop here!"

Saul jammed on the brakes. "Well, really," Heather said, rubbing her neck where the shoulder belt bit into it when she jerked forward. But then she followed Peter's gaze and saw Maya, sitting on a bench in front of the general store. "Oh, well," she said mildly.

"Thanks," Peter said, and was out of the car in an instant.

"Nine o'clock!" Saul called after him. "We're leaving at nine!"

Peter waved over his shoulder, but he was looking at Maya. "Hi," he said.

She stood up. "I thought you weren't coming." She was

140

small and dark, the top of her head barely reaching his chin. Her black hair, cut in straight bangs above solemn black eyes, was held behind her ears by a band of hammered sterling silver, and her long white dress was belted with silver loops. The gauzy fabric made Peter think of a nightgown, especially when she moved. The sun was behind her and her long slim legs were outlined against her dress, and he was struggling to deal with the ideas of nightgown and bare legs and the swelling tightness in his crotch when she came close to him and put both hands on his chest. "I was thinking, if you didn't come, I'd go to your house."

"You'd what?" He was having trouble breathing. She smelled like roses and sage and his arms came up and folded themselves around her. "Why? I mean, how would you get there?"

"Who cares? Hitch-hike. Mama says she wants me to be more Spanish; she wants me to live in Argentina—"

"Argentina! Jesus Christ, that's another continent!"

"—with her cousin in Buenos Aires. Peter, what am I going to do? If I go away you'll forget me. That was why I wanted to go to your house—to tell you this."

Maya's arms were around Peter's neck; her face was turned up to his and Peter, with a long sigh that was more nearly a groan, lifted her in his arms and kissed her. They had kissed and hugged and his hands had wandered about the delicate lines of her body before, but this was different: Maya opened her mouth beneath his, her little tongue danced and licked and curled about his, and then, as he held her against him, she wrapped her legs about his hips, clinging to him as if she were a drowning swimmer.

Peter thought he was going to burst. He was so swollen he hurt, and when Maya tightened her legs to keep from slipping and pressed more firmly against him, he got even harder and he had to do something: get away from her so he could open his pants and relieve the pressure or take her somewhere and get inside her where he'd wanted to be for weeks, lying in bed every night going crazy imagining Maya under him, on top of him, touching him, kissing him . . .

He pulled his mouth from hers. "Listen," he said, but only

141

a strangled sound came out. He set her down on the dusty path and tried to take a breath. "Can we? Go? Somewhere?"

Maya took his hand and they walked across the town to the river on the other side, and a road that followed it up the valley. They walked in silence, hand in hand, Peter taking long ragged breaths, trying to walk steadily and purposefully instead of lurching beside Maya, who seemed so calm he felt like an oaf. They came to a barn—"My father's," Maya said. "He stores grain here in the winter"—and, pushing open the door, they went into its musty coolness. A thin line of sunlight lay across the floor, pointing to a pile of hay in the corner. "No one ever comes here," she said. "It's my special private place."

"I love you," Peter said.

She looked at him solemnly. "You don't have to say that. I already want you to make love to me. I don't need to be—"

"Damn it, I love you! Don't tell me what I can't do!" He stopped. "I'm sorry; I didn't mean to yell."

She smiled. "Do you think we could sit down?"

"God, yes."

A folded plaid blanket lay nearby and they spread it on the hay. "I use it when I come here to read," Maya said. "And think."

"About what?"

"You." She lay her head against his chest, curling her legs under her. "I love you, too. I won't go to Argentina. I'll run away and get a job and when I have enough money I'll go to college wherever you are and get lots of learning so you won't be ashamed—"

Peter kissed her. He unhooked the clasp on her silver belt and then his hand found her leg beneath her skirt and slid up its smooth curve. He wished he were casual and experienced, he wished he weren't so afraid of hurting her, he wished she would help him. But Maya kept her arms around his neck, her head back, eyes closed, lips slightly parted, and he suddenly realized he couldn't tell whether she was in ecstasy or scared to death.

But he couldn't wait to find out. He yanked open his jeans and slid them off, taking his underpants with them, feeling euphoric as the pressure eased. Confidence surged through him; with one motion he pulled Maya's white dress up and over her head. He had never seen such a gloriously beautiful body, smooth, pale bronze, with small pointed breasts and a little triangle of red curly hair—

"Your shirt," Maya said shakily.

"Oh. I forgot . . ." He tore it off, then her arms came up and he held her, their two bodies tight together. Peter's skin burned against hers, and his lips burned when they met hers, but crazily he couldn't feel anything else except his cock between her legs. He didn't seem to have feet or legs or arms; he was all burning skin and feeling that he was going to explode. "Maya," he murmured. *"Please . . ."*

Without a word she lay back on the blanket, looking at him with dark, dark eyes. "I love you," she said. "I love you." Peter touched her triangle of red hair with his hand and as his finger moved into her smooth wet darkness, her legs opened. "Now I'll never have to leave," she said. "Now no one can make me leave." Her breathing came in quick little bursts; her hands fluttered at Peter's chest and he wished she'd grab hold of him but he knew she wouldn't; instead, he pulled out his finger and reached for his pants to find the box he'd been carrying for weeks. His fingers shook as he slipped the thin rubber over his cock and then, while Maya watched him, he lay on her. At the feel of her, a piercing kind of pain tore through his body, a wonderful joy, and then he thought, *Oh, no, please God, not yet, not yet, not yet . . .* and somehow he held himself together while pushing into the tight clinging warmth of this beautiful incredible girl under him, deeper and deeper, until he was all the way in. He felt her flinching, and he wanted to say he was sorry for hurting her, but how could he when he was feeling this wonderful joy? He moved as slowly as he could; he wanted to pound into her but instead he moved his hips in small circles, rubbing against her, wishing she would like it. Then he heard her whisper his name and looking down he saw her eyes tightly closed, her mouth open, her body arching against his. Thank you, he thought; Maya, I love you; thank you . . . It was all right; he didn't have to hold himself in any longer. He thrust into her sweet body, in and out in her fantastic slippery tightness and then at last felt the surge and explosive release he'd been holding back. And then Peter Lovell rested beside his love with a sigh of the most amazing happiness anyone in the whole world had ever known.

Two drinks were on the table when they arrived. "A little touch one appreciates," Rourke told Elizabeth as she and Matt sat down. "I always have the same table, with the same waiters; therefore my simple preferences are met without the dreary repetition of ordering Stolichnaya each time I arrive. A waste of time. Tony's avoids all that, which is why I come here."

"You come here," said Matt, smiling, "because everyone you know comes here, because the food is the best in town, and because you like to feed Wilma tidbits of information."

"Your husband knows all my secrets," Rourke said to Elizabeth. "Wilma has a notable gossip column and she is fond of gathering information at Tony's. What will you drink?"

"Chardonnay, please." Elizabeth looked at Matt. "They know your simple preferences too? I had no idea vodka was one of them."

"I like it now and then," he said briefly. Between them hung the unspoken words—*But not in Santa Fe*.

"Perhaps I like to be here because of my son," Rourke said after ordering wine for Elizabeth. "It amuses me that Houston's most famous restaurant has the same name as my well-known offspring." He paused again to exchange greetings with Tony Vallone, the owner of the restaurant, who stopped at a number of tables, but clearly, Elizabeth saw, not all of them. Vallone moved on, and Rourke asked, "Have you talked to him lately?"

"Tony? Not for a long time," Elizabeth answered. The waiter put a glass of wine in front of her and she held the stem with nervous fingers. She didn't know how Rourke really felt about her being there, since his secretary had announced them on the intercom when they arrived and it was almost ten minutes before they were shown into his office. By then he had hidden whatever annoyance or anger he had felt, and in five hours of meetings that afternoon, he had shown nothing but amiability,

144

explaining reasons behind the budget items she questioned, describing activities of Rourke Enterprises she hadn't known about, asking for her opinion when they were going over editorial policy and news coverage in Albuquerque.

Everything seemed fine; everything should have been fine. Especially now, with business out of the way and nothing to think about but dinner in this lovely restaurant, decorated in soft pastels with modern paintings on burgundy suede walls. It was a spacious room bisected by a long, low planter thick with azaleas. Lavish bouquets were on every table, but they were as low as the planter: nothing was allowed to obstruct the views of the corporate and social elite who came to Tony's specifically to be seen.

"Tony has a new wife," Rourke was saying. Elizabeth turned to him in surprise. "Marion, I think, but perhaps that was his first."

"Ginger," said Elizabeth. "They were at our wedding."

"Ah." He nodded. "I lose track. In any event, they've been married a year, I believe; a record for Tony. He speaks warmly of you. Doesn't miss one of your columns. Neither do I, by the way. I'm sure Matt told you, but it doesn't hurt to repeat it. Yes, two more," he said to the waiter who stood nearby, and to Elizabeth, "More wine, my dear?"

"Yes, thank you."

Rourke nodded, then went on. "We're very excited about you, Elizabeth. I don't know how you do it: two superb columns a week, and you've made the features section of the *Daily News* the most lively in Albuquerque." He sat back as the waiter brought another glass of wine for Elizabeth and two more glasses of vodka embedded in silver bowls of crushed ice. "You know, my dear, I've watched you grow up from a baby into a remarkable woman. I can't tell you how impressed I am."

Elizabeth flushed and began to relax. Why should she look for reasons behind Rourke's words? In the brightly-lit room, she saw only sincerity and pleasure in his eyes, and looking at Matt's proud smile, she felt more of her tension slip away.

Matt put his hand on hers. He had been silent, letting Rourke win Elizabeth's confidence. He was tired of having to defend

Rourke to her; annoyed even when she evaded discussions of him because he knew she was simply keeping her doubts to herself. Strange that he'd never seen the obvious solution: bring her to Houston and let her see Keegan Rourke on his own ground: a shrewd businessman wealthy enough to look for wider horizons; a sophisticated, charming host; a good friend for them to have. Matt tightened his hand on Elizabeth's. All he wanted was that the two of them would be friends.

"Keegan acts like a proud father," he told Elizabeth. "I'm afraid he takes credit for inventing you."

"No, no." Rourke chuckled. "Elizabeth Lovell is definitely her own person. And as of last week, a famous one! My dear Elizabeth, we haven't toasted your triumph!" He lifted his glass. "To a lovely and talented lady and her 'Private Affairs,' especially the one on 'Joey,' which was reprinted in this month's *Good Housekeeping*. You're not a local writer anymore, my dear; you've leaped over all of us."

"It was only one column," Elizabeth protested.

"One is all it takes. Remember that, Elizabeth. One triumph changes everything. When a magazine with such an enormous readership reprints your column, you are a national writer and you must think of yourself as one. That's how I talk about you to my friends when I read your columns to them."

"You what?" She could not imagine him doing that.

"I carry them around with me. Not all of them, of course, but"—he held up a small packet of clippings—"enough to give people their flavor. Not quite as bad as forcing pictures of one's infant on a captive audience, but close." He smiled. "And I agree with *Good Housekeeping*: 'Joey' is one of the best. It reminds me of Tony when he was young; when we still got along. And when my friends read it, especially the part about Joey's rebellion and how he's never sure if he's gone too far and made his parents stop loving him, they ask me how you know *their* teenagers. My dear Elizabeth, Joey is every teenager in America! This is a masterpiece!"

Elizabeth regarded her wine glass, wondering how one responded to such overheated praise. She knew the story was good; she also knew it wasn't a masterpiece. "Thank you," she said. "I know readers liked that piece; we got a lot of mail on it—"

"More than any other story at any time," Matt put in.

"—but it could have been better. I don't have as much time as I'd like to work on each piece."

"I understand. That's a real problem. Here you have a talent, a rare talent, and you can't concentrate on it."

Tino Escobedo, the maitre d', appeared and Rourke said to Matt and Elizabeth, "I'll order for us, if you don't mind; the best dishes aren't on the menu."

The two men plunged into a serious debate and Elizabeth and Matt exchanged a smile. Their hands tightened. "I love you," Elizabeth whispered, her lips close to Matt's ear.

Matt brushed her lips with his. "I'm glad you're here. You were right and I apologize for being a boor and telling you to stay home."

"You were extremely angry," Elizabeth mused. "As if I were horning in on a deal . . . or intruding on a love affair . . ."

"Nonsense." He drained his glass. "I thought we were past that kind of talk."

She studied him. "You never used to have two drinks before dinner."

"Now," Rourke said, turning back. "Where were we? Yes, Elizabeth's writing." He turned his glass thoughtfully in his fingers. "Isn't there a way you could concentrate on it? With the attention you've gotten with 'Joey,' you should be appearing three times a week instead of two."

"I can't do it," Elizabeth replied. "I'd love to, but I can't. I barely have time for two as it is."

"Exactly my point! You don't have time for the one talent which will make you famous. And help make our papers famous as well."

Elizabeth frowned. Why did he exaggerate so? Newspapers don't become famous because of one columnist, and he had the money to buy any columns he wanted from national syndicators. Did he think she was a fool?

"Elizabeth, you're forgetting what I said. The more you appear, the larger your audience and the more likely that other

147

publications will reprint your pieces. Then you'll be syndicated by one of those companies—NEA, Knight-Ridder, Markham Features, I can't remember them all—and you'll appear in three or four hundred papers. Now you're not going to tell me that doesn't appeal to you!"

"Of course it does," said Matt. "You should have seen her face when the *Good Housekeeping* editor called to say they wanted 'Joey' for their series on teenagers. She didn't come down to earth all week."

Rourke nodded. "An exciting step. And well-deserved."

"More than exciting," Matt said. "It was the first time Elizabeth was on a level with professionals who publish nationally. It's a little like being born: suddenly you're for real."

Surprised, Elizabeth said, "I never knew you understood that."

"Because you never knew I felt the same way."

"When?" she asked, then quickly said, "Oh. I see." How strange that she had never realized it was Keegan who made Matt feel like a real newspaper publisher. She'd thought the *Chieftain* and the *Sun* would do it. But if I needed a national magazine to feel like a real writer, she reflected, why wouldn't Matt need more, too?

"The whole *Daily News* staff celebrated," Matt told Rourke. "And Holly and Peter made enough copies of the story to flood the southwest. But more important"—letting go of her hand, he put his arm around her—"it made Elizabeth Lovell the center of attention. And about time, too. She was feeling the lack of it."

For the second time, Elizabeth looked at him in surprise. "I never told you that."

"And you thought I was too dazzled by my own importance to see it."

She looked away—and met Rourke's amused glance. "Yes," she said. "I thought you were."

Tino arrived with a bottle of wine. Rourke read the label, and nodded, and Tino drew out the cork and handed it to him so he could pass it lightly beneath his nose. He nodded again and Tino poured a small amount into Rourke's glass. He swirled it, sipped it, nodded once more, and Tino filled all three glasses and left.

Elizabeth barely watched the ritual; she was thinking about the past four months. Matt was right: it had bothered her that he was the one who got the attention and the credit for improvements they'd worked out together. He was the one Chet Colfax called to report that Rourke was pleased or needed some information or wanted a particular story written; he was the one whom businessmen praised for the new liveliness and brightness of the paper; he was the one—because he wrote the editorials—who was asked to give speeches on local issues. "Private Affairs" was admired; it got mail and telephone calls; but only when it appeared nationally did Elizabeth get the kind of star treatment Matt got.

And Rourke wanted to know if that appealed to her!

"I've wanted you to get more credit from the beginning," Matt told Elizabeth when their dinners were before them. "But there's no glamour in being features editor, and no visibility. Keegan is right; you've got to work on 'Private Affairs' full-time. Three columns a week would be wonderful; you could do that, couldn't you?"

"Of course I could." The wine glowed within her, the pastel birds on the blue chintz chair covers seemed to sing. Most important, Matt's pride and understanding of her feelings, when she'd thought he hadn't even been paying attention, made her feel loved. Dreamily, she watched Rourke wind pasta around his fork and bring it to his mouth without a single dangling end. I'll have to tell Peter about that, she thought; he always says it's impossible. "I'd love to write three a week. But I run the features department and that's a full-time job in itself."

"I thought you understood," said Matt. "It's absurd for anyone with your talent to edit features all day. Keegan and I have talked it over and we both feel, now that you've organized the department, you should do something more important."

It took a minute, in her dreamy mood, for Elizabeth to grasp Matt's words. *Keegan and I have talked it over.* "I don't understand. You and Keegan have already decided this?"

"Of course not," Rourke said with a smile. "We wouldn't

149

decide anything behind your back. We were discussing personnel the other day when I telephoned—"

"And I come under 'Personnel.'"

"Everyone does, my dear, including myself. All we said about you was that we were wasting your talent by forcing you to be part of the daily grind of running a department."

"We said more than that." Matt put down his fork. "We want to use everyone in the best way and it isn't best if your interviewing and writing take second place to another job. We think you should get out of editing. First, because you're too good to be doing it, but more than that: you get too tired, you have no time for yourself, you don't see your friends, and you've been worried about not spending enough time with Holly and Peter."

"I've been worried that neither of us is spending enough time with them."

"I know that and I'm going to see what I can do about it. But right now, if one of us has to cut back, it should be the one who can work anywhere. You can write your column at home; you write it there most of the time as it is, at night, after the rest of us, who only have one job, are asleep."

"I also said we weren't spending enough time with each other."

"We'll do something about that," said Rourke. "I don't want my favorite people to be unhappy. Though of course I'm sure you didn't expect to continue working together much longer."

Of course we did; the whole idea was to work together.

"I see it all the time," Rourke continued. "Teams that start out together eventually move apart as each one finds a niche or a new path. Of course if they trust each other it doesn't matter; they take whatever direction is necessary to succeed, like the two of you. The paper flourishes, the Lovell name is becoming known, Elizabeth even has the *Good Housekeeping* seal of approval." He smiled at his wit. "And Matt, too: making quite a name for himself. That talk you gave in Wyoming the other day—Laramie, wasn't it?—was written up as far away as Phoenix and Oklahoma City."

"Chet's been very thorough," said Matt dryly.

"Chet gets paid for being thorough; how can I know what my executives are up to if he doesn't keep me informed? Well, popularity and success carry a price; it's no wonder you don't have enough time together. But I promise we'll do something about it."

"I think we can work on that ourselves," Elizabeth said coolly, her dreaminess gone. It was strange, she thought, that as clever as Rourke was, he didn't realize when he was going too far and too fast, or how it made her feel to know he kept such close tabs on them.

My father's shadow. The reach of his long arm. In that luxurious restaurant, being given a sample of the kind of life that came with being part of his empire, Elizabeth understood what Tony had meant. She felt a sharp longing for her home and her family. The four of us, she thought, as we were before, with the excitement of owning the *Chieftain.*

But it was too late. It was no longer exciting to Matt. She looked at him thoughtfully: her handsome beloved husband, who wanted to accomplish so much. He had echoed her—"Elizabeth is right, Keegan; we'll handle that problem ourselves"—and then they had begun to talk about the circulation of the *Daily News* and the *Houston Record.* So Matt was involved with Rourke's Houston paper, Elizabeth thought. And probably with other parts of Rourke Enterprises. Too late; too late. The words ran through her head. It was too late to go back to their small success. They had to learn to handle this larger one because it didn't matter whether she wanted part of it or none of it. It was theirs.

She put her hand on Matt's, interrupting his talk. "What do you think? Do you want me to leave the features department? We wouldn't be working together if I did."

A wave of fatigue and frustration swept over Matt. He loved her so much, but Keegan was right: there was a time when people had to go in separate directions. "Yes," he said. "I want you to do it." He turned his hand and clasped hers. "It doesn't make sense for you to do anything but write: it's your strength, it's what you love, and you always say you'd like more time for it. You've trained a good staff: you could promote your assistant to features editor, come in one or two days a week until everything is under control, and write your columns at home where it's quiet and you have all the time you need. And you'll see more of Holly and Peter. You can even keep an eye on Saul; I think he's beginning to believe the *Chieftain* and the *Sun* are his. Elizabeth, it's the right thing to do."

"It's very well thought out," she said quietly.

"It's worth a try, don't you think?"

It sounded like a question, but Elizabeth knew it wasn't. Her husband was telling her he wanted her to agree, because this was something very important to him.

And if I said no, what would I win?

"Of course it's worth a try," Elizabeth said. "We can always change back if it doesn't work out."

"But it will work out," Rourke said. "It's a real breakthrough for you. Wait until you see how much greater your audience will be, especially when we begin to buy new papers. My dear Elizabeth, this is a wonderful thing for you; I'm so pleased. Your parents will be delighted." One of the waiters brought a fruit basket to the table, with a dish of powdered sugar on the side. Rourke took a strawberry, dipped it in the sugar, and said, "Raspberry soufflé for dessert. And while we're waiting, we'll have another bottle of wine. To celebrate."

Tuesday: a hot, dry August morning, the first weekday in months Elizabeth had stayed home. After Matt left alone for Albuquerque, she sat in the kitchen drinking a second cup of coffee. She imagined him driving through the landscape of sand and sage, past the Santo Domingo school silhouetted against the mountains on the horizon, past birds perched on telephone wires, heads tilted as if testing the wind before soaring on its currents, higher and higher, until they could no longer be seen from the road where she and Matt had driven for four months, beginning their day together.

I've got to get out of here, she thought. Just to clear my head. There's so much to get used to. I'll take a drive with Holly and Peter; then I'll come back and get to work.

I can't take a drive. Matt has the car.

Something they'd forgotten: they hadn't needed two cars since buying the *Chieftain* because they'd been working together. Now they were back to separate jobs. And two cars.

Elizabeth picked up the telephone and called Lydia. "Mother, could I borrow your car, just for the morning? It's something we didn't think about. We'll have to buy another one."

"Heather will drive over and you can drive her back," Lydia said. "And why don't you keep it for a few days? I can use Heather's, and your father won't be going anywhere; he's decided to become a cabinetmaker."

"A cabinetmaker? He's never even sawed a piece of wood in half."

"My very words. He says if Matt Lovell can have a midlife crisis and change his life, Spencer Evans can have a late-life crisis and change his. He says he's always wanted to work with wood. He says he's restless and bored and Heather and I can handle the bookshop perfectly well and he wants to get back to nature and use only basic tools, no power saws and so on, and make beautiful things."

"He said all that?"

"All that and more. And if it makes him happy, why not? I won't see him much, since he'll be in the garage—that's why he was cleaning it; he's converted half of it to a woodworking shop—but if he's more pleasant at dinner, it's probably worth it."

"He just left you with the bookshop—"

"It's perfectly all right, dear; I love it and it's what I do best. It will work out and I'm sure we'll both be better for it."

And where have I heard that before? Elizabeth wondered, cleaning up the kitchen. She glanced through the window and saw Holly and Peter, watching for Heather, deep in discussion. They were getting along so well, Elizabeth thought. They were growing up.

"I suppose you'll disappear when we get to Nuevo," Holly was saying, shading her eyes to look up the street.

Peter squinted. "I suppose."

She picked up a branch that had broken off their olive tree

153

and drew a circle in the packed red dirt of the street. "Maya is very pretty."

Peter nodded.

"She has such beautiful hair. It shines in the sun."

A sigh tore loose from Peter as he imagined the small triangle of hair he kept wanting to kiss except he didn't know if she'd like it . . . and then his pants bulged and he turned hastily away from his sister, walking in circles, kicking up puffs of dust.

"And she's so nice," Holly persisted.

"Uh-huh." Peter's back was to her. "She's a good listener," he said, wanting to talk about her but afraid he'd say too much.

"That's what you do? Talk?"

"What's wrong with talking? You don't ask me that about the men I talk to in the pueblos."

"You don't want to make love to the men in the pueblos."

Peter broke into nervous laughter and Holly giggled and then, with relief, Peter saw Heather driving toward them.

Seeing them laughing, Heather thought what a difference it made, having their mother home. Only one day and already they looked happier than they had all summer—although the last couple of weeks Peter had looked dreamy and out of it altogether, lost in some private fantasy. Holly looked wonderful, Heather thought, in shorts and a white shirt, long-legged, tanned, her ash-blond hair like a pale waterfall down her back. Her beauty, like Elizabeth's, always made Heather sigh with envy, but in a rather pleasant way, since you can't really envy people you adore, and anyway, she knew she couldn't look like Elizabeth or Holly unless she woke up one morning with different hair, a different face, and a different figure. Not very likely, she reflected, so I give up. And then, involuntarily, she thought: Saul loves me the way I am.

"Okay, everybody," she said aloud. "Hop in and take me back to work; I have a very strict boss."

"Oh, sure," Peter said as Elizabeth joined them and they all got in the car. "Grandma was never strict in her whole life."

"Probably not," Heather agreed. "Which is why I love her."

"Instead of Saul," Holly said wisely, "who is very strict."

154

Elizabeth, sitting in front with Heather, turned around. "You seem to know a great deal about it."

"We've been with them a lot lately, listening to them fight, while you were in Albuquerque."

"A little more respect, please." Heather's face was red. "We don't fight. We have long talks."

"Right," said Peter.

Elizabeth turned back to Heather. "Not going too well?"

"Sometimes." Heather's lower lip trembled. "He keeps telling me what I should do. He's a lot older and he's been all over the world and won prizes and seen everything, and maybe he does know what's good for me, but I'd like to find out for myself and make up my own mind. Don't you think I ought to? At least try?"

"Yes," Elizabeth said as they pulled up in front of the shop on Canyon Road. "Is it really all right if I keep the car for a while?"

"Sure. Lydia and I will use mine, and Spencer has disappeared in a cloud of sawdust. Keep it until you buy a new one. Make it fancy. And expensive."

"Why?" Elizabeth asked, amused.

"Consolation prize. See you later."

Consolation prize. Because she was the one staying home, while Matt drove off and conquered the world?

But he was right; one of us should spend more time with Peter and Holly. And I have my writing. I don't need consolation.

Still, a fancy car would be nice, she thought, turning on the air conditioning as they left Santa Fe and drove toward the Sangre de Cristo mountains through rolling, reddish-brown hills, dry grazing land, and clumps of scraggly trees. We can afford it now, and why shouldn't I have a nice one? I'll be driving around the state, interviewing people; I might as well be comfortable while I do it.

The divided highway was almost empty and Elizabeth speeded up beyond Canoncito, beginning the climb into the mountains. Holly sat beside her, Peter lounged in back, and they talked about the summer that was coming to an end.

"You know what we sound like?" Holly asked. "Like school, when everybody comes back at the end of vacation and compares notes."

"True," agreed Peter. "And what have you been doing with yourself, my dear Mrs. Lovell? Running a newspaper? How very interesting. We've been busy, too; I have visited my very good friend Maya Solel in Nuevo, and friends in nearby pueblos, learning their legends—in fact, I plan to write a book about them, taking after my famous mother whose work has appeared in *Good Housekeeping* magazine. And my lovely sister also has been active; she takes singing lessons, practices many hours each day, visits her friend Luz Aragon in Nuevo, attends the opera . . . You may know all this, though it is possible word may not have reached Albuquerque—"

"That's enough, Peter," Elizabeth said quietly. "I know I haven't been around much lately, but you don't have to overdo it. I'm here now."

"And maybe it's not so bad," said Holly in her mother's defense. "I mean, maybe families take each other for granted when they're always together. At least now we appreciate having you here."

"I always appreciated having my parents here," Peter said pointedly.

"Peter, will you shut up!" Holly demanded.

"Of course," he said. In the rearview mirror Elizabeth saw the odd, trance-like look that had appeared for the first time a couple of weeks earlier, about the time she was in Houston. Love or worry, she thought. I hope it's love.

"I appreciate you both," she said. "And nothing your father and I have done means we don't appreciate you or love you. We had a job to do; we told you about it; and we asked you to be patient for six months. Was that too much to ask?"

"No," Holly declared. "Peter's just going through sexual anxieties and worrying about being a senior."

"*What?*" Peter demanded.

"It's okay; I understand," Holly said. "Maybe I'll be scared, too, when it's my turn. Last year of high school, getting ready

156

to leave home and face all that competition in college, being alone in the cold, cruel world—"

"Bullshit."

"Peter," Elizabeth said.

"Sorry. But she's wrong."

"She may be. But if she's right, it's nothing to be ashamed of. Give it some thought."

Peter shrugged. "Sure." He wondered whether he should argue about the "sexual anxieties" part and decided to leave it alone. He couldn't beat Holly in a discussion, but he could really get to her by refusing to answer. Pulling off his hiking boots he put stockinged feet against the window and lay back on the seat. Nice being alone; he could dream.

Holly was silent, too, as Elizabeth drove through the main street of Pecos and turned into the Pecos Valley. They climbed steadily on the narrow road, following the Pecos River between steep mountain slopes covered with pine, juniper, gambel oak, and the slender white trunks and quaking leaves of aspens. Above the narrow valley, the sky was a deep blue arch.

Elizabeth drank in the beauty and the stillness. She always forgot how isolated it felt, this close to Santa Fe. Farther on, the valley narrowed even more; they drove through a gap little wider than the road, and then it opened up into broad fields. At its widest, a small sign said Nuevo. Elizabeth turned onto the bumpy dirt road. "What would you like to do?" she asked Holly and Peter. "I'll be at Isabel's."

"Maya's waiting for me," said Peter, trying to be casual.

"Have fun." Holly's voice was suddenly wistful. "I'll go with you," she told Elizabeth as they came to a stop. "*Luz* is waiting for *me*."

Elizabeth put her arm around Holly's shoulders. "I want to leave in a couple of hours, Peter, so meet us at the Aragons' any time before then."

"Right." He loped down the single road that ran from one end of Nuevo to the other as Elizabeth paused beside the car, gazing at the small town: houses of adobe or wood clustered together like tea leaves at the bottom of the cup-shaped valley, each with a vegetable garden and a few flowers; the general

157

store; a repair shop with a gasoline pump at the side; and, some distance away, the small adobe church with a cemetery in back.

On each side of the valley the mountains rose steeply in mixed colors of rock outcroppings amid stands of piñon pine and aspen; the valley floor was planted in corn and wheat, bean and chile plants. The blue ribbon of the Pecos River ran through the center, sparkling from the sun's reflection on ripples made by dragonflies skimming the surface. Zachary's parents had raised horses and cattle on pastures along its banks, and Zachary, when a young man, had bought additional acres and a house, higher up. We should have kept them, Elizabeth thought regretfully, but it had seemed so important at the time to buy the *Sun*. The higher acres, she saw, were planted in corn, but the house looked neglected.

"Elizabeth! Wonderful! I couldn't believe my luck when you called!"

Swept into Isabel's massive hug, Elizabeth laughed. "My luck, too, since I get to see you."

"This makes up for all the missed dinners. I've been praying for you for weeks! Holly, forgive me, Luz is in the garage, repairing our car. She dislikes it, but she does it better than anyone. Where is your handsome brother?"

"He has an assignation with Maya."

Isabel's eyebrows went up. "At ten in the morning? Well, why not? Peter is a man of wisdom. Establish himself firmly in her heart before she is lured by the outside world. How else can we be sure of anything, unless we get there first and then hang on? Come in, come in," she said to Elizabeth as Holly went off. "I'll get us something cold to drink and you'll say hello to Padre; he'll be in talkative ecstasy and we'll have to cut short his long-winded, though of course fascinating, stories or there will be no time to put our heads together and open our hearts. Good Lord, it's been too long . . . I've missed you hugely!"

Isabel Aragon was forty-three, large and plain, with masses of black hair she restlessly wove into a heavy braid as she talked, then loosened, letting it spread like a crinkly cape about her shoulders until she braided it once again. She stood proudly, and her wide smile and unaffected laugh were so warm and welcoming that everyone was drawn to her, and after a few minutes no one thought her plain.

Beside Elizabeth's slender, honey-colored beauty she seemed even larger and darker, and years earlier, when the two of them had walked about the valley with their small children, people in Nuevo had called them *hermanas contrarias*—opposite sisters—which had delighted Isabel. "Every woman needs a sister. Not necessarily next door, but nearby. As for me, I already have too many people next door."

Everyone from the valley, all the way to Pecos, came to Isabel with their problems, receiving brisk, matter-of-fact advice—"that they could think of for themselves if they weren't so knotted up in their worries," she would tell Elizabeth. Her own worries she kept to herself or told to Elizabeth. They had begun the day her husband—young and handsome and such a lover!—was killed when his pickup truck was struck by a tourist van near the old iron mine farther up the valley, leaving her with her father, Cesar; her daughter, Luz, just five at the time; and a small wheel on which she made black pottery with a raised black and ivory design no one could duplicate. It sold well through four galleries in Santa Fe and Taos, and that, plus money Cesar earned with his handwoven rugs, and the vegetables they grew in their garden and canned for winter, kept them going.

"We're doing better and better," she told Elizabeth as they settled into lawn chairs in front of her house. "Tons of tourists discovering Santa Fe—which has only been here since the year 1600 or so—and southwestern arts and crafts . . . Lord, I sell ten times as many pieces as I used to. Where did these people spend their money before?"

"Wherever was 'in,'" Elizabeth said with a smile.

Isabel filled their glasses. "Now tell me everything. Begin at the beginning. How come you're here in the middle of the week? Is it a holiday?"

"I've changed jobs." Elizabeth told her about the dinner in Houston. Sitting in the hot sun in that quiet valley encircled by mountains, sipping lemonade and talking to Isabel, whose

159

concentrated way of listening was so special, Elizabeth relaxed. "This is wonderful. I loved the drive up here, but I had the most awful feeling that it was all wrong: driving in the mountains on a weekday, letting down my staff—"

"And wondering what your husband was doing behind your back?"

Elizabeth smiled. "I didn't put it that way—as if he might be unfaithful."

"He might be. With a newspaper." Isabel's infectious laugh echoed about them. Laughing with her, Elizabeth said, "If he's only unfaithful with a newspaper, I probably can deal with it."

"Well, I wouldn't worry about any other competition," Isabel said. "At least not while he's knocking himself out the way he is. He's really hooked on it, isn't he? Where would he get the energy or time for an affair, even if he wanted one? I'm told the logistics of adultery are devilishly complicated: arranging, rearranging, covering your tracks, lying, remembering which lie you told to which person . . . no way could *I* do it."

Elizabeth's eyes were half closed against the sunlight. "How do you know all that?"

"I'm told by experts. When their logistics get too complicated, they come to me for advice. Me! Ha! If they knew how long it's been since I've had a man in my bed . . . Oh, Elizabeth, I do miss it. Of course no woman ever forgets, so I can talk to them about sex . . . but adultery! What do I know about adultery? I never even thought about it! The way I felt about my husband . . . Well, you know all about that. It's just that I do miss it, you know. There's only so much satisfaction in a grateful father and knowing I've done a good job with Luz . . ." She shook her head. "I've got to stop doing this; I make myself horny and then I can't keep a smooth hand on the clay when I work. Where was I? Oh, my advice-seekers. Well, you wouldn't believe grown-up men could get themselves so messed up. Then they come to me."

"And what do you tell them?"

"That if they dip their pen in too many inkwells they're bound to make a mistake when they try to write with it."

Elizabeth burst out laughing. "Wonderful. Matt will love it."

160

"He'll love it as long as he isn't dipping his pen."

"He's too busy." They laughed again. "And in a few weeks, when the managing editor takes over in Albuquerque, he'll be home again."

"Doing what?"

There was a pause. A bluejay flew past, cawing at something unseen; a hummingbird hovered at a bush, then darted off; children dashed across the fields, chasing a yapping dog. "Working for Keegan," Elizabeth said at last. "Buying newspapers. Managing them. Whatever Keegan wants him to do."

"The company is in Houston," Isabel said.

"Yes."

They were silent again. "You might like Houston," Isabel said.

"I might." Elizabeth turned her eyes from the mountains to Isabel's somber face. "It's a long way from Nuevo."

"Sure is."

A shadow fell across Elizabeth's face and she looked up to see Peter, with Maya slightly behind him. His hair was a flaming halo in the sun; Maya's gleamed like ebony. They were holding hands and their eyes shone. Elizabeth felt a flash of envy. *How wonderful to be young and discovering love.*

"You said a couple of hours," Peter reminded her. "It has been exactly that. However, I was hoping you'd stay longer; my friend here has invited me to lunch. Also, I don't see my sister anywhere."

"Two hours!" Elizabeth exclaimed. "Already?"

Isabel shook her head. "We barely got started."

"I thought I'd work this afternoon," Elizabeth said, "but it could wait until tomorrow."

"Stay for lunch," Isabel urged. "And practice discipline tomorrow."

Elizabeth nodded. She was too content to move. "Will you find Holly and tell her?" she asked Peter. "We'll leave about four. If that's all right," she added to Isabel.

"Perfect." They watched Peter and Maya drift off, clasped hands swinging between them. "Before I forget, do you know anything about the guy who bought your land up here?"

161

"Terry Ballenger? Not much. Why?"

"Do you know how much of this valley he's bought?"

"No. He bought more than Zachary's land?"

"Seems so. He and two other guys. All together they've bought up more than half."

"Half the valley?"

"More than half."

The journalist in Elizabeth stirred. Terry Ballenger had told them he was a car dealer from San Diego looking for a quiet place to spend his summers, maybe do a little fishing. Not a rancher or a farmer or a horseman, not a man who would need more than the thirty acres he'd bought from Elizabeth and Matt.

"We didn't think much about it," Isabel was saying. "Lots of tourists are looking for land in the great southwest; it wasn't until we got together and added up how much was sold that we got to thinking it was pretty damn peculiar."

"It is. I'll look into it, Isabel, and I'll ask Matt about it. If nothing else, it might make a story for 'Private Affairs.'"

"He offered to buy my place, too."

"Ballenger? For how much?"

"Thirty thousand."

"A little high for the valley."

"Right. But Aurelio got sixty and he's got twice as much land."

"Aurelio couldn't have sold. I saw him harvesting when I was driving in."

"That's another odd thing. After they buy, these guys give long-term leases at low rents and tell people to stay where they are, live in their houses, farm their land . . . you'd think nothing had changed."

Elizabeth shook her head. "That can't be the same Ballenger. He said he wanted to spend his summers in the house."

"This is the summer. Does the house look used?"

Elizabeth remembered thinking it looked neglected. "No."

"Same man."

"Did you sell to him?"

"Are you kidding? This is my home! The only one I've got! Besides, we don't need the money right now. He didn't like it

162

when I said no. He likes to get his way." She sighed. "Who doesn't? Luz was furious; she wants me to sell and move into Santa Fe. She wants the high school and the town . . . And so it goes."

She got up lazily and went into the house, returning with more lemonade and a platter of burritos and rice. "Happened to have these in the oven," she said casually, then laughed with Elizabeth. "Well, if Peter hadn't said anything, I would have talked you into staying for lunch. I feel bad about Luz: she's young and lively and ought to have all the fun of Santa Fe, but I can't sell the place out from under Padre, and he won't leave the valley. When Luz goes off on her own, there'll just be the two of us, and I have to think of him, too; he's my family and I like having a man around—even a padre—and he doesn't treat me like a daughter so much anymore. Sometimes we're like friends. Could be worse. I'm glad you're around, Elizabeth my opposite sister. Even when we don't see each other, it helps to know you're close."

She's pretending we didn't talk about Houston, Elizabeth thought. But she said nothing. She didn't want to think about Houston, or Rourke, either. Nothing was settled: Matt might decide he didn't want to work in Rourke's office; something else might come along . . . There was plenty of time.

Cesar joined them for lunch, then went inside for a nap, and Elizabeth and Isabel talked into the afternoon until Peter returned. "Four o'clock on the dot."

Elizabeth looked about. "Where's Maya?"

"Making dinner with her mother. I told her I'd come back tonight. I figured you'd let me use the car. Tomorrow, too. Or you might want to come again yourself."

After another look at his shining eyes, Elizabeth glanced about the peaceful valley, at the farmers harvesting in the distance, at Holly and Luz coming down the path, at Isabel, beside her, solid and comforting. "If not tomorrow, very soon," she said. Lazily, she stood and stretched. "I haven't felt this relaxed in months. Of course we'll come back. Soon."

For a moment, as clearly as the cry of the bluejays, she heard

Zachary talking about the valley, and holding on to his land, and retiring there.

We shouldn't have sold, she thought again. And that reminded her of Ballenger. She'd have to look into that; it was curious. And maybe she and Matt should buy here again. If so many people were selling, they should do it soon. We're a long way from retirement, she reflected as she got into the car. But it would be nice to know it's here, waiting for us, whenever we need it.

The River Oaks section of Houston is an enclave of winding roads shaded by huge pines and lined with bushes and high gates shielding sprawling modern homes and semi-Gothic mansions. Keegan Rourke's twenty-room mansion on Inwood Street was set back in a clipped lawn, but the gardens were behind it. From its rarified atmosphere of Aubusson tapestries, Baccarat chandeliers, and hand-rubbed European antiques, one long wall of windows looked onto floodlit terraced rose gardens, planted so that the eye moved from the darkest wine-colored roses at the base upward to red, pale red, deep pink, pale pink, ivory, and then pale white. Nothing moved in the perfectly manicured garden: guests stayed indoors where the air was cooled, leaving the roses and pines and velvety grass to look like a waxed sculpture framed by the windows.

Looking out, Elizabeth recalled a small abandoned church, a farmer harvesting his fields, the solitary flight of a bluejay. "Only a few inches on the map," Peter had joked when she told him, after her first visit, how far Houston seemed from home. More like a million miles, she thought, and looked up as she felt Matt's hand on her shoulder.

"Stunning," he said.

She nodded. "I was thinking how different it looks from—"

"I meant my wife is stunning."

"Oh." Slowly she smiled. "I like that."

"So do I. Much more than the garden." He kissed her bare shoulder, breathing in the fragrance of bath oil on her smooth

164

skin, and felt a stirring of desire. He touched his crystal wine glass to hers. "To our future."

"To us," Elizabeth responded, and sipped her wine, admiring Matt's black-tie sophistication, so different from his everyday informality of corduroy pants and open-necked shirts. His unruly hair was combed, his shoes polished, his tie straight. "You are the handsomest man at the party."

"I hope so, since my wife is the most beautiful."

"It's not me; it's my pearls. The most exquisite I've ever seen. Have I thanked you for them today?"

"You've thanked me more than enough." He had bought the perfectly matched strand for her forty-second birthday the week before. "Wear them for the party," he had said as she tried them on. "A memorable October. Two celebrations—"

"Two indulgences," Elizabeth had responded. "Except for my luxurious new car last month, we haven't spent this much at one time since we bought the *Chieftain*."

"It's only the beginning," he had said. "No one deserves pearls more. Or that wonderful dress."

Her third indulgence, Elizabeth thought: the most expensive dress at Brock's in Santa Fe. But when she had seen her image in the mirror, she had barely hesitated. The halter top was covered in tiny mother-of-pearl and aventurine beading; the long white skirt of narrow pleats rippled as she moved. She had brushed her honey-colored hair back from one side of her face, letting it curve in a long shining wave on the other side, the ends curling under at her shoulder.

"Dad would be so proud," Matt said suddenly. "He should have lived to see us tonight."

Elizabeth smiled. "He'd strut around the room, beaming, telling everyone he was the father of the famous Matt Lovell—"

"Father-in-law of the even more famous Elizabeth Lovell—"

"My dear Elizabeth," Keegan Rourke said, lifting her hand to his lips. "A month away from office drudgery has made you bloom. And your work has been superb. You do receive the fan mail my secretary sends on from here?"

165

"Yes, thank you. I was going to ask—"

"Wonderful response. Especially the way your readers write to you: as if they know you; as if you're a good friend."

"I was going to ask why you open letters addressed to me."

"Because they are written by people who buy my newspapers. It is useful to me to know who they are, what they are thinking, what makes them buy one paper instead of another. But no business tonight; we should be entirely festive, to celebrate Matt's new position in our little corporate family, and yours too, of course. Matt, I want to introduce Elizabeth to some of my guests. You've already met most of them and Senator Greene wants to have a word with you." Rourke looked around. "Chet?" Instantly, Chet Colfax materialized at his side. "Take Matt to Senator Greene, find them a quiet corner, and get them fresh drinks."

Elizabeth held out her hand and Colfax automatically took it. "How are you?" she asked.

"Quite well," he said shortly, then, facing Matt's outstretched hand, he was forced to repeat the procedure. "Good to see you." His mouth smiled; his eyes were cold and flat. "If you'll come with me, we'll find the senator."

Matt nodded. He touched Elizabeth's arm. "See you at dinner." And before she could respond he and Colfax were making their way through the crowd, their black jackets blending with the men's identical ones, contrasting with the blinding colors worn by the women. Comparing their dresses to hers, Elizabeth felt pale, almost invisible, in her pastel gown, but Rourke, watching her, said, "You have style, my dear. You don't need loud colors or enormous jewels to stand above the rest. Most of the women here haven't learned that taste is more crucial than wealth, and harder to come by. However, you must meet all of them. Not as research—they hardly qualify as the unseen people you write about—but because they are essential to our well-being."

"Whose well-being?" Elizabeth asked.

"Matt's. Mine. Rourke Enterprises and its newest subsidiary, Rourke Publishing. And therefore yours. Come."

In a whirl of introductions, Elizabeth met state senators, U.S.

166

congressmen, two U.S. senators from neighboring states, oilmen, highway and bridge contractors, and real estate developers who had gotten in on the ground floor of the North Belt business district and the communities sprouting across northern Harris County. "Fixin' to be annexed by Houston," one of them explained to Elizabeth. "Which is why we're there."

But though Elizabeth heard much about the city, especially talk of repairs to damage caused by a hurricane four weeks earlier, most of the guests talked to her about "Private Affairs."

"It's just amazin' the way you *get* these people," a striking blond in emerald green said to Elizabeth. "Most especially my favorite, the one about that woman—Charlotte desChampes—who had her ninety-eighth birthday party? And you said how she allowed everybody to kiss her and thank her for starting the family so they can exist? And then you said she looks *piercingly* around so nobody *plays hookey* from thanking her? Now I *know* that is my great-grandmama! Of course you changed her name, but you have absolutely *got* her! What I do not understand is, how ever did you meet her?"

"I didn't." Elizabeth's face glowed. "Charlotte desChampes lives in Taos and she's one of the few people who told me to use her real name. I chose her because she reminded me of other women who behave as if they created their families—"

"By themselves! That is it, that is exactly my great-grandmama! She has absolutely *erased* Great-Grandpapa, who had the sad misfortune of dying early so we none of us knew him. Aren't you the amazing one, though! To do what you do!"

"Thank you." Elizabeth's eyes were shining. This was far different from the compliments of a newspaper staff; different from fan mail; different from a call from an editor of *Good Housekeeping*. These were powerful people, moneyed, not easily impressed since everything was available to them—but they read and remembered her columns!

"And Keegan did choose such good ones to send," the blond woman went on. "I do think he most certainly got your flavor."

Puzzled, Elizabeth asked, "To send?"

"Oh, now I've surely given away a secret. But it was so

sweet of him, whyever shouldn't you know? He sent copies of three of your columns to each of us—"

"To everyone he invited," added another woman.

"In case we hadn't read them," said a third. "So we could talk about them and make you feel right at home. And you know I never do read the newspaper, so wasn't it a good thing he did! Now I look for your column every single day—you're not *there* every day, which I do find unsettling—but I wouldn't even know about you if not for Keegan here. Isn't he a real honey?"

Elizabeth looked at Rourke, standing protectively behind her. "I had no idea . . ."

He nodded a dismissal at the women and took Elizabeth's arm to lead her away. They paused to choose from a tray of lobster hors d'oeuvres offered by a waiter. "I've seen writers embarrassed by people asking what they've written, or saying they hadn't gotten around to reading it yet. I didn't want you to face anything like that."

Elizabeth had never known him to be so thoughtful. If she still couldn't call him a honey, she thought him more considerate than she had ever believed possible. "I'm always thanking you," she said.

"Not necessary. Remember that I profit from your writing, as much as from Matt's expertise. Ah, a new arrival. Tony, you're late."

"Traffic at the airport. Hell of a mess." Anthony Rourke took Elizabeth's hand in both of his. "Hello, stranger. My God, you look magnificent. It's been so long since I've seen you. Ten years? Twenty?"

Elizabeth laughed. "A little over two." His voice was as smooth and warm as ever, his eyes warmer still. "How are you, Tony?"

"Much better than I've been in a little over two years. Come with me to a quiet corner."

Elizabeth glanced at Rourke. "For a few minutes," he said. "I'll want you with me when I make my announcement."

"Plenty of time," Tony said impatiently. He brought Elizabeth's arm through his, and they walked to a corner of the room where they looked out at the rose gardens. "I've missed you. I've never stopped thinking about you. Tried to, but couldn't. Even got married and divorced—well, separated, but it's the same thing. But, good Lord, I couldn't have stayed away at all if my memory had been better; you are incredible. Or have you changed? Of course, I never saw you decked out for one of my father's bashes. Do you watch my show?"

"When I can." A different kind of excitement was running through Elizabeth in the spotlight of his admiration. Even among the most prominent of the people who had been praising her, Tony stood out. Everyone knew him. As they had walked across the room she had heard others say his name; three of the congressmen and one senator had been on his show; others obviously longed to be. But more than his fame set him apart; it was that aura of electricity that Elizabeth remembered—as if, because he was there, something new was going to happen, something tantalizing, something only he could provide.

He had a new sleekness, too, since his hair had turned silver in his forty-eighth year, exactly as Keegan's had. Someone must have told him how striking it looked, Elizabeth thought, since he had not dyed it. And he seemed more relaxed and certain of himself. He exuded confidence: a successful, tanned, superbly groomed California celebrity.

Meeting his expectant smile, Elizabeth knew exactly why she had fallen for him at seventeen and followed him to bed. Few women, especially young, impressionable ones, would be able to resist that electricity, and the warm voice and intimate gaze.

That's enough, she thought abruptly. No more of the past. "We don't watch television much," she said, answering his question. "We're usually working in the evenings." She started to tell him that Holly wouldn't miss one episode of "Anthony," but something made her change her mind. "Peter watches you most weeks, and I catch the show now and then. It's very good. *You're* very good. I like the way you deflate pompous people."

"Nice to hear. I like the way you create word pictures of people and make me want to know them."

"You still read my stories?"

169

"Every one. I also boast that I know you. My clever, wise, most talented good friend, Elizabeth. Now look at that: your eyes are full of gratitude. Don't you get enough praise? Dearest lovely Elizabeth, you should be stroked, cossetted, and rewarded because you are magnificent and people love you. My esteemed father tells me you get more mail than any other writer on his papers. It's not easy for most people to write a letter, but they do when they read your stories. Because they feel less alone; they know there are others like them, with the same problems and fears and dreams. Why do you look surprised?"

"Because you understand that."

"Dearest Elizabeth, you have always underestimated me."

"Yes," she said, "perhaps I have."

A rustle of movement near the doorway caught her attention and she glanced at a cluster of tuxedoed men shifting about, almost, but not quite, shoving. "Like a bunch of ravenous kids in a cafeteria," she observed. "Has Keegan invited royalty tonight?"

"It wouldn't be the first time," Tony said absently. "We were talking about me, remember?"

"Oh."

He followed her gaze and saw, amid the tuxedos, the center of attention: his father's frequent companion, as the gossip columnists said, Nicole Renard, riveting in a strapless black satin gown. White satin was wrapped at an angle around her bodice and tied in a huge pouf over one bare shoulder, diamonds hung around her neck and at her ears, her black hair was swept to the side exactly like Elizabeth's. This time she wore makeup—vivid, striking, almost theatrical. She seemed perfectly at ease in this hothouse of money and power.

And beside her stood Matt.

Elizabeth watched him smile at something Nicole said, then turn to talk to a congressman. In another minute, he and the congressman walked away, deep in conversation. Nicole's look followed them; then she turned to the cluster around her.

And Elizabeth turned back to Tony, who was looking at her inquiringly. "I'm sorry; I didn't hear you," she said.

170

"I was asking if you realize you wouldn't even be here tonight if it weren't for me."

She frowned. "Oh, you mean because you sent Keegan my columns. It seems so long ago. Yes, he wouldn't have known about us otherwise, would he? I should be thanking you for sending them."

"Should? Duty, not pleasure?"

"I didn't mean that."

"I think you did. Aren't you happy about my father's magic wand?"

She gave him a long look. "You ran away from it."

"Yes, dearest Elizabeth, so I did. Frequently he forgets it's a wand and wields it like a whip. But use it while you can, use *him* if you can, until you think he's using you. Then you must run away, as I did. You'll be all right; I have faith in you."

"Does that advice apply to Matt, too?"

"Matt. You know, it's quite astonishing how I keep forgetting him. Yes, of course it applies to Matt. Especially since he's at the magic center of influence, building my father a power base."

"For what?"

"I'll explain it some time. Or you can ask Matt. But that's where he'll be—at the center—while you're at home writing your columns. Are you?"

"Am I what?"

"At home. Or do you have an office?"

"Sometimes I'm at home; most often I've been using Matt's old office at the *Chieftain*. I like feeling I'm part of the newspaper. And Saul and I work together on special projects. And the staff brings me flowers"—she smiled, amused and affectionate—"with little notes about cheering up. As if I—"

"Needed it. Sounds like your staff sees more than you realize. If I know which days you're home, I could come in to keep you company. Bearing flowers and little notes."

"On your way to New York."

"On my way to see you once you move here. It's easy

to commute between Houston and Los Angeles; I could do it—"

"I won't be here. I'll be in Santa Fe."

His eyebrows shot up. "But Matt's joining the company in Houston."

"Part-time. He'll have an office here and one at home."

"I don't believe it. My father—the father I've known all my life—would never allow it."

"He's letting us try it. Peter just began his senior year and a special research project at two pueblos; we talked it over and decided we couldn't ask him to move."

"But it won't work, you know. My father demands devotion, attention, instant response, clicked heels. *Eyeball to eyeball*, Elizabeth."

"Tony, don't exaggerate. I told you: we're doing it this way, at least for eight months, until Peter graduates."

"Then you'll need company more than ever. I'll do better than flowers and notes; I'll bring Belgian chocolates and poetry. I'll bring anything you want. I'll learn to type. I'll be a friend, servant, companion, candlestick maker, lover. Are you smiling at me or with me? Elizabeth, I tend to clown, but I am very serious. Dearest Elizabeth, two years isn't enough to make me forget you; twenty wouldn't be enough. I want—"

"Elizabeth?" Keegan Rourke stood at her elbow. "We need you with us. Tony, if you want to be part of our group . . ."

Tony shook his head. "Thanks. I'd rather be part of the audience."

"It was good to see you again," Elizabeth said coolly, and held out her hand.

He took it and kissed her cheek. "I see I went a little too far. I'll be better next time."

"You'll stand on Matt's right," Rourke said as they crossed the room to a table with a small microphone. Matt was already there; he took Elizabeth's hand in a quick squeeze and held it as she stood beside him. "Friends," Rourke said into the microphone, and the room was silent.

He told them what they already knew: the festivities were in honor of Matthew Lovell, vice-president of Rourke Enterprises and publisher of its new subsidiary, Rourke Publishing, and his wife, Elizabeth Lovell, whose column "Private Affairs" would appear three times a week in all the Rourke newspapers. Elizabeth studied the guests, half-listening as he outlined their background.

"We expect within a year," Rourke concluded, "to have a chain of newspapers, each reflecting its own unique area, but all unmistakably part of Rourke Enterprises. Matt and I don't agree on everything, but our basic ideas coincide and I doubt we'll have many wrestling matches over editorial policy." A ripple of laughter ran through the room. "We also agree on the high standards that will distinguish the Rourke papers, and the special features that will make them profitable. Most important, we agree on our good fortune in finding each other and joining forces. The southwestern United States will never be the same! Ladies and gentlemen, Matt Lovell."

Applause filled the room as Rourke took a step back. For a moment, Matt surveyed the attentive faces, the glittering jewelry, the small smile on Tony's face, the fixed stare of Chet's at the back of the crowd. "Since Keegan and I agree on so many things, I can't contradict anything he's said. He did leave out one important point: the enormity of the challenge he's given me. We're going to be moving very fast and we won't have time for mistakes. I appreciate his confidence; I hope to gain yours, too. I'll be meeting with many of you over the next few months, and by the time Rourke Publishing is well established, I'd like to think we'll have formed some good working relationships, and friendships, too. Elizabeth and I thank you for coming tonight; we look forward to seeing you often. Now I'd like to propose a toast. To Keegan Rourke, who has very big ideas and the courage to entrust them to an unknown, but very grateful, vice-president."

Again there was applause, and murmurs of approval. Everyone drank to Keegan Rourke, who stood quietly, smiling at his guests, until he turned, raised his own glass, and silently toasted Matt. Then, swiftly recovering from his error, he bowed to Elizabeth and included her in his toast.

"Dinner in fifteen minutes," Rourke said into the microphone. "Ask Chet for your seating cards."

The ceremony over, everyone crowded around to shake hands and add more congratulations to those they had been giving for two hours. "Very nice," Chet Colfax murmured to Elizabeth. "It's a nice time for you. It's a pleasure to see that; I always say it's a pleasure to see deserving people get rewards."

"Is that what you always say, Chet?" asked Elizabeth. "That's very generous."

His eyes were blank. "I share Mr. Rourke's pleasure when things go well. We all do. When you live here, you'll share it, too."

"We aren't going to live here, Chet. I thought that would please you."

"Did you?" For a moment his voice slipped and she heard his fury and wondered at it. Because Matt wouldn't be there all the time, where he could be watched? Or because, wherever he lived, Matt was the new favorite, an unknown quantity that had to be considered in everything Chet Colfax did to try to make himself indispensable to Keegan Rourke?

"It will be harder for your husband not to live here," Colfax said. "But if he wants my help I'll be available. Information, you know; it's not as easy as you think to step into a new business."

"I don't think it's easy at all," Elizabeth replied. She looked around for someone to rescue her from the fixed stare and tight voice that had made her uncomfortable ever since she met Colfax in Albuquerque. But everyone seemed occupied; she would have to do it herself. "If you'll excuse me, Chet, I want to—"

"You want to help your husband. I'm telling you how. All these people, you know"—he flicked his glance about the room—"are beholden in some way to Mr. Rourke. You may think it's crude to talk about these things, but it's accurate. Your husband doesn't know how to deal with situations that arise because of it. If he relies on me, I can tell him—"

What makes you think I'd help make my husband dependent on you? "Why don't you do that right now?" Elizabeth asked icily. She grasped his hand in hers and walked rapidly toward Matt. Taken unawares, Colfax let himself be dragged along and in a moment he was facing Matt and Elizabeth was saying, "Matt, Chet wants to help you with some background information on the guests who are here. I thought you'd want to know about it."

Matt saw the bright anger in Elizabeth's eyes and the confusion sweeping across Colfax's face and he knew somehow she'd done in the little weasel. He felt a rush of love for her. She was quick and bright and beautiful—and he didn't tell her that often enough.

"Chet wants to tell you these guests are all beholden to Keegan, but he'll sort them out for you and tell you about situations that arise and how to deal with them. Is that right, Chet? Would you call it crude but accurate?"

"I wanted to help you," Colfax said to Matt through thin lips.

"So I could be beholden, too," Matt said pleasantly. He didn't feel pleasant; he was irritated and tired of going through motions. Play-acting. Making the impression he was supposed to make. He knew it was essential: a major newspaper chain couldn't function without dealing with politicians and corporations. But he was fed up with talk; he wanted to get to work. Instead he was wasting time with this slimy little bastard who—"What?" he asked.

"I said we should be civilized," Colfax repeated. "We have to work together and I want you to call on me as a friend—"

"I'm sure you do. If I need you, I'll call on you."

"But you do need me!" The smooth facade was cracking. "If you'll let me know what you're planning, who you'll be talking to, your schedule and so on, I can give you advance information . . ."

"I'm sure you want me to tell you all that, Chet, but that's not how I operate. I'll call you, I promise, if I need you. Now if you'll excuse us, Elizabeth and I are going in to dinner."

Elizabeth saw the rage in Colfax's face. "You talked to him as if he's a child," she told Matt as they walked away. "I think you should be careful; he could be dangerous."

175

"I doubt it. He's a little man trying to be a big one."

"And you don't think they're ever dangerous?"

He shrugged. "Let Keegan take care of him. He's his lackey, not mine."

They were stopped as they walked through the room by men and women wanting to congratulate them, to ask about their children and where in Houston they planned to live, to invite them to dinner. Matt let Elizabeth answer for both of them. He was exhausted and annoyed—a bad combination—and he had started to fume inside. If Chet Colfax thought he could make trouble for him, he was dead wrong. Anyone who thought Matthew Lovell could be stopped or slowed down was dead wrong. He knew how he'd gotten here and he knew where he was going. For the first time he had all the resources he needed to go as far as he could, to build the kind of empire he'd dreamed of, and no one was going to stop him, now that he was this close.

No one. Not even Keegan Rourke. Or Elizabeth. No one.

176

CHAPTER 7

Keegan Rourke's offices were in the Transco Building, a steel and glass tower in Houston's Magic Circle. Once a patch of empty fields and dirt roads, this part of the city had been transformed in the past few years to a few glittering square blocks of exclusive restaurants, boutiques, theaters, and buildings housing corporations from around the world. In their midst were the enclosed Galleria shopping malls, with international hotels, an indoor ice rink, and a galaxy of more restaurants, shops, and offices.

"How fitting," Elizabeth had said the first time she visited Rourke's headquarters. "Magic Circle. Where else would he be?" But his offices had been a surprise. As richly furnished as they were, there were fewer than she had expected; a handful of trusted people in a small suite of rooms quietly ran Rourke's growing empire. There were vice-presidents for oil leasing, real estate, investment, and development; two accountants; two administrative assistants in an office next to Chet Colfax; and four secretaries in another large office. At the end of the corridor was Matt Lovell's office: Vice-President, Rourke Publishing.

A fifth secretary worked in the reception room, dramatically furnished in chrome, leather, glass, and Art Deco torch lights rising from a plush carpet that reminded Elizabeth of the grass around their courtyard at home when Peter had put off mowing it. A spiral staircase led to the next floor where Rourke's executive secretary sat in a round reception area with beige leather couches, western oil paintings, rare old photographs of the first railway across the plains, and a garden of flowering cactus. Beyond the door, in a spacious office carpeted in deep brown, with suede and rosewood furniture grouped before a fireplace, Rourke was ensconced within the curve of a polished table of red padouk and black walnut. Around him hung the mystical acrylic paintings of Jean Richardson.

"All that's missing," Elizabeth had said at that first visit, "is the feeling that a real person uses the place. No family photos or souvenirs or personal gadgets. Just a high-class decorator. With a high-class budget."

"Someone told me Nicole did the design," Matt had said, and Elizabeth had murmured, "She gave herself away: she's probably as cold as her furnishings."

On the floor below Rourke's office was a windowless conference room with an attached kitchen where caterers prepared lunch for staff meetings, held at least once a month. It was here, two months after the party in Rourke's home, that Matt made his second major progress report to the staff and Rourke's attorneys, who always sat in.

"Last time I gave you details on the Chalmers chain," he said. "I assume the paperwork will be finished soon, in spite of the delay at Thanksgiving"—he looked inquiringly at the lawyers, who nodded—"and the contracts signed. Those six papers cover western New Mexico south from Los Alamos and north to Farmington. You have my memo on the negotiations for the *Phoenix Arizonan* and the *Tucson Call;* in the meantime, there's another group I'm interested in. The prospectus is in front of you: eight newspapers and a television and radio station in southeastern New Mexico. I've spent the last couple of weeks with Jim Graham, who owns the group in partnership with his son. They're losing money, but I'm convinced it's bad management; there's no serious competition and if we can get his price down I'm recommending that we buy it."

"He's asking ten million," read one of the lawyers from the prospectus. "Too high."

"Of course," Matt agreed. "We have to get it down."

The discussion moved around the table. What equipment did Graham have and how soon would it have to be replaced? How much personnel could be let go? How many were close to retirement? Who were the local advertisers? Who were the readers, the viewers, the radio listeners?

Matt had written the prospectus after Chet Colfax had given him data on finances and personnel, and he had made his own inspection trip. Now, standing at one end of the oval table, he answered questions about the eight towns: economics, politics, recreation, geography, what the people were interested in and worried about, prospects for industrial development and tourism.

Matt relished these discussions, working toward a goal fueled by such enormous wealth that the whole process was different from any he had ever known. *The wallet is full.* And now the wallet was Matt's, along with a staff and Rourke's backing, and when he went into a town, that gave him a sense of power so sweeping he sometimes felt like another person.

He remembered sitting at the kitchen table with Elizabeth, figuring out ways to scrape together the money for the *Chieftain*; deciding they had to sell the Nuevo property to finance the *Sun*.

Christ, if only he'd waited! He could have bought any paper they wanted.

But he thought less about the past as he plunged more deeply into building Rourke Publishing. The first newspaper chain, around Los Alamos, added six papers to the two in Albuquerque and Houston. If they bought the Graham chain, it would add eight more. Even without the *Chieftain* and the *Sun*, which Matt and Elizabeth refused to consider part of Rourke's chain, they would have sixteen papers and a television and radio station by the end of the year, less than three months after he'd started. An impressive beginning.

He finished his presentation and the men around the table nodded approvingly. Rourke smiled. For two hours he had

179

watched Matt, occasionally jotting a note on a pad of paper, his eyes noncommittal. And for those two hours Matt had made sure his own eyes were steady when they met Rourke's. He knew he was on trial; for at least the first year he assumed everything would be a test. And he liked that: the feeling of being on edge, tense with energy and purpose, trying a little harder each day. If Rourke had given him the whole wallet with no strings, no watchdog committee, no test runs, Matt would have thought him a fool.

And there was none of the fool about Rourke. Matt had never met a sharper businessman; one who could more swiftly and unerringly judge someone; who could spot a flaw in a situation or a weakness in a man and use them to his own advantage. He knew Rourke's silence was not necessarily approval or disapproval; most of the time it simply meant he was watching, measuring, judging. He would take part when the time was right, to settle a dispute or make a decision.

If my father had been that decisive and single-minded, he could have been anything he wanted, instead of a disappointed old man relying on his son to live out what was left of his dreams.

"So if we can get him to take six million," Rourke's chief accountant was saying, "or, better yet, five and a half; then cut total personnel by fifteen percent and increase circulation by a third . . . I'd have no problem with that."

"No problem!" one of the lawyers repeated, chuckling. "Will he come down to five and a half, Matt?"

"I doubt it. We ought to get it for seven, though. Maybe six and a half. He's trying not to show how desperate he is, so I'm not sure, but it's obvious there's a serious problem—"

"Two of them," Chet Colfax cut in. "One is, he can't keep away from the horses and he bets wrong nine times out of ten. The other is James Junior, known as Jim Bob. He likes horses, too, but even more he favors blackjack at Las Vegas and expensive women anywhere. He and his papa have run through most of their money. And a few months ago Jim Bob started passing bad checks. Which Papa has so far made good on."

No one asked where Colfax got his information or if it was

correct. It was his job to get information; it was his job to be correct. "By borrowing," Rourke said.

"Yes, indeed," Colfax responded. "Ten thousand from one friend, fifty from another, a quarter of a million from a pal in Ohio . . . there's a substantial list."

"Demand notes," said Rourke.

Colfax nodded.

"Matt," Rourke said easily, "let's start with three and a half."

"He won't take it," said Matt. "He knows it's worth more."

"Of course he does. If we know it's irresistible at five and a half, so does he. And of course he'd like six or more; who wouldn't if he had to follow his son around, cleaning up his shit? But my guess is he'll take four and a half rather than wait. So start with three and a half."

"And if I have to go to five?"

"If you play it right, you won't have to."

Matt hesitated. *Play it right*. But he had made it clear he thought six and a half million a good price. If Rourke thought him naive, or incompetent . . . "I'll see what I can do," he said.

"Call me as soon as you know." Rourke moved on to other business and Matt sat back and listened. *We'll be moving very fast*. He should have said, *Learning very fast*. He wondered if they all thought he was out of his league.

But after the meeting, Rourke put his arm around Matt's shoulders as they walked to his office. "Listen, son, I know you can handle Graham. If Chet is right—and Chet is always right about these things—Jim Bob won't be around; you'll just have the old man. A father disappointed by a son." He gave a short laugh, almost a bark. "Take it from me; he's vulnerable."

Matt heard that short laugh again and again as he flew in the small commuter plane to Roswell. *A father disappointed by a son*. Odd: he'd thought of Tony Rourke as a nuisance, possibly a threat, when he kept showing up in Santa Fe to see Elizabeth, and again at Rourke's party when he saw them talking together. But since the day, two years ago, when Tony mocked him about getting away from his father, Matt had never thought of Tony as Rourke's son.

181

A father disappointed by a son. He remembered Rourke's hand on his shoulder as they had walked down the hall. *Listen, son, I know you can handle Graham.*

Gazing at the desert landscape below with its blowing tumbleweed, stretches of pale grass, dry gulleys, and narrow roads like knife strokes across the emptiness, it hit Matt suddenly.

No wonder Chet is in a rage. He wanted Tony's place for himself.

But Chet knew he'd never be a publisher, Matt thought as he walked across the airstrip to meet James Graham, standing beside his car. So all he wanted was the closeness. *Listen, son . . .* And Matt, unknowingly, had shoved him aside. Worse: treated him like a child, Elizabeth had said.

"Matt—glad to see you again." Graham shook Matt's hand. "Get in, get in, we'll grab some lunch, talk business over food, best way, don't you know, full stomach, friendly bargaining." Laughing too heartily, he opened Matt's door, then walked around to his own. He'd lost weight, Matt saw: his jowls sagged; the collar of his shirt was loose; a tightened belt pulled his pants into folds.

Graham followed Matt's look. "My go-to-meetin' pants," he chuckled. "All my jeans, every last one, in the wash. At least so the missus says; my personal opinion is she hid 'em so I'd wear what she calls real clothes and impress you. That's my guess, anyway. They impress you?"

"Your wife hiding your jeans impresses me more," Matt said with a smile. "She sounds like a woman of determination."

"That's her in a nutshell. Fine woman. Not always easy to live with, but I never doubt she has my best interests at heart and we've had forty good years together, which is a kind of record, I guess, with divorce as common as tumbleweed these days. Here we are."

They faced each other in a booth in a small diner on the main street of town. Graham drew small circles on the Formica table with the salt shaker. "I've been thinking, Matt, since you were here last; I'm not sure I made myself clear. I'm kinda tired of working, is the truth, and so is the missus; we've been at it a long time. We figure, you only go around once and we want some time to relax before we're too old to enjoy it. Or before we die; people do, all of sudden, you know: they get sick, hit by a car, whatever. So we want to grab this chance while we have it. What I'm saying is, if you're here to talk business, I'll come down twenty percent. That ain't hay; brings it down to eight million. You'd be getting a steal; me and the missus would get our relaxing; everybody's happy."

Matt shook his head. "I'm sorry, Jim, but it's still more than I had in mind. We should be talking about—"

"Wait, now! Just a minute!"

The waitress brought beer in thick glass mugs. Matt wondered if it was Graham's standing order. "I'm not really hungry—"

"Got to eat! Got to have some lunch! Best way to talk! Chile," Graham said to the waitress.

"All right," Matt agreed. "That sounds fine."

"More than you had in mind?" Graham asked. "Eight million? Now I know you're a young man and new at this, but I did think we got along fine, Matt, last time we talked. I thought we agreed on what it is I've got for sale here, the value of it and all."

"We didn't come to any agreement the last time I was here; I wasn't authorized to make one. I am now. And what I'm offering—"

"Wait!" Graham cried again, trying to put off the moment when Matt named a figure, trying to get him to think higher before he said it aloud and they had to argue about it. "I'm trying to tell you I've been around a long time and I know what we've got going for us, what it's worth, that is, and I'm telling you to give a listen because there's lots you and your people in Houston *don't know*. They send a young fella like you—bird dog, sniffing around—and you act real pleasant first time around, but when things get down to bare ass, talking dollars and all, you get cocky. And you shouldn't, that's no way to do business, which you'd know if you'd been around long as I have, if you wasn't so raw, not knowing anything about—"

"Now *you* wait, Jim." Matt's voice whipped across the table

183

and Graham's stomach sank. He'd said all the wrong things; his wife would tell him so when he recounted the conversation to her, and she'd be right. She'd wanted to come today, to do the negotiating, and he'd said no, but he should have let her; he was so mad inside he'd gone off the deep end, saying the wrong things, and now Matt Lovell, who'd seemed like a nice, simple guy, easy to handle, was furious and Jim Graham knew it was his own fault.

"I'm not here to talk about myself," Matt said. "I came to make an offer for some properties you're trying to sell. If you want to talk about more personal subjects, we can discuss your son."

Graham's head shot up. "Jim Bob? What about him?" Matt was silent. "Well. News sure travels. Well, he'll find a job or something; he's a big boy now, has to make his own way. Like I said, you only go around once and it's me and the missus I worry about; we can't wait on Jim Bob to figure out his life. We can't wait, Matt. I mean, well, it's not like we're desperate, but the missus doesn't want to wait; she's always hockin' at me; your wife probably does the same; women are like that. So that's it. Twenty percent. Two million less."

"It's not enough, Jim."

"Dammit, I came down two million dollars!"

"I'll say it again: it's not enough. You're losing money on every operation. If we paid eight million dollars we couldn't turn the group around and make it profitable."

Graham downed his beer and signaled the waitress by pointing at his glass. "You most definitely can. It might take longer—"

"Jim, I can't sell this deal to my boss by telling him it will take longer than he expected."

A fresh mug of beer materialized on the table and Graham gripped it with both hands. "How long does he expect?"

"We're not talking about that; we're talking about price."

Graham slammed his fist on the table. "All right! What price are we talking about? I don't like games, mister! *What price?*"

"Three and a half million."

184

Graham stared at him, his eyes protruding. "You are out of your mind."

Matt shook his head.

"Three and a half?" Graham's voice went up. "*Three and a half?* You fucking bastard, do you think I'm some hick you can push around? You vultures from Texas come in here trying to ruin people—"

"I'm not from Texas." Matt wondered why he was defending himself; why he cared if Graham hated him. "I'm from New Mexico, just like you. Santa Fe. I work for a man who lives in Texas and he says he'll pay three and a half million."

"Santa Fe. Artsy-fartsy place, doesn't have anything to do with the rest of us. *We* work for a living; you fancy boys sit around and get rich licking tourists' asses."

Remembering what he and Elizabeth had gone through to keep the *Chieftain* alive, Matt burst out laughing. "Jim, you don't know the first thing about it. Are we going to talk business or not?"

"Shit," Graham muttered. "Seven million."

The waitress brought huge bowls of chile and a basket of flour tortillas. "Anything else?"

"More beer," said Graham.

The waitress looked at Matt, who shook his head. When she left, he said, "It's too high, Jim."

"Too—! Goddammit, this is eight newspapers we're talking about, television, radio, people, capital equipment, physical plant . . ." When Matt was silent, he said, "Maybe six and a half. Okay. Six and a half. Shit, Matt, I thought you'd be easier on a guy. But I have my own prob— I have my own affairs to settle, plus the missus to satisfy, and that's as far as I go. Six and a half. If you're smart you'll take it and be grateful I didn't kick you out earlier and send you back to your vulture friends empty-handed. I'm helping you out, see, even though you're acting like a vulture yourself. But I did like you so I'll help you out and if you have a grain of sense in that stupid head of— Shit, forget I said that; sometimes I go too far. But I truly am helping you." He began eating his chile, breathing loudly. "Six and a half. Take it or leave it."

185

Matt ran his finger down the moisture on his beer mug. *Whatever happens, he'll hate me. And so what? Keegan Rourke didn't get where he is because people liked him.* "What happens if your demand notes are called?" he asked casually.

Graham froze, spoon in one hand, beer mug in the other. "What the fuck are you talking about?"

"Otis Kearney, Fred Lepatta, Calvin Sherl, Ordrey Wayland—"

"Jesus Christ, you rattlesnaking son of a bitch, smiling and drinking beer with me and all the time your little spies out there looking under rocks . . . Well it doesn't matter, you hear? Those are my friends, they loaned me money and they'll be paid back when I sell my properties *and they know it*. They're not gonna call those notes and I am not gonna worry about it. If you're trying to scare me, mister, you have another think coming. Six million. Newspapers, TV, radio. That's it. You know about the loans, you know why I want it. Six million. If you say no, there's people who'll say yes. My friends won't call those notes, so I don't have to be in a hurry."

"But you are in a hurry; you told me you couldn't wait." Matt pulled a folded paper from his inside jacket pocket. "This is a list of names and telephone numbers. I talked to Ordrey Wayland this morning. He's heard of the man I work for; he knows his insurance business could double or triple if we steered clients his way."

"You told him that?" Graham demanded.

"He knew it. I reminded him."

"You didn't tell him you'd double or triple his business if he called my note?"

"Why would I tell him that?" Matt asked.

"No, 'course you wouldn't. You wouldn't have to." Graham shoved aside his chile. "You talk to any of the others?"

"No."

"You mean, not yet."

"I haven't talked to any of the others."

"But you would." Graham nodded to himself. "Five million would do it. It's worth—"

"Four."

186

"Now look, dammit, I've dropped from ten to five; you've come up one puny half-million. That is not good-faith negotiating."

"Four, Jim."

"Four and a half."

Matt pulled a typed letter from his briefcase and put it on the table, turning it around so Graham could read it. The only sound in the small diner was the tapping of the salt shaker in Graham's hand. "Shit. All ready and everything. Pretty fucking sure of yourselves. Borrow your pen?"

"You should read it before you sign."

"Do I know what it says?"

"Probably."

"Four and a half million for all capital equipment, subscription lists, advertising contracts, supplies, the works. Contract to be signed at such and such a date."

"Yes. But I'd like you to read it."

"Shit." Graham skimmed the letter. "Pen." Matt handed him one and he scrawled his name. "Congratulations," he said heavily. "Just got yourself a hell of a deal. Your boss promise you a bonus? A mink coat for your missus? A lady for your spare time?"

Matt put the letter away and stood up. "You'll be hearing from us." He hesitated. "I hope you get everything straightened out with your son."

"Bullshit, mister. You don't give a flying fuck what happens to me or my son." Turning his back, Graham drained his beer mug.

Matt waited a moment, then walked to the cash register, paid for their chiles and beer, and left the diner.

I have never done anything like that in my life.

And the fact that James Graham had made his own mess, and then insulted the only buyer who'd shown up in ten months of frantic searching, didn't change the reality that Matt didn't like himself at that moment; he wasn't even sure he recognized Matt Lovell—whom *I've known intimately, he reflected wryly, for forty-two years.*

He stood in front of the diner, realizing he had no way back

187

to the airport. No taxis were in sight; he couldn't ask Graham.
Well, he'd walk; he remembered the way they'd come. He
started up the road. It was only a few miles; he had three hours
before his plane, and a walk was just what he needed. He could
work off some nervous energy, think about what he'd done—
maybe even get acquainted with a Matt Lovell he'd never
known before.

Nicole Renard was married and divorced before she was
twenty-three; at twenty-four she met Keegan Rourke while
skiing in Aspen; a month later she bought a sprawling ranch-
style home in River Oaks, a few blocks from Rourke's; and
by the time she was twenty-six her parties were as well-known
there as in New York, where she owned an apartment in Trump
Tower, and Aspen, where she stayed in Rourke's house on Red
Mountain, across the valley from the ski slopes.

Six years later, when she invited Matt Lovell to her annual
pre-Christmas party, she and Rourke had evolved gradually
from lovers to friends. Occasionally they spent the night together, because they liked each other and it was relaxing to
spend an undemanding evening with someone familiar—"Like
an old bathrobe," Nicole would say, stretching lazily in bed.
"We fit well and we haven't worn each other out"—but they
didn't waste time on possessiveness or jealousy when Rourke
had other women and Nicole other men. Still, the two of them,
though thirty-eight years apart in age, had the special intimacy
that comes from sharing identical ideas about getting and using
the things of the world, and it endured even when they kept
in touch only by phone.

So Nicole was the first outside Rourke Enterprises to know
how well Matt had handled the Graham purchase. And Rourke
was the first to know that Nicole planned to invite Matt to her
December party. "He may not come," Rourke said. "As far as
I know, he doesn't socialize here at all, except for business
dinners."

"Perhaps he'll make an exception," Nicole said, and the first
week in December she called Matt at Rourke's headquarters.
"Pre-Christmas; my own tradition," she said in her husky voice.

"I don't compete with office parties or cozy family gatherings; I give one glorious fete at the precise moment when everyone is dying for a party but dreading the official ones. Do say you'll come. I hear about you all the time, but we've never talked. Keegan monopolized you in Aspen, and I couldn't spring you from all the politicos at that awful party at his house, though I certainly did my best, as you may have noticed. And I'm told my parties are memorable. You will come, won't you? My reputation as a hostess might depend on it. And I am so looking forward to really getting to know you. Please, Matt, do say yes."

"I'd like to," said Matt, intrigued by the contrast between her sultry voice and ingenuous outpouring of words. "I'm not sure I'll be in town."

"Keegan said you didn't socialize in Houston, but just this once I hoped you would. After all, there aren't many pre-Christmases in a year. It's a special occasion for me; it might be one for you, too. And Keegan will be here, in case you're worried about not knowing anyone."

"I'm not worried," Matt replied. "I know you."

"You'll know me better after the twenty-first."

As it turned out, Matt knew a few other guests, but most of those who crowded into the three wings of Nicole's ranch house were like a tossed salad of professions, ages, and life-styles Matt had not expected to find. Television actors, actresses, and newscasters, jazz musicians, stockbrokers, European couturiers, interior designers, and songwriters mingled with oilmen, real estate developers, bankers, resort owners, Olympic swimming medalists, and a magazine publisher who flew in from New York for the party.

They shouted greetings and introductions and wove in and out like dancers, drifting into one pattern and then another. Champagne and hot spiced wine were served in all three wings that extended from the central living and dining room that curved around a swimming pool beneath a domed skylight. Nicole had converted one wing to a huge playroom where guests found games of jacks, marbles, hopscotch, dominoes, pinning a beard on a life-size cardboard politician—a new one every

189

month, Matt learned—a Ping-Pong table, ring toss, and a full swing set. "It's the most popular place in the house," Nicole told Matt when she showed him around. "People tend to scoff, then they sneak up here and have the best time they've had in years."

Everyone had heard of Matt. Word had gotten around that Rourke Enterprises had a new executive and that Nicole— "wouldn't you just *know* Nicole would be the one to do it?" —was the first to get him to come to a Houston party, so when she introduced him he was met with open curiosity and appraisal. The women approved his looks, the men approved his starting out at the top, and they all offered congratulations and urged him to call them if he needed anything.

"Which means they'll call you," Nicole laughed. "They like to think men like Keegan and those close to him can do anything, get around laws and ordinances, swing votes . . ."

"I can't," Matt said.

"But if they want to think it, why stop them?"

By the time they were in the living room again, and she had left him to greet new arrivals, Matt stood alone, wondering about her guests, and her house. It was one of the most beautiful he had ever seen, furnished with elegant sophistication instead of the hard masculinity of Rourke's office.

"She's very good," Rourke said at Matt's elbow.

Matt turned. "I didn't see you come in."

"You were in the playroom. Superb house, isn't it?"

Matt nodded. "Where does she get her money?"

"Real estate."

"In Houston?"

Rourke chuckled. "In the course of three generations, her family has bought several blocks near the Place Vendôme in Paris, a good part of Gray's Inn Road in London, scattered buildings around Columbus Circle in New York, and in downtown Perth and Sidney, Australia. And Nicole is a shrewd investor; she manages her money well. The chandelier, by the way, is a Waterford; the stained glass lamps are Tiffany, and the ones with glass shades painted in country scenes are Handel. Good investments."

Someone called Rourke and he excused himself. Matt contemplated the room, remembering the others in the house. *No personality,* Elizabeth had said. But that had been the Nicole who decorated Rourke's office. This Nicole had used soft textures and bright colors that glowed beneath a sparkling chandelier and glass lamps. Extremely beautiful. And good investments.

The evening was chilly—a cold wave, Houstonians called it, since the temperature had dipped below forty—and fires burned in the living room and dining room and the guest rooms and Nicole's bedroom and study in another wing. Guests sat on silk hassocks, velvet couches, and crewel-worked armchairs. Their voices carried through the house. Matt walked through the rooms, stopped by guests who had heard of him and wanted to meet him, to find out what he was doing for Rourke, and what Rourke was involved in these days. He was invited to speak to three business groups, to join a luncheon club, and to appear as a guest on a television talk show. When someone finally praised "Private Affairs," he felt relieved, as if at last he was sharing something with Elizabeth.

A few minutes later dinner was served at ten round tables, with ten people to a table, and Matt found his place card beside Nicole's. He knew none of the others at the table so he listened to the talk about sports and politics, ski resorts and real estate, European fashions and American designers. Nicole watched over it, heading off disputes, introducing a new subject before the current one flagged, now and then leaving her chair to check on the conversations at the other tables. In the foyer between the living and dining rooms, musicians played waltzes and show tunes; waiters glided in and out refilling wine glasses and bread and butter plates.

Everything was done with a perfection that came from experience and attention to detail. From the pheasant pâté with brandied apples to the white chocolate mousse and espresso, each course was presented on a different pattern of china, each wine in a different pattern of crystal. Where does a woman put six hundred place settings of china and glassware? Matt asked himself. Then he noticed round cut-glass candleholders, four to each table, with candles flickering deep within them; a round cut-glass vase beside each candleholder, with miniature sprays of balsam and red berries, one beside each candleholder, and gold-handled fruit knives at each place. Behind the fruit knives were the place cards: curls of white bark from aspen trees, with guests' names written in a bold script.

Matt admired it as a job superbly done. She knew what she wanted and how to get it. He finished his coffee and dessert, then, groaning inwardly because he had been unable to resist the amaretto truffles, he excused himself, strode the full length of the playroom and then back, to stand at the side of the dining room, watching those who were still eating.

"Lonely?" Nicole asked, coming to stand beside him.

"Recovering," he replied with a smile. "If I hadn't stood and stretched after that meal I wouldn't have been able to get up for a month."

She did not, he noted with approval, make a coy comment about his staying for a month; she merely returned his smile, giving him another chance to admire her beauty. Her black hair was loose and frizzed—each time he saw her it was different—making her face seem smaller and as clear and pale as fine china; her strapless dress was white silk, sinuously molded to her body; around her neck, like a fabulous collar, lay an eight-strand necklace of ebony and ivory. A red camellia nestled in her hair, matching her lipstick: her only dashes of color. "Are you enjoying yourself?" she asked, and she might have been asking about the party or looking at her.

"Very much," Matt answered, letting her decide which he meant. He glanced about the room. "It's quite a collection of people."

"Which surprises you."

Embarrassed, he said, "Am I so obvious?"

"Less than most men. It's one of the reasons I find you interesting. But you are puzzled about me and you didn't expect to be. Am I right? My house has surprised you, my dinner has surprised you, my guests have surprised you."

"You've been watching me."

"I watch all my guests, to make sure they're happy. You've

spent the evening trying to categorize me and put names to the things I own. The rug in the library, by the way, is a Bakhtiari." She laughed. "I'm sorry, Matt; I'm taking advantage of your expressive face. But I like it; I prefer a man who shows his emotions even when he's puzzled because I don't fit into simple categories."

He shook his head. "Unfair. I don't always look for easy explanations."

"Come, now. Men do."

"You pride yourself on knowing enough about men to know that all men don't."

She laughed. "Clever man. Another reason I find you interesting. Not many men are."

"How many have been?" Matt asked curiously.

"I don't keep count," she said, smiling. "Do you, with women?"

"Yes. It's a very small number."

"Ah. Lucky as well as clever. What would you like to know about me?"

"What would you like to tell me?"

She gave a low laugh. "Nothing right now. Someday, when the time is right, I'll tell you the history of the Renards. I'm ahead of you there; I already know yours. Matt Lovell, the brightest star in Keegan Rourke's galaxy."

"An exaggeration. Keegan must have been under a spell. Was it yours?"

Still smiling, she shook her head. "Keegan has been free of my spell for years. You impressed him without sorcery. And why would you need it? You do very well on your own."

"Only a fool turns down help when it's offered."

"Even demonic?"

"If he can control it."

"Ah. A confident man. No wonder Keegan trusts you with one of his biggest jobs."

"If he does. I'm still on trial."

"And covering the whole southwest. Hardly a small stage."

"Hardly a small critic. Keegan isn't easily satisfied."

"Are you?"

193

"Easily satisfied? No."

"The winners of the world never are. I sympathize with you; Keegan isn't easy to work for. But the rewards make it worthwhile."

"You don't mean money."

She gave a small shrug. "Many people make money. It's harder to get power and influence."

"And you think that's what I'm after?"

"I hope so."

"And you?"

"Of course."

He looked at her curiously. "And when you have enough? What will you do then?"

"There is never enough. The stakes get bigger. Keegan knows that, which is why he is never dull. He wants me to design your office. Shall I?"

"I'm not there enough to notice. I like what you did with his."

"I do my best work for my friends. Of course I only work for friends."

"I thought decorating was your business."

"My business is pleasing myself. I decorate offices because it pleases me and keeps me from being bored. And I'm very good at it." She laughed again at his frown. "Matt, your disapproval is showing. What's wrong with wanting to please myself? Isn't that what you want? Why did you buy your first newspaper? Why did you go in with Keegan? You want to please yourself and avoid boredom and do what you're good at. You and I are exactly alike. And because we're like that, we're more interesting, more pleasant to be with—not grouchy from frustration or envy—and more satisfied with ourselves. Is anything more important?"

Matt gazed at her. "You make a good case for it."

"Good case for what?" asked Rourke, joining them. "Excellent dinner, my dear Nicole, as always. Your chef is more innovative than mine. Perhaps mine should come here for lessons. Are you making a case for decorating Matt's office?"

"I offered. I was rejected."

"Matt, you surprise me. Your hostess offers to design your office—"

"And I merely said I wasn't there enough to appreciate it."

"Notice it," corrected Nicole.

"You'll notice and appreciate it, both, if Nicole designs it," Rourke said. "If she'd done it a few months ago you'd have found it more comfortable and been with us more often, available when we needed you, instead of running around the country. If you take my advice, you'll have her start on it right after New Year's."

Matt looked from Rourke to Nicole. It was very neat; as if they'd planned the conversation in advance. *You'd have been with us more often, instead of running around the country.* In other words, in Houston instead of Santa Fe. If Rourke wanted to re-open that discussion, even after agreeing to Matt's working half-time in Santa Fe until Peter graduated, what better way than through Nicole? But Matt couldn't be sure. And he preferred not believing they'd conspired to get him to change his plans.

Nicole was studying him. "I think Matt would rather not have his office decorated," she said softly. "At least not yet. And he's probably right. He should set his own schedule. But I would like to work for you when you're ready, Matt. Will you call on me?"

Her amber eyes were eager and a little anxious. Matt felt a stab of guilt for his thoughts. It wasn't like him to be suspicious. "Of course," he said. "In fact, there's no reason why you shouldn't do it any time, if you really want to. I don't know how much I'll be here, but I might as well enjoy my surroundings when I am."

Nicole touched his hand briefly. "Thank you. I'm not busy in January; I can start right after the holidays. And I'll have sketches for you in a week."

"There's no rush; I'll be in Santa Fe until after the first of the year."

"Oh. Well, they'll be ready, whenever you are."

"Rourke!" a new voice interrupted. "Lookin' fine; not hungry or sleepy or peevish. Must be that ex-cel-lent dinner which

195

certainly sits well; very well. I thank you, Nicole; couldn't have left Houston without one of your spec-tac-u-lar dinners."

"Leaving already, Terry?" Nicole asked.

"I am, and I apologize." He shook hands with Matt. "Terry Ballenger. Don't know if you remember me; I bought—"

"Of course I remember," Matt said. "I'd hoped we could meet when you bought our property, but the realtor and lawyers were too efficient for us. Are you enjoying Nuevo?"

"Haven't had time to set foot in the place. New-ay-vo. Have to get there one of these days. Right now, though, I'm sorry, Nicole honey, but I am indeed sayin' goodbye; I'm flying to Hawaii tonight, looking at some property there—du-ty, you know; du-ty calls, even at holiday time—and then it's on to Japan, so I've got to run."

"How much of Japan are you buying?" Nicole asked, then said in mock warning to Matt, "Watch out for Terry, he'll buy your house out from under you while you're in the shower."

They laughed and chatted lightly until Terry again made his farewells and Rourke walked with him to the door. "I cannot bear to be called honey!" Nicole said in disgust. "And the way he breaks his words into pieces . . . I couldn't live with him five minutes; it would drive me mad."

"He didn't mention other property when he bought my land last spring," Matt said thoughtfully. "In fact, I think he specifically said he was a car dealer."

"He does that, too; he owns four dealerships. Is it important?"

"What does he do with the property he buys?"

"Builds on it, sells it, plants daffodils—who knows? I never can endure him long enough to find out. Somehow Keegan finds such peculiar people. Or dull. Most of them are dull."

Matt forgot Ballenger. He looked at Nicole, waiting for her to tell him he wasn't peculiar or dull. But once again she avoided the obvious. "I'm sorry you won't be here New Year's Eve." Her husky voice was almost lost in the din of the party that was increasing steadily. Matt leaned closer. "I'm having a few friends over, very quiet, nothing like tonight. Keegan will be out of town. I was planning to ask you to join us.

196

Music, conversation, dancing in the playroom, supper at midnight. But you won't be here."

He felt the pull of her amber eyes and half smile; he could almost taste her spicy fragrance on his tongue. But then the party broke in, with its rising decibels, the smell of coffee and candle wax and balsam. "I'm afraid not," he said. He saw the shadow in her eyes—disappointment, he noted, rather than annoyance over not getting her way, which made him like her even more. "My family is counting on me and I'm looking forward to a week with them. We don't have much time together anymore."

She tilted her head slightly. "What are your lucky colors?"

"My what?"

"Lucky colors. I need to know, for designing your office."

"I haven't any."

"Of course you have. You just don't know it. Poor Matt; no superstitions? I'll have to teach you some." She appraised him critically. "Burgundy. Midnight blue. Beige. Definitely not green or orange. What is it?" she asked as his eyebrows went up.

"You just ruled out the two colors I like least. I hope that's as far as your mindreading goes."

"It isn't," she said. "Fair warning."

Just then the party shifted; the foyer filled with people and they were surrounded. Nicole smiled at him. "No more privacy for now. But I do have some ideas for after the first of the year."

"Fair warning?" he asked lightly.

"Fair warning," she repeated, and her hand brushed his as she was swept up by a crowd. Alone for a moment, Matt smiled to himself. As Rourke had said, she was very good. I should be flattered, he thought, especially since I wouldn't have expected her to waste her time on a married man. He watched her move among her guests. He followed her to the playroom where she briefly joined a game of marbles, knocking an agate from the circle with the aim of a ten-year-old on a city sidewalk. "I learned that in Paris," she said casually, and looked directly at Matt, a challenge in her eyes. Without a word, he squatted beside her and sent a Lutz shooter like a missile into two colored

197

sulphides, knocking them out of the circle. "I was born knowing that," he said with a grin.

All evening, when he was not talking or being talked to, Matt found himself near her, or he looked up to find her just behind him, or close by. When he thought about it that night, and the next morning, he realized he had talked to fifty people or more, but remembered only Nicole. Part of the game, he told himself as he sat on the plane watching Houston's vast sprawl and the blue-gray water of the bay disappear below him. Which she obviously likes for its own sake. Like marbles. Spin hard and fast and make an impression and then turn to something else to keep from being bored. A good way to play. No one gets hurt.

Best of all, he thought before opening his morning newspaper, I can be sure I won't come back to a green and orange office.

Snow fell on Christmas Eve, drifting from low clouds and wrapping Santa Fe in feathery white. Churchgoers strolled home at midnight on silent feet, as if walking through a cave, muffled and glowing faintly from pale street lights speckled with falling flakes. In their homes families lit *farolitos*—candles placed in sand inside large paper bags—and many set small bonfires, or *luminarias,* in front of their houses to recall the fires that had warmed the shepherds of Bethlehem.

The next morning the sun blazed and the snow sparkled all over town, even as it began to melt on church domes and sidewalks, streets, lampposts, and the tops of adobe walls. And Christmas bells filled the air.

Holly's pure voice soared through the house, singing carols and folk songs and snatches of operas. All week she had sung in Christmas concerts, and in two Las Posadas pageants telling of Mary and Joseph's search for shelter, one performed in a church, the other in Lydia and Spencer's home in Tesuque for a gathering of friends. She had sung with the school chorus in a Christmas Eve concert in the Plaza, and all Christmas day, while she and Elizabeth cooked and cleaned, she was still so full of music she could not sing enough.

"Maybe because Daddy's home," she told Elizabeth as she swooped into the kitchen and peered into the oven. "I feel so lovely inside. Full of love. When will everybody be here?"

"Five," Elizabeth said. "What time did Peter say he'd be home?"

"About four, but you know he's never on time. Do you worry about me as much as you worry about him?"

"I would if you hitch-hiked all over the place the way he does."

"Mother, he's almost eighteen. He's a *man*."

"Oh. But you say the seniors who ask you out are only boys."

Holly flushed. "They act like boys. I do go out, you know that, but there don't seem to be many real grown-up men in the world."

God knows that's true, Elizabeth mused, thinking of the men she'd met at Rourke's party in Houston—as greedy as children for more money, more influence, more power—and the men at the *Chieftain* and the *Daily News* who seemed to spend half their time working and the other half looking for scapegoats when something went wrong. "But you should go out more often, Holly," she said. "You don't do enough with people your own age."

"You don't go out when Daddy's in Houston."

"Of course not. I wait until he's here."

"Well, I'm waiting, too. When I find somebody I like, I'll go out with him. A lot. I promise."

"What do you promise?" Matt asked, coming into the kitchen.

"I promise to give you a Christmas kiss," said Holly, throwing her arms around Matt. "It's so *lovely* to have you home."

"Yes it is," Matt said, wondering how he could have been away so much in the past months. From the moment he arrived, the day before, he'd felt himself being drawn into his family with a warm sense of belonging he hadn't felt on all the weekends he'd been back. Probably because he'd always brought work with him, he thought, and closeted himself at the *Chieftain* or in his office at home. This was a real holiday: the first week since he'd joined Rourke that he hadn't even brought his briefcase with him.

199

"So if you think it's lovely, why aren't you here more often?" Holly demanded, and that was what they all asked him—the whole family and Saul and Heather—when everyone was at the dinner table watching him carve the turkey.

"I thought I heard you say," Lydia commented, "when you took this new position, you'd be here at least half the time. Though my hearing could be failing with old age."

"Nope." Peter poured honey on puffed triangles of bread called *sopapillas*. "I heard the same thing."

"Well, men have to travel," Spencer put in absently. "Did everyone get a look at the bowl the *posole* is in?"

"Yes, and it's beautiful," Heather said. "The most beautiful you've ever made. I thought Matt was planning to work in his office at the *Chieftain*."

"You didn't travel in *your* job," Lydia pointed out to Spencer.

"I didn't make as much money as Matt, either," he replied. "You know, that *is* a beautiful bowl. I should have gone into woodworking in my youth, instead of spending my best years at a desk shuffling personnel records."

"And ten years owning a bookstore and art gallery?" Lydia asked. "Was that such a sacrifice?"

"What? Good heavens, no. We were working together— very pleasant—restorative after the university. But a man has to move on. Even at seventy-five."

"What about it, Matt?" asked Saul. "You *were* going to work out of Santa Fe, at least until spring."

"I thought I could," Matt said shortly. *In Houston they think I'm in Santa Fe too much; in Santa Fe . . .* "Does everyone have turkey?"

"I don't," Elizabeth said quietly.

"I'm sorry, sweetheart, I passed you up. I should have filled your plate first. Everything looks wonderful."

"Everything is," said Holly. "That wouldn't surprise you if you ate here all the time, like most fathers."

"That's enough, Holly," Elizabeth said. "In fact, that's enough from everyone. Let Matt enjoy his dinner. I want Peter to tell us about college. It's pretty special to get an early acceptance to the place you most want to go."

Peter needed no urging; his excitement was still intact from the day, only a week ago, that the fat envelope had arrived from Stanford and he'd telephoned everyone with the news. He launched into a description of the university and the anthropology courses he planned to take, and that gave Elizabeth the opportunity to ask him another question. "Tell us about *Los Matachines;* I've never seen that dance. Where were you, Peter? Which pueblo?"

He told them about it, describing the Indian Christmas dance with colorful phrases and descriptions that reminded everyone of Elizabeth's writing. He was going to be a fine writer, Matt reflected, watching his son, proud of him but suddenly wondering how well he knew him. He had changed in the past weeks; more unpredictable than ever, swinging from moodiness to a strange radiance, but at the same time more withdrawn, secretive, pulling away from them. Matt thought it was probably a girl—Maya, whom he'd brought to dinner?—and that in the past few months, while he'd been preoccupied, Peter had left boyhood behind.

Elizabeth stepped in again as soon as Peter began to slow down. Skillfully leading the conversation so that no one had a chance to criticize Matt, she led Spencer to tell them about his woodworking, and Heather to talk about her job as assistant editor at the *Chieftain,* and Saul to describe their plans for special coverage of the Bach festival in February.

"That's new," said Matt.

"We just decided," Elizabeth said quickly. "I was going to tell you, but there are so many things I haven't told you yet . . ."

"We're going to sell out at the Ski Basin," Saul announced. "Can't miss. We're calling it *Ski Bach-wards.*"

"Oh, no," groaned Peter.

"Fear not; it won't happen. Elizabeth vetoed it."

"And," Heather added, "she also vetoed *We're Hopi-ng you've Bean to the Dance,* for the Hopi Bean Dance in February, and *There are Deerections to get there . . .* for the Deer dance at San Ildefonso in January—"

"Not to mention," Elizabeth added with dancing eyes,

201

"Dawn't Forget the San Ildefonso Procession which, in case anyone doubts it, takes place at—"

"Dawn!" exclaimed Peter and Holly in unison, and burst out laughing.

"It seems I've missed some lively debates," said Matt. The laughter faded away.

"You should be here," Heather said somberly.

"I think you're right," Matt replied.

In the awkward silence, Heather said, "I have an announcement."

Lydia searched her face. "Oh, how wonderful," she said.

"What?" asked Spencer, then, looking at Saul and Heather, he said, "Oh. Well, that's very good."

"Let Heather *say* it!" cried Holly.

"I guess I don't need to," Heather said. "I mean, it looks like I'm the last to know."

Saul put his arm around her and kissed her. "You were the first to know I love you and want to marry you. You were the first to know you felt the same way. You were the first to know you'd risk it. What else matters?"

"Nothing, really. But I did want to surprise everyone."

"You surprised me," said Matt. "But then I haven't been around to watch love's progress, as people keep reminding me."

"Can I sing at your wedding?" Holly asked. "When is it?"

"Tomorrow," said Saul.

"We haven't decided," said Heather. "But *yes* we want you to sing. We wouldn't have anyone else."

"Well, make it before I go to college," Peter said, "so I don't miss it."

"Good God!" Saul exclaimed. "You're not leaving until next August! Eight months! Is this a Victorian engagement or a modern romance where the hero and heroine get out of bed long enough for the marriage ceremony and get back in as soon as the guests go home?"

"Saul!" protested Heather.

"I apologize," Saul said. "But my darling Heather, we're talking about getting married, not getting engaged."

"I know," she murmured.

Saul sighed. "One step at a time. As for the big date, we'll let everyone know it as soon as we negotiate it ourselves. Is there a dessert to this fabulous feast? And are we soon to exchange gifts?"

"Yes and yes," Elizabeth said. "Which do you want first?"

Matt had been watching her and had seen her gaze at Heather and Saul with a look both wistful and a little curious, as if she were trying to remember how it felt to be in love and planning to get married. Well, it's been a long time, he thought: almost nineteen years. But it isn't really forgotten; we're just under too much pressure. By June, when we're together in Houston, we'll be starting again; it will be exactly the way it was when we bought the *Chieftain*.

"Dad?" asked Peter impatiently.

"Yes," Matt said. "I was thinking."

"We're having presents first and then dessert. Okay?"

"Good idea. Let dinner settle."

Saul pushed back his chair. "About now I could use my New York apartment; I used to jog up and down the stairs after a meal like this. Kept me trim."

"You can jog up the hill to your apartment at Fort Marcy," said Heather as they went into the living room. "All the way to the top."

Matt followed them. *If I hadn't stood and stretched after that meal I wouldn't have been able to get up for a month.*

His life in Houston rushed back: noise, speed, highways; automobile exhausts and humidity blurring the skyscrapers; Rourke's home in tapestries, marble, and glass; Nicole's luxurious ranch house where he'd strode the length of a playroom to work off a rich dinner; his quiet office where he made proposals and decisions that affected four states and millions of people . . .

The brightest star in Keegan Rourke's galaxy.

No wonder Santa Fe seemed backward whenever he returned. It was. And for a long time now it had been too small and quiet for him.

"Do you want to go first, Matt?" Elizabeth asked.

He shook his head as he sat beside her. "I'd rather watch everyone else."

It was the first year Matt and Elizabeth had had enough money for a lavish Christmas. They had shopped together on one of his weekends home, in November, and now they watched the others exclaim in delight over gifts they had always wanted: for Lydia an antique rocking chair for the bookshop, for Spencer a set of chisels from England, for Heather a silver and coral bracelet by Richard Chavez, for Saul a Joseph Lonewolf etching he had admired when they were browsing at the Eagle Dancer Gallery, for Holly her own stereo, and for Peter—"Christmas and graduation," said Matt, giving Peter a tiny box. "Because we're very proud of you."

As Peter turned the box in his hands, Matt and Elizabeth exchanged a smile, knowing he was trying to hide his disappointment, knowing why he felt disappointed, and knowing what was in the box. That shared smile eased the tension from dinner and swept away thoughts of Houston. Matt put his arm around his wife, holding her against him. "He doesn't even guess."

Elizabeth shook her head, smiling, and they watched Peter open the box, slowly unfold a piece of tissue paper, and then let out a whoop as he took out a pair of car keys on a ring. "You did get me one! You did guess what I wanted—!" He stopped as laughter drowned out his voice. "Well, I did hint a little, I guess. Which one did you get? I mean, where is it? I mean, can I see it today or—?"

"You might try looking in the driveway," Matt said.

Peter made a dash for the front door, followed by Holly and then Saul, and the three of them stood in the chill air, gazing at the gleaming Wagoneer four-wheel-drive that would take Peter up any mountain road in any weather, or to any pueblo, or all the way to Stanford in August. He let out a long, ecstatic sigh. "That is a spectacular sight." He started outside, stopped, and came back to put his arms around Matt and Elizabeth. "Thank you, thank you, how can I thank you enough? You're terrific; I love you; I can't tell you how much I thank you—"

"You've told us," said Matt. "Just drive it carefully."

Elizabeth laughed. "I was afraid I'd be the one to say that. How good of you to beat me to it."

"Can I try it out?" Peter asked. "No, it's okay, I'll wait until everybody's had presents."

"And dessert," said Saul. "Then maybe you'll give me a ride."

"Well, actually . . ." Peter said, and hesitated.

"Actually," said Holly, "Peter thought he'd drive up to Nuevo. Right?"

"I did think about it."

"Terrific place for a test drive," Saul observed. "Tell me all about it when you get back."

"I will. Thanks, Saul. What about your presents?" Peter asked his parents. "You haven't given each other anything."

"We're going to do it later," Matt answered. "You'll have to forgive us; we decided to wait till we're alone."

They waited until everyone had left before exchanging their gifts in their bedroom: a robe of burgundy satin embroidered in ivory for Elizabeth, a robe of midnight blue cashmere for Matt. Elizabeth looked from one robe to the other. "What are the chances of two people choosing the same gifts, do you suppose?"

"Evidently pretty good, when you've been married long enough."

"Do you think so?" She took off her terry cloth robe and put on the new one, the satin a cool caress on her skin. "I wonder."

"Why?" Matt was pulling on his robe. "Do you know that this is the sexiest robe I've ever had?"

"Because even though we've been married a long time, we're not as close as we were. That's why we're surprised that we chose the same gifts."

"Well, why don't we try for some closeness now?" Matt asked, reaching for her.

"We used to talk when something was bothering us," Elizabeth said.

"Not always. Sometimes we waited for a better time."

"This seems like a good time to me."

"It doesn't to me. Let it go, Elizabeth. It's Christmas, we've had a family dinner, everyone had a wonderful time, and we have a whole week ahead of us. Let's really spend some time together; can you take a couple of days off from your writing? We'll do the town like tourists, eat out, unwind . . . and talk."

"All right," she said after a moment. He reached for her again and when she opened her mouth beneath his kiss they both knew they were trying to lose themselves in their love-making. Their bodies moved in remembered ways because they knew each other so well; they knew how to arouse and enjoy and satisfy, and they reached their climax in familiar rhythms that peaked together, and together slowly subsided.

But it was not all familiar. Instead of the murmurs and talk that usually ran through their lovemaking, they were silent, and they were silent as they lay beside each other, resting. Finally, Matt said, "I'm sorry."

"So am I," said Elizabeth, and they knew it was because the intimacy and passion of that golden time when they worked together on the *Chieftain* and took a vacation in Aspen, was gone.

But they put off talking about it, though they spent their time together, as Matt had suggested. The first two days they went to the *Chieftain* and the *Daily News*, but both papers were doing well and, though Saul and the managing editor in Albuquerque both made a point of asking Matt's advice about schedules for the next six months, he felt superfluous; after a few hours he couldn't wait to get away.

So they wandered about their favorite parts of Santa Fe, browsing in art galleries, eating lunch at Josie's and dinner at The Haven on Canyon Road after visiting Lydia in the bookshop a few doors away and being given a tour of Spencer's wood-working shop in the garage. And for the first time in years they spent a morning at the Wheelwright Museum, where Peter had first discovered Indian art.

The town was quiet. Skiers were there, but compared to the summer hordes the streets seemed almost empty. The most crowded was Cerillos Road where high school students, with school closed for the holiday, cruised up and down in their cars, looking for action. "Why don't they go skiing?" Matt asked. "Preferably in Switzerland."

"They can't afford it," Elizabeth said, smiling.

"Have you heard from Tony Rourke lately?"

Surprised, she said, "What made you think of him?"

"Switzerland. Didn't he once say he bought a villa there?"

"Italy, I think. Amalfi. He calls now and then."

"And stops by?"

"No. I would have told you if he had."

Matt nodded and changed the subject before Elizabeth could say she and Tony were just friends and didn't he have any friends in Houston?

They stopped for a drink at La Fonda, walking through the crowded hotel lobby that was the town's central meeting place to reach the cavernous dimly-lit bar. At a small corner table, with a frosty pitcher of margaritas and two salt-rimmed glasses, they talked about all the little events of their lives they never seemed to get to in telephone calls or Matt's visits. "You told me you were going to Roswell to talk to someone named Graham," Elizabeth said. "Did that work out?"

"Yes," he said.

She was puzzled. "And?"

"There wasn't much to it. He needed money—he and his son were in pretty deep from gambling—and it was just a question of agreeing on a price."

"So he didn't drive a hard bargain."

"No."

"Keegan must have been pleased."

"He was. It's a good package: a television and radio station and eight papers. Everything's small-scale, but there's room for growth, especially if there's development in that part of the state."

She nodded. "Why weren't you pleased, then?"

"What makes you think I wasn't?"

"Your voice. It sounds as if something about it bothered you."

"You're wrong," he said. "Everything went exactly as it was supposed to go. What you're probably hearing is lack of interest: I'm more concerned about negotiations in Phoenix and Tucson. Those are major papers and if we get them I may stop buying for a while and concentrate on running the chain. I've spent so much time on business I've almost forgotten how to be a publisher. Tell me about your column; Keegan's secretary tells me she sends you stacks of mail."

"She does. It's amazing how it's gone up since I started writing three times a week. And something new: a lot of the writers send photographs of themselves, with their life stories. So I can write about them."

"And do you?"

"Sometimes. It's risky. When people put themselves forward like that, they're usually so anxious to make an impression that truth gets mangled along the way."

"That's very clever," Matt said. "It's not always easy to see. So you still go out and find your own people."

She nodded. "Private ones, who don't advertise themselves. My favorite kind, for friends as well as for 'Private Affairs.'"

Matt started to ask why she liked Tony, if that were true, then let it go. "What else do they send you besides photographs?"

"That's all. But I do get phone calls from people asking for advice. It's very strange; readers seem to think I'm a psychologist or a marriage counselor or an expert on disputes with landlords or office politics . . . I've put together a list of advisers to recommend for every problem imaginable; I don't want to get sued for practicing psychology without a license. The hardest part is convincing people I don't have answers."

"That's because they trust you. Every word you write tells them you like people, you try to understand them, you don't pass judgement, and you're honest. What more could anyone look for in a counselor?"

"Thank you," Elizabeth said. "That's a high compliment."

They were as formal as casual acquaintances, Matt thought. What was it that kept them so far apart?

"Then there's a new assistant pressman at the *Chieftain*," Elizabeth said. "Young and eager and a bit of a problem. I'm afraid he thinks I'm a damsel in distress."

"What kind of distress? Danger?"

She shook her head. "Deserted." She was pouring from the pitcher and missed the expression on Matt's face as she said it. "Of course he hasn't been around this week, with you home, but he's been coming over at least once a day to see if we need help, which of course infuriates Peter. I'll have to talk to him, but he's so earnest I've put it off; I don't want to hurt him."

"Better now than later," Matt said briefly.

"Is it?" Elizabeth asked. "Then why do we put off talking about things important to us? You haven't talked about Keegan all week."

"What about him?"

"How you feel about him. Do you like him, Matt? Now that you know him better?"

"It isn't important whether I like him or not. I like what he offers me."

"But it's important to me, so I can understand what's happening inside you. *Do* you like him?"

"He's very impressive."

"That means you admire him."

"I admire what he's done. He has goals and he achieves them; he knows what he's doing and doesn't let others stop him. He knows what he wants."

"What does he want?"

"Among other things, a chain of newspapers across the southwest."

"Why?"

"To make money, I assume; I haven't asked him. He also owns oil wells and two ski resorts and a couple of hotels; I haven't asked him why he owns them either. Probably because he likes owning them and it's smart to spread investments around. That doesn't satisfy you?"

"I don't know. I've never felt simple explanations fit him."

"You've made that very clear."

"You want me to keep it to myself, is that it? Or pretend I think he's a dear little man who simply likes to play with his money and be a benefactor to unknown small-town journalists."

"I want you to see him as a hard-headed businessman who's

209

making it big in a tough world," Matt said evenly. "Unlike my own father, who never got anywhere, or your father, who worked at a dull job only until he could retire, and then dumped a shop on his wife so he could disappear into a cozy little hobby and get his excitement from wooden bowls."

"Matt!" Elizabeth stared at him. Their waitress, coming to see if they wanted refills, changed direction and went to another table; she wasn't one to get caught in somebody's crossfire. "You've never talked like that about Zachary or my father."

He shrugged slightly. "You make it hard for me. Keegan and I work together and it doesn't help when you talk as if I've sold out to the devil. It's hard enough for me as it is, traveling back and forth between Houston and Santa Fe; sometimes I feel like a stranger here—"

"You've made *that* very clear."

"—and sometimes I feel like a stranger there, but at least when I'm there I can count on sympathetic—" He stopped.

"Oh," Elizabeth said. "Who is she?"

"I'm talking about men who work with me and people I meet. They know what I'm doing; they admire it. I need that as much as you need praise for 'Private Affairs.'"

She nodded. "Matt, the other night I said we're not as close as we were and you said we'd talk about it. Are we going to?"

"Is it necessary? This is all temporary. Once you move to Houston we'll settle down. In fact, why don't you do it now?"

"Because Peter hasn't graduated."

"I know that. This is more important. Everything is changing, Elizabeth, and we ought to be sharing the changes instead of barely keeping up with them. And it's getting too hard for me to commute. Peter can graduate perfectly well in Houston; or if he insists on finishing here, let him live with Lydia and Spencer; they'd love to have him for a few months."

"And Holly? She wants to finish the year here."

"So two teenagers are setting policy for our marriage."

"Those teenagers are our children. And I think they need their parents, or at least one parent."

"For Christ's sake, it's only five months out of their lives!"

"And it's only five months out of yours. So why can't you continue commuting for that short time?"

"Because my work is there, damn it!"

"Well, damn it, my family is here!"

Matt slammed his glass on the table. "It's noisy as hell in here. Shall we go?"

And that was as far as they got in talking about themselves. It simmered inside them but they left it alone because the next day, the last of the year, they took Holly and Peter to Nuevo for cross-country skiing with Isabel, Cesar, Luz, and Maya, and they had no time to themselves. Isabel and Cesar had invited a few friends for dinner; Holly had turned down five dates for New Year's Eve parties, saying she'd rather be with her parents and Luz; Peter had planned all along to be with Maya. "I'll take my car," he said. "Since I'm not sure what time I'll be coming home."

"But you'll ski with us," said Elizabeth. "We'd like it if you would."

"Sure. We'd like it, too."

"And dinner?"

"Uh, no. We're eating at Maya's."

"With her parents?" Holly asked.

"They're in Albuquerque for the weekend," Peter mumbled.

Elizabeth and Matt looked at each other, and then away. Too many reminders of young love, Matt thought.

They arrived in Nuevo early, while the sun was high, and in a few minutes had glided off, following the snow-filled riverbed. The mountain air was sharp, but the valley was protected from the wind and after a few moments of skiing they were warm from their rhythmic strides, and exhilarated by the sense of well-being in the crystal clear day. They skied up the valley, skimming over the snow in friendly competition, picking up speed until the mountains on either side passed in a blur of white and green, brown and black. Finally Peter shouted at them to stop. "I can't see! I need windshield wipers for my eyelids!"

Laughing, breathless, they stopped, and Cesar and Matt built a bonfire of piñon wood in the shelter of a cliff. Isabel and

Luz took wine and cheese, apples and sliced sausage from their backpacks. Maya said shyly, "Peter and I made cookies, if anyone could use them."

"Peter and Daddy eat cookies day or night," Holly said. "Mother and I made bread yesterday morning, but I forgot a knife."

"I have a knife," said Isabel, and they sat on flat stones close to the fire, eating and drinking and watching chipmunks dart in and out of the shadows, leaving long curved lines of tiny prints like beads strung on the snow. The shadows grew longer across the valley. Matt put another log on the fire; there was a hiss, then the flames leaped in silence. In the crystal air, the only sound was an occasional caw of a blue jay or the snapping of a branch as a squirrel leaped from tree to tree. A pure, perfect moment, Elizabeth mused, suspended between yesterday and tomorrow. She remembered she hadn't talked to Matt about buying more land in Nuevo. After today, he'll want to, she thought. Whatever problems we're having, he'll know how right it is to have this waiting for us: a promise for the future.

It was dark when they got back to the Aragons' house, tired and chilled, and they took turns showering and dressing in the three small bedrooms before coming back to the living room where Cesar was ladling out hot spiced wine before a roaring fire while Isabel and Elizabeth made dinner in the kitchen.

When the guests arrived they sat on the floor, on pillows made of fabric woven by Cesar, eating at small low tables near the fire. After dinner, Luz and Holly went off to be alone and the others talked lazily of the weather, new people building summer homes in the Holy Ghost and Grass Mountain areas farther up the valley, next year's crops, and this odd fellow Ballentine who was buying land in the valley and then renting it back to the people he'd bought it from, paying good money for something he never even saw.

"That's not his name," said Isabel, pouring more coffee. "It's Ballenger."

"He's loco," said Cesar. "And bad-tempered. He didn't like it that Isabel wouldn't sell to him."

212

"He bought Zachary's house and land from us," said Elizabeth. "And I was thinking—"

"I met him," Matt said. "I forgot to tell you. He was at a party in Houston. It seems he's not only a car dealer, he also buys property all over the world."

"Does he," Elizabeth murmured thoughtfully. "I was going to find out more about him last August but the column took too much time; I never got around to it."

"What were you looking for?"

"I'm not sure. Isabel says he and two other men have bought up more than half the valley. I thought it was odd."

Matt frowned. "He didn't mention that when we talked. Peculiar guy. Too enthusiastic. And he breaks up his words."

"Like what?" Cesar asked.

"New-ay-vo. Pe-cu-liar. Ar-a-gon."

"That would drive me crazy," Isabel declared.

"So someone said."

One of Isabel's neighbors mentioned a rumor in Pecos about a new road in the area; no one else had heard about it but they debated its merits. Elizabeth, drowsy from the long day outside, and the wine and the warm room, curled up on the rug, her head on Matt's thigh, watching the flames. They were a little distance from the others. "I think we should buy in the valley," she said, her voice low beneath the conversation. "Before Ballenger gets it all."

Matt didn't hear her. The talk about land had recalled a quarrel he'd had with Rourke over whether resorts should be built in wilderness areas. They'd have to resolve that, he thought; he needed a free hand in deciding editorial policies for their papers. Suddenly anxious to get back, to settle the quarrel with Rourke and tackle the other work waiting for him, he heard snatches of conversation about selling the land, irrigating the land, planting the land, finding markets for the pottery and rugs made in the valley. "They never talk about anything else," he murmured.

Elizabeth looked up. "It's their life." Her voice was as low as his. "They feel about it the way you feel about working for Keegan."

213

"Do you think it's the same?" he asked curiously. "These people live in a dying town in a small valley hidden in the mountains. I don't see any connection with what I'm doing; I don't even find much that attracts me anymore."

Elizabeth sat up. "You don't mean that." She'd been about to repeat what she had said about buying land; now she held it back. "All those years we came here with Zachary, we talked about building a second home, spending summers here . . ."

"A long time ago. I hardly remember how I felt about things then. Was that all I wanted? Did I sound like these people?"

"These people are my friends." She studied his face in the firelight. "And they're more like you than you think. They have a passion for this place and the life they've made that keeps them here and sends them out each day to tend their animals and work the land whether they feel like it or not, whether they're sure the valley has a future or not. It's the same kind of passion you have for Keegan, for working for him. The same passion that will make you go back to Houston tomorrow even though we haven't finished anything we began a week ago."

"Fresh wine," Isabel said, handing each of them a mug. "It's midnight. Padre is going to make a toast."

"We wish for health and plenty," Cesar said, and rambled on about love and a place to belong, fertile fields and animals, large families and a prosperous year.

Elizabeth held her mug and leaned forward to kiss Matt. "Happy New Year," she said softly, and neither of them was sure whether it was a prayer or a pledge.

214

CHAPTER 8

Elizabeth sat at Matt's desk in the glass-walled office of the *Chieftain*, writing a "Private Affairs" story about her father.

> He was seventy-five years old when he first picked up a hand saw and made a long cut through a piece of oak, overcoming the resistance of the wood with his own strength. And when he had planed and carved and sanded, and held in his hand something he had made himself, from part of the earth he lived in, he knew that, after fifty years, he was finally doing what he really wanted. And he was content.

She wrote more quickly than usual, looking up absently as she tried to think of the right word or phrase. Through the glass wall she saw the bustle of the newsroom, Saul's smile, Barney Kell's friendly salute, Wally coming toward her. She shook her head to stop him and turned back to the typewriter. Late in the afternoon, she pulled out the last page and read through the whole piece. She stopped at the sentences she had repeated at the end: "He was finally doing what he really wanted. And he was content."

Matt, she thought.

215

But then she shook her head. It wasn't really Matt. He'd been doing what he wanted, and it included both of them. But he'd been sidetracked, caught in his own ambition. And he'd be trapped in it until he found a way to balance ambition with the other things of his life.

That's what we should have talked about at Christmas, she thought: the gap between what we dreamed and what we are now.

Impulsively, she picked up the telephone and called his office in Houston. "He's in a meeting, Mrs. Lovell," his secretary said. "With Mr. Rourke and the governor and some members of the Texas Commission on State Parks. It might last through dinner. Can I take a message?"

"No," Elizabeth said. "Thank you. Just tell him I'll call him at home later."

Not "home"; it's only a rented apartment.

But she never reached him that night, and the next morning his secretary called her. "Mr. Lovell left Houston after dinner last night, Mrs. Lovell; he went to Austin with the parks commissioners. He just called in and I gave him your message and he said to tell you he'll call you when he's back in Houston late this afternoon."

Absently, Elizabeth thanked her. Matt was a newspaperman, a publisher; what was he doing in the Texas state capital with commissioners of parks?

"I just wondered," she said when he called that night. "It seemed odd."

"They were giving me information," he replied. "I had questions and they had answers, so I flew back with them just for the day. We're planning a series on land use in Arizona, New Mexico, and parts of Texas and southern Colorado—"

"Land use?"

"Flood control, irrigation, resorts, state parks—huge projects, Elizabeth; it's incredible what's involved. The landscape of whole states could be transformed. And we're right in the middle of it; we own enough papers now to help shape what happens, build public support, push for new laws . . . can you imagine what that means? The *size* of it—! Of course the

216

states can't afford to do all of it themselves; there will have to be federal and private money, too . . ."

He talked on. *All wound up*, Peter would say, and Elizabeth didn't try to stop him. Their last few telephone calls had been brief and unsatisfactory, with Matt distracted by work and Elizabeth feeling left out, and left behind. It was better to be talking about land use than not talking at all, and it was better to hear her husband sound enthusiastic than vague and brusque.

But when she told her mother about it the next day, Lydia was critical. "You didn't tell him you still felt left out?"

"It wasn't the right time."

"Any time is the right time to tell your husband something important about yourself. If you feel left behind while he dashes around the country playing powerful publisher, you should tell him."

"Mother, do you tell your husband you don't like running the bookshop alone after you began it together?"

"Of course not. He'd get defensive and huff and puff about my trying to stop him from doing something he loves when it's his first chance—Oh. Well. But that's different."

"Why?"

"I don't know, it just is."

"Well, it doesn't matter," Elizabeth said. "Because it's only temporary, our being apart. As soon as I'm in Houston with him, everything will change."

"Did you talk about moving to Houston?"

"No. He was so busy telling me about state parks and flood control, I didn't say any of the things I'd planned to say. I didn't even tell him I bought two lots in Nuevo last week, just outside of town."

"You bought land in the valley? Without even talking it over with Matt?"

"We seem to be doing a lot of things separately these days. It's something I want and I'm not sure he cares about it one way or another. I'll tell him this weekend, when he's home."

But Matt didn't get to Santa Fe that weekend; he had to be in Denver. "Some bright-eyed optimist started a newspaper without knowing the first thing about it," he told Elizabeth

217

when he called on Thursday. "And now he wants to be bailed out. It could be something for us."

"And it has to be this weekend?"

"It was the only time I could fit it in. Was there a special reason you wanted me home?"

She bit back an angry retort. "Is loving you special enough?"

"I'm sorry, sweetheart; I didn't mean that the way it sounded. I just meant—is anything special happening at home?"

"It would be nice if you asked that more often."

"Oh, for God's sake. Listen, Elizabeth—"

"Matt, I'm sorry, but I've done a lot more listening than talking." *Why am I apologizing?* "You've got a family here, with a couple of children who are growing up fast, and you should be part of their lives instead of—"

"Instead of what? Making a better life for them, with more money so they can do what they want?"

"Maybe they want a father. Holly is nervous about her audition; it might help to have a father giving her encouragement."

"The Santa Fe Opera audition? That's a long way off."

"Two weeks from now. And it's the opera chorus. She told you about it."

"I know she did. Two weeks? Well, but I'll be there before then, and give her all the moral support she needs. In fact, why don't I talk to her now? Start my encouragement early. Is she still awake?"

"Of course she is; it's only ten o'clock. Have you forgotten she's seventeen? I'll get her. And then Peter can take over."

"Fine. I talked to him yesterday, though, you know."

"Yesterday?"

"He called me at the office. I thought you knew."

"I know both of them call you; I pay the telephone bills. They don't tell me every time."

"Well, no reason they should. In fact, I was in the middle of a meeting and we only talked a few minutes, so I'd like to talk to him now. And I'll see you the weekend after this. By the way, your column on the audience at the chamber music concert was a gem. We loved the part about the man who snored through the evening—*An uninvited tuba played obbli-*

218

gato from the second row. Keegan's been showing it all over town. I don't know how you turn out three of those a week."

"I turn them out by working ten hours a day. Or night. If you asked more questions about us, you'd know that. Hold on, I'll get Holly."

No more whining, she told herself as she walked down the hall. But she wasn't sure what she would do if he didn't show more interest in them. She didn't want to nag him into it; she wanted it to come from him.

She knocked on the door of Holly's room. "Daddy's on the phone; he wants to talk to you."

I'll find a way, she thought. Something that will get us through the next few months. I'd better; otherwise when I move to Houston I might discover I've gone to live with a stranger.

Holly didn't want Elizabeth at the audition. *"Please,* mother; I can't stand the idea of you sitting there *worrying.* I don't even know if they'd let you in. They probably wouldn't. They don't want hordes of frantic parents wandering around *worrying . . ."*

"I'm not worried," said Elizabeth mildly, understanding who really was worried, wishing she could make it easier for Holly, and knowing she couldn't. "I was worried at my own auditions, the first time we faced the *Chieftain* staff and the first time my column appeared, but I'm not worried about you. You'll do your best, which is superb, and I think you'll make it."

"You really think so?" breathed Holly. "Well . . . but still, please don't come."

"Of course I won't, if you don't want me to. But how will you get to Albuquerque?"

"Peter said he'd drive me."

"And go to the audition?"

"I'm thinking about it. He can wander around the campus if I don't want him there."

Elizabeth nodded. "Call me if you'll be late for dinner."

Sitting beside Peter on the high seat of his new car, cozily warm with the heater on, Holly gazed dreamily at the snowcovered mountains on the horizon. "Mother's so nice these days. Like she's trying to make everything . . . nice."

Peter grunted.

"What does that mean?"

"She's trying to make us not worry about her and Dad."

Holly sighed. "I know. She's trying to make herself not worry, too." They were silent. "I guess we should have moved to Houston last fall; things would be okay then."

"So it's my fault they're going to split!"

"I didn't say it was your—What do you mean, they're going to split? Did mother say that?"

"She doesn't have to; look at them, for Christ's sake. How much are they together? And have you watched them when they are? They used to touch each other, you know, lit- tle . . . touches. And they'd kiss, just quick ones, like Dad'd walk through the kitchen and give her a kiss and a little pinch on her ass—"

"Peter!"

"What?"

"Well, it doesn't seem right to talk about Mother that way."

"Everybody has an ass, Holly. Even mothers."

After a minute, she sighed again. "You're right. They don't do those things anymore. Daddy just . . . visits."

"We're his Santa Fe hotel."

"That's what I meant. We ought to be his Houston family."

"Well, we're moving there in June. It's really not fair to you; I get to graduate here and you don't."

"Peter!" Holly exclaimed suddenly.

"What?"

"My audition!"

"What about it? You afraid we're late? We have plenty of—"

"No. What if I win?"

"I don't get it. Isn't that the whole idea?"

"It's all summer with the opera company. I can't go to Hous- ton!"

He scowled. "Shit."

"Well, you and Mother will go, that's all. And I'll stay here."

"She'd never let you stay alone."

"Of course not. In Grandma and Grandpa's guest house."

"Heather lives there."

"Heather will be married to Saul."

"When?"

"Any day now."

"Heather will never marry Saul," Peter predicted gloomily. "She'll keep putting it off forever. And Mother and Dad will split. And Grandpa will stay in his workshop day and night. Everybody we know has a fucked-up marriage."

"That's not true!"

"It sure is. And I'll go to Stanford and Maya will stay here and find somebody else—"

"Oh, *that's* what's bothering you!"

He shrugged. "Everything seems so . . . useless. Maybe I'll just spend my life being high."

Holly peered at him. "On what?"

"Coke, I suppose."

"Have you ever?"

"A few times."

"You never told me."

"You never asked."

"Did you like it?"

"Sure. It makes everything seem real simple. You never tried it? Even once?"

She shook her head. "I'm scared it might ruin my voice."

"Coke doesn't ruin your voice."

"I don't want to take the chance."

"Well, I can understand that. It's not that you're scared of *coke;* you just want to protect your voice."

"That's exactly right." They were silent. "Why did you only try it a few times, if you liked it?"

He shrugged. "I didn't want it to ruin my research."

"Oh. You mean, it's not that you're scared of *coke;* you just want to protect your brilliant mind."

"That's exactly right."

They burst out laughing. Peter reached over and tapped Holly's shoulder. "You're okay, you know. You and Maya are the

221

only ones I ever told about being scared of it. Actually, it's not coke or pot I'm scared of as much as keeping it under control. I hate the idea of not knowing what's happening inside me—like, letting something besides my brilliant mind be in charge."

Holly nodded. "That's the way I feel."

"I figured. You're not bad to have around, you know, now that you're growing up."

"I'm growing up? You're the one who finally caught up with me! Boys are slower than girls; everybody knows that."

"You tell me often enough. The guys at school think you're a cold fish, you know. And a snob."

She shrugged. "That's too bad. You don't really think Maya will find somebody else, do you? She worships you."

"You think so?"

"You know she does. Peter?"

"What?"

"Do you and Maya make love?"

Peter frowned at the highway. "Sure."

"Really?"

"Sure."

"Is it wonderful?"

"Sure."

"You don't sound very romantic about it."

"Well . . . Christ, Holly, I can't talk about it!"

"Okay."

"It's . . . what you said. Wonderful." He paused. "You never have?"

"No."

"Because you don't want to?"

"Not with anybody I know. I think about it a lot. Did you? Before you and Maya . . . ?"

"Sure. I still do. All the time, seems like. It keeps butting in on my classes and my senior paper and everything. You really can't find anybody you like?"

"I like some of them. But I can't stand the idea of them *pawing* me. I mean, I read about it in novels—every position you can think of, really kinky stuff—but the more I read the

222

more awful it seems that somebody I don't love would
. . . *invade* me." A shudder went through her. "I'm about the
only girl in the junior class who hasn't done it, and sometimes
I feel like they're all grown up and I'm not, but I just can't do
it—not with the boys I know. Did you feel more like a man
when you did it the first time?"

He shrugged. "I guess. Mostly I just felt happy."

"Oh. I like that. Nobody who talks about it in school talks
about being happy. They just talk about *making it,* like it's
fudge or catching a bus. Ordinary. I want it to be beautiful and
glorious and . . . happy. I know they call me a bitch and a
tease at school, but . . . oh, it's so confusing! I want it and
I don't, and it's scary but I'm dying to know what it's really
like . . . Can't you tell me at all what it's like?"

"Close and warm and tight."

"Not for girls, big brother."

They giggled. "Right," Peter said. "I don't know how it feels
to a girl. It depends on the guy. He has to be careful."

"That's another thing. I want somebody who knows what
he's doing and thinks about me. I'm afraid of some *kid* who
just wants to *score,* or find something better than his hand."
She blushed. "Luz and I talk about it a lot; I'm sorry if it makes
you uncomfortable."

"Why should it? I don't treat Maya like that."

"Because you love her. If I loved somebody . . ."

"Well, but you could like somebody a lot. I mean, I love
Maya, but I'm not sure it's forever. Her mother told her she
shouldn't let anybody touch her until they were married."

"Nobody believes that anymore."

"Maya's mother does. I wanted to talk to Dad about it, once.
How he felt about screwing and girls and getting married . . .
But he didn't come home that weekend."

"You could have called him."

"I did. He wasn't there. I thought about driving to Houston
to see him, but, shit, I'm not going to chase him around. If
he cared about being a father, he'd come home and be a father."

Holly nodded. "I think Mother feels the same way. That's
why she doesn't call him so much anymore."

"Shit."

"You say that too much."

"Everybody says it."

"Well, everybody does coke and you don't."

"That's different." He paused. "Would you tolerate hell and damn?"

"Sure." They laughed. "I'm going to miss you when you go to Stanford."

"Some family we'll be. Me in California and you with Grandma and Grandpa . . ."

"Maybe."

"Probably. And Mom in Houston. Probably. And Dad traveling around and popping in now and then for a piece of ass."

"Peter, that's an awful thing to say!"

"Why? Shit, Holly, I'm mad at him."

"Me, too, but you shouldn't talk about him that way."

"A lot he cares about how we talk about him. One thing I've been wondering. About Mom. Do you think she's got somebody else?"

"No! Peter, what is wrong with you? Daddy doesn't have anybody else and neither does Mother! They'll be together in June and everything will be fine."

"Sure." He drove in silence. "We seem to be in Albuquerque. Where's the University of New Mexico?"

Holly unfolded a map and gave him directions. "Oh, God, I'm starting to shake."

"You want me to come with you?"

"I don't know. Yes. No. Oh, Peter, I'm scared to death!"

"You're going to knock them off their chairs. You're going to be sensational. You're going to be the greatest soprano the Santa Fe Opera chorus has ever seen. Heard."

Holly drew a long breath. "You can come with me. I guess I need you, after all."

"If you win, are you going to call Dad and tell him?"

"Of course. Peter, could we not talk about him anymore right now? I've got enough to worry about . . . turn left here . . . let's not talk about him or Mom or anything. Okay?"

224

"Okay." A few minutes later, he said, "Is that the building, up ahead?"

"I think so." A shudder went through her.

Peter touched her shoulder again. "Take it easy. I'm your family and I'll be there. And you're going to win. And everything is going to be fine."

In a pale blue dress of light wool, her shining ash-blond hair falling halfway down her back, Holly stood alone on the stage of the university auditorium, looking at the group of people in the first row of seats. She had no idea that her loveliness had made them catch their breath when she walked out from the wings; she saw on their shadowy faces only the same polite interest they had shown other singers. Far behind them, from the center of rows and rows of empty seats, Peter blew her a kiss.

But she couldn't sing. She couldn't remember her songs. Her throat was blocked. Her stomach was a hard knot and her feet and hands felt like lead and she was going to throw up. *I've got to get out of here. I'm going to die in front of all these people.*

The white-haired man at the piano cleared his throat and she turned toward him. "Everyone freezes at first," he said very softly. He smiled at her. "Shall we begin?"

Holly nodded in desperation. Still looking at her and smiling, he played the first chord of the accompaniment—and Holly remembered everything. With her hands clasped lightly in front of her, she held her head high and let the notes of Mozart's *"Non mi dir"* soar upward. The song told of a woman's love for a man, and in Holly's voice was all the love that was locked inside her, making her feel she'd explode because there was no one to whom she could give it.

Oh, I want to love someone, she thought as the trills and phrases flowed like liquid silver from her throat. I want to be loved and held and made love to. I want to make love to . . . someone.

She held out her hands, filled with love, offering love. Passion and pain were in her voice; the sexuality of a young woman longing to be awakened was in her graceful body as she leaned toward the audience. When she finished there was not a sound in the auditorium.

"Bravo!" Peter shouted. Holly blushed with embarrassment.

"Quite right," said one of the men in the first row. "Have you something in English?"

Quite right. Suddenly radiant, Holly nodded to the accompanist, and when he began to play, she sang "The Little Drummer Boy," a Christmas folk song so different from Mozart in its simple, storytelling cadence it was hard to believe the same young woman was singing.

But in one way it was the same: the song was about someone who longed to be noticed, admired, loved, and, just as in her first song, the longing was so passionate in Holly's pure voice that everyone broke into applause when she finished.

A woman among them nodded to the accompanist, who gave Holly a sheet of music. Nervously, she glanced over it: an aria from *Peter Grimes*, a modern opera she had not studied. But sight reading was a requirement in these auditions and with a deep breath and another glance at the accompanist, she began, making her way carefully through the song until she began to feel its rhythms and emotions. Finally, in the last few bars, she let go, her voice gathering force and volume, reaching a note she had never managed before without difficulty, holding it and gradually letting it fade away. While the reverberations still hung in the air, she made a slow curtsy, though her heart was pounding so she could barely breathe, and forced herself to walk off the stage without a backward glance.

Peter met her there. "I'm the proudest brother in the world." He held her while she tried to stop trembling. "Why didn't you tell me you're a superstar?"

"I'm not," she managed to say.

"You are to me. You will be, to everybody. You're the greatest, most wonderful . . . do you know how you *sounded?*"

"Miss Lovell," said one of the men from the group in the front row. "Would you come with me, please? We'd like to talk to you."

* * *

Elizabeth sat at the head of the dining room table, listening to Holly and Peter tell Maya about the audition. Three weeks had gone by and they'd told the story dozens of times, but each time they added new details. "They said they'd never heard anyone her age with a voice like that," Peter exclaimed as excitedly as the first time, when they came back from Albuquerque and their voices kept climbing over each other as they told Elizabeth about it. "They only take forty apprentices from all over the country, and usually only people at least twenty years old, but sometimes they make exceptions and this was one of them. They said Holly has a brilliant future. They said she didn't have to wait to be notified. They said she starts in June."

"It's like a dream," Maya said.

"Better," said Peter. "It's real."

She nodded. "I meant . . . to get what you've always wanted."

"I don't have it yet," Holly said. "This is just the beginning. Two summers with the opera, and *years* in a music conservatory, and then maybe back here with the opera again . . . a lot of the apprentices do that, they come back and sing with the opera and help new apprentices, like me . . ."

Elizabeth listened to Holly's bubbling voice and Peter's proud one and Maya's envious one. Now and then she suggested they eat their *paella* before it was cold, but mostly she listened, wishing Matt were there, angry that he wasn't.

He had known Peter was bringing Maya to dinner for the first time: a special occasion. But at the last minute he'd called to say he couldn't make it; he'd try to get in on Sunday, even if only for a day. "Tell Maya I'm sorry; the way Peter looks when he talks about her, I really am anxious to get to know her better. Maybe we'll drive to Nuevo on Sunday."

"If you're here," Elizabeth said.

"I'll do my best. By the way, I've been looking at houses for us; you should plan to come down and help choose one."

"All right."

"Not much enthusiasm there."

"That's asking a lot, Matt, when you've just disappointed Peter, and all of us."

"I was there last weekend; I helped celebrate Holly's audition triumph. I do the best I can, Elizabeth. So much is going on here; even Keegan hasn't taken a vacation."

It isn't a vacation to spend weekends with your family.

But she didn't want to quarrel; too many of their calls ended that way. "Fine," she said briskly. "We'll look for you on Sunday."

"And I love you all."

And miss us all?

"We love you, too, Matt. And miss you."

"It won't be much longer. Three months."

Holly was singing a passage from "The Little Drummer Boy." "It's easy," she told Maya. "You keep the rhythm of the drum the whole time. Try it."

Self-consciously, Maya hummed along with Holly, then began to sing the words. Peter joined them, unashamedly off-key. Elizabeth smiled at the three heads close together—Holly's pale blond, Maya's black, Peter's flaming red—like a mosaic, she thought; like my life these days, crowded with different events and people and emotions.

In some ways, she had never been so content. Through Matt's newspaper purchases, her column was carried in twenty papers with hundreds of thousands of new readers, her mail was heavier than ever, and when she was at the *Chieftain* her telephone rang constantly with calls from readers giving suggestions, asking advice about their problems, wanting to argue about something she'd written, telling her how wonderful she was.

He was finally doing what he really wanted. She'd written that about Spencer, then wondered if it was about Matt—but what about her? For the first time she was working full time at writing; she was taken seriously as a writer instead of as a housewife indulging a part-time hobby; she was earning enough from her writing to live on even if Matt weren't there.

But if Matt weren't here, I wouldn't be in twenty papers.

And if *I* weren't here the *Chieftain* wouldn't have been such

228

a success—and Keegan wouldn't have hired Matt—and he wouldn't be buying twenty papers for me to be in.

Elizabeth listened to the young people sing, Holly's pure voice floating above Maya's shy one and Peter's vigorously flat one.

We were so good together; we were such a good team. Doesn't he miss it as much as I do?

And that was the trouble. At long last she was doing what she'd always wanted, but she couldn't be content because Matt wasn't sharing it with her. They weren't partners in anything: not their work, not their marriage.

And it seemed he was too busy and successful to notice.

"Not bad!" Peter exclaimed. "For a couple of amateurs trying to keep up with the star of the Santa Fe Opera, we were pretty good. Well, Maya was good. I was awful."

"You were all good," Elizabeth said, pushing her thoughts away. She'd face them later, as she did every night, when she lay in bed alone, looking at the telephone beside her, debating, and finally deciding—more and more often lately—not to call her husband, because they had so little to say to one another.

"Daddy should have heard us," Holly said. "That's one of his favorite songs."

"Are we going to Nuevo with him on Sunday?" Peter asked.

"I told you we would if he's here," Elizabeth said.

"Yeh. I just wondered if you'd heard any different."

"Not so far. How about dessert? Fresh figs? And Holly and I made a chocolate cake." The doorbell rang. "Peter, would you get that? Holly, if you and Maya clear the table, I'll make coffee."

A moment later Peter came into the kitchen with Saul. "Damnedest thing," Saul said, kissing Elizabeth on the cheek. "I just got around to reading this week's *Capitol Observer*. Look what's here." He handed Elizabeth the daily report from the state legislature, with a small item circled in red: *Pecos Valley: Nuevo State Park and Dam. Committee hearings March 9–10, 9 A.M.*

"Nuevo State Park and Dam?" she said in bewilderment.

"What?" Maya and Holly asked together.

229

"There's no state park at Nuevo," said Peter. "No dam either."

"Yet," said Saul. "Looks like somebody has it in mind."

Maya frowned. "Why do we need a dam?"

"Good question. Another one is how come I don't know anything about it. Usually by the time hearings start the paper's had endless fact sheets and hype about the wonders our legislators are about to perform. This has been kept so quiet my journalist's nose is twitching."

"Somebody wants it kept secret," said Peter.

Saul nodded. "Looks like."

"Dams create reservoirs," Elizabeth said. "Lakes."

"That's what they're for," Saul said.

"But if someone dams the Pecos at Nuevo . . . Well, it can't happen. The town is there."

"It could still be there. Under the lake."

"They can't do that!" Peter said. "You can't drown a whole town!"

"Quite a few towns lying at the bottom of lakes these days," Saul observed.

"But the houses," Maya said, echoing Peter. "And the farms and animals. They couldn't be drowned!"

"Not the animals. Someone buys the land and buildings and the people pack up their animals and worldly goods and find someplace else to live."

"Where? My father has only one farm—in Nuevo. How can someone force him to leave?"

"Maya," Elizabeth said. "Does your father still own his land?"

"Oh." There was a long pause. "No, of course not; I forgot. That Mr. Ballenger bought it from him. But that was two or three years ago! And he's rented it to us ever since. He never said he wanted it; we have a lease—"

"Ballenger," Saul mused. "Two or three years ago. First name?"

"I don't know. But we have a—"

"Terry," said Elizabeth. "He bought our land, too."

"Anybody else been buying around there?"

"Two other men, I'm told. Do you know their names, Maya?"

Maya shook her head. "My father might, but I wanted to say—"

"How much have they bought?"

"More than half the valley," Elizabeth replied.

"Will somebody let Maya finish a sentence!" Peter thundered.

"I'm sorry," Saul said. "What is it, Maya?"

"We have a lease—Ballenger rents us the land and the house. It's for twenty years."

"Twenty years?" Saul echoed.

She nodded. "My father said it would be time for him to retire by then and since Ballenger was offering good money and letting him stay, it was a very good deal."

"Too good." Saul put back his head and gazed at the ceiling. "It looks to my aging and cynical eyes as if somebody is trying to sneak something big through the legislature with no publicity. Now I ask myself—why would that be? And how could someone accomplish it? My nose is twitching because something smells putrid. And my journalist's instincts tell me I should go to those hearings."

Elizabeth looked at Maya's troubled face and Peter's indignant one. "I'll go with you," she said. "Nothing could keep me away."

But first they went to Nuevo. Maya had told her father the news and it had spread to everyone in the valley. When Elizabeth and Saul arrived on Sunday, with Holly and Peter but not Matt, who had called to say he couldn't get there after all, they found people clustered in small groups, talking, gesturing, some of them pacing, others standing with heads bowed, drawing circles in the dust with the points of their boots. All of them were moving gradually toward the old church where Cesar was wrestling open the heavy door.

"Elizabeth!" Isabel cried when she saw the four of them. "What the devil is going on?"

"We're not sure yet. I brought a friend to help. Saul Milgrim, managing editor of the *Chieftain*—Isabel Aragon; Cesar Aragon."

231

They shook hands and Saul looked at the open door of the church. "Looks like someone's called a meeting."

"I did," Isabel said. "I wanted Padre to do it, but he said he was too old."

"Too old to get into a battle," said Cesar. Barrel-chested, with broad shoulders, he had heavy eyebrows and a thick, downturned mustache. "Young people should fight. Old, tired ones should help but stay in the background."

Isabel shrugged. "I tried to talk him into it. He's too stubborn for me."

"Talk him into what?" Elizabeth asked.

"Firing up the town. Saul, I'm glad to meet you; Elizabeth's talked about you. Maybe I could call on you to talk to us. Could I? To tell us what's going on in that state capital of yours."

"It's yours, too," said Saul. "But I'm not a public speaker."

"Saul, they need information," Elizabeth said. "You know how helpless people feel when they're in the dark. Please help them."

"You only want information?" Saul asked Isabel. "Not a leader from the big city?"

"Information," Isabel said.

Elizabeth studied her friend. "I think the people of Nuevo already have a leader."

Isabel spread her hands. "Somebody had to do it. I'll see you inside. Sit in the front row, if you can find seats."

"Saul, you will help them, won't you?" Elizabeth asked. "Just tell them what's likely to happen. You can use it all in the story you're going to write."

"Writers are impartial observers."

"Be impartial later. Can't you think about them instead of yourself? You'll get your story. I'll take notes for you, if you want, while you talk to them."

He looked curiously at her. "Do they mean so much to you?"

"They're my friends. And you don't like to see anyone get hurt any more than I do."

He nodded thoughtfully. "Elizabeth, people who are having

232

marriage problems tend to throw themselves into other people's battles. Be careful."

"You don't know anything about my marriage, Saul."

"Bullshit. It's all over your face. Look, I'm not telling you to turn your back on your friends; I'm just saying you might think about saving some of your energy for your own problems. Friendly advice; that's all it is."

He went inside. Slowly, Elizabeth followed. Holly and Peter were already there, with Maya, Luz, and Cesar; Isabel stood at the pulpit. Wearing a long, blue denim skirt and a white blouse with a drawstring at the low neckline, her hair in a thick braid, she looked almost formal: a strong woman with a magnetic smile, regal posture, and powerful voice. She waited for everyone to find places. Sunlight came faintly through dusty windows; the wooden pews were thick with dust that flew up when people whipped bandanas and handkerchiefs about before they sat down. Elizabeth counted eighty people and others were still coming in as Isabel began to talk.

"We took a poll. Three-fourths of the farmers and ranchers have sold their land; none of us in the town have sold; we don't know who owns this church or the land under it. We don't know what's going on in the state legislature. Some of you still own your land, others have leases, but now there's this business of a dam—a possible dam—which would flood part of the valley. Now I'm not ready to lie down and let somebody pour a million gallons of water, or more, over my house and land, but I'm not even sure who I should be mad at. We have a friend here who knows more about it"—she held out her hand to Saul—"and I'd like to introduce him. Saul Milgrim, the man who runs the Santa Fe *Chieftain*."

Saul glanced at Elizabeth. "*Runs* it?"

"Let them believe it," she said in a low voice. "It's mostly the truth, isn't it?"

He smiled and touched her hand, then walked up to the pulpit. "I really don't know much more than you do," he told the intent faces looking up at him. "I tried to get some information yesterday, but nobody's around the statehouse on Saturday. My suggestion, for what it's worth, is that you hold your anger until you know your opponent, and what's being proposed for the valley. I think you should send someone to testify at the hearings this week, with copies of your leases and a statement on the hardships you'll suffer if you have to leave: what you'd have to pay for new land and houses, the cost of moving your stock, and so on. At the very least, you should ask for time; this has been sprung on you and you deserve a chance to find out what's going on so you can respond intelligently and share in the final decision. If you need help finding information, I'll do what I can." He looked about. "That's all I can say right now."

"No answers," grunted Cesar.

"Sure, it's an answer," said Isabel. Standing, she sent her voice ringing through the church. "I nominate Cesar Aragon to go to Santa Fe and fight anyone who means to flood our valley."

Cesar shook his head. "I already said no; I'm too old to deal with these things. Isabel should go."

"Nominate her," Elizabeth whispered to him.

He leaped to his feet. "I nominate Isabel Aragon to go to Santa Fe and fight any bastards who mean to flood our valley!"

All the women shouted, "Yes!" They glared at the men and the men nodded. "Is it a vote?" Isabel asked.

"Unanimous," Saul said. "You're their leader."

"Well, then." Isabel looked at her neighbors. "I don't have any idea what I'll do there, but I promise to do it very forcefully."

Someone applauded; others picked it up. The sound echoed through the church like a hailstorm. Isabel looked at Elizabeth and laughed. "I could get to like this," she said.

Elizabeth laughed with her, but her eyes were thoughtful. Then Peter leaned over. "Can I go to the hearing? Maya wants to go, too."

"I think you both should be in school," Elizabeth said. "I'll tell you everything that happens. And Saul will write about it."

At the end of the row, Luz whispered to Holly, "I wish Mom would be quiet. If they flood the place, we'd get out with a pile of money. Why can't she just let it happen? Nobody cares about an old valley; money's a lot more important."

"Hush," said Holly. "Someone will hear you."

But no one was listening; they were leaving the church, talking among themselves. Elizabeth waited for Saul and they walked out together. "It's too bad you didn't have anything definite for them," she said.

He shook his head. "Damnedest thing. Everything is under wraps. Whoever Ballenger and the others are, they've got clout."

"We'll meet them at the hearings."

"I can't wait."

On the drive back to Santa Fe, everyone was quiet. Once Holly said, "I keep seeing all the houses and farms at the bottom of a lake . . ."

"Like ghosts," Peter said moodily. "Rooms full of water, things floating around . . ."

Holly shivered. "It's awful. Our land, too, that Mother just bought . . ."

They were silent again until Saul stopped in front of their house. "See you Wednesday at the statehouse," he told Elizabeth. But her attention was on their front door. Saul followed her gaze through the gate in the adobe wall; so did Holly and Peter.

"Tony!" Holly cried ecstatically, and leaped from the car to dash up the driveway. Peter followed more slowly.

Saul turned to Elizabeth. "A pleasant surprise?"

"A complicated one." She got out of the car and leaned down to kiss Saul's cheek. "Thank you for driving. I'll see you Wednesday."

Tony was contemplating Holly's radiant face as she told him about her audition. "I'll have you on my show yet," Elizabeth heard him say as she approached. He moved toward her. "Dear Elizabeth, how wonderful to see you again."

His look was open and admiring, as innocent as a boy's. Smoothly handsome, silver-haired, dark-eyed, he wore a sheepskin jacket over a dark turtleneck shirt: the image of a star, Elizabeth thought. But she felt a rush of pleasure at the look in his eyes, and she suddenly realized that, except for

Saul, she hadn't spent time with a man since Matt's last visit, two weekends ago—and even then he'd worked for hours at the *Chieftain*, making phone calls and dictating letters.

"You'll stay for dinner," she said.

"I was hoping I could take you somewhere. It's been so long since we stepped out together."

"I'd like that." Elizabeth looked at Holly and Peter. "You two have homework, don't you?"

"You know we do," Holly said angrily.

"What's your problem?" Peter asked.

"Nothing." Looking at the ground, Holly said to Elizabeth, "I'm sorry. I guess I . . . I'd rather go out than do homework."

"It's all right, love," Elizabeth said gently. "I'm sorry I made you feel left out. There's *paella* in the refrigerator—"

"We'll be okay," Peter said. He was frowning, trying to figure out his sister.

"I'll have to shower and change," Elizabeth told Tony.

"Then Holly and Peter will keep me entertained," he said, and she went to her bedroom, leaving the three of them in the kitchen. When she returned, Peter was slicing tomatoes, Tony was drinking Scotch, and Holly was answering his question about the *paella*.

"Chicken, sausage, shrimp, clams, rice, saffron, tomatoes, onions, chiles . . . You could stay for dinner; there's plenty here."

"Not this time." Tony looked up as Elizabeth came in, and drew in his breath. She had changed from jeans and a khaki shirt to a handwoven dress of white wool and a necklace of thin discs of petrified wood polished until they shone like agate. Her hair framed her face in long waves of golden bronze; her eyes were a smoky gray in the light from the kitchen chandelier. "An elegant lady," Tony said. "Is Rancho Encantado all right? I made reservations."

She hesitated briefly; it was a place she and Matt especially liked. But after all, it was only a restaurant. "Fine," she said, and kissed Holly and Peter goodbye. "I won't be late. If anyone calls . . ." She paused.

"Yes?" asked Holly shrewdly.

"Just say I'll be back about ten. Have a good dinner, you two."

As the front door closed, Peter said to Holly, "What do you think?"

"About what?"

"About Mom and Tony. I was wondering if we should call Dad and tell him."

"There's nothing to tell!" Holly said and burst into tears.

"What's your *problem?*" Peter demanded.

"*Nothing!*" In a moment, she wiped her eyes and sniffed. "Why aren't you setting the table? You never do any work around here!"

"Jee-sus," Peter muttered, and pulled plates and glasses from the hutch beside the table. He began to sing one of Holly's songs, every note flat, humming where he forgot the words.

"Okay," Holly said, laughing as she wiped her eyes again. "You convinced me; it's better to talk than listen to you sing. Thanks," she added, putting the *paella* on the table. "I'm fine now. I guess I was just upset . . . flooding Nuevo, and everything . . ."

"Sure," said Peter. He heaped his plate. "Well, here we are, the Lovell family. Shrunk but hardy." He lifted his glass of soda. "Cheers."

Tony took Elizabeth's hand and kissed the palm. "I've missed you. As usual."

She moved her hand to pick up her water glass. "Are you on your way to or from Los Angeles?"

"To. I've been in Houston."

She looked up quickly. "Did you see Matt?"

"Last night. He was at my father's house for dinner. A busy man, Matt. Meeting politicians, buying newspapers, writing editorials . . . And very good at everything he does. My father thinks the world of him."

And that bothers you, Elizabeth thought. You and Keegan haven't gotten along for years, but still you'd like him to think the world of you, not Matt.

But now she knew why Tony had come to Santa Fe: he knew Matt was spending weekends in Houston.

"He'll be here next weekend," she said. "And we're moving to Houston in June, after Peter graduates."

"Are you indeed." He opened the menu. "What's good here?"

"Everything."

When they had given their order, Tony talked about Los Angeles, his show, his travels. "I've taped interviews in the most god-awful places. Do you have any idea how hot it gets sitting next to a Sphinx? Can you imagine how frigid it gets in Quebec in February? Then there was the submarine off the coast of someplace, where I got claustrophobia and in order to finish interviewing the actor playing the captain of that submerged coffin I had to pour five martinis down my throat so I could believe I was really home in bed, dreaming the whole hideous experience . . ."

Elizabeth laughed. Then, curious, she said, "You never talk about the people you interview."

"You know, it's odd, but I hardly remember them; they're a blur, all talking about the same things: sex and money. Making it big in films or Broadway or clothes design or condominiums—whatever it is, it's always the same. Money and sex. Money, success, and sex. Did you ever notice how alike 'sex' and 'success' sound? Try saying sex-success ten times, fast. You laugh. But most of the celebrities I interview say it twenty or a hundred times, very fast, and very successfully. Sex-cessfully. There. I put them together like the good celebrity I am."

She smiled. "I've noticed they interest you, too."

"They do; I admit it. However"—his face turned melancholy—"I have success but very little sex-cess these days." He waited. "You don't ask why. I'll tell you anyway. Because only one woman appeals to me. I wander around my lonely house looking for her. 'Elizabeth,' I call softly, and she doesn't come, so I raise my voice. 'Elizabeth, come here!' I demand, but still she is nowhere to be seen, so I shout—"

"You don't, but it makes a touching story. I thought you'd outgrown your dramatics."

"Most of the time. You bring out the best in me. Which

238

reminds me, I do enjoy your columns; I look forward to them. You get better and better."

"I like that. It means more to me than all your dramatics."

"I don't use dramatics; I tell the truth. Sometimes, when I'm especially lonely in that Malibu mausoleum, I take your columns from my bedside table and pretend you're lying beside me—"

"That's enough, Tony."

He spread out his hands. "As you wish. I do think of you; ask any of my lady friends who wonder about the photograph next to my bed."

She laughed in relief. "Much better. I was afraid you'd become a monk."

"Therapy, dear Elizabeth; a man needs comfort." He pondered the plate that had been put before him. "Everything in that house is new; I couldn't stand being alone and shabby at the same time. But in my villa at Amalfi everything is antique, faintly moldy, glowing eerily with furniture polish. Like an aunt you'd thought was dead for years who suddenly shows up with a face lift."

Elizabeth laughed again. "But you're not alone in Los Angeles and you're not alone in Italy, either."

"True," he admitted. "I can't endure it. The echo of my voice and footsteps . . . I feel empty. Invisible."

"So the rest of us are your mirrors, making you feel real."

He gave her an admiring look. "That's very clever. You could do a story on it: people who feel real only when they're reflected in other people's eyes."

"Do you want me to do a story on you?"

"You can't. I'm too famous for your 'Private Affairs.'"

"I'm afraid you are. But if I ever expand to famous people who feel invisible, you'll be the first."

"I don't feel invisible with you. I feel potent and powerful."

"Potent?"

"Because I make you laugh."

"And that's why you like to be with me," Elizabeth said. "Every man wants to feel potent."

"I like to be with you because you are bewitching and beautiful and full of life. You make jaded television stars feel young."

"You're not jaded; you're just tired from chasing will o' the wisps."

"You mean Elizabeth Lovell, *Mrs*. Matthew Lovell, who is forever beyond my reach?"

"And others, I assume. You can't be chasing only me."

"Only one. And you are not forever beyond my reach, dear Elizabeth. That's why I'm here. I'm courting you."

"A courtship takes two people, Tony. All I want is friendship and laughter."

"For now."

"You're dramatizing again. You have so many other women, Tony, and your work. Doesn't that give you pleasure? And contentment?"

"Does your writing give you contentment?"

"Often. But we're talking about you."

"All right, we'll talk about me. Does my work give me pleasure? Of course. Leaving aside the Sphinx and the submarine, I love every minute of it, especially the power of asking questions that make people squirm but come back for more because an audience of millions is more important to them than dignity or privacy. But do you know the one moment I love best? When the red light on the camera lights up, telling me I'm *on*."

"And you're no longer just Tony Rourke," Elizabeth observed. "But the famous 'Anthony,' watched by millions. Millions of mirrors, making him feel real. And potent, when they love and applaud you."

"Dearest Elizabeth, are you making fun of me?"

"No," she said seriously. "We all need love and applause."

"Well, I give you both. I love Elizabeth Lovell; I applaud 'Private Affairs.' Do you know we have eaten our trout and I haven't the faintest idea what it tasted like?"

She laughed. "Shall we order seconds?"

"Alas, no; television cameras show every extra pound. But I am allowed dessert now and then." He beckoned to the waiter and they ordered apple pie with rum, followed by coffee and cognac. Then they bantered and reminisced, close and comfortable as the candles burned low on their table.

It was then that Elizabeth found herself thinking, I am having a very good time, the best time I've had in months. "Tell me about Keegan's dinner," she said abruptly. "What did you talk about?"

"Politics." Tony watched the waiter refill his coffee cup. "My father thinks I ought to make it my new career. I told him I'm happy in television."

"Did Matt think you should go into politics?"

"We didn't discuss it. We only saw each other at dinner and other people were there. Oh, I did talk for a few minutes to someone else who knows you; I met him in the newsroom at the *Record*. I was returning Chet's car, which I'd been using, and found him talking to someone who used to work for you. Artner. Something Artner."

"Cal? Cal Artner in Houston? With Chet?"

"That's the name. He said he was working at the *Chieftain* when you bought it, and a few months ago Chet found him working at a paper Matt bought from a guy named Graham, in Roswell, and brought him to Houston. Small world."

"Yes." Elizabeth thought back to the last time she'd seen Cal, emptying out his desk after Matt had fired him. Cal and Chet. "Does Matt know Cal is there?"

"I have no idea. Should he?"

"I think so. I'll tell him. What else did you do in Houston?"

"Met beautiful women and thought of you." He leaned forward. "Could we talk about you? All I know is you write wonderful newspaper stories about people I'd like to meet. What else do you do with your time?"

"Oh, I'm as busy as Matt," she said. "I'm going to help fight for a town."

"A town? What's happening to it?"

"It seems someone wants to build a dam and flood it."

"And you want to save it so you can write about it?"

"I want to save it because my friends live there. Not everything is done for money, Tony."

241

He sat back, contemplating her. "Elizabeth the crusader. You're the first one I've ever known."

"I'm not crusading. I told you: I'm helping my friends."

"Whatever it is, it sounds diverting. Shall I get involved?"

"How?"

"I have no idea. Command me; I'll do what you say."

"I will, if I think of something. We don't know what's going to happen yet."

"Well, I like the sound of it. Better than a Sphinx and a Quebec winter. And any friends of yours are friends of mine."

"I warn you: I might really take you up on that."

"My dear, I'm always looking for ways to prevent boredom and being alone. If I can do that and also help you, it would be paradise. Ask my help; make use of my vast powers. Whatever you care about, I care about. Shall we drink to that?" He raised his cognac glass. "To Elizabeth. And Tony: her most loyal follower."

It was almost one in the morning before Matt answered his telephone; Elizabeth had been calling him since saying good night to Tony at eleven. "I thought you might be out of town again," she said when she heard his voice.

"A long and very dull dinner," he replied.

"You sound tired."

"Worn out. It's been a hellish week. We're revamping the paper in Phoenix, new type, new layout—"

"I know what revamping means; we did it at the *Chieftain*, if you recall."

There was a pause. "If I felt like a quarrel, I'd say that was a nasty crack."

"It was. I'm sorry, Matt. It's just that I get the feeling a lot of the time that you forget who I am, or at least what we did together."

"I don't forget. If I explain things to you it's because I'm in the habit of explaining things all day, every day. There aren't many people around here I can talk to the way I can talk to you."

"What about Keegan?"

"He doesn't know newspapers; he doesn't pretend to. If he

242

did, he wouldn't need me. I saw your friend Tony, by the way. He was at Keegan's for dinner last night, talking about becoming a senator. He thinks that's what his new career ought to be."

"Who thinks that?"

"I told you, Tony. I gather it's something he wants for a rainy day. He says there's no such thing as permanent popularity for television stars, so the smart ones have a second career in reserve. What are you laughing about?"

"It didn't come out that way when he told me about it."

"He called you? Tonight?"

Elizabeth hesitated. "He was here. We went out for dinner."

"You went out for dinner. And where is he now?"

"I beg your pardon?"

"I asked, where is he now?"

"I know you did," she said coldly. "I wish you hadn't."

"Don't use that tone with me!"

"Why not? You ask me an insulting question—"

"Which you have not answered."

She took a deep breath. "He is at La Fonda, no doubt asleep because he has an early flight to Los Angeles in the morning. And speaking of sleep, I'm very tired. Good night, Matt—"

"God damn it, don't you hang up on me. If you feel I've insulted you—"

"I *know* you've insulted me. If you think I'm sleeping with Tony, say so. We went through this a couple of years ago, remember? You accuse me of sleeping with Tony as if that explains whatever problems we're having. But it never does. I didn't have to tell you Tony was in town; I could have said we talked on the phone, or never mentioned him at all—but I don't lie to you, Matt, and you know it. Now I really am tired . . ."

"All right, I'm sorry," he said. "It's been a lousy week— but I've already told you that, haven't I? Don't hang up yet; I want to ask you something; I was going to call you tomorrow, in fact. There are two houses I want you to see and I'm going to be in New York for four days—"

"Over the weekend?"

243

"Probably. It can't be helped. But I want you to come here Wednesday and Thursday. I'll cancel everything else so we can be together; we'll look at houses and then go down to Galveston and walk on the beach and have dinner at the Wentletrap. Elizabeth? Are you listening?"

"Yes. I can't come on Wednesday, Matt."

"You can schedule your writing around a two-day trip. If I can juggle a dozen meetings, you can fit in your column."

"It isn't that. Saul and I are going to a hearing on Nuevo. Something's going on there—"

"Saul can tell you about it; you don't have to be there."

"I want to be there."

"More than you want to come to Houston."

"If I come to Houston, will you come home this weekend?"

"Are we playing games? I told you I have to be in New York."

"Well, I guess I want to go to the hearings as much as you want to be in New York."

"God damn it—!" She heard him take a long breath. "I'm sorry. That's about all I'm saying tonight, isn't it? Look, think about Wednesday. You can let me know tomorrow."

"Or the next day?"

"If you call early. I'll need time to juggle my schedule." When she was silent, he became exasperated. "I have a job. You have a job. Until we're together—and even afterward— we're going to have to fit our schedules around our jobs; you know that. You do it now, don't you? Even with Holly and Peter."

"Whom you will not see for another week."

"I don't like it any better than you do."

"I wasn't thinking of me. I was thinking of them."

"For Christ's sake . . ."

"Matt, I'm going to sleep. I'll talk to you soon."

"Call me tomorrow."

"I'll try."

"Elizabeth, did you hear me? I want you to call me tomorrow."

"Goodnight, Matt."

She hung up. They hadn't said *I love you*. They hadn't said *I miss you*. And she'd forgotten to mention Cal Artner.

I'll call him tomorrow. If I have time.

On the Sunday after the hearings, the people of Nuevo once more assembled in the church. Many sat in the same seats they had taken the week before, including Elizabeth in the front row with Peter and Maya, Holly and Luz, and a scowling Cesar. Isabel and Saul stood in the pulpit.

"I asked Isabel to let me say something before she begins," Saul told them. "She's going to apologize to you for failing. She shouldn't. She was as forceful as she promised; in fact, she was damned impressive, even with no time to prepare her case. But I'm sure nothing could have made a difference: they'd made up their minds. It was cut and dried."

Elizabeth, taking notes as she had the first time, recalled the overheated room, the bored faces of the members of the State Committee on Land Use and Recreation as they fidgeted and scribbled and whispered together while Isabel talked. When she had finished, they thanked her for her concise presentation, and Terry Ballenger for his, and Thaddeus Bent, their chairman, for his explanation of studies on the environment, resorts, state parks, water conservation, and job opportunities which had been researched and prepared over the past four years.

"Four years!" Saul had whispered furiously to Elizabeth. "And we didn't know about them. Which means they lumped them under State Parks, with no other identification. Why the secrecy? Never mind," he added. "I know the answer. As long as it was secret, nobody else would be interested in land around Nuevo, so Ballenger and his pals could buy what they wanted. But I would like to know why this committee should help them by keeping things quiet. And who the hell Ballenger and his crew are fronting for."

Standing in the pulpit of the church, Saul looked at the townspeople in the pews. "Isabel did her best. She did you proud. Remember that." He stepped down, and Isabel took his place.

"This is how it is." Her hands gripped the sides of the lectern;

her eyes smoldered. "The Committee decided that a state park and reservoir for flood control and recreation would benefit the entire state. They voted unanimously to recommend that the legislature vote the funding to dam the Pecos River at the narrows below Nuevo to create a two-thousand-acre lake—about a mile wide and three miles long—and to develop the Nuevo State Park."

"But what about Ballenger?" asked Maya's father.

"Ballenger, that snake, owns more than half of the valley. It turns out those other two men were buying for him. He's donating the land along one shore of the lake for a state park. His company also will pay for a new road through the valley, since the one we have now will be partly under the lake. Also, his company will pay for cutting a road ten miles through the mountains to the Pecos Ski Area."

"But *why?*" someone shouted.

"Because Ballenger, that reptile, wants a year-round resort. In winter, cross-country and downhill skiing; in summer, golf, horseback riding, boating, swimming, fishing. He's bought the land for his resort, but he needs a lake. And to get the lake he needs a dam. And to get the dam he needs state approval. And because Ballenger is a very shrewd reptile, he makes sure of state approval by donating land for a state park and paying for a new road around the flooded part, the lake."

The church was hushed. "But we have leases!" Maya's father protested. "The state can't make a park or a lake—they can't even build a dam—as long as we have leases for the land!"

Isabel shook her head. "If a state government decides a project is good for the whole state, it can cancel private leases."

A sigh swept through the people like a heavy wind. "Wait!" Cesar said. "It won't work. Who does this worm think he is, anyway? He doesn't own the town—we didn't sell to him—or the rest of the land in the valley, so he can't flood it."

Looking down, Isabel met Elizabeth's eyes. The bearer of bad news, Elizabeth thought, knowing how hard this was for her. But Isabel gave it to them without softening it. "The state can condemn land. It can cancel leases and it can buy land if it decides it's for all the people of the state."

"For Ballenger, you mean!" Peter said angrily.

"The resort is Ballenger's. But the state park will be on one side of the lake, so even if Ballenger's resort is on the other side, the lake is there for the people of the state. They made one concession: they extended the time we can stay here while we look for new places to live. We've got twelve months—until next March. Then we have to get out."

"Why?" Peter shouted. "It's up to the legislature, and if they don't vote for it—"

Isabel's lips tightened. "They did. This morning. Our land will be theirs next March." Her voice rose over the sudden rush of protests from the pews. *"But construction on the dam begins this spring, as soon as the weather—"*

A tumult of voices drowned out her last words.

"That's it? Just like that?"

"They'll take our houses—?"

"—and Gaspar's store—?"

"—*and this church?*"

Isabel nodded. "They buy them from us."

"Buy!" Cesar spat. "But they decide for how much!"

"Yes, but Saul says it's usually a fair price," Isabel responded. "Fair market value."

"Fair! To make us leave when we don't want to?"

The voices rose again. Elizabeth wrote swiftly, describing the people, their arguments, and Isabel's dignity and determination to keep the meeting orderly instead of a jumble of squabbling angry voices. She heard Maya say to Peter, "Now maybe I can't go to Stanford after all, even if Mama would let me. Maybe I have to stay and help my family."

"Help them do what?" Peter asked.

"I don't know. Fight."

"How?"

She shook her head. Tears were in her eyes. Peter stood up and shouted, "What can we do?"

Isabel put up her hand to quiet the crowd. "We'll try to get an injunction to stop construction until next January, when the legislature meets again. If that doesn't work—and Saul doesn't

247

think the chances are very good—then the only thing we can do is to try to get the bill rescinded next January."

"After they've already started work on the dam?" Maya asked.

"You can always stop something that isn't finished."

"How?" Peter demanded. "What the hell can we do?"

Elizabeth put her hand on his arm. "We'll think of something. I already have some ideas. After all, we have the whole summer to figure out how to make the legislature pay attention to us."

It was not until two hours later, when they were back home in Santa Fe, that she realized what she had said. *The whole summer.*

But weren't they moving to Houston, in June, to be with Matt?

Tony sat in a corner of the low-ceilinged room, unnaturally quiet, listening to Elizabeth interview Isabel. They'd been there since early morning, sharing coffee and *sopapillas* with honey, while Isabel talked about growing up in the valley, learning to make pottery in high school in Pecos, selling her first piece when she was twelve. "You must have been so excited and proud," Elizabeth said.

"Ecstatic." Isabel gazed through the window at the frail new aspen leaves trembling in the April breeze. "I thought I was really somebody; not just a little mountain girl, but somebody important. I expected to make us rich, and then leave the valley."

"For good?"

"Of course. All the young people want to leave. You've heard Luz; she can't wait to get out."

"But you didn't leave."

Isabel shook her head with a rueful laugh. "Didn't get rich. I gave it four years, then decided I had to live closer to where the galleries were. So I went to Denver. But I hated it; I'm not made for cities. So I went into the mountains—Central City and Estes Park—and I sold everything I made to the tourists. I was on top of the world." She laughed. "Really was, in those incredible mountains. Higher than ours, you know; more rugged, more spectacular."

"But you came back to Nuevo."

Isabel nodded. "I guess there was no way I wouldn't. I got married in Central City; I was pregnant with Luz. Her father was a gallery owner who told me I was the greatest artist in the west, and he made it seem an honor that he chose me to take to bed. But he hadn't figured on fatherhood and when I couldn't hide my round stomach he sent me on my way. Later, back here, I met my husband. The best father and husband in the world."

"But when you were in Central City, and pregnant and alone . . . ?"

"Luz was born there and then I started making the rounds of the tourist towns with my wheel and my pottery and my baby in a sling across my chest. I remember how her fuzzy little head kept knocking against my chin. But I knew I didn't want to keep that up: traipsing back and forth with no home for my little girl except under my chin, and no family—and Padre was asking me to come back and live with him after Madre died. Then there were all those pretty-boy ski bums who thought I was fair game. I was prettier then, and I had my figure, and God knows I needed a man, and I bedded down with some of them, but they weren't serious about anything except skiing, certainly not a Hispanic girl with a baby. It was always a one-night thing . . ."

Her voice trailed off. "What was it you hoped for from them?" Elizabeth asked softly.

"Mostly to say they wanted me, Isabel Aragon, not just a body they could take their pleasure from and then forget."

"You didn't want to marry again?"

"Sure, if I loved somebody. But friendships would have been fine, too, if they'd been real. I wanted somebody to care about me. And it turned out the only ones who did were in Nuevo."

"So you came home."

"That was it. Home. Sanctuary, almost. I knew it the minute I walked into this house and sat down. I belonged."

She talked on as Elizabeth asked about her father and Luz,

her neighbors and her work. She brought out her new pottery and briefly described her experiments with glazes and raised patterns using ancient designs—"I can't say much about them; they'll get stolen"—and showed sketches of pieces she had sold. "But I'll tell you something," she added as she slipped them back into a leather portfolio. "I'm thinking about getting out of the pottery business."

"I see," said Elizabeth.

"*You see?* That's all you have to say? You're not surprised? Good Lord, you already know what I'm going to say!"

"Tell me. Then I'll know if I'm right."

"You probably are, my opposite sister. It started in the church, with all that applause . . ."

"And you said you could get to like it."

"Right. And then at the hearings, when I saw those shifty-eyed bastards deciding what was good for us, and not giving a damn *or even knowing anything about us,* I thought, why not? I'd be a hell of a lot better representative than they are."

"So you're going to run for the legislature."

"By God, you *are* my sister; you understand me better than anyone. Well, you're right. I'm giving politics some thought. What would you say my chances are?"

"I think you'd knock out the opposition. You were wonderful at the hearings; you look like everybody's mother, so a lot of men will vote for you; and you've been helping people with their problems for thirteen years, which means everyone knows you. I don't see how you can lose. What about Tom Ortiz? Will he run again?"

"He's getting old. He's represented this district—if you can call it that—for thirty years. I think he's tired. And if he isn't, people are tired of *him.* You really think I can't lose?"

"I'm not an expert. But I think you can't lose."

"Nice words. I haven't decided, you know. I just think about it while I make my pottery. But I must say, that was one good feeling, standing there, being applauded. I think about it a lot."

"What else do you think about?"

"Oh, what happens when Luz is gone, how Padre is starting

to forget things, the fact that I'm for sure not going to find another man, which changes the way I think about my life . . ."

Their low voices, soft and intimate, asking and answering, wove around each other until midafternoon, when Elizabeth finally closed her notebook. "Thank you," she said. "You've been wonderful."

Isabel put her arms around Elizabeth. "Real friends are even harder to find than good men. You keep the loneliness away. I'd do anything for you." Tony stood up and she jumped. "You were so quiet I forgot all about you. Come again; we'll let you do some talking."

"You and Elizabeth do it much better than I," he said, and ducked his head as he went through the low doorway. He waited in the car while the women kissed each other goodbye; then Elizabeth got in behind the wheel and drove off.

He watched her in silence, admiring her profile. Keeping her eyes on the road, Elizabeth said, "You're supposed to be watching the scenery."

"I prefer watching you. Besides, I saw the scenery driving up here."

"It's different when you see it from the other direction."

"That's what I keep telling you. If you see things from my point of view, everything looks quite different."

She laughed. "My single-minded Tony. I am not going with you to your Italian villa; I am not going with you to your mansion in California. Let's talk about Isabel."

"Let's talk about why you called me your Tony."

"Did I? But you know I meant my friend Tony. Now tell me: did you like her?"

"Of course. A good woman. Dull, but how can one dislike her?"

"She is not dull."

"She is to me. She's dedicated to her father, her daughter, her pottery, her valley. She's not beautiful or clever or sophisticated; she's not sexually arousing or bitchy. She's a very good, honest, direct woman whom we both like. She is also dull." When Elizabeth was silent, he asked, "What difference does it make? She's your friend, not mine; I'll never see her again.

251

What I really want to talk about is you. No, don't frown. I mean I want to talk about your interview with her. Do you know how good you were?"

"I know I'm good at interviewing, Tony. I've been doing it for a long time. This one was special, though. Isabel and I cooked it up to make trouble for Ballenger."

"I don't give a damn about Ballenger, whoever he is; I'm talking about Elizabeth Lovell. You got her talking, you controlled the interview, you got intimate revelations that she wasn't always aware she was telling you. And when she did know you were on personal territory, it didn't bother her, because you were interested and sympathetic, not curious or prying." He gave a long sigh. "If I could do that, I'd be popular forever. You are wasting a brilliant talent on a handful of newspapers. You should be sharing it with the world."

Elizabeth looked at him briefly before turning back to the narrow road. "What does that mean?"

"It means you should be on television."

"I'm a writer, Tony. I don't like television. It's too fast, too superficial."

"You wouldn't be on television if someone offered you a show?"

"What kind of show? How can I answer? It doesn't matter; I probably wouldn't. I really do love to make words appear on paper in the right order, not toss them at a camera and never see them again. Anyway, I'm not about to move to Los Angeles, or anywhere, to chase the fantasy of an audience of millions. I like what I'm doing, and it's real: I'm in twenty papers; that's more than I ever dreamed of." She made the turn at Pecos and picked up speed on the empty road. "What did you mean about someone offering me a show?"

"I didn't mean your own. I meant being part of mine. Didn't I offer that long ago? I don't recall whether I was serious or not, but now that I've seen you in action I am very serious. Elizabeth, let me talk to my producer about you. Just to get his opinion. The show could use some jazzing up—oh, Christ, I didn't mean that, don't frown again, you're so much more beautiful when you smile—all I meant was, next fall, after summer reruns, we're going to want something new and different, for variety, for sparkle . . ."

"To postpone the rainy day when you go into politics?"

There was a pause. "Who said that?"

"My husband."

"I see. He got it wrong."

"Did he? A few minutes ago you talked about being popular forever."

"No one is popular forever. Even God gets bad ratings."

"Then what did you say at Keegan's dinner?"

"That television and politics are alike. They both give top rewards to people who can convince an audience that the bullshit they're spouting is genuine conviction, coming from their own brains. But you *are* genuine," he went on. "And since your talented husband is the latest to fall victim to my father's charm, there is all the more reason for you to expand your career to include television. After all, what will you do when your offspring are gone? Nobody to clean house or cook for, no young ones to keep on the straight and narrow . . . what will you do for excitement? Sit alone all day at a typewriter? You could do that part of the time—there's no need for you to give up your writing—but for the rest . . . some live action, a challenge for your interviewing skills, new people . . . Are you listening?"

"Yes," Elizabeth said.

"Then you will notice I'm not talking about Italian villas or California mansions. I'm talking about one slot of ten or fifteen minutes a week, on 'Anthony.' You'd be amazed how much information can be packed into fifteen minutes. More than in one of your columns. Let me talk to my producer. That's all I ask. He may not like the idea, in which case I'll probably have to give it up, at least for a while. A producer is like a spouse: you compromise or you get a divorce; and I can't handle divorces from wives and my producer as well. So we can talk about it again next time I'm in Santa Fe; by then I'll know what he thinks. Is that all right?"

"Yes," Elizabeth said again. Tony made a small sound, almost a hum of satisfaction, and settled back to enjoy the scenery.

As proudly as a queen, Isabel Aragon stands beside the Pecos River that flows through Nuevo. When she stretches out her arms they are like the mountains around her, embracing the valley where she was born. "This is what they want to destroy," she says. "Restless people in a restless country, forever tearing down, throwing away the past, like orphans who don't recall their roots and don't know the meaning of *home*. Little men who only feel strong when they're shoving somebody around and ripping things apart. Listen, you little men out there! This is our home! Our roots are three centuries deep in this valley! Fifteen generations are buried here and we hold in our hearts their dreams and jokes and sadnesses, and our own, that grow from the soil of this valley. Some of us sold our land, lured by money and promises. But now we're going to show you how people fight for their home. *We are going to buy back our land*. You think we can't? Watch us. We'll work every day, every night until we have enough money, and until then we're going to hold up your project by making a stink in the legislature that will make the manure on our farms smell like gardenias. Because *we will not let you drown our town . . .*"

Elizabeth's story included Isabel's earthy retelling of Indian and Spanish legends, and modern tales of the people in the valley who brought her their problems, and it ended with Isabel standing before the old church.

"Too many of those little men think they can crunch other people underfoot like centipedes. But I'm telling them it won't work! Too many legs! Too many of us! They'll see whether it's so easy to stamp us out . . . !"

Elizabeth knew it was the best story she had ever written. And on May 10, three weeks after it appeared in the Rourke chain to an outpouring of mail and telephone calls, it was reprinted by the *Los Angeles Times* as part of a two-page article on vacation resorts in the southwest. Tony tore it out and sent it to his producer, with a scrawled note. "Please read! You turned thumbs down on my brilliant idea of having Elizabeth Lovell interview her non-famous people on 'Anthony.' Kindly explain why she's good enough for the *Times,* but not good enough for us."

"We're not talking 'good,'" his producer said on the telephone the next day. "We're talking audience. Nobody cares about people they never heard of."

"Call the *Times,*" Tony ordered. "Ask them about their mail."

A week later his producer called again. "How did you know?"

"I'm a fan. How many letters did they get?"

"Fifty letters, ninety-two phone calls, eighty-one offers of money to help that woman fight for her valley."

"Ha! Do we try her on my show?"

"Tony, are you fucking her? I don't want hysterical women on this show, and when you're through with them they always get—"

"Not to worry; she isn't the hysterical type."

"You haven't answered my question."

"My love life is not part of my contract," Tony said sweetly. "It's not something we discuss."

"But we do discuss your ratings. Which are slipping. Probably because you're not as sharp as you were five years ago—"

"Nobody is as sharp as they were five years ago. Including you."

"—or because audiences are tired of celebrities—which I doubt—or we're picking the wrong celebrities. Or all of the above. Okay, I'm willing to let your girl friend do a few pilot tapes, but if you turn this place into a sexual stew—"

"I told you not to worry," Tony retorted. "I'll handle her."

"As long as you understand that you're responsible. One more thing. I know you don't pick dogs, but I'm asking anyway: how will she look on camera?"

"Like it was invented for her. Also she's got class. Why

don't you trust me in these matters? I'm a connoisseur and you know it."

"I know you often get carried away."

"I pretend to when it's useful. And you know that too. Now listen: she doesn't know about my ratings. She thinks I'm at the top of the heap. There's no reason to tell her otherwise."

"She thinks you're doing this out of the generosity of your corrupt heart?"

"Don't try to be clever. She doesn't think it's corrupt. Are you going to be careful how you talk to her, or not?"

"Of course I am. As long as she helps the show."

"I applaud your wise decision." Tony hung up and immediately called Elizabeth. "I have news," he told her the minute she answered. "My producer, unlovable but shrewd, will soon call to offer you a place on 'Anthony.' That is, he'll ask for a few pilot interviews. If he likes them, we'll run them this fall, to see what the response is. Do you know about the offers of money at the *Times?*"

"Yes, they sent me the letters. They want to buy more of my stories, Tony. Should I let them?"

"Not until you have an agent. I'll help you find one. Did you hear what I said about my show?"

"Yes. How often would I have to be in Los Angeles?"

"It depends. You can tape interviews on location with crews from local affiliates, or we fly your people here and you interview them in the studio. Plus one day a week for editing and conferences on planning and scheduling. You'd enjoy being part of that, wouldn't you? And Los Angeles? It would be a homecoming for you. And I'd be here, to lend a helping hand."

"I don't know, Tony. I'll think about it."

"That's what you're going to tell my producer?"

"It depends on what I've decided when he calls."

"What can I do to convince you? Swoop in and take you to dinner? How about the M & J Sanitary Tortilla Factory in Albuquerque for Bea Montoya's famous burritos?"

She laughed. "How do you know about Bea's place?"

"I watch television. It made her famous; it will make you famous. Shall I come and take you to dinner?"

"Not tonight."

"Soon, then. And you'll let me know as soon as you decide?"

"Of course. And thank you, Tony." Hanging up, Elizabeth contemplated the television set in the corner of the den. *It will make you famous.*

For Peter's graduation, on the last Sunday in May, Elizabeth and Matt, Spencer and Lydia, Holly and Maya squeezed into the tightly-packed stadium bleachers, sitting halfway above the field and halfway below the sign announcing "Demon Country." Eight hundred students in caps and gowns marched into the stadium, their names called in pairs as they entered. When Maya heard Peter's name she let out her breath in a sigh. "It's like he's taken a big jump and left me behind."

"I know," Holly said. "He's changed so much." Later, when Peter stood to give the class address and the seniors gave him a lusty cheer, she shook her head in wonder. For four years he'd never fit in; he'd been mocked for his shyness and his love of Indian art and legends instead of sports. He hadn't gone on the senior class trip, or to the senior prom; he'd taken Maya to dinner and the Taos Spring Arts Celebration instead. And although he had joined the photo club and the French club, he was still uncomfortable and he left the campus as soon as he could each afternoon. "Why are they cheering him?" Holly asked Elizabeth.

"Because he's their top student," Elizabeth replied. "And he makes all of them look good by being smart."

"He makes the whole school look good," Matt said. "Besides, people cheer a handsome man who makes something of himself whether they like him or not. They cheer because he's shown them success is possible."

"That's very clever," Elizabeth said. "Is that why people cheer you in Houston?"

"Some of them," he replied evenly.

"And the others?"

"The others think I'm doing a good job."

A few minutes later the ceremony ended, the field swarmed with students and their relatives, and Peter's family took him off for a festive dinner with Saul and Heather, Maya, and some friends from the *Chieftain* staff.

"It was perfect," Elizabeth said later to Matt as they sat in their courtyard sharing iced tea and cookies. "Just the kind of celebration Peter wanted. And best of all, you were here."

"You couldn't have doubted I would be."

"Once I couldn't have."

"But this time you did."

"Yes."

He inspected the decorations on one of the cookies. "Eight months," he murmured. "It's gone so fast I can't believe it's been that long. But it was long enough to make you stop trusting me."

"I think you gave me reasons." Elizabeth leaned forward and put her hand on his. "Matt, maybe you ought to slow down. You've done far more than we ever dreamed: twenty papers—"

"Twenty-one," he interrupted automatically.

"Twenty-one, then; I didn't know you'd bought another."

"I was going to tell you about it tonight. It's not big yet, but there's tremendous potential—"

"Matt, I'm trying to talk to you."

"I heard you. You're telling me I should give up what I'm still building and turn my back on the biggest job I ever had. What would you like me to do? Come back to Santa Fe and run the *Chieftain*?"

"Not if you don't want to. I didn't ask you to give up everything. A year ago this week we owned two newspapers and were just starting out at the *Daily News*. Now you're running twenty-one papers, you give speeches all over the country, you're influencing legislation on land use . . . how much do you need to feel satisfied?"

Must there be a limit at the outset?

They looked at each other, both of them remembering Rourke's asking that seductively vague question, in Aspen.

"I don't have a number," Matt said. "But we want influence in certain states and that means owning key papers in those states. Until we've done that, we keep buying."

"Twenty-one isn't enough for you? Just you, Matt. Not Keegan or his corporation; just you. I remember when we talked about owning one or two papers—"

"And you wanted your column to be in one or two papers. Are you unhappy with twenty-one?"

"Of course not. But no one asked me if I would have been happy with ten or fifteen."

"Would you have been?"

"Yes. Just as I'm happy now with twenty and don't need thirty. Matt, there are other things I care about. I thought you did, too. What good is making a lot of money if we can't enjoy it together? What good is paying off our debts if we're not free to travel with Peter and Holly, or alone—or just be together, all of us? We shuttle back and forth between Houston and Santa Fe on little visits, and not many of those, lately; we're all going in different directions; we're not sharing; we've lost the idea we started out with of being partners. We're not working together at anything, not even our marriage. Matt, are you listening?"

He was gazing over the adobe wall, at the branches of an olive tree faintly outlined against the starlit sky. The scent of primroses filled the air. He took a deep breath. "Yes, of course I was listening. I've had regrets in the past months, too, but I thought we'd make up for them. I thought I was building a future for the two of us—"

"Alone. Not with me."

"It worked out that way. You wanted to stay here until Peter graduated and that seemed logical to me."

"I think I was wrong. It sounded so simple, but how could we believe we could stay close while we were so far apart? It's a romantic idea that couldn't work, at least while our lives are changing—while we're changing. We were wrong to think it was a good idea."

"I don't think so. It was good for Peter, and I've been on the move so much we wouldn't have seen a lot more of each

259

other than we did with you here. Anyway, it's done. And I've made a start at something enormous—and you want me to quit."

"I didn't say quit. I said slow down so we can make a life together again."

"I thought we were planning to make a life together in Houston. In fact, if you'd come to choose a house when I asked, we'd be packing now instead of talking. Do you know how many times you've come to Houston since Keegan's party?"

"Three."

"In eight months."

"I don't enjoy it, Matt. And you don't enjoy having me there. You may have been on the move a lot, but you've managed to make friends and build your own life, and they're not my friends and it's not my life."

"Because you've always been visiting. If you lived there, you'd make them your friends."

"Because they're all I'd have? Because I'd find out how lovable they are underneath? Or because they're important to your empire?"

He made a gesture of impatience. "You'd pick and choose and find those you like. Are you saying you couldn't find a friend in all of Houston? You were more adventurous once."

"Do you really want an adventurous wife? Or do you want one who will help you be the head of Rourke Publishing? Hostess, companion, good listener; well-groomed, sexually attractive . . ."

"What's wrong with that? We'd be working together—"

"That's not the job I want!"

"It's not a job; it's something we'd do together. I don't want you to stop writing; you know I'm proud of what you're doing. But the more you help me, the faster we'll build the kind of life that will give us everything we want."

"Matt, will you listen to what I'm saying? I'm not sure I want that kind of life!"

"That's because you don't understand it."

"I understand that you're changing in ways that bother

me, either because of the people you're with or the work you do—"

"You've never approved of the work I do because it's come from Keegan. You don't understand how important it is—"

"And how important you are in doing it."

"What's wrong with that? Elizabeth, listen to me. Small groups of people run the affairs of this country. Why shouldn't I be part of them? Why shouldn't I take advantage of the greatest opportunity I've ever had and give it all I've got? How many times does the brass ring come around? Once—if we're lucky. If I hadn't grabbed it in Aspen, or if I walk away from it now, it would be gone; it won't come again. I'd go back to being a small-town editor with no influence and no importance; not even on the fringes of power. I'd be one of the people you write about who go through life with no say in the decisions that shape the country. Do you think I could go back to that after these past months?"

Ambition is eating you up inside.

They both remembered Rourke saying that, too.

Matt stood, and leaned forward, with both hands on the table. "How often does anyone get a chance to climb above everyone else? Most people never even dare dream about it. But when a man does get it, and knows he has to go after it, he'd like his wife at his side. But my wife wants me to give it up. That's what 'slow down' really means, isn't it? You never wanted me to go after it; you've tried to hold me back since the day Keegan made his offer. And now, after I've spent months working twenty hours a day to get a handle on this job, learning how to use the money and power at my disposal, all you can say is you want us to have some time together. Though I'm not sure why you want that, since you also say you don't like the way I've changed."

"I want it because you're my husband and I love you."

"If that's really true, if you really gave a damn about our future—"

"Whose future? Yours or mine?"

"Our future, damn it. When a wife helps her husband win a race he's waited for all his life, it's their future."

261

"I've helped you from the beginning. Or don't you remember that?"

"I've never denied it. I probably wouldn't have bought the *Chieftain* without you; I couldn't have made it a success without you. But you've built that into some kind of fairy tale. Have you forgotten how hard we worked there? And for what? To double a circulation of ten thousand! Millions of readers in this country and we cheered for twenty thousand!" He straightened up, looking down at her. "I can't understand why you're fighting me on this. You're getting what you've always wanted, too. You're becoming known, appearing in more papers, making more money . . . Christ, Elizabeth, it's not as if I'm asking you to stay home while I get all the excitement and attention; you have a tremendous talent and a career that I'll make bigger with every step I take—"

"And that's all that matters, isn't it, Matt? Big, bigger, biggest."

"Why not? When was it ever possible before?"

"When was it the main thing in our life before?"

There was a sudden silence. Matt pulled out his chair with his foot and sat down. Elizabeth added ice and mint leaves to their glasses and poured tea from a glazed pitcher Isabel had made her for Christmas the year before. "Matt, do you really think I don't want you to succeed?"

"I don't know what you want. I've been trying to figure it out. We understood each other, once; we wanted everything we could get. But this past year you haven't given me any real help or support; in fact, every chance you get you tell me you don't like Keegan, you don't like Chet, you don't like Cal Artner knowing Chet—as if it makes a damn bit of difference!—you don't like the way I've changed . . . Would you please tell me what you do like?"

"I like what you used to be. I like what we used to have. I like the determination you had a couple of years ago to work only for yourself, no one else. What happened to that? Doesn't it bother you to work for Keegan, to be at his beck and call—"

"He isn't that way. I've tried to tell you: he gives me all the space I need. I do what I want."

"Well, while you're doing what you want, he's getting to you somehow. Because a lot of your ideas sound like Keegan Rourke, not Matt Lovell."

"You don't know anything about his ideas. Unless . . ." He frowned. "Unless Tony is telling tales of his terrible father. Is that it? How often does friend Tony stop by Santa Fe these days?"

"Two or three times a month."

"By God, almost as much as your husband. That fills your time nicely, doesn't it?"

"He never came when we were working together!" Elizabeth cried. "Leave him out of it; he has nothing to do with what we're talking about. I've known Keegan longer than you have—"

"But not better. I've seen him or talked to him every day for the past year, and I trust him. I have no reason not to. Do you?"

She was silent.

"Then you don't have much right to criticize. But you'd rather do that than come with me. You'd rather dream about what we used to have—which was pale and insignificant compared to what we can have now—than take a chance on Keegan Rourke and the future." When Elizabeth was still silent, he said "You told me what you like about the way things were. What do you like about the way they are now?"

"Between us? Nothing."

Matt shoved his chair back. "I'll ask you one more time. Will you move to Houston and be part of my life there?"

"Do you want me to?"

"I've never said I didn't."

"That's not an answer, Matt. Are you beginning to wonder whether it would work? You'll still be traveling a lot of the time; is that right?"

"For a while."

"A month? Six months? A year?"

"I don't know."

"So we might have weekends, if we're lucky. Of course, I'll be going various places to interview for my column; maybe our paths would cross once a month. That leaves Holly alone in Houston, where she has no grandparents and no friends."

"She'd make friends."

"Of course. Then when you and I manage to be home at the same time, I'll be that hostess and good listener and sexual companion you want, while typing my stories with my free hand—"

"Stop it."

"Tell me I'm wrong. Tell me you'll make sure we have time together. Tell me you really want me to share your life, which means telling you my feelings about it. Because I couldn't go to Houston and stand by in silence without telling you how I feel about what you and Keegan, and even Chet and Cal, are doing."

"Then you don't have to stand by at all."

The words echoed in the fragrant courtyard. "I didn't mean that," Matt said. "I wish I could make you understand how important this is to me. I know I talk about the excitement of being close to power and having my own . . . but it's not fun and games, Elizabeth; it's not the simple problems we had at the *Chieftain*. It's fighting to prove I can hold my own; it's maneuvering around sharks who think they can run the world—and many of them can, damn it, and they're more ruthless because they know it; it's building walls to protect what I have so no one can take it away . . ." He leaned forward. "I need you to stand with me, help me believe in myself and what I'm doing, help me fight to get all I can. When we've got our newspaper chain and a uniform policy and people under me I can trust—then I can relax, be a publisher, and spend time with my wife, with all the money we need and the whole world to play in. And you'll be building up your own readership helping me secure our future."

"Very neat," Elizabeth murmured. "I can't imagine a happier couple."

He gazed at her somberly. "We could be very happy."

Elizabeth ran her finger around the rim of her glass. "What

would you think if I did interviews on television in addition to the ones in newspapers?"

"Television?" He grew thoughtful. "It would be perfect. Every viewer would connect your name to the local paper that carries your column: the best kind of advertising. Of course you'd have to insist on keeping the name 'Private Affairs'—"

Elizabeth flung herself from her chair and almost ran into the house. Matt found her pacing back and forth in the kitchen, holding herself tightly with folded arms. "What the hell is it now?"

She threw him a look. "I wanted to know what you thought about me in television. Me, Matt, and you, too, because one of the questions I had was how much it might interfere with our marriage—what's left of it. I was asking about me, not the Rourke chain. Can you think about me for a minute separate from your beloved newspapers and powerful boss? I don't give a damn about the Rourke chain—"

"You've made that clear all too often."

"Not clear enough. Not often enough. I want you to make me and your children at least as important as that company. Maybe even put us first. Can you understand that? Have you forgotten how to do it?"

"As much as you've forgotten to put me first. I keep telling you what's happening in my life and all you think about is yourself. Now listen to me. Damn it, sit down and listen!"

"I don't want to sit down."

He shrugged. "Fine." They stood on opposite sides of the kitchen as if an earthquake had ripped apart the floor between them. "I'll try once more to explain this. For the first time in years I'm controlling my own life. I'm not living my father's life; I'm living my own life, my own dream, the one I had when we were married. Do you remember it?"

"Remember it! We lived it! What were we doing at the *Chieftain?* Weren't you in control of your life then?"

There was a pause. "Yes. But that was—"

"*We* were in charge of *our* life!"

"Let me finish. What we had at the *Chieftain* was a schoolboy's dream; the one I had when I was twenty-three. It seemed

265

so grand, then: I was going to own a newspaper! My God—
a single paper! Sometimes I'd whisper a prayer for two papers.
I really thought that would satisfy me!"

"Maybe it would have. If we'd done it then, together, the
way we planned."

"Maybe. But the reason Saul is content is that he has his
big time behind him. I haven't had mine. I'm just beginning
it. And I'll do anything it takes—however many hours a day,
however many days a year—but I'm going to make it. I am
not going to crawl back to this town a failure. Keegan's given
me the chance to do everything and be everything I could ever
want, and all you've given me are arguments to hold me back.
You tried to convince me not to trust him. *You wondered why
he'd chosen me.* You could have had enough faith in your
husband to believe he chose me because I was good at my job!
Every time you've come to Houston you've criticized the people I work with. And now you want me to quit—sorry, *slow
down,* be satisfied with what I've got, ignore what I might
achieve and how far I might go, settle back in my rocking chair
and declare myself a happy man."

Elizabeth shook her head. "No, you wouldn't be happy. It's
too late. You'd always think the great exciting world was passing you by. And you'd blame me."

"Not if you—"

"Not if I agreed with you and accepted the life you make.
But it's too late for that, too. I didn't think I was trying to hold
you back, Matt. I always believed in you. But I wanted to be
realistic, understand what was happening, go a little slowly so
we'd really be in control of our direction. *We,* Matt. Together.
That's what you left out of your story. We had those dreams
together, and maybe they were timid and young, but I was
excited about them because they were about two people who
were in love and getting married and planning to work together
as partners. And when we came back here to take care of
Zachary, you weren't the only one to give up a dream; I did,
too. I waited, too. But Keegan wasn't looking for me in Aspen;
he came for you and you went along, as starry-eyed as a teenager, and got busy remaking the world, and that put an end to

266

what we were building together: a new partnership, a new marriage. By now we can't even talk about my interviewing on television. Did you ask me how I feel about it? Did you ask how many days I'd have to be in Los Angeles—?"

"Los Angeles?"

"It doesn't matter where. New York, Berlin, Moscow—what difference does it make? You weren't curious enough to ask. All you thought about was the impact it might have on your newspapers. You weren't so preoccupied with grabbing your brass ring a couple of years ago—you had time for the rest of us, then—but Keegan has always thought of grabbing opportunities for himself first. It must please him to see how well you've learned his lessons."

Her throat was tight. She turned away, putting her palms on the cool tiles of the countertop. "You said I didn't have to stand by. You meant that. You try to pretend that you want me, probably because you think a man *ought* to want his wife, but I think you'd be happiest if I stayed out of your way. And I'd rather do that, Matt: stay out of the way while you and Keegan go after all the money and power and influence you can get, in any way you can, without my questions or criticism. It's probably best for you: sometimes people travel fastest and farthest alone." She moved toward the door, her back to Matt, to get out of there before the tightness in her throat turned to tears. "I wish we could have found a way . . . some way to—"

"Elizabeth, damn it, I love you." Matt was behind her, holding her with her back against him, his face in her hair. "Come with me. You helped me before; help me again. And then we'll have everything. There's nothing we can't do if we do it together."

His arms were strong and warm around her, and she put her hands on his, remembering all the times their bodies had been so close, closer, joined. "I'll live with you in Houston if you want me to stand with you when I think you're right and disagree when I think you're wrong, and try to slow you down if I think what you're doing is destroying what we have. Do you want that?"

"A loaded question," he said wryly. "You answer for me."

"Your answer is no. You don't want me there. I think you still love me . . . or maybe what you love is the idea of the perfect woman: loving wife, mother, helpmate, successful career woman with her own newspaper column, maybe even a television show. The ideal companion for Keegan Rourke's publisher. Why do you hold me this way, so we can't see each other or kiss each other?"

After a moment, his lips still in her hair, he said, "I don't want you to see my eyes."

She nodded. She felt empty and cold. "I'd hoped I was wrong, but I wasn't, was I?" Loosening his clasp around her waist, she turned within his arms to face him, her hands on his shoulders, her eyes searching his, and she knew he agreed with her: he could go farthest and fastest alone. "I love you, Matt. But I want you to go. Now."

He touched her hair, then dropped his arms. "Will you tell Peter and Holly I . . . had to leave early? I'll call them. I'd like them to come to Houston. You could come with them. We'll work that out, don't you think? I'll call you. You'll be here?"

"Yes."

"I'll call you. Tell Peter and Holly . . ."

Elizabeth nodded. There was a long silence. And then he turned and left.

"Wait," Elizabeth said. "You didn't pack." But there was no one to hear her. And then she realized it didn't matter. He had a closet full of clothes in Houston. And work and friends and challenges and dreams.

He had another life. And when she got used to that idea, and figured out what it meant to both of them, she'd have to find a life of her own that didn't include him. At least for a while. At least until they decided whether this arrangement—whatever it was, exactly—was what they wanted.

On the table beside the telephone was a picture of them in Matt's office at the *Chieftain*. She picked it up and ran her sleeve over the glass. She rubbed it harder and harder, her arm

268

moving as fast as it could, polishing the glass above those smiling faces until she realized they were blurred because of her tears. Carefully she put it down and turned away. And as she did, she caught a glimpse through the doorway of the television set in the corner of the den—and once again heard Tony's voice. *It can make you famous.*

Part
III

CHAPTER 9

Bo Boyle had been the producer of "Anthony" since its premiere, hitching his career to its popularity, building a new personality for himself as he and the show became more successful. From Booton Eamon O'Boyle, choir boy and playground coward at St. Joseph's Grammar and High School in Newark, New Jersey, he had transformed himself, beneath the shimmering Los Angeles sun, into Bo Boyle, who was climbing to the top in television with astonishing speed. He was beginning to attract notice for making lackluster game shows more lively, when, out of the blue, he was plucked from a dozen contenders with better backgrounds and named producer of "Anthony."

Insulted by his new producer's lack of glamorous credits, Tony Rourke ignored him, but Bo Boyle, amiable and tenacious, outwaited him and within six months they had settled into a friendly, if wary, partnership. It was good for both of them: Boyle's changes in lighting, stage set, and pacing made Tony look better, and when the ratings went up, that made Boyle look good.

Tony had the visibility—Tony Rourke, with the sleekest of good looks, a quick tongue, and a unique talent for making women viewers feel motherly and sexy at the same time, without making male viewers resent him—but Bo Boyle was beyond jealousy: he was too busy gathering power into his hands. Tony was the perfect perch for a producer who would stop at nothing to get to the top, and when Tony and his show ultimately faded, as happens to all television hosts and shows, Bo Boyle would lose nothing but a perch—and perches, he liked to say, had only one purpose: to become launching points for flying to even greater heights.

But for now, "Anthony" was the right place for him. And it might be about to get better, Bo thought, contemplating Elizabeth Lovell's profile across the studio as he finished a telephone call, it might be about to get better. "Tony will be late," he said, his voice echoing in the cavernous room as he picked his way over the heavy power cables stretching across the floor. Grabbing a folding chair, he opened it beside Elizabeth's and straddled it, folding his arms along its back, gazing at her with bland eyes that seemed half-asleep but saw everything. Christ, the son of a bitch had done it again. Even in the middle of the goddam New Mexican desert, where Bo Boyle would be lucky to find lizards and prairie dogs, Tony Rourke comes up with this incredible creature with a face and a pair of legs that would keep half of America from switching channels. How the fuck did he always do it? "He said to start without him."

"I'd rather—" Elizabeth caught herself. "Fine. What would you like me to do?"

"Well now, Lizzie, let's think about that." He saw the shadow cross her face. "Something wrong with Lizzie?"

"Yes."

He sighed. "We live in a fast-moving world. Elizabeth is a long name. All those syllables. Liz? Liza? Betsy? Bets! None of them? Elizabeth, then. How formal. How proper. Well, Elizabeth, what will you do for us while our Tony is absent? Let's wing it, shall we? Find out how you think on your feet. Let's have you interview"—drumming his fingertips on his knee, he glanced about the studio—"Greg Roscov. Any problem with that?" Elizabeth followed his glance and met the startled eyes of a burly cameraman a few feet behind them. "Of course there's no problem with that," Bo answered himself cheerfully. "In fact, it's perfect. Greg helps bring "Anthony" into millions of living rooms, but no one ever sees him. The invisible man! Now is that perfect or is that perfect! You come here to interview people the rest of the world doesn't see and I hand you one on a silver platter! Greg, you'll help us, won't you, in our hour of need? Be on the other side of the camera for once."

There was a pause. Damn it, Tony, Elizabeth fumed silently. You got me into this; where are you now, when I need you?

It seemed she was doing everything herself, these days. Only two weeks since Matt had gone back to Houston, but already everything had changed. She was alone most of the time. Peter had a summer job at an art gallery on Palace Avenue, and spent his spare hours with Maya. Holly had begun her apprenticeship with the Santa Fe Opera, and her day stretched from nine in the morning until late at night. Lydia was getting ready for the first tourists who would arrive in June, and Spencer was in his workshop, having recklessly promised carved wooden candlesticks, his latest triumph, to everyone who admired the pair he had placed beside the coffee and tea service in the bookshop.

Elizabeth wrote. In a kind of fury, she interviewed two and three, sometimes four people a day, then sat at her typewriter until early morning, for the first time getting ahead of her schedule. It was a good thing she did. Because within that same fourteen days, she said yes to Tony when he offered again to give her a spot on his show; Bo Boyle telephoned to say they required a camera test; Tony called back to promise her there was nothing to it; and two days later she flew to Los Angeles where a studio limousine drove her to Television City in Hollywood. Once there, she was led to a cavernous studio hung with lights and cluttered with cables, equipment, and battered desks and chairs. In an odd way, it reminded Elizabeth of a newspaper office.

Fourteen days ago Matt had left. And was anything in her life the same?

Behind her, the cameraman shrugged. "I don't have anything to talk about. I'm not good at acting or anything like that."

"Acting!" exclaimed Bo Boyle. "You just be your own sweet

274

self. Elizabeth will take care of the rest." He stood. "We'll use Tony's set, but I want the armchair and couch closer together, and the coffee table pulled forward . . ." He stepped onto the raised platform where half of a lavish mahogany and leather study faced the cameras. It was a room designed to portray Anthony Rourke as a man of wealth and lightly stuffy tradition but also—because the couch was so deep, the carpets and drapes faintly Arabian, the cognac accessible, and a silk robe just visible on a hassock near the fireplace—a man who used the privacy of his retreat for sports other than reading and interviewing occasional guests. Bo, who had helped design it, stood beside the couch, directing two stagehands, seeing in his mind the angles of Elizabeth's face he wanted the cameras to capture. Another thought came to him. "Makeup," he called to Elizabeth. "Tell Roberta ten minutes."

Elizabeth caught Greg Roscov's eye. "Why not?" she asked, smiling. "Since the whole thing is made up from start to finish. Roberta can do both of us."

He shook his head. "Boyle'd hit the ceiling. Nobody cares what I look like."

"I do," Elizabeth said. "Tell me something. If I'm plastered up with creams and powders, how will the lights make you look, next to me?"

"Like something fished out of the water," he said.

"That's what I thought. Come on, Greg; we're in this together. We both glow with health or we both look like drowned rats."

He grinned, beginning to feel better about the whole crazy business. Maybe she was okay and not out to make an ass of him.

"Come on. We won't give them time to wash it off." She took his hand and led him from the studio and up the stairs to the makeup room she had seen earlier that afternoon. A step behind her, he looked at her long legs, the curve of her rear end under her silky skirt, and her shining hair lying in long waves like dark honey against the jade green of her silk suit, and he knew he'd do anything she said. The hell with Boyle. The hell with everything.

275

But he became worried again when he was sitting close to her in the luxurious study he'd seen every week from behind his camera. He didn't belong there and he was miserably uncomfortable. The goddam leather was slippery; he kept sliding forward on his ass, digging his heels into the Arabian carpet to keep from going all the way to the floor, trying to wriggle back into position while one of the crew was bending over him, clipping the microphone to his shirt.

Elizabeth knew she should be setting him at his ease, creating the relaxed and friendly atmosphere that led people to reveal the private person behind their public defenses, but she couldn't do it. It was one of her greatest skills in interviewing for her column, and she knew she couldn't succeed in television without it, but at that moment she couldn't concentrate. Everything was too new. The lights were blinding, making her feel exposed and vulnerable; beneath their white heat she felt she was melting into the leather chair. The cameras leered at her like black one-eyed monsters; her silk suit clung to her back; damp tendrils of hair curled on her forehead; her heart was pounding.

Turning her head, she saw a television set off to one side, and on the screen a woman's face, fearful, tense, trapped. Poor thing, Elizabeth thought involuntarily, and then realized she was looking at herself.

It couldn't be! Where was the beautiful Elizabeth Lovell people were always talking about? This woman looked like a squirrel being chased into hiding . . . no, a panda, she thought with a flash of humor. A sun-tanned panda. Too much eyeliner; too much makeup. Roberta overdid it: *this isn't me!*

Someone was clipping a small piece of metal to her suit lapel. "Microphone," said a quiet voice. "Relax; you look great. Dynamite. Now if you'll sit still, I'm not getting fresh, I'm just hiding the mike wire under your jacket, pull it behind you . . . no sweat. Thanks."

"Thank you," Elizabeth murmured.

"Voice level," a disembodied voice said.

"Elizabeth, can you say a few words?" Bo Boyle asked, his voice floating in from beyond the blinding lights. "Talk about the weather, list the kings of France, anything. We're just checking your microphone."

"What about Greg's microphone?" Elizabeth asked.

"We'll make it as exquisite as his makeup," Boyle said dryly.

Elizabeth saw embarrassment sweep across Greg's face and she forgot the lights, the dampness across her back, the confusion of seeing her unfamiliar image on the television screen. She leaned forward. "I heard you talking to the other cameramen earlier; you seem to know every inch of this place. How long have you worked here?"

Startled, Greg dug his heels into the carpet and sat straight. "Ten years."

"We're not taping," said Boyle. "I asked for a few sentences."

Still looking at Greg, Elizabeth said softly, "I'm sorry, Bo. It's just that Greg is much more interesting than the kings of France. And isn't this a good time for us to begin talking? You can check both our microphones while we get acquainted."

There was a brief pause. "Suit yourself," Bo said and pulled his folding chair forward so he could watch her and the television monitor at the same time.

"Did you start out as a cameraman?" Elizabeth asked Greg.

He shook his head. "Gaffer."

Elizabeth made a mental note to find out later what a gaffer was; now she didn't want to interrupt Greg's thoughts. "Not everybody can be a cameraman?"

"Right."

"Why not?" Elizabeth asked when he said no more.

"It's complicated."

She sighed. "What makes it complicated?"

"There's a lot to it."

There was a silence. This is awful, she thought desperately. Dull, slow, dead. It's not for a newspaper; I won't be writing it up later in a lively way; it has to be lively right now.

From the corner of her eye, Elizabeth saw a red light on one of the cameras. They're taping, she thought, and to her other desperation she added worries about her looks. Which was better—profile, full face, three-quarters? And how could she control it, how could she decide how to sit, if she didn't know which camera shot which angle? How would she know if she were on the screen, or Greg, or both of them?

The palms of her hands were moist. She was going to fail. She'd never done anything like this before and she was going to fail.

Who says I am? Matt did something new and he succeeded. Why should he be the only one?

She took a deep breath. "Okay, Greg," she said firmly, holding his eyes with hers. "Let's say your bosses tell me I can't handle a television camera; it's a man's world, they say. I want to prove they're wrong. I ask you to teach me everything a good cameramen knows. How do you do it?"

He grinned. "It *is* a man's world."

"Baloney." Elizabeth stood up. "Microphone!" someone yelled just as she felt the tug of the wire beneath her jacket. She unclipped it from her lapel, putting it on the arm of the couch, and then strode to the nearest camera. She saw another camera following her as she grabbed it, ignoring the yelp of surprise from the man behind it, and began to maneuver it closer to the set. It was unexpectedly difficult. The wheels seemed to go their own direction, like a grocery cart with a bad wheel. It was only when the cameraman told her that while she was pushing it she had to turn a huge steering wheel encircling it horizontally, that she was able to move it smoothly on its rubber wheels to the edge of the rug.

"Okay," she said, coming back to her chair and clipping her microphone on. "It's heavy and clumsy and I had to be shown how to handle it, but obviously the technique can be learned, and if it's a question of muscle, there are lots of strong women around. Who says it's a man's world?"

"I do." He was still grinning, but this time with admiration, and then he began to talk. He talked about producers and directors who sat in control rooms and told cameramen where to move their cameras and where to focus them; he talked about the headset he wore that connected him to the control room; he began to ramble about cross shots and close-ups, dollies and microphones, booms and teleprompters.

278

But Elizabeth, concentrating on his voice, heard it change every time he talked about— "The camera," she said, cutting him off. "Tell me about the camera."

"Which one? My first? You wouldn't believe it—a little Brownie; remember them?" And then he was talking about Greg Roscov, who had wanted to be a photographer but finally had to admit he wasn't good enough to stand out amid all the competition. "Everybody could afford a camera, and the chances of people getting good pictures kept going up and if you weren't a genius . . . Well anyway, I gave it up. And then I found this little station in Chicago, one camera, one director, and people doing shows in Polish, Lithuanian, Italian, Spanish— you name it, they had it. Anybody who couldn't get on any other station could get on that one, and I don't know who the hell watched it—maybe just the relatives of whoever was on— but it didn't matter because they let me have the camera."

"*Have* the camera?" Elizabeth repeated softly. "The way you *have* a woman?"

"Well, yeh, that's the feeling . . . She can be a tricky mother, you know."

Elizabeth kept her face calm and interested, but excitement was running through her. There was always this perfect moment in an interview when she found the secret center that made each person special. "So it's a contest?" she asked quietly. "To see who's in charge?"

"No contest." His voice was scornful. "You push that mother around, you get her where you want her—doing what you want her to do—and it's the same when you get things right with your woman, getting her where you want her. And that's what life is all about, right? I mean you *feel* it."

"And I wouldn't, is that it?" Elizabeth asked. "That's what you mean by a man's world?"

He grinned again. "You got it. Be unnatural to see you wrestling . . . well, you wouldn't want to, right?"

"What about your wife?" she asked. "Do you treat her the same way?"

He shrugged. "Home and work . . . if you're smart you keep 'em separate. My wife would think I was some kind of

279

frigging idiot if she heard me talk this way." A slow frown sliced two deep lines between his eyes. "Shit." He looked around. "I forgot. They been running the tape?"

"It's only a test," Elizabeth said. Shading her eyes, she peered beyond the platform. "We have enough, don't we?" she asked in Boyle's direction.

"Plenty," his voice replied, but it was Tony who walked onto the set while workmen dimmed the lights and cameramen pulled back their cameras and someone appeared to take the microphone Elizabeth removed from her lapel.

Tony knelt before her chair. "You have made me the happiest man in the world. Dearest Elizabeth, you are an enchantress. Greg"—he turned and held out his hand and Greg automatically shook it—"you're a prince of a cameraman and you've made my day. We won't use it if you don't want, but I want to talk to you later; perhaps we can convince you what a gem you've given us. Thank you, Greg." His voice was dismissive. "I mean that. You've been enormously helpful to the show."

Standing, Greg looked down at Elizabeth. "Did I make an ass of myself?"

She stood beside him and kissed his cheek. "You were wonderful. You paid me the greatest compliment of all: you were honest. That's why I'm so grateful. And we won't do anything without your permission. I promise."

He nodded. "I believe that." He hesitated, then kissed Elizabeth as she had kissed him. "Thanks. I had a good time. You made me feel like you really cared about what I said."

Elizabeth watched him walk away. Tony, still on his knees, leaned an elbow on the leather chair and propped his head on his hand, watching her quizzically. "You're more impressed with honest Greg than with me. Whose idea was it to use makeup on him?"

"Mine. Tony, please stand up. I need the chair."

"Why?"

"Because I'm shaking all over. Was it really all right?"

"You know it was more than all right."

She nodded, sitting down as Tony perched on the arm of the

chair. "I'm looking for compliments. I know it was good. But it started badly and I was afraid—"

He kissed the top of her head. "Here comes Bo, full of energy. He'll be a pompous prig and pretend he knew all along how wonderful you are. You were sensational; you got honest Greg to bare every macho inch and you did it in a way that made everybody, *including Greg*, love you. From this moment, my enchanting Elizabeth, you are part of my show. And we are going to be the greatest team the world has ever seen."

"The way I heard it," Peter said, slamming an apple back and forth from one hand to the other, "or the way I *thought* I heard it, you and Dad were the ones who were working together, going off hand in hand into the sunset of a happy old age—"

"Peter, we've been through this," Elizabeth said evenly. She pushed harder against the rolling pin, stretching the pastry dough from the center into a large circle.

"Right, but that was before you hooked up with Tony the Twit. Television's Terrible Tasteless Twit."

"Cut it out, Peter. It's a good job."

"Oh, for—!" He slammed the apple from his right hand to his left. "A job? An ordinary job? This guy's been hanging around like a leech for years, and he finally gets you on his show, working with him, and you expect anybody to believe it's just a little old job like secretary or grocery clerk—"

"I expect you to believe what I say," Elizabeth snapped. She turned to look at him. "I have enough to think about these days without having to listen to insinuations from my son, who could be helping me get through a pretty bad time instead of making me feel even worse."

"I'm sorry; Christ, Mom, I'm sorry; I'm a dumb shit, a rotten bastard, a half-assed idiot—"

Elizabeth broke into laughter. "That's enough; you've convinced me. Now do you want to hear about my new job or shall we talk about something else?"

"Something else. You and Dad."

She sighed and turned back to the pastry, cutting small circles from the large one. "We've been talking about that for two weeks. I've told you all I can."

"Sure you have. The two of you've got different goals and different ideas about how to go after them so you decided to try doing it on your own for a while, but maybe everything will be back to normal by Christmas. Bull." He shot the apple back to his right hand. "Nobody'd be stupid enough to be-lieve—Okay, okay, I'm sorry; I believe you. I believe whatever you say. It's just that it's awful . . . *flat.*"

"Would you rather I made something up? Your father and another woman? Me and another man? Wife beating? Husband beating? Guns, knives, quarrels?"

"I'd rather you told me how you feel."

"Oh." She paused, then, concentrating, put a spoonful of cooked meat and spices in the center of one of the small circles, folded it over, and crimped the edges. She made four more, then said, "I feel lousy. I miss Matt and I'm scared because I don't know what he's thinking or how he might be changing or what he'll want in a month or two, and I'm worried about how this is affecting you and Holly and the way you feel about both of us, and I'm excited about being on Tony's show, and then I feel guilty because I'm not sure I should be happy about anything without Matt, and then I'm annoyed with myself be-cause men assume they'll have their own separate career, so why shouldn't I assume the same? Also," she added recklessly, "I miss making love to my husband; I don't like sleeping alone or going places alone—it's a lot easier being part of a couple—and I don't like lying awake at night wondering what I should have done differently to prevent all this from happening."

There was a silence. "Jesus," Peter whispered.

Over her shoulder, Elizabeth said gravely, "More compli-cated than you gave me credit for?"

He nodded, scowling at the apple in his hand. "I guess sometimes I forget other people besides me are mixed up."

She turned. "Peter, I'm sorry. We haven't talked about you at all. Mixed up how?"

He took a determined bite from the apple. "Nothing that can't be cured by ten years of rapid aging."

Elizabeth smiled. "Maya? Your Dad and me? Going to Stanford this fall? The job at the gallery? All of the above? None of the above?"

"All of the above. Don't worry about it, Mom. You've got enough on your mind."

"Part of what I've got on my mind is you. Where is Maya going in September? Stanford?"

"We don't know yet."

"Do you know if you want her to?"

"I told her I did."

"But people change."

"She thinks they should stay the same."

"So that's a problem."

Peter shrugged.

What's wrong with me? I'm so good at getting Greg Roscov to talk; why can't I be as good with my own son?

"Saw Luz yesterday," Peter said abruptly. "In the Plaza, getting signatures on a petition."

Elizabeth knew he was changing the subject, but her curiosity was piqued. "Petitions for what?"

"For her mother to run for the state legislature. Luz says if you run as an independent you need petitions."

"Oh, good for her," Elizabeth said. "She told me the other day she'd about made up her mind. Won't she be wonderful? She'll wake everybody up—"

"Luz doesn't think it's so great. She says Isabel's going to campaign against the dam, and probably mess up their chance to sell their land for a pile of money and get out. It's hard to tell Luz she's wrong, isn't it? I mean, I don't have to live there. I might like to, some day, but I have a choice; to me it's a nice town and to her it's a prison."

"That's just seventeen-year-old moaning. Luz isn't in a prison; she's already planning to go to the College of Santa Fe next year. And she's known for a long time that Isabel won't sell out or leave the valley, especially now, with a battle to fight. Would you really like to live in Nuevo?"

"Maybe someday. Since you bought that land there I've thought about it some. Will Holly be home for dinner?"

283

"She'll be here about eight-thirty; I told her we'd wait. Is that too late for you?"

"No, I'll munch something." He finished the apple and tossed it into the waste basket. "Mom."

Elizabeth looked at him, realizing with a pang how much he looked like his father. Except for his red hair, he could be Matt just a few years before they were married. Matt at twenty-three: tall, lean, serious, his deep blue eyes so full of love—

"Yes," she said hastily, to Peter. "What is it?"

"I didn't mean there was anything wrong about you and what's-his-name working together. I just think you got a raw deal from my father and I worry about—"

"Wait a minute." *Why am I always defending Matt—except when I'm alone at night?* "Let's get this straight, Peter. Your father and I made our decision together. We both agreed it was the best thing to do."

Peter scrutinized her. "He left you and us and the house and went off to live in the big city, and you thought it was the best thing to do?"

"Yes," she said steadily.

"Is he paying our bills?"

"The last time you asked that question I told you he is. Why should it change?"

"I thought it might have," he mumbled.

"You thought you'd catch me out. But I wasn't lying then and I'm not now. Why can't you trust us?"

"Because that bastard's gone off—"

"Peter!"

"—as if he's as free as a bird and you're left behind with everything on your shoulders—"

"That's enough, Peter!"

"—and it isn't fair—!"

"Probably not," Elizabeth said, surprising him into silence. "But it's the way things are right now and I'm not whining about it and I don't expect you to either, or to talk about your father the way you just did. Ever. Is that clear? I appreciate your trying to protect me—"

"Well, goddamit, somebody has to!"

284

"Then protect me by taking out the garbage without being nagged into it every day!" At the sudden hurt in his eyes, she said quickly, "I'm sorry, I'm sorry, Peter; I didn't mean that; I do appreciate you; it's just that there are different ways of protecting people and you could protect me best by being my friend. Holly won't be here much—her schedule is so heavy—and I do need help around the house and someone to keep me company. That would be enough. And it would be good for both of us, to be friends."

He nodded. "I guess. But it seems like I'm letting him off the hook by doing the things he should be doing."

Elizabeth opened her mouth, then closed it. In a minute she turned back to the counter and began filling and sealing the remaining *empanadas*. "Why don't you go talk to him about that?" she asked casually.

"I talked to him about it on the phone. He said the same things you did. Different goals. All that shit. Sorry."

"But if you were with him, you could get more personal—don't you think?—than on the telephone."

"He asked me to come. Both of us. I said no."

Elizabeth's hands stilled. "I think you should go, Peter. You can't shut him out."

"He shut us out."

"But he's asking you to come to Houston."

"You want me to go? Us? You want us to go?"

"I want you to have a father. Of course I want you to go."

There was a long silence. Peter pulled the garbage bag out of the wastebasket and twisted the top into a knot. Elizabeth started to say she wasn't ready to have it taken out, then stopped, smiling to herself. *Serves me right; he'll probably take it out ten times a day.* He went through the house to the garbage cans at the side of the driveway, then came back. "Well," he said, stretching the word into a drawl, as if it really weren't all that important, "I guess it wouldn't hurt for Holly and me to visit the old man. Check out what's going on, and all. Only thing is: would you mind paying for the tickets? Otherwise I'd have to just about clean out my savings account, and then I might not get to college and I'd still be here when I'm old and gray, taking out the garbage on feeble feet . . . ."

Elizabeth turned and rested her arms on his shoulders, keeping her floury hands away from his shirt. "Of course I'll buy the tickets. And I love you, Peter; you're very special. I don't know what"—she stopped and swallowed hard, fighting back sudden tears—"I don't know what I'd do without you, my dear, dear protector."

Peter and Holly sat stiffly, hands in their laps, faces turned toward the window, as the plane descended over Houston's Intercontinental Airport. "I just think you ought to try to understand him," Holly murmured. "Instead of acting as if everything is his fault."

"It is his fault."

The plane touched the runway and, as it taxied to the gate, clicks like popping corn were heard as seat belts were sprung apart. "Please keep your seats," the steward said into his microphone, "until the captain has stopped at the jetway." But everywhere people were standing, taking briefcases and sports jackets from overhead bins, pulling baggage from beneath their seats. Holly and Peter sat still. "You'll kiss him hello, won't you?" Holly asked.

Peter shrugged. "You can do that part. I've outgrown it."

"Fathers and sons kiss each other if they love each other," Holly observed.

"Well." He shrugged again.

The plane had stopped. Watching everyone stand packed together in the aisle, going nowhere, Holly resumed their earlier argument. "Daddy *did* have to get out of Santa Fe. It's too small for him and too slow, and Mother doesn't seem to care that he needs—"

"*Doesn't seem to care?* What the hell does that mean? He's in Houston because he's not appreciated in little old Santa Fe? Is that it?"

"No—!"

"Mom drove him away, then. Is that what you mean? She's

sitting at home, missing him like crazy, worrying about the future, but according to you she drove him away!"

"I didn't say that! I said she doesn't seem to understand him."

"Oh, for Christ's sake. She's been married to him for nineteen years; she understands him better than anybody in the world."

"Who says? People change and the people around them don't always change with them."

At the obvious truth of that, thinking of his latest disagreement with Maya, Peter hesitated.

"And," Holly went on, "even if she does understand him, she doesn't seem to realize how much he wants to *do!*"

"He told you all this, of course," Peter said, his voice heavy with sarcasm. "Explained his feelings and intentions in detail before leaving our happy home."

Holly looked at her hands. "You know he didn't. But he called us from Houston the next day."

"And explained his feelings and intentions in detail . . ."

"All right, he didn't! He never has, not really. Isn't that the reason we came here? To ask him ourselves instead of only hearing it from Mother?"

As the aisle began to clear, Peter stood up and yanked his duffle from the overhead bin. "I'll be damned if I'm sure why we came. Probably shouldn't have . . ."

"Oh, stop it," Holly said wearily. Reaching down, she pulled her overnight bag from beneath the seat in front of her. "Could you shut up, just for the weekend, so we could try to have a good time? And maybe learn something? Our own parents, and sometimes I think we don't know them at all. Maybe we could find out some things . . ."

"Why not?" Peter asked, abruptly switching moods. He put an arm around Holly. "Here we are in the golden buckle of the sun belt, as the local cheerleaders like to call it; we'll put on golden smiles and have a golden time and everything we touch will turn to gold."

"Nice idea," Holly said with a wistful smile, and then they were moving up the aisle and out of the plane, and in a moment

287

they saw Matt, taller than everyone else, his eyes scanning the passengers and lighting in quick warmth when Holly waved.

"My apartment first," he said, holding Holly as she hugged him. "Then I thought we'd spend the afternoon in Galveston. Unless you had something special in mind?"

"Just to be with you," said Holly. She gave Peter a sharp look.

"Hi, Dad," Peter said. Awkwardly, he put his hand on Matt's arm, feeling the pleasurable shock it always gave him when he realized the two of them were the same height. Then, seemingly by itself, his hand moved across Matt's shoulders until he was embracing his father and Matt's arms were around him and they were holding each other and kissing each other's cheek. And Peter, unexpectedly, felt a surge of relief.

Matt talked about Galveston as they walked through the terminal to the parking deck, describing the hurricane and tidal waves of 1900 that had killed six thousand people and destroyed the port and the town. "That's when they built the seawall. Wide enough for cars to drive and people to walk—"

"Is this *yours?*" Peter exclaimed.

Matt looked from the car he was unlocking to Peter's awe-struck face. "It belongs to Rourke Enterprises. I get to use it."

"Is that the thing around here?" Peter asked. "For the company car to be a forty thousand dollar Mercedes?"

"Cars," Matt said briefly, putting Peter's duffle and Holly's overnight bag in the trunk and slamming it shut as Holly got in the back seat. "Rourke has four. Other companies have a dozen or more. And yes, that's the thing around here." He leaned against the hood. "There are five hundred and fifty square miles to Houston, so people spend a lot of time in their cars. And they develop a deep, intimate, often passionate relationship with them." As he talked, he stroked the car with long, delicate passes of his fingertips. Peter began to grin. Finally he burst out laughing, and then they were laughing together. "So you see why it's the thing to have Mercedes or Cadillacs as company cars." They sat in the front seat, and Matt turned the key and then the air conditioning controls. "Give it a minute and it will be fine in here."

"Is it always this hot?" Holly asked. Ever since they left the terminal, she'd felt as if she'd walked into a wall of humid heat. "How do people stand it?"

"It's like this only about half the year, and people stand it because they live here, just as we accept the dust in Santa Fe. And there are the winter months to look forward to."

"How hot is it?" Peter asked.

"Now? About ninety, I suppose." Matt turned onto the expressway. "But what makes Houston memorable is that the humidity is ninety percent or more. It's a climate beloved of mosquitos, and, before air conditioning, not much else."

"I like Santa Fe better," Holly said. "You don't feel like you're sagging."

Matt smiled. "A dry desert is definitely better than a soggy bayou. But you won't sag too far, Holly; everything *is* air conditioned. Speaking of which, I should warn you: I have a new apartment."

"Warn?" Peter echoed. "It's like the Mercedes?"

Matt looked at him sharply. "A little bit. It's a bigger place than I need, and the building is a little intimidating, but I'll be doing some entertaining, so it's probably not a bad place for me to be, at least for a while." Silence fell. Then he began talking about Houston's history and its future, telling the anecdotes he'd been storing up just for this moment, so he could put off the accusations of his children.

Though they were hardly children anymore, he thought, driving through the black wrought-iron gates of his building. They were a man and woman, beautiful and bright, with intelligence and charm and the right to make certain demands on him. But that describes my wife, too, he thought, and it hasn't been enough to stop the changes in our lives. He wished Elizabeth had come, too. He should have called her, invited her himself, instead of that casual suggestion tossed out to Peter on the telephone, almost as if he didn't quite mean it. Well, maybe he really hadn't quite meant it, and Peter picked that up. Maybe he'd really wanted a weekend alone with his kids. Maybe he thought they could learn something about each other if they had time to relax and talk.

Holly and Peter had been eyeing the building, tall and white with terraces at every corner. It stood alone, separated from the nearby townhouses by landscaped grounds and gardens behind a high stone wall. Matt had driven through the gates and straight ahead to the garage ramp, bypassing the branch of the driveway that curved around a fountain and beneath a canopy sheltering the smoked glass entrance doors, but Peter and Holly had glimpsed the uniformed doorman at his desk. "Keeps out the riffraff," Peter murmured. But he said nothing to his father, following silently as they took the elevator to the thirty-second floor.

Matt still wasn't used to the apartment, and when he heard Holly's exclamations of wonder, and saw Peter's stony face, he felt as if he too were seeing it for the first time, as he had three weeks earlier when he'd mentioned to Nicole he'd be looking for a place of his own instead of the furnished apartment he'd been renting. She had told him Rourke owned three, for visitors, and she'd just finished decorating one of them. "It's a little big, but of course you'll be entertaining, so you can use the space, and the colors are perfect for you. In fact, it seems made for you."

"Was it?" Matt asked abruptly.

She smiled. "Not exclusively. But Keegan did mention that you'd likely be here most of the time, after a while, and it would be nice to have something in keeping with your position waiting for you, and since the apartment did need redecorating, it seemed like a good idea . . ." She had looked at him with the combination of honesty and calculation that always piqued his interest because it left him wondering what she was really thinking behind those magnificent amber eyes. "Well, of course I decorated it for you," she said. "I was thinking of you the whole time. But if you decide not to use it, my feelings won't be hurt. I'll even help you find something else, if you'd like."

He hadn't needed to find anything else. Once past the marble-floored lobby, paneled in butternut and hung with crystal chandeliers, he'd been unable to resist the luxurious rooms, especially the space, three times larger than the apartment he'd been renting, and the combination of lightness and solid comfort Nicole had achieved with shades of blue, gray, and rust, and flashes of white, against walls of serene, pale gray. The apartment, taking one whole floor of the building, was wrapped in glass walls, and when Matt walked in with Peter and Holly all the blinds were partially closed against the relentless June sun, but, still, light was everywhere, brightening the huge living room, dining room, and study, reflecting off oak and brass, so there seemed no barrier between the brightness of the Texas sky and the earth-and-sky colors of the rooms.

His lips tight, Peter followed Matt and Holly. Years of studying art made him respond to the paintings and silver and gold sculptures, and the elegance of the rooms, but he didn't feel comfortable in them: they were too perfect, everything matching everything else, everything in its place. He thought of their low-ceilinged house in Santa Fe, with its vivid colors and casual air, always sort of rumpled because somebody hadn't put something away, cool because of thick adobe walls rather than air conditioning hissing at you. It wasn't perfect, but at least it looked like people really lived in it. Just then they came to the larger of the two bedrooms and he saw his Dad's slippers, side by side next to the bed. Suddenly he felt like crying. Shit, he thought; I'll be damned if he'll see me *cry*. He turned and left the room, and in a flat voice said, "I guess you're making a lot of money now."

"Two hundred thousand a year," Matt replied just as flatly. "Your mother knows that; there's no reason why you shouldn't. Holly, here's your room; Peter gets the study. The sofa bed's ready for you, Peter; I made it up earlier."

"No maid?" Peter asked. He tried to sneer but he was still having trouble with a lump in his throat.

"I have a maid. She doesn't come on Saturday." Matt opened doors. "Holly's bathroom. Peter's. Kitchen. I stocked the refrigerator; help yourself whenever you like. Now I have a couple of quick phone calls to make, and then we'll get going. Did you bring jeans? Why don't you change while I make my calls; you'll be more comfortable. Sound okay?"

"Of course," Holly said, feeling sorry for him because he was even more nervous than they were. But she felt sorry for

291

Peter, too: angry Peter, trying so hard not to love his father. I'm the only one who understands everybody, Holly thought. I know Daddy's here because you can't let a really big chance go by when it comes, and I know Mother wanted to keep our family together, but she shouldn't have tried to hold Daddy back because that only pushed him away and I wonder if he's got any—

But Holly didn't want to think about Matt and other women; she would rather believe there was no one else in his life but his wife, who didn't understand him, and his daughter, who did. And when Matt gave her a quick hug as they went down in the elevator, and asked her to sit in front while they drove so she could tell him about the opera company, it was easy to believe she was right.

"We start at nine," she said as they drove out of the densely crowded city. On the highway, Matt set the cruise control and they glided in their air-conditioned cocoon between flat fields dotted with small oil and gas wells, their arms pumping rhythmically above the green fields. "My first class is Body Movement. Walking, sitting, turning, all the things you never think about but there are so many ways to do them! And to show how you feel with your body instead of always using your voice and your face . . . !"

Matt smiled. "You walk like a dancer."

"I'm learning, I'm practicing, but I have so much to learn! Where was I? Oh, Body Movement. After that we have classes in makeup and hair styling and languages and how to move and stand on stage; we have voice lessons and also we have individual coaching; we go to master classes taught by visiting singers and experts on the operas . . . what did I leave out?"

"Rehearsals," said Peter dryly from the back seat. "They're so dull you forgot them."

They all laughed and Holly thought what a lovely sound it was; it made everything seem fine. "They're more exciting than anything," she told Matt. "It's all new and I've never done anything like it, but, it's the funniest thing, in a way it's like I've been getting ready for it all my life. Do you know what I mean?" Matt gave her a brief look and a nod; he was listening intently. "We're doing six operas, in repertory—we're learning them all at once!—and you can't imagine what it's like, Daddy . . . everything feels so . . . *bright,* and exciting, even the hard work, because you're with professionals—and they've been all over the world and they know so much and they're so good!—and it's like you're sort of on trial but everybody's helping you, too, because we all want the same thing—a perfect performance—and you're always stretching to be better than you are because there's always sort of a new test coming up, not a test, really, it's more like a new challenge, and you want to be perfect and impress everybody and do all the things you've always dreamed about . . ."

Her voice trailed away as she watched Matt's face. She glanced behind her, at Peter, scowling as he contemplated his father's profile. "That's how you feel," she said to Matt. "Working for Mr. Rourke and meeting all those other newspaper people and politicians. You feel the same way, don't you?"

"In a nutshell," Matt said quietly. His face was somber.

Holly looked out the window. She didn't really want to hear about *his* exciting life. "Look at that," she said, gesturing toward a landscaped shopping plaza. "Palm trees and cactus, side by side. How can they both grow in the same place?"

"And holly," Matt added. "Those hedges are holly, bright and beautiful, like their namesake." He put out his hand and smoothed the back of her head. "And they all grow here because they're hardy breeds. It doesn't take long for them to adapt to a foreign environment and begin to thrive."

"Like newspaper publishers," said Peter.

The car was silent. "And even after the season starts," Holly said, as if there had been no break in her description of her schedule, "when we have performances every night, we still have classes and lectures all day, and, sometimes, auditions for new parts in the operas. And that goes on for three months."

"A busy summer," said Matt. "And I can't imagine a more wonderful one." The silence returned. "Peter," he said, "we'll talk in Galveston."

"Sure," Peter said.

For the rest of the drive, Matt and Holly talked, until they

293

drove across the long bridge to the island and Matt gave them a sightseeing tour along streets lined with oleander, past houses built in the 1840s, and enormous Victorian mansions being restored and opened to the public. They drove to the beach and Matt parked on the sand. The tide was coming in, splashing in long gray waves that broke slowly and slowly receded, leaving a thin outline of foam that faded and disappeared. Egrets and spoonbills rose on huge wings, settling back on the sand a few feet from where they began. Gulls cried to each other; slanting rays of sunlight glinted off shells at the water line.

Holly pulled off her loafers and socks. "You too, Peter," she said, her voice gentle but insistent. "Because I thought we'd have a race, but if you're groaning about sand in your shoes, and stopping to shake them out, you'll lose. Of course you'll lose anyway, because I'm faster than you and my Body Movement Class has taught me the proper way to run, but if you're barefoot you might have a *chance*—"

"Ha!" snorted Peter. He knew she was trying to distract him and cheer him up, and he appreciated it, but since when did she think she could beat him? And what was this shit about the "proper way to run"? Without another word, he pulled off his shoes and socks and ran past her to the beach.

He heard Holly's outraged cry and lengthened his stride, but he didn't really care who won; he took deep breaths of the fresh smell of the ocean and heard the calls of a dozen different birds, and as his muscles stretched and his bare soles slapped against the ridges in the hard, wet sand, all of a sudden he felt so free and joyous he wanted to shout. Even when Holly's shadow appeared beside him, and he knew she really *had* learned to run, he felt wonderful, and he turned and grinned at her to show her that everything was fine.

Matt watched them: his two long-limbed, beautiful youngsters, laughing together as they raced, kicking up small spurts of sand and sprays of water as they dodged the incoming tide. Loving them, he ached for them. *I wish they could keep this all their lives: laughter and freedom and the whole world stretching in front of them* . . .

But later, after the three of them had walked together and

294

found a place to sit on the dry sand farthest from the water, he said, "The trouble is, we can't hold onto the freedom we have when we're young. The minute we decide where we're going, what we want to do with our lives, what we want to be, our choices get narrower: the steps we have to take, the rules we have to follow, the connections we have to make with other people, whether we want to or not . . ."

"You mean you're living in Houston and hating every minute of it," Peter said.

"I mean I'm living in Houston because that's the only choice I had, to be what I want to be."

Peter tried to recapture his anger, but he couldn't do it. The sun beat down, mixed with a cool ocean breeze and saltwater smell, and he sifted warm sand through his fingers. Slowly, he said to Matt, "Maybe you shouldn't be . . . whatever you want to be. Not if you've got a family to think about."

"Well, let's talk about that." Matt leaned back, his hands in the warm sand, and gazed at a quartet of white pelicans standing in the foam of breaking waves, looking like a group of politicians debating which direction to go. "I have two children, but they're grown up now. My son is leaving for college in a couple of months; my daughter leaves next year. And for a long time they've been building their own lives, pulling away from their parents, not needing them in the ways they used to. Even if I still lived with you, you'd be the ones to go away—"

"Mother isn't going anywhere!"

"She could have; I asked her to. She made a different choice."

"Why?" Holly asked.

"That's something she should tell you herself. I'm surprised you haven't asked her."

"We have," Holly said. "She said you have different goals."

"She's right. And the goals I've set for myself—"

"Goals!" growled Peter. "You two sound like a college catalogue."

Matt chuckled. "Maybe we do." He became serious. "I know, what you want to hear about are feelings. Well, I feel your mother wants to hold me back from the goals—sorry—from

295

going as far as I can in running a newspaper chain that can give me the kind of power and influence I've always dreamed of. And your mother doesn't like it when I say I intend to concentrate on that and put off other things until I'm established; at least until I know how far I can go. She doesn't like what I'm doing; she doesn't like the people I'm doing it with; she doesn't like the decisions I'm making; she doesn't like the way I think about the future; she doesn't like the way I remember the past."

"But she likes you," Holly said in a small voice.

At that, a sense of loss swept over Matt, and his fingers clenched in the loose sand. But he kept his voice even. "We like each other. But it isn't enough, Holly. Look: what would you have done if we'd told you to give up the opera this summer and move to Houston?"

"I wouldn't do it."

"Of course you wouldn't. It would have been the wrong thing for you to do. And we would have been terribly wrong if we told you to. No one should tell another person to give up a great chance. They come too rarely."

"Then what do you do when you disagree?"

"You compromise."

"Which means doing it your way," said Peter.

"Maybe. At least trying it for a while."

"Mother needs to be taken care of!" Peter said flatly. "You left her to handle the house and a job—two jobs—"

"Two?"

"Her column and what's-his-name's show."

"Why do you always pretend to forget it?" Holly exclaimed. "Tony Rourke. And his show is 'Anthony,' and Mother does one interview a week on it." She looked at Matt. "I thought you knew."

"She said something about it, in May." His eyes were on the horizon. "I guess I wasn't paying much attention."

"Well, anyway," Peter went on insistently, "she's got the house and two jobs and our problems to listen to, and she still works with Saul sometimes at the *Chieftain*, and I don't know what else, but she's all alone—!"

"She has you and Holly. She has her parents, her friends—"

"She doesn't have a husband living with her! When I leave, who's going to take care of her?"

Matt's eyebrows went up. "You don't have much confidence in your mother, do you?"

"What the hell does that mean?"

"You don't think your mother can take care of herself. I do. I trust her to know what she's doing, and make her own decisions."

"Shit!" Peter flung himself away and strode to the water's edge.

"Daddy, that wasn't nice," Holly said hesitantly.

Matt watched his son's lanky figure bending and straightening as he picked up stones and skipped them across the surface of the water. "He has to understand that we're old enough to manage our own lives."

"But he thinks you're managing Mother's."

"Then he's wrong."

Holly looked the other way, gazing pensively at the pelicans, still grouped in serious discussion. "Do you think you'll be home by Christmas?"

"Home? You mean living in Santa Fe?"

She nodded.

"Holly, I can't . . . why do you ask?"

"Mother thinks you will."

Matt sat up, his arms around his knees. "I don't know whether she really believes that or not. But she knows how much is at stake here—so do you and Peter, because I've told you often enough—and she knows I can't just walk away from it. Not now; not at Christmas. Sweetheart"—he put his arm around Holly and she rested her head on his shoulder—"I love you and Peter and I love to be with you. I'm proud to be your father; I'm proud to be your friend. And I expect us to visit and write letters and talk on the telephone. But I'm not moving back to Santa Fe. A long time ago I changed direction for my father, and then I stayed where I was because you and Peter were young and needed security—and we did, too, I guess. But you're not young anymore, and your mother and I don't need the kind of security we clung to for so many years . . . we have more money than ever before, for one thing. So I can't go backward. There's room for your mother in that enormous apartment I have, if she decides to share my life again. You can tell her that; it's hardly a secret."

Holly sat straight. "You want her to come to Houston? You miss her? You need her?"

There was a barely perceptible pause. "Of course."

"And you want me to tell her that, too?" Holly asked shrewdly.

Matt sighed. "Holly, give us time. Are you and Peter so sure your mother is really unhappy about this? She's never had a life of her own; she's never even had any time to herself. Neither have I. Maybe we both need it, to explore on our own. Then we'll see. Give us time; don't push us."

Holly's eyes met his. "That sounds like the kind of thing you'd say to make yourself feel better about what you've done."

Matt felt as if he'd been punched in the stomach. "I'll have to think about that," he began, then saw with relief that Peter was coming toward them, scuffing sand with his toes.

He stopped in front of Matt. "I guess you're right. I was thinking about Maya—she's already worrying about when I go to Stanford—and I just thought Mother must feel the same way because she's a woman and she's staying home . . . I just want her to be happy."

"I know," Matt said gently.

"It's not that I don't want *you* to be happy, too, but . . ."

"I know," Matt said again. "And I'm proud of you, because you care so much about your family, even when you're about to go off to make your own life. And Holly, too: both of you ought to be all wrapped up in yourselves and the exciting things happening to you, but you still worry about us. That means a great deal to me." There was a pause. He slid a few inches to the right. "Need some room?"

Looking to left and right along the thirty-six miles of beach, Peter broke into a grin. "I *was* thinking it was a little crowded . . ."

They laughed, and as Peter sat down, Matt said, "Why is

Maya worried about your leaving? I thought she was planning to go to Stanford with you."

"It's too late," Peter replied. "She kept arguing with her mother about Argentina, but now that she's won and her mother says she doesn't have to go, it's past the deadline for fall. I'm not sure she could even make it for winter. She needs a scholarship, too."

"Maybe I could help. Sometimes a phone call to the right person . . ." He paused. "Or would you rather I stayed out of it?"

"No, it's just that . . . Shit, it's a lousy thing to say, but—"

"But you think you'd like to be free for this new adventure."

Peter grunted. "I don't like to say it. Or even think it. Like I'm betraying her. I guess you know what that feels like."

"I guess in a way I do."

Holly listened to the two voices weaving together like the notes of a song. After a while she joined them, her musical voice a counterpoint to their deep ones. And it was like that all weekend. They had dinner at the Wentletrap, changing in the restrooms from jeans and T-shirts to a white summer dress for Holly and slacks, jackets and ties for Peter and Matt, and Holly thought what a handsome family they made, sitting in the dining room of the restored building that looked more European than American, eating fish caught that day right off the island and drinking white wine.

Matt had made so many plans for Sunday they had to choose among them. Peter chose a tour of outdoor sculptures and they spent the morning driving through empty streets connecting the cluster of dramatic skyscrapers that were Houston's downtown, to see works of Miro, Dubuffet, Nevelson, even Claus Oldenburg's "Geometric Mouse X" that he'd heard about but had seen only in books. Holly chose brunch amid the marble and silks and tapestries of the Remington Hotel, and they lingered over quail and snapper and hot almond cake with amaretto in the greenhouse off the dining room. Their table was near a harpist and flutist whose music floated about them like bright crystals in the sun and they talked as if they had all the time in the world and had never been apart.

That evening, after an afternoon of museums and Hermann Park's planetarium and zoological gardens, and what Matt called a down-home dinner at the Confederate House, Peter said, "It was a better weekend than I expected."

"For me, too," Matt said, echoing his son's honesty. They were driving again—it seemed to Peter and Holly that most of what they'd done all weekend was drive; everything was so far from everything else—and he said, "We'll stop at home to pick up your luggage and then go straight to the airport."

"Home," Peter said pointedly.

"My home," said Matt. He drove through the wrought-iron gate. "I live here." In the apartment, Matt went to the study where Peter had slept and turned on his telephone answering machine. "As soon as you're finished packing, we'll go."

Stuffing their bags with clothes and new books and shells from the beach at Galveston, Holly and Peter half-listened to the recorded voices greeting Matt: a man with a problem about circulation in Denver; another with a question about an editorial on a new ski resort at Pagosa Springs; and then a woman's warm, husky voice. "Matt, I've reserved Tony's wine cellar for next Thursday night, to say goodbye to my friends before I leave for cooler climates. Please come; it won't be a proper going-away party unless everyone I'll miss most is part of it. Call me soon."

Peter's face was like stone when Matt looked up and met his eyes. "'Tony's wine cellar'?" Holly asked from the doorway. "Does Tony Rourke have a house here?"

"Tony's is a restaurant," Matt said. "No relation to Tony Rourke. The wine cellar is a good place for lunch, and it's reserved for private parties at night. Peter, when your mother is invited to parties—"

"She hasn't been."

"She will be. Will you tell her to stay home?"

Peter looked at his feet. *My mother doesn't know anybody with a voice like that.* "I guess not."

"I hope not. Both of us need friends." He reset the answering machine and picked up their luggage. "Ready to go?"

When they were in the car, retracing their route of the day before, this time with Holly in the back seat, Matt said, "You'll come back soon, won't you? I want to be as much a part of your lives as I can."

"Double lives," Peter mumbled.

"What?" asked Holly, leaning forward.

"Double lives, double families, double homes, double cities. We used to have one family. Now we've got two."

"When that happens," Matt said, pulling into a parking place at the airport, "make the best of both of them."

"Sure," Peter said. He thought about it while they walked through the terminal to their gate. And when it came time to board the plane and Holly hugged and kissed her father goodbye and Peter self-consciously shook hands with him, he couldn't keep from saying, "You're really cold-blooded about the whole thing, aren't you?"

"No," said Matt. He pulled Peter to him and hugged him. "I have a lot of second thoughts, and I miss you all. But this is what I have to do."

"Are you going to call that woman back?"

"Yes. She's a friend. But listen to me, both of you." He held their hands in his. *"We're* going to be friends, more than ever before, I promise that, and we're going to help each other. And I'll try to make you understand what I'm doing and why I think it's important. I'd like your approval. And your love."

"Well, you've got *that,"* Holly said. They walked to the gate. "We'll give your love to Mother, too."

And they went through the doorway to the plane, their last view of Matt the same as the one yesterday morning: taller than everyone else, standing alone, hoping for their smile.

CHAPTER 10

Nicole let the chiffon stole slip from her bare shoulders and settled with a sigh into the curve of the wing-backed chair. "My favorite place to relax," she said in her husky voice, and smiled at Matt as he turned back to her from a quick study of the antiques and fine paintings that had furnished La Colombe d'Or since its days as a private home. "The Fondrens built it; they were one of the founders of Exxon. They called it Humble Oil, then, though not much in Houston is humble—"

"Or stays that way," Matt finished, smiling with her. "But you're right; it's a beautiful place."

"And nicer than usual, with good company after a weekend entertaining an extremely dull crowd. How was yours? Work or play?"

"A little of both," Matt replied wryly. "I entertained my offspring and fended off criticism."

"Surely not the whole weekend."

"No, mostly we had a good time. It's wonderful being with them. But now and then, without warning, there were jabs."

She tilted her head. "Mostly from your son, I'd bet. Protecting his mother."

Matt picked up the oversize wine list. "What would you like? Wine? Cognac?"

"Amontillado, please." She seemed about to say more, then was silent, and Matt admired her for it. He'd made it clear they were not to discuss his family, and she accepted it without comment.

He put the wine list aside. "Who was the dull crowd you entertained this weekend?"

"Some investors Keegan is wooing for a hotel and conference center in Breckenridge. I learned more about square footage and tax revenues and Colorado politics than I ever wanted to know. You and I can find more interesting subjects to talk about."

"Your trip, then. I didn't know you were going out of town." A waiter approached, and he ordered the same sherry for both of them. "You didn't mention it last week."

"I'm sorry; I suppose I assume everyone knows. No one stays in Houston in July and August, Matt."

"Except a few working people."

"But you could get away, couldn't you? Keegan wouldn't crack such a mean whip—"

"What does he have to do with it? I make my own schedule; I know how much work I have to do."

"I'm sorry. I shouldn't have said that." The waiter put their drinks on the table. "All of a sudden we seem to be angry with each other."

"I'm the one who should apologize. I'm jealous because you're getting out of this muggy metropolis. Where are you going?"

"Maine. I own a small place there."

Matt thought of her sprawling house and the apartment she had decorated for him. "You have your own definition of 'small.' A small house? A small hotel? A small town?"

"A small island." She looked quizzically at him and they laughed. "With a rather small house, and a truly small motor boat to get to the small town on the shore."

"Plus a small staff."

"Two people. In the summer my needs are simple, my wants are few."

"Nothing about you is simple."

She gave him a long, slow smile, then raised her glass. "To simple desires."

He touched her glass with his, and she sat perfectly still, letting him look at her, as she had at her party. In the muted light from antique glass fixtures, her bare shoulders were pale against a black strapless dress embroidered in black roses. At her throat was an ebony rose on a silver chain; her hair was a cloud of black darkening her amber eyes. Her scent was elusive, faintly spicy; her fingers long, with polished nails; the corners of her mouth curved with pleasure at the look in his eyes. "I'm glad I meet with your approval."

"And if you didn't?" Matt asked.

"I'd change what you didn't approve . . . or change your mind about approving it."

He chuckled. "Which would be easier?"

"It would depend on where we were, and what we were doing."

The spiciness of her perfume blended with the heady aroma of his sherry and, instinctively, Matt sat back in his chair, putting distance between them. "Tell me about Maine," he said. "I've never been there."

"Cool and forested," she replied, once more letting him guide their conversation, once more doing it without visible disappointment or anger. "Rocky soil and shoreline, high waves, chilly nights with black shadows from a white moon. Wild and beautiful and the perfect antidote to the bayou and a season of parties."

"You enjoy parties."

"I couldn't live without them. But Maine is like the day after an all-night bash: a cool place to stretch out and relax, relive the night before, plan the next one . . ."

"Plot the future."

"Plots are for writers and spies. I dream. And try to make my plans match my dreams."

The waiter paused at their table. Matt ordered two more sherries, then, smiling easily, said, "Well put. Now tell me more about your small island."

A shadow crossed her eyes, gone the instant Matt identified

304

it as her first betrayal of impatience. But then she did as he asked, talking pleasantly about her ten-room house and gazebo surrounded by pines; the gardens tended by a local gardener who grew snapdragons, asters, and dahlias in planters atop the shallow soil, as well as cherry tomatoes and bibb lettuce for her table; days spent swimming off the rocks, water skiing, shopping for handcrafts in the towns along the coast. Undemanding, amusing, worldly, she told him in a dozen unspoken ways how attractive she found him. The perfect companion, Matt thought, and was thinking of extending his original invitation for a drink to include dinner when, as if anticipating him, she mentioned a dinner party where she was expected at eight-thirty. "And I'd better get home or I won't have time to change." She slipped out of her chair. "I've enjoyed this. If you wait too long to call again, I'll call you, so we can repeat it."

Peter would have snorted, Matt thought as they parted in front of the hotel; he'd have said she was playing games. And he would have been right. But even Peter had been captivated by Nicole's voice on the recorder. Peter would understand her attraction, and the pleasure a man would take in her games— and in being pursued.

Though, even understanding that, Peter still would have found a way to make a pointed comment about his mother—to make sure his father hadn't forgotten her.

His father hadn't forgotten.

Matt thought about Elizabeth more now, it seemed, than before their break at the end of May. By the beginning of July, he still found himself frequently reaching for the telephone to call her. But often there was no answer. She was probably shopping, he thought. Or interviewing for her column, or that damn television show. Or visiting Isabel or her parents. Or talking shop with Saul at the *Chieftain*. How the hell could he keep track of what she did with her days? Or her nights? Sometimes she was there and they exchanged a few words; other times he talked to his children or Lydia, who frequently answered to say she and Spencer were taking Peter and Holly to dinner because Elizabeth was in Los Angeles.

But his own days and nights were so crowded he couldn't think about Elizabeth for long before something broke in. As soon as it became known that he was living in Houston, his calendar filled up with meetings, paperwork piled high on his desk, his hours at the office grew longer. He was still buying papers, based on Chet's reports; he talked every week to each of his twenty-one editors and tried to keep up with the politics in all twenty-one cities and whatever local issues got people aroused enough to fork over twenty-five cents a day to read about them. Between telephone calls he read reports on circulation campaigns, contests to capture new readers, plans for changes in layout, whether using color would attract enough new readers to justify the expense, how important readers thought bigger weather maps and longer television listings were since they left less space for local stories—dozens of reports, dozens of questions that someone had to answer.

"You can't do it all," Chet told him as he added a folder to the stack on Matt's desk. "New people always think they can, but of course they fail. You should tell Mr. Rourke you need an assistant, maybe two or—"

"Thank you," Matt said curtly. "I'll tell Mr. Rourke what I need when I need to. Is that the financial report on the *Austin Star?*"

"Right." His face blank, Chet turned to go. "They're anxious to sell. If you have any questions, don't hesitate to call me."

Absently, Matt nodded. Elizabeth would say he should be more careful with Chet. And she'd be right. But he didn't have the patience; lately his temper was more erratic than ever. And he didn't have time, either, to tiptoe around Chet. Not only because of paperwork and phone calls and traveling two or three days a week, but also because he still was being tested, his decisions scrutinized, his activities monitored. He saw Rourke daily, and was part of everything that affected his newspapers, yet he felt he had to tread carefully, constantly proving himself.

"I'd better do something about this," he said to Rourke a few weeks after Peter and Holly's visit. Houston wilted under the heat of late July and everything seemed to have slowed down except the work pouring across his desk, which included the memo he brought to Rourke from the editor of the *Tucson Call*.

"We might be in for a strike," it said. "No one died in the pressroom accident, but Dugan thinks we're in a weak position because of it, and he's demanding we begin negotiating a new contract now, six months before the old one expires; otherwise he's hinting about a strike over unsafe working conditions. We barely broke even in the first six months; I don't think we could weather a strike."

"I'll be there Monday," Matt told Rourke, showing him the memo. "I've already rearranged my schedule for next week."

Rourke frowned. "We had good relations with Dugan. What happened?"

"Damned if I know. Negotiations were set to begin in a couple of months; everybody was happy. Something tore it apart, and it wasn't that accident. That's one of the things I'm looking into."

Rourke nodded thoughtfully. "What's wrong with the *Call*, Matt? You've had it seven months; long enough to show some progress."

"I don't know what's wrong. Equipment and morale were in bad shape when we bought it, but—"

"But it was the same with Graham's chain. Half the papers you buy are in trouble and you pull them out. Why not this one?"

Matt shook his head. "I can't get the staff moving. It's sluggish, as if it's determined to prove the paper won't make it. The other day I had the crazy idea they'd been bribed to throw it, like a baseball team throwing a game. But of course that *is* crazy: they'd be doing themselves out of a job."

Rourke leaned back in his chair. "I understand they're getting mail for 'Private Affairs.'"

"It's the only part of the paper that's working. I don't know where we'd be without it."

"You'd be finding a way to succeed. You're the one who turns these papers around, Matt; no one else. And you'll succeed in Tucson; you've never failed yet. I suggest you send

307

Chet there first. He can fill you in before you talk to them. You have more important things to do than digging up background information."

"I don't think we need Chet in Tucson."

"I think we do. He has a way of sizing up situations, and you've used enough of his reports to know he's thorough. He can save you a week of listening to everyone lie about everyone else. And, Matt, when you get there, don't give that bunch any leeway. We don't negotiate at gunpoint. Fire Dugan, fire the whole staff if necessary; you can always bring in people from other papers until you hire new ones. You've given them a new printing press—they know it's on order—you don't have to give anything else, at least until the contract is up."

Matt felt a flash of dislike. "I didn't 'give' them a printing press. I ordered one because two men were injured on the old one. And of course I'm going to negotiate. But I can do it informally; Ernie Dugan and I understand each other. I sit in on his poker games when I'm in town and we've gone drinking together, and we have an equal stake in the *Call*. He's right about our being in a weak position if they talk about striking over unsafe conditions; I gambled that I could wait a year before spending money on new equipment. I was wrong. But I don't think he'll push that; he knows we're not making a profit yet."

"If you think you know Dugan, I won't argue," Rourke said pleasantly. "But I'd like Chet to do the advance work. Indulge me, Matt. I don't think you'll regret it."

Matt hesitated, then nodded. He didn't want to meet Ernie Dugan with Chet nosing around in the background, but whining wasn't his job; getting along with Keegan Rourke was.

Ernie Dugan, just under five feet tall, with a dense tangle of black beard that was his special pride, claimed he had only two sports, poker and negotiating contracts, and he played them both with passion. From the first time he invited Matt to sit in on his weekly poker game, and the two of them had sat up afterward, drinking and comparing their different lives, he'd called Matt the only honest publisher he'd ever met. But something had changed by the time Matt arrived in Tucson and Chet met his plane. "All his officers," Chet said as they drove in from the airport. "And two from national headquarters. They're all waiting for you."

"I told Ernie on the phone I wanted a private talk," Matt said.

Chet put out his hand, palm up. "I didn't know that. I put together a team of our own people so we wouldn't be outnumbered. By the way, I'd rather you didn't tell him I told you about his crew; he thinks he's going to surprise us."

"*Surprise* us? That's not the way Ernie plays; what's got into him?"

"He thinks he has us by the balls and he's going to get all he can. Just don't tell him I said anything; I don't want to lose my sources of information."

That was twice in two minutes Chet had told him to keep quiet. Matt looked at him thoughtfully, but Chet was concentrating on his driving and they made the rest of the trip in silence.

"I'll be in the editor's office," Matt said when they arrived. "Tell him to meet me there. And the business manager. No one else. And tell Ernie to come in when they leave."

"But everyone's waiting for—"

"Chet."

"Right. Give me a minute . . ."

"Not too long." Matt waited in the bare office the editor had never redecorated, thinking the paper could fold at any time. When the editor and business manager came in, he gave them barely time to sit down. "I'm going to talk to Dugan myself, and try to find out what the hell is going on around here; can you give me any reason why I shouldn't?"

The editor, knowing he was being bypassed, shrugged. "I haven't been able to talk to him for weeks; he looks past me."

"Have you asked him why?"

"Of course not; it would make me sound weak."

"He already knows you're weak. I've been pushing you for months to get the paper moving, and you haven't been able to do it, and he knows it." He looked at his watch. "I want to talk to him, so we're going to have to make this fast. I'm

309

bringing in a new editorial staff. I can find jobs for both of you on one of my New Mexico papers; that goes for the features and news editors, too. If any of you don't want them, you're on your own; my new people will be here next week."

"Next week!" They barraged him with angry excuses and defenses, voices rising, faces red.

"That's enough," Matt said.

"You could have given us some warning!" the business manager blurted.

"I've given all of you seven months of warnings. What did you think I meant when I said I expected a profit?"

The two men looked at each other. "Not many major papers in New Mexico," the business manager said.

"They're not major." Matt handed them an accordion folder. "These are descriptions of the papers and the towns they're in. If you take the jobs and get used to the way I run a newspaper, I may be able to shift you to larger ones in a few years. Think about it while I talk to Dugan."

The editor put out his hand. As Matt took it, he said, "I'm sorry. I wanted to make it work, but it was like a brick wall."

Matt nodded, thinking he'd probably been too harsh. "Let me know what you decide."

"You can't do this—" the business manager snorted, but the editor maneuvered him from the office, and in a few minutes Dugan arrived.

"Thanks for coming in, Ernie," Matt said as they shook hands. "It's too crowded out there for poker and a quiet talk. Who called up the troops?"

"Seems we both did," said Dugan. "Because of the love and trust we have for each other."

Matt shook his head. "You know damn well I wouldn't do that to you. I told you on the phone we could handle our problems informally. This isn't a battlefield, Ernie."

"Well, now, Matt, I guess it's beginning to look like one. You and I've taken care of little things in the past, but this looks like it's getting too big for that. You called your friends; I called mine. What did you want to talk about?"

"Damn it, Ernie, calm down. I want to talk about anything

310

that's bothering you. But get this straight: I didn't call my friends, as you put it." A thought struck him. "Did Chet tell you I called that meeting in the conference room?"

"Now, Matt, listen, I don't talk about other people. You and I can still get along; all it takes is some honest negotiating. If you really want to talk, maybe we should get started?"

Matt took a folding chair and poured coffee into two Styrofoam cups on a table beside him. Helpful Chet. *I'd rather you didn't tell him I told you about his crew . . . don't tell him I said anything . . .* And the son of a bitch probably said the same thing to Ernie. *Don't tell Matt I told you about the army he's going to hit you with . . .*

But what was in it for Chet? After more than twenty years with Rourke, why would he play both sides? Matt watched Dugan blow on his hot coffee. All Chet had managed to do was make it a damn sight harder for Matt Lovell to prevent a strike—

All he'd managed to do? That was quite a bit.

Matt felt his anger build. If Elizabeth were there, she would have been able to defuse it, as she had so often with her sharp comments that helped him understand others because she was better with people than he was. But for months he'd been without her steady presence, and though he was getting better at holding himself back, he still found himself often wishing she were there to help him—especially with Chet. Somehow, she'd always known just what to say about Chet to make Matt smile and calm down.

But of course she wasn't there; he was on his own. He had to calm down and he had to be patient, because at the moment there was nothing he could do about Chet. The two of them worked for Rourke and had no business squabbling in front of Ernie Dugan, who was on the other side, however much Matt once thought they had in common. He drank his coffee, burned his tongue, and in a black mood said, "All right, Ernie. You've got a list?"

"I do. And you know where it starts, Matt. The accident in the pressroom shouldn't have happened. The reason it

311

happened, no one was willing to spend money on new presses—"

"Agreed."

"—so two men . . . what?"

"I said I agreed. Don't give me this bullshit, Ernie. We took a chance and postponed buying new presses; we made a mistake and we're doing all we can to make up for it. We've made a cash settlement to both men; we're picking up medical expenses not covered by insurance; we're holding their jobs for them; we've ordered new equipment for the pressroom. We've also started a phased purchase of a new computer system. You haven't got a grievance, Ernie. You've got past history."

"Well. Not quite." Dugan tugged at his beard, avoiding Matt's eyes. "Too many things postponed around here. Not just the presses, but also salaries, bonuses, overtime, profit sharing—"

"We've never talked about profit sharing, Ernie."

"Don't I know it. I'm saying if we want peace and harmony around here it's about time we did. Then there's the pension plan—"

"We have the best of any paper in Tucson."

"Which isn't saying much. And we have to look at vacations, sick leave, overtime, assignment schedules—"

"All right."

"What?"

"Tell me if I understand you correctly. You want to negotiate everything after you'd pledged to freeze benefits for two years, or until the *Call* is profitable. You want to get more of everything, and the hell with making the paper stronger. Is that right, or did I leave something out?"

"What the fuck, Matt, you've never talked to me like that!"

"You've never brought me ultimatums. What the hell has gotten into you, Ernie? In all the times we've talked and played poker, we've never threatened each other."

"Poker's fine when people are friends," said Dugan heavily. "Not when one of them is putting on a good-buddy act to get the other one to sell out."

"You son of a bitch," Matt said quietly.

312

"Fuck it, Matt, we're not working for the same people. I have a membership to answer to; you've got a corporation. I didn't think of it at the time, but when the owner of a paper cozies up to the head of the union there has to be a reason."

I didn't think of it at the time. The image of Chet Colfax came to Matt as clearly as if Dugan had said his name. "And somebody helped you think of it, Ernie. Right?"

Dugan ran furious fingers through his beard. "Labor and management don't sleep in the same bed; if they do, somebody's getting screwed. I can think for myself."

"Were you thinking for yourself all these months when you said I was honest and we understood each other and could work together?"

There was a silence. "Are we going to start talking about our contract, or not?" Dugan asked.

"We're not." Matt poured more coffee, spilling some on the table. He felt cold. Stupid, he thought. A babe in the woods, believing in Ernie. Rourke had seen that. *If you think you know Dugan, I can't argue.* Whether Chet had put him up to it, or Ernie had decided on his own that they were adversaries, Matt Lovell had been stupid and naive. Looking for a friend, for Christ's sake, when in fact they stood on opposite sides of a war zone.

But he hadn't completely lost his wits: he'd made contingency plans. What made him feel cold was that he had to use them.

"Let's go out and talk to the others," he said, moving to the door. "I want them to hear this."

"You're going around your editor?" Ernie demanded.

"I've cleared what I'm going to say with my editor and business manager. Come on, Ernie, you asked for this."

At the head of the table, with Ernie glowering at him from a seat halfway down one side, Matt stood and faced the two rows of men. Chet sat apart, in a far corner of the room. "We made progress the first couple of months after I bought the *Call;* since then, we've barely held our own, and the place is about as lively as the dugout of a losing team. In fact, I mentioned to someone last week that the staff acts like it's throwing the paper the way a team throws a game."

"Just a fucking minute—!" Dugan burst out.

"Not yet, Ernie. You'll have your turn when I say so. I'm not making accusations; I'm telling you how it looks to *management*. I came here to talk and find out what you're worried about and find a way to work together to put some life into this paper. In other words, I came here to cooperate, and I find my friend Ernie Dugan expecting me to negotiate at gunpoint. Ernie"—he focused on Dugan—"you must have some friends over at the *Sentinel;* you've been trying to organize that paper for years."

When he paused, Dugan growled, "What's that supposed to mean?"

"Gunpoint, Ernie." Matt's voice was like steel. "I've been talking all week to Bill Falworth about buying the *Sentinel*. He hadn't intended to sell, but he's been rethinking that, and it looks like we'll be able to reach an agreement. And I'm not sure whether I want to own two papers in Tucson."

When it sank in, Dugan was on his feet, his face dark with rage. "You fucking bastard! You're saying you'd shut down the *Call!*"

Matt's face was expressionless. "With labor problems at the *Call*, especially after months of poor performance, I'd be a fool to put money into bigger benefits for a gang that's holding me up when I can buy the *Sentinel* and run it my own way."

Dugan began to pace, skirting the chair in the corner where Chet sat rigidly, alarm in his round eyes. "Three papers in this town and you want to close one of them down. Take jobs away from people, knowing they couldn't get other jobs because there'd only be two papers left, and you'd own one of them."

"That's the picture," Matt said evenly.

"Goddammit. *Goddammit*. You planned this! You started talking to Falworth before we even knew you were coming to Tucson! You'd destroy this paper to get your way!"

"No. I'd shut down the *Call* because it isn't profitable and the union's demands will make it impossible to turn it around."

"We don't have demands! We have an agenda!"

"You have demands. I didn't hear anything about greater productivity, longer hours, more aggressive investigating, better reporting, more careful editing. I didn't hear any ideas from you about helping the people of the state or helping the *Call* survive. All I heard were demands. And not one of them had anything to do with the fact that *this paper doesn't have enough readers to make a profit.*"

"Goddammit, we can work all that out in negotiations! We understand each other; we can *talk*, dammit—"

"In the same bed? With one of us getting screwed? Sit down, Ernie; I'll tell you exactly what we can work out."

Dugan stopped pacing. "My job is negotiating, not sitting and listening."

"My job is making this paper profitable. When you sit down, I'll tell you how we're going to do that."

Dugan gave a furious kick to the leg of an empty chair, sending it skidding, then came back to his place and sat down. "We'll start with the contract," Matt said. "If you demand a new one with different terms, we'll go on negotiating with the *Sentinel*. If you'd rather we didn't do that, we'll stay with the current contract, but we'll extend it for eighteen months with the same terms and no new negotiations. Don't say anything, Ernie; you'll waste your energy. I've only started. I'll say it again: we're freezing salaries and benefits for eighteen months. That goes for everybody: editors, management, staff. But we have to cut other costs, too. We'll find more efficient ways to do everything and we'll cut out waste and perks, but at most that will save about five percent, and I'm aiming for twenty. That means reducing the staff. We'll work it out together, or you work it out alone; I don't care, as long as costs are down twenty percent in six months. No one will be hired to replace workers who quit or retire or die; the least essential workers will be let go; reporters who insist on writing the kind of mediocre crap you've been turning out lately will be out. The same goes for photographers. I'm bringing in a new editor and top staff from some of my other papers—"

A rustle ran down the table; the men looked at Dugan, then

quickly away. They might have had a weapon if Matt had kept his old team, but now they had nothing.

"—because I'm sick and tired of the *Call* being second-rate. I can't believe you aren't, too. If the paper shows a profit, we'll negotiate a new contract in a year and a half, with pay increases directly related to performance. We'll do our share to help: we're starting a new contest right after Labor Day; we'll have billboards, radio and television advertising, a telephone circulation drive, and a larger bonus for bringing in advertisements. But we can only bring readers to the paper once or twice; the way to keep them is by giving them a superior product. I expect the *Call* to be superior; I expect it to be profitable in eighteen months. Are there any questions?"

A chair scraped; Matt turned and saw Chet Colfax leave the room. Ernie stared at his hands and was silent. Someone asked about overtime, someone else asked about medical insurance, and finally the science editor said carefully, "About improving stories . . . There's been a . . . feeling that if we didn't knock ourselves out, if we just did an okay job, we could bargain for a better contract."

Matt kept his face still. "How?"

"By trading better work for better pay. The feeling was that if we were already doing top work, we had no leverage. But if we're keeping the current contract for a year and a half—and we'll have to vote on that, but we don't seem to have any alternative—I'd like to talk about using more photos, more graphics, maybe color?"

Others began to make comments and suggestions; the discussion caught fire. Matt listened, putting in a word now and then but mostly letting the others talk while he thought about Chet. How often had Chet been in Tucson in the last seven months? While Matt Lovell had been running around the southwest, buying newspapers or visiting his family in Santa Fe, how often had Chet been helping the staff of the *Call* think about trading better work for better pay? How many times had Chet hopped over to Tucson to make sure there was a feeling that reporters and photographers should only do an okay job?

He sat quietly, letting the discussion build its own momentum. One side of the table had been beaten; the other side had won; now they were talking and working together as if there'd been no war. Elizabeth wouldn't like the way he'd done it, he thought. He could almost see her puzzled frown and hear her voice. *I know you had to avoid a strike; I know you want the paper to grow; but did you really have to hit them with a wage freeze and all those staff cuts? And did you have to humiliate Ernie in front of everyone, instead of telling him privately what you were going to do?*

Matt shook his head like a dog shaking off a sudden drenching. He didn't need Elizabeth's voice; he knew he'd gone farther than he intended. He'd been angry at Dugan, and at himself, and worried that Rourke would think he was too soft on employees. He was changing, even more than he'd changed when he'd forced Graham into a corner on selling his papers, because this time he was sending a message to unions and employees in twenty-five cities. He didn't much like the brutality of what he'd done, and his skill in being brutal. But he couldn't spend time worrying about it, because he could see the results. He'd have to keep track of Chet's game-playing, but in everything else he'd gotten peace and harmony, on his terms, and a staff that was finally talking about ways to bring the *Call* to life.

And he'd been naive enough for one day. It was about time he understood that a certain amount of brutality went with the job.

The plane descended over the hazy sprawl of Houston, coming in over pine forests that were familiar now, no longer the surprise they'd been the first time Matt saw them. He debated calling Rourke at home, then decided against it. He didn't like making reports on the phone; he liked watching people's faces, seeing their reactions as he talked. And especially with Rourke, whose legendary silences on the telephone unnerved all but the most confident, Matt would go out of his way to be in the same room when reporting on a trip.

He had talked to Rourke from Tucson, saying only that there would be no strike at the *Call*; then he'd gone on to his papers in Phoenix and Durango and San Antonio, looking for signs

317

of sluggish performance or deliberate slowdowns. But he found nothing. So the *Call* had been a practice run, he thought; and from now on I can't ever relax with Chet.

And where have I heard that before?

Everything else on that trip was smoother than he had expected. Even in July, usually a slow month, the papers were making money and the staffs were happy. In fact, happiness was all Matt heard in the ten days after he left Tucson. As his plane taxied to Houston's terminal and he fastened the top button of his shirt and tightened his tie, he reviewed all that happiness: three newspapers turning a profit, everything under control, a brave new world of journalists as amiable as pussycats.

And that was no good, he thought, swinging his suiter over his shoulder and walking toward the cabstand. A vigorous press couldn't function with pussycats. He'd have to weed out most of them and turn the firebrands loose on investigations and exposés. Without them, papers withered away or turned into comic books, and readers lost their only protection against corruption and waste in government and insidious dangers like those at Love Canal and Times Beach.

The best news he'd heard on his trip was the success of "Private Affairs." Staffs loved it because it upgraded their papers; readers argued or agreed with Elizabeth in letters and phone calls, hundreds adding that they clipped her columns and saved them. She must have enough by now to make a book, Matt thought. I'll have to talk to her about that; she probably wouldn't think of it her—

"Want a ride, mister?" a voice asked at his elbow. "Nothin' better, I always say, than a handsome publisher to give my hack some class."

He laughed at Nicole's cockney twang and the cap she wore low over one eye. "How did you know I'd be here?"

"Keegan mentioned it. Are you going to let me drive you home?"

"Of course I am. There's nothing worse than a Texan taxi driver at rush hour."

But he had never driven with Nicole. "It's all right, Matt,"

318

she laughed, seeing him close his eyes as she swerved her white Cadillac to the next lane at seventy miles an hour, cutting off another car with barely an inch to spare. "I've been driving since I was ten and am considered extremely competent. If you don't relax after your arduous trip, you won't be a stimulating dinner companion, and I've been planning this dinner for two weeks."

He opened his eyes to look at her, thinking her striking beauty would have made it a pleasure even if his purpose were not to avoid seeing how she drove. "Planning it for two weeks but not mentioning it? We've talked on the telephone three times."

"Four. I did tell you I'd canceled my party and postponed my departure to Maine."

"You didn't postpone it to have dinner with me."

"I never do anything for only one reason. And don't ask what the others are; I won't tell you. As you should know after all these months, I dote on secrets and surprises. Now will you please relax?"

With a quick look at the traffic becoming heavier and forcing Nicole to slow down in spite of herself, Matt shrugged and put his head back. The hell with it. He'd probably been safer at thirty-eight thousand feet, but he was on the ground now, Nicole was driving, and either they'd make it or they wouldn't. As for dinner—"I'm not scintillating," he warned her. "Arduous is a mild word for the past ten days. But I'll take you to La Reserve and then we'll call it a night."

"You're not taking me anywhere. I'm feeding you at home. We've gone out so often lately I owe you at least a dozen dinners."

"I don't keep tabs. We'll go out, Nicole."

"Matt, if I don't practice my cooking now and then—or any other sport, for that matter—I'll lose my touch."

He smiled. "I've never seen you out of practice and if you were, you'd take care that no one saw it. And we are going out for dinner."

"And you are extraordinarily stubborn."

"So I've been told."

"Which you cannot soften by flattery."

319

"Can't I?"

She laughed. "Yes you can and you know it. All right. We'll go out tonight, but next time I feed you. Agreed?"

"I'll think about it. I appreciate the invitation."

"Matt! I thought you played fair!"

"I'm very good at surprises."

She smiled. "That's true. How are you at compromise?"

"The newspaper union in Tucson would say I'm rotten at it. But I'm not. Not always. All right, Nicole. Next time you cook."

"Much better. And I don't want La Reserve tonight. Do you mind? Let's go to Don's for crawfish."

"Noisy, crowded, and a long wait for dinner."

"And too casual for a stuffy someone who says *I appreciate the invitation?*"

Chuckling, Matt felt his fatigue begin to lift. Her light banter, the cool perfection of her black hair and alabaster skin set off by a white sundress, her aggressive driving, and the brightness of her eyes when she looked at him, all replaced the bad taste left by Tucson and then those other cities where too many men and women had jockeyed for his favor. And in the air-conditioned car, as she changed lanes, speeding where she could, slowing when she had to, her sexuality was less powerful than in the close confines of dimly-lit restaurants and piano bars. She was a pleasant companion and he was grateful. "I apologize for my stuffiness. If we can get near the oyster bar, I don't mind waiting for a table at Don's."

"Thank you. I'll take you home first, so you can refresh yourself. We have plenty of time. Now tell me about your trip. Did they all cozy up and tell you they've been *waiting* for someone *just* like *you* who *understands* them, and how every-thing is *smooth* and *well-oiled* and thank God they can finally do a *good job?*"

Matt burst into laughter. "You're a wonder. You sound like every one of them. How did you know?"

"I've met a few of them. Tell me all about it."

He told her, the stories and descriptions pouring out as she asked questions and laughed with him. It was the first time in

320

over a year Matt had talked so easily about himself. Not since the days when he and Elizabeth had worked together had he felt so comfortable in sharing his experiences.

But when they were at dinner, she asked, "Is there something you can't tell me about?"

He put down the menu. "Why?"

"I get the feeling you're leaving something out. And I want to hear it all."

"I left out Tucson," he said, and after they ordered he told her, briefly, what had happened. "I suppose the poker games have ended, and I'm sorry about that. But the rest of it was all right."

"*All right?* Listen to the man. It was *wonderful*, Matt; you were playing to win and you had to make everyone understand that from the start. If you'd given Ernie or any of them a leg to stand on they would have kicked you with it. You did exactly what you had to do. And I'll bet those poker games haven't ended. You wait; everything will settle back. You have power, Matt. People won't give up the chance to be close to you."

He smiled, brushing her words aside. "I thought it was my charm and wit that brought you here tonight."

"I am aware of them," she said, returning his smile, and then changed the subject, asking him about other Rourke papers. All through dinner they talked about his trip. It wasn't until he left her, after she had pulled up in the circular drive at his building and leaned over to kiss his cheek, that he realized she had led him through a discussion so complete he had already organized his report to Rourke.

Impressive, he thought, pulling off his tie in his apartment. And then, just before he fell asleep, he realized something else about Nicole Renard: she had said almost nothing about herself since picking him up that afternoon.

He'd done the talking; she'd urged him on. And listened. And not mentioned bed, though both of them wanted it and made no attempt to hide it. Briefly, he wondered why they were waiting. But he knew enough about Nicole by now to know the answer. They were waiting because she wanted to wait. Because she was showing him everything else she could do, first. Impressive, he thought again with a smile. Requiring good timing and a sure touch. And she hasn't lost it. Any more than she probably has in cooking. Or in anything else.

Keegan Rourke was sitting on the couch in Matt's office, leafing through a magazine on southwestern art, when Matt came in. "Article here on Hopi Indian wood sculptures by Peter Lovell," he said, looking up. "Your son?"

Matt grinned. "Not bad for eighteen, is it?"

"It's a fast start. He takes after his father."

"He takes after his mother. He's a damn good writer." Matt went to a credenza behind his desk and turned on the Braun coffeemaker. "I called Tucson before I left home this morning; they're putting together a schedule of layoffs and economies to cut expenditures by twenty percent. I'll have it by the end of the week."

"Layoffs." Rourke put down the magazine. "What did you do to Dugan? Beat him up? Hypnotize him?"

"Neither." There was a knock at the door and Chet Colfax walked in. Matt looked at Rourke.

"I asked Chet to join us," Rourke said. "I assumed you'd expect it. You were both there."

"Don't let me interrupt," said Chet.

The Braun gave a final sigh and gurgle and Matt pulled out the carafe. "Coffee?"

Rourke nodded. "What did you do to him?"

Perched on the corner of his desk, Matt described his meeting with Dugan and the one in the conference room, leaving out all mention of Chet. As he talked, he watched Rourke's face change from interest to delight. At the end, he was smiling as broadly as Matt had ever seen him.

"Brilliant," he said. "Eighteen months of stability. And reduced costs. And to transform a confrontation into a dialogue on improving the paper . . . a masterstroke. Congratulations, my boy." He went to Matt and put his hands on his shoulders. "Imagination and a good aim: go for the jugular so neatly no one is left bloodied." He chuckled. "I'm glad we have you on our side. Of course, I never doubted you'd succeed. Did I, Chet? Even when you were worried."

"Worried?" Matt echoed. "What were you worried about, Chet?"

Rourke answered for him as he went to the coffeemaker. "Chet's an old woman sometimes; thinks the sky's about to fall. He was afraid you might be outflanked by Dugan and his crowd and give too much away. Of course we all knew you'd never faced a situation like it before, but I'd put money on you against Dugan any time. You've got brains and class. Dugan hasn't. That's what Chet forgot."

"Chet doesn't forget much," Matt said.

"And a good thing," Rourke responded. "Coffee, Matt?"

"Thanks. Chet, was there anything else you were worried about?"

Chet shook his head.

"Nothing else?" Matt pressed.

"What did you have in mind?" Rourke asked.

"Chet's trips to Tucson. Before I left, I was told he'd been there six times in the last eight months and I wondered why, if he wasn't worried about something. I also wondered why he made them without mentioning them to me."

Rourke dismissed it. "Chet visits all our operations from time to time on my orders; I like independent reports, Matt, you know that. I'm sure if he made six trips he thought they were necessary. Chet, is there anything we should know?"

Chet's rigid features had relaxed. He looked blandly from Rourke to Matt. "Not at this time."

"There was unrest at that paper," Matt said sharply. "In six trips, Chet should have seen it coming."

Rourke raised an eyebrow. "What about that, Chet? No hints or inklings?"

"Nothing big enough to bother you about."

"He was tripping all over them," said Matt. "Either he decided to ignore them or he was more interested in digging into Dugan's sex life."

"He was there for that, too. We couldn't know you'd find a

better way of handling him. And speaking of that: what would you have done if he'd called your bluff on the *Sentinel?*"

"I was sure he wouldn't."

"But if he had. Would you have recommended to the board that we buy it?"

"No. Falworth wants too much for it."

"Then I'll ask it again. What would you have done if he'd called your bluff?"

"I'd have dealt with it when it happened."

Rourke's smile returned. "You had no specific plan?"

"I knew I didn't need one."

"By God." He began to laugh. "Pure faith. That's what gets you through. There's a kind of innocence to you, Matt, but you're not afraid to use power. No wonder you get what you want; no one knows what to expect from you. Or is it innocence? If it's an act, you should be giving lessons to all of us."

Matt's lips tightened. "I don't put on acts, and I don't think innocence is the right word. I knew what I was doing."

"I'm sure you did." Rourke paused, and then a new note crept into his voice. "But I would have liked to be in at the beginning, Matt. Approaching Falworth was a brilliant idea, but it was a gamble that could have cost us more than a strike at the *Call.* And when you plan something like that, I like to be kept informed."

"It was a contingency; I might not have used it."

"I realize that. I'm making a simple request for future situations."

There was a small silence. Matt saw the three of them, frozen for a moment: round-eyed Chet in a cautious dark suit and somber tie, Rourke in lightweight gray wool as sleek and elegant as his silver hair and manicured nails, Matt himself in identical lightweight gray, but feeling less than elegant, thinking he needed a haircut and never had had a manicure in his life, knowing he was thinking about them only because they were symbols of Rourke's dominance.

You have power, Matt. Nicole's voice lingered in his memory. But in this office, though Matthew Lovell's name was on the door, only one man had real power and could expect to be kept informed.

Matt nodded. "I'll remember," he said to Rourke. He picked up a piece of paper from his desk. "I'll send you a report on the rest of my trip. If we've finished with Tucson, I'd like to talk about your memo on the New Mexico senate race."

Rourke turned to Chet. "We won't need you anymore this morning. You'll find a list on my desk of items I'd like taken care of."

Instantly, Chet put down his cup and went to the door. His hand on the knob, he hesitated, then said tightly, "Matt, I agree with Mr. Rourke. That was a fine job you did in Tucson. Fine job. I hope you'll call on me again, whenever you need me. I want to help as much as I can." He nodded to both of them and then he was gone.

"Now, what about the election?" Rourke asked, returning to the couch.

"I don't understand why you want to support Greene. He's a tired old man who's not even interested in New Mexico anymore; he spends most of his time in Florida or telling amusing stories at your dinner table. I've talked to some business people around the state; there's a lot of interest in a congressman from Albuquerque—Dan Heller, young, agressive, very sharp. I've read up on him; I like his politics; I like his ideas on land use; and he's got some key people behind him. I brought a file on him; when you've read it, I'd like to give our editors the go-ahead to start supporting him for November."

"You're going a little fast for me, Matt. Is there anything wrong with Greene's voting record on land use?"

"There's nothing wrong with Greene except age and fatigue. But why support him if there's someone better?"

"You're sure this congressman is better."

"I think so. Read his file; I think you will, too."

"A file only gives the public side of a man."

"You mean I should send Chet to dig into his sex life."

"Eventually we may want that. But not this year. If he's as young and sharp as you say, he'll know enough to wait until the right time. Andy Greene has worked for every piece of

325

legislation I've been interested in; he's pushed for exploration rights and development of public lands and private recreation areas; he's worked behind the scenes for highways and roads. He's also a personal friend, Matt, and I've already promised him our support."

Matt paced to the center of the room, then to the windows, looking across the city to the downtown skyscrapers where other meetings were being held, determining the shapes of campaigns, companies, jobs, lives . . . "You didn't consult me about that."

"I should have. I apologize. Andy and I were playing tennis a while back and it came up. He wants one more term; that's all. Then he'll retire. I have his word on that. And I gave him mine. I can't go back on it."

Still looking out the window, Matt said, "Will you get his word he'll endorse our candidate when he retires?"

"I have his word on that, too."

It was said too quickly. Matt turned. "You have someone lined up for six years from now?"

"There are always a few people on the horizon. We'll take a good look at Congressman Heller when the time comes. No one could promise more than that, this far ahead. By the way, since we're talking about New Mexico, make a note, would you, on a man named Tom Ortiz? He's running for re-election to the state legislature. He's been in it so long he's practically a fixture; never had any real opposition; but this year some Hispanic woman crawled out of the woodwork to run against him, and I hear she broke all the records on signatures on her petitions. Tom did me a favor once; I'd like to help him out by having the *Chieftain* support him. A light touch on his opponent, of course—a woman *and* Hispanic; she's practically untouchable. Except on experience—she hasn't any, and that's the direction Milgrim should take. He'll know how to handle it." He paused, then looked closely at Matt. "Is something wrong?"

"I hope not. Since when is the *Chieftain* part of Rourke Enterprises?"

"Contractually it's not," Rourke said easily. "But I think of

326

it as part of your chain; when we discussed our coverage of New Mexico, didn't you include the *Chieftain* and the *Sun?*"

"If I did, I made a mistake. Those papers are independent. Editorial decisions are made by my wife and Saul."

"That doesn't mean they wouldn't favor a suggestion from you."

"They might. I've never tried to find out."

"Milgrim's done a couple of stories opposing development of wilderness areas. You've seen them, of course."

"No. I'm behind in my reading. I trust Saul more than my other editors, so the *Chieftain* gets shoved to the bottom of the pile. I'll look into those stories, but they have nothing to do with the election. If Saul and Elizabeth decide to support this woman—do you know her name?"

"I did; I've forgotten it. Matt, it's too small an issue to quarrel over."

"I'd like to keep it small by dropping it."

Rourke stood and looked at his watch. "I'm due at a meeting downtown. I'm sorry we can't agree on this; I'd like you to give it some more thought."

"I will, but I don't see a reason to change my mind."

"Peace and harmony," Rourke said with a smile. "If it's good enough for Tucson, it's good enough for Rourke Enterprises. Congratulations again on that job, Matt; I'm proud of you. Come to dinner on Saturday; a couple of governors are in town; it might be an interesting evening. Bring Nicole; then if it turns out to be dull, you won't be bored." He put his hand lightly on Matt's shoulder, one of those gestures he made with no one else, setting Matt apart as a kind of favored son. Matt felt the familiar pleasure it always gave him. But this time it occurred to him that there was more than warmth in Rourke's touch: there was also pressure.

The jazz was soft and slow at Birdwatcher's, curling around their table as Nicole's hand rested briefly on Matt's. "Feeling better?"

"Much. I'm already forgetting the kind of week it was. You couldn't have picked a better place." Idly, he pulled the flickering candle closer to them, looking at her in its light. "Or looked more beautiful. What have you done to your hair?"

"Rearranged it. The dress required something dramatic."

The dress was black; in the dim light it seemed to Matt to be made of floating layers. Luminous against it, a single strand of pearls wound once around Nicole's neck, then hung to her waist. Her hair was pulled back and coiled at the back of her head. Amused, Matt said, "When are you less than dramatic?"

"When I wake up," she replied. "Drama requires an alert mind and in the mornings I am languid and slow. All feeling; no thought."

In his mind Matt saw the image of Nicole in bed, long legs and slender arms stretching lazily between smooth sheets. *Languid, slow, all feeling*. A wave of desire swept him. And Nicole knew it. Looking up, her eyes caught his before he could look away, and she smiled. "You have a wonderful face, Matt; so much more alive than most men's. Don't you ever pretend? Haven't you even once tried to look like the stalwart ship's captain, stern and undaunted, single-handedly bringing your passengers safely through a fierce and terrible storm?"

Matt laughed. "Not once. And neither has anyone else I know."

"Oh, I'd wager they have. You don't see it because they only put on their masks for women—to impress us and pique our curiosity. Who can resist the challenge of finding out what a man is really thinking behind that stern look of perfect control?"

"You don't sound impressed by it."

She tilted her head and studied him. "No," she said. "Masks bore me, and the fearful men who wear them bore me even more. I prefer a revealing face."

"But there's no challenge to it," he said.

"Oh, indeed there is."

He waited.

Nicole shook her head. "Not now. Ask me again. If it's the right time, I'll tell you what it is."

The musicians finished their set and casually accepted the applause of the crowd before putting down their instruments and leaving the small stage. The room filled with conversation, the clink of ice in glasses, the scraping of chairs. Matt finished his vodka and looked at Nicole's glass. "Do you want to stay?"

"If you don't mind. Let's hear at least one more set. I like to feel it build."

He ordered two more drinks and sat back, wondering what it was that Nicole liked to feel building: sexual desire or the intensity of jazz. She was still setting the pace, controlling their times together, choosing where they went, what they did, what they talked about, and he went along because she was undemanding and intriguing, and because she never judged or competed with him.

But tonight she'd done more than set the pace. Tonight she had aroused him, then made him laugh, then engaged him in conversation that kept his desire under control. *I like to feel it build.* And so do I, Matt thought. After weeks at the center of Rourke Enterprises where he could not let down his guard, it was a luxury to let something build gradually, to savor anticipation. For the first time it was as exciting to slow down as to speed ahead.

Clever woman; to make herself as unpredictable and desirable as any dream I might pursue.

The musicians returned; once more the music coiled about them; and Nicole plucked a conversation from an hour earlier, continuing it as if nothing had intervened. "Do you truly think you and Keegan disagree on important things?"

"I don't know," Matt said shortly, unwilling to talk about work.

"I wondered how much it might change your feelings about him, and working here, if you do find you disagree."

"Not much. I admire him; I think he admires me . . ."

"He does. You know he does."

"Then we can get along. Two people can't work together without occasional disagreements; I don't mind giving in when it's important to him if he does the same for me. We'll work it out."

"Keegan has very definite ideas," Nicole said thoughtfully. "But frequently he doesn't make them clear. He likes to do

329

things in roundabout ways. It pleases him to keep people at a distance; make them guess what he's up to."

A memory caught at Matt. A long time ago—in Aspen?— Elizabeth had described Rourke in almost identical words. "Maybe that's the mask he puts on for women," Matt said. "I don't see him that way."

"Oh, my dear," said Nicole. "Keegan is a man who wears masks for everyone, men and women alike. Though not for me, which is why he doesn't bore me. But, Matt"—she put her hand on his—"don't change your mind about him. Even when you discover things you don't like, stay with him; let him open doors for you. I know you could do it on your own; you're as brilliant as he is; you could go as far on your own as he has, and equal his power and wealth, but if he can make it easier and faster, do let him. *He* had help, you know: all those oil wells that sprouted like weeds on his father's land."

She saw Matt's quick frown. "No one ever told you that? His father bought hundreds of thousands of acres all over the South in the early 1900s, at absolutely bargain prices. He was building a house somewhere in Arkansas and got terribly annoyed because when he tried to pump underground water into his new swimming pool it kept streaking with filthy black oil. He spent thousands to get a nice clear swimming pool. Poor man; he died before he knew what he had. Keegan knew. And he built an empire from it. You would have done the same, Matt."

Her hand had been lying lightly on his as she talked. She sat back and picked up her glass. "Now that's enough of Keegan for one night. I know I brought him up, but now I'm banishing him. We don't need him at our table."

"We don't need anyone. You have a way of making everyone else seem unnecessary."

The clarinet reached a high note and drew it out, long and sweet. Nicole caught her breath. "May I propose a toast to a most wonderful companion?"

"We'll drink to each other. And to Maine."

"Why Maine?" she asked curiously.

"Because it relinquished you. No lobstermen came to drag

330

you to your island when you decided to spend the summer in Houston—even though, as we know, *no one does*."

She laughed softly. "I believe in experiencing everything, at least once. I do thank the Lord daily for air conditioning, but otherwise I seem to have struggled through to mid-August in fairly good shape."

"Fairly good," he repeated gravely.

Her laughter rippled again. "Thanks to you. You're the only person who could keep me here, and in good shape at that. I'm grateful for you, Matt." Her amber eyes held his; her voice curled around him like the long notes of the clarinet; and Matt wanted her with a force that stopped his breath. The room blurred behind her; the music reached a high syncopated pitch that worked its way into his blood. He pushed back his chair. "But I have a favor to ask," she said suddenly, breaking the mood. "I want to choose the evening's entertainment."

Matt let out a long breath. A few minutes ago, he reminded himself, he'd been amused and intrigued by her unpredictability. "I thought you already had. You chose jazz. And Bird-watcher's. And a black dress."

"And I want more," she said. "May I choose again?"

"Whatever you want."

She put her elbows on the table and rested her chin on her clasped hands. "I'd like to play a game of Ping-Pong. If I recall correctly, you once claimed to be an expert."

Momentarily silenced, he said after a moment, "You want to follow jazz and vodka and simple desires with Ping-Pong?"

She nodded, her smile challenging him.

Finally the absurdity caught him and he chuckled. "Why not? What else could I have wanted to do? Is it important that I haven't been an expert since the prehistoric era of my college years?"

"Not at all. It simply means I shall win."

"Possibly." He put his hand on the gossamer fabric molding her shoulder. "Shall we go?"

"If you like."

By the time they reached her house, none of the past week's corporate infighting remained in Matt's thoughts. There was

331

only Nicole's beauty beneath the white light at her front door. "Of course I don't want to force anything on you," she was saying as she turned her key in the lock. "We can change our mind, if you'd rather not play."

"I said you could choose."

He caught her small, pleased smile as he followed her through the silent house to the playroom. She switched on a hanging light over the Ping-Pong table, leaving the rest of the room in shadows, and slipped off her shoes. "Ties are not allowed in the playroom," she said. "Shoes are optional."

Matt took off his jacket and tie and unbuttoned the neck of his shirt. He left his shoes on. Hefting the paddle at his end of the table, he flexed his wrist. "Do you want to warm up first?"

"I thought we'd been doing that for the past three hours."

He laughed, feeling boyish, reckless, free. At the other end of the table, lit from above, Nicole's beauty was subtly changed, shadows making her cheekbones seem higher, the line of her neck longer, her breasts barely outlined beneath layers of black lace and chiffon. She picked up the small plastic ball and looked inquiringly at Matt. "Ready," he said, and she sent the ball smashing across the table.

She played the way she drove: fast, aggressive, daring. She played to win. It took Matt a few minutes to get accustomed to the small paddle and table after years of tennis, and a few minutes more to recall the tricks he'd known in college. They all came back, and he used them all, but Nicole had her own tricks, and an uncanny ability to anticipate him: time after time she stepped back and slammed the ball across the net in an impossible return.

"Volley for serve?" she asked after ten minutes. "I think we ought to be keeping score."

"I thought we'd been doing that for the past three hours," Matt said.

She burst out laughing. "I asked for that. And I didn't see it coming. Would you like something to drink before we begin a game?"

"I would. I seem to need all the help I can get."

Smiling, she went to the refrigerator built into a cabinet along one wall. "Napoleon?"

"Fine."

She poured the cognac into two snifters and brought him one. "Does the winner get to choose the prize?"

"Of course." He took a drink, then put the glass on a counter behind him as Nicole walked around the table. "Where did you learn to play like that?"

"From two older brothers who thought female meant inferior. They allowed me to watch them at everything." She picked up the paddle. "I memorized what they did, practiced in secret, then challenged them to a game. They lost. It went on for years. They never caught on that they were my teachers. Ready?"

They volleyed until Nicole missed a shot and Matt served. They were very fast, beginning to know each other's moves, whipping the ball between them. It was only a few minutes before Matt tossed Nicole the ball so she could take over the serve. "Three-two," he said. "You watched your brothers at everything?"

"Everything." She served a slicing shot that caught the corner of the table. "Three-three." As Matt retrieved the ball from the shadows she said, "There was a maple tree outside their bedroom windows. I'd been climbing trees since I was five. And when I was ten they began sneaking girls into their rooms. Are you going to serve?"

He played for a few minutes in silence. When it was her serve again, Matt said, "So you learned from girls, too."

"I learned not to giggle and not to pout."

"That's all?"

"That's all. The rest I learned from my brothers. To know what I want, to go after it, to make sure I'm satisfied. Don't you see? They had it all. I sat outside, looking through a pane of glass at their power, their smug confidence, their maleness. Do you remember those picture books that showed Atlas holding up the world? I thought of my father and brothers that way: chests out, muscles bulging, holding up the world. They had it all."

"They didn't have your beauty."

333

"Beauty is a weakness. May I have the ball? I believe it's my serve." He tossed it to her and she served again, giving the ball a treacherous spin. But Matt had seen it coming and he returned it with an opposite spin, making it bounce sideways, past her. "Ten-eleven," she said. "I didn't know you could do that."

"Neither did I. I've never done it before. Why is beauty a weakness?"

"Because people believe it's all a woman needs. If she has beauty, no one wants to waste time teaching her anything; what could she need, since she already has the greatest treasure of all? Everyone wants beauty; everyone thinks it will bring fame, fortune, happiness, whatever anyone could want. A lie, of course, but try making people believe that. Tell them beauty is an obstacle to power and they'll tell you you're just being coy."

She served again and they played in silence: fast, furious, concentrating. "Twenty-all," Matt said at last, taking over the serve. "You're a formidable opponent."

She smiled. "When I choose to be."

He studied her. "You could have minimized your beauty."

"I was afraid to. I didn't know how good my other weapons would be."

Struck by her honesty, he paused, still studying her. The amber of her eyes darkened; the tip of her tongue touched her upper lip. He took a step toward her.

"Matt," she said softly. "The game isn't over."

"It's barely begun," he said, but he stepped back and served the ball, and in another few moments Nicole won on a lazy return that sent the ball just over the net and off the edge of the table.

"Yours," Matt said with a laugh. "I should have guessed you'd pull something I hadn't seen before."

"I practice doing that." She picked up the bottle of cognac. "You're wonderful, Matt. Your eyebrows get fierce and your mouth determined . . ."

"I'm pretending to be a ship's captain getting you safely through a storm."

334

She gave a small laugh. "I'd trust you to do that."

Matt went to her as she filled their glasses and took the bottle from her hand. His arm circled her shoulders and his other hand covered her breast. Nicole leaned against him and raised her face. "Of course," she said, the words barely audible as her arms came up and circled his neck. "You did say the winner gets to pick the prize." Her mouth was full and soft beneath his, opening to let their tongues twist together; then, turning within his arm, she pressed the length of her body against his.

She held the kiss before slowly pulling away. Holding his hand on her breast she led him past the swing set and dart board, past stuffed animals and a hopscotch diagram on the floor, past jump ropes and pick-up-sticks and Lego sets, past the corner where he had once watched her shoot marbles, to a deep couch at the far end of the room. She drew him with her into the depths of its cushions. "If you knew how I've wanted you," she murmured. "Since that first night, at my party, when you looked wide-eyed at every room . . ."

"But tonight you chose Ping-Pong," he said, his lips against hers. He was above her as she half-lay against the arm of the couch; his hands moved from her breasts to her smooth skin and the long line of her throat. "All those damned games . . ."

Her eyes were closed, but her lips curved. "Everything is a game, Matt. Different names, different ways of playing, but it's always a game."

"And this?" His mouth came down on hers with a kind of fury at the passion pounding inside him while she talked of games. He raised his head. "Was that another one?"

"The best of all. Dear Matt, you play so beautifully, we're so well-matched, we'll be wonderful together. I promise. Whatever you want, however you want to play it . . ."

Roughly he turned her and pulled down the thin zipper that reached her waist. The dress seemed to float off her shoulders, and he ran his hands over her bare skin, sliding them around her to cup her breasts, the nipples hard and pointed beneath his fingers. She made a low sound, like a long purr, and raised herself against him so he could pull off her dress and pantyhose, and his hands moved over her, discovering the taut lines of her body, as lean as his, before they reached the silkiness of her thighs and the soft darkness between them.

He felt a slow shudder through her body, then she curved above him like a reed floating free in the water. "Your turn, dear Matt," she murmured, and bent her head to run her tongue along his neck, taking small bites while her quick fingers opened his shirt.

Her tongue followed her hands, the pointed tip licking small circles down his chest. He felt her warm breath as she reached his belt buckle and zipper and then her tongue moved down in long strokes as her hands slid off his clothes. Four months, he thought; no one for four months . . . But the words dissolved beneath Nicole's tongue; his hands held her breasts as her fingers curved around him, and then she took him deep into her throat, sending desire surging through his veins like a flood of molten silver.

He had to take her; the rest, the slow playing, would have to wait. He pulled himself out of her mouth and began to turn her so he could lie on her. But with a smile, as if it were still her serve, she stayed above him, moving smoothly, sinuously, upward, along his body. He saw the faint light reflected in her amber eyes; he saw the luster of her long pearls against her breasts; he watched her firm white body cover his darker one. His burning skin felt the marble coolness of hers, and fleetingly he thought of the strangeness of that, but then she was astride him, lowering herself onto him. Her breasts were above his face; he brought one and then the other into his mouth. He heard her say his name in a long whisper, like a breeze lifting their locked bodies, and then the playroom, like the past, disappeared.

336

C H A P T E R 11

I'm inviting you to dinner," Tony said on the telephone. "I'll be there by four o'clock; five at the latest—"

"I'm sorry, Tony; we won't be here. In fact, we'll be in Los Angeles."

"You told me you weren't coming in this weekend."

"I wasn't. We decided at the last minute—"

"We?"

"My children and I. Peter is driving to college and we're going with him as far as Los Angeles for a couple of days. I've been promising them a trip for a long time, but Holly had to wait until the opera season ended."

"Wonderful. I'm a superb tour guide; we'll give them a visit they won't forget."

"That's sweet of you, Tony, but I know my way around by now. We won't bother you."

"I want you to bother me. I want to see you. I was coming to Santa Fe this weekend, remember? Call me when you get in. You're staying in the cottage at the Beverly Hills? Elizabeth? Will you call me or shall I call you?"

"I'll call you if we have time, Tony. This really is a weekend for the three of us."

"I'd like to make it four. Think about it. Please."

She thought about it while taking turns at the wheel with Peter and Holly on the drive from Santa Fe to Los Angeles. The desert shimmered with heat waves rising from metallic brown sand to a pale sky, and when she was not driving she put her head back, eyes closed, playing word games with Peter and Holly or listening to Holly sing snatches of folk songs or operatic arias, or thinking of Tony.

"Are we going to see Tony?" Holly asked as they drove past the outskirts of Palm Springs, a sudden oasis, sharply defined, like a picture neatly cut out and pasted on the sand.

"I don't think we'll have time," Elizabeth replied.

"But won't he be at the television studios when you take us there?"

"Probably not. He doesn't come in on Friday."

"We could call him."

"I don't think so," Elizabeth said sharply. Then, more gently, she added, "We'll see how the weekend goes, Holly."

They did not mention Tony again, though later, as she led them through the different buildings of the television center, past dressing rooms and makeup rooms and along a corridor lined with studios, Elizabeth knew Holly was looking for him, and Peter was alert for anyone who looked at all familiar. "This is where we tape 'Anthony,'" she told them, and pulled open a high door, standing back to let Holly and Peter walk in ahead of her. "Tony's set," she said, gesturing toward the cut-away library where she had done her first on-camera interview, with Greg Roscov, in June. Almost three months ago, she thought. It was so fresh it seemed like yesterday, but at the same time it felt like years ago: so much had happened since then.

"You'd never know it's the same room you see on television," Peter said. "It feels fake when you stand in it and half of it isn't here."

Elizabeth smiled. "Television would collapse if it weren't for people's imaginations. Everyone would see it for the mirage it is. That's my set, in the other corner."

Holly was already walking toward it. The feel of the studio, dim, mysterious, romantic, sent shivers of excitement through her. Applause was best—an audience on its feet, cheering and clapping and calling for encores—but that was only a few thousand people. Television! Holly thought, stepping up to the platform where Elizabeth interviewed her guests. *Millions of people!*

On the platform, she sat down and looked around. It was a rustic porch, with a wood railing and deep-cushioned bent-twig chairs drawn up to a round olive-wood table that usually held glasses and a pitcher of lemonade, or pottery mugs and a matching coffee pot. Behind the porch was a painted backdrop of green mountains fading into the distance. "It's exactly like our sets at the opera," Holly said. "Nothing looks real when you get up close."

"You waiting for Mom to interview you?" Peter asked, joining her.

"No, she should do you, you're the one leaving for college. Don't you have profound thoughts on life and love to pass on to the vast viewing audience of 'Private Affairs'?"

Peter tipped back his head and contemplated the thicket of canister lights hanging at all angles above them, covering the ceiling. "I'd tell them that no one knows if love will last and they shouldn't look for guarantees, but that doesn't mean they shouldn't take a chance because unhappiness doesn't last, either."

"Cynical," Holly observed. "But vague. Why don't you say what you mean? You told Maya you don't want her in Stanford."

"That's not for television," Peter said. "That is really and truly private. And since Mother has a way of getting people to tell her their secrets, that is why I am not one of her guests."

"Maybe you will be when you're becoming a famous anthropologist and writer," Elizabeth said. "People will want to know what's behind your success."

"Would you be a guest on Mother's show?" Peter asked Holly.

She shook her head. "I'd be afraid of blurting things out. Like you. You don't want to talk about going off to your exciting campus and leaving Maya behind."

"You don't know anything about it. She thinks I should start

339

fresh in a new place, without being tied down. She thinks I can go faster by myself and she doesn't want to slow me down."

"She thinks or you think?"

"We both do! And she's got a job at home, helping run Isabel's campaign—"

"That's just volunteer stuff. Everybody in Nuevo is doing it."

"She's being paid; she's organizing the volunteers. She's terrific. When Isabel's elected she'll be her administrative assistant. She's got a career!"

"And maybe someday you'll get together again?"

"I DON'T KNOW! Damn it, I told you: there aren't any guarantees!"

"What about our tour?" Elizabeth asked. She had been watching them, wondering how well she knew these two adults who had been children such a short time ago. "Shall we go on?"

"I didn't *enjoy* telling her goodbye," Peter said. "It wasn't easy, you know."

"We know," Elizabeth said gently. "Come on, now. You haven't seen the control room. Holly?"

Holly came down from the porch. "I'm sorry," she said to Peter.

He shrugged. "You were only doing it to keep me from asking you about your own private affairs."

She looked at him mischievously. "It worked, didn't it?"

He laughed and they left the studio and walked down a long, wide hall, stopping now and then to examine painted flats and props stacked against the walls: sewing machines, rocking chairs, beds, fabric flowers, desks, bathroom scales, dishes, silverware, wine glasses, even a spinning wheel. Crew members were consulting prop lists and gathering items for different shows, and as Holly and Peter eavesdropped, taking it all in, Elizabeth watched them as she had before. It's hard to grow up, she thought ruefully. My talented, beautiful offspring are having trouble doing it, and sometimes I think, so am I.

They turned corners, peeked into makeup and costume rooms, slipped quietly into studios. In one, they watched a cast rehearse a segment of a soap opera; in another they listened to a comedian tell jokes to an audience, warming it up for the game show that was about to begin. After a few minutes, Elizabeth led them from the building, across a parking lot to another with a long hall running between small rooms, each with a glass window cut in the wall. "I feel like I'm in an aquarium," Holly said, watching technicians setting up satellite transmissions, working on sound equipment, remastering tapes of movies and miniseries to fit them on larger reels, and editing tapes of talk shows, newscasts, and sitcoms.

"It's like a whole town," Peter said as they crossed a grassy stretch to still another building. "All these people, and nobody sees them, or even knows they exist—but here they are, all working away just to get one face on a television screen—"

"And well worth it if the face is your mother's," said Tony Rourke, coming up to them at the door of the green room.

In the flurry of greetings and Tony's flamboyant kiss on the back of Elizabeth's and Holly's hands, Elizabeth missed the sudden change in Holly's face and the brightness of her eyes. Tony saw it, but gave no sign that he did, and Peter scowled, but in an instant her face was calm again and her eyes had the distant look they had on the opera stage when she was concentrating.

Inside the green room, a television set was tuned to the game show going on at that moment in a studio downstairs. A group of contestants waiting for the quiz show that would follow it sat nervously shuffling their feet, sipping coffee, staring hypnotically at the screen. Tony and Elizabeth led the way to the lavish buffet where the four of them chose from an assortment of coffee cakes and cookies, and then to a pair of leather couches. Peter was talking all the while. "Mother told us you don't come in on Friday."

"She's right. But I change my schedule when I suspect we might have interesting visitors. Will you let me help you see Los Angeles? Starting with dinner tonight? I'd love to take all of you to some local spot, and tomorrow I'll dedicate myself to acting like a guide who thinks Los Angeles is paradise on earth."

"Oh, Mother, please," Holly begged.

341

"Not tomorrow," Elizabeth said. "It's the last day Peter will be with us for quite a while, and I'd like it to be just the three of us. But dinner tonight would be lovely, Tony. Thank you."

"Someplace where we can recognize people?" Holly asked Tony.

"Trust me," Tony said, and took them that night to Ma Maison. As they sat down, he watched in open amusement as Holly and Peter gazed around them with faces lengthening in disappointment. "Problems?" he asked.

"It's . . . not what I expected . . ." Holly said feebly.

"After seeing a parking lot filled with Rolls-Royces and Mercedes," Tony finished. "That, of course, is part of the charm of the place."

Holly was having trouble finding charm. Tony had called it one of the city's best-known restaurants, but all she saw was a small room with a low, faded canvas tent for a ceiling, white plastic chairs with small cushions, and a thin carpet covering the hard floor. Recalling the restaurants Matt had taken them to in Houston, she looked for glittering women in silks and satins, but there were none: the women were casually dressed, and few of them wore jewels. They looked quite ordinary.

"Dear Holly," said Tony, and took her hand for a moment. "Ma Maison poses. That does have a certain charm when it is not overdone. And if you'll look carefully, you'll see that nothing is overdone. A bud vase with a single perfect rose. A small candle. Waiters in tuxedoes, but with the homey touch of white aprons hanging to their knees. Fine china and silver, simple, not gauche. Now look again at the faces around you. I guarantee they're recognizable, though not as easily as if they were made up for television. Look closely, relax, and let the place grow on you. I recommend the lobster salad as a first course. And wine. Do you drink wine?"

"A little," Holly breathed.

"Elizabeth?" Tony turned in his chair, giving her all his attention. "My dear, you look exquisite. I haven't seen that dress."

"From a modest corner of Rodeo Drive," Elizabeth said, her color high as his eyes moved slowly over her face and body.

"If you found a modest corner on Rodeo Drive, you're the only one who ever did. Jonquil silk; perfect for you. And of course I recognize the necklace—"

Glancingly, Elizabeth saw Peter's eyes narrow in suspicion. "It was a gift from the staff of 'Anthony,'" she told him and Holly. "To welcome me to the show."

"It was indeed," Tony said promptly, picking up her cue. "Though they asked my help in picking it out—in a not-so-modest corner of Rodeo Drive. It's wonderful with that dress: you have a glow that dims the candles at Ma Maison."

Elizabeth smiled again, but picked up the wine list and handed it to him, to let him know to stop. "Wine," he said immediately. "Thank you for reminding me. A bottle of Montrachet? Perhaps two. The offspring can join us."

Holly sucked in her breath. *Offspring.* And the way Tony's face had changed when he looked at her mother! She felt Peter's hand on hers and looked up to meet his sympathetic eyes. "Ignore it," he said under his breath. "He's an actor; it doesn't mean anything."

Holly nodded. "Sure. Thanks," she added. "That was nice."

"I'm a nice brother," he said, and grinned. Holly smiled back, suddenly very grateful for him. "Yes, you are," she agreed, and then settled back, looking around the restaurant, trying to see it with Tony's eyes—posing as a casual little summer place with food and prices that hardly matched. Charming, she reminded herself. And to add to the charm, the owner came from the small bar on the other side of the entrance to greet Tony, to shake hands with all of them, to admire Elizabeth.

That was the moment when Holly, looking beyond him, began to recognize other diners—and to see that some of them were casting sidelong glances at *her*. Well, not really, she thought; they're really wondering about Mother and Tony and how come Tony Rourke brings *offspring* on a date. But it didn't matter; it was fun to be watched; she liked it. *And someday they'll watch me and know I'm Holly Lovell, the great singer, and they'll wonder who my guests are, that I liked enough to treat to a dinner at Ma Maison.*

The owner left their table; waiters brought their dinner, and a soft wine that lay on Holly's tongue like a warm caress. She ate and drank slowly, savoring each bite, each sip, listening to Tony and Elizabeth answer Peter's questions about television and talk about "Anthony" and people they knew. She was silent, listening to Tony's voice, low and smooth, and she pretended it was just for her.

"—confusion of *my* first year at college," he was saying to Peter. "I didn't like my father, so I didn't miss him, but I missed my familiar routines; I hated starting from scratch. I was terrified I'd do the wrong thing: insult the guy who hated Texans and kept a gun hidden under his mattress or say the wrong words to the most beautiful girl on campus—"

"You must have said the right ones," Elizabeth commented, smiling. "You married her."

"No, I said the wrong ones, exactly as I feared. *Will you marry me?* Of course, I was out of college by then, but they were still wrong because it was the wrong girl. I was in love with a girl back home, you see, but I didn't know it until after I'd uttered those disastrous words."

Tony went on about his college years and the years following when he worked for his father in Houston while dreaming of television, and then his first years in Hollywood—"when I was right back where I started; worrying about men with guns and saying the wrong words to beautiful women."

"And marrying them?" Peter asked.

"And marrying them. Though not lately."

Holly ate more and more slowly, and lingered over a dessert she was too full to eat, trying to make dinner last forever, but finally Tony was paying the check and he and Elizabeth were definitely getting ready to go. "It's so lovely here," Holly said desperately. "I hate to go back to the hotel."

"Hotel!" Tony exclaimed. "At this early hour? In Los Angeles, the city of dreams?"

Elizabeth watched Holly, enthralled, and Peter, his hostility gone, listen as Tony told them about a place called Mercutio. He'd thought of everything, she reflected. He planned the weekend so she could choose what she wanted from it. But as he drove them there, pointing out sights from the Hollywood

Freeway, Elizabeth knew she was enjoying herself not only because of his thoughtfulness, but mainly because she liked being with a man who paid her compliments, admired her with his eyes, and let her know, in dozens of little ways, that he was waiting for her.

To be what? she wondered that night in one of the cottages on the grounds of the Beverly Hills Hotel that "Anthony" kept for its guests. Friend, companion, co-worker, she told herself as she had told Tony—how many times?—since beginning to make regular trips to Los Angeles. And he had been more patient and charming than in all the years she'd known him. He had said nothing about Matt after a brief remark that it seemed he'd found a way to deal with Rourke better than Tony ever had. "But sons seldom do well with their own fathers, do they?" he'd added lightly, and that was all he said about Matt.

But he said a great deal about Elizabeth, especially her increased sophistication before the camera in the six interviews she had completed. Each interview was more relaxed than the one before; each was more revealing of the person she drew out with her questions and her ability to respond quickly to an unexpected response, changing direction with a smoothness and sensitivity that took everyone, including her guests, by surprise. Bo Boyle, though he would never overdo his praise in public, was privately ecstatic when describing her over candlelit dinners with the young man who shared his Laurel Canyon home.

And Tony heard all of it and passed it on to Elizabeth. Which was very thoughtful of him, Elizabeth told herself, turning out the light in the room at the Beverly Hills Cottages; another sign of how far he'd come from being an overly-dramatic, self-centered boy to a pleasant companion. *Oh stop being so cool and boring about him. Admit it: he's fun to be with; he makes you feel desirable; he's a handsome, successful, exciting man. He's a Tony you haven't known since you were seventeen.*

But I was taken in by him when I was seventeen, she reminded herself. He forgot me and married someone else . . . *said the wrong words and married the wrong girl.*

But of course Tony always did have a good line, she thought drowsily. And I'm old enough now to recognize it when I hear it. And then she was asleep, and barely stirred until she heard Peter's knock on her door the next morning. "I thought we should get an early start," he said through the closed door. "It's just the three of us, right? You haven't changed that?"

"No; it's just us. Give me ten minutes to get ready."

They had a quick breakfast; then Peter allowed Elizabeth to drive his Wagoneer—"so I can gawk," he said, and that was what he and Holly did as they toured the city that stretched over green hills and into flower-filled valleys. Over and over, they exclaimed at the lush green, so different from home. Even with its pink-brown adobe and dark green pines, Santa Fe paled in memory as they drove past dense lawns glistening beneath sprinklers, tall flowering cacti, skinny palms topped by head-dresses of drooping leaves, and coral trees with long branches parallel to the ground, massed with dark leaves and huge, vivid red flowers, each petal as big as a child's hand.

After some searching they found Olvera Street, thinking it would remind them of home, but, like much of Los Angeles, it was more like a stage set for a Hispanic neighborhood than the real thing. "But it's all very colorful," said Holly. "It makes Houston seem rather *square*."

"Los Angeles is *wild*, when you think about it," said Peter.

"Houston is solid, like gas and oil wells," Holly responded sagely.

"Los Angeles is curlicues and minarets and statues."

"Houston is flat and rich and modern—"

"Los Angeles is hedges clipped to look like animals, mush-rooms, arches, and permanent erections—"

"Houston is elegant women, humidity, and men in cowboy hats—"

"Los Angeles is elegant women, humidity, green lipstick, and men in cowboy hats."

They dissolved in laughter. Their two worlds, Elizabeth thought. Their two families.

"Where's UCLA?" Peter asked her. "We want to help you relive your youth."

Elizabeth drove up Westwood to a neighborhood of low buildings with bookstores, restaurants, and shops that was the first part of Los Angeles that looked like a small town. At the far end were the gates of the Los Angeles campus of the University of California, and they drove up the curving street, higher and higher, passing dormitories in the hills to their left and athletic fields in a sunken amphitheater to their right. "That was our side of the campus," Elizabeth said, pointing to older, Spanish style buildings on the far side of the athletic fields. "I think there's a parking lot at the top of this hill."

She was swept by memories. There were new buildings, but she recognized old ones and she felt again the comfort of a campus separate from the rest of the world, shaded by huge trees, the roads lined with red brick buildings mellow and warm under the hot sun. We didn't appreciate it when we were here, she thought as the campus seemed to wrap itself around her, making the world she lived in as unreal as the sets she and Tony used in television.

From the parking lot they strolled into the shade of a vast sculpture garden. "Most of this is new," Elizabeth murmured. "They've bought so many pieces."

Peter was darting from one sculpture to the other, exclaiming in delight at familiar names. "Henry Moore and Jean Arp and Giacometti . . ." Looking up, he saw Elizabeth starting up the broad steps of a brick building. He loped back to her. "What's this place?"

"Dodd Hall; the school of journalism. Where your father and I met, and worked together on the campus paper, and passed love notes back and forth in class." The corridor seemed dark, after the sunlight, and she paused. "It doesn't look the same." Frowning, she read the names beside the doors and looked into the classrooms. "Excuse me," she said at last, stopping a professor coming out of a classroom. "Isn't this the school of journalism?"

"Oh, my, no," he said. "That was phased out some time ago."

"Phased out?" Elizabeth looked down the corridor at the rectangle of sun that was the front entrance. "Why did they get rid of it?" she asked the professor.

"You know, my dear, I don't know. I never knew much about

it, though I believe some of the school's graduates have become rather distinguished in the newspaper world."

"Yes," Elizabeth said, "I believe they have." She walked on, belatedly remembering to turn and thank him, but she was distracted by an overwhelming sense of change and loss. *I thought it would be here forever. I thought a lot of things would last forever.*

They shared their leftover lunch in a corner of the sculpture garden, then drove down Sunset Boulevard to the white gates of Bel Air. Elizabeth drove slowly up the steep twisting road to the top, catching panoramic glimpses of the city, fading into mist on the horizon. Wildflowers grew along the road and trailing leafy branches brushed the Wagoneer when they pulled close to high gates where Peter and Holly craned their necks, trying to see the mansions hidden behind thick shrubs and huge trees. "I wish we could go inside," Holly said, gazing at the corner of a terrace beneath an arbor of riotous flowering vines. "Does Tony live up here?"

"No," Elizabeth said. "He lives in Malibu. We can drive over there, if you'd like."

"Oh, please."

They drove to the Pacific Coast Highway and then turned to follow the ocean where Peter and Holly exclaimed at white sand beaches and the sun-splashed ocean with dark figures of swimmers and sailboats skimming past. Thinking of the hundreds of miles they had driven that day, Holly sighed. "There's so *much*. Santa Fe seems awfully . . . small."

"It is small," Elizabeth agreed. "But it has its own beauty and its own pleasures. No city has a monopoly on those."

"You mean Houston has them, too?" Holly asked, almost slyly.

"Yes," Elizabeth said after a moment. "Houston probably has them, too. I haven't been there long enough to find out. We're coming into Malibu; we ought to stop talking and admire the scenery."

Mountains were on one side; the ocean on the other. "How do we get to the beach?" Peter asked as they rounded a curve and saw a gatekeeper guarding the road.

"We don't," Elizabeth answered. "This stretch is private."

"People own the beach?"

"In this part of Malibu."

"Is Tony one of them?" Holly asked.

"Yes," Elizabeth said.

"You mean we can't see his house? The gatekeeper would let us by, wouldn't he? If he knew we were Tony's friends?"

"The gatekeeper meets people every day who call themselves Tony's friends," Elizabeth said.

"But we really are!"

"Even so, we're not going to try. Maybe next time you come here we'll arrange it."

"You've been there," Holly said flatly.

"Yes, and someday you will be, too. Right now, though, we're going to stay on the public part of the beach; we'll be there in a few minutes."

They drove down an access road beyond the row of private homes and then walked along the water, while Holly's mood swung from disappointment to delight in the beauty around them. But later some of her prickliness returned when they finally began to talk about their family.

It was when they were eating dinner, their second picnic of the day, though this time, instead of leftovers, it was an assortment of pâtés and smoked fish Elizabeth had bought at Mon Grenier, in Malibu. They sat on the grass of the Hollywood Bowl, surrounded by the Santa Monica mountains. Thousands of people around them were sprawled on blankets or sitting on folding chairs at tables set with cloths, crystal, and candles, while children shouted and played tag until hauled in by their parents, only to begin again a few minutes later.

The night was warm, the breeze brisk as the sun went down, and then, as they finished dinner, Peter remembered aloud the days when they'd all picnicked at the open-air Santa Fe Opera, and Holly thought aloud how much her father would like this spectacular place, and then they were talking about Matt.

"I don't think he's really happy," said Holly. "I mean, he's busy and he's doing lots of interesting things, but when we talk on the phone he always says he misses us—and I don't

349

understand how you can be having such a good time and running around with Tony when Daddy's in another city, alone and lonesome . . ."

Her voice faded away. Around them, many of the picnickers were packing up to sit on the wooden benches closer to the stage. Others remained on their blankets and, like them, Peter lay back, staring at the sky, listening to his sister and his mother.

"If your father is lonesome, he knows where to find me," Elizabeth said at last. "But I haven't heard anything from you or him that makes me think he's unhappy. Holly, he chose to go to Houston alone; he chose what he's doing. We talked about it and that was what he wanted. I've told you everything I can about what's happened to us. Nothing has changed. You talk to him more than I do; you know better than I what he's thinking. But as far as I can tell, he's making his own way at his own speed and he still thinks he can do that best if I'm not with him. When he changes his mind, he'll tell me. And I'll tell you."

"And Tony?" Holly asked after a moment.

"Tony is my friend. I've known him for twenty-five years; he's made it possible for me to be on television; he likes me, he tells me so, and he's fun to be with. Would you rather I didn't have fun? What do you think I should do? Sit at home with the doors and windows locked while my husband decides what he wants to do with his life?"

Holly squirmed uncomfortably. Peter turned his head and looked at Elizabeth. "Isn't there anything in between? Couldn't you have fun with Isabel and Heather and Saul?"

Elizabeth smiled. "I do."

"But you're not really happy without a man," Holly said. "Telling you how perfect you are in jonquil silk."

Elizabeth gave her a long silent look until Holly dropped her eyes. "It's nice to be admired by a man. It's nice to share a dinner with a man. It's nice to talk about your work with a man. You know all that; you want the same things. I hope you find them with a man you love. If you don't, I hope you find them with a man who is a friend."

The music began. The lilting melodies of a Strauss waltz

350

danced through the natural amphitheater. Dreamily, Peter said, "I wonder how many friends Dad has in Houston."

"Peter!" Holly cried, and vehement shushes came from the people around them.

"I don't know," Elizabeth said in a low voice. She was uncomfortable and unwilling to admit it. "I'm sure he has some. He needs companionship as much as anyone, and you know how attractive he is . . . I'm sure he has a lot of—a few— casual friends . . ."

She was being shushed as vigorously as Holly had been, and she fell silent, sitting quietly with her arms folded about her knees, her thoughts far from waltzes, far from Los Angeles. She hadn't let herself put it into words, but why wouldn't Matt sleep with other women? He was a sexual man who wasn't used to sleeping alone after twenty years of marriage . . . especially after the two years that followed their purchase of the *Chieftain*, when they'd been so close.

The music reached a crescendo and as it ended, the audience burst into applause, breaking into her thoughts. I'll deal with it later, she told herself, and it almost worked. Her thoughts about Matt lay just below the surface all evening, and into the next day when the three of them had breakfast before Peter left for Stanford.

"You'll sort of keep an eye on Maya, won't you?" he asked as he got up from the table. "You'll be there, anyway, with Isabel; could you just stop in once in a while and see that she's okay?"

"Of course," Elizabeth said.

"I will, too," Holly said. "Luz and I will keep her too busy to be unfaithful."

"I didn't mean that," Peter said, flushing. "When people are apart for a long time, you can't expect them to . . . Oh, shit, I'm sorry, Mom."

Elizabeth ignored it. "Are you all packed?"

"Sure."

"And everything is in the car?"

"Mom, stop worrying. I've got everything. I am fully prepared to face the world. And"—he grinned a little lopsidedly—

351

"it's only a trifle scary." He gave Holly a quick hug, then put his arms around Elizabeth, holding her so tightly she was breathless. "I wish I could stay home with you, Mom. I hate to leave you alone."

With her hands on his chest Elizabeth put a few inches between them. "I'm not alone, Peter; I'll be fine. You're the one who's going off among strangers. But I predict you'll take the place by storm." She kissed him on both cheeks and held him. "I'm so proud of you, dearest Peter; I'm going to miss you."

Against her cheek she felt the muscles of Peter's face tighten and knew he was facing the reality for the first time of *leaving;* of never living at home again in the same way; of no longer being able to hide behind youth or helplessness when things got rough.

"But I like knowing you'll be doing what you most want to do," she went on, giving him no time to ponder the fears that surged up when least expected. "And I'll feel close to you when I read your letters. Because you are going to write, aren't you, Peter?" She held him away again. "Regularly."

"Sure." He grinned that lopsided grin again. "Or I'll find the front door locked when I come home for Christmas, right?"

"Wrong. The front door will never be locked to you. But write anyway. I love to get mail."

Peter grinned again, then dropped his arms. Elizabeth had gotten him past the shaky part and he was ready to leave. "I'll call you tonight, okay? When I get my room and phone number and everything. You and Holly'll be home by then, won't you?"

Elizabeth saw that he was ready, but suddenly she was the one to hold him back. *My family is shrinking. Just two of us left—Holly and I—in all the rooms of our house where there were four not very long ago. And in a year Holly will be gone, too. But by then . . . maybe Matt and I . . .*

Peter was looking toward the Wagoneer and she stepped back, setting him free. "I'm pretty sure we'll be home. If there's no answer, keep trying."

He gave Holly a quick hug. "Take care of everybody. I may call you up now and then. If you don't mind."

Holly shook her head, biting her lip. "I think I might miss you, too, like Mother."

Peter looked at the two of them standing side by side. He coughed and bent to kiss Elizabeth again. "I love you, Mom." He coughed again because his voice was sounding weird and he wasn't sure he could trust it. He got behind the wheel and leaned out the window.

"Drive—" Elizabeth bit her tongue. Do not tell him to drive carefully, she ordered herself, and then heard herself say, "Watch out for the other drivers."

Holly and Peter burst into laughter, and Elizabeth joined them, and so, with laughter buoying him up, Peter pushed in the clutch, shifted gears, and drove away.

The dust was thick and choking on the road to Nuevo and heavy trucks rumbled around the narrow curves that led to the town. Dynamite blasts echoed off the mountains; pneumatic drills, like deafening machine guns, rattled through the valley; the roar of engines and warning beeps of trucks as they backed up was heard all day long.

Elizabeth hated to make the trip—a drive she had once looked forward to as an escape into a lovely timeless serenity— but she knew it was worse for Isabel and Maya and the others who lived beside the construction site. And so, at least once a week through the red and gold days of September, she gritted her teeth, rolled up the car windows to keep out as much dust as possible, and went to see them.

In almost every way, Nuevo was being transformed. Saul had kept his promise and hired a lawyer to try to get the court to stop construction until the dam could be studied more fully, but that had failed: reports on four years of study had been submitted to the Committee on Land Use and Development; it had studied them further, then recommended approval to the legislature, which had duly approved it. There was no reason, the judge said, to grant an injunction. The work could proceed.

And so construction headquarters were set up on the high ground at the narrow end of the valley, where an abandoned farm had been sold long ago to Terry Ballenger. Office trailers,

353

equipment sheds, portable toilets, and fuel tanks sat helter-skelter near a bulldozed parking area for cars and trucks. Below the headquarters, crews were digging a channel to divert the Pecos River from its normal course through the town. The channel would lead the river in a sweeping turn around the town and the dam site, forcing it into a tunnel blasted through the rocks on one side of the narrow exit from the valley. From there the river would connect with the riverbed below the Nuevo Valley. The following summer, when the dam was built, if all went according to plan, the diversion channel would be closed, the river would return to its original course—and when it was stopped by the dam it would overflow its banks, flooding the town and the lowest part of the valley, and form a lake.

"But of course nothing will go 'according to plan,'" Cesar told Elizabeth. "We're taking care of that."

And that was another way Nuevo was being transformed: it had become Isabel's campaign team. In almost every house, in Gaspar's General Store, in Roybal's Maintenance Shop and Gas Station, the people of Nuevo were mimeographing letters to voters, addressing and stuffing envelopes, lettering posters, lining up private homes where Isabel could meet voters and talk to them, arranging campaign appearances in village squares and crossroads of small towns.

Cesar was in charge of the campaign, but in a few weeks Maya had become his best helper. She knew nothing of political campaigns, but she knew everyone in the valley and she soon learned that her small wistful smile could convince someone to work another hour or seal another hundred envelopes and her solemn black eyes could make someone willing to do the dullest job. Soon, with the ideas she picked up from Saul and Elizabeth, the newspapers she read every day, and her fierce belief in Isabel, she became more confident, taking on whatever tasks she was given. She was finding a place for herself.

Nuevo worked for Isabel and fought the dam, but in other towns and valleys voices were raised in argument. As the summer wore on, Isabel campaigned in a district that was becoming sharply divided, because for the first time in years there were jobs in the valley.

Most of the people in Nuevo knew nothing of the politics behind the dam, the new roads, and the resort; what was important to them was that the companies doing the work were New Mexican, using local workers. Months earlier, in the spring, hiring had begun; young people, hearing of jobs, came back to Pecos and Nuevo and other small towns that had been dying, and engineers and foremen from Albuquerque added to the growing population by setting up house trailers for the season. Roybal was making twice as much money in his gas station as the year before; business tripled in Gaspar's General Store; and in July Hector Corona re-opened the restaurant and bar he had closed five years earlier.

"Boom time in Nuevo," said Isabel wryly, handing a paper plate to Elizabeth and settling with a sigh on the grass beside the river. They were at the far end of the valley, away from the town. No longer could they eat in lawn chairs beside Isabel's house, talking in low voices and listening to the cry of a jay overhead; the jay and their voices were drowned out by the noise of construction. Even where they sat, more than a mile from the site, they had to stop talking when the warning siren sounded, and, a few minutes later, when dynamite was set off.

"It could lose me the election," Isabel went on, gazing at the cloud of dust over the distant town. "Even if I win, I might have to support the dam and everything that goes with it because that's what the voters are beginning to want."

"Enough of them?" Elizabeth asked.

"Maybe. Most people in the district think we're being screwed and they're sorry, but in private they probably thank the Lord it's us and not them. Almost everybody in Nuevo wants me in the legislature so I can stop these guys from destroying a town just so they can get rich from a private resort—"

A siren sliced through the valley, short high bursts of sound warning everyone away. "Here comes another one," Isabel said. "And every explosion changes the shape of the valley. That's something we'll never be able to undo."

A few minutes after the siren, the dynamite blast shattered the rock, seeming to rattle whole mountains, making the ground tremble. Elizabeth refilled their glasses from the thermos of lemonade. The deafening noise, the army of trucks and workers, and the fact that Isabel was right—mountains that had seemed eternal were being reshaped before their eyes—made the immensity of the forces at work very real and seemingly unstoppable. "You're only one person, Isabel," she said. "Do people really think you can stop all this if you're elected?"

"Some do. But I've stopped making promises because I'm stuck. I don't know what to say. Isn't that something? Isabel Aragon stumped for words! But what the hell do I say to people in the towns and valleys where they're getting jobs without losing their homes and farms? They won't fight the dam; why should they? Nuevo loses everything—even the ones who are making money now, Roybal and the others, will be gone by next spring when our twelve-month grace period is up—so of course it fights the dam. And I'm in the middle. Which is nowhere."

Elizabeth stood up for a better view of the trucks and the small figures of workers scurrying about. "I wonder if there is a middle," she said thoughtfully. "Something we've missed. A way to have the dam and the resort and still have the town. And jobs and money coming to the townspeople . . ."

"What is this? A fairy tale? Nobody but fish will live in Nuevo when the dam is built. And money . . . what the hell, Elizabeth, you know the compensation they'll pay us won't be enough—"

"I didn't mean compensation."

"Then what did you mean?"

"I meant maybe we ought to think about using the dam instead of fighting it."

"Another convert—my dearest friend, who owns land in Nuevo which, of course, will be flooded. How can I hold out if even you switch sides?"

"I'm not; I'm looking for a compromise. I'm thinking about the real world, Isabel: what we do when things don't turn out the way we'd like. What we can salvage when it seems we won't get our heart's desire."

"Are those the words of an expert?"

"Those are the words of experience." Elizabeth sat down

again and drank her lemonade. "Now tell me about your campaign, and what I can do to help. I wanted to interview you on television but my interviews have to be completely different from Tony's, and since his guests are all in the public eye, mine can't be anywhere near it. Maybe later, if people like me, I can interview anyone I want."

"No mail yet? You've been on two weeks."

"A few phone calls. Nothing much. Tony says it takes a while. Matt said the same thing about newspaper columns."

"Speaking of Matt——"

"Let's not."

"Oh. Sorry."

Elizabeth put her hand on Isabel's. "*I'm* sorry; I didn't mean to cut you off. I've been so jumpy lately: I can't get used to the house with just Holly and me in it, and I never seem to have enough time for everything. I could handle three columns a week and a taped interview, but I've been going to Los Angeles every week, just overnight——"

"Holly told us. On a private jet, no less."

"It belongs to the show; Tony uses it more than anyone. And it saves time, because I don't have to go to Albuquerque; it lands at the municipal airport in Santa Fe. But I have less time with Holly, and my mother expects us to have dinner at least once a week, and Heather wants to talk about Saul, and on top of everything it's so awful coming here and seeing what's happening to the valley . . ."

"Yes indeed." Isabel put her arms around Elizabeth. "We'll have to cheer each other up. Shall we go to a singles bar and check out the scene?"

Elizabeth burst out laughing. "Where did you get that?"

"Luz and Holly were talking the other day——"

"Luz and Holly! They aren't planning to do it!"

"Far from it; they said they'd never consider it unless they were old and hadn't found anybody interesting."

"How old?"

"Twenty-five."

Their laughter drowned out the sounds of trucks and drills, and for that moment, when they could pretend everything was

357

the way it had always been, they felt better; they felt that whatever was wrong could be made right.

And maybe it can, Elizabeth thought later, driving back to Santa Fe to pack for a flight to Los Angeles. Why not? Give us time to plan, and to choose the right direction, and if we really believe in ourselves, who's to say we can't make things right?

Before she left, she called Saul to tell him she'd be back the next day for their weekly meeting. "In the afternoon, unless something is urgent enough for the morning."

"Nothing is urgent," he said. "You know how quiet it is after the Fiesta. I may even take a vacation, if I can convince my fiancée to come along."

"Why don't you marry her?" Elizabeth asked abruptly.

"I beg your pardon?"

"You stopped talking about setting a date a long time ago, didn't you?"

"I did. I communed with nature in the forest near Nuevo, before dynamite made communing impossible, and concluded that one person can't force another to feel desire. You can perhaps make someone like you, feel grateful to you, even love you. You cannot make someone desire you or your presence on a permanent basis. I don't want Heather marrying me because I've exhausted her or made her feel guilty about putting me off. I want her to want me on a full-time basis. If she doesn't desire that enough to overcome her reluctance, I don't desire it either."

"Not true," Elizabeth said.

"Of course not. But I'll grow old waiting until she wants it as much as I do. And she was right, you know, a long time back when she said we have good times together. We're great in bed and we're good friends. I count myself lucky; how many married people have all that? Or am I asking the wrong person?"

"Probably. I'll see you tomorrow, Saul."

She'd sounded wistful, Saul thought, and was wishing he could tell Matt what he thought of him, when he saw the assistant printer through the glass wall and went out to meet him. "The repairman showed up?"

"He just . . . appeared," the assistant said. "I was in the other room and when I came back, he was there, working on it."

"How'd he get past the front desk?"

"Search me. The back door, maybe?"

Scowling, Saul walked down the hall to the pressroom. "How the hell did you get in?" he demanded of the two legs stretched out on the floor behind the printing press. "You're a day late as it is, goddam it, and then to prance in here as if you own the joint—" He stopped short as the repairman stood up and he found himself face to face with Matt, holding out his hand with a grin.

"I do own it—I think. Anyway, my key still opens the back door."

"I'll be damned." Saul shook Matt's hand. "You just happened to wander in when we needed a repairman?"

"That was just luck. I wanted to look around without running the gauntlet of the newsroom and the kid who was here thought I was the repairman and cheerfully answered all my questions about the presses. Lousy security, Saul; he didn't know me from Adam. He's not very bright, either; wouldn't he wonder why a repairman would be wearing a pinstripe suit? Where's the pressman?"

"Home with the flu. I knew that kid wouldn't last. Did you fix the press?"

Matt grinned again. "A true editor; worry first about the press. I think so. Shall we try it?"

"Sure." Saul looked at him as they pulled out the crumpled paper that had been caught in the press and adjusted a rack of new paper. "Your pinstripe suit may never be the same."

Matt glanced at his sleeve. "Probably not. But it's a good idea to get grease on a suit now and then; otherwise you can forget what a pressroom feels like, smells like . . ."

"Maybe you can. I can't."

Matt set a lever and pressed a button and they watched the press begin to run. "I guess I haven't lost my touch. Was that a criticism, Saul?"

"You're damn right it was. Your wife is a friend of mine, Matt. I care about her."

"Saul. You're out of your territory."

"Bullshit. If a friend can't talk to you about your wife, who can?"

"My wife."

"Your wife is on her way to Los Angeles and I've been itching to tell you—"

"Saul, we'll stay better friends if you drop it."

"We'd stay better friends if we talked more often. Or wrote. I'd even settle for smoke signals. Do you ever read the reports I send you?"

"Not often enough. I don't even read the *Chieftain* as often as I'd like. I have too many editors who need direction; you're not one of them. I'm sorry if you feel ignored."

"Don't make me sound like a cast-off mistress. I don't want instructions shot at me from Houston; I like a free hand. I was only questioning your idea of friendship."

Matt looked around the pressroom, remembering. All those weeks, after they fired Artner and Axel Chase quit, when he'd run the press and Elizabeth did paste-up. All those months when the two of them had worked late into each night, coming home to coffee at the kitchen table and then bed, where they'd found just enough energy to make love. So long ago. One newspaper, one marriage. Simple goals. And when Saul had come, that had been simple, too. He and Elizabeth had more time together; he had a friend.

"I've missed you," he said at last to Saul. He paused. "Is there any reason to keep this press running?"

"You can turn it off," Saul said absently. "Matt," he said abruptly, "I'd like to buy the *Chieftain*. Hold on, don't say anything yet. I've been running it pretty much by myself since you went to Houston; Elizabeth has tried to keep up, but she only has so much time, although I'd want her as consulting editor—"

"She's agreed to this?"

"Calm down; she hasn't agreed to anything. I told her about it last week; she listened politely and said she'd think about it.

I want you to think about it, too. You've got other papers; Elizabeth has her column and her television show. I'd like the *Chieftain*. Trouble is, I don't have much money, but I've worked it out that if the two of you agree to be minority shareholders—"

"No." Matt felt as if he were smothering. He didn't know why, but his throat felt constricted, his muscles knotted, as if he were in a cramped cell, with no room to move. "I'm sorry, Saul; I understand how you feel, but I can't sell it."

"Can't or won't?"

"Can't."

Saul contemplated him. "It's a very tiny part of your empire."

"God damn it, I said no! It's not part of any empire; it's separate and it's mine and it's going to stay that way."

"Yours and Elizabeth's. Or did you forget?"

"Listen, you son of a bitch, that's enough. Just run my newspapers; I can run my own life!" Saul gave a low whistle and Matt closed his eyes, running his hand roughly over them. "Christ, I'm sorry, Saul. Hell of a thing to say; I didn't mean it."

"You don't have to apologize; you know I won't quit. I gave that away, didn't I? I told you I want to buy the paper; this is where I want to be."

Matt paced to the end of the pressroom and stared out the window at the *Chieftain* trucks parked near the loading dock. He shouldn't have come back. It had been a sudden impulse— Peter had called from Stanford and they'd had a long talk and then Matt had had a terrible longing to see Holly and he'd thought he could make a quick stop at the *Chieftain* building; it was his, after all, and he hadn't set foot in it for months— but it was a mistake. He should have sent Holly an airline ticket and stayed in Houston. Something about the place was making him say all the wrong things.

Saul, maybe. Wanting the paper. *Running it pretty much by myself since you went to Houston*. Working with Elizabeth. Deciding editorial policy and whom to endorse—

He turned from the window. "I meant to ask you, Saul: who's

the woman you've endorsed for Tom Ortiz's seat in the legislature?"

Saul stared at him, then began to laugh. "You really don't know? You've made my day, Matt. Isabel Aragon."

"*Isabel*—?" It sank in, and then Matt was laughing with him. "By God, that's wonderful. Of all people! The legislature will never be the same. I wish someone had told me."

"Maybe no one thought you'd be interested."

Matt ignored it. "I'll ask Holly about it at dinner."

"Is that why you're in town?"

"Mostly. I didn't realize how good it would be to see you again." He looked again about the familiar room. "I spend too much time talking about business and not enough wandering around newsrooms."

"I've missed you, too, you know; we had some good times. You were a hell of a publisher. I'm not sure how much we have to share anymore. But I'll give it some thought. Do you have time to say hello to Heather?"

"Of course. Is she here?"

"In my office. Sorry. Yours."

"Yours, Saul. For now."

Through the glass wall they saw Heather look up from the book she was reading and her face light in a smile when she saw Matt. Poor love, Saul thought. She thinks all is well, but she's about to discover once again that men are often unreliable.

"I found a friend in the pressroom," he said, opening the door.

"Matt, how wonderful to have you back!" Heather said, kissing his cheek. "There's grease on your sleeve; what have you been doing? Elizabeth's on her way to—"

"Heather," said Saul quietly.

She looked from his face to Matt's. "Oh. How long are you staying?"

"Through dinner." Her green eyes, losing their warmth, made him uncomfortable. "I'm on my way to Phoenix and I stopped off to—" He caught himself as Saul and Heather exchanged a glance, and he knew they were remembering all the times he'd been annoyed at Tony's "stopping off" in Santa Fe.

Heather's eyes had become as glittering as emeralds. "Saul," she said, "I have some questions about the special section on the opera. When can we talk about it?"

Saul gazed at her thoughtfully, wanting to kiss her. He knew what she had in mind and he loved her for it, but it wouldn't work; Matt might be interested in what they were doing, but not interested enough to change his mind all of a sudden and move back to Santa Fe. They were small potatoes next to what he had in Houston.

But what the hell, he thought; what did they have to lose? "Let's talk about it now," he said. He pulled his desk chair across the room, next to a pair of faded armchairs. "Want to sit in, Matt? Give us the benefit of big city thinking?" Without waiting for an answer, he sat down and when Heather sat in one of the armchairs and handed him a folder, he said, "Elizabeth thought this up a few months ago . . ."

He and Heather began to talk, glancing at Matt without bringing him into the discussion. But after a while he couldn't resist it. The ideas were good; best of all, they were ideas he knew he could use for all his other papers, and soon he was caught up in their talk. He leaned forward, offering a tentative suggestion. "Good thinking," Saul said casually, and added one of his own.

With that, suddenly, the two men were talking at the same time, challenging each other, topping each other, jumping from thought to thought, idea to idea. Now and then Heather asked a question, but mostly it was Matt and Saul, reaching into their store of knowledge for new ways to do traditional things, chuckling as they tossed in impossibly expensive gimmicks or story ideas they'd never put in a family newspaper. Watching them, Heather knew, from the look of contentment on their faces, that only Elizabeth was missing to make this exactly like the wonderful give-and-take sessions they'd had in the years before Matt left.

Matt knew it, too. As he and Saul talked rapidly, voices overlapping, he felt the joy of creating, sharing his experience and skills with the one man whose thoughts most closely matched his. Then, in the middle of a sentence, Saul said, "I have a lot

363

to do before the end of the day. Matt, how about staying over until tomorrow? I don't want to cut in on your dinner with Holly, but in the morning we could—"

The spell was broken. Matt sat back and shook his head. "I'm expected in Phoenix. I'd like a raincheck, though."

Saul nodded, disappointment and nostalgia sweeping through him, even though they'd only been recapturing the past for an hour. Don't act like a cast-off mistress, he ordered himself. We're too small for Matt; I knew that. Small potatoes compared to Rourke Publishing. "We'll be using some of those ideas you've just given us," he said.

"I hope so," Matt replied. "I'm going to do the same. Modified, of course." He hesitated, reluctant to move. "I've enjoyed this."

Saul nodded, then stood up. "So did I. It's fun to look back now and then."

It was polite, but it was a dismissal. Matt kissed Heather, shook hands with Saul, promising to keep in touch, and then he went into the newsroom and talked to the staff, making conversation about Houston and Elizabeth and the *Chieftain*'s success under Saul.

And all the time, beneath the friendly banter, he was telling himself that his joy in one small discussion wasn't important. Nothing he did in Santa Fe could be as far-reaching, or have the same impact, as his work in Houston. The afternoon had been only a reminder of what was gone, like a footprint on a beach or the wake of a boat in a quiet lake. Time didn't stop; people didn't go backward.

He used Barney Kell's telephone to call home—Elizabeth's home—and Holly answered. "I finished early, sweetheart," he said. "Can you spare an extra hour?"

"Oh, yes," Holly said. "How lovely. Mother's not here—"

"I know. I'll see her next time. But I want lots of time with you. Can I pick you up in ten minutes?"

"I'll be ready. I'll be waiting in front."

"I'll see you soon. I'm looking forward to it."

Too formal, he thought. Somewhere between a father and a date. He stood beside Barney's desk, absently gazing through

364

the glass wall of the corner office where Saul Milgrim sat at Matt Lovell's desk. Heather sat nearby, making notes on a page from one of her folders. Watching them, Matt realized they were more harmonious than he had ever seen them. They were working together and they'd already forgotten him; they were busy putting out a paper. And all around him, the newsroom was busy; everyone intent, concentrating . . . it's Wednesday, he thought. Tomorrow they go to press. He was an outsider, watching. And then, he heard Nicole's voice. *You were wonderful. You did exactly what you had to. You have power, Matt.*

The feeling of being an outsider left him. He'd been right; this wasn't his place anymore; it wasn't where he belonged.

The trouble was, he thought as he waved good-bye to the staff and went outside to his rented car, he didn't know exactly where he did belong. The give-and-take with Saul, the brief feeling of a close-knit group he'd had in the newsroom, were part of what he'd given up for Rourke Enterprises. He'd done it because there was a bigger job to do there than any in Santa Fe, but it left him with an empty space that nothing else quite filled, and that odd question of where he belonged.

Maybe nowhere, he thought disconcertingly. But as he drove the familiar route to Camino Rancheros, he brushed it aside. At least in Houston, he knew the direction he was going. He knew what was expected of him; he knew what power he had and how to use it. And Nicole was there, approving what he did. Houston was the closest he could come, at the moment, to being home.

C H A P T E R 12

O n stormy days when the surf was high, waves thundered
against the wall at the base of Tony's Malibu house; when the
wind was calm and the ocean tame, the water lapped in playful
curls and ripples of foam along the glistening sand of his beach.
From the low window seat that spanned the width of his glass-
fronted living room, Elizabeth had watched storms roll across
the sky, and waves rise into huge silver walls hundreds of feet
from shore. When they crested, the top of the waves curved
over, then plunged straight down, like waterfalls along the faces
of the advancing walls that grew smaller as they ran down
themselves until what was left crashed with a roar against the
piled stones protecting Tony's house.

On other nights the ocean was quiet, reflecting vivid sunsets
that lit the room behind Elizabeth in shades of salmon, coral,
burnt umber, violet, and purple. The colors blended imperceptibly into each other until darkness swept them all away, flinging
stars in their place.

On the night of Tony's party in her honor, no one paid
attention to the stars outside: the important ones were in the
house. Tony and Bo Boyle had made up the guest list in the
first week of October; invitations had been printed; envelopes
were stuffed, addressed, and stamped—and tucked away in a

drawer, to be mailed only if "Anthony"'s ratings were up at the end of the month.

They were up three and a half points, moving "Anthony" to second place in its time slot. Television critics across the land wrote solemn analyses of Elizabeth Lovell, "Private Affairs," and the new American passion for the secret lives of "invisible" people. And Bo Boyle, in a reckless moment of uncharacteristic generosity, promised to supply cases of Dom Perignon for Tony's party—the invitations to which had been mailed two minutes after the ratings were in.

"Tony, you're making me feel like the debutante of the year," Elizabeth said as she listened to the two men go over the guest list a final time. She looked at the papers scattered on the round, glass-topped table, with names starred, checked, or crossed out. A breeze off the ocean, reaching the deck where they sat, riffled the sheets of paper, and the rustling mingled with the cries of gulls and the steady rhythm of the waves that slid lazily up the beach and then withdrew. The afternoon sun was low; the three of them wore slacks and cotton shirts and dark glasses, and Elizabeth had trouble believing it was the end of October and she'd worn a wool suit when she left Santa Fe that morning. "If you give this kind of party for me after only two months on your show, what's left? I have nowhere to go but down."

"Give us another five points in the ratings," Bo said in answer, "and we'll charter the Concorde for you. Just to prove you can always go higher."

Higher, she repeated to herself. Big, bigger, biggest. She knew exactly why it tugged at Matt; it tugged her in the same way. She remembered when she had been stopped in grocery aisles in Santa Fe. Now she was stopped in restaurants in Los Angeles, and recognized in the boutiques of Rodeo Drive and Melrose Avenue, and greeted with pleasure by executives and crews of the television network who had long ago stopped being impressed with most celebrities.

And then Tony told her he was giving her a party, to present her to the most important people of television and movies, because she was now one of them.

367

"Paul Markham," said Tony, skimming one of the guest lists on the glass-topped table. "He isn't here."

"Why should he be?" Bo asked. "We're not inviting any newspaper syndicators."

"I want him."

"We already have one hundred and thirty-two—"

"If you're worried about champagne, I'll buy Markham's bottle. Bo, think a minute. We want 'Private Affairs' to appear in as many newspapers as possible, do we not?"

"No question. But we send copies of every one to the syndicators, three times a week, week in and week out—"

"With no results. Markham's different from the others; he likes off-beat pieces. I want him to meet Elizabeth; I want to ply him with your champagne."

Bo shrugged and added the name to a short list before him. "Any more?"

"Not that I can think of. These people should be called; not enough time to use the mail."

"I know. The girls will do it tomorrow." He stood and planted a casual kiss on the top of Elizabeth's head. "I'm off. Some fancy do at the Wilshire tonight and I should make an appearance. You're bringing us luck, Elizabeth. I only wish you'd relent and let me call you Lizzie."

"She's not a Lizzie type," said Tony. "Can you find your own way out?"

"You know I can. Goodbye, E-liz-a-beth."

She smiled. "Goodbye, Bo. I'll remember the Concorde."

"Did I mention the Concorde? It must have been a slip of the tongue. Early taping tomorrow, Tony; I'll see you at eight."

Tony waved a careless hand. "An abominable hour to be upright, much less witty and charming. But I'll do my best. As always." He turned to Elizabeth as soon as Bo was gone. "What can I get you? Three hours until dinner, according to my tyrannical cook. Another drink? Snacks? French hors d'oeuvres?"

"French hors d'oeuvres."

"Done. You thought I was joking." With his toe, he pushed a buzzer in the floor beneath the table, and in a moment the

368

houseboy appeared. "Hors d'oeuvres, two bottles of the Margaux, and no phone calls. You see?" he said to Elizabeth. "My suggestions are not to be taken lightly."

"I take you very seriously, Tony," she said.

"Not true, at least not completely true, but we're getting there. As for the party, dearest Elizabeth, you deserve everything we do for you, and more. When you do an interview you don't just talk to one person, you talk to everyone out there, and you make them feel they're not alone. That's the key, dearest Elizabeth: *Other people are like me; I'm not alone.* You're the only one who does it. That's why our ratings are going up; that's why we raised you to eighty thou a year; and that's why we're throwing a party next weekend. Elizabeth, are you listening?"

She nodded. "Yes. Thank you, Tony." But she was thinking of something else: the first time Tony had praised her for her story on Heather. That night she'd decided not to talk to him again because she and Matt were so content, with each other and their family.

"Elizabeth," Tony said. She had been looking at the ocean, a frown between her eyes; when she turned back, he was offering her a glass of wine and a plate of small triangles of toast covered with pearl-gray caviar. "You requested these."

"Thank you. I'm sorry, Tony; something you said reminded me of . . . another time."

"I'll try not to be guilty of that again." He put some hors d'oeuvres on his own plate. "I didn't finish telling you the main reason I'm giving this party. It brings you to my house. You have a standing invitation, but you've been here exactly five times; I had a key made for you, but you refused it; I've offered you my guest suite as your own whenever you're in Los Angeles. The guest suite instead of my bed! To the most beautiful, desirable woman I've ever met! My God, do you know what that would do to my reputation if it got out?"

Elizabeth laughed. "No one will know. I promise. It's better if I stay at the hotel, Tony."

"Better for whom?"

"For me."

369

"We could debate that."

"But we won't. Because we're having a wonderful time and you don't want to ruin it."

"How can I argue with that? My very clever Elizabeth. But some day, dearest Elizabeth, you won't want to be clever with me; you'll want to be loving. I predict that. It's what I'm waiting for. Now try some of these: they're either roasted peppers with melted chèvre or lobster mousse with paprika—I can never tell them apart. Why do you laugh?"

"Because they look nothing like each other and a two-year-old could tell them apart. Who's being clever, now? You make a declaration you know I don't want to hear and then you sneak in some silliness that makes me laugh."

"The lady sees through me," Tony said conversationally to a seagull soaring at the water's edge. "I'll have to think up new mysteries to keep her intrigued." He took a box from his pocket. "What color are you wearing to your party?"

"I haven't decided, but put that away, Tony, please. You've already given me a necklace—"

"That was from the staff."

"Everyone gave ten dollars; you paid the rest."

"You're not supposed to know that."

"It doesn't matter. I love it and I wear it, but I won't take any more jewelry from you. Don't argue, Tony—"

"Because we're having a wonderful time and I wouldn't want to ruin it?" She smiled and he sighed deeply, contemplating the box in his hand. "A gold bracelet. What shall I do with it? Never mind; I don't want to hear your answer. I'll put it away for the time you no longer want to be clever with me." He replaced it in his pocket. "Now you can relax; I'll be very good for the rest of the evening. We have wine and hors d'oeuvres and in a little while we will have the sunset. Tomorrow we work, but the evening is ours."

He stretched out his legs and leaned back in his chair. "You are the only woman I've ever known who is quiet. You don't fidget. You don't curl your hair around a finger or examine your nails or consult a mirror to see if your lipstick is sufficiently glutinous to satisfy the entire cosmetics industry. You sit quietly; you speak quietly. You make it very pleasant to sit on the deck and look at the ocean. I never do it when I'm alone; it bores me. I begin to tremble in five minutes, shake in six, go into convulsions in seven, and then go running through the house in a desperate search for entertainment. You laugh, but I am telling the truth. Yet right now I feel perfectly peaceful. However, I'm talking too much. Tell me what you do in Santa Fe on those dreary days when you're not here with me. Tell me your dreams. Tell me anything you like."

Elizabeth told him very little about her feelings, but it was more than she would have told him a year, or even six months, earlier. And as they sat together, talking about themselves and then the interviews they would tape the next day, she thought how pleasant Tony could be, how comfortable she felt with him, and how well they worked together.

How well we work together.

It had happened so gradually, she hadn't thought of it until now. For two months—three, if she counted August, when she'd begun taping interviews for the fall season—she and Tony had been working together. As Bo let her participate more fully in their planning sessions and editing her interviews, she'd begun coming to Los Angeles for a day or two every week, taping more of her interviews in the studio than on location, since she was there anyway, and expanding the time she spent with Tony. Together, they were thinking of new ideas for a show that would reach as many people as possible, attract advertisers, and be remembered and looked for when the same day came around next week.

Exactly what I dreamed of doing. Except that I thought it would be with someone else.

The thought was like a thorn that pricked her at unexpected moments that evening, the next day in the studio, and all week, before she returned to Los Angeles for Tony's party. And when she stood in the two-story living room, wearing a cloth of gold dress with long sleeves, a deep V both back and front, and a full skirt falling to the floor in deep folds that seemed to catch the sun and its shadows, the thorn was still there.

"My lovely Elizabeth," Tony said, holding her hands as he

stood back to gaze at her. His eyes went to her wrist. "You need the gold bracelet."

"All I need is that look in your eyes," she said lightly. "You are a very handsome host. Have I seen that navy blazer before?"

"You haven't seen a third of my Brioni blazers. We'll have to do more gala evenings together. Look at us: have you ever seen a more perfect couple?"

Elizabeth looked with him at their reflection, then turned away. Because Tony was right: in their finery, beneath track lights that lit the house like a stage set, they made a magnificent couple: her glowing, honey-blond beauty beside his sleek dark handsomeness; his lean frame, pale eyes, square clefted chin, and patrician nose—the image of his father's—complementing Elizabeth's gentler curves, her dark brows above wide-spaced gray eyes, the soft shadows beneath her high cheekbones, the silken fall of her hair.

"Sensational," Tony said, facing the mirror.

Elizabeth still looked the other way. *Matt and I were sensational once.*

But how long had it been since they stood before a mirror, admiring themselves as a couple?

Voices filled Tony's house; the guests had arrived, all two hundred of them within a few minutes. They greeted Tony and Elizabeth with cries of congratulations, invitations, and knowing looks: nowhere do ratings and box office numbers translate into intimacy more quickly than in that small stretch of California from Malibu to Hollywood. The voices rose to the highest point of the pitched ceiling; a small orchestra in a corner of the enormous room played show tunes, with a tuxedoed baritone and a sequined soprano singing into hand-held microphones; beautiful young men and women passed champagne and hors d'oeuvres, working to earn money "between shows," silently praying to be noticed by producers, directors, stars, influential hangers-on. A row of photographs of Elizabeth and Tony, blown up to life-size, stood along one wall.

"Success," Bo said to Tony as they watched guests unerringly spot Elizabeth in the crowd, and move to her side for a few

372

words. "If anyone knows who has a chance to make it, they do; celebrity is their food and drink."

Elizabeth was smiling—quiet, poised, gracious—but there was a gleam in her eyes and Tony knew she was reveling in every minute: it was a new experience for her to be the center of attention in a room filled with famous, wealthy, never-quite-satisfied people who usually demanded, and got, the kind of attention they were giving her. It was partly her beauty, Tony thought. There was, of course, more beauty per square inch in Los Angeles than anywhere in the world, but in this crowd of professional beauties, Elizabeth stood out, not only because she had worn cloth of gold, which few women could wear without looking brassy, but also because she used less makeup and stood still, her eyes on the person talking to her instead of darting about the room to see who was there, who was watching her, and which women others were watching. Amused, Tony decided it was Santa Fe. She still had the natural beauty and self-possession of a child of the desert.

"Isn't that Markham?" Bo asked him.

Tony's smile broadened. "It is." He watched Paul Markham take Elizabeth's arm and walk with her to the small dance floor on the other side of the orchestra. "All is well, Bo. You may drink champagne and relax. We have nothing to worry about."

"Tony Rourke is watching us," Markham said to Elizabeth, his arm around her waist. "I hope he's not jealous; I'm a poor duelist."

Elizabeth laughed as they moved onto the dance floor. "Tony would be the first to run from a duel. But there wouldn't be one; he wants me to enjoy myself. It's my party, after all."

"So it is. And from what I hear, you've earned it. Stopped his ratings from plummeting."

Elizabeth frowned. "I've heard that before. It's an exaggeration. They'd dipped lower; that's all. It often happens when a show has been on for years."

He smiled. "I admire that. Loyalty is rare in the television industry." His hair was brown, his eyes blue, his brown beard streaked with gray. He wore a gold wedding band and his eyes admired Elizabeth, but when he talked it was as if he were in a business meeting. "I've been thinking about you for six months," he said as they glided farther from the orchestra where it was quieter. "I read your columns; I watch you on television. You've got a rare talent for making people think you care about them."

"I do care about them."

"If that's true, you're the first television interviewer who does. Maybe that's why they open up to you. Could you travel around the country, if necessary, to interview for your column?"

Elizabeth felt a quick rush of excitement and anticipation. "Yes," she replied. "Not too much, but some. My daughter is still at home and I won't leave her for more than a day or two at a time."

"We can work that out," Markham said as the music stopped and they stood still in the middle of the dance floor. "It shouldn't be a problem. Elizabeth, I want you to sign with Markham Features and let us syndicate 'Private Affairs.' You've impressed me. You're a fine writer and interviewer and a remarkable woman. I've never seen you demean anyone to get a laugh or make a point, you're never salacious to increase ratings, you never cause pain to make yourself seem in control. And you never let your audience see too much; you know when to stop. Also—and this is not a small detail—you're extraordinarily lovely. We'll expect you to give talks now and then; good speakers are in great demand and you help both yourself and us by keeping a high visibility, but the main thing is your writing. We want to offer three columns a week to our subscribers; four hundred papers, from New York to—"

"Four-hundred—?"

"Give or take a few. From New York to Hawaii, Toronto to Bermuda. This isn't the place to talk about money, but I guarantee you'll do extremely well."

It was the dream of every newspaper writer, but most of them dreamed—if they let themselves—of fifty, seventy, perhaps a hundred papers. Four hundred, Elizabeth repeated to herself. The orchestra began a waltz and she and Markham were dancing and she was still saying the number to herself. They whirled about the floor, revolving in small circles past

374

guests clustered in conversations, past Tony, talking to a willowy raven-haired beauty while his eyes followed Elizabeth and he wondered what had caused her to have that stunned look.

"No answer?" Markham asked. "If you're waiting for more specific details—"

"No. I mean, of course I'll want those, but not now." Elizabeth took a deep breath. "I'm sorry; I'm a little dizzy. You've reminded me of someone else who was offered a great chance, the kind people dream of, and when he grabbed it, his whole life changed."

"And you're afraid yours will change."

"Perhaps . . . Yes, I think that's what I'm afraid of."

"So afraid you can't enjoy your good fortune?"

She looked at him. His smile was warm, his eyes were like pale blue pools, hiding nothing. Elizabeth floated on the music and let herself believe it. He was real; he was serious; he wasn't an illusion. *Four hundred papers! Wait until I tell Matt!*

She missed a step in the dance, almost stumbling, then caught herself. Tell Matt? The last time she'd told him about herself—that she had a chance to do her interviews on television—all he'd thought of was how much it would increase her value as a columnist in Rourke's papers.

Anyway, when had they last shared news of their triumphs, or setbacks? Why hadn't she gotten over wanting to do it?

Why should I get over it?

"Lost in thought," Markham observed. "Anything I can share?"

Elizabeth met his eyes again: warm and admiring. "Not yet," she said. "I'm getting used to it."

Four hundred papers. The only way a newspaper writer could break out of home territory and enter millions of households all over the country.

Of course she did that now, on television. And television had that exciting glamour that nothing else matched. But still, newspapers were different. They were tangible; they could be held, savored, clipped, filed. Long after the television set had been turned off, a newspaper story, like a book, could be picked up, re-read, brought to life again.

It all fell into place—her own treasure, her own pot of gold at the end of the rainbow—and Elizabeth laughed, a joyous peal that caused others to turn, smiling, because her delight was infectious. "Thank you, Paul. Of course I can enjoy it. I've been dreaming of it since college."

"I'm glad," he said. "I thought I might have to talk you into it. Now tell me about yourself. I've been curious. Where did you learn to talk to people? Where did you learn to *listen?* Almost no one listens, these days. Most people are so busy thinking about what they'll say next, they can't hear what's going on around them. You're every man's dream: a beautiful woman who listens."

"And what do women dream of?" Elizabeth asked.

"The same thing in reverse. I've never met a woman who thinks a man listens to her with the attention and sympathy she deserves. You do. And you're a stranger, so your beauty isn't threatening."

"If you really believe all that," said Tony, coming up behind them, "how could you wait so long to offer Elizabeth a contract?"

Markham smiled easily. "I had to be convinced that the public would care about people no one ever heard of. I know how many people buy books about Bette Davis, Lee Iacocca, Joan Collins, Jane Fonda, John Belushi; I know how many people turn on their television sets to watch the glamorous, the notorious, the ridiculously wealthy, the criminal . . . or all the above. You should know, Tony; they're your guests."

"That's what I'm known for," Tony said. "And why should I change? I have Elizabeth to delve into the secret thoughts of those waiters over there, and my gardener, and the man who presses my pants, and all those other people I can never tell apart because they all look exactly alike to me."

Elizabeth gave him a quick look. "Do you really mean that?"

"I do; I can't help it. I was brought up to divide the world into those who are worth knowing—and all the rest. I'm sat-

376

isfied if all of them know *me*. Shall we eat? I see by the caterer's autocratic nod that I am to lead the way to dinner."

Twenty round tables covered with blue linen and set with crystal and cobalt-rimmed china formed two rows along the front of the great room, overlooking the deck and a starry sky vaulting over the dark ocean. At the center table, Tony was on Elizabeth's right; Paul Markham was on her left. Seven other guests had been chosen to sit with them, although everyone at the party seemed equally famous to Elizabeth; she had been recognizing actors and actresses, singers and musicians all evening. It was exactly what she had called it: a coming-out party to introduce Elizabeth Lovell as one of them: famous, recognizable, envied.

And just three years ago, she thought involuntarily, she and Matt had been jubilant over thirteen letters from readers of her first "Private Affairs" column, on Edward Ortega, in the Santa Fe *Chieftain*, circulation ten thousand.

Tony had given Elizabeth capsule descriptions of everyone at the table: two lead characters in a detective series, the red-headed beauty who played the villain's first wife in a series about a wealthy shipbuilding family, the anchorman of an evening news program, a screenwriter on a steamy soap opera, an actress being considered for a morning talk show. "And Polly Perritt," Tony finished up, knowing Polly was listening, "who terrorizes us with the gossip she puts in her syndicated column. Be gentle with her, be diplomatic, and never let down your guard."

"Dear me, I do sound dreadful," sighed Polly, dissecting her quail. "Don't believe him, Elizabeth; I'm tender-hearted and I cry easily at movies." She crunched a small bone between her teeth. "I'm a faithful follower of 'Private Affairs' and I'd feel privileged if you could give me five minutes tonight; a quick interview for tomorrow's column."

"What a good idea," Tony said smoothly. "May I sit in?"

Polly twinkled at him. "You know me better than that, my sweet. Elizabeth and I will become good friends without any help."

"Turning the tables," said the television detective. "Ever been interviewed, Elizabeth?"

"Not by an expert," she replied. "I'm looking forward to it. Over coffee?" she asked Polly. "We can sit in the library."

"Lovely," Polly hummed, and turned back to her quail, listening, as the others talked of television and feature films, for the small tidbits of information from which she wove her tapestry of the lives and loves and litigation of Hollywood. Elizabeth watched her as she finished the quail, downed several glasses of wine, and dug into the salad of watercress and arugula as soon as it was placed before her. She took no part in the conversation; she seemed interested only in food and wine; but her hand stilled when something caught her attention, her head tilted, her whole body tensed with listening. She doesn't want good news, Elizabeth thought, unless it's titillating. And Tony's voice echoed in her mind: *be diplomatic; never let down your guard.*

"Tony's a love," Polly said as they left the table after finishing their salad. A waiter followed them to the library, bringing dessert and coffee. "My, my, he is indeed a love. Amaretto cheesecake! My favorite." She speared it with her fork.

Elizabeth sipped her steaming coffee. "What would you like to know about me?"

"Oh, everything, of course." Polly used her fingertip to pick up crumbs from the plate. "How you feel about fame and fortune and having one of the most desirable bachelors between the Mississippi and the Pacific at your beck and call. The usual things." She drank from her cup, eyeing Elizabeth over the rim. "The truth is, I know a good bit about you. But not exactly what I'm looking for. So what I want to know is, how come you're so tolerant?"

"In what? Politics? Religion? Books for teenagers?"

"Husbands humping in Houston was what I had in mind."

A silence fell. From the other room, Elizabeth heard the orchestra slide smoothly from "Smoke Gets in Your Eyes" to "Send in the Clowns."

"Crude," she said evenly. "I'd like you to explain it."

"That was my surprise gambit," Polly said. "Being crude

helps the surprise. As a fellow interviewer, you know all about that: it's wonderful for tripping people up and making them pour their guts out. How else would you and I get real stories? I wondered if you'd fall for it, but of course you're too smart. Anyway, your Matt is playing around, honey, and it looks more serious than a toss in the hay—everybody knows it—and I want to know what you *think* about it. You and I can talk to each other because we're in the same business, we understand each other, we like to get inside people. Now that's as honest as I can get. I don't beat around bushes, you know."

"I imagine you spend more time in them than around them," Elizabeth said, her voice like a whip. Hearing Matt's name on those crumb-covered lips made her sick, and having "Private Affairs" compared to the sleazy gossip of this bone-crunching peeping Tom made her so furious, she didn't care what she said.

Polly's eyes narrowed. "My, my, aren't we brave. After lover told you specifically to be gentle and diplomatic."

"Diplomacy works when everyone follows the same rules," Elizabeth said. "I'm waiting to hear what you were implying."

"I don't imply, my sweet. I state facts." Polly drank coffee, searched nearsightedly for crumbs on her plate, let the silence drag out. "The word from Houston is that the hottest couple in town is the star publisher and the lady with the playroom. She's a well-known hostess; he's—as I said—a star and he's got her. She's his." When Elizabeth was silent, she said, "Your turn."

"For what?"

"To talk, honey. This is an interview. You know what that is?"

"Questions and answers. I haven't heard a question yet."

"Well, then, I'll ask one. Is your hubby the luckiest man between the Mississippi and the Pacific because he has a famous wife keeping the home fires burning while he slides between the sheets with a happy homebreaker named Nicole Renard?"

"Nicole?" Elizabeth swallowed the bile in her throat and made her face a mask, bland and faintly amused. "She's an old friend of the family. We ski together in Aspen. She's very beautiful, isn't she, Polly? Or haven't you met her?"

She had succeeded in flustering her. Polly tilted her wine glass and found it empty. "Aspen," she said, casting about.

"And, yes, of course my husband is pleased to have a famous wife; he's encouraged me in my writing from the beginning. We ran a newspaper together for a couple of years, which you know, of course, and when our daughter goes to college next fall we'll combine our careers again and buy a house somewhere. Nicole will no doubt be a frequent dinner guest. With her companions. She has a number of them, but of course you know that, too, don't you, because you're careful to collect facts, you don't imply, and you're never crude except when you're being surprising. I find you surprising all the time. Is there any other information I can give you? If not, I'll rejoin my host and good friend, whose only mistake tonight was seating you at our table."

She swept from the room, her gold gown rustling as it brushed the doorway. *It's a lie, all of it. Matt wouldn't . . . not before we've decided anything.*

Tony was standing at her chair, waiting for her. His smile faded as she came closer. "Something wrong?" he asked. "Elizabeth? There isn't anything wrong between you and Polly, is there?"

"She said we're in the same business and we understand each other," Elizabeth said.

"Did she mean it?" Elizabeth did not answer. "Well, of course this isn't the place to discuss it." He put his arm around her and led her to the dance floor. The music was a slow sweet version of "Summertime" and Elizabeth put her cheek against Tony's shoulder, closing her eyes, letting her body move with his as she thought about Matt.

How could you give people a chance to talk about us? If you had to have a woman, did you have to choose one who advertises herself? Didn't you know that by flaunting her, you'd hurt me?

Or didn't you care?

Tony's cashmere blazer was soft beneath her cheek; the bright

380

lights burned through her closed eyelids; the music wove about her as the soprano crooned the words. *Hush, little baby; don't you cry.*

And don't complain either, Elizabeth thought, remembering what she had told Isabel, if things don't go the way you want. Do something about it.

And that was when she knew she was going to Houston.

Tony offered her the use of the network jet, and himself as companion. She accepted the plane. "I have to go alone, Tony; I can't share this with you. Or anyone."

"Will you just tell me—she left before I could talk to her—did you make Polly angry?"

"Polly made me angry. I returned the favor. Tony, please don't go on about her."

"You don't understand her power, Elizabeth; I am trying to tell you—"

"Tell me when I get back. Please. You gave me a lovely party last night and you cared enough about me to invite Paul and I'm very grateful, Tony; please don't spoil it by talking about that woman."

"Oh, God; *that woman.* Is that how she's talking about you?"

"I have no idea." She gave him a quick kiss, the kind he had resigned himself to when he realized everything would take longer with Elizabeth than he had anticipated, and then she left.

She was stopping first in Santa Fe, taking the time on the short flight to shift, as she always did, from the fast pace of Los Angeles to the slow tempo of home. She had the plane to herself: space for ten on two leather couches and four armchairs surrounding an oval rosewood table; a galley kitchen and cabinets stocked with smoked pheasant, caviar, shrimp, French crackers, pâtés, liquor and wine; a telephone and television set; and a soft carpet woven with the names of the network's top shows. "Anthony" was in front of one of the couches, and Elizabeth gazed at it absently on the flight to Santa Fe, remembering what Saul and Holly had told her about Matt's quick visit. A modern marriage, she thought wryly: each of us flying into Santa Fe on different corporate planes.

Lydia was waiting, with her car, and they hugged each other. "Luxury," Lydia said, looking at the plane. "And so convenient to fly in here instead of Albuquerque. You look pale."

"Do I?" Elizabeth's arm was around her mother's waist as they walked to the car. "Maybe you just think I should because you could tell by my voice on the telephone I was upset."

"It's so difficult when one's children see through one," Lydia said to a cloud drifting in an azure sky. "One doesn't know how much to say."

"One could simply say what one feels," Elizabeth said. "Do you want me to drive?"

"If you please, dear. I have trouble with the glare. What did he do? Find another woman?"

"Yes."

"You must have expected that."

"I did. But I didn't expect it to be serious."

"It can't be. He's married to you. He loves you. It's just recreation, Elizabeth. What else would it be?"

"That's what I'm going to find out." She drove fast and straight along Airport Road, turning north on St. Francis, thinking of Holly when she passed the high school. "You didn't tell Holly, did you?"

"Of course not. It's for you to tell her about her father."

"I'm only going to tell her I'm going there. That's all I know for sure."

"If you're not sure," Lydia said, "why not pretend there's no woman at all—or just a casual friend—and have a reconciliation and begin again?"

Elizabeth took her eyes from the road long enough to give her mother a wondering look. "Are you serious?"

"My dear, more marriages are saved by pretending than by confronting. You believe in compromise, don't you? I'm just giving it a prettier name."

"I don't want pretty names. I want honesty."

Lydia sighed. "You're a dreamer, Elizabeth. You always have been."

Elizabeth drove in silence until she pulled up at the door of the Evans Bookshop and Art Gallery. "So were you," she said to her mother. "You were a dreamer. That's how you got this shop."

"But my husband is at his workbench this very minute, making rocking chairs; he gets more ambitious with each project, and I've stopped reminding him we were supposed to run this business together. Come in for tea; Heather's minding the shop and she wants to see you. Elizabeth, my dear"—she turned in the front seat and put her hands on her daughter's shoulders— "I'm very proud of you. You make me jealous, almost, when I think of what I might have done when I was your age; but then I think it's all right, really; my daughter is going farther and faster than I did and that's the way it should be with each generation. But I'm ahead of you in marriage, my dear; I still have a husband."

"So do I," Elizabeth said. "Are we having a contest, Mother?"

"No, no, Lord no." Lydia opened the car door and stepped out. "I just wanted to pass on the wisdom of my advanced years."

Elizabeth laughed, and was still laughing as they walked into the bookshop.

"What a happy sight," Heather said, coming up to kiss her. "We thought you were desperate. Flying to Houston in a private plane, stopping for the night in Santa Fe . . ."

Elizabeth sat at the table and watched Heather pour tea for the two of them while Lydia helped a customer. "Talk to me about you."

"Why?"

"Because my mother just advised me to pretend nothing's changed between Matt and me."

Heather frowned into her cup. "Why?"

"To save my marriage."

"Oh. Well, it might. But I didn't think that was the kind of marriage you wanted. Was she talking about another woman? We wondered if he'd found one. Has he?"

"So I hear."

"And you're going to Houston to find the truth?"

383

"I'm going to Houston to find out what we have left. If he's changed so much that he's having a serious affair—not just a casual fling, which I'd expect—"

"Have you had a casual fling?"

"No, but that has nothing to do with it. I thought I'd wait to see . . . I chose to wait, that's all. But I realized last month that it was silly to think Matt would go on, month after month, with no one; he's a sexual man and he's never felt deprived; especially for a couple of years, when we had such a wonderful—" She stopped, her throat tight. "Damn. It isn't as easy to talk about as I thought."

"Or to be casual about. 'Of course my husband will have his little affairs . . . what's it to me?' Did you really think that was how you felt? Didn't you know you were hurting inside? You don't have to hide it as if it's shameful or old-fashioned. It's okay to hurt inside."

There was a silence. "Heather," Elizabeth said, "you've never mothered me before."

Heather grinned. "Maybe I'm growing up. Paying attention to somebody besides me and my own problems. Saul would say it means I'm ready to get married."

"Would he be right?"

"He might—oh, don't get me started again. We're talking about you. What if you find you and Matt don't have anything anymore?"

"I don't know. I haven't thought that far."

"I don't think it will happen. He refused to sell the *Chieftain* to Saul, you know; he was vehement about it. We think he's clinging to Sante Fe. Afraid to let go."

A slow smile lit Elizabeth's face. "I hadn't thought of that. You could be right. If he wants a place waiting for him . . . something to replace the Rourke papers. . . . But how could the *Chieftain* ever do that?"

Heather was frowning. "I think I shouldn't have said any—"

"No, it's all right. It's an idea and you may be right. This may be his way of telling us he hasn't really made up his mind."

"Elizabeth, I wouldn't jump to—"

"I'm not, I'm just thinking. Thank you, Heather, you're wonderful; you've given me something new to think about. And thank you for the tea." She stood up and slipped into her suit jacket. "I want to be home when Holly gets there. I want to explain why I'm not taking her to Houston, and I want to have the evening with her. Thank you again; I'll talk to you when I get back."

She waved to her mother in the back of the store, and once again to Heather, who sat quite still, wishing she'd kept her mouth shut until—as Saul was fond of saying—she had a few facts to back up what she was talking about.

Matt was in his office when Elizabeth arrived. She had called his secretary the day before and left a message telling him she would be there. "No, don't disturb him," she said when the secretary wanted to ring him. "Just tell him I'm coming in. No, I don't know exactly what time. Probably in the morning."

So Matt was prepared, but only barely, and when he came out to greet Elizabeth in the reception room, his smile showed his uncertainty as he held her hands and kissed her lightly on the lips. "You're looking well," he said formally.

It's because he doesn't like uncertainty, Elizabeth told herself; he likes knowing his options in advance. Anyway, the receptionist is listening: discreet but very alert, like Polly Perritt. "So are you," she replied as they went to his office. "Holly told me your hair was turning gray; it seems she exaggerated."

He chuckled. "She counted three gray hairs. I pulled them out."

"To please her or yourself?"

"Probably my own vanity. Are you ready for lunch? I'm free for the rest of the day."

"I'm not really hungry; could we go to your apartment first?"

"If that's what you'd like. I made reservations—"

"Later. If you don't mind."

Matt told his secretary to change their reservation at the Remington, and he and Elizabeth rode the elevator in silence to the lobby.

385

The vast space was crowded with workers on their lunch break, their chatter and hurrying footsteps echoing off massive marble pillars and window walls, filling the silence between Matt and Elizabeth as they made their way to the parking deck. Even when they reached his car, Elizabeth said nothing; Peter and Holly had already told her about the white Mercedes and she stubbornly refused to comment on it, even though both of them were conscious of how it contrasted with all the other cars they'd owned. "I never gave you that tour of Houston we talked about," Matt said as he drove out and merged with the traffic on Westheimer.

"I know." Elizabeth looked behind them at the sprawling white buildings of the Galleria. Everything in Houston seemed oversized, like the city itself, and its state, and Elizabeth wondered if anyone who came to take that for granted ever could be content with life on a smaller scale. She turned back. "We'll have the tour some other time, perhaps."

"How is Holly?" Matt asked after a moment.

"Fine. She has a new voice teacher, someone from New York—"

"Yes, she told me on the phone."

"Oh. Did she tell you about Juilliard, too?"

"No. She's decided that's where she wants to go to college? She'd be starting at the top."

"Her voice teacher thinks there's no question she'd be accepted."

"New York. A long way from home."

"Yes."

They withdrew again into their own thoughts until Matt drove through open wrought-iron gates to the glass entrance where the doorman waited. "Keep the car here, Johnnie," he said. "We won't be long enough to put it in the garage."

Through Elizabeth's eyes, he saw the lobby as it had appeared to him the first time, its chandeliers, butternut paneling, and Oriental carpets making it seem more like a hotel than a residence. But she made no comment about it, nor about the mirrored elevator they took to the thirtieth floor, and Matt was the first to break the silence, as he unlocked the door to his apartment. "Of course, it's bigger than I need, but it's convenient—"

"—and you need the space for entertaining. Holly and Peter told me." Elizabeth walked through the foyer into the living room, struck again by excess: oversize furniture, huge modern paintings, vivid flashes of color, a striking arrangement of cattails, bare branches, and wheat stalks in an antique Black Mesa floor vase near the windows that stretched, unobstructed, across two walls. Reluctantly, she admired it: overdone, not the style she would have predicted for Matt, but sophisticated, with a sense of excitement.

"Do you want to see the rest of the place?" Matt asked.

"Of course," Elizabeth said, and followed him on a swift tour of the two bedrooms, his study, and the kitchen—not used much, she saw, but fully equipped for anyone with a sudden urge for domesticity.

When they returned to the living room, Matt opened the door to the terrace. "We wouldn't do this in the summer," he said. "But it's pleasant, now." They walked out into the late October warmth, shading their eyes, looking down at the flat, densely crowded city and, in the distance, a cluster of buildings with the Transco Building towering over them.

"Something to drink?" Matt asked.

"Sherry, please."

They sat in cushioned wrought-iron chairs on the terrace, a little distance from each other. "You look wonderful," Matt said. "I like that suit."

"Thank you."

"Did you get it in Santa Fe?"

"No."

"In Los Angeles?"

"Beverly Hills."

"Where in Beverly Hills?"

"The Rodeo Collection. Ungaro."

His eyebrows rose. "A long way from the Plaza. Good for you; you deserve the best. 'Private Affairs' is superb, Elizabeth; of course it always has been, but you get better all the time. You're very fine on television, too, but I have a special feeling about the columns. Nothing in any of our papers gets the reader response they do."

She smiled coolly; it was the kind of compliment she got from strangers.

"And congratulations on Markham Features," Matt said. "It's a real triumph."

Elizabeth's eyes widened. "That only happened night before last."

He smiled. "Paul Markham called me last week to ask about your status with us. I told him we'd rewrite your contract with Rourke Enterprises so it wouldn't conflict with his."

"You didn't tell me."

"He said he hadn't made up his mind. I think he probably had, but he asked me not to say anything until he saw you in Los Angeles. I'm so pleased for you; it's a dream come true, isn't it?"

She studied him. "Yes. Is Nicole your dream come true?"

In the sudden silence, the hum of traffic from Post Oak Boulevard drifted up to them. "Nicole is a friend," Matt said finally. "And a companion."

"Steady companion. And hostess. And, according to people in Houston, yours."

"Who the hell said that?"

"Does it matter?"

"No. She's not mine. Nicole is not the kind of woman to belong to any man." He stood. "More sherry?"

"No thank you."

"Then we should go to lunch."

"Could we just eat here? It doesn't have to be elaborate. Whatever you have in the refrigerator."

He hesitated. "I chose a restaurant I thought would please you."

"I'd rather talk where it's quiet. Please, Matt." She stood. "Let me see what I can put together for lunch."

"No. I'll take care of it. You relax; you're the guest. Magazines in the study, if you want."

I don't want a magazine. I want to know why you won't let me cook for you.

But she didn't ask him; instead, while he was in the kitchen she unashamedly took another, more careful look at his apartment. Books were everywhere; he was reading as much as ever. The bar was stocked with Scotch, sherry, Stolichnaya and Absolut vodkas, and a dozen kinds of cognac. A brass magazine rack held newspapers from New York, London, Paris, Rome, and Jerusalem; a cabinet held an enormous television set, a video recorder, and a compact disc player, with a collection of concertos and quartets that included most of the ones they had collected together over the years. *He's been here five months, and he owns almost as much as we had after nineteen years.*

The master bedroom closet was open an inch so she felt guiltless in opening it wider. Alongside a wardrobe of men's clothes she had never seen, hung a woman's black cashmere robe piped in white velvet, with an R embroidered in white silk on the cuff. My size, Elizabeth thought. What a coincidence. Quietly she shut the closet door and went to Matt's study.

At the back of his desk, behind a clutter of computer-printed reports, hand-written notes, memos, and newspaper clippings, stood a small silver-framed photograph of Nicole, looking just as Elizabeth remembered her from Aspen and from Rourke's party. Her lips were curved in a small smile; her eyes were dark amber; she wore a dress of layered black lace and a long strand of pearls. Across the bodice she had written in silver ink: "For Matt—a champion at Ping-Pong and other games."

Raising her eyes, Elizabeth saw herself in the full-length mirror in the adjoining bathroom. She put back the picture, exactly where she had found it, and walked slowly toward her reflection. She was slender, well-dressed, beautiful. Everyone told her so. *But I'm forty-three years old. She's ten years younger; she doesn't have children in college, reminding her that she's getting older; she doesn't have children at all. She's perpetually young.*

"Did you find everything you need?" Matt asked, his reflection suddenly appearing beside Elizabeth's in the mirror. Her eyes met his. *Does Nicole make you feel perpetually young?*

"Is there anything I can get you?" he asked.

Love, cherishing, sharing, a marriage, home.

"Nothing, thank you. But I'd like to help in the kitchen."

"It's all done. You can help me carry, if you'd like to eat on the terrace."

"Fine. How efficient you are."

"You said you didn't mind a simple lunch. I took you at your word."

"I took you at yours," Elizabeth said, carrying a tray to the terrace. "When you said you could go fastest alone."

"I am alone. And I'm going as fast as I want. Did you come to Houston to play the betrayed wife?"

"That's the first time you've asked me why I came to Houston."

"I was sure you would tell me."

They set the table with plates and silverware, glasses, a bottle of Sauvignon Blanc, and a platter of cheeses, grapes, sliced nectarines, and English water biscuits. "Napkins?" Elizabeth asked.

"I'll get them. I always forgot the napkins, didn't I?"

"Yes." She closed her eyes briefly. "You always did."

He left and was back in a moment. "Did I forget anything else?"

"No. It's a lovely lunch. Thank you."

"I should thank you. You taught me how to function in a kitchen. I remember when I couldn't slice a nectarine without mangling it."

"Do you really remember that?"

"Why shouldn't I?"

"It doesn't look as if you kept anything of the past."

"You mean the apartment." He shrugged. "It isn't what I would have chosen, but I've gotten used to it. Did you come to Houston because of Nicole?"

"Of course I did. You can't be surprised."

"Can't I? You didn't come when I asked you to move here; you didn't come with Peter and Holly on their visits; why should you come when you hear I've found a companion? Did you expect me to commute to Rourke Enterprises from a monastery?"

390

"No. I expected you to sleep around."

"You what? When have you ever known me to 'sleep around'?"

"Never. That's why I thought you'd do it now." She leaned forward, elbows on the table, her chin on her clasped hands. "Aren't you doing a lot of things you never did before? We met in our first year of college, Matt; you had one year of dating in your senior year of high school and then you met me. You never slept with anyone but me, you never lived alone, you never made your way in the big world without either your father or your wife as a partner. Now you're doing it all. You're finally getting the adolescence you never had."

"Adolescence."

"That may not be the best word—"

"How clever of you to recognize that."

"How clever of you to talk about one word you don't like instead of facing what I'm saying."

"I know what you're saying. You don't like what I'm doing so you give it a name that makes you feel superior."

"It makes me feel rotten," Elizabeth said bluntly. "After you left, last May, I thought maybe it wasn't such a bad idea for us to have some time apart, maybe we needed it, but I also made a lot of predictions about you and none of them has come—"

"Predictions?"

"How else do you think I could watch you walk away from our house? I predicted you'd do all those things you'd never done before and then you'd grow—" She caught herself. "—Wake up and think differently about things. I predicted you'd see through Keegan and stop idolizing him; I predicted you'd want to be your own boss again. I was sure you'd miss your family, and working with your wife. And I predicted you'd get tired of casual screwing and remember how loving we were . . ." The words hung in the air between them. "I bought a couple of lots in Nuevo—did Holly and Peter tell you? It was a silly thing to do—sentimental—it helped me believe you'd remember what we once dreamed of, and want it back. But none of that has happened. I can't believe how wrong I was. You're all snug and settled with that cold bitch who slid out of Keegan's bed and into yours—"

"That's enough. You don't know what you're talking about."

"I know as much as I see. As much as I hear."

"You see and hear what you want. I'm not snug and settled with Nicole, but I'm damn lucky she's here. She's attractive and stimulating and supportive of me—"

"Clean, brave, reverent, and loyal. Just a good little Texas girl scout."

"You can't make her disappear by being sarcastic. She's a good friend who doesn't criticize me, or my work, or the man I work for. Can't you understand what it was like when I came here? I was learning, I was on trial, I was being watched by Rourke and his executives, I had more work than I could handle. *But I was making it.* I was buying papers and making them pay; I was reaching millions of people; I was getting supplements into the schools and working with community leaders . . . damn it, *I was beginning to have some influence!* That was my dream; you knew it; and every time I took a step forward or won a battle I turned around to tell my wife—to share, damn it!—and where the hell were you? At my side, making the days easier and the triumphs more satisfying? Hell, no, my wife was in Santa Fe or the playgrounds of California, thinking what a son of a bitch her husband was for wanting to grab his brass ring while he was young enough to take it for all it was worth."

He poured more wine into their glasses. "I was so busy and tired I could hardly think straight when I got home at night, but I was awake enough to know I missed you and wanted you and you didn't give a damn. I kept expecting you to show up, apologizing for not standing with me, telling me you missed me and loved me and we'd work out our two lives. I missed Saul, too, but that's another story. I missed a lot; but *I wasn't going to miss the chance Rourke gave me.*"

"Of course not," Elizabeth murmured, feeling closer to him than she had in months. She looked at his dark unruly hair, wanting to touch it; her hand almost reached out to smooth away the lines between his eyes that had not been there before.

392

Damn it, she cried silently. Smile at me the way you used to; show me the warmth I know is there; don't pretend you're someone else.

Unless you are.

"I wasn't going to miss it," he repeated. "And that was all I spent my time on for four months; I barely saw Nicole or anyone else outside the company in all that time. I waited like a good little scout, as you put it, until I didn't know what the hell I was waiting for. And Nicole gave me what I'd been wanting from you: she listened, she admired, she encouraged me. She even changed her plans last summer to be with me. You could learn a few—"

"How dare you!" The closeness was shattered. "Don't you ever tell me I could learn from—"

"I wouldn't have to if you'd try to understand what I'm talking about!"

"You're a misunderstood husband? Is that the line you gave Nicole? Or did she need one? Was she lying in wait? Who found this apartment? Who decorated it? Who plays hostess in it?"

"Nicole found it, decorated it, and plays hostess in it *because my wife refused!* What do you think I've been saying? If you'd come here five months ago, when Peter graduated—"

"All right! I should have! Are you satisfied? You didn't want me—you've forgotten that part, haven't you—but I should have come anyway. Holly would have managed with her grandparents, and I could have kept up my column at least once a week, in between hostessing, and I probably could have kept my mouth shut about anything I didn't like in your work and Keegan and the rest of it . . . but do you know what I think? Nothing would be any better between us. Because you want your own way—"

"Like an adolescent."

"Exactly. And adolescents don't have wives and—"

"That's enough, damn it! If you want to talk about adolescents, talk about Elizabeth Lovell. No husband around, free to do what she wants, making her way in the big world all by

393

herself—as far as the Rodeo Collection, by God!—a social butterfly winging her way to Malibu—"

"How do you know about—"

"Hardly noticing her husband is gone—and when she does she's damn glad of it—"

"That's not true! What are you talking about? I've missed you for five months!"

"Not enough to live with me. Talk about wanting things your own way! If I won't conform to what you want, you write me off. Much more satisfying to posture in front of television cameras . . . you're not even with your daughter, for Christ's sake: the only reason you gave for not moving to Houston!"

"It wasn't the only reason, and you know it. And I'm never away from Holly more than one night a week; you're the one who dropped that responsibility—"

"And if you really want to talk about adolescents, *I'm* not the one who's still sleeping with the lover I had when I was seventeen!"

The sudden silence settled over them like a cloak, muffling the sounds of traffic, the drone of a plane, the clink of Elizabeth's glass as she set it on the table. "Your spies seem to be working overtime. But they're not—"

"I don't want excuses or denials."

"I wouldn't even try. I came here to find out how far apart we were, what we had left—"

"You pretended you came because of Nicole. But it had nothing to do with her, did it? You came from a bed in Malibu to tell me we don't have much left."

"I came to ask you that. You just gave me the answer."

A wave of shame surged through Matt. He turned away, gazing over the parapet at the skyline of the Galleria and the Transco Building. Strange, to be looking at it with Elizabeth beside him; he was accustomed to seeing it with Nicole, telling her what went on behind its closed doors. He started to tell Elizabeth he was sorry, but no words came. Because, he suddenly realized, he didn't know what he wanted. Except time. More time to see what he could accomplish, more time to think about the demands others had on him

"Will you stop seeing her?" Elizabeth asked. "Until we know where we are?"

"No," he said without turning.

"Then . . . do you want a divorce?"

"No," he said immediately.

"Matt, please sit down. I'd like to have one quiet glass of wine together before I leave." He met her eyes, wide, clear gray touched with the blue of the sky. "Please," she said.

He returned to his chair and filled their glasses, emptying the bottle. "Are you sleeping with him?"

"What difference would it make, since you have Nicole?"

He gave a rueful smile. "I'm not in love with Nicole."

"I'm not in love with Tony. Matt, I asked you if you want a divorce."

"And I said no."

"Why not? You said we don't have anything left."

"I didn't mean that."

"What did you mean?"

"I don't know."

"You can't be that vague about yourself—"

"*I don't know!* There are too many unanswered questions. What about you? Do you want a divorce?"

"No."

"Do you want to live with me?"

"Yes. But not here. Not as part of Keegan's empire."

He shrugged. "Nothing's changed."

"Oh, no, a lot has changed. You're very successful; you still look up to Keegan—"

"Not in the—" Matt stopped. He wanted to tell her about those brief feelings of dislike for Rourke, of the pressure of that hand on his shoulder, little seeds of discord over political candidates . . . but he couldn't. He could tell Nicole, but he couldn't give Elizabeth a chance to say she'd been right. And he wasn't sure of that, either. "Not in the same way. We're more equal than before."

"Then everything is fine." She heard the quaver in her voice and forced herself to smile, sitting straight in her chair. But when she tried to drink her wine her throat closed against it.

"It's difficult to enjoy wine on foreign territory," she said almost inaudibly and walked across the terrace to a wooden tub of azaleas, their flowering season long past, and deliberately emptied the glass over it. "You don't want me," she told Matt. "You just think you've burned too many bridges already and you don't want anything else to change for a while. That's why you wouldn't talk to Saul about selling the *Chieftain*, isn't it? You like the thought of a place waiting for you. Even though you don't plan to come back, you like knowing we're all there. Just in case."

"I don't want to sell the *Chieftain* because it's part of me."

"Part of us."

"I haven't forgotten," he said.

"The hell you haven't."

"I haven't forgotten, but I've gone beyond it! I don't dote on the past! If you could ever learn that, if you could let yourself face the fact that people change, goals change, marriage changes . . . we might have something to share again!"

"If I could face it! You haven't let me face anything else! But I could ask you to learn a few things, too. That people can share their goals, even while they're changing, if they want to; that they can build their marriage in a new way together *if they really want to.*"

Matt's voice hardened. "Is that your explanation for everything? That I haven't wanted to protect our marriage?"

"Have you?" she asked. "Has it ever had a chance, next to the prizes Keegan offered?"

"It's not a contest! Damn it, does it have to come down to winners and losers?"

"Maybe . . . If the stakes are big enough. What if it did? Who would win?"

Once more, silence fell between them. It stretched out until Elizabeth couldn't stand it. She walked through the terrace doors into the living room, and then stopped in bewilderment because she wasn't sure what she would do next. Matt was still on the terrace, only a few feet away, but he had gone so far from her that those few feet might as well have been miles. She looked back, and all she saw, silhouetted against the glare

396

of the Texas sky, was a tall form, a well-dressed businessman, a stranger.

Somehow, through all the past months, Elizabeth had always believed that if she needed to stretch out her hand to her husband, she could reach him. There was no way she could believe it any longer. He had walked out of the place in her life that had been his, and for the first time in all the years she had known him, Elizabeth felt alone and unprotected.

She had to get away; she couldn't look at the stranger on the terrace. Walking carefully, afraid of stumbling, she made her way to the foyer and took her purse from the small table near the door. But as she began to open it, Matt appeared beside her. "I'm sorry," he said. "I didn't mean to make it a contest."

"Neither did I," she replied. "But maybe that's all that's left when a partnership ends." He was standing so close to her their hands touched, and suddenly she wanted his arms around her so intensely she ached all over. Instinctively she reached up, as she had wanted to do earlier, and smoothed the lines between his eyes, but that made the aching worse.

"I have to get away," she said, almost inaudibly and opened the door. "I hope you find—" She stopped, then pushed the words from her, one by one. "I hope you find everything you want." She looked at him once more, at the lines she hadn't smoothed away after all, and his shadowed eyes. "I love you, Matt," she said, and quickly left, pulling the door closed behind her.

She ran to the elevator, shivering with the ache inside her, nervous because she thought he might follow her and she didn't know what else to say to him. But his door remained closed and that was what stayed in her memory as she took a taxi to the airport and flew back to Santa Fe: Matt Lovell's closed door, separating them.

It stayed with her, as solid and real in her thoughts as it had been when she closed it, and it was so vivid that when she walked in her own door, at home, and heard the telephone ringing, she thought it had to be Matt, because how could he not have felt exactly what she was feeling?

But it was not Matt; it was Tony. "I can't talk now," she said. "I just walked in, Tony, and I can't—"

"I know. I've been calling. Elizabeth, just tell me what happened. I couldn't stand not knowing. If you're packing your bags to return to Houston and live happily ever after, I'll say goodbye. If you're about to join the great army of the divorced, I offer myself as comforter and adoring companion. Please tell me, Elizabeth; I have to know."

"I'm not packing for Houston. But I don't want to talk, Tony—"

"You don't have to. Just listen. Now that you've told me you're not packing I have something else to say. Are you listening?"

She closed her eyes. "Yes."

"Well, then. Bo and I have been working on a schedule of interviews of wildly famous people who are living or filming or writing or whatever in Europe. We decided yesterday to pair mine with yours, the way we do in America. What do you think?"

"About what?"

"I told you to listen. 'Private Affairs' would focus on American tourists or temporary workers who want the experience of living in Europe. Probably Paris and Rome; we're still ironing out the details. Are you following me? My famous people and your unknown ones—in Europe. How the world looks when you're famous; how it looks when you're unknown; how it treats you; how you feel about being an American, famous or unknown . . . and so on, limited only by our fertile imaginations. When we're finished, Bo wants to turn it into a book. I don't care a hoot about that, but it's right up your alley, isn't it? And you could write your column from Europe, too; is there any rule that says 'Private Affairs' has to be done only in America? I need you, Elizabeth; you're wonderful on my show; the contrast between your people and mine is so damned exciting, to everybody . . . and I work better when you're near me. I promise I will be a gentleman, but I also remind you that I adore you. What do you think?"

The rush of his words had cut through her other thoughts. "You're asking me to come to Europe with you."

"How well you put it."

Behind her closed eyes, Elizabeth saw Matt standing on his terrace with the Transco Building in the distance. She saw his study with Nicole's amber eyes and small smile framed in silver; she remembered his silence and closed door. She held the telephone tightly in her hand. "Yes," she said.

C H A P T E R 13

The Plaza Athénée has a warm grandeur that overcomes even
the grayest rain of Paris in November, and Tony sighed with
exaggerated relief as he and Elizabeth walked to the registration
desk in the corner of the lobby. "May and June are the best
months, and September, of course; why did we choose November for this caper? Never mind; I know the answer." He
handed Elizabeth's passport to the official behind the ormolu
desk. "We want to devastate the competition in the ratings
sweeps in February. More important, it gave me an excuse to
lure you to exotic spots where I am irresistible. And you see,
here we are, registering at the Plaza."

"Only one of us," said Elizabeth lightly. "You're staying at
the Ritz."

"True, that was the plan. How quickly one forgets."

She smiled, liking him for his easy companionship. In the
week since she had agreed to go to Europe with him—*the first
time since I was seventeen that I said yes to Tony*—he had not
said a word to show that he knew that *yes* meant everything
would be different between them. Even now, in the silken
luxury of the Plaza's lobby, he waited. And Elizabeth, keyed-
up by the strangeness of a city and a continent she had never

seen, lightheaded from twenty-four hours without sleep, felt grateful and, once again, affectionate.

For days, preparing for the trip in Santa Fe and then meeting Tony in Los Angeles, she had felt no affection at all; in fact, she wasn't even sure she liked Tony Rourke. Why in heaven's name had she agreed to go to Europe with him? But at the same time, she was excited about the trip, a new adventure that she wanted more and more the longer she thought about it. On the plane her doubts grew stronger; she didn't know what she wanted. And then she heard Matt's voice in her mind, as she had since leaving Houston. . . . *she gave me what I'd been wanting from you: she listened, she admired, she encouraged me.*

Fourteen hours later, when they landed, her thoughts were going in circles. It was almost a relief to discover they barely had time to stop at their hotels to change before plunging into work.

It was morning in Paris, and they were met at the airport by Bo Boyle, who had been there for three days with a television crew, filming background shots and confirming interviews. "Your schedule for today," Boyle said as they walked through the terminal. "Tony interviews Sidney Kidd, world-famous author of novels of terror, in Paris to study ancient torture chambers for his next book. The interview is in a dungeon; if his descriptions get too gory, cut him off and ask him about scenes with sex and beautiful people. Lizz—Elizabeth—has a young man from Vermont who came here to be the world's greatest painter; works instead in a meat market on the Rue de Buci. I know you like to choose your own people, Elizabeth, but we have so much to do and so little time that I risked choosing one for you. I have names for the rest of the time in Paris, and then for Rome; you can select from them after today. Now, as far as Kidd and the Vermont meat cutter, I have background notes for both of you; I have photos, I have lists of suggested questions—"

"But no heart in that sunken chest," Tony said. "Elizabeth and I have spent fourteen cramped hours aloft. When do we take a nap, wash our weary bodies, comb our rumpled hair, and drink gallons of restorative coffee?"

"You weren't cramped; you lounged in first-class comfort. You have an hour for combing your hair and downing gallons of coffee; you can take a nap before dinner. But when have you ever needed a nap?"

He never did, Elizabeth thought. In Paris even more than Los Angeles, Tony Rourke exuded an inexhaustible nervous energy. Even when he rebelled against Boyle's schedule, after the taping of his dungeon interview and Elizabeth's with the young man from Vermont, he did it light-heartedly, as if nothing could spoil his mood. "Enough for today," he said, watching Boyle drive off in one car while he and Elizabeth sat back in their limousine. "It's raining and we've done our duty. We are now going to transform ourselves from working people to civilized citizens of Paris. I wangled a reservation at Taillevent for dinner and though you don't know what a miracle that is, I expect to be admired, nonetheless. The Plaza," he said to their driver, and they drove through the steady gray downpour to the glowing warmth of the hotel where Tony escorted Elizabeth to the reception desk.

"If Madame will follow me," the official said, and led them through the lobby, past palm trees and vases of bright gladioli that seemed to blend into the murals of the walls, to an elevator, and then along a hushed corridor. "Madame's suite," he said.

"Madame's suite," Tony repeated when they were alone. "And what of monsieur? Of course the Ritz is quite pleasant— I have nothing against it—and my room there will certainly help keep the rumors down, but I thought we would—"

"So did I," Elizabeth said. The day of work, the atmosphere so far from home, Tony's closeness, and the recurring memory of Matt's voice had wiped away her confusion and reluctance. She was barely aware of the beauty of the rooms, with their cut-velvet wall panels and silk taffeta drapes and, in the bedroom, flowered silk drapes and bedcovering and two enormous armoires awaiting her clothes; far more powerful was an inner voice saying, *Damn it, why not?* Her fingers shook as she unbuckled her raincoat. Then Tony's hands were on her shoulders, removing the coat, and as quickly as it began the shaking stopped.

"Let me look at you," he said. "My damned producer has kept us so busy I haven't had a minute to gaze at you in private." She wore a burgundy suit and amethyst silk blouse—warm colors and simple lines chosen for television, but also perfect for the warmth of her golden beauty. "Exquisite. A little paler than usual, but that only makes your loveliness more bewitching. Dearest Elizabeth, I have waited for you so long."

He slipped her suit jacket back from her shoulders and Elizabeth let it fall to the floor as she moved into his arms. She felt a brief shock of surprise as she put her arms around him—the shoulders were not as broad as she was used to, the muscles of the upper arms not as strong, the mouth pressing on hers not as firm—but then it was gone. Of course everything was different, but it wasn't important; she was so hungry for the warmth of arms holding her close, of urgent lips on hers and the murmured endearments that made her feel young and desirable that nothing could interfere, nothing else mattered.

With one hand, Tony unbuttoned her blouse and bent his head to kiss her throat and move his lips in small kisses to the shadow between her breasts. He undressed her slowly, his mouth following his hands, refusing to let her do anything for him. "Let me," he murmured. "I've dreamed of this so often; next time we'll do what you want . . ."

She lay on the bed, watching him pull off his clothes. "I feel as if I'm seventeen again," she said. "You did the same thing then, undressing me first, only I was afraid to look at you. I'd never seen a naked man."

"Did it frighten you?"

"I didn't look."

He paused, looking down at her. "Didn't you? I'd forgotten that. What did you do?"

"Closed my eyes, of course. Tony, you're taking a very long time."

He smiled. "I'm prolonging it."

"How you've changed."

"Not nearly as much as you." Naked, he bent over her,

looking at her pale, faintly shadowed curves and rose nipples and the small patch of golden hair where her thighs met. He drew in his breath. "Exquisite woman . . . unreachable for so long . . . except in my dreams; fresh and lovely and seventeen . . ." Kneeling on the bed, he kissed the soles of her feet and spread her legs, caressing the insides of her thighs and around her hips. With his hands spanning her waist, he moved his tongue across the firm silken skin of her stomach, around the golden patch of hair and below it, licking with slow strokes as his hands had stroked her thighs.

Elizabeth's fingers were in his hair. "Tony," she said, her voice husky, almost a whisper.

"Lie still," he murmured. "Let me—"

"No. I want you."

He raised his head and smiled. "Yes, my sweet."

He moved upward, covering her, and Elizabeth pulled him into her, thrusting against him, filling the emptiness inside her. Her arms were around him, her palms against the sharpness of his shoulder blades, her nipples crushed by the thick black curls on his chest. His waist had thickened over the years; lying on her, he felt heavier than—*Stop it! Don't compare . . . don't remember.* She repeated it until the words were drowned out by the dark roaring in her ears and at last there was no inner voice to remind her of anything else and she could lose herself in the rhythm of their bodies and the steady drumming of the November rain.

Bo Boyle had organized every hour of every day. "No way around it," he said. "We have to tape twice as many interviews as we need so we can choose the best, and Elizabeth insisted on being back for Thanksgiving. You cramp my style, I have to cramp yours."

So the days and nights quickly fell into a pattern of sharing work, sharing their evenings, sharing their bed. Each day began with croissants and fresh fruit jam and café au lait in their room, as they read Boyle's notes to prepare for the day's interviews. Then Tony would tape his first interview while Elizabeth watched. He was not as sharp with his guests as he had been when his show was new, and though he had always refused to talk about it in Los Angeles, on their second morning in Europe he casually asked her advice about questions he might use in that afternoon's interview. Later, after he used them and the interview went well, he asked more easily, and Elizabeth was more confident in making suggestions. Soon, as she watched his tapings, she heard him using as many of her questions as his own to skewer self-important celebrities. And at the end of each interview, he would look her way, and wink conspiratorially.

He watched her interviews, too, smiling his approval, throwing an admiring kiss as her questions slid beneath the protective masks most people wear in public. Between tapings, they ate lunch together and, much later, dinner, always at intimate restaurants Tony frequented whenever he was in Paris, where he was known and addressed by name. And after a brief visit to one or another night club, they returned to their dimly-lit room and turned-down bed and came together with the same hunger of their first day in Paris.

Longing for love and comfort, Elizabeth thought she would never have enough of it. And as Tony held and caressed her, murmuring how lovely she was, how he adored the sensuality that was a woman's, the body that was a girl's, she found it easier to close off whole areas of her thoughts, let desire build, and give herself to pleasure.

Her body woke to all the joys she had locked away for five months; she was strung as tightly as a high-wire, responding to the sound of Tony's voice, the lightest brush of his sleeve against her arm, the touch of his hand on her breast when he took off her dress at night. She was young and alive, her senses heightened, her appetite growing as Tony's skilled hands and mouth brought her to a pitch and a fulfillment she had forgotten she'd ever known.

"Wonderful woman," he murmured when they came back to the hotel early on their third day in Paris and lay on the silk coverlet, in too much of a hurry even to pull it aside. "You're a man's dream. My dream." He lay on Elizabeth, sliding into her, and she held his hips with her hands, eyes closed, listening

405

to the deep velvet of his voice, feeling him move inside her. "I need you at work, I need you in bed, I need you over croissants . . . beautiful, adored Elizabeth . . ." He brought his mouth to hers, their tongues thrusting together as their bodies did, and a small moan of pure pleasure escaped Elizabeth's lips beneath his. "Perfect," Tony said.

But the next morning he frowned when she said she wanted to see Colette's apartment on the Palais Royale. They were at breakfast, sitting on a striped silk loveseat in the French windows of their sitting room. The table was set with a single rose and thin Limoges china; steam rose from the coffee cups, making the wrought-iron balcony waver in the morning sun. Tony shook his head. "No time for sightseeing, my love. Bo thinks we're here to work."

"You don't care about sightseeing," Elizabeth pointed out.

"True enough. I've been here too often. And I never could pump up enthusiasm for museums or buildings smelling of the past; I want only the best restaurants and front-row-center theater tickets. Anyway, why do you care about a dead writer's apartment? She's not even there to talk to."

"It's all right, Tony," Elizabeth said coolly. "You go to your interview without me; I'll go to Colette's apartment alone."

"You really want to do it? Well, but we'll meet for lunch; you don't want to miss Jamin."

"Don't count on me. I'm going to browse in bookstores on the Left Bank, and I'm going to do some writing this afternoon."

"But dinner! You do plan to join me for dinner?"

She laughed. "Of course I'm joining you for dinner. And anything you want to do afterward. We don't have to be together every minute, Tony. I'd like some time to myself."

"And you shall have it." He left his chair and sat on the arm of hers, holding her against him. "You shall have anything you want. Have I told you how I feel about your being here?"

"Yes," she said. "But that's no reason not to tell me again."

"You make me feel I can do anything. You make the days bright and the nights even brighter, you are my warm, delicious, most lovely Elizabeth and I adore every moment with you.

Didn't you notice that the rain stopped the day after we arrived? You make Paris beautiful."

Elizabeth laughed again. "Paris manages to look beautiful without me. But thank you, Tony; I love the kind words."

"Is that all you love?"

Instead of answering, she said, "Isn't your appointment in forty minutes?"

"Oh, my God, it is. And on the other side of town. Damn Bo; he said he'd call to remind me. What the hell happened to him?"

"Wouldn't he be calling you at the Ritz?"

"No. I told him I'm here."

There was a silence. "I see," Elizabeth said quietly.

"I was going to tell you. He's known from the first day, Elizabeth; he has to be able to reach me."

"You've been calling him every morning."

"You were so uptight, it was easier to pretend he didn't know. But it was clumsy, and we decided it was ridiculous to keep pretending. I understand that you're worried about people knowing, but I'm officially at the Ritz as far as everyone else is concerned. It's just that Bo is different."

"And how many people does Bo confide in?"

"His boyfriend. No one else, as far as I know. But my God, Elizabeth, we're not doing anything the rest of the world isn't doing. Why do we have to be secret?"

"Because it's important to me. Do we have to go public to please you?"

"We have to be together to please me. I'll do whatever you say." He ran a comb through his silver hair. "How do I look?"

"Sleek and satisfied."

"Because of you." He kissed her again. "I'm off. If Bo calls, I'll be at the Musée Rodin."

"Tony Rourke at a museum?"

"Columbia's filming a chase scene there for their latest Parisian thriller: two people trying to skewer each other in the shadow of 'The Thinker.' I interview them when they take a break from lurching through the garden. Don't blame me; it's Bo's brainstorm. Goodbye, my sweet, see you at dinner."

Elizabeth took an hour for sightseeing that morning, and an hour the next, finding Colette's apartment and the house where Edith Wharton had lived in St. Germain des Prés, and then Gertrude Stein's house on the Rue Christine and the one Picasso shared with Fernande Olivier in Montmartre. And then, abruptly, she stopped. She had been happily wandering an ancient street, map in hand, when she began to feel uneasy, and by the time she stood in a small chapel in the church of St. Sulpice, gazing at the Delacroix fresco of "Jacob Wrestling with the Angel," her heart was racing and she knew she couldn't go on. I'm the one who's wrestling with something, she thought, looking at the fresco. I just wish I knew what it is.

Whatever it was, she stopped sightseeing. It's all right, she told herself, taking a taxi back to the hotel. I have too much to do to waste time sightseeing. Four hundred papers—so many new readers—and I want to do some magazine articles, too. I have to work harder than ever. If I don't put everything I have into succeeding now, when I have the chance, I never will.

From that moment, Elizabeth buried herself in work and the warmth of Tony's companionship. They shared the television crew, but because Tony taped two interviews a day and Elizabeth only one, she had time to cram in all the work she wanted, taping her television interview, writing to Peter and Holly and her parents, and spending four to five hours a day on her columns, interviewing Americans from Boyle's list and meeting others they recommended.

She had worked out a system of taking notes in longhand, then writing the story on an antique desk in her hotel room, using a portable computer she had brought with her to Europe that stored the text on small disks. She sent one disk to Markham Features in New York where a printout was made and distributed to their four hundred subscribing papers and the Rourke papers with whom they had worked out an agreement, and the other disk to Saul, who did the same for the *Chieftain* and the Alameda *Sun*.

"We just got the first one," Saul told Elizabeth on the telephone as she and Tony sat at breakfast on their sixth morning in Paris. "The Vermont painter whose palette is a side of beef. I like the way you caught the feeling of somebody in transition—not sure where he belongs or what he'll do next. We'll run it next week. You've got more coming?"

"Three a week, as usual. Did you think I was loafing?"

"I hoped you were at least sightseeing."

"Oh. Well, I was, but I've been busy. Have you seen Holly?"

"Last night. She's fine and she's going to call you in five minutes, so I'm going to hang up."

"She's going to call me? Do you know why?"

"I'll let her tell you. Talk to you soon."

Tony put his arms around Elizabeth as she hung up. "He liked the story and wants you to stay in Europe for six months with your current companion and keep writing. Yes?"

She smiled. "He likes the story."

He cupped her breasts with his hands. "I like the lady who writes them."

The telephone rang again and she picked it up. "Mother!" Holly cried. "Isabel won!"

"Won?" Elizabeth pulled away from Tony's hands, closing her robe about her as if Holly could see through the telephone. "The election," she said. "I lost track of the date. How wonderful, Holly. But we never really doubted it, did we?"

"No, but it was so exciting—you should have been here! We were all at La Fonda and people were running in and out, shouting numbers and cheering, and then Tom Ortiz called and said he was conceding because it looked like Isabel was getting seventy percent of the vote—actually she got seventy-four—Mother, are you all right?"

"Yes, of course. Don't I sound all right?"

"You sounded odd. Your voice is different."

"It's probably the five thousand miles between us. I'm fine, Holly. Tell me about you."

Holly talked about the final days of the campaign, after Elizabeth left: hundreds of volunteers handing out brochures on street corners and plazas, and ringing doorbells to ask people to vote for Isabel. "And they did! Isabel thinks they were mostly disgusted with old Tom Ortiz, who never did anything; she says everybody's still divided on the dam and she doesn't know what she'll do in January when the legislature meets."

"We'll talk about it when I get back; I told her I had some ideas. Give her a kiss and a hug for me, Holly; I'm so proud of her. Did you have a big celebration?"

"Until four in the morning! Grandpa fell asleep in the middle of a sentence about sanding a rocking chair, and I sang ten songs, and Maya and Luz and I had two margaritas each and got headaches, and Saul and Heather looked deep into each other's eyes. They're changing; they used to just love each other; now they like each other, too. It was the most wonderful party! We missed you and Peter."

"I miss you, too. And I'm sorry I missed the party. You still haven't told me much about you."

"There's nothing new, Mother; you've only been gone a week."

"A week? I can't believe . . . it seems like more."

"Because everything you're doing is new. Everything I do is the same, except for the election, and a week feels like a month. I wish I was with you. *Are* you doing lots of new things?"

I'm sleeping with a man who isn't my husband and that is certainly new, and I'm enjoying it, which is something I never thought I could do . . . "There are lots of things I don't have time for. Next time you'll come with me and we'll do all the sightseeing I'm not doing now; we'll go around the whole city—"

"Aren't you doing that with Tony?"

"He's not interested and we're really much too busy. It will all be new when you and I do it."

"He's not interested?"

"Only in restaurants and theaters—"

"And an exquisite, exciting, passionate woman," Tony murmured in Elizabeth's ear. He ran his lips across the back of her neck and she shivered and shook her head.

"Tell me about school," she said to Holly.

"It's the same as ever. How long will you be in Paris?"

"Three more days. Don't you have my schedule?"

410

"Yes, but I like to hear myself say the word. Paris. Paris. Paris. Is it as beautiful as it sounds?"

"It is, and you'll love it. There's music everywhere . . . and grandeur, even in everyday things, that's so different from home. The whole city is like an art book; when you turn a corner it's like turning a page to a new painting. The streets are laid out so you can see down long avenues to a building or monument, as if you're looking through a telescope in a museum. Except of course it's not a museum; it's a place where people live and work and gendarmes direct traffic as if they're conducting an orchestra . . ." She heard Holly sigh. "You'll be here before long, and it will all be waiting for you. For us. We'll discover it together."

Abruptly, she stopped. *And that's why I couldn't do any more sightseeing. Because Matt and I always planned to go to Europe and it was all wrong that I was exploring Paris alone.*

"Mother?" Holly asked.

Elizabeth cleared her throat. "We'll discover all of it together. We won't put it off; we'll make time. I promise." They talked a few minutes more; then Elizabeth hung up. "Everything seems so far away."

"But I'm right here," Tony said and put his arms around her.

"No, Tony; give me a few minutes. I'm having trouble switching from one person to another."

"From Holly to me?"

"From the old Elizabeth Lovell to the new one."

He shrugged. "We all change, my sweet. It just took you longer, tucked away in the desert, settled in your snug—"

"Tony. I don't want to talk about it."

"Well, then. Let's go over today's schedule. Can you meet me here at five? Tea in the Galerie des Gobelins with some newspaper people from *Le Monde* and *Figaro*. And tomorrow I've planned a dinner at L'Archestrate with a bunch of writers. Does that interest you?"

"You know it does. Tony, how sweet of you."

"I am a very sweet fellow. Keep that in mind."

"I will," she said, and smiled.

* * *

In Rome, while Tony interviewed a former model who had married into the exiled royal family of Rumania, Elizabeth was introduced to Genghis Gold. That afternoon she wrote a column about him.

Genghis Gold sketches portraits of tourists in the Piazza Navona in Rome, plays the saxophone in London's underground stations, and sings folk songs while playing his guitar near the Opéra in Paris. He is tall and gangly and slightly stooped, like a scavenging stork; his blue eyes have a bright, puzzled look in the small clearing between his dark hair and beard; his fingers are slender and quick. He dresses like an international conference: his raincoat a Burberry, his hat Russian sable, his jeans American, his scarf Irish, his pointed shoes Italian. He hasn't been home— a gray-shingled house in Baltimore where his parents still live—in ten years; last month he turned thirty and next month he will have a new name. "Genghis Gold is only for a while," he says. "Every name is only for a while. Last time I was Balfour Brie, and before that Morgan Massive. Sometimes I have trouble remembering the name my parents gave me."

He sits on the edge of the fountain of the four rivers in the Piazza Navona. Behind him, in stepped pools of water, are lifesize horses and cherubs, gods and goddesses, frozen in marble. Genghis Gold shakes his head. "I'll never be like them: always and forever the same. I change my name, I change my face. Some weeks I have a beard, or just a mustache, sometimes black hair or blond or red. And I talk in different ways: loud, soft, tough-guy, British gent, American southerner, cockney, Russian immigrant, Chinese-American. I'm very good at it; nobody can tell it's not really me."

Leaning back, hands in pockets, he looks at the sky. In the protective thicket of his beard, his mouth turns down; his eyes grow more puzzled. "But once in a while . . . once in a while I wonder what it would be like to be the same person all the time. Maybe then somebody would fall in

412

love with me. I'm not sure I could keep it up because I'm
so used to pretending, but now that I'm thirty, getting old,
I do think about it. Quite a bit." He gets up, stretches
until he finds a posture he likes, and starts to walk away.
He pauses, and looks back over his shoulder. "In fact,"
he says softly, "if you want to know the truth, I think
about it all the time." Then Genghis Gold crosses the
piazza, and is gone.

Elizabeth was still writing when Tony came in and kissed
the top of her head. "You're early," she said, typing the end
of the sentence.

"The idiot couldn't say three words in a row. All he can do
is ride a horse, but who expects a jockey to do anything else?
We canceled it." He leaned forward and read the lines on the
computer screen. "Can I see all of it?"

Elizabeth scrolled the text to the beginning and moved away
so Tony could sit in her chair. He read in silence. "Good piece.
Terrifically visual. How come you're wasting him on a newspaper story?"

"Wasting?"

"Sorry; I didn't mean that. I meant, he's perfect for the
screen. Stands like a stork, thicket of beard, international
clothes . . . I'd like him on the show."

Elizabeth shook her head. "I don't want to make a fool of
him."

"He wouldn't be a fool; he'd be himself."

"He'd be performing. Demonstrating his cockney accent, or
how he walks or shuffles or acts like a tough-guy—"

"That makes a good show, Elizabeth. Why does it bother
you?"

"He's not a performer. He's a sad little man who doesn't
have a real life, only one fantasy blurring into another, and I
don't want to have him stand in front of a camera, all alone,
and . . . lonely."

"My sweet, he really got to you."

"I cared about him. And I don't want to take advantage of
him, or have his parents turn on their television set and see

413

their son for the first time in ten years, and discover he isn't really their son anymore; he isn't anybody."

"But that's the kind of character who gets viewers off their collective asses to call their station and say we're wonderful—"

"Tony. I don't want to use him."

After a moment, he shrugged. "It's your decision. But I wish you'd think it over and remember that viewers like us better when we give them a chance to feel superior to some character on the screen."

Elizabeth gave him a long look. "You don't feel sorry for him."

"No; did you want me to?"

"Of course I did; if that didn't come across, the story fails."

"Don't say that. Your stories don't fail. It didn't work for me; he just made me uncomfortable; but you mustn't worry about it, Elizabeth; you have millions of readers who'll probably feel just what you hope they'll feel."

He was wandering about the room, glancing at magazines and newspapers on the low coffee table, and Elizabeth gazed pensively at him. Maybe he's uncomfortable because he and Genghis are brothers under the skin, she reflected. Tony used to play-act all the time; maybe he doesn't like to be reminded.

Or maybe he's still that way, and what he is now—sweet, thoughtful, the perfect lover—is just the current pose, for Europe, for me.

Tony looked up and found her watching him. "Dearest Elizabeth," he said, and came to her and took her in his arms. "I wanted to tell you how I felt, coming back to the hotel and finding you here; like a suburban husband coming back to hearth and home at the end of a long day." Beneath his lips Elizabeth's mouth opened and her body curved along his, warm, melting, shaping itself to his. "I want to make love to you," he murmured. "And then ask you to help me do some work."

She drew back, then began to laugh. He's not acting, she thought as they walked through the suite to the bedroom, their arms around each other. He's changed. We don't feel the same way about a lot of things, but he's tender and he cares about me and he makes me feel wonderfully young and desirable. He's just what I want: an amusing, exciting lover who's learned to care about someone other than himself—just when that's exactly what I needed more than anything else.

"And I meant it about work," Tony said when they were dressing for dinner. "I have to make some decisions about next spring and I want you to help me."

"Of course," Elizabeth said, but she was distracted by her image in the tall, gilt-framed mirror. Tony had gone shopping with her the afternoon before, on Via Condotti, where prices were even more numbing than on Rodeo Drive but the clothes more dramatic, and though he knew better than to ask her to let him pay for anything, he had freely offered advice. In front of the mirror, studying the white satin blouse with plunging neckline, the narrow ruby red skirt, and shocking pink silk sash with the ends trailing almost to her hem, Elizabeth thought briefly of blue jeans and a plaid shirt, sleeves rolled to the elbow, and construction dust covering her shoes. She hadn't thought of Nuevo other times she'd worn finery; why now? she wondered.

Because now I'm in Europe. So far from home. In every way.

"—famous but just at the beginning of being known everywhere," Tony was saying. "My lovely Elizabeth, you're stunning; you should always buy Italian clothes; but are you listening to me?"

She laughed. "Yes. Just getting known everywhere. And what am I to do?"

"Help me choose some of our new celebrities for next spring. Bo's given me backgrounds and photos on a few dozen and I trust your judgment; can you spare an hour or two for the next few days, to help with this very dull chore?"

"I'd love to help you."

So it became part of the pattern of their days to spend a quiet hour or two before dinner talking about the work they'd done that day, and planning future shows. Tony's best interviews were now the ones built around Elizabeth's questions. Neither of them talked about it but both of them knew it, and so they chose celebrities whom she knew, or knew about, or could learn about quickly so she could think of sharp, probing questions for him to ask. Once she got him started, he thought of his own, and then they would bat one-liners and tough questions back and forth, laughing as Elizabeth pretended to be Tony's guest, until he knew them by heart. Even so, he would write the best ones on a small card and carry it with him, in case he forgot them on camera.

Elizabeth looked forward to those close times: the hushed room letting in only faint sounds from the traffic on the Via Veneto below; the two of them sitting together on the cut-velvet sofa, making notes on clipboards, talking in the private language of two people who share work and play, drinking a soft red Spanna Gattinara and sharing antipasti of baked oysters with Parmesan, shrimp with oil and lemon, and roasted peppers with anchovies.

Then they would change for dinner, and at nine o'clock go to one of Rome's grand restaurants with journalists and television writers whom Boyle had found, on Tony's instructions, and told in advance about "Private Affairs" and Elizabeth's television interviews. All of them were prepared to greet her as a fellow professional, but when they saw her, the men let out a long Italian sigh, vocally admiring this lovely woman whose honey blond hair was like a flame among all the black curls at the table, and whose clear gray eyes they compared in Italian and English to rare opalescent pearls.

The women greeted Elizabeth with curiosity and comradeship, liking her best when she laughed comfortably at the men's exaggerated praise and returned their compliments by comparing them to charming princes and errant knights. Then they talked into the late hours about writing and interviewing, television and radio, gaily comparing jokes and superstitions in their countries, and the peculiarities of the rich and powerful who controlled their jobs. Elizabeth's descriptions, as colorful as those she wrote in her columns, drew laughter and praise, and at the end of each evening her head was reeling from the attention she received for her beauty, her clever way with words,

416

and also the success of syndication in four hundred papers and a place on television.

I have it all, she thought. Everything I dreamed of. Doing what I love, working and living with a man, sharing our work, sharing new friends. And my children, who call me, even in Europe, and who, amazingly, write to me regularly. There is nothing I don't have.

The thought was dreamlike, but it gave her none of the pleasure she expected. Later, when Tony slept, she repeated it to herself—*I have it all*—but it kept slipping away from her. I'll think about it later, she told herself. Some other time when I'm not so busy. I'm happy, and that's enough for now.

And if there was a thorn in the happiness, she didn't want to look for it; she preferred keeping it out of the way by filling her time with work and pleasure and planning.

"I'd like to interview Isabel, Tony," Elizabeth said on a dark afternoon as they sat in their suite. The drapes were pulled but the sounds of traffic seemed louder than usual, and rain and wind shook the windows.

"I'm thinking of Amalfi and warm sun," Tony said, closing his eyes. "Flowers. White, white houses and dark green trees. The corniche to Ravello. Swimming with you in the bay. And—"

"All that in two days?" Elizabeth asked.

"—and making love to you in my own bed in my own villa," he finished and they were silent, listening to the wind, while Elizabeth tried to imagine an Italian coast she had never seen, where it would feel like summer.

"Tony," she said after a minute, "did you hear me about Isabel?"

"Of course. You've already done her. In a column."

"Yes, but she'd be wonderful on television. And I told you she's been elected to the state legislature."

"You're supposed to do invisible people, not politicians."

"She's not a politician, she's an elected official."

"Same thing."

"Tony, open your eyes."

He looked at her. "Why is it so important?"

417

"*Isabel* is important. How many Hispanic women get elected to public office and—"

"Does it matter? Who cares?"

"I care. Women care. Women from traditional cultures hardly ever make waves in public, and now here's Isabel Aragon trying to fight off a bunch of people who want to drown her town. Even if you don't care—and why don't you?—isn't that just the kind of drama you're looking for? You always say you want viewers to get off their collective asses and call their stations to say how wonderful 'Anthony' is. Isn't that what happened in Los Angeles after my column on Isabel? Or don't you remember?"

"Of course I remember; it convinced Bo to bring you on the show. And I know what she's doing; if *you* remember, I was there when you interviewed her. Do you want her on the show to inspire other women or to give a speech for stopping . . . what was it? A dam?"

"Yes. She won't give a speech. I want her because she's a wonderful personality; she reels off anecdotes about the people of the valley like a storyteller; and she may not be as unknown as the others I've interviewed, but she's only a state representative from New Mexico, Tony; that hardly qualifies her as a celebrity."

"And what about her crusade against this dam?"

"What about it? If she talks about it, maybe she'll get some attention. It can't hurt us if somebody proves the power of television or, better yet, 'Anthony.'"

He sighed. "I'll talk to Bo. I don't think he'll like it, but if it's important to you—"

"It is."

"Then I suppose we'll manage it, to keep you happy. Maybe I'll put my father on the show with her; he'd bulldoze River Oaks for a resort if he thought he'd make money at it. Wouldn't that be something? A homely, middle-aged Hispanic woman putting the great manipulator and Lord of River Oaks on the spot."

"Don't call her a— Would you really put Keegan on the show?"

418

"Of course not. I don't want him near my show. Anyway, we've never had debates on 'Anthony'; there's no reason to start now. Have we finished Bo's lists? Our last night in Rome; a farewell party with your adoring admirers, and one or two of mine; I don't see why we should work at all."

"We've finished," Elizabeth said. "We can play all we want."

But the next day, when they had finished their last interviews and were having a drink in the hotel bar, Bo Boyle handed them a folder. "A few more notables I thought of . . ."

Tony shook his head. "Not this time, Bo. We are leaving in one hour for Amalfi, land of sunlight and love, to recover from three grueling weeks of doing your bidding. We intend to do nothing but swim and eat."

"And frolic," Boyle said, contemplating the two of them as they sat together. He ignored the folder Tony was returning to him. "Slip it into your overnight bag; it doesn't take any room, and if you get a few minutes, you can go through it."

"If we get a few minutes we won't spend them on your assignments."

"I'll see you in Los Angeles on Monday," Boyle said. Unexpectedly, he leaned over the table and kissed Elizabeth's cheek. "You've been terrific, Lizzie; much better than I could have hoped. No temper tantrums over the schedule, lovely interviews, and you turned Tony into a human being for three solid weeks. You're quite a lady."

"How kind of you, Bo," Elizabeth said coolly. "I'm always pleased when I exceed expectations." She looked at him curiously. "What did you mean about Tony?"

"Don't talk over my head, my sweet," Tony said, an edge in his voice. "Bo didn't mean anything, did you, Bo? It was a little joke to convince me to do some work on Amalfi."

Boyle shrugged. "Probably." He finished his drink and stood. "I'll see you in LA. Have a good weekend."

Tony put his fingers on Elizabeth's lips. "No questions about Bo. No talk of work. From this moment, we are on vacation. I've only been waiting for three years to take you to Amalfi." He took his fingers from her lips and held her hand. "Have you ever met anyone so patient?"

"No," she said, smiling.

"Or as adoring?"

"Not lately." Abruptly pushing back her chair, she said, "I'm going to clean up. Should I change before we leave?"

He was looking at her closely. "Not unless you want to."

"Then I won't be long."

Tony went with her to their suite and while they packed the few things they had not left with Boyle to take back to America, he talked lightly and ramblingly about the chess players of Amalfi and the hand-carved cameos in Ravello. "But I have an important gift for you before I buy you a cameo," he said, and handed her a small box.

His undemanding chatter always got her past the moments when the past crept in, and Elizabeth was smiling as she opened the box and took out a wide gold bracelet. "Oh, Tony, it's beautiful. Did you find it here?"

"I found it at Fred Joaillier on Rodeo Drive. Two months ago. You turned it down."

"But I've never even seen— Oh. Just before your party."

"I told you, if you recall, that I'd keep it until you no longer want to be clever with me."

Elizabeth held the bracelet to the light; it gleamed in her hand. Matt had given her a Zuni necklace of coral and silver, in Aspen. And pearls for her forty-second birthday, on the night of Keegan's party in his honor. And what was he buying now, for Nicole?

"I don't feel very clever," she murmured.

"Good," Tony said, misunderstanding her. "Three weeks in Europe changes one's perspective on everything. Will you wear it?"

"Of course," she said, and slipped it on her wrist, thinking how strange it was that after years of hearing her say *no*, Tony seemed not at all surprised to hear her, suddenly, and often, say *yes*.

But it came to her when they were in Amalfi that Tony almost never seemed surprised; he masked it, as he did most of his emotions. He allowed only declarations of love and adoration, and an occasional flare of anger at Bo—but did anyone know

420

how deeply he really felt those?—and kept the rest of himself hidden.

But for three weeks he had tried to please her, and on their first morning in Amalfi she thought there was nothing else she could ask of him; it was more important than all his declarations of eternal love. They were sitting at breakfast on the terrace of his villa, drinking espresso and eating soft, ripe melons. Elizabeth sat back, taking deep breaths of the cool early morning air that smelled faintly of the sea, and delighting in the view of the town above and below the terrace, unlike any she had ever seen.

Pure white houses, tall and narrow, with symmetrical narrow windows, climbed steeply from the brilliant blue Bay of Amalfi to craggy cliffs high above, topped by crumbling spires and monasteries abandoned five hundred years earlier. Below, in narrow streets, townspeople shopped, gossiped, played chess, put to sea in fishing boats, gathered firewood, cooked, baked, cleaned. The town was slow and easygoing, a little drowsy, even in the morning, suspended above the sea in mellow sunlight, fragrant with lemon and olive groves, vineyards, and tumbling sprays of bougainvillea covering rocks and garden walls in vivid purple.

Why was Tony here? Elizabeth wondered. Of all the resorts on the Italian coastline, Amalfi was the one place ignored by the international set. There were no three-star restaurants or boutiques, no glistening white beach or yachts or sailboats, no local branch of a New York or London stockbroker. There was only the quiet town—as simple and off the beaten path as Nuevo, Elizabeth thought whimsically—with a rocky strip along the shore of the bay where the still, clear water was disturbed only by local fishing tugs and a few boys from town, windsurfing. Yet Tony had bought, and lavishly rebuilt, a house high up the hill, expanding it to an airy, three-level villa far different from its neighbors.

"Why do you like it here?" Elizabeth asked him. "You like nightclubs and restaurants and parties. The most exciting activity in Amalfi is watching the windsurfers."

"The most exciting activity is being in bed with you." He

421

paused. "I'll tell you why I like Amalfi. It's quiet and uncomplicated, it's completely different from Los Angeles, and not a soul here has ever heard of me." He paused again and gave a small smile. "I don't have to watch myself every minute to make sure I'm acting like Tony Rourke."

"Acting."

"Being 'on.' A personality. A star."

"Can you really tell when you're not?" she asked.

"Can't you?" he countered. When she hesitated, he brushed her cheek with the back of his hand. "You are so lovely. Believe in me, Elizabeth. I often tell you the truth. I told you the truth about why I'm in Amalfi."

"I believe that," she said. For once he didn't want to talk about himself, so she said, "But you didn't mention its beauty."

Tony shrugged. "The world is full of beauty; it all looks the same to me. I'm satisfied to have you; your beauty is special."

"You don't 'have' me, Tony," Elizabeth said quietly.

He sighed and stood up. "Come for a drive with me. We'll go to Ravello and eat ice cream and pretend we're in love. Can you do that?"

"Pretend?" She shook her head. "You don't want me to."

"The hell I don't."

"Well it doesn't matter. Tony, we're having a wonderful time; don't spoil it."

"You said that in Malibu, the day you refused my bracelet."

"Yes, I remember."

"But you're wearing the bracelet."

She gave him a quick look. "It's not a dog collar, Tony. I can't wear it if that's how you think of it."

"I don't . . . Elizabeth, listen to me. I love you. How many times in my life do you think I've said those words?"

"Five or six hundred."

"Oh, Christ, you're not taking me seriously. I've only said it *and meant it* once. You're the only woman I have ever loved. I love you. I need you. I want to marry you. You make every day bright and the nights even brighter—"

"Wait, Tony. You've already used that line."

"What does that mean?"

"In Paris you said I make your days bright and your nights even brighter."

He flung out a hand. "I'm not a writer; forgive me if I sometimes say the same thing twice. If you'd think kindly of me, you'd realize it means I feel something so deeply I repeat it."

It might be true, she thought. It might also be true that she would never know, for sure. "You're right; I'm not being very nice. I'm sorry, Tony; I believe you."

"Then you might answer me."

"No, Tony."

"You won't marry me?"

"I'm already married. Tony, this is too dramatic for me. I like it when we're good friends and have a good time and give each other pleasure."

"I want more than that, and people do get divorced these days."

"But I'm not. Matt hasn't asked for a divorce; neither have I."

"Why not?"

Elizabeth left the table and stood looking over the edge of the terrace at the smooth water of the bay. "I suppose because we're both concentrating on being very successful—and waiting to see what happens next."

"But you're not still in love with him. Elizabeth, I've made love to you for three weeks; you can't tell me you haven't been falling in love with me."

Below them, a man in a small tug cast a fishing net in a graceful arc over the water. Elizabeth watched it sink without a trace.

Watching her, Tony said, "You are still in love with him."

"I don't know." She turned and ran her hand over his silver hair, smoothing the frown between his eyes. "I've had the most wonderful three weeks, Tony; we work so well together, and enjoy each other, and need each other. Can't that be enough?"

"Do I have a choice?" He stopped her hand and held it. "Best friends. Just as we have been. Unless . . . Listen, my sweet, you may not realize it, but Europe makes everything different.

423

It's like a bottle of wine; it lowers people's resistance. That's why I was so anxious to bring you here. What if you change when we get back?"

She smiled. "It wasn't Europe, Tony; I wanted to make love to you. I suppose the trip made it easier, but I'd already made up my mind." She paused. "You see, the change came before I ever got here." She walked across the terrace to a steep stairway that descended to the road. "Shall we take that drive?"

"What a good idea." He followed her down the steps and when they were in the small Alfa Romeo he kept at the villa, he leaned over and kissed her. "Don't worry about anything, my sweet. Just stay close to me and everything will be fine."

She sat back as Tony followed the signs for Salerno, climbing the twisting Corniche until they were high above the sea. He drove easily, almost carelessly, on the narrow road that made hairpin turns, plunged in and out of natural rock tunnels, clung to the rims of spectacular gorges, and cut through steep rock, allowing a brief view of the sea, like a picture framed by cliffs.

Elizabeth held her breath, almost standing on her right foot, as if she were instinctively putting on the brake. "Sit back, dearest Elizabeth," Tony said with a sidelong smile. "I am not going to endanger your life, or mine. We're both far too precious to me."

Elizabeth laughed and began again to enjoy the startling scenery all along the coast, most of it as wild and precarious as if it had just been created, untouched, unreachable, unchangeable. When they reached the small town of Ravello, human touches appeared: masses of hydrangeas and tea roses, their scent so keen Elizabeth could taste it, and small houses clinging to the cliffs. Tony stopped the car in the center of the town, and when they stepped out she slipped off her jacket and half-closed her eyes against the blazing sun. She felt as if she floated at the top of the world.

In the sparkling air, cooler than in Amalfi, they turned in place to look around the square at the Villa Rufolo, famous for its guests—"I've taped interviews there," Tony said—the ancient cathedral, the gardens, and the outdoor cafés and shops. Perched on top of the ridge of mountains along the coast,

Ravello was completely at peace. A small cloud drifted lazily across the limpid sky; its shadow followed it on the ground, passing over Elizabeth and Tony and then out to sea. "Hazelnut ice cream," Tony said. "And then a cameo for you if I can find the little man who makes them."

They sat in the small café, savoring pale, silken ice cream. Tomorrow they would fly home, with enough interviews for two months and enough notes for Elizabeth to write still more columns and some magazine articles. The sun lay heavy and golden upon them, the air was fragrant with flowers and lemon trees, Tony's hand was upon hers. What more could she want? What more could anyone want?

"Elizabeth," Tony said. He raised her hand and kissed her palm, slowly, caressing it with the tip of his tongue, sending small shocks of desire through her. "Tell me you'll think about marrying me. Just think about it. I don't ask anything more than that and I'll never push you for an answer."

Elizabeth lay her other hand along his cheek, beside his dark eyes, sincere, unwavering, intent on hers.

"All right, Tony," she said. "I'll think about it."

He pulled his chair to hers and pulled her to him, kissing her. "Dearest Elizabeth, dearest partner, I adore you, I admire you, I desire you, I am yours. Command me: anything you want. From now on you have but to speak. A safari in Africa, the Tsar's jewels in the Kremlin, the perfume of Arabia . . . what can I place at your feet? Where would it please you to go?"

"Across the square," Elizabeth laughed. "I'd like to see the garden behind the hotel and look down at the Bay of Salerno."

"A cheap date," he said, shaking his head. "I hope you'll demand more in the future." Arm in arm, they walked across the plaza. Tony's step was light—because of her, Elizabeth thought. And why not believe it? Why not believe everything he said?

Every day, every night, he made her feel like a young woman caught up in the beginnings of desire; he surrounded her with people who praised her; he made her the center of attention. And he was helping her become more successful than she had

425

ever dreamed—more than most people ever dreamed—by giving her a place, every week, on television.

She probably never would know for sure whether he was acting or not, but why not believe the best, the most comforting, the most loving? Why not relax in his embrace and let his words flow over her like warm, perfumed oils that made her feel adored, desired, needed? Why not? It would make them both happy.

And wasn't that what they both wanted? Just to be happy?

Keegan Rourke's house sat near the top of Red Mountain, catching the last rays of sun that had long since left Aspen in shadow. The angled window walls of the two-story living room met in a point, like the prow of a glass ship and through them Matt watched the last few skiers coming down the mountain across the valley: diehards braving the December cold that plunged to near zero once the sun left the slopes. He sat in a deep chair of royal blue Egyptian cotton, one of several groups of chairs and couches in hunter's green, burnt orange, and blue, arranged throughout the room, each group surrounding a table of petrified wood polished to a marble gloss. Matt stretched his legs, relaxing after six hours of hard skiing. It was his first vacation since his last time in Aspen. March, he thought. Over a year and a half ago. Involuntarily, he looked across the valley again, this time at the Aspen Alps condominium complex, and the corner apartment where he and Elizabeth had stayed for a week, ending with dinner at Krabloonik with Rourke. And Nicole.

"Matt, darling," Nicole said from the doorway, "do you mind a cocktail party before Mort and Lita Heller's dinner party?"

"Where?" he asked absently.

"The Formans'. You haven't met them. They have a house in Starwood."

"Whatever you want. But if I drink too much, I won't be interesting to ski with tomorrow."

"You are always interesting, Matt. Maybe not always fast, but always interesting."

He chuckled, watching her walk away. She wore a black

426

satin caftan slit to the thigh, and his gaze stayed with her as she went through the study to their bedroom, an enormous room with a stepped-down sitting area facing the same view as the living room and a king-size bed on a raised platform with pushbutton controls for lights and appliances throughout the house. A few minutes later he followed her and went into his bath-and-dressing room; Nicole was in hers, on the other side of the bedroom. "Who are the Formans?" he called across the empty room.

"They own a baseball team and some race horses in Kentucky, and a racetrack. They've got some dispute with a congressman over racetrack revenues; they're trying to force him out of office. They're not wonderful—he's rather a boor and she's boring—but they might be useful to you."

"I have nothing to do with Kentucky."

"Today. How do you know what you'll need tomorrow?"

"You mean other than you?" he asked lightly. He pulled on the cashmere turtleneck she had bought him the day before, on her daily shopping tour of Aspen, and picked up the tortoise-shell comb on the dressing table.

"Very handsome," Nicole said, standing in the doorway of his dressing room.

Matt studied her reflection in his mirror. "No one will notice me when they see you." Her hair was pulled sleekly back; she wore narrow black leather pants and a wool and silk tunic woven of black and white nubbly threads; at her throat were twisted strands of freshwater pearls. "But this is a wonderful sweater, Nicole. Thank you."

She gave him a long, slow kiss and he pulled her against him, his hands moving down the silky tunic to her leather pants. She pulled away, smiling. "I'll try to keep you in cashmere; it suits you. Shall we go?"

They drove down the winding road, their headlights illuminating chalets of rustic barn siding and stained glass windows, glass-fronted ranches with swimming pools and tennis courts shrouded in deep snow, and massive four-level cedar homes tucked into the mountain. Below, the lighted town seemed to grow larger as they descended. It was cold and still in the early evening, reflecting the glow of Victorian street lamps, trees bending to the ground beneath heavy snow, and behind it all, Aspen Mountain's ghostly ski runs and black trees against the cloudy sky.

While Nicole browsed in her favorite boutiques, Matt wandered through the mall, buying a Jim Hayes silver belt buckle for Peter and another for himself; he bought a turquoise pin for Holly and, impulsively—because she was trying so hard to make this trip special for him—a hammered silver bracelet for Nicole.

He gave it to her in the car. "Thank you for everything you're doing," he said, and slipped it on her wrist.

"I'm just hitting my stride," she said with a smile, then gave him directions to Starwood. As he drove down Main Street she turned her wrist, letting light from the street lamps gleam on the bracelet. "It's lovely. How thoughtful you are."

"The word is grateful. I wouldn't be here if it weren't for you. I wouldn't have taken time off—"

"—though you clearly needed it, tense and moody as you were."

"—and I wouldn't have asked Keegan to loan us his house; I would have rented one."

"But you wouldn't have found one as lovely. You're too proper, Matt: I've borrowed that house dozens of times. Keegan loves being generous when it doesn't interfere with his plans, and he dislikes Aspen in December. He told me to check with him whenever we want to get away; especially March; he won't be using it then."

"I didn't know that. When did he tell you?"

"We had dinner last week, while you were in Denver. Turn right at the stoplight on the other side of the bridge. Now let me tell you about some of the people you'll be meeting; it's a different crowd from last night."

Each night it was a different crowd, at a different party, and each day a larger group joined them on the slopes. Nicole seemed to know everyone, and she'd filled their calendar for all ten days of the vacation. She had suggested the trip after

428

the November elections, when Matt was working every night to catch up on work left over from the hectic campaign weeks.

He'd been unprepared for the demands on him. Besides the normal routine of keeping track of thirty papers, he had to follow their political coverage; work with his editors on which issues and candidates, both local and national, they would support; and take telephone calls from morning to night from candidates asking for his editorial endorsement or legislators urging him to support candidates who would vote for their favorite bills.

And after election day, his telephone still rang. Newly-elected congressmen wanted his papers' support for bills in congress; city council members urged him to take this or that position on local problems with police and firemen, garbage collection, mass transportation, school lunches, new highways and state parks.

He and Rourke went over the list once a week, deciding which causes and political figures would get special attention. "There's that firebrand congressman in Tulsa," Rourke said thoughtfully. "I want him out two years from now."

Matt frowned. "I endorsed him."

"I know that. We couldn't beat him this time, so I didn't raise the issue. But he isn't what we want in Oklahoma, Matt. Read up on him and we'll talk about it again."

"I've already read up on him. I don't make endorsements until I read up on candidates."

Rourke nodded. "I'd like you to take another look. Now, where do we stand on that dam and state park in New Mexico—Nuevo, isn't it? Can we control that woman when she's in the legislature?"

Matt smiled, picturing anyone trying to control Isabel. "No. But there's been a change; I think the people are beginning to want the dam. I'll have editorials and stories in the Albuquerque *Daily News* and the smaller chains. We have until January, when the legislature meets; we can do a lot by then."

The meetings went on, the telephone calls came in, the work piled up. But Matt reveled in it. He had an empire of thirty newspapers, four television stations and plans for buying more with the backing of Keegan Rourke, and a national network of corporate executives whom he called regularly to share information and advice. It was the headiest time he'd ever known; it seemed nothing was beyond his grasp. But he was also worn out and when Nicole told him he was moody, irritable, and needed a vacation, and she'd arranged for a house in Aspen, he was ready to go.

"Wonderful people for you to meet," she said with satisfaction as she finished filling their social schedule. "They detest tourists, so they come here now, when it's quiet."

She organized everything but breakfast; Matt drew the line there. "If I want an extra hour in bed with you, I don't want to be told we're due somewhere for orange juice and socializing."

Nicole conceded with a low laugh. "No dates for breakfast. I like that extra hour, too."

But in every other way she kept things moving, and the hours sped by in a kaleidoscope of people and talk, skiing, drinks before roaring fires, lavish dinners, late-night dancing, and early-morning lovemaking. By the time they were halfway through their stay, Matt had met as many political and corporate figures as he had in a year and a half with Rourke. "It's much easier when they're all in one place," Nicole said. "That's why I knew you should be here."

He'd been there before, Matt thought. But he and Elizabeth had seen no one. He felt a brief moment of nostalgia for that quiet anonymity, but it vanished in the blinding glare of this new side of Aspen that pulled Matt to its center. Tall, tanned, handsome, radiating vitality, his dark hair newly shot with gray, his blue eyes deeper and more intense than ever, he was the season's star attraction. And with Nicole's striking beauty beside him, they became the most sought-after couple in that group of the world's rich and powerful who made Aspen part of their yearly peregrinations.

At the Formans' cocktail party Matt was greeted everywhere by name, even by those whose faces were new to him. When Nicole left him to talk to a stockbroker from New York, he made his way through the crowd, holding his vodka with one

430

hand, shaking hands with the other, exchanging pleasantries with worldly men in cashmere and suede, and confident women in silk jumpsuits with snakeskin belts, or velvet pants and fur-trimmed angora sweaters.

At the end of the long room a buffet table had been set up beside the pianist who was pounding out chords in a vain attempt to be heard. From the corner of his eye he glimpsed Nicole's black and white tunic in the crowd and turned to see her talking to a tall red-faced man, deftly taking small dance steps backward each time he tried to put his arms around her. Matt pushed his way to her side.

"Matt, how lovely!" Nicole exclaimed with a little skip that took her almost into his arms. "I thought I'd lost you. May I introduce our host? Roy Forman, Matt Lovell."

"How do," Forman said. "Heard about you from everybody and his cousin. And Nicole talks favorably about you. She's a lovely lady, Nicole. You're a lucky fellow to have her."

"I don't 'have' her," Matt said, shaking the damp hand Forman held out. "But I'm lucky to have her friendship."

"Well, now, if that's the way you want it, senator. I could use a *friendship* like that, myself."

"Publisher, Roy," said Nicole sweetly. "Not senator."

"What's to choose? He prints lies; senators tell them." He contemplated Matt. "Which would you rather be?"

"Publisher," replied Matt in amusement.

"Then you're one of a kind. Odd breed, newspaper folk. Don't trust 'em, don't read 'em: that's my motto. Glad you could come tonight; look forward to skiing with you tomorrow."

He turned and was swallowed up by the crowd. Matt and Nicole looked at each other, laughing. "Polished and sophisticated," Matt said.

"I warned you. But it doesn't hurt to keep him friendly. Shall we circulate, *senator?*"

"I think you should know I'm forgetting names faster than I'm learning them."

"Don't worry. I remember them all. Just stay close to me and you have nothing to worry about."

431

"I'm discovering that," Matt said, and they followed Forman into the maelstrom of guests.

Forman was part of the group awaiting them the next morning when they arrived at the Little Nell lift. The group grew larger each day, and they rode the chairlifts in shifting combinations that gave everyone a chance to talk to everyone else. Musical chairs, Matt thought, amused, but it was exhilarating to be sought out by these powerful men and drawn into their turbulent lives.

"Damn good place to talk," said Seth Vaughn, chairman of Vaughn Electronics, as he settled himself beside Matt on the Bell Mountain lift. "How many places do you get fourteen solid minutes of privacy these days?"

"Not many," Matt said. "And if you try to sell the Aspen Ski Company on putting mobile phones on these chairs I'll oppose you in every one of my newspapers."

Vaughn chuckled, then began to talk of a breakthrough in high fidelity speakers as they moved up the mountain. The day was brilliantly clear, the air cold but windless beneath a blazing sun. Matt turned briefly to look at the receding town. The roofs of Aspen were mounded in white; white steam and smoke rose from the chimneys; the streets were white with packed-down snow.

"Nice place," Vaughn said. Matt turned back to him. "You know, Matt, I've been taking note of you, enjoying our talks, watching you ski. You can tell a lot about a man by the way he skis; you're confident and fast, you take chances but not crazy ones, and you like to know where you're going. I like that. I like to know where I'm going, too." When Matt nodded, Vaughn put a gloved hand on his shoulder. "I think we ought to see more of each other. I'm going to have my wife invite you and Nicole to our place in Palm Beach for a week in January. Think you can make it?"

Matt kept his face still while triumph swept through him. Seth Vaughn, close friend of three presidents, former ambassador to England, gave few invitations. "I'd enjoy a few days, Seth," he replied. "A week is usually more than I can take. I work for a strict boss."

Vaughn's laugh echoed off the mountainside and from the chair in front of them Nicole turned and smiled at Matt. "Sure you do," Vaughn said. "He's so strict he talks to everybody about how great you are. Well, you work it out with my wife. A few days, a week, whatever you want. Already time to get off? Fastest damn ride on the mountain."

They stood and skied away from the chair to a flat area where the rest of the group awaited them. "Are we skiing from here?" someone asked. "Or taking the next chair to the top?"

"Now where else would Matt Lovell go but to the top?" Seth Vaughn asked.

They laughed and gave Matt mock salutes, then skied toward the next lift. Matt stayed behind, waiting for Nicole and thinking of what Vaughn might want. Everyone wants something, Rourke was fond of saying. They prance around for a while, but there's always something behind the stroking and the praise.

"Something wrong, senator?" Nicole asked, beside him.

He put his arm around her. "You're very beautiful this morning. Is that the new outfit?"

She nodded. "Elli's finest." It was a sleek one-piece suit of black piped in heavy white braid, and with it she wore white mittens and a white fur hat pulled close about her face. Her cheeks and lips provided the only color. "I'm glad you approve. Now what caused that frown between your eyes?"

"Vaughn. He wants us to come to Palm Beach as his guests. And of course he wants more. Probably fierce editorials pushing import quotas."

"Probably. But it's not all business, Matt; he likes you. He told Russ Garson he wishes he had a son like you."

"Too late; I've already been adopted by Rourke. Let's ski by ourselves for a while. Are you ready?"

"Always, dearest Matt." She threw him a smile and pushed off, to beat him down the slope. Matt deliberately held back, skiing just behind her. He enjoyed watching the fluid lines of her body as she swept down the mountain, her skis together, her body swaying like a long reed. She skied as she did everything from Ping-Pong to socializing: with hard determination, staying close to the fall line, in perfect control but descending at an aggressive speed that would have left Elizabeth far behind and often beat Matt by several seconds. No one else in the group could challenge her and for their first few days the group had hired an instructor who specialized in leading the glamorous and the famous around the mountain. "We reserve Tommy every December," Lita Heller told Matt as they rode the chair to the sundeck. "Everyone enjoys him and he's very good with the ones who can't admit they have anything left to learn."

Matt smiled. "What's my share of his fee?"

"Nothing," she said easily. "You're our guest; the rest of us divide it up."

At once serene and vivacious, she and her husband had welcomed Matt into their circle of friends—all year-round residents of Aspen—with a natural openness that drew him to them, but now he shook his head. "I like to pay my own way, Lita. I'll take care of it at lunch, when I can get at my wallet."

As easily as before, she nodded. "Whatever you like." They rode in silence for a moment, then, eyes bright, she smiled gaily at him. "As long as we're here, let me tell you about our ballet season. We're having a benefit in the spring and since you're so anxious to reach for your wallet . . ."

He burst out laughing and leaned back to admire her warm attractiveness with its disarming blend of ingenuousnes and sophistication. She was the opposite of Nicole, he thought, drawing him into a part of Aspen where the arts, and raising money to support them, were as important as sports and material possessions.

But it was Nicole's Aspen that pulled him in. It filled his vision as he rode up the mountain, and skied down, with men whose talk was of business, power plays, and—suddenly—personal offers of financial backing if he decided to look into new ventures.

"They don't bet on losers," Nicole said in bed after a dinner party where Matt had found himself seated beside a Chicago banker who offered to help him buy newspapers in the midwest. "Every one of them would back you if you wanted them to. They have more money than they know what to do with, and they like you."

"And I like you," he said, reaching for her. "No more business, Nicole; I've heard more proposals today than a debutante."

He heard different ones each day, from investment portfolios to joining limited partnerships buying condominiums in France. He heard gossip and business deals, propositions and stock tips, and the plans of men whose companies could absorb his newspaper empire twenty times over, but who still sought him out. "They know you're going to do great things," Nicole said as they dressed for skiing on their last day. "And they can help you."

"If I help them."

"Of course. They're all quite agreeable, Matt."

"You haven't talked to Tom Powell." He pulled a heavy sweater over his head. "His agreeable offer was to increase his company's advertising in exchange for my editorials supporting his right to dump chemical wastes wherever and whenever he wants."

"What did you tell him?"

"Nothing. It was more diplomatic than what I felt like saying." Nicole gazed at him. "You didn't answer him at all?"

"No. I was thinking." Matt sat on the edge of the bed. "It was yesterday morning, when it turned so damn cold, and his teeth were chattering and he kept wiping his nose with the back of his glove, and I was thinking: if we buried Tom Powell at the top of the ski run, would he poison the soil of Aspen Mountain and perhaps even change the color of the snow? What do you think?"

"Matt, be serious."

"Serious? I'm telling you he made me sick and I couldn't even answer him, much less take him seriously. Do you find something wrong with that?"

"Not if that's the way you felt." She turned away. "I'm about ready; are you?"

"Is it as cold as yesterday?"

"Yes. Do you want to make it a short day?"

"Very short."

Some of the group had already left town; twelve remained,

435

and they skied fast and hard, almost alone on the mountain. "Lunch," Matt said when he and Nicole were on the lift. "Isn't anybody else hungry? Or cold?"

"We all are. We're going to Ruthie's after this run. Sit-down in the restaurant instead of the cafeteria so we can take our time and get warm. And I fear, in a weak moment, I invited everyone to share the jacuzzi later as a farewell party. Do you mind?"

"I prefer the jacuzzi alone with you. Are we going to feed them all?"

"Wine and hors d'oeuvres. I called the houseman; he'll have everything ready. You don't have to do anything but enjoy yourself and pay attention to me."

"Those always go together."

Lunch was long and leisurely in the cushioned mauve and beige of Ruthie's dining room. Looking down the mountain at the midday stillness of Aspen, and across the valley at Red Mountain, Matt and Nicole picked out Rourke's house, near the top. The high, pointed windows flamed with the reflection of the sun.

Afterward they skied on Bell Mountain as the sun dipped lower. Nicole led the way in the increasing cold; Matt was behind her, skiing just on the edge of control. The mountain was a blur of pines and firs, snow and shadow, and his body sang with the exhilaration of flying. When he came to a skidding stop, he realized he had kept up with her all the way.

"Magnificent," she said, her eyes shining. "You made me work." She shivered. "It's cold, when we aren't moving."

"I'm ready to ski down," Matt told her, knowing she would not be the first to suggest it; sometimes she was like a child, needing someone to take care of her. But once he said it, she couldn't wait to get warm, and she skied off without warning, leaving him to follow. Somehow she always managed to keep control.

They reached Rourke's house ahead of the others and began to strip off their ski clothes almost as soon as they were inside, leaving a trail across the bedroom to the door leading to the deck. The houseman had removed the cover of the jacuzzi and turned up the heat; steam was rising from it against the backdrop of the ski runs across the valley. Peeling off her long silk underpants and silk undershirt, Nicole took a deep breath. "Here goes," she said, and opened the door to dash through the frigid air and slip into the steaming water of the enormous tub.

Matt heard her gasp; then he joined her, feeling his own dizzying shock as he submerged himself in the one-hundred-four-degree water. He sat on the ledge that ran around the huge tub and waited for his heart to slow.

"Lovely," Nicole said.

"It will be in a minute." The intense heat seemed to be inside him; his body seemed to be part of it. When he raised his legs and watched them float beside Nicole's, it was as if they belonged to someone else.

"It's snowing," murmured Nicole. "Lovelier every minute."

The snow was falling lightly, then more heavily, the flakes forming clusters that drifted from the darkening sky. When the guests arrived, their nude figures appeared palely in the bedroom doorway, paused, then dashed across the deck through a curtain of snow to slide into the water with a gasp or a stifled yelp. Twelve in all sat on the ledge and then Nicole flicked a switch and jets began pulsing the water against their legs and thighs, hot water pounding them, massaging their muscles, running like quick fingers along their breasts and stomachs. A long sigh ran around the tub. It grew dark and lanterns came on, casting a yellow-orange glow on the steam rising from the hot water and the large lazy flakes and the nude bodies floating like pale tendrils near the surface.

Amid murmurs and low laughter, the houseman walked silently around the tub with glasses of chilled white wine. He left opened bottles on the deck near Nicole, then made a second trip with silver trays of crackers and cheese, bread rounds, goose and duck pâtés, and ice cold grapes. He left a tray behind each couple and left as silently as he had come.

Nicole put back her head, eyes closed, catching snowflakes on the tip of her tongue. Matt leaned over her and kissed her, running his tongue along hers. It was as cold as if the snowflakes were still there. Around them indistinct words rose and fell with the clink of glasses; lanterns shone dimly through the swirling steam and thickly-falling flakes; pale bodies shifted, couples merging and weaving like entwined water lilies. Their hair was damp from the steam and ice formed on it in the freezing air.

Matt thrust his tongue deeper into Nicole's mouth. He tasted cold wine and warmed her tongue with his and felt her hand, underwater, move up his thigh to hold and stroke him. Water splashed onto the deck, and froze into small shining eyes reflecting the lantern light. Matt closed his eyes against them and gave himself up to the pounding water, the hissing of snowflakes on its surface, and Nicole's sinuous body beside his, showing him, as she had all week, that she was the perfect woman to be with him in a fast-moving, high-pressure world that was the only one he wanted.

Heather called Elizabeth, and Saul called Matt, and so, after almost twenty years, they found themselves together once again at a wedding given by Lydia and Spencer. This time it was in a candlelit living room in Tesuque rather than a garden in Los Angeles; it was a cold evening between Christmas and New Year's instead of a sunny June afternoon; their eighteen-year-old son sat in the first row, and their seventeen-year-old daughter stood near the bride and groom, singing two arias before the ceremony and a Catalan love song at its conclusion; and Elizabeth stood beside Heather, and Matt beside Saul, where before they had stood together.

Still, they were part of the same ceremony. And as it ended, Elizabeth remembered the cool greeting she and Matt had exchanged an hour before, and compared it to the look Saul and Heather exchanged as Holly's voice let the long final note of the love song fade away, and she was swept by memories so powerful she thought she could not stand up against them.

Where did we go wrong? We had so much; how could we lose it?

Her eyes burning, her throat tight, she escaped to the library as everyone crowded around Saul and Heather with congratulations and kisses. She wanted to put her head on her mother's

438

shoulder and cry. But Lydia was busy with wedding guests and keeping an eye on the caterer's staff, and Isabel, whose shoulder was the only other one Elizabeth could imagine using, was somewhere among the wellwishers.

"Mom?" Peter had followed her. "You all right?"

"Sure." She gave a small smile. "Just a little overtaken with memories."

"I bet." Sitting beside her on the couch, he took her hand. "What can I do?"

He's become a man, Elizabeth thought. Only three months away at school, but he's taken a leap greater than any single one he took before he left. We don't lose our children when they leave home; we lose them the first time they come back and we discover they've vanished and adults have taken their place. "Help keep everyone talking," she said, returning the solid pressure of his hand. "Heather's parents look lost and so do Saul's. Since they're here even though they're not pleased, we should try to make them happy. Which pair do you want to tackle? I'll take the other one."

"It's not your party, Mom. Grandma does that sort of thing just fine. You should relax and enjoy . . . but you're not enjoying it, are you? Okay; you take Heather's Mayflower descendants from Minnesota, and I'll take Saul's New York Jews one generation from Austria. How did those lovers get together, anyway? They weren't exactly falling into each other's arms when I left."

"I did it with my little bow and arrow," Saul said from the doorway. "Captured my bride and carried her off through battlefields mined with parental disapproval. How come you two are hiding from my wedding?"

"I needed a breather," Peter said quickly. "I felt faint from my sister's glorious singing."

"Good try," said Saul. "But your mother led the way. What's wrong, Elizabeth? Do you want me to punch our Houston visitor in the nose? I would, even though he made a respectable best man."

"That's my job," said Peter.

"It's nobody's job." Elizabeth shook her head, but she was

439

smiling. "My two champions. I don't want either of you to play boxer. I'll be all right in a minute and then I'm going to take your parents under my wing, Saul."

"No, they go under my wing," Peter said. "We divided them up, remember?"

"Divided who up?" Heather asked. "What's going on in here? I've been married ten minutes and I'm already trying to keep my husband from wandering."

"Not far," Saul murmured, his arm around her. He kissed the tip of her nose. "Is she not the most astonishing woman?" he asked Elizabeth and Peter. "Did I ever think this day would come? Occasionally. Did I want it with all my heart? Constantly."

Heather smiled, a softer smile than Elizabeth had ever seen on that small, fiercely determined face. Peter saw it too, and sighed. "Constantly. If you were in college, you wouldn't have time for constantly anything. But wanting something whenever you relax and think about her—it—that I understand." He glanced quickly at Elizabeth and met her questioning eyes. "Well, I do think about her," he said. "I think about her a lot." Self-consciously he cleared his throat and held out his hand to Saul. "I haven't congratulated you. It's terrific you worked it out; you've restored my faith in young love. Too bad about your parents, though."

"They'll adjust," Saul observed wryly as he and Peter gripped each other's hand. "Come to dinner; we'll talk about young love."

"Let's help the parents adjust," Elizabeth said, standing up. "Thank you." She kissed each of them, thinking how lucky she was. "Let's join the party before people think the ceremony made us sick or we're hatching a plot or just being rude."

They walked to the door. "Do you want me to say anything to Dad?" Peter asked.

"You mean take him a message? No thank you, Peter; it's sweet of you, but we still do talk to each other."

"Not often."

"No, but very politely."

"Shit."

440

"We're really fine, Peter; we're doing what we want."

"That's not true. You're putting up this brave front—"

"A lot of it isn't a front. Peter, dear, I know you worry about me, but I'm doing some pretty exciting things and having a good time . . . a lot of the time. If we're going to talk about brave fronts, what about you and Maya? I've told you about her in all of my letters, but you almost never mention her in yours. Do you want to talk about her?"

"Sometime, maybe. We're going out later, after the wedding dinner. I don't know about us. I was . . . awfully glad to see her."

"You've got a lot of years—" Elizabeth began, when she saw Matt coming toward them. She gave Peter another quick kiss. "Thank you again; you were just what I needed."

Matt put his arm around Peter's shoulders and said to both of them, "Holly stole the show, didn't she? I haven't heard her sing for a while; it's astonishing how her voice has grown. Peter, I'm going to be in San Francisco in mid-January. Can we spend a weekend together? I can come to Stanford or you can come to the city. It will be our first chance to talk in a long time."

"Stanford's better. But here I am, Dad; we can talk now and at dinner."

"I'm not staying. I'm sorry, but—"

"You're not staying for dinner? Why not? You can't face everybody for more than half an hour?"

"If you don't know what you're talking about," Matt said evenly, "I suggest you keep your mouth shut."

"Wow!" said Peter. "You've gotten real tough around all those Texas cowboys."

"Peter!" Elizabeth exclaimed.

"Sorry," he muttered. "If you'll excuse me, I'm going to take some New Yorkers under my wing."

As he walked off, Elizabeth looked at Matt. "I'm sorry, too. He doesn't mean—"

"Of course he does. He's being protective. We'll talk when I'm at Stanford, maybe straighten out some feelings." He paused, gazing at her, trying to hide his surprise at her beauty. It was softer than he remembered, and warmer: in an apricot velvet dress that clung to her figure in one curving line from the V-neck to a hem higher in front than in back, she looked like the flower he remembered someone calling her years before.

He met her clear gray eyes and, unexpectedly, remembered how they looked when she was beneath him, bright with desire and love; and at other times, when anyone criticized the *Chieftain* or tried to injure it, or Matt, the way the laughter in them would turn to scorn. *She wouldn't have shrugged her shoulders at Tom Powell's bullshit offer to trade advertising for editorials defending his right to poison the world. She would have made mincemeat of him.*

He thought of telling her about Powell, and how he wished he'd been free to tell the son of a bitch what he thought of him instead of remaining silent, but in the same instant he knew he would not. He couldn't tell her any of his doubts any more than he could tell her about the exhilarating sense of power he felt, most of the time. He became aware of her raised eyebrows and realized how long he had stood there in silence. "I like your stories from Europe," he said.

"Thank you."

"Especially Genghis Gold. Sad, lonely man, but touching in his bravado; you made me like him."

Elizabeth's eyes brightened. "You did get that from it? I'm glad."

"No one could miss it. At least, no one who cares about people." Once more he paused. "Did you enjoy your trip?"

"Very much."

"Were you doing interviews for television, too?"

"Yes."

"Just in Paris and Rome?"

"Yes. Matt, I want to ask you something. Last week Saul showed me the stories and editorials your papers have been running on Nuevo."

"And?"

"Are they being written on your orders?"

"I work with the editors . . ." He shrugged. "Yes."

"Why?"

"Because that project is good for the whole state. I know how you and Saul feel about it, and Isabel whipped it to death to get elected, but the fact is, you're all wrong. I've read dozens of environmental and economic reports on Nuevo and other proposed developments—"

"Nuevo isn't 'proposed'; it's been passed. The bill was rammed through and construction began last summer. The valley is torn up right behind the town; they've dynamited a diversion channel for the river; they're cutting new roads—"

"Well, what did you expect them to do? The bill passed, the money was allocated, the state will benefit . . . it would be a crime if construction didn't begin."

"It's a crime that construction did! No one considered the people who will lose their homes and stores and farms—"

"They're getting compensation; you know that."

"I know they're getting a lake they don't want, and a state park they don't want, and a private resort they don't want, and compensation that won't pay adequately for what they're losing. Matt, these are people you know! Doesn't any of this bother you?"

"I'm sorry when anyone has to be uprooted—I'm even sorrier that you and I are on opposite sides on this—but a handful of families can't dictate to an entire state. They'll go somewhere else. If they're smart, they'll use their energy to make new homes instead of clinging to land that should be for all the people instead of a selfish few. That park will be there long after they're dead and forgotten."

"And you said you cared about people!"

"I care about the greatest number."

"Because they vote for your candidates and that's where the power is. You don't give a damn what happens to small groups, because they don't have any influence. You sound just like Keegan Rourke."

"I don't, but it doesn't matter; nothing will convince you he isn't the devil. You don't understand a word I've been saying. I do care about large numbers, but that doesn't mean I abandon small groups. You know damn well everyone in Nuevo has been given a list of places to live that are similar to Nuevo, and they've been offered extra financial help in resettlement."

Elizabeth stared at him. "What did you say?" He repeated it, and she shook her head. "They haven't been given any such thing. Or told any such thing."

"That's a lie."

Elizabeth drew a sharp breath. "I don't lie. If anyone should know that, my former partner should."

"I'm sorry; I shouldn't have said that. But you've been misinformed, Elizabeth. I have a report on that offer; it was one of the reasons I ordered those stories and editorials."

She frowned. "Would you send me a copy of the report?"

"Of course." He looked at his watch. "I'm due back tonight; I have to get started."

"I'm not ready to be dismissed," Elizabeth said coldly. "Holly says you're giving her a graduation party."

"I am. The last week in May."

"I thought we'd have one here for her friends and family, in June, when Peter is home."

"There's no reason you can't."

"I think you and I should give it together. Other parents are giving parties—"

Matt shook his head. "It won't bother Holly if she's different; there's never been a time when she was like everybody else. How many others were accepted by a school like Juilliard? How many others have her talent? And her beauty?" He smiled. "She's got enough going for her for three or four parties."

Elizabeth did not smile. "Shall we ask her what she would like?"

"No." Matt threw a quick look around the room, at the clusters of people who were talking animatedly but also casting surreptitious looks at Matt and Elizabeth Lovell, so deep in discussion near the front door. Once these people had been his whole world. It seemed a lifetime ago. "Two parties will be fine. If Holly wants to talk to me about it, ask her to call. She's coming to Houston on her spring break; we decided that just before the wedding." He leaned forward and touched Elizabeth's cheek with his lips. "I'm going to say a few goodbyes and slip out. I'll send you that report tomorrow."

Elizabeth watched his tall figure move among the guests. He kissed Heather and shook Saul's hand, exchanged a word with Spencer and Lydia, talked briefly to Peter, then walked to the back door with Holly, his arm around her shoulders.

"Champagne," Isabel said, and handed her a glass. "And perhaps you'll join the rest of us. We miss you."

Elizabeth put her hand on Isabel's. "How dear you are, to say just the right words to me."

They walked toward the other end of the room. "Elizabeth, do you know that he still loves you?"

"No. I don't know anything of the—"

"Well, neither does he. But someday he will. You'll have to give it considerable thought. So you'll know what to do when the time comes."

Elizabeth shook her head. "Thank you, Isabel, but I'm better off getting used to the idea that he doesn't."

"You used to think I knew a great deal about men."

"I still do. But even if I thought . . . He's changing, Isabel; I don't think I like him as much as I used to."

"But you love him."

"That's separate. I can't change that. But I can't cling to dreams, either. I have to face what's real." They reached the guests and Elizabeth moved toward the center of the group, raising her voice. "Saul? Heather?" When the room fell silent, she said, "I haven't made my wedding toast to you. You're so dear to me, to all of us, such a special part of our lives . . ." She felt tears prick her eyes and blinked them back. "I wish you years of joy. I'm so glad you found each other; I'm so glad you took each other's hands . . ." The tears filled her eyes. She saw the wavery forms of Peter and Holly come quickly to stand on either side of her and she smiled at them as she stretched out her hand and Saul and Heather held it with theirs. "A lifetime of happiness. We all love you, and the way you've made us part of your laughter and your fun, even your disagreements—which is probably why we all feel we had a share in this wedding." Saul grinned and low laughter rippled

445

through the group around them. "We love your curiosity and persistence and your honesty, with us and each other, and especially your strong friendship . . . That's what has meant so much to me"—she stopped again, to steady her voice—"and I wish you a lifetime of love and fulfillment and delight in each other . . . the best of what marriage can be."

"Thank you," Heather said softly. Saul kissed Elizabeth and all the guests lifted their glasses to drink. And in the flickering candlelight, the bubbles of champagne were like shooting stars.

446

C H A P T E R 14

Polly Perritt led off her post-New Year's gossip column with an item that Elizabeth found on Saul's desk when she arrived for their weekly meeting.

> What tantalizing television twosome is tenderly tucked in after traipsing through Europe together? Let's have a round of applause for rosy romance and sexy serendipity and the skyrocketing success and fantastic fame of the fabulously lovely Liz . . . but isn't the lady's legal link to a notable newspaper nabob a bothersome barrier to permanent partnership?

Polly Perritt. *Be gentle with her and never let down your guard*. I should have taken Tony's advice, she thought. Her column appears in more papers than mine.

"Bitch," muttered Saul, reading over her shoulder. "Does she hire out-of-work actors as her private CIA?"

"I wouldn't be surprised," Elizabeth said. "Do you think Holly and Peter will see this?"

"Doubtful. I clipped it from the Los Angeles *Trumpet*, which I'm sure they don't read, and she isn't carried in Santa Fe or anywhere around Stanford. I don't think they'll see it."

"Unless someone shows it to them."

"It's only gossip, Elizabeth. Just tell them it's wrong."

She nodded, waiting for Saul to ask if it was indeed wrong. But of course he wouldn't, first because he wouldn't pry, and second because he assumed it was true. Everyone will assume it's true, she thought; and why shouldn't they? And why was she so naive that she never realized the sex lives of public people like Tony Rourke always made newspapers from coast to coast?

Not only Tony Rourke. Now that Elizabeth Lovell appears on television, she's news, too.

Carefully, she folded the item into a tiny square and slipped it into her briefcase. "Shall we get to work? I'm sure you have February all scheduled, but I'd like to see what you've done."

"I have a tentative schedule; I don't make final decisions without you." They sat on the wobbly leather couch that had been there since Matt's first day in the office, and Saul spread out his penciled schedule for the next month's stories and special sections.

Elizabeth read through it rapidly. "I like it all, but I think you'd appeal to more people if you added cross-country skiing. What if you combined the cross-country race in Chama with the veterans' downhill race in Taos? Put them together in a full-page spread, with photos from last year. And then why don't you send it to Paul Markham? If he likes it, the story could be all over the country and you'd be a hero for getting publicity for the *Chieftain,* not to mention the state of New Mexico."

"Clever on all counts. Any other suggestions?"

"No. I told you: I like it all." She stood up. "Can I work in your old office for a while? I like to get away from mine at home now and then."

"My old office? That closet? Work in here; more room to spread out."

Elizabeth shook her head. "You're running the paper, Saul; you deserve the elegant office."

He gazed at the tilted, torn couch, the shabby chairs and

448

scratched desk, the worn patches in the linoleum floor. "Slightly less than elegant. Heather thinks I should have a carpet."

"I do, too. And new furniture. In fact, why don't you get the whole office redecorated? There's no reason to keep it this way."

"I'd rather wait. Its rightful owner may come back and disapprove of my choice of colors."

"Saul. Please have it redecorated. In whatever colors you want." She gathered up her coat and briefcase. "I'll be in your cubicle if you need me."

"Hold on, I almost forgot; are you free for dinner tonight? Heather invited some people; she says you'd like them. Holly, too."

"I'd love to come. Thank you, Saul. I'll have to let you know about Holly."

"I wish we had a dashing prince to offer her as a first course, or for dessert."

"She could use one. Or a concert hall or opera house. Maybe just college. She's terribly restless lately. I'll call Heather later, to let her know."

In the small cubicle Saul had used when he first arrived, Elizabeth spread out her notes for a magazine article on a group of young people she had met in Rome, who had quit high school to go around the world.

"Mrs. Lovell," the receptionist said from the doorway, "do you want to talk to the people who call about your column?"

Elizabeth looked up. "How many are there?"

"Eight so far today, and I thought as long as you're here . . ."

"I don't think so; I can't take the time. Just keep a list, as usual, and I'll write to them later."

"You write to all of them? Forty or fifty a week?"

"Closer to three hundred, from all the newspapers and television. But I have two people helping me." She turned back to her notes. At first Heather had helped, until the job got too big; then Elizabeth had hired a full-time secretary and a student from Santa Fe State College, who worked at two small desks she had bought and moved into the study. When she worked at home she used a desk and computer she had set up in Peter's room; when Peter was home from college she moved into the living room.

"I'll give you an office here," Saul had said. "With new furniture and a door that locks." But Elizabeth had put off that decision. She liked getting out of the house and working near the camaraderie and bustle of the newsroom, but she still got a shock when she looked up and saw Saul, not Matt, in the corner office, and she could not bring herself to make a permanent change.

"Mrs. Lovell," the receptionist said on the intercom, "an editor at *Good Housekeeping* is on the phone."

Elizabeth took the call and answered questions about her story. As she hung up, there was a knock on the doorframe and she looked around to see Maya's tentative smile. "Come in," she said, and listened to Maya's jumbled talk about Peter and political campaigns and Nuevo. "Maya, this isn't a good place to talk," she broke in at last. "I can't speak for Peter any more than I can tell you what to do, but maybe it will help you sort things out if I just listen and ask questions. I'll come to Nuevo on Saturday."

Maya bent and kissed her. "I wish I had a mother like you."

And Holly, short-tempered and restless these days, probably wishes she had someone else's mother. As Maya left, Elizabeth turned to the computer and worked for a few minutes before the telephone rang. "Damn," she muttered, but answered it. "Elizabeth," her secretary said, calling from her house. "The New York Press Women are on the other line; they want you to speak at their annual convention in March."

"Don't I have Tulsa in March? The Junior League?"

"Yes, but New York is three weeks later. And Tulsa wants you to tell them how you juggle writing and television with being a wife and mother."

Plus a lover and a gossip columnist, she thought. And the girl my son left behind, and a difficult high school daughter, not to mention Isabel and the others who want help in figuring out what to do . . . and a husband I can't stop thinking about, no matter how much I squeeze into each day.

"They're very keen to have you in New York," her secretary

went on. "They said you're the first speaker they've ever invited who doesn't write on government or foreign policy. And in their last survey, 'Private Affairs' got the highest recognition factor of any national column except for Ann Landers. I must say I've never heard a New York media person sound so enthusiastic."

It ran through Elizabeth like a fine wine: the excitement of being recognized. The wonderful feeling of being sought out.

"All right; say yes to the press women and tell them I'm grateful for their enthusiasm. And while I'm there I'll do some interviews for my column and 'Anthony'—would you pull out the files on New York and New Jersey? And call our New York television station and give them the dates—I'll stay two days, no more—so they'll have a taping crew ready."

"Shall I call you back to confirm all that?"

"No. I'll be home about four."

She turned back to the notes for her magazine story. Beside them was the letter commissioning the story; the editor admired ". . . your special flair with men and women, particularly young people, who don't know how much they have to say until you draw them out."

The excitement of being praised. The thrill of being wanted. The sound of applause.

It's the next best thing to being loved.

The next hour was peaceful, with the newsroom activity a pleasant background to the quiet click of her computer keys, until the telephone rang again. "Elizabeth, I want to talk to you," Spencer said. "How about lunch today?"

"I'd love it." Elizabeth looked at the small calendar she always carried with her. A dress fitting at two and an interview at two-thirty. "Is twelve-thirty all right?"

"Fine. The Haven at twelve-thirty."

She typed rapidly for fifteen minutes and then once again the telephone rang. She tried to ignore it, then, exasperated, answered it.

"Don't blame the receptionist," Tony said. "I told her it was a matter of psychological desperation, with the future of American television hanging in the balance."

She laughed. "I'm sure she had no idea what that means, and neither do you. Tony, I came here to escape the telephone so I could get some work done."

"There is no escape from your adoring public. What time shall I send the plane for you tomorrow?"

"About six."

"That late? I hoped we'd have the afternoon."

"We'll have all day Friday. I can't leave until I finish the first draft of this article, and I want to write a column on the interview I have this afternoon, and Holly's leaving school early so we can go shopping. I'll be lucky to make it by six."

"Then let's eat in tomorrow night. On Friday you'll edit your tape and we'll meet with Bo and then we'll buy clothes and trinkets on Rodeo and elsewhere, but tomorrow night we'll stay home. Would you mind? My chef has mastered Cajun and Thai; you have your choice."

"Wonderful. Thank you, Tony; I'd much rather have privacy."

"Is there a reason for that?" he asked after a pause. "Polly's prattle, for instance?"

"It wasn't prattle; it was mostly the truth."

"Including the part about only your marriage standing between us?"

"No. That part wasn't. Tony, I have to get back to work. We can talk tomorrow."

"Oh, yes, work. Bo has the rest of January and all of February blocked out; he wants your ideas for March. He's joining us for breakfast Friday morning. And the publicity department wants background material on the Americans in Europe you're using in February, so bring your notes. Also we have an interview set up for you here, if you want to do it: some joker who's written thirty books and hasn't had one of them published, so he's putting them in a time capsule because he says people appreciate dead authors more than live ones. Don't laugh; he's serious. Think about whether you want him. Oh, and I can't find your red velvet skirt; did you take it home last week?"

"Yes. Why were you looking for it?"

452

"I was going through your closet and I couldn't find it."

"Going through my closet?"

"I do it once a day, to make sure I didn't dream you. Good-bye, sweet Elizabeth; I'll see you tomorrow."

Elizabeth paused to contemplate the image of Tony Rourke going through the clothes she kept at his Malibu house. *It isn't true, of course; he just likes the way it sounds. Why does he think he has to dramatize everything to keep me fond of him, and in his bed?*

"I've been brooding," Spencer said at lunch at The Haven, just up the road from his wife's bookshop and his woodworking shop. "Your mother says things didn't work out the way she expected them to. It occurred to me that was the way you felt, too."

"A lot of people feel that way, don't you think?" Elizabeth asked mildly.

"You see," he said, going on with his thought, "I'm seventy-seven and I thought that was old enough to do whatever made me happiest. But I'm not old enough to make your mother unhappy; I probably never will be. I love her, you know."

Elizabeth smiled. "What started you thinking about this after all this time?"

"You mean after all this time hiding in my workshop. Saul and Heather's wedding. And seeing you and Matt, standing there, talking, your heads close together and your hearts a thousand miles apart. It made me melancholy. I don't like to think of you as not settled."

"Settled," Elizabeth repeated. She set her wine glass on the table and gazed at him. "I'm forty-two years old, with a son in college and a daughter graduating high school; I've paid off the mortgage on my home; I do work that I love; I'm admired and well-known; and I have an income in excess of a hundred thousand dollars a year, not including my husband's contribution—"

"What husband?" Spencer took her hand and contemplated her gold wedding band. "Do you have one or not?"

"I'm not sure." Elizabeth looked through the window beside their table. The front porch of the low adobe building had been

453

swept clean, but snow covered the small yard and the steps of art galleries and craft shops up and down Canyon Road. Everything was very still; the narrow street of low adobe buildings set in snowcovered yards seemed frozen in its serenity. The hard-edged skyscrapers of Houston, the lush gaudiness of Los Angeles, the ancient stones and grand monuments of Europe were far away. "But whether I have one or not, I'm securely settled on my own. You don't have to worry about me."

"I don't worry about money or work." Spencer picked moodily at his smoked trout. "I worry about somebody to keep you warm at night. That's what your mother complained about: she missed it."

"I miss it, too," Elizabeth said quietly.

"Then, damn it, tell me what you want me to do! A father ought to help his daughter. I've been slow getting to it, but here I am; what can I do? Talk to Matt? Drag him back here? Convince you to get a divorce? Maybe you just need someone to listen to your problems. I know, I know, I haven't been around. But I'm around now. Tell me about Tony Rourke. He called one day when we were at your house; you were off somewhere on an interview. Would he take better care of you than Matt?"

Elizabeth laughed. "I don't need taking care of. I like Tony; we work together and we have a good time. But I'm not planning to marry him. I don't want you to do anything for me but make Mother happy. Are you going to spend more time in the bookshop?"

"Some of the time. But for the rest, we're going to find a manager. Lydia ought to be able to get out once in a while too, you know."

"What a good idea," Elizabeth said, smiling. "And what will the two of you do after you've gotten out?"

"Travel, go to concerts and movies, work together in the bookshop some of the time, share my woodworking. Lydia says she wants to learn all about varnish. I told her with her light touch she'd be an expert in no time."

Is it possible that if we wait long enough, we'll get everything we want?

Elizabeth stretched her hand across the table. Spencer took it and for a few minutes they sat in silence. "I'm really all right," she said. "There isn't anything I want you to do but show me that the two of you are happy."

"That's not a problem anymore. We're taking care of it. We still have to take care of yours."

Elizabeth bit back a retort. "Let me handle my problems," she said gently. "Maybe if you knew some of the things I'm doing, you'd feel better. It's been so long since we really talked . . ." And through the rest of their lunch, while they ate their trout and finished a bottle of wine and shared a dessert, she amused him with stories about Europe and Los Angeles, readers' comments on "Private Affairs," quotes from Peter's letters from school, and praise from Holly's voice teacher.

Spencer listened; he nodded, smiled, and chuckled. And then, as they walked out into the sharp clear air where powdery snowflakes caught the sun as they danced in the breeze, he took Elizabeth's arm. "Of course if you don't love Tony, that's that. But what about this fellow Paul Markham? Your mother said Heather said Saul said he's called you at the paper a number of times—why are you laughing?"

"Because I love you." Elizabeth kissed him. "Would you make a jewelry box for Holly's graduation? She's been wanting one made of rosewood. Oval, hinged, with red felt inside."

"And varnished by your Mother."

"Perfect. It would be from both of you. Thank you for lunch; I'll talk to you soon."

When she flew to Los Angeles the next day, Elizabeth tried to tell Tony about it—*he's seventy-seven and she's seventy and they're finally getting themselves straightened out*—but Tony didn't want to talk. As soon as the limousine brought her from the Santa Monica airport, he took her in his arms, his mouth and hands rousing her in an instant. "My God, I missed you," he said. "A whole week without you . . . I dreamed of you; I wanted you every minute. I can't stand this house when you're not here; it's so empty. I'm so empty . . ." Undressing her, his hands moved over her body, touching, stroking, exploring, with an intensity that made Elizabeth dizzy. "Once a week," he murmured. "My God, I go crazy wanting you." And he took her to his bed for the hour before dinner and again later, when the ocean was dark and the thunder of the waves seemed to lift the house above the sand, and beneath the urgency of his hands and fingertips and whispering mouth Tony gave her no time to think.

Late that night, when he slept, Elizabeth lay awake, wondering why she could not love him. They had everything she had ever wanted: they worked together and slept together; they were known as a couple in Los Angeles—and in Polly Perritt's column—and nationally as partners on "Anthony"; they had a good time together.

She moved her head restlessly on the pillow. She was grateful for his desire and his lovemaking; when they were apart she missed the words he scattered over her like soft, scented rose petals—telling her she was exquisite and sensual, as slender as a girl, as warm and strong as a woman, as sexy as a fantasy, as haunting as a dream. And what woman doesn't long for those words? Elizabeth asked herself. But there was too much drama in Tony and no room for simple emotions; too much striving to win and no sharing of feelings. I can't love him, she thought, unless I could see behind the facade. Then, perhaps . . .

The next morning, before Boyle joined them for breakfast, Tony again asked her to marry him. He caught her as she climbed out of his pool. "Enough is enough," he said. He paused to watch her graceful nude figure disappear within the long blue robe that matched his own. "How long can this go on? We want each other, we want the security, we're not happy when we're apart. There's no reason to wait."

She sat beside him on the chaise. "You remind me of Peter: he used to think that if he repeated something often enough I'd believe it. Tony, I'm already married and I don't want to marry anyone else."

"But I'm not anyone else. I am specific and unique."

She laughed. "So you are. But you're not about to be my husband. Now we'd better get dressed before Bo gets here.

Oh, Tony, did you ask him about Isabel? I want to set that up—"

"No, no, and no. Don't ask me why, my sweet, but he wouldn't give an inch on this one. Forgive me; I truly tried. He gave it two and a half seconds and then nixed it. Said she's a public figure; he wants new people, not someone you've done in your column; he wants the unknown people you've proved yourself on; you should stick with what you do best, especially when it makes our ratings go up. And he's right, you know; the politicos really belong in my part of the show."

Reluctantly, Elizabeth nodded. "I suppose so."

"Do her daughter," he said carelessly. "Young Girl Loses Mommy to New Mexico Legislature."

Elizabeth smiled with him, but her eyes were thoughtful. "Sometimes you have very interesting ideas, Tony. Good lord, look at the time! Come and get dressed; we have so much to do and I want to be home by ten tonight."

"Tonight? You're not staying over?"

"I stayed last night. I told you, Tony, no more than one night a week."

"After three solid weeks in Europe, how can you be satisfied with that? If you'd allow me to set foot in your house in Santa Fe—"

"I won't. I told you that, too. I am not going to sleep with you with my daughter down the hall and my son calling to make sure we're all right." She put her hand on his hair, still damp from their swim. "Breakfast. And I promise I won't leave until after dinner."

"If I didn't let you use our plane, you couldn't even leave then."

She became impatient. "If you want me to use a regular airline, I will. It will mean I have less time here than I do now. If you want me to stop coming to your house, I'll stay in the cottage at the Beverly Hills, the way I used to, and then we'd have even less time together. What would you like?"

"I'd like you to marry me and stop this goddam running back and forth to Santa Fe like a yo-yo, hiding from your offspring, who probably know what's going on anyway. I'm

457

sorry; don't get angry; I won't say any more. Let's go to work like good little scouts and then have a peaceful dinner in some exotic spot and perhaps you'll let me kiss you chastely on the brow when it's time for you to take off in our network's winged chariot."

Even after he was most petulant he always recovered swiftly enough to make her smile. But that night Elizabeth was glad to get home, and the next day she had put him out of her mind, because she was driving to Nuevo.

The valley was soft and white, the gashes and scars of construction hidden under deep, wind-swept snow. Even the hulking earth-moving equipment and construction trailers looked like fat white toys scattered behind the town. Beneath the snow, everything was still, everything slumbered.

Elizabeth and Isabel sat with Cesar at a table near leaping flames in the fireplace, drinking coffee with cinnamon and eating freshly-made sopapillas with honey. Upstairs, Luz and Holly read issues of *Elle* and *Paris Vogue* that Holly had brought from Santa Fe, fervently wishing for something spectacular to happen to them. "It's as if everyone is waiting for construction to start again," Elizabeth said. "And destruction, too; they go together."

"Also jobs," mused Isabel. "And customers. And excitement for the young people."

"Tell Elizabeth about the legislature," Cesar urged. "They do not give a goddam hoot in hell for the people of this town."

"True," Isabel said. "But it would be extremely stupid to batter our heads against brick walls. One wall, maybe. Forty walls, no."

"What does that mean?" Elizabeth asked.

"It's too late to change anything. They notice me, now that I'm elected, but they don't listen, they just want to straighten me out about how there's no way the committee will start this debate again. They're too busy spending this year's millions to think about last year's, and the work's already gone on for a whole summer. Nuevo is like yesterday's newspaper, and there's nothing I can do about it."

Elizabeth put down her coffee. "Isabel, Matt told me the townspeople were given a list of places to move, and promised extra money and help in resettling."

"Promised—!" growled Cesar.

"We were promised a kick in the rear if we didn't get out when we were told to," said Isabel. "What made him think that?"

"Some report. I've asked for a copy of it. I should have had it by now."

"There is no report!"

Elizabeth was silent, her eyes troubled.

The door opened and a gust of cold air bent the flames in the fireplace. "If I'm not intruding—?" Maya said.

"Of course not," Isabel said. "Elizabeth will pour you coffee; give me your coat, your boots, your gloves, your hat—" She looked at Maya closely. "Something wonderful has happened: your eyes are shining like pebbles in the bottom of a stream. Come have coffee and tell us the news."

"I had a letter today," Maya said. She smiled at Elizabeth, trying to be demure, but her eyes were dancing. "The words are very beautiful. And I couldn't wait for you to come to my house for lunch. I hope you don't mind, but I thought I would explode if I couldn't talk about it—"

"So you will do what?" demanded Isabel. Cesar had dozed off, and she lowered her voice; she was pretending to be stern, but a smile broke through her words. "Move to California? Study politics at Stanford? Work on someone else's campaign? I'm losing my assistant—is that what you're saying?"

Her color high, Maya shook her head. "I don't know. I wanted to ask you," she said to Elizabeth. "Because you know Peter. He gets very enthusiastic, and says wonderful things, but maybe besides all that feeling, there should be a little more thinking. When he studies and writes his articles he plans and thinks and organizes, but with personal things, he . . . leaps. Do you know what I mean? The way he told me last fall that he wanted to be alone at the university, and I was hurt, but I thought, well, he believes it and it's important to him. Now he says he was wrong; he can do even better with me there, because he'll be happier. And it's much nicer to be loved than hurt, and I've prayed for a letter like this, but maybe . . . maybe I should say let's wait until spring when he knows better if he really wants me all tangled up in his life . . . or maybe even summer, when he's home for a while. I mean, is it good for a woman to change her whole life because a man leaps? What if later he leaps in a new direction? I would hate to be worrying about that if I've turned my life upside down for him. But then I wonder, should I say yes because this time it may be smart to leap and if I don't, he may never want to again and then I would be miserable for the rest of my life."

It was the longest speech she had ever made and she stopped abruptly, out of breath. Elizabeth met Isabel's eyes, but Isabel gave a tiny shake of the head; she wouldn't touch it; let Peter's mother handle the question of whether Peter and Maya should live together now, or later, or at all.

Elizabeth started to reply; then she looked closely at Maya. "But that isn't all, is it? Something else is bothering you."

"Oh, you are very smart." Maya spread her hands. "I'm ashamed to say this, but . . . I love Peter and I want to live with him, but I also loved working on Isabel's campaign and I love working in her office in the statehouse and I love talking about fighting for our town, and I don't want to miss whatever happens . . ." Her voice trailed away. "That's not nice, is it? To think of other loves instead of just Peter."

Once again Elizabeth met Isabel's eyes. "It's fine," Isabel said, adding dryly, "At eighteen you have a few years to think about what's most important to you. But you haven't got a problem about Nuevo, Maya, because it looks like there won't be a fight after all."

"You haven't given in to those robbers!"

"I've given in to the facts of life. The legislature isn't going to budge. And to tell the truth, I don't think enough people want to fight. Jobs, business, money, excitement . . . who the hell would fight all that?"

"But it isn't right!" Maya exclaimed. "I mean, of course jobs are good, and it's good that people are coming back to the valley, and tourists are good, and the new road to the ski area means they'll be here year-round so there will be jobs even after the dam and all the buildings are finished—"

"You're making the speech for the opposition," Isabel said.

"No, I'm saying that all those good things certainly will happen, but it's not right that they won't help us a bit!"

"Jobs," Isabel said.

"So my father can work in a hotel instead of his own farm. Wonderful. And Gaspar can work in somebody else's store, and Roybal can pump gas in somebody else's station. How grateful we should be! And where do we live while we work for other people? In places we rent from them, or in other towns and drive back and forth each day. So rich people who probably won't even live here, and don't give a single damn about this valley, will get richer and richer from our work, on land they practically stole from us. *And that is not right!*"

Astonished, Elizabeth watched the change in Maya from a bewildered girl uncertain about her future to a fierce woman willing to fight for what she thought was right. If everyone was that determined, Elizabeth thought, they could move mountains.

Move mountains? It would be better if they could move a town.

What a good idea, she thought. Find a friendly giant to pick up the town and put it somewhere away from the dam and the center of the valley that was going to be flooded.

No, even a giant wouldn't help; he'd have no place to put it down. All the land was bought up long ago, and no one would give up enough acres for—

She sat straight, her mind racing. "Maya, Isabel, listen." She'd wondered last summer if they could build a new town, but she'd been thinking of nearby valleys. Now, Maya's words changed everything. *Rich people will get richer from our work* . . . "Listen," she said again. "What if we can find a way to keep the town and also have the lake and a state park and a resort?"

"There is no way," Isabel said. "We'll be under a hundred feet of water."

"You won't be here." Elizabeth took her notebook from her

461

shoulder bag and sketched the valley, with the town at the narrow end, the dam, the long oval that would be Lake Nuevo, the state park on one shore and the resort on the other. She drew the new road that was being cut on the high ground overlooking the future lake, making a wide arc around the dam and the resort, and out the valley at the other end. And finally, as Isabel and Maya watched, she drew a town, straddling the new road.

Maya let out a small cry. "Build Nuevo higher up—?"

"Can't," Isabel said shortly. "That land isn't ours. I saw the plans last week; that whole area is for future expansion of the resort."

Elizabeth nodded. "So they say. But if Nuevo could be built there . . ." She darkened the new road on her sketch, connecting the town, the resort, and the state park.

"Well, wouldn't that be something," Isabel murmured. "Nobody could get anywhere without going through the town—"

"—shopping at Gaspar's store," said Maya.

"—tanking up at Roybal's gas station," Isabel went on.

"Buying souvenirs," Elizabeth said. "Picnic baskets. Tennis balls. Underwater watches. Postcards. Aspirin. Suntan lotion. Ski goggles. T-shirts."

"Tourists!" Isabel exclaimed. "Spending carelessly, as tourists do. My God, wouldn't that be something! Except, of course, that it's impossible."

"Who says it is?" Elizabeth asked. "Has anyone suggested it?"

"Of course not. *We don't own the land!*"

"We would if someone gave it to us."

"You've found a saint? Or an idiot? Who else would give up a hundred acres because we ask nicely?"

"That's what we're going to work on. We're going to find some pressure points."

"Pressure points," Maya said thoughtfully. "Is that like blackmail?"

"Persuasion," Elizabeth said with a smile.

Isabel reached across the table, putting her hand on Elizabeth's. "I love you for wanting to help. I admire the devious workings of your mind. But if you do anything for us now, you'll be going public against your husband and his newspapers."

"I know," Elizabeth said briefly. She turned to a fresh page of her notebook. "Let's make a list of what we're going to do."

Isabel squeezed her hand. "Okay, you don't want to talk about it. You want to plan strategy. Who am I to refuse, when I see that glint in your eye?" She put her other hand on Cesar's shoulder. "Padre! Wake up! Things are getting interesting around here."

"Try to forget the camera," Elizabeth told Jock Olson. A technician was clipping a tiny microphone to the pocket of his denim shirt, and Olson was looking at it warily, as if waiting for it to bite. "After a while you won't even notice it. You weren't nervous when we talked yesterday; you wanted to get acquainted first and we had an ordinary conversation. This is no different."

"Except for a few million people who'll be seeing it."

Elizabeth gave him her warmest smile and watched him respond almost automatically with his own smile and an easing of his tense shoulders. "No one wants to make you look foolish," she said. "We all want you to be as wonderful as you were yesterday."

They sat in armchairs in a studio in Albuquerque, where Olson was working for the winter. Behind them was a backdrop of an enlarged photograph of Nuevo as it had looked the previous summer, with two hundred trucks kicking up dust, construction equipment biting into the mountainside, and clouds of dirt and debris blasted into the air by dynamite.

Elizabeth nodded to the cameraman, then led Olson through a description of his farm background, his first job as a worker at Albuquerque Construction, and his new job, beginning last summer, as crew chief on the Nuevo Dam. Relaxing, he answered Elizabeth's questions about how he felt about construction work and being crew chief; he became animated and joked about "this dam job we're doing at Nuevo."

463

Elizabeth laughed, then said curiously, "What damn job? Is something wrong with it?"

"No," Olson said immediately. "It's fine. Lots of guys would give their eye teeth to have it."

"But it can't all be fun."

"It's not supposed to be fun; it's work. Hard work, with lots of hassles. But the pay's good and it's a steady job. Something always needs to be built somewhere."

"What kind of hassles? Bosses looking over your shoulder—?"

"No, what are you talking about? Nobody looks over my shoulder; I'm a professional. Me and the engineers and the general contractor—we work together."

"But then who's hassling you? Not your workers; they know you're in charge. So who else is there?"

"Look, Mrs. Lovell—"

"Elizabeth."

"Right. Elizabeth. Look, there's a *town* there. People *live* there. They don't like us."

"But they don't even know you."

"We buy things in town, we eat there, we talk to them; there's some cute chicks around . . ."

"They don't want you to talk to the chicks? The young girls?"

"Right. But that's not the main thing. Shit, they don't—sorry, I forgot; shouldn't say that—they don't like us because we're building a dam that will flood their town."

"But that's your job."

"Tell *them* that. They think if we disappeared the dam wouldn't get built."

"But someone would build it."

"That's the thing. You see that; I see it; they don't want to. But there's too much money at stake. There's gonna be condominiums there, a club house, golf course, boating docks . . . This is big, big money, and ain't nobody in the world gonna let anything stop the dam because if it's not there, there's no lake or anything else. The people in that town don't know shit from shinola—sorry, I forgot—the people can't stop it. Last summer some of 'em tried: stood in the road, you know, when the trucks were coming, but nobody got hurt. Mostly they talked; damn if they didn't about yak us to death. Between the ones who wanted us gone and the ones who wanted jobs, I damn near went nuts. I kinda felt sorry for a lot of 'em; they were so sure everything would be hunky-dory if we'd just get the hell out and leave them alone."

"Why should you feel sorry for them? It sounds to me like they were nothing but trouble."

"Well, no question, they were a pain in the ass. But, funny thing: when you got to know them they were okay. Just . . . people. Like everybody else."

"And you liked them?"

"Well, sure. Some I did, some I didn't. Like everywhere."

"And they liked you?"

"Yeh. We got along."

"Did they make you an honorary citizen of Nuevo?"

"How the hell did—? Well, Cesar joked about giving me a piece of land in town, but it wasn't like I was a *citizen*."

"Cesar? One of the people in town?"

"Right. Decent old guy. Everybody's old man, sort of."

"But how did that happen? How could you make friends with them while you're building a dam that's going to flood their town?"

"I just . . . hung around. Damn it, I *liked* the place! I've been all the hell over the country, every state just about, but this place I really liked—the town, the valley, the people. So I'd hang around and we'd rap and after a while there were a lot of us . . ."

"How many?"

"Fifteen, twenty, sometimes more; they'd come and go, but there was usually a bunch telling stories, rapping . . . like Cesar . . . he'd talk about years ago when the place was a jumping town; he and his friend, a guy named Zachary, dead now, used to hunt rabbits, chase 'em into the—well, that's a long story. And this guy Gaspar? Owns the general store; knows everybody all the way to Pecos, and all the gossip; used to listen at the window when people dumped their problems on Cesar's daughter. You probably heard of her—Isabel Aragon—

465

she was elected to the legislature in the last election. Isn't that something? I wasn't around; we'd shut down for the winter and I was on another job, but I'll bet they were so damn proud . . ."

Elizabeth let the interview unfold at its own pace. Her eyes never left Olson's face; the warmth of her smile and the intimate line of her body, leaning forward in her chair, made him forget the camera: it was as if they were alone.

When Tony watched the uncut tape with her the next day, in Los Angeles, he let out a sigh. "Dynamite. You are a wizard, my sweet. How did you find him?"

"Cesar told me about him. I'd thought of interviewing Cesar and Maya and a few others, but I wanted someone from outside who cared about them."

"Well, you found him. Pity you can't use him for three months."

"I'm using him next week, Tony."

"My sweet, you can't. We've scheduled the European interviews into April."

"I know, but they can all be moved back a week." She was rewinding the tape. "Why did you think I came in today to edit it?"

"I thought you came in to see me."

"Not now, Tony; I'll see you for dinner."

"You'll have to tell Bo you're using this guy next week."

"I know. I'm seeing him this afternoon."

"Well, then. Dinner. L'Orangerie, and wear something special."

"Why?"

"You and I are going to make a potential sponsor fall in love with us."

"Do we need a new sponsor?"

"Bo says we lost one," he said carelessly. "I don't pay attention, but tonight's a big one. Japanese cars. Or is it German cameras? Whatever it is, we're supposed to be our most beautiful and charming selves. I'll be back at six to pick you up."

As he left, Elizabeth rewound the tape and began running it again, in spurts, cutting it to fifteen minutes and editing out the words unsuitable for television. As she reached the end, Bo Boyle came in and watched the last few minutes.

ELIZABETH: Why isn't it a good idea to have a lake in that valley? We can always use more places for recreation, can't we?

OLSON: Depends on the place. I don't like the way they're doing this one, is all. Look, I've worked on a lot of these fancy resorts and nobody builds them out of the goodness of their heart—they build them to make big bucks. Which is okay—everybody likes to make money—but you shouldn't do it by hurting decent people like Cesar and the rest.

ELIZABETH: You mean they should be able to stay?

OLSON: Sure. Why not?

ELIZABETH: But their town will be gone.

OLSON: Build a new one. There's lots of room—we're not doing any work at all in one whole section of the valley. It'll just sit there, empty.

ELIZABETH: Build a new town?

OLSON: It's not such a big deal; people do it all the time. Tornadoes, hurricanes, earthquakes—people rebuild. They could take some of that land—nobody'd miss it—and then everybody'd be happy. I'd even work for nothing, after hours, to help them. And build myself a place, too, a real home, for between jobs. This is a damn nice valley we're talking about; and nobody should be kicked out of it! Listen, this is a terrific idea! Everybody can be there because *damn it, there is room in that valley for everybody!*

At the last word, Boyle turned and slipped out of the room. His office was a few steps away; once at his desk he punched the numbers on his telephone and drummed his fingers while waiting. "Boyle," he told Rourke's secretary and waited again until Rourke was on the line. "It may not be anything, but I thought you'd want to know about it. Lovell's just taped an interview with a guy named Olson, construction chief on a dam in that place in New Mexico, and he came up with the idea that the townspeople ought to be given land high up to build a new town. Did you say something?"

"No," Rourke replied. "Go on."

"That's about it. You told me to watch for stories on mining and resorts, so I thought you'd want to know about this one."

"Did she prime him to say what he did?" Rourke asked.

"Not clear. But she always does preliminary interviews, so it's likely she knew what he'd say."

"Kill it," Rourke said.

"No problem. Do you want a copy of the tape?"

"I want the original. No copies. Is that clear?"

"Sure thing."

"And let me know what she does next."

"About what?"

"About anything. Is she there now?"

"Yeh. Editing her tape."

"And staying the night at Tony's?"

"I presume. She doesn't inform me, but she hasn't stayed in the Beverly Hills cottage since they got back from Europe."

"All right. How is Tony's mail?"

"Fair. Up and down. He's slow, though; he just doesn't knife people the way he used to."

"What were last week's ratings?"

"Twenty. Not as low as before we had her, but not where we'd like them. We lost the greeting card company; I've lined up a couple of possible new ones to fill in."

"All right. Keep in touch. And kill that interview."

Boyle started back to the editing room, then slowed. Why do it now, when he'd have to give reasons and see those gray eyes change from friendliness to anger? There was a better way to handle it.

* * *

468

Isabel, Cesar, and Luz brought Maya with them to Elizabeth's house to watch the February 6 edition of "Anthony." Holly rescheduled her voice lesson to be with them and they all ate dinner together, then moved to the den and sat in a semicircle in front of the television set, waiting for Elizabeth to introduce Jock Olson.

"This is Elizabeth Lovell and 'Private Affairs,'" said Elizabeth on the screen, after Tony had finished his opening interview. "Introducing you tonight to an apprentice chef, Terry Pelz of Butte, Montana, whose private dream was to study in Paris with the great—"

"Chef?" asked Maya in bewilderment.

"Mother, what happened?" Holly demanded.

Elizabeth stared at the screen where she sat in an empty restaurant in the sixteenth arrondissement of Paris with a gangly boy who talked fervently of food as art and love. "Someone made a mistake," she said angrily. "I scheduled Terry for next week. I left five notes on five different desks; I told Bo, I told Tony. And I put the tape in the box for tonight."

She switched off the television set. "If you'll excuse me, I'm going to make a telephone call."

She went to her bedroom and closed the door. "Al," she said when the engineer answered, "who mixed up my tapes?"

"Mixed up? Nobody. There were only four tapes in tonight's box—three of Tony's and yours on this guy Pelz. Is something wrong?"

"Yes, but it's not your fault. I'll see you tomorrow."

She stood in the doorway of the den. "Holly, do you mind if I go to Los Angeles tonight? Somebody deliberately switched those tapes and I can't wait to find out who did it. And why."

"There's no plane tonight," Isabel said. Her mouth drooped with disappointment. She and Elizabeth had planned to pressure key legislators with the mail they expected to come in after Olson's interview. Maya had written a pamphlet telling how a new town would have historical value, since the oldest buildings, including the church, would be moved to the new site; how it would create goodwill by showing that progress didn't have to steamroll people; how it would provide jobs for New Mexicans.

Now they couldn't use any of it. They'd have to wait—and the legislature would be in session only through March. Seven more weeks.

"The network plane is at the airport," Elizabeth said. "I was going to fly in early tomorrow. What do you think, Holly?"

"I think you should go. And take me. Will you? I'd only miss one day of school."

"This isn't the best time. It may be a battle royal. I will next week, if you can miss rehearsal."

"I can miss anything just to go somewhere else for a while."

"Tell me about it," Luz muttered. She turned to Isabel. "Can we go with Elizabeth to the airport?"

"We'll all go. Padre? Wake up."

Thinking of them, Elizabeth smiled to herself as the plane climbed above Santa Fe's small splash of bright lights on the dark plateau. Then the smile faded. It was bad enough that someone had switched her tapes without consulting her, but then no one had bothered to tell her about it. What was going on?

"Who was it?" she demanded of Tony. He had been out to dinner when she arrived at his house, and when he came home to find her in the living room it had taken her ten minutes to convince him that neither love nor desire had brought her to Malibu twelve hours early: she wanted to talk.

"I don't know," he said. "Word of honor, my sweet, I have no idea. I didn't even know your sensitive macho was dropped; you know I never see the show until the next day when you and I can watch it together. Somebody probably mixed up the tapes after a night of too much booze or coke or both; we'll run it next week and all will be well." He put his arms around her. "But it's a blessing in disguise; it brought you to me tonight. Oh, don't frown, dearest Elizabeth; it hurts me to see you frown."

"Why didn't anyone call me to tell me a mistake had been made?"

470

"How do I know? They knew you'd be here tomorrow and they could tell you then."

"I should have been consulted before air time. 'They' didn't want me to know in advance. Who are 'they'?"

"I don't know! Do you doubt my absolute innocence in this? It was somebody's simple mistake—"

Elizabeth slipped out of his arms and picked up her suede jacket. "It was not simple and I doubt very much it was a mistake. I'm going to talk to Bo."

"Bo! Elizabeth, Bo lives in Laurel Canyon. It's an hour's drive, at least. He is no doubt happily in bed with his young man, just as you could be much more happily in bed with me. This can wait until morning!"

"No it can't. I've got to talk to him, Tony. 'Private Affairs' is mine; it's my part of the show. That was our agreement. And as long as I'm in charge of it, no one is going to do anything to it behind my back."

"You're right. No question about it. But you can make that clear in the morning when we're all more alert. Sleepy people are not good in discussions, Elizabeth; they misunderstand each other and get angry and I've had a good deal to drink and I can't handle this. It's not the right time for you to have a face-off—"

"May I use your car?"

He sighed deeply and loudly. "I'll drive you. Eleven o'clock; we'll be there at midnight. The witching hour. How pleased Bo will be to see us on his doorstep. God, you're lovely when you're fierce. Like a goddess who's been betrayed by a mortal. All right, let's go; at least there's a moon; Laurel Canyon will be pleasant to behold."

Elizabeth did not notice the moon or Laurel Canyon; she was brooding. And by the time she faced Bo, scowling darkly in his satin and velvet dressing gown, filling their glasses with Scotch though he knew she disliked it, she was angrier than ever. "Just tell me how it happened," she said coldly. "And that it won't happen when I schedule Olson next week. Not much gets past you in that place; you can make sure it doesn't happen again."

471

"If I so desired." Boyle downed his Scotch and poured another. "Which I don't. That interview with Olson was inflammatory: a political polemic that has no place on 'Anthony' or any other entertainment show. I wouldn't allow it and neither would our legal department."

"Legal—?" Elizabeth's voice wavered. "They said we were vulnerable because of what Jock Olson said?"

"Inflammatory," repeated Boyle, and poured a third drink.

Tony was looking at him curiously. "Bo, dear Bo," he said amiably. "I've known you a long time; I always know when your imagination is percolating. You did not go to our legal beagles."

"Bullshit."

"And that is very odd," Tony continued. "Because if you didn't go to legal, why did you switch the tapes?"

Elizabeth swung her glance to Tony. "Bo switched them?"

"Oh, I'm sure he did. Nobody else has the authority."

"You've known that since I first told you about it."

"Dearest Elizabeth, of course. But I detest quarrels and I wanted to be in bed with you instead of standing in the middle of Bo's dreary living room in the wee hours wondering why he's lying about the legal department. But since we're here . . . why are you lying, little Bo Peep?"

"Tony, don't be a bore," Boyle said. "You're horny and you've had too much to drink. Crawl into bed with your inflammatory lady; take two fucks, and call me in the morning."

Tony's face darkened. "You son of a bitch, you can't talk to me like that! And you won't talk about Elizabeth at all! Just tell us you won't fool around with her tapes again without her permission, and we'll go home and forget that anything happened."

"I'd like to know why it happened," Elizabeth put in quietly.

Looking at Tony, Boyle said, "Keep out of it, Lizzie; the great lover wants this between us."

"Bo, what the hell's gotten into you!" Tony exclaimed. "You've never talked like—"

"You've never gotten me up at midnight to tell me how to do my job. I've got pressures from all directions; I don't need

472

any from you or your little lady." He splashed more Scotch into Tony's glass.

"Stop; I don't want your goddam liquor—" Glancing at Elizabeth, Tony drew himself up and became suave. "You've disappointed me, Bo. We came here with a simple question and I never doubted we could discuss it like gentlemen, but you talk like somebody from the gutter. I don't drink with gutter rats." Absently he drained his glass and automatically held it out to be refilled. His words rolled out. "You work for me, Bo; don't forget that! And don't forget what I've done for you. You should be on your knees in gratitude; you haven't got the talent"—the dignified facade began to crack—"to make it to Laurel Canyon or anywhere else—television, radio, walkie-talkies—without riding on my coattails; you've been hanging onto them for years!"

"Your coattails! Fuck it, you pathetic bastard, you don't know your ass from a hole in the ground. You'd be a deejay on a thirty-watt station without me. Even with everything I do, we can't jack up your ratings; we have to scrounge for sponsors and then pay *them*—"

"ENOUGH! THAT'S ENOUGH! YOU'RE FIRED! I don't listen to vermin puking out lies—"

"You'll listen to *me*, you stupid bastard! You can't fire me—you can't tell me what to do—because I don't work for you; I work for someone else. *And I don't lie about sponsors!*"

Confused, Tony paused, looking at the dark, heavy furniture crammed into the square room. His glance passed over Elizabeth as if he did not recognize her. She was standing in a corner, leaning against a long library table and watching the two men who were barely recognizable in their anger. She'd started something that had grown into a monster; she didn't understand it, but its ugliness appalled her and she wanted to run from it, but she couldn't move: she had to stay and hear the rest of it because somehow she was part of it.

"'Work for someone else,'" Tony repeated finally. His voice deepened in scorn. 'Scrounge for sponsors . . . *pay* them.' You'd love to believe lies like that; you've always been jealous

473

of my popularity. But everyone knows sponsors line up to get on my show."

"Everyone knows you're going downhill. You're talking ancient history, fella; there's nothing for me to be jealous of. We would have lost the show five years ago if . . . somebody hadn't reimbursed—that means *paid*—Gardner Insurance to sponsor three fifteen-minute segments. That only left us the fourth to sell; a cinch, we thought, but we're having trouble keeping it sold."

Tony's lips stretched; he was trying to grin. "Good old Bo; always joking. But it's not a joke; it's pure shit. So what the hell is going on? You're trying out for Johnny Carson or Polly Perritt? Or you've flipped and you're a dangerous maniac. YOU SON OF A BITCH, YOU'RE THROUGH!" His voice came in breathless spurts, as if he had been running. "You've practically ruined my show—goddam it, you drove down the ratings! I've never liked you—I would have fired you years ago, but I felt sorry for you, poor bastard, I kept you in clothes and shelter and pocket money to hire little boys because they're the only ones in town willing to get on all fours for you—"

Boyle flung the empty bottle of Scotch at him; it struck him in the chest and he doubled over with a grunt of pain and surprised rage. Elizabeth ran to him. "Tony, let's go; let's get out of here—"

"Not yet, God damn it; I'm going to teach this"—he started for Bo, but Elizabeth was clinging to his arm and he turned a contorted face to her—"LEAVE ME ALONE!"

"No! Tony, listen to me, *don't listen to Bo, listen to me!* Don't say any more, don't listen to any more . . . Tony, *let's go home!*"

"Fucking bastard!" he said to Boyle, jerking his arm out of Elizabeth's grasp and starting again for the other side of the room. "So fucking jealous you try to ruin my show—tell lies about—"

"Listen you little shit, your show would be dead and buried if it wasn't for me and your Daddy."

Tony stopped. "That's a lie. He doesn't have anything to do with my show. He never did. *You fucking liar!*"

"Daddy, Daddy, Daddy," Boyle chanted. He was holding another bottle, and he took a swig from it, watching Tony. "Daddy pays Gardner to sponsor your show; Daddy's kept you alive for five years; Daddy pays me to watch over you and edit your interviews so they're good enough to—"

With a roar, Tony threw himself at Boyle, knocking him to the floor, his fists slamming Boyle's face. "Bastard! Lying, fucking bastard!" He was stronger than Boyle and pinned him down, half-lying on him, trying to get his hands around Boyle's neck, but Boyle fended him off, twisting under him, his arms straining as he kept Tony's hands from his neck. "Working for . . . DADDY," he gasped and tried to laugh, but it came out a wheezing grunt. *"All these . . . years . . . shit, Tony . . . get the hell off! . . . even Lizzie knows . . . you need help . . . too weak—"* Tony's fist slammed into his mouth; blood covered Boyle's teeth and Tony's knuckles, and as Boyle gagged Tony got his hands around his throat. Eyes bulging, Boyle scratched at Tony's hands and pried one finger up and jerked it back. Through their gasps and strangled curses came a sharp crack; Tony screamed and sat up, holding his hand, his face black with rage and pain. He stood and kicked Boyle in the ribs, then aimed again, but Boyle had rolled away and was on all fours, wiping the blood from his mouth. He stood and pulled his robe tight around him and tied it. "You dumb ass, you stupid fart." Head down, holding his ribs with his folded arms, he glowered at Tony. *"Where the fuck do you think you'd go on your own?"*

Breathing raggedly, his broken finger held inside his jacket, Tony looked in his direction, his eyes unfocused. The color had drained from his face, leaving it pasty and old. "Shut up," he said, but the words had no force.

Carefully stretching out one hand, Boyle grasped a bottle on the table and drank from it. "Get out." He spat and blood spattered on the front of his robe. *"Out."*

"Tony, we're going." Elizabeth had her arm around his waist. "We can find out if it's true about your father in the—"

"It's true," Tony said dully. "Bo wouldn't make it up. It's true, isn't it, Bo?"

"Yes."

Elizabeth tightened her arm, to turn Tony in the direction of the front door. She had watched the fight without moving, rigid with fear at the violence they had unleashed, afraid Tony would succeed in strangling Boyle, caught between pity for Tony and astonishment at his contorted face and the venom spewing from his mouth. And through it all, like a dark thread, ran the thought, It can't be true, I haven't been working for Keegan; I haven't; *I haven't been working for Tony's father!* "Come on," she urged Tony, trying to get him moving, trying to get him out of the house.

"I want to know about it," he said hoarsely. "Why do you keep interfering?" He pulled away from Elizabeth's embrace; his shoulders slumped and his arm twitched, as if he were a puppet that someone had tossed aside, its strings broken, its stuffing gone. *"I want to know about my show!"*

"Your Daddy's show," Boyle said. He leaned against the table, breathing hard. "He subsidizes it; it's his."

"Subsidi—" Tony cleared his throat. "You knew I was . . . working for him and you never told me."

"He told me to keep it quiet."

"For a price."

Boyle shrugged, then winced and held his ribs again. "I don't come cheap. Your Daddy is going to back me as a miniseries producer as soon as I've run out of ways to prop you up."

"Why?"

"Why is he backing me? Because I'm a superb producer."

"Why did he . . ."—Tony choked on the word—"subsidize my show?"

"I didn't ask him and he didn't tell me." Boyle's voice had become stronger as Tony's grew weaker. "Any other questions?"

Silently Tony shook his head.

"Tony," Elizabeth said. "That's enough. You've heard enough. We're going."

476

"He's ignoring you, Lizzie," said Boyle. "He has to make up to me. You should see that. You've lost him. You lost Olson, too. You should be clear on that, so listen carefully." He started to drink from the bottle, then poured Scotch into a glass instead, and drank from it. "This is for the future. You can do what you want when I approve it. That means you'll clear everything with me: every interview, every editing job, every tape that goes on the air. And you won't argue when I put my foot down. You're good, but it's my show and I didn't like the Olson interview so I killed it. Them's the rules. I wouldn't like to lose you, but I don't tolerate insolence; television is teamwork. You stay on our team; you'll be very happy. Don't think Mr. Rourke and I don't know that the ratings are up because of you; we're planning a nice raise and your own house and car for when you're in town. You're a valued part of 'Anthony.' Who knows? Someday 'Anthony' may even become 'Private Affairs.'"

Elizabeth's stomach was churning; she was so angry the room was blurred and red, as if her blood rushed hot and fuming just behind her eyes. "Not your 'Private Affairs,' Bo; not ever. You won't ever have a chance to kill anything of mine again." She took Tony's hand in both of hers. "Tony, I'm leaving. Please come with me."

He turned to her, his mouth rigid. "Why are you fighting him? Don't argue; just say you'll go along!"

"Go along?" She let his hand drop. Boyle was watching, a small smile on his face, but she spoke only to Tony. "Go along with what?"

"With whatever he says! Do you have to be so goddam . . . proud? It's not important enough! He killed one lousy interview! *That's all we're talking about!*"

"We're talking about my work!" she cried. "It comes from my mind; I create it; and you're damned right I'm proud! I'm proud of what I create; it's part of me and it's very important! Can't you see that? Can't you understand it and stand up for me?"

"Did you hear what he said about my father?"

"Of course I did; that's part of it. Do you think I want to

work for Keegan any more than you do? But how can we talk about it—how can we talk about anything—if you can't understand what I'm saying and at least support me—"

"*There's nothing I can do.* What the hell do you want me to do? Risk my whole future because you don't like taking orders? Nobody likes taking orders! Are you so special I'm supposed to destroy myself so you don't have to take them? I'm the one who needs support, not you! One interview, Elizabeth! One tiny fucking interview!"

Elizabeth closed her eyes briefly. "I can't believe you're saying this. Where's all the brave talk I've heard for months? Tony, we can find other sponsors. If our ratings are up, that's not a secret. If we believe in what we can do—"

"No. You don't know what you're talking about. It's a jungle, this business, and I won't go out there looking for a job, getting chewed up . . ." He looked at her, his eyes pleading. "Do what Bo says. It's not so terrible, is it? And you're famous, Elizabeth! Nothing else is important if you have that! Christ, Elizabeth, don't make trouble! I don't know how the hell I got into this—I knew we shouldn't come tonight—then I wouldn't have found out—I'd never have known—I don't give a damn about sponsors! I do interviews; I don't worry about money! *Sponsors are not my problem!*"

"Tony, stop!" Elizabeth cried. "You keep making things worse!" She went to a chair near the doorway and picked up her jacket. "I know how terrible it's been for you, Tony, finding out about your father, and I'd like to help you handle that, but I can't, at least not here, not now. All I can do is ask you to come with me. You've been wonderful to me and I'm grateful, and I'll work with you, if you want, and help you get away from your father. We'll start another show—people know us, we have an audience—we'll put a program together, Tony! And I'll be with you."

"I can't do it! Damn it to hell, Elizabeth, don't you understand? I'm a famous person, not somebody just starting out! I don't go around begging for a show, hiring a producer, worrying about sponsors . . . Why the hell do you think I'd get involved in all that?"

"You wouldn't. I was wrong to think you would. I'm sorry, Tony—"

"Lizzie, we want you on the show!" Boyle said, his voice riding over hers. "Don't try to be Joan of Arc; you'll regret it. You've got one hell of a brilliant future—"

"I won't see you again, Tony."

"You can't leave me!" Tony cried. "I need you! Elizabeth, my God, you can't leave me! You can't leave the show! Look what it's done for you! Look what I've done for you! Damn it, I made you! You were buried in the desert! Nobody knew you; nobody cared about you; even your husband wouldn't stay with you; I was the only one—"

The last of Elizabeth's control slipped. Enraged, she lashed at him. "How dare you! You don't know the first thing about me, or my husband—you have no right to say anything about us! You're having a tantrum, Tony—my God, why won't you grow up! You've been exaggerating and dramatizing for years— I kept thinking maybe you weren't, or it didn't make any difference, but it makes all the difference in the world because you can't live any other way, can you? Hiding yourself, playing your little games, scared to death of being honest because maybe no one would love you if you were just . . . you. And maybe no one would; I don't know and I don't care. I don't love you, Tony—I never did—I suppose because there isn't anyone to love: only a hollow little boy trying to be a man. How are you going to live with yourself after tonight? Your big chance to stand up to your father and his rotten little flunky— his *spy*—your chance to defend my integrity, and your own, and grow up; and you threw it away. You'd rather have your crib: nice and warm and secure, with no danger of falling. Failing. I hope you're happy in it, Tony; I even hope you find someone to share it. But it won't be me. It isn't big enough for me. And neither are you."

She opened the door and ran to the car parked in the circular drive. The tires screeched as she turned into the road and drove away. It was only when she was halfway down the canyon that she remembered it was Tony's car; she'd left him behind, with Boyle. A small laugh broke through the red anger still churning inside her.

Let them work it out; they make a fine pair.

Part
IV

CHAPTER 15

In the smoke-filled, windowless conference room of the *Dallas Post*, Matt opened that morning's paper, fighting off boredom as talk of advertising lineage droned on. The fourth conference of the day; the eighth day of what Chet cheerfully called wall-to-wall meetings in cities from San Diego to Dallas; he'd had more than enough. He turned to the second page to read 'Private Affairs.' Elizabeth's picture was at the top, as usual, but beneath it was an odd sentence, in italics. *This interview was intended for television. For unknown reasons it was canceled, and so it appears here, almost exactly as in its original form when it was taped three weeks ago on February 6.*

What the hell, Matt thought, but before he could begin to read he heard his name. "—need your opinion on that," the managing editor was saying.

Matt struggled to recall his name; by now everyone in every meeting looked and sounded the same, and so did the discussions. They were part of his job, and he didn't try to delegate them; even if he wanted to, there was no one to whom he could delegate the job of stroking corporate advertisers, keeping track of fluctuating readership, and dealing with Keegan Rourke's unexpectedly frequent suggestions, criticisms, requests for explanations, and changes in plans that Matt had to accept if he couldn't get them changed back. All of it was a long way from his idea of newspapering, and too much of the time it frustrated or bored the hell out of him.

He remembered the managing editor's name, dealt with the question he'd asked, then did what he'd ordered himself not to do: barely concealing his impatience, he took control of the meeting away from his editor, got everyone talking on the same subject, and led the discussion to the conclusion he'd wanted in the beginning. And then he told them he was calling it a day.

He refused several invitations to adjourn to a local bar, folded his copy of the *Post* to read on the plane to Houston, and strolled through the building. Six-thirty: the third- and fourth-floor offices were almost empty; only the executives who had been in the meeting were still there, closing up to go home. In the second floor bullpen, some reporters on the graveyard shift were coming in early, meeting those on the daytime shift who were leaving late. Matt stood in the doorway, watching the men and women sort through the clutter on their desks, talk on the telephone, pound the silent keys on their computers as if they were still working on typewriters.

Even at this time of night, the room had a vitality and sense of purpose that awoke memories; Matt could feel the urgency that had knotted his muscles years ago when he and Elizabeth and their small staff raced to get the *Chieftain* printed and onto the waiting delivery trucks. He turned away, then turned back and found his way to the pressroom.

The huge room was quiet now; in a few hours it would be rumbling and crackling with the sounds of thousands of sheets of paper rolling through ceiling-high presses, eight pages at a time being printed, folded and collated, stacked, tied, and sent on conveyer belts to the loading dock. Now, only one press was running as two pressmen freed a mass of paper chewed up within the gears and worked on a lever mechanism. Instinctively, Matt moved forward, then stopped, smiling ruefully at himself. Only at the *Chieftain,* he thought, remembering his elation at working with his hands the day Saul had mistaken

483

him for the repairman. He and Saul had laughed together. The pressmen of the *Dallas Post* probably would not be amused to find the publisher of Rourke Enterprises muscling in on their territory.

I've lost all the fun of it. I've forgotten what it's like to roll up my sleeves and work in a newsroom. I'm not a newspaperman; I'm a goddam executive. I might as well be running a bank or a manufacturing company; I wouldn't be much farther from real newspaper work than I am now.

But what the hell could he do about it? He sat on the plane, leaning back and staring out the window at dull flashes of distant lightning in the immense black sky. He'd wanted power; he had it, and it was a full-time job. And when he wasn't frustrated or bored, he could get back the feeling that it was what he'd dreamed it would be. When he was alone behind the closed door of his hushed, comfortable office, writing his own memos that would set the future course of his newspapers on national and state issues, then he felt a surge of power that made him forget everything else. Or when he spoke at conferences where he was sought out for his support and he could choose which programs and candidates would be endorsed by his papers: then he was satisfied. Or when he heard from contacts in state legislatures, and in Washington, that legislation he had fought for had been passed, and he knew he'd helped shape the lives and fortunes of the people in half a dozen states, then once again, as in Aspen with Nicole, he knew this was what he wanted.

The steward brought his vodka. He lowered the tray table in front of him and ordered a second drink, knowing how long it always took to arrive; then he pulled out the morning paper and turned again to Elizabeth's column.

Construction crew chief Jock Olson has powerful shoulders, blue eyes under shaggy brows, a gravelly voice, and a broad grin that makes him look like a kid who's built his first tree house and feels on top of the world. "This is a damn nice valley we're talking about!" he says, looking into the distance, as if he could see that peaceful valley, and its small town of Nuevo, isolated in the mountains of New Mexico.

"And the people there care about it!" But he frowns as he says it. Because the people of Nuevo are being forced out by developers who will flood the valley for a lake and private resort. And the reason Jock Olson frowns is that he's come to love Nuevo.

"I've been all over the country, but I really like that place, especially the people. And somebody's gonna clean up there without those people getting one damn thing out of it. They've lived there all their lives—their parents and grandparents, too—so how come they can't share in it? Listen, I know that place: *Nobody should be kicked out of there because there's room for everybody in that valley!*"

"I'll be goddamned," Matt muttered.

Beside him, a man in a pin-stripe suit looked up from his yellow legal pad and saw Elizabeth's picture. "Good, isn't she? We get her in Phoenix. Which one is that?" He peered at it. "Oh, the construction guy. I read that a couple days ago. Damn shame, isn't it, what's happening to those people? My wife and I sent a check; so did my secretary."

Matt contemplated him. "Did you?"

"Why not? They need help, don't they? Least we can do; nobody's kicking us out of *our* home."

Matt nodded thoughtfully. "You're right. And, yes, she's very good." He turned back to the column and read Elizabeth's description of Olson's work as crew chief, his slow acceptance by the townspeople, his feeling of belonging in Nuevo, and his desire to build a house of his own there.

"I'd even work for nothing, after hours, to help them," he says, but he knows the town is doomed. "They're gonna drown it and the people don't have the money to buy land higher up, even if whoever owns it would sell. No money to build new houses, either, or move some of the old ones, and the old church, to save them, you know, because they *should* be saved, they're terrific: like something out of a story book."

He lets loose with a few four-letter words, and some a little longer, and then goes back to work. This winter it's an office building in Albuquerque, but next summer Jock Olson will be crew chief again in Nuevo: forced, because it's his job, to build a dam that will drown the place he loves, and take a town and a valley away from people he loves, whose only crime is that they happen to live in the path of a posh resort.

At first Matt was stunned by the boldness of it; then a surge of pride swept through him. The column was wonderfully done, bringing Olson and Nuevo to life while throwing down the gauntlet to the developers by offering a solution—all of it without preaching or sounding shrill. He had never felt so proud of her.

He wondered if the idea of moving the town was Olson's, or if she'd put it in his head. It didn't much matter. Olson was right: the idea was terrific. And Matt strongly suspected that Elizabeth had some ideas on how it might be worked. And Isabel, he thought, and others in Nuevo, and probably Saul and Heather, too.

The same nostalgia that had swept him in the pressroom of the *Post* tugged at him again, this time for that group of friends in Santa Fe and Nuevo working together to keep the town alive. He wished for a moment he could join them; they were helping people in just the way he'd hoped to do with his newspapers. And they'd found a better solution than the only one he'd known of: the offer of financial aid for resettlement—

He frowned. Where the hell was that report? He'd promised it to Elizabeth at Saul and Heather's wedding, in December; she'd called a couple of times since then, asking about it; he'd said they hadn't found it yet, and then told Chet, again, he wanted it. He'd have to get after Chet, he thought; no reason for a simple request to take this long.

The plane began its descent into Houston. On impulse, Matt opened his briefcase, pulled out a sheet of stationery, and wrote a short note to Elizabeth. He'd mail it at the airport, on his way to the lower level, where Nicole would be waiting to take him home.

Elizabeth read the note two days later, on a plane to New York. In her rush to get out of the house to drive to the airport in Albuquerque, she'd stuffed the mail in her briefcase, opening it only when she had settled back and lowered her tray table as the stewardess brought her sherry. The handwriting gave her a shock as it always did, even though Matt regularly sent a check with a brief note. *I ought to be used to it after eight months.* But the check had come last week; this was something else. She tore it open. "Dear Elizabeth," he had written in his bold scrawl with strong, slanted lines. "You've made Olson a hero and Nuevo everybody's idea of home. It's a wonderful, moving piece and proves (though no one could have doubted it) that you're the best there is. With love, Matt."

She read the note over and over, her anger growing with each re-reading until she was trembling. *The best there is.* But evidently not better than Nicole. Not better than Keegan Rourke. Not better than that fawning crowd in Houston. Not better than glamour and wealth and a very fast track.

She crumpled the note, letting it fall to the floor, and accepted a second sherry from the stewardess, though she never had more than one. But it's been quite a month, she thought. First the blow-up with Bo and Tony, then, as word spread through the industry that she had left "Anthony," without warning and with sixteen weeks still left in the season, she began receiving invitations to radio and television talk shows—and she began to travel.

Now it was more than a speech in New York or Philadelphia or Tulsa, and perhaps a night away from home; now the appearances were stacked up by Elizabeth's agent and she was away two or three nights in a row. In between, she fit in interviews and wrote her column on planes or on the days she was in Santa Fe. She never prepared for her appearances; she answered questions spontaneously about her taped interviews and those for Markham Features, in Europe and America, using anecdotes and charm and the on-camera skills she had learned in Los Angeles.

She never talked about "Anthony" or about Tony Rourke. "Why not?" Heather asked after Elizabeth's second week of travel, as they sat in the bookshop unpacking cartons from publishers. "If you tell the truth, you could puncture his whole fake image!"

"Nothing I could say is as devastating as silence," Elizabeth answered. "It gives Bo nothing to contradict."

"That's very clever." After a moment's hesitation, Heather said, "Elizabeth, how long will you go on with these shows?"

"I don't know. I hate living out of a suitcase, but I'm afraid to give up being in front of a camera, and being treated like a star. I'll probably get enough of it one of these days, Heather, and then I'll settle down with my column and the little bit of work I do at the *Chieftain*."

"And live happily ever after?"

"No, that's for you and Saul. You both look so *content* these days. Don't you ever quarrel anymore?"

"We'll always quarrel. But we have a huge amount of fun when we're getting along, which seems to be more and more often lately. It's harder than I thought, living with someone, and for some reason it's even harder when you're married."

" 'Husband' has a different meaning than 'lover,' " Elizabeth murmured.

"Yes. That's true." Heather opened a new carton and removed some paperbacks. "Elizabeth, I know you like the camera and the attention, but I want to talk to you . . . ask you . . . it's none of my business, of course, except that we're like your family, Saul and I, and . . Elizabeth, you've been home *two days* this week."

"I've only been gone three nights."

"But I want to talk to you about that, too."

"Heather, if you're going to talk about Holly—"

"Which I am—"

"—don't. She understands that my crazy schedule won't last. I'll have a few weeks of talk shows and press interviews and then I'll be replaced by a chef who murdered his wife because she told him his veal needed salt, or a Japanese couturier whose fall sportsclothes are made entirely of rusted automobile fenders."

"I don't think you should joke about leaving Holly alone."

"I'm not joking about leaving Holly alone. Heather, how much do you know about young women who are almost eighteen?"

"I was one."

"So was I. But I'm not expert at being a mother of one, and neither are you. Holly's going through some stage these days, in between a child and a woman, and she's so restless she nearly drives both of us crazy. She doesn't confide in me the way she used to; she's uncomfortable with me—"

"But you know she's not."

"I know she is. We're two women; we share a house; each of us has a talent. But I'm an adult, living by my talent, seeing adult men . . . and Holly has to live as if she's still a little girl, in her mommy's house, with no audience for her talent. She probably hates me sometimes for what I have."

"She doesn't hate you."

"I know that. But she's ready to be grown up and these last few months before she can go to college and really be on her own are hard for her. Anyway, she's been avoiding me, staying late at school for rehearsals or practicing in the music room, and driving out to see Luz, and eating with you and Saul—do you know, she sees more of you than she does me?"

"Because we're here. I'm not trying to take your place, Elizabeth; Holly doesn't love us more than you—"

"I know that. Good heavens, Heather, I'm not accusing you; I'm glad you're here. You're close enough to Holly's age to be her friend and she needs somebody older who isn't a mother. Who knows that better than you?"

"Oh. You mean the way I feel about Lydia. Isn't that odd? I never thought of it. I love her because she's wonderful, but it's even more wonderful that she's not my mother."

"That's what I meant. And it's good for Holly to be with Saul, too. So just enjoy her; I wish she was as nice to me as she is to you."

489

"But you talk, don't you? You don't ignore each other."

"Of course not; we talk about a lot of things, just not very personal ones. I told her about quitting Tony's show and why I'm traveling so much——"

"What did you tell her?"

"Just that Bo canceled my interview with Jock and that Tony and I disagreed about it and about how the show should be run. I'm sure she wonders about the two of us, but she must not want to know for sure, because she's never asked. I told you: we don't talk about personal things. But she knows that everything will settle down pretty soon and I'll be home most days and nights. Though that seems to be the last thing she wants."

"Isabel says young women always need their mothers more than they admit."

"Probably true. But I'm here a lot, Heather. More than Holly is, if you want to count hours."

"Maybe. But, still, if you could slow down a little bit——?"

"I can't; not yet." *I can't slow down; I have to be admired by people in my profession, be one of them, to make up for failing. I didn't handle myself like a professional on "Anthony"—I should have known I needed Bo as an ally—I treated it like a hobby, not a job. Matt wouldn't have failed; Matt succeeds at everything; he has control of his life. And I've got to have control of mine.* "I just have to keep moving," she said to Heather. "At least for now."

"How will you know when to stop?" Heather asked.

"I suppose when I feel all right about myself again." She hesitated. "Damn it, Heather, don't you see? I'm ashamed of myself. I'm ashamed of sleeping with Tony and thinking I might learn to love him; I'm ashamed that I *wanted* to love him."

"Oh, stop whipping yourself," Heather said calmly. "We've all lied to ourselves to make it all right to sleep with somebody; there wouldn't be any affairs at all if we couldn't close our eyes to the truth about a lot of men. But you don't have to wallow in it."

"Thank you," Elizabeth said gravely. "I didn't think I was wallowing. I just thought I was being suitably ashamed."

490

After that, she'd talked briefly to Isabel, who was working late every night with Maya, preparing the speech she hoped to give on moving their town, and then to her parents, but she didn't try to explain herself to any of them; she just kept moving.

On the plane to New York, holding a glass of sherry in her hand as her thoughts floated free, Elizabeth's foot touched the crumpled letter under her seat. Matt must know that she wasn't on "Anthony" anymore; she'd been on too many network shows for him not to have seen or heard about her. He must even know—or did he?—that she'd been working for Rourke all along. Just like her husband. But this note was the first she'd heard from him, and he'd written only about Jock Olson.

She leaned back and gazed out the window at the dark sky. Lightning flashed on the horizon and as she watched it she recalled an electrical storm one night when she and Matt were driving home from Taos. They had stopped the car at the side of the road while thunder rolled about them and they watched the spectacular display of jagged streaks leaping through the sky, illuminating every rock and clump of sagebrush on the desert. Matt's arm had been around her, Elizabeth's head on his shoulder; they had watched in silence, and when the last drumroll of thunder died away, and the sky and desert were again dark and still, they had kissed, a long kiss as intense and lingering as the lightning.

Where did we go wrong? When did everything change? Was there one single moment when we could have said, No, we won't take this step, make this turn, go this direction? Couldn't we have seen what was happening before everything got away from us?

The plane had left the lightning behind. Elizabeth bent down and retrieved the crumpled letter at her feet. She held it in her clenched hand, then, as it was, still wadded up, she put it in her briefcase and after a moment pulled out her appointment book to go over her schedule for the next day.

The "Today" Show. Interview with Sam Burnell of the *New York Times*. Interview with Rose Ulmer of *Newsweek*. Lunch at the Four Seasons with three network executives anxious, so

491

they said, to give Elizabeth her own show. A "Private Affairs" interview with the floor maid in Elizabeth's room at the Mayfair Regent. Cocktails with Paul Markham. Seven-thirty plane to Albuquerque, where she'd left her car.

It was the kind of schedule she preferred these days: the hours crammed so full there was no room for memories of Matt or Tony or the violence of that night in Boyle's living room, that still haunted her dreams. She forced herself to concentrate on everything she was doing at the moment she was doing it, shutting out everything else, and so, when she was alone in her hotel room late the next afternoon, writing a "Private Affairs" story on the hotel maid, the ring of the telephone was an intrusion, and she frowned as she picked it up.

"Elizabeth!" Isabel cried. "You can't imagine what you've done! Letters—money—offers of help! *Volunteers*—can you imagine?—wanting to come to Nuevo to help move the houses and the church! You should hear Saul! He's in ecstasy; he roars, *"They wanted a flood! They got a flood!"* And no one will be able to stop it, he says. You should be here to share it; when will you be home?"

"Tomorrow night. Money, too? And volunteers? There was some money after the Los Angeles *Times* ran my story on you, do you remember? But—volunteers! Isabel, it might work!"

"Might! It will! I believe everything Saul says!"

"When are you going to make your speech? I want to be there to hear it."

"In a week, I think. Give me time to buttonhole everybody and wave your column at them—and now I can tell them about the letters, too!—and I guarantee the legislature will take a new look at Nuevo. And for a change, condemn somebody else's land instead of ours. But you must be here for all of it! Can you stay in town for a while?"

"I'll try." In her mind she saw all of them at her dining room table—Saul and Heather, Isabel, Luz and Cesar, Maya, Holly, perhaps Lydia and Spencer, and herself—reading the letters forwarded from newspapers all around the country, putting the money aside for depositing in a special account for the new town. Her favorite people: her family. "I'll definitely see you day after tomorrow, Isabel. And if you don't mind, I want to be lurking in the corridors of the statehouse when you button-hole the legislators. It just occurred to me that seeing one of my columns in action may be as exciting as being in front of a camera."

The newspaper was open on Keegan Rourke's desk, with Elizabeth's picture and "Private Affairs" in the upper left corner. *"Four—hundred—papers,"* he said, each word a hammer blow. "And every one of them getting mail?"

Chet Colfax spread his hands. "Most of them, it looks like. Mail and phone calls. I'll know more when my friend at Markham Features calls again."

Rourke nodded. He stood tautly beside his desk, keeping his rage clamped down with an effort that made him grind his teeth. He did it from habit—he never showed his feelings unless there was a benefit to be gained from it—but he also held his control because rage would have seemed a peculiar reaction to a story about a resort in some valley in New Mexico, and he couldn't afford to have people wonder about him and Nuevo these days.

Chet, of course, knew he was angry, and why, but even Chet, who'd been watching and imitating Rourke for years, didn't know the depth and destructiveness of his anger. "Money, too," he said. "I don't know how much; I'll try to get that. The craziest part is the people volunteering to help move the town. That I can't figure—"

"Because you're a fool," Rourke lashed out, but immediately drew back into cold rigidity. "You don't understand, even after all this time, the emotional pull of that woman's writing. She can be very dangerous."

His intercom buzzed and he answered it. "Mr. Boyle insists you want to see him," his secretary said. "He says he flew in from Los Angeles on your orders—"

"He'll wait; I'm in conference." Rourke turned back to Chet. "Where's Ballenger?"

"Montana, looking at property. I called him earlier; he'll be here tomorrow."

"Call him again. Tell him to meet you in Santa Fe."

"All right. Of course."

Rourke drummed two fingers on his desk. "The two of you will make sure the legislature holds the line until the end of March, when they adjourn. That's all we need: three more weeks. By the next session the dam will be finished, the flooding will have started, the town will be gone. Those people will be gone." He forced his fingers to be still. "You've dealt with the key ones down there . . . Thaddeus Bent and Fowles—Jim or John—who else?"

Chet read five names from a pocket-size spiral notebook. "Those are the main ones."

"Not too many; you and Ballenger can take care of them in a few days. How much will you need?"

"Twenty-five thousand, fifty at the most, depending on whether they want cash or campaign contributions from the PAC we've set up there. Since the next election is a year and a half away, they'll probably want cash, in which case five to ten thousand apiece will be plenty. They tend to be less greedy than in other states."

Rourke shrugged; he was interested in taking advantage of greed, not measuring it. "You'll make it clear: *no changes*. We spent five years making sure the committee would vote an entire package and the legislature would approve it and no ragtag mob of agitators is going to interfere with that."

"Right. Absolutely."

"You'll call in every day. Do it from your own room; I don't want Ballenger to hear your reports."

Chet nodded; his face was flushed.

"I don't need to tell you to stay in the background; I don't want you to run into that woman or the Hispanic one . . ."

"Isabel Aragon. She doesn't know me."

"Must I repeat myself? You will stay in the background; you will see no one but those six men. You and Ballenger divide them up or each of you will see all six, whichever is best. You know all this; I shouldn't have to go through it." He turned away. "That's all; I'll expect to hear from you tomorrow evening. Call my home number."

"Right." He went to the door. "Thank you."

Rourke nodded absently. He was looking down at his desk, reading the column on Jock Olson. The fiftieth time, Chet thought with a flash of contempt. One fucking woman, one whining construction worker. Small potatoes.

As the door closed behind him, Rourke picked up the telephone. "Get Ballenger on the phone," he said. "He's in Montana; his secretary will have his number." He waited, gazing at Elizabeth's picture, until his secretary buzzed him. "Terry," he said without preamble, "Chet will be calling you about spending a few days in Santa Fe. I want your reports, every day, and I don't want him to know you're making them. Call me from your room and keep it to yourself. Any problems with that?" He listened, smiling thinly. "Of course he's going to be calling me; that's what he's paid for. But I want you to tell me how he's doing. I'll talk to you tomorrow night. Have a successful trip."

Hanging up, he found himself skimming Elizabeth's column again. He almost knew it by heart, but still, when he came to the last line, he could feel the bile rise in his throat. While it was there, his anger at a pure and perfect pitch, he told his secretary to send in Boyle.

"Knocked myself out to get here," Boyle said cheerfully. He felt powerful and poised for the future. He'd kept the Olson interview off the air and cowed Tony into submission. And Rourke had called him to Houston for a private meeting. He smiled as he took a seat on the couch, ready to discuss his new position as miniseries producer. "Don't want you to think I'm late; your dragon of a secretary kept me cooling my heels out there for half an hour."

"My secretary does what she is told."

The cold words jolted Boyle's aura of good feeling, but he was too absorbed to let it do any damage. He was pulling typed pages from an envelope—a list of proposed films, two to ten hours long, based on novels, newspaper scandals, and foreign intrigue—and he was still smiling as he held it out to Rourke.

Rourke did not move; he stood beside his desk looking expressionlessly at Boyle. Half a minute of silence went by;

then it dawned on Boyle that he had sat down while Rourke was standing. Hastily, he stood. "Ideas for movies," he said, holding out the papers again. When Rourke's silence dragged on, Boyle dropped his arm. "Of course I'll leave them with you so you can go over them at your leisure."

"It occurs to me," Rourke said at last, "that you do not read newspapers."

"Never," Boyle said. It was an odd question, but Rourke was wealthy and powerful and therefore had a right to be odd. "I read Polly Perritt, of course, since I plant items with her, and once in a while I read Lizzie Lovell, but I don't have to anymore, since she's gone—"

"Not quite gone. She wrote a column on Jock Olson, which, obviously, you did not read."

Boyle's face underwent a series of transformations. *"Jock Olson?"*

Rourke indicated with a tilt of his head the newspaper on his desk and Boyle went to read the story, standing over it, leaning on his hands. "Jesus Christ," he muttered. "Jesus. What a shit. To go behind our backs and put it in the paper after I told her—"

"Told her what? You stupid, half-assed prick, what the hell did you think she'd do when you killed her interview?"

"Now just a minute; I have great respect for you, but let's not get confused here; you specifically told me to kill that interview and that's exactly what I did."

"And made her furious."

"Well, you wouldn't expect her to dance for joy."

"What I expected, you damned idiot, was that you'd mollify her, coddle her, make her feel smart and beautiful instead of kicked in the teeth. Do you know what you've done? Do you have any idea what your amateurish bungling has done? You had enough sense to call me about that interview—you knew I wouldn't like it—why the fuck couldn't you use a little of that sense when you killed it? Read that line again: *For unknown reasons it was canceled* . . . What the hell did you say to her? Did you take her to dinner and give her the reasons the Olson interview wasn't right for the show? Did you ask her suggestions on what to replace it with? Did you bribe my son to buy her a fur coat and take her back to Amalfi for a week so she'd forget that one of her gems was pulled off the air? Did it occur to you that her column appears in *four—hundred—newspapers*? Are you aware that television is not her only means of communication with the world—that she's a powerful writer with a huge and adoring following? You empty-headed son of a bitch, what the hell did you do to make that woman so angry she wrote that column and made it clear that it was canceled by 'Anthony' so everyone would pay even closer attention to it?"

Boyle shriveled. The sheaf of papers fell unnoticed from his hand. His cheeks were hollow, his eyes blank, his mouth slack as he watched his future disappear, swept away in the torrent of Rourke's rage.

"And what did you do to make her quit the show? What did you and Tony do to make her walk out? The best talk segment on television; you had it in the palm of your hand, Tony had his cock in it, and the two of you threw it away. WHAT THE FUCK DID YOU DO TO HER?"

"I don't know! We had a fight . . ."

"Who had a fight?"

"Tony and me. I. Not Lizzie; she stayed out of it. She got mad at Tony and told him off, but it didn't have anything to do with me. The truth is, I don't remember too much about any of—"

"You and Tony had a fight and Elizabeth told you off and walked out and you don't remember it."

"Told Tony off! Not me! And that's right, I don't remember! It was late—they woke me up—and I was drinking—I was very upset! And I don't remember! And what the fuck difference does it make anyway? She's off the show and we have enough tapes for the rest of the season—almost, anyway, we'll re-run two or three from last fall—and if we line up a couple of sponsors we'll be fine for next year. I'll put off the mini-series, since you'll need me to keep Tony going for another season—that's getting harder, but I have him under control now—I really do know how to handle him, you know, and get

497

him to do his best—no one knows him the way I do, no one could produce him better than—"

"Stop whining. You're through and you know it. I hired you for two simple jobs: to keep an eye on Tony and to keep his ratings up until I was ready for him to do something else. You bungled both of them. I gave you an even simpler job—to keep one interview from the light of day—and you fell apart. You're a useless piece of shit and you're through. Get out. And get out of your office by tonight; I'll have someone else in it tomorrow morning."

"You don't mean that! Mr. Rourke, you need me . . . no, wait, I meant to say, listen, I've lived up to my part; I've watched over Tony, I've reported everything he did, here and in Europe, I've cleared his interviews—and Lizzie's!—with you. I did everything you told me; I had as many politicians on the show as I could and Tony scored points with all of them—if he ever wants to go into politics he has more friends and people beholden to him—" At the expression on Rourke's face, Boyle stopped abruptly.

"If you're quite through," Rourke said flatly, "my secretary has a check for you. I don't want to see or hear from you again. If you ever repeat any part of this conversation, or decide to write a book about your experiences as Tony's producer, or about anything at all that has to do with Tony or me, I will destroy you. You can get a job tomorrow in any television station in the world—I don't give a fuck what you do—but the day you talk about Tony or me is your last day in television. Is that clear?"

Boyle's face worked but no words came out.

"I asked you a question."

"Yes. It's . . . clear."

"Then get out."

Boyle dragged himself to the door, turned back to pick up his lists of ideas for films, then disappeared.

Rourke picked up the intercom. "Call my son and tell him he's to be at my home tonight. If he asks for me, I'm not here. But first get Nat Pollock on the telephone."

He stood by the desk, drumming the same two fingers, until

his telephone rang. "Mr. Rourke," Pollock said. "This is a pleasure. Been a long time—"

"Nat, I need a producer for three months. Nothing fancy; most of the show is already taped. I heard you weren't doing anything right now; can you handle it?"

"Word gets around. What show?"

"'Anthony.'"

Pollock whistled. "Bo died?"

"You might say that. He's left the show and Tony needs someone to keep it going for the rest of the season."

"And Daddy's helping out."

"That's what we're for, Nat."

"How did you know I'm not working?"

"I had someone check around. I don't intend to talk about your private life—you've done a good job of hushing it up—and I'll find you a show next season if you'll do this now, no questions asked."

"Just three months? To the end of the season?"

"That's all. The show is being canceled."

Pollock whistled again. "The ratings were going up. Something to do with the disappearance of the gorgeous lady?"

"I said no questions asked."

"So you did. Can I ask when I start?"

"Tomorrow morning. Twenty thousand for the three months; Tony will do a few live interviews; they're already scheduled. The rest is on tape."

"Enough for three months?"

"Close. When they run out, use re-runs. Any other questions?"

"Which office do I use?"

"Boyle's. It will be empty."

"Okay. That takes care of it."

"Keep in touch; I'll expect regular reports."

"On what?"

"Anything that strikes you as interesting. And let me know what kind of show you want for next year."

"I'll do that. Talk to you soon. And thanks." Rourke did not answer; Pollock heard the telephone click as it was hung up.

Slowly he put his own telephone down. "Anthony" had lasted ten years, a long time for any television show. Something peculiar had happened over there and no one had the whole story; even Polly Perritt was frustrated—not satisfied with the official word that Lovell had been let go for insubordination— and poking around town like a beaver, looking for dirt. Maybe we'll never know, thought Pollock. But isn't that something? After all these years. With no warning. No more "Anthony".

The last light was fading from the sky when Holly walked home after dinner with Saul and Heather. At her front door, she lingered, reluctant to go inside. The evening was clear and perfectly still and in the darkening sky stars were beginning to appear, becoming brighter as she watched. The magic of their appearance, just out of reach beyond the treetops, made her feel crazily happy, but then she caught the scent of pines and it made her feel melancholy, and so restless she thought she would jump out of her skin.

I want everything. I want to do everything and see every-thing, sing every song, taste every food, love ecstatically and be passionately loved . . . I want everything and I want it now . . . why do I have to go a step at a time when I want to fly?

The air had turned chilly. She unlocked her front door, but before she could go in she heard behind her the sound of tires on the gravel drive. She turned, and saw Tony Rourke stopping his car a few feet away.

She caught her breath. He was so beautiful and he was like a dream—someone she knew but hadn't seen for so long, except on television—and she could only stare at him as he got out of the car and came up to her, smiling a little crooked smile that seemed so sad she almost couldn't bear it. He took her hand and kissed her cheek, and he said her name, and then, through the jumbled thoughts in her head she heard herself say, "I'm sorry . . . I mean I'm not sorry, but . . . mother isn't . . . here."

"But can't I wait?" he asked, still with that sad little smile.

"She's not *here*. She's in San Francisco."

The smile disappeared. "San Francisco?"

"Taping . . ." She swallowed; it was so hard to talk because she wanted to tell him how beautiful he was and she'd missed him and she thought about him so much and he made all the boys at school seem like children and why did he look so sad? But finally she said only, "They're taping her on the Sherry Todd show tomorrow morning; she'll be home in the afternoon."

"Sherry Todd." He nodded. "Very big." His mouth drooped. "I was so sure . . . Sunday night, you know; I was so sure she'd be home . . . and I wanted so much to apologize . . ."

"Apologize? Apologize for what?"

Tony's brows drew together. "She didn't tell you?"

"You mean about your show? She said she was mad at Bo and you didn't agree with her about what he'd done and how the show should be handled, and so she decided not to be on it anymore. But it sounded like she was mad at *Bo*. Did you *fight* with her?"

"No . . . oh, no, we'd never fight, we were good friends, you know, and we worked together, we were partners, but I said some things that your mother really didn't understand and she did seem angry at me and I've felt so *alone*, Holly, because I thought she didn't like me anymore and I had to come and tell her how sorry I—" He looked down as if only then realizing he still held Holly's hand. "I never thought she wouldn't be home, you know."

Blushing, Holly pulled her hand away, then wished she could put it back; it had felt so warm and lovely in his. "She'll be here tomorrow. You could stay in town and wait for her."

He shook his head. "My father has ordered me to Houston." He gave her a small boy's smile. "When he does that, I always wonder what I've done wrong."

Holly felt a rush of protectiveness. "You could go to Houston tomorrow."

Again he shook his head. "I've already disobeyed my orders; I was supposed to be in Houston by now. Holly, could I ask you for something to drink? Are you allowed to offer Scotch to a friend, or would I be corrupting a minor?"

501

"Don't be ridiculous," Holly said angrily. "Come in. You're probably hungry, too; wouldn't you like something to eat? There's lots of leftovers—"

The telephone rang and Holly ran through the living room into the den to answer it. "Just making sure you're there," Saul said. "When a beautiful young woman refuses my offer to accompany her home—"

"You follow up with a chivalrous phone call. You're sweet, Saul, but you always say exactly the same thing."

"I always feel exactly the same way about letting a woman walk home alone. You forget, I'm from New York."

"I don't forget; you keep reminding me. Anyway, this isn't New York, I only walked four blocks, and I'm fine."

"You're sure?"

"Of course."

"You sound breathless."

"I was outside . . . looking at the stars, and I ran in to answer the phone. Saul, stop worrying. You're worse than Mother."

"Could be. Okay sweetheart, we'll see you soon. We loved having you, as usual. Come any time."

"I had a good time, too. Thank Heather for me. And thank you." She hung up and looked through the doorway and met Tony's eyes. He had followed her as far as the living room and had been listening as she avoided mentioning him to Saul.

We have a secret, she thought.

"Leftovers," she said, leading the way to the kitchen. "You probably don't remember, but I offered you leftovers a long time ago. You and Mother were going out and I wanted you to stay and I tried to tempt you with *paella*. I suppose you don't remember. *Do* you want some dinner?"

"I would love dinner." He was smiling at her, but it wasn't a sad smile anymore; it was bright, as if he were thinking about something new. "And of course I remember that night; I wanted to stay here but your mother wanted to go out. What I don't remember is where we went."

"Rancho Encantado." Holly went to the refrigerator, trying to be calm, but she was so excited she was almost shaking.

502

For years she'd dreamed about being alone with Tony and she'd made up all the things they would say to each other, but nothing she had ever imagined had been anything like this: warm and exciting and so *happy*.

Drinking his Scotch, Tony sat at the round table where, long, long ago, he had watched Elizabeth fix a lunch for him and Matt. This time he watched Holly fill a platter with cold sliced meat and jalapeño cheese, slices of avocado fanned out with circles of red pepper, and, in the center, a pile of fresh tortilla chips. "How wonderful you are," he said when she put it before him. "But part of this is for you."

"I ate with friends, just before you got here."

"The phone call just now?"

She nodded. "We ate early so I could come back and practice my music."

"For . . . ?"

"The senior musical. I have the lead."

"You always have the lead, as I recall."

She flushed and nodded. "So far."

He was eating ravenously, as if he'd been starving for weeks, but he kept looking up at her with that curious brightness in his eyes. "Holly, would you sing something for me?"

"Of course. Shall I play the piano or sing without it?"

"Without."

So, sitting where she was, with no accompaniment and no self-consciousness, Holly sang, in French, one of the Songs of the Auvergne. Lush and sensuous, the long notes rose and fell, the melody lingering, then fading slowly to silence. Tony never took his eyes from hers and she held his look through the whole song, completely poised for the first time since he had appeared. He was stunned by her loveliness. He'd always thought of her as a child, but as he watched her, sitting straight, her head high, so confident in her singing that she looked directly at him instead of fearfully left and right and at the floor, she was a woman. She was a young Elizabeth, with no experience in her face. Her ash-blond hair fell like silk about her shoulders, her mouth was wide, exquisite, and vulnerable, her gray eyes were . . . her gray eyes, fixed on his, were adoring.

He forgot the emptiness and helpless anger of the past month, when he could not drink enough to wipe out Elizabeth's words and the contempt on her face. He forgot his fears about "Anthony"'s future, the humiliation of dealing with Bo now that he knew Bo represented his father, and his father's peremptory order to come to Houston. In the bright kitchen, everything disappeared but the lovely girl across the table. The blush in her translucent skin was caused, he knew, by Tony Rourke, nothing else.

But she's Elizabeth daughter. She's only seventeen or eighteen, still in high school—and Elizabeth's daughter.

Of course.

"Dearest Holly," Tony said, and a tremor came into his voice. "I've never been so moved by a song. You almost made me weep."

"Oh." Her face was radiant. "Thank you. I can't tell you what that means to me."

"I can't tell you what your singing means to me. And I thank *you*." He leaned forward. "May I ask just one more favor?"

"Of course. Anything."

"If I could have one more drink before I leave—"

"But you're not leaving for a long time!"

"I have my marching orders, remember."

"But . . . wouldn't you like coffee? You can help yourself to Scotch, but you must want some coffee, too!" Jumping up, she filled the coffeemaker. "Would you like cookies? Or ice cream?"

"No, my dear. You're taking very good care of me. But I would like to sit in the living room. Would that be all right?"

"Oh, yes, of course, it's much more comfortable. Do you want some coffee?"

"If you'll share it with me."

"Of course."

He carried the Scotch; she carried the coffee carafe and two mugs, and they sat at either end of the couch. Holly switched on the lights on the *placita*, just beyond the sliding glass doors, and the trees and tubs of green plants sprang into view. "It's too bad it's so bright in here," Tony said. "It dims that lovely picture through the glass."

Without a word, Holly rose and turned off the living room lights. They sat in the soft glow that reached them from the outside lanterns and Tony sighed, loosening his tie and stretching out his legs. "This is the first time I've relaxed in over a month. Thank you for that, dear Holly. You've made me feel wonderful."

"I'm glad." Her face was hot, her voice almost inaudible. Her hands were clenched in her lap to hide their trembling.

"Tell me about yourself," he said. "I heard you're going to the Juilliard School. What will you study? What do you want to do?"

"Everything."

"Good. Tell me."

She poured coffee into their mugs and talked, hesitantly at first, then more easily, about college and travel, her favorite books and music, the concerts and operas she dreamed of. She made no mention of high school graduation in two months.

"Go on," Tony said when she stopped. He refilled his glass, then put his arm along the back of the couch, leaning toward her. "I have to know all about you. You are the most extraordinary woman—unbelievably lovely—and your voice—! I want to know you, dearest Holly; everything about you."

Holly was dizzy. His voice was dark velvet, wrapping her in soft muffling folds. She sank into it. "I don't know what else—"

"What kind of jewelry do you like? And clothes? And perfume? What do you dream of? Whom do you love?"

There was no more talk of his leaving for Houston. It was a dream, Holly thought: Tony Rourke, alone with her, neither bored nor impatient, but interested, admiring, intent on everything she said, wanting to stay. He took off his jacket and rolled up his sleeves, and, with his elbow on the back of the couch, leaned his head on his hand, watching Holly's face grow animated as she talked.

"I feel like everything's just waiting for me; the future—all

505

of it—foggy, you know, not really clear, but I *know* that it's all going to be amazing and incredibly wonderful . . ."

"To believe in that," he said. "A fairy tale . . ."

"But I know it's there, waiting for me—it's mine and it's real, waiting for me to find it. I just can't get there yet. It takes so long and I get impatient because it hurts to want something so much and not know exactly how to get it . . ."

"You want someone to teach you about the world," Tony said very softly.

"Yes, all of it: everything there is to learn and see and *feel* . . ." She was giving away secrets she'd told only Luz—and some she hadn't told anyone. But she was floating in the embrace of Tony's eyes and his dark velvet voice and it was almost like talking to herself: he was so quiet and so absorbed in her he made her feel safe. He made it seem they were the only two people who were real; the rest of the world was distant and shadowy, but he could lead her through it; he would take care of her.

The lantern light cast shadows on his face, hollowing his cheeks, deepening his eyes, making his thin lips seem fuller. His eyes never left hers, his smile was only for her. I wish he'd kiss me, Holly thought; why does he sit so far away?

Unexpectedly, the thought frightened her, and she gave her head a little shake. "I'm talking too much about myself. You're hardly talking at all."

"Later," he said. "I've never talked to you; you wouldn't deny me the chance now, would you? What if I asked you"—his voice became casual—"to appear on my show? A young woman at the beginning of her career . . ."

"Oh . . ." The word drew out into a long sigh. "Could I? I'm not a famous person; no one knows me . . ."

"I know you."

"But your producer—Bo—doesn't he decide—?"

"I make the decisions. No one else. The show is 'Anthony,' remember? Leave it to me, my lovely Holly; I'll make you famous. People will forget about me—all they'll remember is that I'm the man who discovered Holly Lovell. My bewitching

Holly; lovely and so very sweet, so full of life and excitement . . ."

"Oh, don't," Holly whispered. For some reason she felt like crying even though she was breathing rapidly and her heart was pounding. "Don't tell me things you don't mean . . ."

"I would never lie to you. You're a dream I've longed for all my life. I came to this house and found a vision, more exquisite, more warm and welcoming than I ever could have imagined; a desert flower, hidden away, waiting to be found. Thank God I found you. Dearest Holly, you would make the days bright and the nights even brighter for any man lucky enough—"

"Not any man," she whispered.

Tony moved along the couch until he sat beside her. "No, you're too precious to love any man . . . you have the whole world to choose from . . ." He touched his fingertips to her eyebrows, and lightly stroked them, again and again, following their curve to the soft skin beside her eyes and along the sides of her face to her chin, then moving back to her eyebrows, his light touch stroking the delicate outline of her face, past her mouth quivering at the corners, and down to her small chin.

Holly closed her eyes. She was melting; her body flowed toward Tony's. She began to lift her arms, to embrace him, but she was not sure, she didn't know what he wanted, so she lowered them, her hands in her lap, waiting. She felt heavy, barely able to move, sinking, as if a door had opened below her and she was falling through it into a darkness that had nothing in it but the touch of his fingers sending pulsing ripples through her body, to the soles of her feet and the palms of her hands and her mouth, open, waiting for him. "Tony," she whispered, loving the sound of it. "Tony . . . Tony . . ."

Slipping his arm around her shoulders, he eased her back until she lay full length on the couch. He leaned over her, brushing her lips with his, forcing himself to go slowly. Very lightly, he brushed them again, barely a kiss, feeling them quiver beneath his. With feathery fingers, almost imperceptibly, he began unbuttoning the long row of tiny buttons that ran from her throat to the hem of her white dress, cursing the number of them, but patiently taking them one at a time. "Tony," Holly whispered, and made a slight move to sit up.

"Dearest Holly," he murmured. His hands held her down. "My sweet enchantress; you've woven a spell around both of us . . . I won't hurt you, my lovely, lovely one; I promise I would never hurt you . . . I only want to love you . . ."

The top of the dress was unbuttoned and he slipped it back over her shoulders, sliding his hands slowly around her back, her skin warm and silken beneath his palms. She shuddered as he unhooked her brassiere, freeing her breasts, small and firm with a slight curve hinting at fullness. *Just like Elizabeth's* . . .

For Holly the room had turned dark; there was a roaring in her ears like the sea when it thundered just before a storm. She was trembling; sighing in little bursts; not thinking, just feeling. The cool air on her breasts was a caress and she waited for Tony's hands to hold them. In her mind she could feel his hands and his lips; she had never let any boy touch her breasts, but she had imagined an unknown, perfect man doing it—she had imagined Tony Rourke doing it—and now she waited, her nipples taut and puckered as if his hands and mouth were on them . . .

But he did not touch her. Holly thought she would burst from the trembling of every nerve. *Touch me, please touch me, Tony. Please kiss me; I can't stand it if you don't* . . .

She opened her eyes and saw him watching her, holding his hands above her breasts, curved to match their curve. It gave her a little shock to see him, his eyes dark on hers, his hands held above her, refusing the caress she ached for, but she was barely aware of the shock before he gave her a small smile and bent again to her buttons, those tiny buttons that marched down the pure white of her dress. He slipped them from the small loops that held them, his hand moving slowly from one to the next until the dress lay opened on either side of Holly like the petals of a flower spread apart to expose its hidden center.

"My God," he murmured. "So fragile and perfect, like porcelain . . ." He slipped his hands beneath the waistband of her pantyhose, lifting her and pulling them down, his hands burning on Holly's skin as, very slowly, he drew the sheer nylon down her thighs, her legs, and over her slender feet.

Silently he studied her, from her silken hair to her long legs. He was as taut as a wire, wanting to bite and tear into her, to pound her, but he devoured her first with his eyes, watching, with the faint smile that never left his face, the ripples of her muscles, the arched back that lifted her breasts to him, the plea in her eyes. She wanted him; she was begging him to take her.

He stood and tore off his clothes. When he turned back, Holly's eyes were closed—*Just like Elizabeth, the first time*—and he lay beside her, whispering her name as his tongue played in her ear, then kissing her nipples, taking them into his mouth, rolling his tongue over them, sucking until she was making small breathless gasps. He raised himself on his elbow and parted her legs, stroking the inside of her thighs, exploring her wetness with his finger. And then at last Tony Rourke lay on Holly Lovell's slender body. *Elizabeth*, he thought, and ruthlessly thrust himself into her.

Holly cried out at the pain, like a knife twisting inside her. Desire fled; languor and sensuality vanished. Her eyes filled with tears, pain radiating through her as Tony moved inside her. *What am I doing?*

But then, through the pain, his name rang in her mind like a song. *Tony.* Tony was making love to her. For years she had dreamed it, and her dream had come true. So it *had* to be all right, it had to be wonderful and ecstatic and passionate. Because Tony loved her. She just had to wait for it to be wonderful; she had to be careful not to disappoint him, and then everything would be perfect, as it always was in her dreams.

She spread her legs wider and lifted her hips, even though that drew him in more deeply and made the pain worse. It didn't matter; this was what she had dreamed of. Opening her eyes, she tried to smile into his dark look. "Tony," she whispered. "I love you."

CHAPTER 16

"They've asked me to stay over another day," Elizabeth told Holly on the telephone. "I'd rather not, but as long as I'm here, it probably makes sense. I'd be home late tonight or early tomorrow morning; what do you think? If you want me home, I'll be there this afternoon; I still have my ticket. Maybe that would be best; I haven't had a chance to spend much time with you this week, and anyway I'm awfully tired. I think I'll tell them I can't do it now; maybe another time."

"No, stay," Holly said. She shuddered as Tony's hand slid from her breast to her stomach and probed between her legs. She'd wanted him to leave last night so she could be alone and think, but the most he'd done was to slip outside and drive his car into the garage, closing the door behind it. Then he was beside her again, holding her, begging her to let him stay. "I didn't reserve a room because I thought I'd be going on to Houston . . . how could I know I would find you and my whole life would change? Dearest Holly, I can't bear the thought of leaving you; please don't send me away."

So they had gone to bed in her room, where Tony fell asleep in an instant and Holly didn't sleep at all. She hurt and her mind churned, and all night long she felt tears running down her face before she even realized she was crying. Once she slipped out of bed and went to her mother's room and crawled between the cool, smooth sheets of her mother's bed, but as she lay there, she realized that what she really wanted was to curl up in her mother's lap, and that confused her so much she carefully remade the bed and went back to her own room where Tony sprawled across her bed and she had to tuck herself in a corner, staring at the rectangles of her deep-set windows as they grew light with the morning.

When Tony woke, the sun was shining and he looked at Holly as if he didn't recognize her. But in a minute his eyes brightened, a huge smile broke over his face, and he said her name over and over, not just "Holly" but "Holly Lovell, Holly Lovell, Holly Lovell." And then he caressed her and lay on her as he had the night before. But no matter how hard she tried she couldn't get back that wonderful warm feeling of languor and longing that had made her strain toward him; she had to pretend, and she really didn't know how, and when he was inside her it hurt just as much as the first time and she didn't want him to see that, either, because she thought he'd be disgusted with her and leave.

But she'd wanted him to leave, she reminded herself. The churning in her stomach, and her confusion, made her want to cry again, even while Tony thrust deeper into her, harder and faster, until he groaned and finally lay still. He turned his head and grinned at her, without moving. But a little later, when the telephone rang, his hand was exploring her again.

"Stay another day," Holly said to her mother on the telephone by her bed. She swallowed hard. "There's no reason for you to hurry."

"Holly, what's wrong?" Elizabeth asked. "Did I wake you? I thought you'd be getting ready for school. Are you sick?"

"No, I . . . I don't know. Maybe just a cold. I think I'll stay home today."

"Just a cold? Holly, something's wrong and I'm coming home this morning."

"No! I don't want you to! There's no reason! You don't have to come running home because of me; I don't want you to! Tomorrow is fine; I'll be fine; don't *worry* about me!"

511

"Well, if you're really sure . . ."

Holly heard the hurt in her mother's voice. *Please come home. No, you mustn't . . . Oh, I wish I could ask you . . .* But Tony's hand was between her legs and his mouth was on her breast and for the first time she felt some of the stirrings of the night before—and then she began to cry. "I just have this stuffy nose," she said into the telephone. "But I'll be fine. And I'll see you tomorrow."

"I'll call again later," Elizabeth said, and as soon as she hung up, she called Heather. "Something's wrong with Holly and she won't tell me and she doesn't want me to come home."

"But she was here for dinner last night and she was wonderful," Heather said. "And later Saul called to make sure she got home all right and she was fine. Are you sure she's not just sleepy or maybe annoyed because she thinks you're checking up on her?"

"Something's wrong, Heather. But I don't want to come rushing home when she's told me to stay away; I don't want her to think I don't trust her. Would you call her? Or would you mind going over there, just to see how she is?"

"Of course I will. Shall I call you back?"

"Yes, at the Stanford Court. Have them page me in the restaurant; I invited someone to breakfast to interview her for a column."

"Give me half an hour; I'm not dressed."

When Heather called, forty minutes later, she told Elizabeth there was no answer at her house. "I peered in the windows and couldn't see any sign of life. I'm sure she went to school. Do you want me to go check? I know her schedule."

"No; she'd think I was spying; she's so sensitive about her privacy . . . Either she's in school or she's in bed. Sleeping, probably; she said she had a cold. I'll call again in an hour . . ."

"Listen, you've got a job to do. *I'll* call again and I'll keep trying. Don't worry, Elizabeth; everything is under control."

Thaddeus Bent, in his fifth term as a New Mexico state legislator, had visions of the governor's mansion dancing in his head. He considered himself shrewd, intelligent, discreet,

512

a perfect judge of men. He liked power, though not responsibility, so he got reflected power by mingling with powerful men. Terry Ballenger boasted of knowing Rupert Murdoch, William Randolph Hearst, Barry Goldwater, and Keegan Rourke. Since it might be true, Thaddeus Bent was flattered when Ballenger began to pay attention to him.

Thaddeus was the first person Chet Colfax called when he and Ballenger arrived in Santa Fe. "Actually we're in La Cienega," he said on the telephone. "Sunrise Springs Inn. Away from the hustle of the city."

This was a joke, as they both knew how quiet Santa Fe was in March. But over the years Chet and Ballenger had let it be known that they sought privacy, especially the kind of privacy found in one of the stone and wood cottages scattered about the thirty-five acres of Sunrise Springs, ten miles south of Santa Fe. "Dinner at seven," Chet said. "Been too long since we've seen you; we'll catch up on all the news."

"Do you want me to bring anyone else?" Thaddeus asked, reluctant, but thinking it was a proper question.

"Of course not; we want some private time with you."

"Ah." It was a sigh. Pride and thoughts of the governorship, with the right people behind him, sent a rush of good-fellowship through Thaddeus Bent. And it lasted all through dinner in the main dining room of the lodge, a friendly room where three men who understood each other had a friendly meal.

"No question, it caught us by surprise," Thaddeus said, rolling the fine bourbon on his tongue. "One lousy newspaper story; who would have guessed? Came through like a bulldozer; flattened half the members; shook up the rest. Everybody had a copy, seemed like, and then what's-her-name, the Aragon broad, came around waving the damn thing like a banner, saying public opinion would knock us off our butts and into the street if we didn't vote to move the town."

"What public opinion?" Chet asked. "Do-gooders in New York or Chicago have nothing to do with you."

Thaddeus dipped a cactus fritter into sauce. "You'd be surprised. People sending money, you know, *and volunteering to come here!* They come into our state, get a lot of publicity,

513

tell us how to run our affairs, give us a bad name! Who the hell do they think they are?"

"Only out of state?" Chet asked. "No one from New Mexico?"

"Well," Thaddeus conceded, "some. These kids, you know, call themselves idealists, think they'll help the little guy, whoever the hell the little guy is—anybody with guts can make it in this great country, is what I say, if you just put your mind to it and don't lie around asking for handouts—and what the hell, you can't stop progress, right? Problem is, though—"

"We know the problem," said Ballenger. "You're being pressured. Volunteers. Money coming in. Mail. We understand; we sympathize. However, Chet has assured me he has utmost confidence in your ability to hold everyone in line for three more weeks, until adjournment."

"Well . . ." Thaddeus looked modestly at his plate. "I like to think I merit Chet's confidence. And yours, too."

"Which is why Mr. Ballenger's Political Action Committee contributes to your campaigns," Chet said.

"Well, now." Thaddeus looked doubtful. "The election is a long way off. What I have to think of now is keeping in touch with my constituents and learning how other states solve problems. Countries, too. The Europeans deal with a lot of the issues we face . . . we could learn from them."

"Absolutely. You should be able to travel wherever you think you can broaden your knowledge. And that requires money, and dedicated legislators often have trouble making ends meet. Mr. Ballenger believes, of course, that helping legislators do their best is part of our civic responsibility. And since it's cumbersome having to funnel money through a PAC all the time, he feels it would be appropriate for him to contribute five thousand dollars to your education fund, for studying new methods of governing in the years between elections."

"*Five thousand* dollars?"

"Ten," Ballenger said. "I'm afraid Chet confused you with our United Way donation, Thaddeus."

"Well, I'd think so. These are delicate matters; they require diplomacy, brains, a sense of duty, a love of the people of our great state . . . nothing comes easy, gentlemen."

"I also have a little place on Maui that doesn't get enough use," Ballenger added. "I'd be glad to have you take it over for a month or two; better if it's lived in." He pulled from his pocket a glossy folder of lavish grounds with private homes almost hidden by flowers and lush foliage. It lay on the table like a tantalizing centerpiece while the men sped up their eating and ordered coffee.

"How many are undecided?" Chet asked.

"It's close. I can't call it yet. The ones whose relatives got sweet deals on restaurant and gift shop leases are solid; they don't want competition. The ones who want more state parks are afraid controversy might delay the whole thing, so they'll probably stand firm. My committee believed the reports—they never checked to see if they were genuine or not—and of course a few of them found it worth their while to help push the vote along, so it's a safe bet they're okay. But everybody else—" He turned his hand over, palm up, palm down, a few times. "It's iffy. They've got so many bills to vote on before adjournment, they'll go however the wind blows, and that broad is making like a tornado with copies of that stinking column and letters from all over the country, and checks—! Jesus, you should see them. Five dollars, fifty, five hundred . . ."

"All right," said Chet, sounding like Rourke when he'd learned enough, and they chatted of other things through the rest of dinner and then sent Thaddeus home.

In the following afternoons and evenings, he and Ballenger met with Horacio Montoya and Jay Fowles and the others on their list, and Ballenger made contributions to their education funds for a trip to Spain, one to Tahiti to inspect the workings of local government, and one to send a failing offspring of a legislator to a college where he would be sure to graduate. There were also promises that other legislators would receive special attention on the purchase of choice condominiums in the Nuevo Resort.

At the end of five days Ballenger returned to Montana, satisfied he'd done his part. Chet stayed on, and three days later, in the midst of his daily massage, received a phone call from Thaddeus Bent. "We're making progress—God, I've talked till I'm blue in the face!—but now there's an emergency bill on the floor and I wouldn't put money on—"

"Who introduced it?"

"It's called the Aragon Bill; does that answer your question? Can you believe the nerve of that woman? Asking for a hundred acres—as a gift! To nobodies—and funds to move some buildings. A bunch of shacks, can you believe it?"

"I believe the world is full of crazy people. You can't predict the vote?"

"Like I said, I wouldn't put any money on it, either way."

Chet handed the telephone to the masseuse and put his head back down on the table, his arms dangling over the sides. Iron hands kneaded and pummeled his back and neck, worked down to his waist and farther down, along his spine. He barely noticed; he had a problem. Mr. Rourke was not going to be happy.

But it had helped after all, he thought when he was back in his stone cottage; he knew he always had his best ideas on the massage table. Showered, freshly dressed, his skin pink, his hair neatly combed, he embraced a tall vodka and ice and punched numbers on his telephone. And when the receptionist at the *Houston Record* answered, he asked for Cal Artner.

On March 15, the banner headline of the Albuquerque *Daily News* blared,

ATTACKS STATE PARK PROJECT
FOR PERSONAL GAIN
Columnist a Secret Landowner in Disputed State Park
by Cal Artner

Elizabeth Lovell, syndicated author of "Private Affairs," is using her column to attack a new state park and force a bill through the legislature that would rob the people of New Mexico while lining her own pockets, it was alleged today.

In an exclusive investigation, the *Daily News* has learned

that Lovell, whose "Private Affairs" column appears in 400 newspapers, secretly bought land, and is on close terms with other former landowners, in Nuevo, a mountain town on the Pecos River, where the state of New Mexico is building a dam and flood control reservoir and a state park.

Construction of the dam began last summer after the townspeople sold their land and were offered further compensation for resettlement elsewhere. Recently, egged on by outside agitators, they began demanding they be given back some of the most valuable land they sold.

To force the legislature to give them the land, they are attempting to ram the Aragon Bill through the legislature. The stated purpose of the bill is to allow the townspeople to stay in the valley but the real purpose, it is alleged, is to reap huge profits from the tenfold increase in land values that came once the state park was announced, and also from the increased tourism.

Lovell was recently removed from the popular talk show "Anthony" for "insubordination," according to network sources. Last year she used her column to launch the political career of Isabel Aragon, newly-elected state legislator and sponsor of the Aragon Bill; currently she is using it to disseminate the views of the Nuevo residents, to promote the Aragon Bill, and to attack the dam and the flood control reservoir.

In Los Angeles, the *Daily News* spoke to a technician on "Anthony," who reports that Jock Olson, a construction worker on the Nuevo dam, was rehearsed by Lovell, the day before she interviewed him, to attack developers for taking advantage of the people and to claim that lakeshore land is abundant, and should be given to residents for a new town.

The *Daily News* has learned, however, that Olson, like Lovell, is a landowner in Nuevo, having been given land and made an "honorary citizen" by the townspeople last summer. This would entitle him, like Lovell, to some of the more valuable land being demanded by the people.

The investigation into those who would reap huge benefits from the Aragon Bill is continuing.

Elizabeth called Matt. *How could he? How could he?* But his secretary said he was out of town. "He'll be calling in, Mrs. Lovell, but I don't know just when."

"Tell him to call me," Elizabeth said shortly and hung up, trying to control her furious shaking. *After everything we had— even if it's not the same anymore—how could he?*

And to use Cal, of all people. How did he find him? How could he—?

I don't ever want to talk to him again.

Then why are you calling him?

Because I want to hear what he has to say; and to tell him it's over. I'm getting a divorce.

But there was more to come. Artner's story had been aimed at the New Mexico legislature, but Polly Perritt knew a good scandal when she heard one, and the day after she heard about the story from her contact in Santa Fe, she had an item in her column.

And Saul was the one who showed it to Elizabeth, so she would be with a friend when she read it.

Nasty news for Elizabeth the Lovelly, whose splendid star seems to be sinking. The Private Affairs lady is accused of using her column to skyrocket her savings account. One wonders: If our clever columnist has been using tricks, was it beddie-bye bouncings with her handsome host that got her on "Anthony" . . . and the same with powerful Paul that climaxed a contract for 400 papers? After all, hubby got her started—and don't we know how helpful handsome he-men soon become a habit?

"Don't say anything," Saul cautioned. "Let me talk while you get your murderous emotions under control." He paced about her sunny living room, now and then glancing at Elizabeth's stony face and the rigid set of her shoulders. Sitting crosslegged on the couch, barefoot, in white jeans and a blue cotton sweater, she looked young and vulnerable, but he saw faint lines in her face that had not been there a year ago, and

518

as he paced and talked he was silently cursing Matt and everything he had brought down on his house.

"Ignore Polly the parrot; she has a short attention span and tomorrow she'll be screwing somebody else. Don't even talk about Matt for a minute. Let's talk about Artner. First, we take his story seriously; it's damaging and we have to counter it. Second, most of it seems at least partially true, except the rehearsing of Olson. I assume you did some preliminary get-acquainted stuff, right? And Artner probably bribed someone who was there. What I most want to know is, who the hell does Artner work for? That story didn't come from his minuscule brain; someone fed him the idea and the facts and then made it worth his while to write it. Are you calm enough to talk? I assume he's the helicopter boy-wonder you and Matt booted for sneaking Indian dancers onto the front page of the *Chieftain*."

Elizabeth nodded.

"What else do you know about him?"

She took long breaths, steadying herself against the onslaught of anger and frustration churning inside her. She'd thought she'd reached a height of anger the night she walked out on Boyle and Tony, but this time her emotions seemed to go in so many directions: at Polly Perritt, at Cal Artner and whoever it was who gave him small bits of information that added up to one big lie, but mostly, and most devastatingly, at Matt, who must have approved Artner's story, because no editor would commit professional suicide by printing an attack on his publisher's wife, unless given permission to do so.

What's happened to him that he could do this?

"I don't know much about Cal," she told Saul. "A long time ago I heard something about him and Chet Colfax at that Graham newspaper chain Matt bought. I remember telling Matt it seemed odd, and he said I was imagining conspiracies, or some such thing. That's all . . . oh, no, at dinner one night Tony mentioned seeing Cal at the *Houston Record*. Other than that, I haven't heard a word about him."

"Quietly nursing his grudge and biding his time. Colfax works for Rourke."

"Of course; that was why I told Matt about it."

"And Rourke owns the *Houston Record*."

"I know, Saul, but that's a coincidence. There's no reason for Keegan to be involved in this; he doesn't care about me; he never did. He only wanted Matt."

"And a resort at Nuevo?"

Elizabeth stared at him. "Did someone tell you that? Terry Ballenger is behind Nuevo."

"So he is; the question is, who's behind Terry Ballenger?" Saul shrugged. "You're a journalist; you know how suspicious we get when we see lots of signposts; we figure they're probably pointing to something around the corner—maybe all the way to Houston. I'm thinking of talking to Matt about it."

There was a pause. "Are you asking me what I think of that?" Elizabeth asked.

"I guess I am."

"I'd rather you didn't. At least, until I've talked to him myself. Keegan may own those papers, Saul, but Matt runs them—"

"And nobody would smear the boss's wife unless the boss said okay. That's what you're thinking, right? But didn't Artner sneak a photograph past you once?"

"Oh." She thought about it, then shook her head. "If you knew he'd done it once, would you give orders to someone to keep a very close eye on him?"

"I would," Saul conceded.

"So would I. So would Matt. That's why I want to talk to him."

"To tell him what?"

"That I want a divorce." The word shook her like a gust of wind. "We've been living apart almost a year, and whatever I thought might happen to get us together again . . . isn't going to happen. I don't even care; I don't want it anymore; I don't want him anymore—"

"Hold on a minute." Saul sprawled in an armchair opposite her, trying to find the right words. She was lying to herself; all the wise women around him—Heather, Isabel, Maya—said she still cared for Matt. But he had no right quoting them to Elizabeth.

520

"—why should I be married to a man who doesn't give a damn about me? There's nothing left of what we had."

She paused, remembering a note she had read on an airplane. *Olson is a hero . . . you're the best there is.* But then she dismissed it. The note was brief and impulsive: a momentary lapse. Artner's story was different; it had taken time and careful planning.

"If he can send a reporter to do a hatchet job on me, it means he doesn't care about people anymore; only about his newspapers and the power they give him to build and destroy, to make careers and break them, to—how did he put it?—change the shape of the land. None of that impresses me and he doesn't either, not anymore, and I don't want to have anything to do with him."

"Hold on," Saul said again. "I agree it looks rotten, but we don't really know what happened. In fact, a lot of peculiar things seem to be happening around that Olson interview. Have you heard anything about your friend Tony Rourke losing his show?"

Elizabeth's brows drew together. "Losing his show? He wouldn't lose it even if every sponsor pulled out. His father subsidizes it."

"He what?"

"Underwrites the sponsors; they don't pay full rates. He likes to have control, Saul, you know that, and that's one way of controlling Tony."

"Maybe he's controlling him into oblivion. There's a rumor going around LA about the show being canceled; I got a whiff of it from an editor out there; maybe I'll ask around. And I'd like to ask around about Artner's story, too, if you don't mind, to see if I can find out who assigned it and gave him his information."

"If you want. I don't really care, because however the story got its start, it ended up being approved by Matt, and he's going to hear from me about that. You do what you want, Saul, and later you can ask him about Keegan or anything else. But let me at him first."

The telegram from Paul Markham was curt: EXECUTIVE COMMITTEE MEETING FRIDAY 10 A.M. PLEASE ATTEND.

It arrived while Isabel was sitting at the kitchen table, drinking hot chocolate and telling Elizabeth her bill was dead for the current session. "And that means forever. The next session isn't until January; by then the dam will be built and we'll all be gone, with whatever money they give us. Some of the people have left already; they've gone to Pecos and Belen and Chama . . . it's like petals scattering when the flowers die in the fall." Her mouth drooped, her shoulders sagged. Then, remembering Elizabeth, she straightened up. "Well, what the hell. We put up a nice fight, made a few politicians lose some sleep, and then our time ran out. We don't have a right to be there: the land belongs to the state; our twelve months is up. Jock told me yesterday that right after my bill was killed, his boss told him to knock down anything in his way—that means the town—because part of it's on land they need for the base of the dam and anyway it costs extra to work around us."

"Not while you're living there!" Elizabeth exclaimed.

"He'll try not to, and we trust him—he's one hell of a guy—but we don't expect miracles anymore. We're renting places in Pecos, most of us, and pretty soon we'll move. Some of the men want to stay and force the sheriff to carry them out, but the rest of us . . . I don't know why we're waiting, to tell you the truth; all I know is everybody's legs feel like stone when we talk about really moving."

"If it weren't for me, and Artner's story," Elizabeth said, "your bill would have passed."

"My God, that is not certain! You can't blame yourself; nobody did more than you to help us!" Isabel put her hand over Elizabeth's. "You were grand. You're our heroine, don't you know that? We wouldn't have had any chance at all if it weren't for your column on Jock. And I'll tell you, something funny was going on, even before that Artner story came out: people were changing their minds right and left. One minute Thaddeus Bent was wavering; the next he was against us. And Horacio Montoya, too, and a bunch of others. It wasn't just Artner, although we were close; we might have pulled it off, because they were still talking about Olson, too . . . well, what the hell. I keep telling myself: no more postmortems."

522

She finished her chocolate and stood up, her hand on Elizabeth's shoulder. "Luz isn't unhappy; she'll be in college next fall. The other young ones are already looking to buy mobile homes downvalley and work in the restaurants and shops the bastards will build in the resort. Nobody's unhappy but eighty or ninety stubborn people who wanted to keep their town and have a share of the wealth their land will bring. And we don't count; we're not strong enough or rich enough to make people sit up and take notice. We'll vanish; Nuevo will become a posh resort next to a pretty state park that will probably get squeezed smaller and smaller and eventually disappear, and the only record of the story will be in old clippings of the *Chieftain*."

There were tears in her eyes as she bent to kiss Elizabeth's cheek. "I love you. And I'll see you later; I'm due back to vote on about forty bills that are supposed to make New Mexico a better place to live. Was the telegram you got a while ago something I should know about, to share a joy or a worry?"

"No, it's just a meeting in New York at Markham Features. I'll have to go, but probably only for a day."

There was more to it, but she kept it to herself. As long as Isabel had her own worries, she wouldn't add to them with her own . . . which included a curt telegram from a man who, until today, always telephoned, and invited her to lunch or dinner while she was there. So Paul was feeling pressured and was ordering her to New York to discuss Artner's story . . . and whatever he and his board had decided.

"Why don't you come with me?" she asked Holly that afternoon as she packed her overnight bag. "I'll be busy part of the time, but you can browse on your own, and then we can do some museums together, or shopping, and have dinner, and maybe get to Lincoln Center or Carnegie Hall. Or a show; I'd love to see the new Sondheim. You wouldn't miss much school."

Holly shook her head. "I can't."

"That time you wanted to come to Los Angeles you said you could miss anything to get out of town."

"Well, now I can't."

"Why not?"

Curled up in a rocking chair in her mother's bedroom, Holly

523

examined her fingernails. "Mother, when you were in San Francisco, did you send Heather to spy on me?"

"No," Elizabeth said. "I asked her to telephone or come to the house to make sure you were all right. Do you call that spying?"

Holly flushed. "She snuck around and peered in the windows like I was a criminal or something!"

In the midst of folding a blouse, Elizabeth's hands grew still. "You saw her? And didn't talk to her?"

"I was in bed."

"But you could have called later, to say you were all right."

"I don't like being spied on!"

"Holly, you're not being very pleasant or easy to talk to."

"*I'm sorry.*"

"Can you tell me what's wrong? If something serious is bothering you, couldn't we talk about it? I might be able to—"

"No!"

"Hey," Elizabeth said lightly, "don't jump down my throat. That was an offer, not an attack. Sometimes it helps to talk about problems, even to a mother—"

"NO!" Holly burst into tears. "Can't you leave me alone? I'm trying to handle things and I can't do it if you keep yelling at me all the time!"

"Yelling?" Elizabeth raised her eyebrows. "Do I yell at you?"

Wiping her nose, Holly shook her head. "Not really. I just wish you'd leave me alone."

"Well, I can do that, if it's what you want. But I thought now that I'm home more, we'd talk and learn to be better friends."

"Were you good friends with Grandma?"

"Yes. Most of the time. And you and I were friends, too, until recently."

"It's probably just a stage," Holly said, tossing it off. She paused. "Mother—when you fell in love with Daddy, was it all wonderful? Or only parts of it? I mean, did you keep waiting for it to get better?"

"It was wonderful from the first day." Elizabeth looked closely

524

at Holly, watching her lovely face close up in confusion and stubbornness. "We had more fun with each other than we'd ever had with anyone else; we couldn't wait for the times we'd be together; there was a glow in the world when we . . ." She stopped, a sudden rush of tears flooding her throat, stinging her nose and eyes. "It was wonderful, Holly."

"You never talked to me about it."

"I should have. I'm sorry. For a long time it hurt . . . I guess it still does. But we can, any time you want . . . are you telling me you've fallen in love and that's why you're having problems?"

"I guess." Airily, Holly said, "All lovers have problems, you know; you and Daddy waited twenty years to have yours, but you really got a bundle when you did. I mean, you never talked before, and you don't now, very much, but the two of you certainly aren't a romantic novel, are you?"

Elizabeth's eyes were troubled and she tilted her head, studying her daughter. That wasn't the kind of phrase Holly used; she'd picked it up somewhere. "Who's the lucky man?" she asked. "Is he in the school musical with you?"

Holly gave a wild laugh. "Right. We make beautiful music together."

There was a long silence. Trying to say the right thing, Elizabeth asked casually, "Well, does he have a name or do I have to wait to read it in the program?"

"That's what I mean! You keep asking questions! You don't leave me alone! I tell you one thing about me, I try to confide in you, but you just keep pushing for more. I don't ask you how you feel about Daddy and Nicole, do I?" At the look on her mother's face, Holly felt sick and said in a rush, "I'm sorry; *I'm sorry.* I don't really *know* anything; it's just that I saw her picture on his desk and he gave me the usual story about a good friend, but he told me about ten times that she wouldn't be the hostess at my graduation party, and I shouldn't think about her, she's just a good friend . . . Mother, don't pay any attention to me; I don't mean half the things I say; just go to your meeting and if you meet a tall beautiful man in New

York and have a good time with him I won't ask any questions and I'd appreciate it if you don't ask me any, either."

And without waiting for an answer, she left the room.

I can't go to New York. I can't go anywhere until I know what I can do for Holly.

"Mother?" Holly was in the doorway. "I apologize; I didn't mean to get hysterical. Please don't worry about me; I'm fine; I just have a lot on my mind. I can't go to New York, but thank you for asking me. I'd like to, next time, if that's all right."

She was so calm, and so lovely, even with reddened eyes, that Elizabeth felt better. "If you're sure . . . I'm afraid this is one meeting I really shouldn't miss."

"I'm sure." She came to Elizabeth and put her head on her shoulder, like a little girl, though they were the same height. "I'm all right, really. Just a little confused. But everybody gets that way, you know. At least some of the time."

"Yes," said Elizabeth, "I know." She held her daughter close until Holly moved away. Then, snapping shut her overnight bag, she said, "I'll be gone tomorrow and tomorrow night; back early Saturday morning. We'll have the weekend together. All right?"

"Fine." Holly brushed her mother's cheek with her lips. "Shall I drive you to Albuquerque?"

"No, Saul offered. He wants to talk to the editor of the *Daily News,* about a story they published. But I might call you to meet me on Saturday. Oh, one thing; I've been trying to reach your father; I've left messages, but he hasn't called. Do you know where he is?"

After a moment, reluctantly, Holly said, "I think he's sailing off the Florida Keys."

"Oh. I see." And both of them knew it was not necessary to ask with whom.

Paul Markham had never fired anyone. It had been done to him once, and he never forgot the humiliation and helplessness he'd felt as he left, sneaking out after everyone had gone home to avoid facing anyone. He'd vowed then that he would one day own his company, be his own boss, and never fire anyone.

Elizabeth knew that; he had told her one night at dinner in the Russian Tea Room, confessing his weaknesses while a waiter deftly slit open their chicken Kiev, letting melted butter flow onto the plate. So she was not surprised that he was a silent observer at the meeting of the Executive Committee of Markham Features, looking grimly at his sharpened pencils while his senior vice-president did the talking.

"In a nutshell, we've weighed your enormous popularity against the possibility of lawsuits. You're the apple of our readers' eyes, but local editors are scared out of their gourd; the minute the AP spread the Artner story all over the country they were in a stew; they never thought there was anything fishy about your column; now all they think about is, have they been selling tainted stuff when they thought they were buying prime material they could count on? We've tried buttering them up, it won't work; their meat and potatoes is readers' trust; if they lost that, they lose everything. We're not canceling your column, Elizabeth, but we're putting a hold on it until you've cleared your name. There are vultures out there who'll milk a story for all it's worth and you can't duck it; you have to be aggressive. We'll help all we can—we do have confidence in you—and if you need an investigator, for instance, to prove you've been villified, we'll find one for you and share his fee. None of us relishes the idea of losing you, but you must understand our position. Please let us know your plans, and what we can do, so that everyone gets his—and her—just desserts."

Markham and the others chimed in, expressing their regrets, hoping Elizabeth would be able to clear everything up in a short time, but it was not a discussion: they'd made up their minds. And half an hour later, Elizabeth was out of the building, walking past Rockefeller Center.

Automatically, she began thinking ahead to the interviews she had scheduled for the rest of the day. And then it struck her: what would she do with them? All she had left was one column a week, for the *Chieftain* and the *Sun*. Her three-times-a-week column in four hundred papers had been canceled—no, put on hold, whatever that meant, exactly—by someone who could barely say a sentence without talking about food.

No television show, no syndicated column. And not much hope of new ones: the offers of television shows she was receiving would surely be withdrawn for the same reason Markham's food-loving vicepresident had put her on hold. She felt empty. When would she get angry? Maybe she'd used up all her anger. When would she be depressed? Whenever it really sank in. When would she be worried about the future? Not for a while: she'd put a good bit of money away and maybe she'd finally get the time to put together a book of "Private Affairs"— if anyone would publish it as long as she was suspected of using her column to line her pockets.

I think I'd better find Cal Artner and string him up by his ankles until he confesses he lied.

Find Cal Artner? Find his boss, first. She stopped at a pay telephone near Central Park and called Matt. "I'm expecting him to call in, Mrs. Lovell," his secretary said.

"Doesn't he have a telephone on that boat?" Elizabeth demanded, then quickly said, "Never mind. Just tell him to call me at home tomorrow." She hung up, staring at the graffiti-covered walls of the telephone booth. *You can't tell the world you know your husband is so busy sailing with another woman he doesn't get your messages.*

She walked into the park; it was a warm day and she sat on a flat rock outcropping in the sun, watching women pushing baby carriages, old men playing chess on park benches, and a young couple throwing a Frisbee for an ecstatic dog to catch and return to them. *I'm going home now,* she thought. *I don't want to be here; I want to be home.* There was no reason to stay: she'd have to leave the Mayfair Regent in any case, since the suite was kept by Markham Features, and she was sure anyone on hold with them wouldn't be welcome in their suite.

She was beginning to feel angry, at Matt on his boat, at Markham and its suite. *Good,* she thought. *As long as I can get angry, I'm alive.* She took a cab to her hotel to pack her small bag and was at LaGuardia within an hour.

Then she waited for a plane to Albuquerque. She bought a paperback and used her Markham Features membership card one last time to gain admittance to the travelers' club where she sank into an armchair with a glass of sherry and her book. A telephone was at her elbow, but there was no one she wanted to call. The only person she might have confided in was Matt—and he had done this to her.

Enough of that, she told herself, and looked purposefully at the page before her. She read for two hours. Later, she could not remember the name of the book or a word in it.

She set her watch back two hours as her plane landed at Albuquerque. Two o'clock; she'd rent a car and be home before four. And once she was beyond the town and driving through the desert, she felt calmer. She rolled down her window to breathe the sage-scented air, and drove more slowly, feeling herself relax, surrounded by desert and brush, the endless sky, misty purple mountains on the horizon, the solitary call of a jay. Home. Everything will be all right. Saul will find out who Artner works for; we'll get him to write a retraction; Paul will tell me I have my papers back again; Polly Perritt will be stalking someone else; I'll find a way to talk to Matt and to forget him. Everything will be fine.

And I can use a rest. I'll call this a vacation. Why not?

She was almost smiling by the time she reached her house, after repeating *Everything will be fine* in a rhythm that matched her tires as she got closer to Santa Fe. The smile faded when she pulled into her driveway and found a car already there—a rented one, she saw—and then she felt a lurch within her as she saw that it had been rented at the municipal airport.

She flung herself from the car and ran to the house, turning her key in the lock and pushing open the front door in one motion. She was down the hall and standing in the doorway of Holly's room before either Holly or Tony had a chance to move.

Tony, tieless, shoeless, his shirt unbuttoned to his waist, stood behind Holly, his hands around her, holding her breasts, his mouth on the back of her neck. Holly was motionless. Wearing a plaid skirt and white blouse that made her look like a schoolgirl, she stood with her arms hanging at her sides, her head down, her long ash-blond hair falling like a curtain around her face. "Of course it's all right," Tony was murmuring urgently. "Stop worrying, you must come, I'll take care of—"

Then they heard Elizabeth's heels on the tile floor, and sprang apart. And that was when Elizabeth saw the open suitcase on the bed, with Holly's clothes folded inside it.

Oh, Matt, my God, what have we done to our family?

They were all frozen; it seemed they did not even breathe. Tony's eyes darted around the room. "Listen—" he began.

"*Get out.*" Elizabeth's voice sliced across Tony's soft flesh. "*Get out of this house.*"

"Elizabeth, you don't under—"

"I told you to get out!"

"But it was you I wanted! You! The whole time—!"

Holly made a whimpering sound. "You said you wanted me! You promised to put me on your show."

Elizabeth burned; she wanted to strike out, to pound her fist into Tony's face. But she kept her hands clenched, the nails biting her palms. She looked at her daughter's wide, bewildered eyes and tremulous mouth, and she was consumed by an inferno of rage at the man who stood there, his face working as he tried to find the right expression. "He doesn't have a show," she said contemptuously. "It was taken away from him. He has nothing to promise."

"You're lying! You fucking bitch, nobody knows that—!"

"Tony!" Holly cried, looking at him for the first time.

"*Get out!*" Elizabeth came into the room and stood beside Holly. "Get out of this house and out of town, and if you ever come near us again I swear to God, Tony, I'll kill you."

He took a step back from her fury, staring at her, trying to talk. His breezy handsomeness was gone, his face was fleshy and slack, his mouth sagged at one corner. "How did you know about—"

"*Did you hear me?*"

His hands were making little clutching movements; his head wagged slowly as he looked around the floor. "I do have a show," he muttered. "I'm working it out . . ." He sat on the edge of a chair and picked up one of his shoes.

"Get out of that chair! You despicable—*creature*"—she spat it out—"you'll never touch anything in this house again! I'm

530

warning you; I'm telling you for the last time . . . *get out of my house!*"

Her voice and face finally terrified him. He scuttled around her, like a crab. His stockinged feet slipped on the smooth tile floor and he grabbed at furniture as he went. Holding the doorjamb, he swung himself through the doorway, his other hand still making those clutching motions, as if grasping at something in the room. "I do have a show," he said defiantly. "You'll be sorry; you'll wish you'd been nicer to me—" He looked at Elizabeth wildly and then he was gone.

Elizabeth heard the front door open and slam shut, but she stood without moving until, a moment later, she heard a car engine starting up, wheels skidding on gravel, and then silence.

Holly's shoulders were shaking; she had covered her face with her hands. Elizabeth put her arms around her and held her as tightly as she could. "Holly, dear. Dearest Holly . . ."

Holly stood rigidly within her mother's tight embrace. "I'm not a baby! You didn't have to come in here and . . . I didn't need to be . . . *rescued* from the big bad—"

"I thought you did." Elizabeth's throat was tight; her stomach was knotted with anger and fear for what might have happened. "I don't think you're a baby—I don't, Holly; I think you're a woman, and a fine, strong one. Sit down with me and we'll talk." Holly shook her head. Elizabeth sighed, staying where she was, holding one arm around her daughter's unyielding shoulders. *Where do I start? I'm not going to come out of this covered with glory, the way mothers would like to: wise, calm, pure. Oh, Holly, forgive me.*

She took a long breath, and quietly, almost casually, asked, "When did this start?"

"When you were in San Francisco."

"Three weeks ago. That was when you were crying when I called?"

"And you sent Heather to spy on me!"

"Holly, why were you crying?"

"A lot was happening! I was being emotional . . ."

"You sounded unhappy to me."

"I was happy! It was the most wonderful evening! We talked

531

and talked and he asked me all my dreams and he listened to me sing and said it almost made him cry . . . And I loved him! I still do! And he loves me!"

"You think so? After what he said—about me?"

Holly closed her eyes. "He probably said that so you wouldn't be mad and make him leave . . . or . . . something. He says things—sometimes—that he doesn't mean . . ."

"He says a lot he doesn't mean. The trick with Tony is to sort out the acting from the truth."

"That's not fair! I know he was telling the truth! He said such wonderful things . . . he told me my loveliness was . . . bewitching . . . and he said I made his days bright—"

"And his nights even brighter."

Holly flung herself from her mother's arms. Her face was deeply flushed. "How did you know that?"

"Because he said the same thing to me," Elizabeth said bluntly. "I suppose he also told you you're an exquisite, exciting—"

"—passionate woman," Holly finished, looking at the door. She put her head up and stared accusingly at her mother. *"You went to bed with him!* How can you even talk to me? You betrayed Daddy—!"

"Now just a—"

"I thought you probably did, but I wasn't sure, and then you never stayed in Los Angeles more than one night so I decided you couldn't be. Because I knew if it was me I couldn't just be with him one night a week if he made love to me . . . and then when he told me how I'd changed his life I was sure he never made love to you because you're much more beautiful than I am, and much more sophisticated and fascinating, and he'd never look at me if the two of you . . . I don't believe you! *He never said all those things to you!"*

"He probably says them to all his women," Elizabeth said. "And each time he probably believes he means it, or at least most of it."

Holly stood in the middle of the room, her body as rigid as when Elizabeth had first arrived. Suddenly she went limp and began to cry, shaking silently, then breaking into great gulping sobs that wracked her slender body. "Oh, *Mommy!*" She put her arms around Elizabeth's waist and rested her forehead on Elizabeth's shoulder. "I'm glad you're here; I'm so glad I didn't . . ." The words came jerkily, between her sobs. "I wanted you . . . but I didn't . . . I got in your bed one night when you were gone . . . but that wasn't what I . . ." She drew a ragged breath. *"I didn't know what I wanted!"*

Elizabeth put her arms around her. "Hush, sweetheart. My sweet Holly, I know it hurts . . ." Her murderous rage came back—*that bastard!*—but she pushed it away. "It will be all right, Holly; everything will be all right." She led her to a deep armchair and cradled her grown daughter on her lap. "We'll talk about it in a few minutes. Not now. Give yourself a little time."

"No, I want to. I have to!" Holly wiped her nose with the back of her hand. "I don't know why I'm crying . . ."

Elizabeth set a box of tissues in Holly's lap. "Use them up."

Holly pulled out a handful and held them to her eyes. A long sigh shuddered through her. "You're not mad at me?"

"I couldn't be mad at you. I love you. And we both fell for the same line." Holly shuddered again. Elizabeth kissed her forehead and held her slender form, remembering holding her as a baby, thinking how fragile and strong she was, and what a remarkable thing Elizabeth Lovell had done to have such an amazingly perfect daughter. She ran her hand over Holly's head and the silken hair that looked exactly like her own when she was just Holly's age—and sleeping with Tony Rourke. "Let me tell you about Tony," she said, and told Holly the whole story, beginning with that long-ago summer, when she was almost eighteen.

"He was six years older than I, so sure of himself—at least he acted that way—and he made me feel grown up and free. Grandma and Grandpa were so afraid of taking risks—they were always making lists and schedules, worrying about all the things that could go wrong, planning far ahead—and then Tony came along and swooped me up and it was like a roller coaster ride: fast, exciting, dangerous, never planned, never scheduled, different from anything in my whole life. Of course there was more: I was crazy about him and I also felt tied to him because he'd taught me what it meant to be sensual, what kinds of feelings I could have, and what to do with them, and I thought he was the only one I could ever be with, in that way . . ."

Holly stirred in her lap. *What am I saying? Is this the way a mother talks to a daughter?*

"Go on," Holly said, when Elizabeth hesitated. "Please. How long were you lovers?"

"A whole summer." *All I can do is be honest with her; I don't know what else to do.* "And then he went back east and found someone else and married her."

Holly drew a sharp breath. "But you must have quarreled—or you found someone *you* liked better—?"

"No. Tony found someone. And I thought I'd die."

Cuddled against her mother, damp tissues wadded in her hand, Holly was very still. "But he came back," she said at last. "He kept coming to Santa Fe, to see you."

"I've told you, Holly: Tony likes drama. Somewhere between his third and fourth, or fourth and fifth marriages, he decided I was the love of his life. A dream love, unattainable because I was married. Happily married. But for Tony that set the stage for exaggerated sighs and declarations that were perfectly safe because they couldn't lead to anything serious. Those visits were just part of a role he was playing. Until"—her voice slowed—"he saw that my life had changed. Tony is very good at spotting people who are vulnerable, and he's at his best with them because it's the weaknesses of others that make him feel strong. That doesn't show at first, because he's an actor and very good, even at fooling himself, which actors often do."

Elizabeth looked over Holly's head, at tree branches barely visible in the darkness beyond the window. "He saw that I needed someone to make me feel loved and desired. And young. You think I betrayed your father, Holly, but we were already apart, and he'd made another life, and I felt . . . old. And unwanted . . ."

"So you went to bed with him."

"It wasn't quite that simple, but that's close." Elizabeth thought she might as well hear all of it. "He knew what to say and how to say it; he knew what I needed. He took me to Europe where everything seemed new, even Tony Rourke, even lovemaking. And we were working together in that strange, wonderful place; and he made that seem new, too, so it didn't matter if I didn't always like the things he said or if there were things we didn't share at all, because he's not always nice or lovable . . ." She stopped. "I think you must have seen that. But you were so excited and everything was new—"

"Just the way you said." Holly's voice was muffled. "I didn't know you could feel like that when you're older and know everything."

Elizabeth bit back a laugh. "You can always feel that, Holly. It's nicest when you feel it with somebody who makes you happy."

"*He did.*"

"Really? You were happy with him?"

Holly's tears started again, quiet this time, streaming down her face as they had that first night with Tony. "I wanted to be happy. But things kept getting in the way. He'd say something, or . . . hurt me . . . or I'd think how awful it would be, leaving you and Daddy . . ."

Elizabeth remembered the suitcase on the bed. "Where were you going?"

"To Malibu, and then Amalfi. He said his house in Malibu was cold and empty without a woman in it and the only thing he had to talk to was his refrigerator and I'd bring the house to life. He said we'd swim in his pool and he had a blue bathrobe that matched his, and would make my eyes as blue as the sky . . . it was so *lovely* when he said things like that . . . And even when he didn't seem . . . nice . . . when it wasn't as wonderful as I thought it would be, I still was so full of love and wanting . . . wanting to love and be loved, and share . . . do you know what I mean?"

Elizabeth nodded, her cheek brushing against Holly's hair. "I know what it is to be full of love and wanting."

"From Tony?"

"From your father."

"Oh. But it didn't last, between you."

535

"Because of other things. But it's still most wonderful, most joyful, when you find someone you really love, not someone you have to pretend with."

"I wasn't pretending!"

Elizabeth let the sound of the words fade before she said, "Were you really going to leave school for him, and Juilliard, and everything you've been working toward?"

"I didn't want to, not at first, but Tony said I didn't need anybody but him. He said even after years of college I'd still have to know the right people to get anywhere and he could find them for me now. He said he'd introduce me to people in television and the movies, and he said when he went into politics and became a senator—"

"Senator? *Tony?*"

"That's what he said. He was going to move to New Mexico—something else for us to share, he said—and then he'd move to Washington when he got elected, and he'd meet other important people, and . . . make me famous."

Fairy tales, Elizabeth thought, to impress Holly in case she somehow heard about his show being canceled. "And you believed him?" she asked.

"I wanted to." Holly's voice was almost inaudible and Elizabeth bent her head closer, to hear. "When he touched me I believed everything he said. I loved it when he touched me. It was scary but it was wonderful because he said I was perfect and bewitching and he made me feel beautiful—not just pretty—really beautiful, like you. And he kept saying my name, as if there wasn't anybody in the world like me . . . Nobody else ever made me feel that way . . ."

Her words poured out; she couldn't talk fast enough. At first her mother's confidences about Tony had shocked and embarrassed her, but then they made her feel wonderful; she'd never loved her mother so much, she wanted to talk and talk and tell her everything that she hadn't been able to tell anybody, even Luz—or even think about, to herself! Holly felt so grateful—she had her mother back—maybe now she could get rid of the awful feeling inside her, like a rocket in her stomach, and feel good about herself again.

536

"I mean, you and Daddy always made me feel special, and Peter too, and Grandma and Grandpa, and Luz—but I wanted to be loved in a different way—I wanted somebody to make me feel special, not like a girl in high school, but like a woman who had these *feelings* . . . I wanted to know the things I felt *and wanted* were the way a woman ought to feel, and when he . . . when he undressed me"—her voice dropped even lower—"he didn't like me to undress myself, he'd always undress me and he'd look at me and say I was the most beautiful, desirable woman in the world . . ."

Elizabeth shrank inside, contempt for Tony mixed with a feeling of loss for Holly: *She should have discovered this with someone who would leave her with happy memories . . .*

"And nobody else ever did that," Holly was saying. "Nobody else I ever met—"

"But you didn't give the boys at school a chance," Elizabeth murmured.

"Sleep with *them*?"

"You don't *have* to sleep with anyone, Holly."

"You did."

"Yes. But later I was sorry. Not just because Tony broke my heart—and I really thought he did, for a while—but mainly because I never got to know boys slowly, as friends first, and then as lovers. After Tony, I didn't know what I wanted from boys. They all seemed too young, after him, until I met your father—"

"But that's the whole point! They *are* too young! You kept telling me to go out with boys my own age and I did, but they don't care about music—Tony asked me to sing for him!—and most of them don't want to talk about anything serious; all they care about is sex—fumbling around in the back seats of cars, trying to get their hands inside my blouse or up my skirt and they're clumsy and in such a *hurry* . . . They're babies! And Tony is a man. We talked and talked; he said lovely things; he told me I'd enchanted him . . . oh. Did he say that to you, too?"

"Something like it. Holly, are you asking me to tell you it was all right to sleep with Tony because it's better to learn about sex from a man than a boy?"

Holly chewed the corner of her fingernail. "You don't think it was all right."

"No." Elizabeth shifted a little so the two of them could look at each other. "It's not hard to sleep with a man, Holly, and it doesn't make you grown up. Understanding yourself, learning to balance all the parts of your life, including a love affair . . . those are the things that make you grown up. Right now you don't really understand yourself because you're going through so many changes; you don't know how to handle an affair; and you certainly don't understand Tony. You never did because he made sure you wouldn't. He took terrible advantage of—"

"He didn't! I wanted him to make love to me!"

"But you said it wasn't always what you dreamed it would be."

Holly dropped her eyes. "Sometimes I hated him. But other times I loved him. Sometimes I loved him and hated him in the same afternoon . . . or night." She looked at her mother. "But then, the last week, I felt . . . trapped. I didn't know what to do. I loved him—I love him!—but sometimes I wanted to get away from him because he was always here—he stayed in town—"

"When I was here?" Elizabeth asked.

Holly nodded. "He said he'd been given a few weeks off by his father and he stayed in Taos and drove in—we spent afternoons at the Taos Inn—"

"You told me you were in rehearsals."

"I was with Tony in Taos; I haven't been . . . I haven't been singing very much. It's so hard, all of a sudden—can't I tell you about Tony?"

"Yes," Elizabeth said, hating it, but knowing they had to get through it.

"He was always *around*. And I loved it—I mean, Tony Rourke wanted to be with me all the time! That was a dream and I couldn't believe it, but then all of a sudden one day I felt trapped. We were in Taos, at the Inn, sitting in the courtyard outside our room—his room—and he told me I was going away with him. I *did* believe him when he said he'd make me

538

famous, but I was afraid to leave everybody, but he wouldn't give me time to think about it, he kept talking and talking and then yesterday, when you went to New York, he took my suitcase down so I could look at it and get used to the idea and then *he started packing my clothes and I couldn't stop him!* I wanted to ask you what to do, I've been wanting to ask you all this time, but I didn't know how and anyway, you were gone so much—"

Elizabeth winced, and Holly said quickly, "I didn't mean that."

"Yes, you did," Elizabeth said. "And you're right. I wasn't here. I was running around, not paying attention . . . Holly, it's all my fault; I'm so sorry—"

"No, don't do that, don't blame yourself. You can't say it's your fault as if I'm three or four or something; *I'm grown up.*"

Holly began to cry again. She wasn't sobbing or anything; the tears just came. "I didn't need you," she said through her tears. "I mean, of course I needed you, but I didn't know it until later. And you were excited about the things you were doing, and people saying you were wonderful and that was very important to you—you needed that."

Elizabeth felt her own tears come. *My lovely, loving daughter is comforting me.* "I owed you some attention too," she said.

"I wanted you to leave me alone. I thought. Anyway, that's what I told you . . . I can't exactly complain because you did what I wanted." Impatiently, Holly wiped her eyes. "I wouldn't have talked to you even if you were here every minute of every day. That's the truth. I knew if I told you about Tony you'd tell me I couldn't see him anymore—and I was happy! At least I was happy until I started feeling trapped. And then he said I'd be on his show *next month—April!*—and why shouldn't I want that? What was wrong with my sleeping with him and letting him do things for me? I was afraid you'd stop all of it—"

"You're right; I would have. Holly, listen to me. Tony Rourke is forty-eight years old and you're seventeen. The two of you have nothing in common but a few fantasies that he recognized and took advantage of. And you're asking me what's wrong

539

with your sleeping with him? Everything was wrong with it. And I think that's what you really want me to tell you: not that it was right to sleep with Tony, but that it was wrong. You want me to tell you never to get yourself in that kind of mess again. Well, that's what I'm telling you. If you can't find a man whom you care deeply about and wouldn't be ashamed to marry—then sleep alone. It's cleaner and in the long run a lot more satisfying."

After a moment, in a small voice, Holly asked, "Did you follow your own advice?"

"I tried to convince myself that I cared for Tony. It didn't work."

Holly met her eyes. "Did he really lie about putting me on his show?"

"I'm sure he did. A television critic in Los Angeles called to tell me his show had been canceled, but even if that story is wrong, you know he never features unknown people. And if that weren't enough, he'd have to clear you with Bo Boyle and Bo would never allow my daughter on the show."

"I asked Tony about that because I knew you'd quarreled with Bo. He said it's his show; it's called 'Anthony,' you know."

"It's his father's show. He and Bo control it. That was why I left; because Bo and Keegan have final approval on everything. And Tony wouldn't stand up with me, against that."

Holly was silent. "Why didn't you ever tell me?"

"I'm not sure. I think I didn't want to admit to you that my good friend Tony let me down. I should have; then you wouldn't have greeted him so warmly."

"Maybe I would have been even warmer. Thinking I'd show my mother the right way to handle him."

A small chuckle broke from the two of them. They put their arms around each other and sat quietly in the silent house. Two women, Elizabeth thought, finally open and honest with each other. My daughter is growing up. And so am I.

CHAPTER 17

Matt read a report on Cal Artner's story in Key Largo, where he and Nicole had docked for the night. While she browsed in a sportswear shop, he flipped through a Miami newspaper, his eye caught by a headline: "Columnist Accused of Conflict of Interest."

> (AP) ALBUQUERQUE, NM, MARCH 19. Elizabeth Lovell, nationally syndicated columnist, has been accused of using her column, "Private Affairs," to advance her own interests by rousing public opposition to a state park and resort being developed in the mountains near Santa Fe, New Mexico.

The story was a brief review of Artner's charges, picked up by the wire service and reprinted around the country. Matt read and re-read it, disbelieving and infuriated. Elizabeth! The most honest person he had ever known, stubbornly refusing to do anything unscrupulous from her first stories in high school and college, through all their work together, from the time they fired Cal Artner for—

Artner, for Christ's sake. Since when did he work at the *Daily News?* And who the hell let this trash go to press?

541

"Matt, good gracious," said Nicole, coming up to him. "Has someone accused you of murder? Piracy? Hijacking a plane to Majorca?"

"Worse." He ripped the page from the paper and stuffed it in his pocket. "I'll be right back; I'm going to call the office."

"Darling, it's eight o'clock; seven in Houston. No one will be there."

He paused. "I'd forgotten." Then he said, "But it's only six in Albuquerque. I'll be back in a few minutes."

In a telephone booth, he struggled to remember the name of the editor of the *Daily News,* and when it came to him he placed the call. "Just tell me," he said when the editor answered. "Who authorized that story on Elizabeth Lovell?"

"Oh, Christ, Matt, you didn't know about it? Shit. I thought it was kind of peculiar—in fact, tell the truth, I wanted to call you before we ran it, but Chet said you knew all about—"

"Chet?"

"Well, who else would I listen to except you? He said you knew about it and Mr. Rourke knew about it. He said both of you were hopping mad, worried about opposition to land development all over the southwest if people like Aragon were allowed to sway public opinion and ride roughshod over the will of legislatures—those were his words—I wrote down everything he said. You know, just in case."

"Send me a copy."

"I sure will. Always glad to—"

"Now tell me why you never called to check that story with me."

"Chet said you weren't available. He said you were off sailing somewhere and you'd put Artner on the story and then sent him—Chet—to tell us to run it, since it was the New Mexico legislature you wanted to reach. Of course, you knew the AP would pick up a local story —'course your wife's so famous, we should have guessed . . . but it wouldn't matter if you already knew about it, except I guess you didn't . . . Christ, Matt, I'm sorry as hell, but Chet said you'd fire me, or Mr. Rourke would, if I didn't run it. What was I supposed to do?"

"Call me. How many times have I told you to call me any time you have the slightest doubt about a story?"

"That's what I told Chet! He said you were sailing!"

"Wherever I am, I call in for messages. You know that."

"He said there was a rush on it."

Matt nodded, though there was no one to see him. It wouldn't have made a difference, he thought; on this trip, for the first time, he hadn't called in every day. Nicole had been like summer wine—heady, warm, lulling, so that he thought of nothing else. They'd gone swimming off the boat in waters as clear as shimmering sunlit air; they'd rented diving gear and photographed vivid fish and coral at inky depths; they'd lain naked on the teak deck of Rourke's sailboat, drinking margaritas, tasting the salt on each other's lips, mingling sex and seawater and sunlight. And whenever they felt like it, they ate from the lavish picnic baskets Nicole bought at every stop. They never cooked or prepared anything, but they always had food and drink: salmon bisque, Szechuan pasta, cold curried scallops, goose liver pâté, salade Niçoise, dark sourdough and Russian rye breads with Normandy butter, French and Danish cheeses, white and red wines and Belgian chocolates with centers of mousse or liqueurs. It was the closest Matt ever had been to a fairyland where genies anticipated his wants before he was even aware of them and the days passed in a haze of sunlit sensuality.

Until he bought a newspaper: the first in a week. "I'm going to write a new version of that story," he told the editor. "As soon as you get it, I want it run."

"Uh . . . Matt, would you mind . . . would you talk to Mr. Rourke about that? Chet told me—"

"Print it when you get it," Matt said shortly. "I don't need to be told when to speak to Rourke." He hung up. Of course he was going to speak to Rourke. As soon as he could get a flight to Houston.

Nicole was annoyed when he told her; it was one of the few times she had let him see it. "I'm only cutting two days off the trip," he said the next morning, dressing in slacks and a shirt. He'd made arrangements for them to fly to Miami in a private plane that would be leaving in half an hour. He pulled

543

on his sport coat, then tilted her chin up, forcing her eyes to meet his. "After I talk to Rourke, we'll find a way to finish our vacation. All right?"

She shrugged. "I thought a vacation meant getting away from everybody and everything."

"We've done that, for a week."

"And now you're ending it. Because of one newspaper article. Can't your wife take care of herself? Do you have to be her shining knight, dashing into combat to protect her poor little reputation—?"

"What the hell are you talking about?"

"I'm sorry, oh, damn it, Matt, I'm sorry, that was stupid. I didn't mean it." She put her hands on his shoulders. "Please say I'm forgiven. I don't say stupid things so often, do I, that you can't forget this one? Matt? Are you listening? Am I forgiven?"

"Of course." She'd sounded jealous, which was odd, for her, but she'd also sounded worried. "We'll talk about it later," he said. "Are you ready? We should be on time when we're hitching a ride and it's almost noon."

"Yes," she said, very subdued, and they barely spoke on the way to the small airstrip, or later, on the plane to Houston, or later still, driving in from the airport. Matt gave Nicole's address to the driver of the limousine, but he stayed in the car when they pulled up at her house. "I'm going straight to the office; I'll call you when I'm through."

"I'll be waiting to hear how it went. Shall we have dinner here?"

"Whatever you like."

Settling back as the driver wove through the traffic from River Oaks to the Transco Building, Matt thought about what he would say. It wasn't complicated; he was just looking for information. And he had a few small demands to make.

"Chet has to go," he said to Rourke, pacing in the circular office. For the first time in a year, the shape of the room bothered him; he felt imprisoned within the seamless walls, as if they were closing in, with no corners to keep them in their place, and he found himself pacing in a large circle.

544

Chet had been in the office when he walked in unannounced; he and Rourke had looked up together, surprised into silence by Matt's abrupt appearance two days before he was expected. In that silence, Matt told Rourke he wanted to talk to him alone. Rourke's face had already smoothed out, all signs of surprise gone. He tilted his head at Chet and immediately Chet gathered up his papers and left the office, nodding at Matt as he passed.

"He has to go," Matt repeated. He slapped the page from the Miami newspaper on Rourke's desk. "He ordered this story; he claimed he was speaking for me. I don't know what the hell made him think he could play publisher, but he's not going to get away with it."

"I'm sure he wasn't trying to take your place, Matt," Rourke said easily. "I'll talk to him; it sounds like there was some confusion in assignments."

"Chet doesn't confuse assignments you give him," Matt said bluntly.

Rourke shook his head. "I don't know anything about this. I agree with you: the story shouldn't have been written and it shouldn't have run. But for whatever reason he did it, Chet always acts from zeal, not evil; we don't fire people for that."

"We fire them for overstepping the bounds of their authority, for acting irresponsibly and giving someone cause to sue us for libel, *for lying,* God damn it!—"

"Matt, Matt, talk about overstepping bounds! We're dealing with a loyal worker! Someone who's been with Rourke Enterprises for over twenty years! Now I agree that he did something he should not have done, but let's keep it in perspective. Chet was trying to protect the concept of free and open development of private and public land. He knows I'm concerned about it; he knows I have investments in a number of these places—"

"In Nuevo?" Matt asked suddenly.

"We're talking about the entire southwest; Chet knows I'm always interested in new properties; he knows I want land opened up for mining and lumbering, for housing, ranching, recreation . . . I don't believe in government owning too much land, and Chet knows that. You know it, too. You've written editorials on opening up more land; you ran a brilliant series of articles on the subject last year and we've talked about a new series for this year. We're not in disagreement on that. Our small disagreement at the moment is over one single decision that Chet made independently. Of course he thought he was helping us, but he went too far. He ignored the fact that Elizabeth is your wife, and I confess I'm surprised that he took it upon himself to allow criticism of her in our paper. Of course I intend to speak to him about it, but I must say I'm surprised at your overreaction, Matt: flying back from Florida, rushing in here demanding Chet's head on a platter because the man made the mistake of working too hard for our interests—"

This man is lying. After telling me for months how much he trusts and relies on me, he's telling me a pack of lies. "Listen to me," Matt said, his voice hard and cold as it never had been with Rourke. "This isn't an overreaction and I'm not overstepping my bounds; I'm defining them. First, I will not have Elizabeth or anyone else smeared in a paper of mine: I don't run that kind of operation. Second, as publisher I decide what is printed in my papers. I can't force you to fire Chet; he works for you, not me. But I expect you to tell him that never again will he talk to anyone but me about my newspapers; he will never again go near my papers or my editors; he'll never again attempt in any way to influence what goes in my papers—"

"I think you'd better stop there, Matt. Whose papers are you talking about?"

"Mine. I bought them; I'm publisher of them. I was given complete control of—"

"You weren't, but the important word there is *given*. You were given those papers by me. And since I gave them, I can take them away." Rourke leaned back in his chair. A stranger would have said he was relaxed, but Matt knew those half-closed eyes hid a glint that made powerful men quail. "If you think you can behave as if those are your newspapers, and order me to tell one of my staff how to conduct himself, you don't know the meaning of bounds, much less overstepping them. God damn it, I made you! I freed you from that piddling rag you were turning out once a week behind a cactus somewhere; I widened your boundaries, I made them limitless, I made you known and respected not in an adobe wasteland but in the whole country!"

Matt had stopped pacing. "You didn't make me anything. *I've* been running those papers; I've made my own reputation."

"You fool. If you have a reputation, it comes from working for Keegan Rourke."

"It comes in spite of working for Keegan Rourke. You gave me my start—God knows, I've never denied that—but do you know how often I've been hampered by you? I should have supported Dan Heller for senator in New Mexico, gotten in on the ground floor with him, but I lost that chance because you insisted on backing Andy Greene—poor, tired Andy, who shouldn't have run again, much less been supported. And our readers know it. So now I have to work at getting back the confidence they had in us before. And I shouldn't have given in on that highway in Colorado; I knew it wasn't necessary and would damn near destroy a wildlife area, but I gave in when you asked me to, and now I have to deal with readers who know what I've always known: that nobody benefited except a handful of men who owned land along—"

Rourke lunged forward, sending his chair skidding backward until it bounced off the marble window ledge. "Who the hell do you think you are to make accusations in this office?"

There was a sudden silence. *Accusations?* Matt plunged his hands into his pockets and contemplated Rourke's sleek figure at the far side of the circular room—not quite so sleek now, hunched over the desk, leaning on his hands, returning Matt's look through those half-closed eyes. *Accusations.* If he says I'm accusing him of supporting a highway because his friends own land along the right of way, it's a good bet his friends own land along the right of way. Or he does. And he's probably lined up someone for Andy Greene's senate seat; I asked him about it once, and he dodged it. And it's a good bet he owns some or all of the new Durango ski area. And skipping past a few other developments—how close is he to Terry Ballenger?

Watching Matt's face, Rourke knew he had made a mistake. "Listen, son," he said, and Matt heard the echoes of that phrase

547

go back over the years. Rourke walked around the desk so that nothing stood between the two of them. "We tend to get overexcited about issues that aren't as important as our relationship. A very special relationship. We both went too far in some of the things we said; I think we ought to exchange apologies." He paused, but Matt was silent. "I'll talk to Chet; no question he touched on subjects and people, a person, he had no right to touch; no question he went too far. But so did you, my boy. We all have to follow orders, you know; you think I don't hop on a plane when the President of the United States calls and tells me to come to Washington?" He chuckled. Matt remained silent. "All right, that's enough, we don't have to wring this turkey's neck long after it's dead. We know where we stand and there's no reason to go around again. All I want is to hear you tell me you're part of Rourke Enterprises, and that you understand that means teamwork and no indulging in sentiment."

"It isn't sentiment. It's a question of justice."

"I don't know what that word means, and neither do you. Your wife got treated roughly in a newspaper story; we all regret it, but if there are errors in it, I'm sure she'll correct them. The story was written from the best motives, and as far as I'm concerned that's all that counts. And it ends there."

"Not for me. That wasn't a news story; it was a smear. It was written by someone who's had a grudge against both of us for years, and I'm not going to allow him to get away with it; I'm not going to let that story stand without correction—"

"You're not going to let it stand? I thought I made it clear who owns that paper, and I'm telling you there will be no retraction, no new story. *I decide what's in my papers.* Matt, this has gone on far too long. We had no trouble before this came along; if your wife weren't involved we wouldn't be having any trouble now."

"We're having 'trouble,' as you call it, because a pack of lies was published in my—in a newspaper with my name on the masthead. But in one way you're right: I compromised in the past, on Andy Greene and dozens of other issues, but I won't compromise on Elizabeth. I won't see her name dragged

548

in the mud. She's been through a lot lately, largely because of me; she's made a brilliant reputation on her own and I won't be a party to anything that damages it." He walked toward the door. "I'm a journalist, you know. I'd almost forgotten it, I was so busy being an executive, but it's coming back to me, and I'm going to find the truth behind that story, and write it the way it should have been written the first time."

"Stay right there!" Rourke's face was dark; in contrast, his silver hair and eyebrows had a metallic sheen. "If you write one word on that story, you're through. Your career is over. You'll never work for this corporation again and I'll see to it that you don't get a job on any other paper in the country. In the world, damn it! I have connections! Is that clear? Did you hear me?"

Matt paused, but all that came through the pounding thoughts in his head was a sick feeling of betrayal with every word Rourke flung at him. Almost automatically, he went on toward the door. "I'll send you an advance copy of the paper when the story comes out."

"*Sit down!* You fool, you're not walking out of here! Where would you go? You're bluffing; trying to make me bend. You ought to know by now that I don't bend. I gave you the dream that's dominated you all your life; you wouldn't walk away from it. Listen to me! I'm giving you one more chance to become the most powerful publisher in America! All you have to do is say you're with me! That's all—your word that you won't fight me. There are so many things we can accomplish, Matt; you don't even know yet all the uses of power; there's so much I still have to teach you. But only if I'm sure of you! Matt, my boy . . . *Do you hear me?*"

Matt had opened the door. "I hear you more clearly, Mr. Rourke, than I've heard you for two years." Very gently, he closed the door behind him and walked through the reception room, down the spiral staircase, and along the hallway to the office at the end, with the brass plate beside the door that read, "Matthew Lovell, Publisher."

* * *

It was after six; everyone had left. The corridors were empty, the offices silent behind closed doors. Matt sat at his desk, looking through his own door, left open, down the hallway lined with offices of the other vice-presidents of Rourke Enterprises—all of whom, he surmised, understood exactly where the center of power was and never made assumptions about control over their own departments.

He pulled a sheet of his personal stationery from his desk and unscrewed the top of his pen—Mont Blanc, heavy, black, successful-looking; a gift from Nicole—and swiftly wrote a single-sentence letter of resignation from Rourke Publishing and Rourke Enterprises. His pen stuck briefly on *Publishing*— the dream of a lifetime, as Rourke had put it—then moved on, finishing the sentence. Without reading it over, he put it in an envelope, wrote Rourke's name on the front, and placed it precisely in the center of his desk, beside the wrinkled page he'd ripped from the Miami paper.

What now?

You mean this minute? Tomorrow? Six months from now? All of the above.

Irresolute, he looked about the plush office so skillfully decorated by Nicole. Then he shrugged. He wanted to get away from there before he began to doubt himself, and that meant he had to clean out his desk.

It was surprisingly easy; he hadn't realized how few personal items he had brought to that office. Two photographs in a hinged frame: one of Peter and Holly at Peter's graduation almost a year ago, the other of himself and Zachary in front of the printing plant, Zachary grinning widely because he was alive and out of the hospital, with his son beside him; an antique silver letter opener Matt had found in Zachary's desk after his death; a brass pen holder with a quill pen that Elizabeth had given him the first time the *Chieftain* showed a profit. He put them in his briefcase and opened the top drawer.

Automatic pencil, pocket calculator, business cards, a Kundera novel he hadn't finished, a Ross McDonald mystery he hadn't begun, personal stationery, private address book, a bottle of aspirin. And a note he'd scrawled in early January, when he'd returned from Saul and Heather's wedding: "Send Elizabeth Chet's report on resettlement help for Nuevo residents."

He'd never sent it, because he'd never found it. And Chet had never responded to his requests to get him a copy. Suddenly the report seemed too important to ignore: another example, like Artner's story, of something that should have been in his control, and wasn't. He riffled through his files, clearing out personal letters and memoranda as he looked once more for the three stapled pages headed "Nuevo: Compensation and Resettlement." He remembered it, remembered the map of settled valleys within fifty miles of Nuevo, remembered the budget showing moving and resettlement costs, farming start-up costs, even an amount for replacement of damaged equipment.

It was not among his papers. The only other material on Nuevo, that he knew of, was in Chet's office. He found a box in the closet, crammed it with files and records he intended to keep, and the possessions from his desk, set it beside the door, and walked down the hallway toward Chet's office.

The cleaning crew was working in Rourke's office upstairs; Matt heard the rattle of miniblinds being dusted, the clatter of objects moved about—and then Rourke's voice, raised in anger, drowned out almost immediately by a vacuum cleaner starting up.

What the hell, he thought; I saw him leave an hour ago. But the voice came from down the hall. Frowning, Matt walked on, past closed office doors, until he came to Chet's, where he heard, beneath the hum of the vacuum cleaner, Rourke's voice—and then his own.

"You'll never work for this corporation again and I'll see to it that you don't get a job on any other paper in the country. In the world, damn it! I have connections! Is that clear? Did you hear me?"

There was a pause. "I'll send you an advance copy of the paper when the story comes out."

"*Sit down!* You fool, you're not walking out of here! Where would you go?"

The voices went on. Matt stood outside the closed door, his hand clenched on the doorknob, shaking his head in disbelief.

The little son of a bitch! The loyal employee of twenty years—gopher, righthand man, advance man, Rourke-worshipper—bugging his boss's office! And no one suspected; not a rumor, not a word of suspicion, in all the time Matt had been there. Clever Chet: covering his tracks like the weasel that he was.

And now he sat behind a closed door, listening to a tape of Matt and Rourke's conversation after Rourke told him to leave. And this is what he does every night, Matt thought grimly. Sits in his little nest, listening in on the day's events so he can plan tomorrow. A worried, frightened little man. Even after twenty years, unable to trust himself or his revered chief, stockpiling information in case he ever needed to blackmail someone to keep his job.

A frightened, dangerous little man. And Matt remembered that Elizabeth had seen that the first time she met him.

He listened to the last few moments of the conversation, heard himself on tape open and close the door of Rourke's office, and then, tight with anger, he thrust open Chet's door and strode in.

Chet was hunched over his desk, reaching out to turn off the recorder. He froze when he saw Matt bearing down on him, then leaped to his feet. "What the fuck do you think you're doing—coming in here without knocking—spying like a goddam peeping Tom—?"

"Sit down!" Matt's voice lashed across the desk. "I want to talk to you and I want you where I can see you."

"You can't order me around! You don't even work here anymore! You've been fired!"

"*Sit down!*" Matt stood over him, six inches taller and thirty pounds heavier, lean and muscular to Chet's pudgy softness. Chet looked at him, tried to look past him, failed, and sat. Matt looked down at him, his hands at his sides, and watched him begin to squirm as the silence lengthened.

Except for the faint hum of the vacuum cleaner, the office was very quiet. It was sparsely furnished, with a teak desk, a black swivel chair, two black leather armchairs, three black file cabinets, and a single picture on the wall, of Chet and Rourke. It was cold and cheerless, lacking any identifiable personality. Exactly like Chet. "You're a busy fellow, Chet," Matt said at last, still looming over him. "And you're going to tell me all about the things you do. The hatchet job you assigned to Artner; using my name to give orders in Albuquerque; bugging your leader's office—"

"It's not true!"

"What isn't true?"

"That I . . . *any of it!* Cal. Artner. Cal dug up his own information. He was very unhappy about it because it was your wife, but wrongdoing is wrong whoever does—"

"You puny sanctimonious bastard!" Matt thundered. "Who the hell do you think you are to pass judgment on my wife? You spoonfed that story to Artner and he had a ball with it; the two of you probably sat up all night giggling over it. You've been pals since you dredged him up from Graham's old chain and added him to your collection, the way you add tapes of Rourke's conversations. You stinking little scavenger—"

"Goddammit, you can't talk to me like . . . listen, you son of a—Wait!" he cried as he saw the look on Matt's face. "Don't you touch me! You don't work here anymore; you can't—you have no right—"

"Keep your mouth shut! From now on, the only time you'll open your mouth is to answer my questions." Matt leaned against the desk a few inches from Chet. "Why did Artner write that smear?"

"It wasn't a smear—it was a straight news story—!"

"Damn it, I told you I want answers! I flew in today to get the truth, not your usual bullshit, and you knew it the minute you saw me. That wasn't a news story; it was a lying piece of—"

"Every word in that story was true! I made sure of that before—" He stopped, then struck the desk with his fist. "I told him to check his facts! They're all true!"

"They're a pack of innuendoes. But you're not answering my question. I'll ask it again: *Why did you order that story?*"

"I didn't! I keep telling you! I wasn't even there!"

"You were in Albuquerque; you told the editor of the *Daily News* I'd fire him if he didn't print the story." Matt looked him

553

up and down. "I could beat you to a pulp," he said softly, and those soft tones were more terrifying to Chet than shouting. "God knows I've wanted to often enough. But right now I need answers." He leaned forward and, so casually Chet was slow to realize what he was doing, he opened the tape recorder, removed the cassette, and dropped it in his pocket. "Why did you order that story?"

Chet's eyes bulged. "Give that back!"

"I asked you a question."

"Give it back! Jesus Christ, do you know what you're doing?"

"Did you, when you made it? There are always dangers in bugging an office, Chet. Being found out is one of them. I'm still waiting for your answer and I'm getting goddamned tired of asking."

Chet licked his lips; he chewed the inside of his cheek. In the silence, they heard the high-pitched whine of the cordless vacuum cleaner a worker was using on the spiral staircase as she made her way a step at a time to the lower floor. The whine stopped; there was a knock at the door. "Cleaners!" a woman's voice shouted.

Matt went to the door and opened it. "We won't be long. Can you do the other offices first?"

The woman shrugged. "Sure, but we're fast. We'll be back in maybe half an hour."

"We'll be out of your way by then." He closed the door. "Rourke and I kept you later than usual tonight, didn't we? All right, let's wind this up. Why was the story written?"

"Will you give me that tape?"

"I'll consider it. Why was it written?"

Chet let out a long breath. "I tried to protect him," he said to the ceiling. "I'm not sure why; lately he hasn't been very nice to me. He even had Terry report to him from Santa Fe after he told me I'd be the *only one* reporting, after he told me he trusted me. That wasn't honorable."

Matt watched him, wondering what the hell he was talking to himself about. Terry was probably Terry Ballenger, but when was he in Santa Fe—and reporting on what?

Chet looked at the outline of the tape cassette in Matt's

554

pocket. He shrugged and looked up, meeting Matt's eyes. "Her Olson interview was a threat and I decided we had to discredit it. Sometimes I need to make on-the-spot decisions; this was one of them."

"To ruin Elizabeth's reputation. What was the threat?" Chet looked at him blankly. "That was a question, Chet. Who needed protection? Who was threatened?"

Once more Chet shrugged. "There was a lot of public pressure on the legislature, because of what Olson said, to take land from Mr. Rourke and give it to those people for a new—"

"From Rourke?"

"It's his land. He owns Nuevo."

Matt gazed at Chet's round glasses, reflecting the fluorescent lights in the ceiling. *I asked Rourke half a dozen times if he was involved in that project; he denied it in half a dozen convincing ways. And this afternoon he dodged it.* "What about Ballenger?"

"Terry owns two percent of Ballenger Associates. Mr. Rourke owns the rest. Terry buys land all over the world for Mr. Rourke. He sets up corporations under his name, because if it got out that Keegan Rourke was buying land, prices would skyrocket or people would refuse to sell, or whatever. He stays in the background and gets people like Terry to go out and buy the land."

"The whole Nuevo valley. And no one knew."

"Right."

"How was it kept so quiet?"

"You know how. Privately held corporations don't have to reveal the names of their shareholders. Milgrim, Saul Milgrim, was asking around but he couldn't find any—"

"I know all about corporations. How was it kept quiet in the legislature? When the dam was approved, did anyone mention Ballenger buying the whole valley? And having the government build him a dam?"

"I don't know! I don't know anything about that! All I know is, Terry bought the land, and Mr. Rourke isn't getting the dam for nothing; he's paying for it; not in dollars, not directly, but he donated the land for the state park; he's building new roads around the dam and the lake, and to the ski area—and he's paying for the resort and the docks and beaches on that side of the lake . . ."

"And he doesn't want to give any of it up."

"He won't give it up. He's already planning to expand the resort if it takes off the way he expects—and he won't allow those people to have restaurants and shops competing with his. He doesn't like trouble. He planned—*we* planned it—for more than ten years. Do you know when he first heard about Nuevo? At your wedding! From your father! And nobody's going to come along after all this time and throw a wrench in it. Now will you give me that tape? It doesn't mean anything to you."

"I'm still considering it. The resort area covers over a thousand acres. You decided to destroy Elizabeth's reputation so that Rourke wouldn't lose a hundred of them. Is that correct?"

"Well, no, that's not—I wouldn't put it that—"

"I would. And so will our readers when I tell them the story."

"You won't do that! Christ, you can't—! Mr. Rourke told you not to! He fired you! Said you wouldn't get a job anywhere in the world! I knew that would happen, you know. He liked you best, but I knew I'd outlast you because I know him better than you. Better than anyone. Now look; we can work together. I'll talk to him—there's a technique to it—and he won't stand in your way when you look for another job. I can even promise a reference . . . *if* you give me that tape. Now. Then I'll take care of things upstairs and you'll find a job in no time . . . you've made a nice reputation for yourself. I hear about you wherever I go; people talk about you . . ."

Matt contemplated him. "Last year you gave me a stack of reports to use in our series on land use. Where are they?"

"On file. In Santa Fe; the state legislature."

"I'll ask it once more, since you're having trouble. There's a stack of reports, including one on resettlement help for the people of Nuevo. Where are the originals, and where are the copies?"

"I don't know."

"Goddam it, do we have to go through this farce every time

I ask a question? Stop this bullshit or I'll give in to my worst instincts and beat the hell out of you." The thought flashed through Matt's mind that the real farce was that he had never struck anyone in his life and doubted that he'd have the stomach to beat the hell out of anyone, even Chet. *"I want those reports. Where are they?"*

Chet sat still for a moment, his face blank, his eyes glazed, then shrugged one more time. "It's not my fault," he mumbled. As if he were sleepwalking, he moved to one of the black file cabinets, unlocked a drawer, and pulled out a folder. He began to leaf through the papers inside it.

"Don't bother," Matt said, lifting the folder from his hands. "I'm interested in all of it."

"Look." Chet's shoulders slumped; his voice was dull. "Nobody's supposed to see that stuff; it's my job to keep it safe. You're creating a situation I can't handle. Let's be reasonable. What about my offer to speak up for you with Mr. Rourke? This is your future we're talking about! You want to protect it, don't you? I'm not asking much. Go ahead and read that stuff—I can't stop you—read it here and give it back, and give me the tape—you've got to give me the tape!—and then I'll go to Mr. Rourke and get him to change his mind about you; I promise I can deliver on that!"

There was another knock at the door. "Cleaning!" the woman's voice cried. She opened the door and peered around it. "I'm sorry, sirs, but we get in trouble if we miss an office, and we have the other floors to do—"

"It's all right," Matt said. "We're finished."

"We're not!" Chet cried. "Goddammit, Matt! Those papers! The tape—!"

"They're safe," Matt said shortly. "I hope I won't have to tell anyone about the tape. It will help if you don't tell Rourke I have the papers. Take heart, Chet; I'm more trustworthy than you are."

"Nobody is!" Chet scurried into the hallway behind Matt as the cleaning woman went into his office. "Nobody's trustworthy; you know that! Matt, goddammit, if he ever finds out—"

557

"Yes, that would be a problem, wouldn't it?" He looked with contempt at Chet's bulging eyes, thinking how amazingly consistent it was that rats never had the guts to face their own tricks turned against them. "You were the one who wanted to be reasonable and make a deal, Chet. I'm making one. I don't want Rourke to know I've taken anything from the office. It's in your interest not to tell him. I'm aware that it's hard for you, after twenty years of getting dirt on other people, to know that someone has something on you, but you'll get used to it. And after a while I may give serious thought, again, to returning your tape."

With a few long strides he reached his office, where he picked up his briefcase and the cardboard box heavy with files and memorabilia. When he returned, Chet had not moved. "You'll be all right, Chet. And if you cooperate, you may even do some good for once, even if it's against your better judgement."

He walked to the elevator a few feet away and pressed the call button. "You'll be hearing from me."

And then, as the vacuum cleaner started up again, the elevator arrived and he stepped in. His last sight before the doors closed was of Chet, eyes wide and staring in the empty reception room, with the whine of the vacuum cleaner filling the air.

In the study in his apartment, he opened the folder and fanned the papers on the desk, like playing cards. He recognized the reports Chet had given him—saying they'd come from the legislature in Santa Fe—on job opportunities created by the Nuevo Dam and State Park, tourism and increased business in the entire valley, flood control, irrigation, and a reservoir for future water needs. He'd only skimmed them the first time; ten different projects were included in the series on land use and there'd been no reason, or time, to study all of them closely before passing them along to the editor who was writing the series. This was the first time Matt really had looked at how the Nuevo Dam got approved.

And how the people were compensated. He found the report

headed "Compensation and Resettlement" and pulled it out. And with it came another, just beneath, with the same title: a draft version of the resettlement report peppered with typing errors, phrases crossed out and rewritten in Chet's precise handwriting, penciled comments in the margins, three versions of a resettlement budget scribbled across the bottom of the second page, a note at the top of the third page saying "Check time schedule with Bent," and, at the end, the notation, "Mallard Typing Service," with a telephone number.

The little bastard wrote it himself. Typed it himself, edited it, then sent it out of the office for final typing.

And brought it to me with other reports supposedly from the New Mexico state legislature, as research background for our series on development.

Research.

How many of the "research" documents we used in that series were written fifty feet from my office?

His telephone rang and he picked it up, "Yes," he said absently, looking at the report before him.

"It's Elizabeth."

Caught by the iciness of her voice, he looked up from his desk, at the starlit sky behind his windows. "How are you? I was going to call you later to—"

"Were you. I can't imagine why. You couldn't possibly want to hear anything I have to say; it might interfere with your faith in that simple-minded smear you published."

"I published? Elizabeth, you can't believe I had anything to do with that garbage?"

"Of course I believe it. What did you think I'd believe? That your minions are running the Rourke papers themselves? That they'd try to destroy the reputation of their publisher's wife on their own? That they're slipping stories into your papers behind your back?"

"Artner did that once before, if you recall."

"Yes, Saul made the same point. And I told him I couldn't believe that you'd let Artner, of all people, work without supervision after he'd pulled that trick once. You don't need two lessons, Matt; you've always learned very quickly from one.

I hope I can do the same. I don't want your explanations or excuses; I can't think of anything you could say that would soften what you did. It was so destructive I couldn't believe you'd do it to anyone, much less to me. It had only one purpose: to make me seem venal and unreliable, and it worked; Markham has stopped syndicating 'Private Affairs'—"

"Oh, my God."

"You can't be surprised; you're an expert on the power of the press—your power with your press, to get what you want. And you want progress, don't you? I read your series on land use—someone else wrote it but it was in all your papers, so the direction came from you; I do remember how you work. Bigger and better resorts, ski areas, timbering, mining—and the hell with the people."

"I never said that or felt it; I always—"

"When did that series mention the people who live in all those areas you want to develop? Once in a while there were a few words about compensation; that was it. The rest was progress, and the people be damned. And your family, too, for that matter"—he heard her voice tighten—"there are things happening here because of what you've done, what I've done—"

"What? What's happening? No one's called me—"

"Because you're not part of it anymore. I shouldn't have said anything; it just came out; it shouldn't have. You left me with this family and I'm dealing with it. You don't care enough; you haven't talked to me about your work or anything personal for months. And the one favor I asked you got ignored, because you'd lied. You said you had a report on helping the people of Nuevo and you'd send it to me. In December. This is the end of March and I still haven't—"

"I couldn't find it. I have it now—"

"Do you? How convenient. It doesn't matter anymore. All you care about is having the power to change the shape of the land and push your privately chosen people into office to run it, and you'll do anything to get what you want. You and Keegan. I said that once before, didn't I? You make a good pair. Like a married couple. Like partners in crime. I haven't—"

"That's enough, damn it, be quiet and listen to—"

"If you interrupt again I'll hang up. I haven't liked what you've been doing for a long time, but I kept thinking one of these days we'd talk about it. Maybe I still thought you'd go back to the way you used to be. I don't anymore. If you can watch Cal Artner drag my name through the mud to turn the legislature against Isabel—that worked too, by the way; you'll be delighted to hear her bill is dead—then you're capable of anything and I don't want to have anything more to do with you. I'm filing for divorce next week. You're hearing it from me instead of reading it in Polly's column, not because I'm doing you a courtesy, but because I had to tell you how I felt and I've been calling you for a week, trying to reach you. I understand you were sailing. I hope it was pleasant; I assume you'll be rich and powerful enough to do much more of it in the future."

"God damn it—!"

"I told you I'd hang up, Matt. It seems I've passed the boundaries of whatever courteous behavior my parents taught me. You'll hear from my lawyer."

The phone went dead in his hand.

Matt slammed it down. She might have asked him what he knew about the story, what he thought about it, what he was going to do about it, what he—

But why should she? She'd told him what she thought: the story appeared on the front page of one of Matt Lovell's papers and Matt Lovell runs his empire with a firm hand. It would never occur to her that he ran it at the whim of Keegan Rourke.

I would have told her the whole damn story if she'd calmed down long enough to listen. She would have understood: she had Chet pegged from the beginning.

But maybe she wouldn't have understood—or taken the trouble to try. The Elizabeth who had just hung up on him was an Elizabeth he had never known: more assertive, less pliable, not as warm.

But I can't expect . . . how the hell could I expect her to

561

be warm and pliable, when she thinks I did my damndest to ruin her?

We keep going around in circles, he thought; we don't learn about each other. He'd watched her on a dozen or more talk shows, steadfastly refusing to discuss her sudden unexplained departure from "Anthony," and he'd wanted to ask her about it, and whether it included leaving Tony Rourke. He'd wanted to tell her about Rourke's ownership of Nuevo and the faked report lying on his desk and his resignation from Rourke's company. *No longer a power at the press. No longer a power anywhere.*

He reached for the telephone. He'd call her back and tell her she had to listen to him. He wanted to know what she meant about "things happening at home." He wanted her to understand that he intended to write a retraction of Artner's story, with the truth about Nuevo, and publish it, if only in the *Chieftain*.

And what else? Do I want her to divorce me?

In the silence, he heard the sound of a key, and his front door opening. Nicole. Damn, he'd forgotten to phone her. "Matt?" she called. "In the study," he answered, and stood up. Maybe it was a good thing she'd decided to show up; he could use some comforting, and he probably wouldn't have asked for it on his own.

"Darling, I was worried," she said, brushing his lips with hers. "When you didn't call I thought you and Keegan must be at each other's throats. I could see headlines: POWER BARONS FOUND BLOODY BUT UNBOWED. What happened?"

"One of us bowed," he said with a short laugh. Putting his arms around her, he pulled her close and kissed her, holding her mouth beneath his with an intensity that he knew was not passion but a search for reassurance. He raised his head and took in with a grateful look the perfection of her face; her cool, amber eyes with a shadow of anxiety; the black halo of her hair above a white wool suit and black silk blouse open at the top to reveal her smooth skin and choker of jet and pearls. "Come and sit with me; I need a beautiful woman to tell me I'm better than I think I am and that I have a brilliant future."

"You know that already, darling." She went to the kitchen and found a bottle of vodka in the refrigerator. Dropping a curl of lemon zest and an ice cube in each of two glasses, she called out, "Have you had dinner?"

"No. I'm not hungry."

"You need something besides vodka or you'll pass out and that would make our bedtime extremely boring. Are there any leftovers? Or shall I send out for something?"

"Nothing. Damn it, Nicole, come sit with me. I need to talk."

"That must have been quite a meeting," she said lightly. He had moved to the living room and she sat beside him on the couch and handed him a glass. "Give me the details later; just tell me how it ended."

"I resigned."

"My God, you didn't! You couldn't! Matt, that's a terrible joke! Now tell me the truth."

"That is the truth." He drained his glass and went to the kitchen to get the bottle she had left on the counter. "Why did you say I couldn't do it?"

"Because you'd never do anything to destroy your future; you're the kind of man who'll do whatever you have to do to get to the top by the shortest route in the fastest time. That's why I love you. Now will you please stop playing this silly game? Are you testing me, to see if I'll still love you? Whatever you're doing, I don't find it amusing, and I'd appreciate it if you'd get serious and tell me what you and Keegan talked about."

He gazed at her thoughtfully. "You'd rather not know."

"Nonsense, I have to know! I want to know everything you do—it makes me part of you! Don't you like it at the end of the day when you come to me and talk about everything that happened? And I listen and ask the right questions *and give you support!* I thought you liked that. I work at it, you know. Being what you need."

"Yes." He was still scrutinizing her. "And I do like it. But right now I'm not sure whether you do it for me or for yourself."

"Oh, Matt, of course I do it for you!" She took off her suit jacket and leaned back, crossing her legs. Her breasts were outlined beneath the sheer silk of the blouse. "What would you like me to say, to convince you?"

"I want you to tell me whatever I do is all right; that it doesn't matter whether I'm publisher of Rourke Publishing or editor of the *Chieftain* or a reporter on the *Los Angeles Times*— you'll still feel the same way about me and be at my side, pouring vodka and showing off your figure . . . even telling me I'm a great success."

"Don't be silly, darling, you wouldn't be a great success if you were a reporter or just an editor. You wouldn't want me to lie. The man I love isn't content to be third rate; he has to be first." She gave him a small smile. "Matt, you're making me worry. Tell me you didn't resign."

"I can't do that," he said quietly.

The smile faded. "You really did it."

"Yes."

"You're a fool."

"You and Rourke agree on that. Is that all you have to say?"

"Go back to him. Tell him you made a mistake but you've thought it over and there's no reason for both of you to throw away everything you've built—and a whole future—just because you got upset and lost your head. He'll understand; he knows people get emotional and can't keep things in perspective—"

"That's another of Rourke's favorite words. Damn it, Nicole, I don't need you here to repeat Rourke's arguments; I need you to give me some support. This isn't easy for me; I've got an investment of time and energy in that company, and a sense of accomplishment and a future with no limits—I thought there were no limits, until tonight—and now I have to pick up the pieces and figure out what I'm going to do next, and I want you to help me do it."

"Why should I? I liked the way things were. We were having such a nice time! Eight months, Matt, that's a long time for me to stay with a man. We have good times together, you told me yourself I'm a perfect hostess for you, and we have a lovely time in bed. And I've watched you fit into Keegan's group;

I've watched you make them respect you and listen to you . . . poor Chet's so jealous, worried about you and Keegan being so close—that alone should tell you how far you've come! It was all there for you; all you had to do was keep on the way you were and nothing could stop you! You and Keegan were a team! There was nothing the two of you couldn't have done! Everything was perfect! Why do you have to go and ruin it?"

"Everything wasn't perfect. He wanted a front man to run his newspaper chain the way he wanted people like Ballenger to buy land while he stays in the background, pulling strings. But I won't—"

"*Terry* Ballenger?"

"It doesn't matter. I won't be his puppet; can't you understand that? If I'm publisher of one newspaper or twenty or a hundred, I have to be able to run them in my own way. That was my dream; not sitting in a luxurious office looking important while decisions on what goes in them, or what doesn't, are made upstairs, in Rourke's office."

"What difference does it make? The rewards are enormous! You can't just throw them away because you don't agree with Keegan on something as unimportant as how you define publisher!"

"Unimportant!"

"Damn it, of course it is! In the long run you'll be in charge of your papers: Keegan's almost seventy, Matt; one of these days he'll start turning things over to you—if he trusts you. And meanwhile you've got influence and wealth and recognition . . . my God, how can you even talk about being a puppet when you have those! So you don't make every little decision; so what? It's ridiculous that you ever thought you could. Keegan has to have final authority; it's his company. You've always known he gave you the newspapers; he can take them away—"

"So he told me. Do you two get together periodically to run through your lines?"

"That's not funny. Of course we don't."

Matt gave her a long look. "Of course you do. The two of you discuss everything, don't you? Including me."

"We're friends, Matt. You've known that from the beginning. We talk about anything that interests us."

"Including me."

"Matt, he's very fond of you! He needs you! Go back to him! Don't throw everything away!"

He stood up and paced to the windows, then to the door of his study where the papers were spread out on the desk. He wondered if Nicole knew about them. It didn't seem to matter anymore. He turned and looked at her across the room. "Let me ask you the same: don't throw everything away. You were right about our time together; we've had eight good months. Why don't we have eight more? Wherever I am, you'd still be my hostess, we'd still have good times together, we'd still have lovely times in bed. Why not, Nicole?"

"Because that isn't what I want! I can't do it! Oh, damn it, damn it, can't you understand?" She was sitting straight now, head back, eyes blazing. "Couldn't you be satisfied with what you had? You had more than most men ever dream of, much less get close to! Why couldn't you be content and protect what you have instead of throwing it away? And on top of it, ask me to wander around with you while you look for a job . . . Damn it, Matt, we could have been so happy! And now we can't, we won't, and damn you to hell for that!"

She waited, but he was silent, watching her from the doorway of his study.

"I can't go with you!" she cried. "I can't! How many times do I have to say it! I need a man who's already powerful! I thought you understood that. Matt, don't you see, I don't feel *real* unless I'm with a man everybody knows! I'm afraid there isn't any *me* unless I'm connected to somebody who opens doors and people clear a path for. Can't you see that?"

Her hand was trembling and the ice cubes shook in her glass as she drank, tilting back her head. "Some people *do* things—my God, I've kept track of what Elizabeth has done and I can't believe it! She writes and she's so damned good, and she was marvelous on television, much better than Tony, and she's got

566

children, and I suppose friends—women friends—and she's always doing something that makes her Elizabeth Lovell! By herself, without anyone else! *I can't do that!* I can't do anything but be a perfect companion!"

"That's not easy to be," Matt said gently. She had never been so exposed and vulnerable and he wanted to take her in his arms and comfort her and tell her she was beautiful . . . but of course she knew that and she'd already said it wasn't enough. "And you're leaving out the homes and offices you decorate."

"I dabble in it. I can't do it alone; I get advice from experts. I never told you that, but it's true. I don't need the money— I know Keegan told you about how well my family has done and how I don't have to worry—and that's why I could devote myself to you and make it easier for you to be everything a man should be. You see, Matt, I could never be a sweet little woman for a man who's struggling. I could never cook whole- some dinners for him and work at making him feel big even though he's a little cog working for some corporate mogul. I can't help it; that's the way I am. But it was lovely with you because I do care for you—you're a nice man and that's rather charming and rare—and we do have good times, in bed and out . . . Matt, I don't want to lose you. Please, please go back to Keegan, be somebody again, stay with him, stay with me."

Be somebody again. Matt's gaze went past Nicole to the wall of windows, with the lights of Houston stretching below. A memory came to him: Elizabeth, laughing into his eyes in a noisy room. *The women are all wondering where they can find a husband like mine.*

She'd said it in Aspen, he remembered. When he was a small-town publisher of one paper. No, two; that trip was to celebrate their purchase of the Alameda *Sun.* But another time, when they'd bought the *Chieftain* and toured it for the first time, she'd pointed to the corner office and said, *It's yours, Matt. Publisher and editor-in-chief.* And she'd said it with pride.

"Matt?" Nicole asked. "Tell me what you're thinking."

"I was wondering what it means to 'be somebody again.' What am I now?"

"Powerless. When it comes to shaping the world, you're nobody."

He thought about it. "There are so many worlds to shape," he said at last. "Of course some are bigger and noisier than others, but what if that really doesn't make any difference? Maybe the only important thing is being visible in our own world, whatever its size."

"I don't believe that. And you don't either; I know you better than that. Those little worlds are like the ones Elizabeth writes about; nobody pays any attention to them; the people in them live and die and get trampled by men like Keegan Rourke. And Keegan's big world—and yours, too, Matt, if you have any sense!—never knows the difference. When she writes about those people, they're real for a minute and then they're gone. The newspaper wraps the garbage and that's all. Nothing is left. But what you were doing—! You were creating something that will last! Matt, you got angry and you lost sight of what's at stake. Think about it tonight, that's all I ask. Then tomorrow you can call Keegan—"

"Do you think *he's* thinking about it tonight? And deciding to call me tomorrow to tell me I can run my—those papers without interference?"

"That's not his style, Matt; you know that as well as I do. Good Lord, can't you admit that he *owns* those papers and that means you aren't equal? You work for him!" She poured vodka into her glass. "Do you want some more?"

"No, I've had enough."

She looked at him as she drank. "You know how much he admires you; he gives you more leeway than most people he hires. He thinks of you as his son; you're the one he wants to take his place eventually, no one else. How many men have a mentor like Keegan Rourke? Matt, *think!* You've got to take what he can offer; you'll never have a chance like it again!"

"He thought of me as his son, once; that only made it easier for him to think of me as his puppet. That's the trade-off, Nicole, and there's nothing I'd take—"

"Nonsense. Everyone has a price; it's just a matter of finding out what drives them."

It struck Matt like a blow. "Another line of Keegan's. He's taught you well." He walked to the couch and picked up her suit jacket. "Forgive me, Nicole. I can't be what you want. There isn't anything I can do for you."

She stared up at him. "You're telling me to leave?"

"I'm asking you to leave. I want to make a telephone call and then I have a great deal of work to do."

"I can't believe you're doing this. I'm trying to help you— you said you wanted help—"

"I said I wanted comfort and support. We don't agree on what that means."

"If you would listen to me—!"

"I listened to you. I'd like to help you feel better about yourself, but I can't—"

"Feel better about myself! That sounds dangerously close to pity, Matt. And I do not need pity. I do what I want; I'm close to some of the most powerful men in the world; and I do not need pity!"

"Then I'll keep my feelings to myself. But I can't help you, any more, it seems, than you can help me. I wish we could end this with some affection—"

"It's all right, Matt; don't overdo your solicitude. I'm quite able to find affection when I want it." Deliberately, she finished her drink, set the empty glass on the table, and stood. "You'll miss me."

"Yes, I think I might. But it won't change anything." He put his arm around her shoulders, she allowed it to rest there briefly, then turned her back, waiting, and when he held her jacket she slipped it on.

They walked toward the door together; halfway there, she stopped, opened her purse, and pulled out a key on a small ring. "You'll need this for the little woman who cooks your wholesome dinners."

He felt again the desire to comfort her in her vulnerability, and put his hand on hers. But she snatched it away.

"I'm not usually this wrong," she said coldly. "But you

fooled us all. Shrewd, ambitious, aggressive Matt Lovell, or so we thought. Instead, you're short-sighted, narrow-minded, self-destructive . . . My God, what you are giving up! No one will believe it!"

"They'll believe what they want, no matter what they hear." Matt kissed her briefly. "I wish you good fortune, Nicole."

Her eyes glistened; the first time Matt had ever seen her even close to tears. "Matt, call him! Call him tomorrow! He'll understand . . . he'll take you back!"

Matt shook his head and opened the door. "Good night, Nicole."

"I'm thinking of what's best for you!"

He smiled faintly. "If you were, my dear, it would be out of character."

Her tears were gone; the amber of her eyes was cool as she studied him for some last sign that he was wavering. Then she gave the tiniest of shrugs and walked down the short hallway to the elevator. She turned to him as it arrived and the mahogany doors slid noiselessly open. "If you call him, call me right afterward. I'll wait for a little while. Not long, but for a little while."

"Goodbye, Nicole," he said, and in another moment he was alone, gazing at the smooth mahogany surface of the elevator doors.

When he returned to his study, he turned off the light and sat in the darkness. Leaning back in his chair, feet crossed on the window sill, he gazed out the window at the panorama some thirty stories below. Houston: a network of tiny blazing lights, dark patches that were parks and neighborhoods, highways like great desert snakes flung across the sprawling city. In the distance, its windows lit against the star-studded sky, the black Transco Building stood alone, looking across the city at Matt's white, balconied apartment building. His two towers, he thought. Beacons of home and work. Symbols of power, symbols of the huge exciting dream that had beckoned all his life, until Rourke offered to make it come true. Now he'd lost it. He'd left his wife and family behind in the pursuit of it and now all of them, and the dream as well, were gone.

But the longer Matt contemplated it, the smaller the Transco Building looked, like a toy tower in a miniaturized town. And he knew his own imposing building looked as small and fragile from the Transco Building. And the city itself, though he knew it to be a restless and energetic place where fortunes were made and failure was larger than life, looked from his windows like a scale model, wired and motorized to convince skeptics that it was alive: a place where dreams came true.

Images, he thought. Nicole had wanted images. As long as she clung to the arm of a powerful man, or dressed for one or slept with one, she could look in a mirror and believe she was powerful. And real. Whatever was the reality of Nicole Renard, whatever substance she had, she couldn't trust it: she was too afraid of the dark beyond the spotlight that followed dominant, powerful men.

And what about Matt Lovell? he asked himself silently. He'd thought he was fulfilling his own dream, after so many years . . . but all he'd done was replace one father with another: building Rourke's dream instead of Zachary's. He'd thought he finally had everything, and it turned out he'd had only images. A woman whose reality came from someone else. A job with someone else pulling the strings. Newspaper stories written from faked reports. Friendships as instant and shallow as conversations on a chairlift.

I've been chasing mirages all this time.

In the city below, tiny cars scurried around the 610 Loop and its branches, whipping around each other to pick up a few seconds here or there. He'd been one of them. He remembered that urgency, like a disease gnawing his insides, making him feel he had to go faster and farther, pushing aside anyone who seemed to be in his way. But something had happened to it. It had shrunk. It wasn't overwhelming anymore. It no longer drove him.

Sour grapes, he thought with a smile. Maybe I'm just disappointed at not having what I thought I had, so I tell myself it no longer seems important. Or maybe I'm angry at myself for being fooled by image and mirages. Or maybe I'm sorry. Maybe I think that if I'd taken everything a little slower over the past three years, and looked around, I would have seen what was happening—and maybe salvaged something from it, instead of being left with nothing.

He sat without moving for a long time; he didn't look at his watch. But at last he began to think of all he had to do, and he swiveled and faced his desk. The first step was learning the truth about Nuevo; the second was writing it and publishing it in a way that would clear Elizabeth's name. But it had been a long time since he rolled up his sleeves and plunged into investigative journalism; a long time since he got down to the real work of newspapering. He didn't want to do it alone: he needed a friend.

And he had a friend. Maybe. If he could get in his explanation a lot faster than he had with Elizabeth. He turned on his green-shaded desk lamp, picked up his telephone, and dialed Saul Milgrim's number, at home.

CHAPTER 18

"**Y**ou son of a bitch," Saul growled into the telephone. "Whatever you're looking for, I don't have it; you picked the wrong—"

"Who's somebody named Bent?"

"What?"

"Bent. Possibly in Houston; more likely in New Mexico. Does it ring a bell?"

Saul struggled between curiosity and outrage. Curiosity won. "Why do you want to know?"

"Chet Colfax wrote the name Bent in the margin of a faked report on Nuevo; I'm assuming whoever he is, he knows about it, possibly even helped write it."

"Faked? Which report?"

"Resettlement help. I just got hold of a draft version and the final one."

"I'll be damned." After a pause, Saul said, "There's a Thaddeus Bent in the New Mexico legislature. Chairman of the State Committee on Land Use and Recreation."

"The one that recommended funding the dam?"

"The very one." He paused again, long enough for his simmering anger to surface. "Listen, you bastard, you've probably found what I've been scrounging for and I'd give almost anything to see it, but I can't work with you. I have a friend, and you've fucked up her life—"

"Wait a minute; I want to talk about that and don't hang up on me! That's what Elizabeth did, and God damn it, at least listen for thirty seconds! I didn't know Artner worked for the *Daily News;* I had nothing to do with that rotten story; the first I knew of it was an AP report that I read in Florida; I'm going to write my own version of it when I get the real story; and I resigned from Rourke's outfit this afternoon."

Saul dropped into his desk chair. "Resigned. Why?"

"What the hell difference does it make why I resigned? I'm not there anymore. I'm working on a story. I need help in getting information so I can write it. What else do you need to know?"

"Need? Nothing. Am I curious? You're damned right." He began to draw stick figures on a pad of paper. "Who's going to publish the story when you've finished it?"

"You are."

He grinned. "If I like it."

"If you do the research at that end, I'll make it a double byline. We've never written a story together."

"It's a possibility. And then what are you going to do?"

"I don't know. There are newspaper chains all over the country . . . magazines . . . I have to look around. I don't know what I want."

"Did you, with Rourke?"

"I thought I did. It's a long story and I'll tell you some time if you want to hear it, but not on the phone and not now. Saul, I'm asking for your help."

Saul drew a stick figure hanging from a gallows. "No close friends in Houston to help?"

There was the briefest hesitation. "I don't owe you any explanations; I wish to hell you'd stop passing judgment on things you don't understand."

"I understand everything I need to."

"You don't, but I don't give a damn. I want to write a story that will help Elizabeth; if you're really her friend, you'll work with me."

"You're doing it for Elizabeth?"

"Damn it, why else would I do it?"

"Maybe you want to make a name as an investigative reporter. How the hell do I know why you want to write it? You haven't been doing a whole lot of favors for Elizabeth in the last year. Have you talked to Holly recently?"

"No. I'll be calling her tomorrow, and Peter, too."

"She's stopped singing."

"She's what? Stopped? Why, for God's sake?"

"I don't know. I suppose her mother does, but we don't. She withdrew from the senior musical and she stopped her voice lessons."

"I'm going to call her now. I'll call you back after I've talked to her."

"She's not here; Elizabeth took her to Denver for the weekend. Anyway, why bother? Damn it, Matt, stop fucking around; either be a part of that family or disappear. It may not be my place to say it—"

"It's not."

Saul was silent, angry and frustrated. *God damn it, who else is there, besides Spencer and Lydia? And they won't tackle Matt; afraid they'll make things worse. But there are limits to what a friend can do, and maybe I've reached them.* "You may be right," he said. He drew a guillotine and a stick figure with its neck beneath the descending blade. "Okay, I'll work on the story with you. To help Elizabeth." *And because the damn thing has been driving me crazy since I first heard about it and this may be my only chance to find out what the hell has been going on.* "Tell me about the resettlement report. Who faked it? Was it the only one? I saw the others, on jobs and all the rest, and they looked okay to me."

"I don't know about them, yet. When will Elizabeth and Holly be back?"

"Sunday night or Monday morning. I'll tell Elizabeth you called. Now are we going to get to work?"

"Yes. Thanks. First let me tell you about my conversation with Chet Colfax—who's been bugging his leader's office by the way—"

"Rourke's office? I'll be damned. Blessed are the weasels, for they shall use tape recorders to cover their asses."

Matt chuckled. "My God, I've missed talking to you."

"A pity Houston has no telephones. Otherwise you could have called me any time."

There was a pause. "I was talking about Chet, wasn't I?" Matt said evenly. "But maybe I'll start somewhere else, with a small revelation. Do you know who owns ninety-eight percent of Nuevo?"

"Ballenger. And his company. And unknown backers. I checked on him; he couldn't afford to do it on his own, but I couldn't get the names of—"

"Keegan Rourke."

Saul sat very still. "I will be goddamned," he said softly. "Very, very neat. First he buys the newspapers, then the valley, then the resort. And does he also buy the legislature? To make sure it all goes through without a hitch?"

"It's the kind of thing a thorough man would do. Will you check on Thaddeus Bent? And any others who might have been on the take? I'd look for PAC contributions, trips to Europe, college scholarships for offspring—you know how to look for them. First, let me give you the gist of my talk with Chet; I'll send the rest in a letter. And I want to know what else you got from the scrounging you said you'd been doing."

Heather passed the open door and glanced in. Saul must be talking to one of the reporters, she thought; his voice was intense and involved, as it only was when he talked to a colleague about an investigative story. And the way he was scribbling notes meant it was a big one. Saul looked up and met her eyes. "Matt," he said, his hand over the mouthpiece. "He left Rourke. We're doing a story on Nuevo; it should help Elizabeth." And he returned to his conversation.

Stunned, Heather walked to the desk. "Is he coming back?"

Writing, Saul shook his head.

"Why not?"

But Saul was hunched over, talking. Heather picked up the page of stick figures he had torn off to make his notes. They're all getting clobbered, she thought. Are Saul and Matt going to

576

clobber someone? Or we're going to get clobbered—Saul and I—if Matt does come back and takes our newspaper away from us.

She smiled ruefully. *Our newspaper.* She was as bad as Saul; loving the paper, wanting to help him run it forever. She looked down at her trim waist. Somewhere beneath that flat, girl's stomach, a baby had begun. If she could have all her wishes, the first would be that by the time the baby was born she and Saul would own the *Chieftain*. Then she would have put all the pieces of herself together: Heather Farrell Milgrim: wife of Saul Milgrim; mother of Jacqueline or Stephen—both, if she were lucky enough to have one of each; associate publisher of the *Chieftain;* friend of Elizabeth, Isabel, Lydia, Spencer, Holly, Maya, Peter, the staff of the newspaper, especially Barney Kell, who treated her like a favorite daughter . . .

I'm content, she thought. I know how much I have and it's more—and more wonderful—than I ever dreamed.

"My God, he's changed," said Saul, hanging up. "His voice was melancholy. Honest-to-God, genuine, fourteen-carat disillusionment. Think of that. The great awakening."

"Will he come back?" Heather asked.

"Depends on the stars in his eyes. He's talking about looking for other newspapers, maybe magazines . . . says he doesn't know what he wants. It depends on how much he needs the fast life, or what he and Elizabeth do, or what his lady wants. I gave him a chance to say he wasn't good friends with her anymore, but he passed. I'll tell you what I think: you and I shouldn't speculate on it. We could grow old and feeble analyzing a future that may never come. He says Elizabeth is going to divorce him."

"Since when?"

"Tonight. He talked to her before he called me. She didn't give him a chance to say a word; just told him he was a little lower and more untrustworthy than a viper and she was divorcing him. I told him it was high time she did."

Saul pulled her to his lap. "I remember when I was eaten up with envy for what those two had together. Now look at me: is any man more fortunate? But what can we do for Eliz-

577

abeth? Can we find her a scintillating, handsome, wise, passionate man for companionship?"

Heather kissed him. "I only know two. One I was smart enough to marry; the other isn't really wise, or he'd be here, instead of Houston. But I'll keep looking. What are you going to do for Matt?"

"Blow the lid off Thaddeus Bent. And I'm going to ask Elizabeth to help. She knows Bent; she wrote the story of his son's wedding when she was a reporter on the *Examiner,* and she did a 'Private Affairs' column on his daughter-in-law a while back. I want her in on this anyway; if we do blow it open, it'll show why Artner wrote that smear, and she ought to be part of that. She deserves it, don't you think? I'm going to call her in Denver; do you want to pick up the extension and join the conversation?"

"Yes," said Heather. "I want to be in on it, too."

Four years earlier, Elizabeth had danced with Thaddeus Bent at his son's wedding. She had been remembering her own wedding that day, thinking about the passage of sixteen years, and Bent had gallantly told her she was too lovely to work as he held her carefully and led her through one dance. Since then, she had seen him occasionally as his public appearances became more frequent; it was common knowledge that he was chafing to get out of the state legislature and into what he called the big time.

Elizabeth had written about Bent's daughter-in-law, using pseudonyms, in a "Private Affairs" story about what it was like to live with politicians and be the only family member who had no political ambitions of her own.

"She was very discreet about Bent," Elizabeth told Saul as they walked through the statehouse corridors on Monday morning. "But she did say he was traveling a lot and having meetings at home on weekends. Probably looking for campaign funds."

Saul nodded. "He leaks tidbits of information every few weeks. Did you call Matt this morning?"

"No."

"And you don't want to talk about him?"

578

"No. Saul, even if he told the truth about Artner's story, and leaving Keegan, he's still off on his own journey and we're not part of it. I did think about what you and Heather said, but I don't want to call him. If he wants company in his job hunting, he has Nicole. If he wants to talk to me, he knows where I am."

She stopped before a closed door. "Here's Bent's office. Listen, dear, dear Saul; I love you and Heather, and I love having you worry about me, but I have a few things to take care of right now and that's what I'm thinking about. What Matt does is his business; I can't wait for him, or anyone else. I want to clear my name and get back my contract with Markham—which means I have to find out what was behind Artner's story—and I want to spend as much time with Holly as I can before she leaves for college. That's even more important. She's had some troubles and for the first time in years we're close enough to talk about them."

"About why she's not sing—" Saul broke off.

"Thank you for not asking," Elizabeth said. "I can't talk about it right now. And," she went on, "I want to help Isabel and the others in Nuevo; if there's some way, from this meeting with Bent, or anything else, that we can get that town rebuilt on higher ground, I'm going to do what I can to help make it happen. That's a full schedule; I can't be bothered by Matt right now. If he's having troubles, I'm sorry, but they're his troubles, not mine. He went to Keegan with his eyes wide open and I assume he'll keep them open when he deals with whatever happened between them. I haven't got time to weep for him." With her hand on the doorknob, she said, "Is there anything else we should talk about before I go into my act in there?"

"Not a thing. Can I say *bravo* to a very special speech by a very special lady? I'm proud to be your friend and your colleague. Now I'm going into that office and watch you take care of our would-be senator. Who probably takes bribes. Maybe we ought to work for his election: at least then he'd move to Washington. Ready?"

"Saul."

"What?"

579

"Just a minute. I have to think about something."

"Okay. Can you share it?"

"Not yet." Elizabeth leaned against the door and gazed unseeingly down the corridor, remembering Holly's low voice as she sat in her mother's lap. *He was going to move to New Mexico—something else for us to share, he said—and then he'd move to Washington when he got elected, and he'd meet important people and make me famous.* The words repeated themselves. "Tony Rourke thinks he's going to be a senator from New Mexico," she said to Saul.

"I beg your pardon?"

"Don't ask me how I know, but he's planning to establish residency here and run for the senate, probably in a few years, probably about the same time—"

"—Thaddeus Bent will be running. My God, what a choice. Bent or Tony. I may relocate." He looked at Elizabeth. "You think you can use it in there?"

"I don't know yet. But it's always nice to have bombshells handy; it's wonderful how they liven up an interview. All right, I'm ready."

"I can't wait," said Saul, and they went in.

Thaddeus Bent had fired his secretary and hired a new one to fit his idea of what a national statesman's secretary should look like: one-third the age and twice as pretty as his former one. Foolish, Elizabeth thought; he just lost a good part of the women's vote. But she smiled pleasantly as the secretary led them into Bent's office and he rose to shake hands. "My dear Elizabeth, it's been such a long time. How lovely you look; as exquisite as the day we danced at my son's wedding . . . I hope you remember that interlude as clearly as I."

Still smiling, Elizabeth nodded. "You know Saul Milgrim."

"I do. A pleasure, sir." Firmly, Bent shook Saul's hand. "Sit down—my secretary will bring us coffee—and tell me what this is about. A newspaper story, you said. I'm glad to see, Elizabeth, that you're still writing and not letting that mean-spirited story get you down. I like spunk in a lady—that is true—and I say, Good for you. So. Are you here about your column?"

580

Elizabeth shook her head. "You're too famous and influential, Thaddeus." She watched him preen, then said, "Once in a while I like to write about people who don't fit 'Private Affairs' and Saul has offered me space in the *Chieftain* for a profile on you. I like to beat the competition, you know, and since it looks like you're about to become one of our most powerful representatives, I want to be the first to do your story."

Bent tried to be indifferent, but he failed. He beamed. "Recognition. It's the name of the game. What can I tell you?"

Elizabeth began with casual questions that became a friendly talk more than an interview as she led him to describe his father's move from Detroit to Sante Fe almost forty-five years earlier, his athletic prowess at Santa Fe High and at college, his part-time jobs and early years as a lawyer, his wife and four children, and his election to the legislature and his chairmanship of the Committee on Land Use and Recreation. As the answers rolled out, Bent leaned back in his chair, enjoying the sound of his voice, and Elizabeth's murmured comments as she took notes; since both of them were concentrating on him, he was having a wonderful time.

Behind Elizabeth, Saul sat perfectly still to avoid breaking the mellow mood, watching as she wove her web. Her soft voice murmured innocuous questions in a rhythm almost hypnotic, and then, so casually Saul almost missed it, she changed her questions from the past to the future. "Of course the U.S. Senate is an awesome place, especially for someone from a small western state . . ."

"No, no! Well, now, awesome. That is true. The Senate of the United States of America. But you're not suggesting that someone from New Mexico, specifically Thaddeus Bent, experienced and respected, can't handle the responsibility."

"I'd never suggest any such thing," Elizabeth said warmly. "You know your way around. I'm sure everyone thinks you'll be a superb senator."

"That is true. They're lining up to help, in fact. Big people, big money. We'll send out the standard campaign letters, of course, and the dollar bills and sawbucks will come drifting in, but that's mainly to know who's going to vote for us. The real money, in the hundreds of thousands, comes from the big men."

"Big men are attracted to big candidates, Thaddeus."

"By God, that's good! Can I use that? Can I put it in my brochures and posters? And speeches?"

"It's yours," Elizabeth said graciously. "My small contribution to your campaign. What about my co-contributors? Are they from New Mexico, too, or have you swept the southwest?"

"Well, now, of course we like to be supported by fellow New Mexicans, but so far the biggest contributor—confidential, now, off the record—is from *California.*"

"I know some political brokers in California," Elizabeth said. "Some of them are notoriously fickle . . ."

"Ah, but not this one! I have his word! You wouldn't know him; he keeps very quiet."

"Could you tell me his name? You're probably right that I don't know him, but if by chance I do, it might be helpful to you. I've spent a lot of time lately in Los Angeles, you know, meeting a few people in television and movie circles . . ."

"Ah. That is true. Well. Ballenger. Terry Ballenger. He is quite big, I am told; in fact, his associate, a Texas businessman, Chester Colfax by name, tells me Ballenger is big in the entire southwest. Very solid, Colfax assures me. And solidly behind Thaddeus Bent."

"Terry Ballenger." Elizabeth frowned slightly to hide the excitement of discovery running through her. "I do know the name. But I don't think he has much money, Thaddeus. He buys land for others. And how can Chet Colfax work with him? He works in Houston."

Bent scowled. "No, no, my information is impeccable. Terry Ballenger bought the whole Nuevo Valley; he's building a resort there; that takes more than a few pennies. And Chester is working with him. You have your facts wrong. But that isn't what we were talking about. We were talking about . . . what were we talking about?"

"Your contributors. Thaddeus, this is confusing. The reason I've heard of Chet Colfax is that he and my husband both work

582

for Rourke Enterprises in Houston. I can't believe Chet didn't tell you that."

"Well. Most likely he mentioned it and it slipped my mind. Rourke Enterprises. Houston. That's Keegan Rourke, isn't it, a very big man. Chester and Rourke . . . well, of course he told me. That's not a small thing, after all."

"But there are still some things I don't understand, Thaddeus; maybe you can help me. You see, we found out the other day that Chet was the one who ordered that article on me in the Albuquerque *Daily News*. He did it so the legislators wouldn't take my story on Jock Olson seriously—you know the one; it suggested the legislature set aside part of the valley for a new town. The editor has confirmed that Chet ordered Artner to write it and ordered the editor to print it. As you said, it was mean-spirited. Now, if Chet represents Rourke—"

"Now wait! Elizabeth! I have great respect for you, but you have got your facts wrong! That is true! I know the facts and you are wrong! I'd like to go on to another subject and finish the interview quickly. As you know, I am a busy man."

"I do know it, Thaddeus; I don't like to keep you from your work. But I want to have my story correct. I'm in trouble over that *Daily News* story, and I can't take any chances. May I tell you what else I know? Then you can correct me where I've got my facts wrong."

Reluctantly, he nodded. His body had withdrawn into his chair. Besieged, Saul thought.

"Well, then." Elizabeth leafed through her notebook. "This is what I understand so far. Terry Ballenger's company, Ballenger and Associates, bought up most of the land in Nuevo, to build a resort, and he's donating the land along one shore of the future lake for a state park."

"That is true. You have that part right."

"But according to Chet Colfax, Keegan Rourke owns ninety-eight percent of Ballenger and Associates, which means—"

"WHAT? WHAT'S THAT?" Bent was out of his chair, his face working. "Terry owns that company!"

"I don't think so, Thaddeus. We can double-check it—I could be wrong—but I think—"

583

"WELL YOU'D BETTER DOUBLE-CHECK IT, YOUNG LADY!"

"I will," said Elizabeth softly. "But for now, shall I go on with what I've put together?" Without waiting for an answer, she continued, "If Keegan Rourke owns most of Ballenger and Associates, he owns most of Nuevo and he's the one building the resort. So, when Jock Olson suggested a hundred acres be given to the people, and when voters began sending money, and volunteering to help build a new town, Rourke would be concerned that the legislature might do just that: take some of his land, and he'd probably try to convince key legislators to prevent it. He might even try some form of bribery, but of course you would never tolerate that. So what else could he do? He could make me, and my interview of Olson, look bad by having someone on his staff plant a story smearing me. Chet came and planted it. Chet works for Rourke."

"Stop. Just stop a minute." Bent was pacing, his face contorted with a scowl. "Forget all the shit about a story; it doesn't affect me and I don't care about it. All I care about is Chet's promises. He said Terry was behind me; said he'd formed a Political Action Committee—"Land Free for All" it's called—and when the time came they'd take out paid ads, do mailings, arrange transportation for my campaign . . . *I believed him!* Does he have the money to do all that or not?"

"Chet? Or Terry?"

"Terry! Terry! Chet said if I made sure that—" He missed a step in his pacing, caught himself, and went on. "Chet said when the time came, Terry would support me. That is true!"

"If you made sure of what, Thaddeus?"

"Nothing. Some minor matters; nothing to talk about."

"Well, that's surprising," Elizabeth observed. "Terry Ballenger and Keegan Rourke don't usually leave anything to chance. I would have thought they'd have approached you last year about helping along the Nuevo dam. After all, they know how much power you have—everyone does. I imagine you're inundated by people who know how many bills and recommendations you could control if you thought they were good for the state."

"Inundated." Bent frowned, trying to adjust to Elizabeth's swift transition from the present time to a year ago. "That is true."

"It must be difficult. All that pressure . . ."

"Well. It goes with the job; you get used to it. If you know what you're doing, you can handle it."

"But didn't Chet or Ballenger or Rourke know that? I mean, if they didn't ask you for help on Nuevo, years ago when the studies began, and last year when it was voted on, they must not have recognized how much power you have, and what you could do for them."

"Of course they recognized it! You said it yourself: everybody does! I don't know why you'd say that when you know how well-known I am. That was why they came to me in the first place—not to make a deal, I never make deals, a man in my position doesn't make deals—but to discuss how Nuevo would help the state: jobs, tourism, flood control—and how we could get it approved without problems—"

"Or publicity," Elizabeth slipped in quietly.

"Publicity has harmed more worthy projects than you can shake a stick at, Elizabeth. It might have killed this one."

"But you didn't let that happen."

"There are ways," Bent said vaguely. Elizabeth said nothing; she watched him pace, her clear eyes direct, fascinated, unwavering. Bent found the silence excruciating. "If you know your way around, you can get research studies lumped in with other bills, nothing wrong with that, of course, just a method to keep things moving along. Otherwise people slow them up . . . slow them down . . . whatever . . ." He cleared his throat. "So we did all that, but now I ask myself, *How can Terry finance my campaign* if he doesn't have money or even his own company?"

"I don't know, Thaddeus. What do you think?"

Bent pondered it. "Chet was absolutely positive. So he knew the money was there." His face brightened. "Rourke! If you're right, and he owns Ballenger and Associates, then Chet was speaking for him! I don't know why he couldn't just come out and say so, but it's Rourke who's going to support me! That

585

is true! I should have seen it right away. And he is a hell of a lot bigger than Terry!"

Elizabeth looked up curiously. "You're talking about the next election?"

"No, no, too soon. I'm just getting started. The one five years from now. We need to line up money, delegates, endorsements . . . Chet admired me for that: knowing how to bide my time. I'm running for Greene's seat, when he retires."

"But Thaddeus, didn't you know?" Elizabeth hesitated. "I feel terrible. I don't know how to tell you . . ."

Saul held his breath. How nice to have a bombshell, he thought.

Bent's eyes were narrowed. "Tell me what?"

"About Rourke's support," Elizabeth replied. "I'd think if he supported anyone, it would be his son."

"His son?"

"Tony Rourke," Elizabeth said helpfully.

"I know his name! But what the hell are you talking about? His son's on television; he's a big star with his own show; I don't have to tell you that; you were on it. I used to watch you."

"But I'm not on it anymore. It isn't doing well, you see. I was told it's being canceled at the end of the season. Then I understand Tony will move to New Mexico to establish residency . . . Good heavens!" she exclaimed abruptly. "The resort! I didn't think of that! He'll probably run it for a few years, meet all the local politicians, make a name for himself in the state . . . he's an actor; he could do it superbly."

"Canceling?" Bent asked. "Canceling his show?"

"That's what I heard," Elizabeth said. "Of course with television no one ever knows until the last minute, but as far as I know, it's being canceled. And Tony will be ready for a new job."

A heavy silence fell. Saul's foot kept doing a little dance and he kept pulling it back under his chair, telling himself to be calm. Elizabeth sat quietly, head bowed, writing nonsense words on her notepad. Bent leaned against the wall, supporting his suddenly shaky body and fumbling in a pocket for the cigars he used to keep there, before his wife talked him into quitting.

Suddenly, into the silence, his voice burst out. "Goddam son of a bitch!" He took three steps to his desk and rang the intercom for his secretary. "Get me Andrew Greene in Washington. You're wrong!" he roared to Elizabeth. "You'll see! Hear! You'll hear it for yourself!"

He slammed his fist into his palm while he waited. "Never heard a whisper about Rourke," he said to no one in particular. "Hard as hell to keep secrets in politics; he sure knows something I don't."

He turned to Elizabeth. "Where's that husband of yours? Working for Rourke, you said. In Houston? Without you?"

"At the moment," Elizabeth said evenly.

Bent shook his head. "Doesn't sound good. He the only one in the family working for Rourke? You're not?"

"No," she replied.

"Who *are* you working for?"

"Myself, Thaddeus. You may not be interested in Artner's story, but it damaged me and I'm going to do something about it. I'm proud of the work I do and the name I've made for myself and he dragged my work and my reputation through the mud, trying to make me look like something I'm not. And I intend to get the truth out, and my name cleared."

"What truth?" he asked, peering at her.

"I'll tell you when I'm sure of it."

"You're doing it for yourself? You just work for yourself?"

"And the *Chieftain*. And the people of Nuevo. I'd like to see justice done."

"There's no such— They had justice. Compensation. Help in resettlement."

"Of course," Elizabeth said demurely, and waited.

The intercom rang. "About time! Now you listen to this!" Bent switched on the speaker phone and paced as he talked, raising his voice to reach the speaker. "Andy? How are you? Listen, I've got—"

"How've you been, Thaddeus?" Greene's voice, slightly metallic, echoed through the office.

"Fine, just fine, listen, I've got——"

"Good. It's good to talk to you. Been too long. What's new in your part of the world? Cherry blossoms are gone here; too bad you couldn't see them . . ."

"I've got a question! I'm talking to somebody in my office about the election, you know, when you retire, and I said, because I remember this clear as day, I said you gave me your word you'd endorse me and tell the party leadership to back me. Right?"

No answer came from the speaker. The small black box with its black grill seemed to stare at them from a dozen blank eyes.

"Andy? *That's right, isn't it?*"

"Well, now, Thaddeus." The joviality was gone from the metallic voice. "I do recall we talked about it, last year, before the election. But surely you don't think I'd promise an endorsement this early in the game."

"I don't think! I know! You gave me your word!"

"Well, now, no need to argue. Everybody hears what they want to hear, you know that, Thaddeus. First lesson of politics."

"I hear what I hear and I remember what I remember! Listen! Do you know . . . do you talk to Keegan Rourke?"

"Well, of course I do; his papers have always supported me. Even last year, old and feeble as I was"—his chuckle echoed through Bent's office—"Keegan helped me stay in action instead of rotting away in a home for has-beens. He's a friend; I'm indebted to him."

"Right. Indebted. A friend." The pencil in Bent's fingers snapped and he threw the pieces at the wastebasket; they missed and bounced on the floor. "And he's got a son."

"Indeed yes, fine young man, made a real name for himself on television. One of our finest young——"

"He's fifty if he's a day, Andy!"

"We're all at least fifty, Thaddeus. Tony is an excellent young man; I've known him since he was a toddler; he's outstanding at whatever he undertakes. Does his father proud."

"And he will in politics? Is that what you're getting at?"

"Wasn't 'getting at' anything, Thaddeus. But if young Tony

588

ever chooses politics, he'll be a credit to any state he represents."

"And you'll endorse him."

"Did I say that? I told you I'm not making any commitments; it's too early—"

"You gave me your word!"

"—and I don't like being pushed. I'm a statesman, Thaddeus; statesmen aren't accustomed to being pushed or accused of going back on their word. I'm a man of honor. And right now I'm being noncommittal on who takes my seat in this proud chamber."

"It's not enough! Dammit to hell, being noncommittal isn't enough! You promised me; now you're backing out. Just because Keegan Rourke pushed your wheelchair back to Washington and plugged in your hearing aid and pacemaker and whatever else holds you together, you think you owe his fucking *son*—" A loud click came from the speaker. "Andy? Andy, *goddammit!*"

Bent grabbed the speaker and flung it at the wall; its wires jerked it back and it fell to the floor and shattered. His face was beet-colored and his breathing was harsh as he kicked the plastic pieces in all directions. "Maybe the son of a bitch had a heart attack." Pacing, breathing in gasps, he looked at Elizabeth from under lowering brows. "I didn't—handle him—right."

"He was very provoking," she said sympathetically. "What will you do now?"

"Son of a bitch. Son—of—a—bitch. *The only thing I ever wanted was to be a senator.* You didn't know that—nobody does—but that's it, that's my whole life, and that fucking bastard has just—thrown it in the trash can. God, I'd like to kill him, but I can't. I'm a peaceful man. Son of a bitch! Took my life, everything I've done . . . you remember my son's wedding? And my daughter-in-law? Sweet girl, but what I liked best about that marriage was her background; she's related to all the right people in this town. Everything I've done . . . all these years. . . . *Jesus.*"

"And now?" Elizabeth asked.

589

"It's gone! That's what I'm telling you! There isn't a fucking thing I can do without Andy Greene; nobody's going to promise anything until that bastard gives somebody the nod, and we know who's going to get it, right? And it ain't me! Right? Right. So I'm out. Just like that. Years of service to my state and concern for my fellow citizens, and somebody else gets the prize."

He paced to the window. "Christ, what I did for them!" He spun around and met Elizabeth's eyes. "Knocked myself out for them and the whole time *they knew* they weren't going to keep their promises. Can you believe it? How can men be so dishonorable?"

Softly, Elizabeth said, "Did they make their promises before or after you helped them write the resettlement report on Nuevo?"

"Before. A long time before. We'd already hired people to write the ones on irrigation and flood con—" It was as if a knife blade had sliced the word neatly in two. The beet color faded from Bent's face. "Who told you about that report?"

"Chet."

"Chet? He didn't. He couldn't. He was always so afraid somebody'd find out; always talking about locked file cabinets and safes . . . The little fart! What did he tell you?"

Elizabeth evaded the question. "He even kept the draft version, with your name on it; we have it now. And he bugs offices; have you searched yours lately? His hobby seems to be collecting information he can use on everyone."

Bent's glance darted about the office as if he could see microphones everywhere. "That mother . . ." The words died away; his energy had run out. He looked at his hands, opening and closing them, and then at the brave gleam of his polished shoes. "You didn't come here to interview me for a story, did you?"

"Yes, we did," Elizabeth said. "But not the kind you think. I'm sorry; I don't like trickery. But we didn't know how else to do it."

"We." Bent looked at Saul as if for the first time, then back to Elizabeth. "You're going to tear me to pieces."

"Thaddeus," she said quietly, "a minute ago you talked about dishonorable behavior. What would you call yours?"

He gazed at her in silence. "It grew," he said finally.

"It always does," Saul observed dryly. It felt good to talk, after pretending to be invisible. "Tell us about it."

"Why should I? You'll send me to prison."

Saul met Elizabeth's quick glance and gave a long sigh. That was the last piece of information they needed. "You wouldn't worry about prison if money weren't involved. You could claim you didn't know the reports were faked, but you can't deny payments if records were kept. From what I know of Chet, I assume he has evidence galore tucked in his files." Bent was silent, his eyes darting in all directions. "You can force us to talk to Chet, or you can tell us what you know. If you do, it might earn a reduced sentence. And you'll be helping Elizabeth clear her name; that might ease the pain." He waited once more. "You'll also be keeping Tony Rourke out of the Senate. What better reason could you want?"

"None. You're right. You're damned right. They think they can do what they want because they're rich and powerful and people kowtow to them . . . Shit, they're not even from New Mexico. A pretty face and a rich father . . . if he thinks that's all he needs, he'll find out different. I'll see him in hell before he sits in the United States Senate. Whatever it takes." Bent strode to a corner closet and took out a bottle of bourbon. "Anybody?" Saul and Elizabeth shook their heads. He found a plastic cup, filled it, and drained it. "I'll tell you about it, but you can only print the parts about Rourke."

"Don't be an ass," said Saul. "You can't cook him or his son without burning yourself, and you know it. You took bribes from men who work for Rourke, you faked legislative reports to push through his project . . . how the hell could we leave you out? Why should we? This is the truth we're writing, not a campaign pamphlet."

Bent gazed at him expressionlessly. "You know, I like your newspaper. It's one of the best around. But I don't like you."

"It's not required," Saul replied casually.

"I like Elizabeth," Bent said. He turned his back on Saul. "I'll tell you, is that all right?"

He was like a child, Elizabeth thought. His dreams had crumbled around him, and he had become like a child. "That's fine, Thaddeus."

He nodded. "It seemed very simple, you know. Everybody knew Andy was going to retire, even though he hadn't announced it, and Chet came by one day, introduced himself as an associate of this rich used car dealer from San Diego, Terry Ballenger, who was building a resort at Nuevo, and said Ballenger and some other powerful men thought I should have Andy's seat. And he said Ballenger was concerned about Nuevo: wanted to make sure the proceedings went smoothly. We drove up there, Chet and I, and he talked about the lake and the park and the resort—a man'd be crazy not to want them for his state—and he said Terry wanted to give me one of the condos that'd be built on the lakefront. That's all there was to it."

"And then it grew," Elizabeth said.

Bent spread his hands. "Ballenger had already funded the impact reports. The ones on jobs and tourism showed the project was a good deal for the state; they were legitimate and everybody was happy. But then the preliminary ones on the environment came in and they were a disaster. Animal habitats gone; plant life destroyed; and the water experts said no way in hell did that area need flood control or irrigation. Chet took them back and in a few weeks the final reports came in and they said nothing serious or long-term would impact the environment, and the valley was a perfect watershed for flood control and irrigation. By that time Ballenger's PAC had made a couple of major contributions to my campaign fund and I thought it would be damned ungrateful if I started being suspicious about a couple of reports. Then, later, the people of the town started making noises, having meetings in the church, we heard, and then that woman, Aragon, was running for the legislature, so they quick wanted an official report on resettlement help—to convince newspaper editors the people were taken care of. And Chet asked me to write it."

"And you did," Elizabeth said when he stopped.

"I did after Andy Greene called and promised me the moon. And then some other donations came in from the PAC, and a pile of cash from Ballenger for what he called my discretionary fund."

Saul had been taking notes; he slipped the pad of paper into his inside jacket and re-entered the conversation. "You'll have to tell that story a few times. And give the names of everyone else on your committee or in the rest of the legislature who got political contributions. And name Colfax and Ballenger. You won't forget the details, I suppose."

Bent grimaced. "Shit, I'd forget the whole thing if I could, but then I think about the Senate . . . Goddammit, I told my whole family I'd be elected! My son already started calling me Senator Bent! *Goddammit!*" He glared at Saul. "I want Rourke identified. I want his plans and his picture all over the newspapers and television; I want everybody to know he's a lousy crook."

"Father or son?" Saul asked.

"Both of them! I'll be damned if I'll let either of them come out clean! And that pretty boy won't ever be called Senator!"

"It's a safe bet he won't be," said Saul, standing up. "I'd guess he'll spend the rest of his life working for his daddy. But that's not your problem, or ours. We'll bring Rourke into it; you'll bring in Colfax and Ballenger and your committee. And yourself. That'll clean out a lot of dingy corners and sweep Tony away with the rest of the dirt." He turned to Elizabeth. "Anything else?"

She was replacing her notebook and pen in her briefcase. She held out her hand. "Goodbye, Thaddeus."

He took her hand. "I guess I should have been interested in that story on you. Chet shouldn't have done that."

"None of you should have done what you did." Withdrawing her hand, she walked to the door where Saul waited. "Will you be in town this week? We may have questions, to check our facts."

"I'll be here. Where would I go?"

They left him standing alone in his office. "I'm going to the office and call Matt," Saul said to Elizabeth. "I promised I'd call in, like the good reporter I am. Why don't you come along? The three of us can have an editorial conference on the phone."

"No thank you, Saul. You'll make a very thorough report without me. But let me know what he's planning; he got on the story first and I won't write anything until I know what he's going to do."

Saul opened his car door for her. "I'll tell him you said that; we don't see much courtesy among journalists these days." He got in on his side and started the car, then, before pulling away from the curb, he leaned over and kissed her. "You were terrific in there, Elizabeth. You got everything you wanted. May it always be so."

Keegan Rourke had tried to get the governor to be more specific, but all he would say was that he wanted Rourke to meet him as soon as possible, in absolute secrecy. And so, because Mitchell Laidlaw, governor of New Mexico, was not a man Rourke could ignore, he found himself two days later sitting in the luxurious interior of a small jet parked at the side of the tarmac in the Las Cruces airport. Chet was on his left ("Bring that clever assistant of yours," the governor had said), and, on a couch across the aisle, Mitch Laidlaw and Andrew Greene, who had flown in together from Santa Fe.

The governor's jet was furnished like a Santa Fe living room; the carpet was woven in geometric Indian designs; the upholstery on the oak couch and armchairs was a tapestry-like fabric striped in blue and maroon, beige and black. Outside, the airport baked in the early April sun; inside, the plane's air conditioning worked overtime and the men had tall glasses of gin and tonic, and bowls of piñon nuts and sunflower seeds on the tables beside them. Laidlaw, Rourke noted, had a bulging soft-leather briefcase at his feet.

"Well, Mitch," Rourke said after they had made their own drinks. "You've aroused my curiosity. Shall we begin? I'm flying from here to visit my son in Los Angeles and I told him I'd be there this afternoon."

Laidlaw nodded gloomily. An enormous man with dark eyes, a square jaw, and leathery skin, he wore a cowboy shirt and faded blue jeans that somehow, because of his size and authority, made the other men, even Rourke, look stiff and uncomfortable in their dark business suits. "I appreciate your coming in, Keegan. I think you'll understand why I insisted on secrecy as soon as we—" He was looking through the window and suddenly stood. "This makes our group complete." He opened the door of the plane, letting in a blast of hot air.

Rourke heard a whimper. He saw Chet's eyes glaze with fear, and he followed his look to see Matt Lovell duck his head and step into the plane, shaking Laidlaw's hand, calling him Mitch, apologizing for being late. "The flight was delayed and there weren't others to choose from." He wore casual pants and an open-necked shirt with the sleeves rolled up to his elbows. Nodding briefly to Rourke and Chet, he shook hands with Senator Greene. "How are you, Andy?"

"Not too well, Matt, but I expect I'll survive to choose my successor. We're serving ourselves; help yourself."

The governor resumed his seat. "Now that Matt's here, I want to get started—"

"Not with me," Rourke said flatly, standing up. "I fired this man from my organization two weeks ago; I have no intention of sitting in a meeting with him. I'm surprised at you, Mitch, springing this on me without warning—"

"Keegan, get your ass back in that chair," Greene said wearily. "It's too late for you to call the shots."

Chet sat fixed and rigid. The others heard a slight sound and looked at him. He was grinding his teeth.

Rourke wavered. "What the hell does that mean?"

"Sit down and we'll tell you," said Laidlaw. "I won't begin, Keegan, until you're sitting down."

Rourke took his chair. "I don't like this, Mitch. You and I don't operate this way; we've always gotten along well. And I don't have to remind you of my help in your campaigns."

Laidlaw was opening his briefcase. "I have a campaign coming up; that's why I'm worried." He pulled out a page of handwritten notes. "This meeting is Matt's idea and I've asked him to run it, but I want it understood that he speaks for both of us. A few days ago he called to tell me about a newspaper

595

story he's writing. He wouldn't send me a copy but he told me the gist of it—that's why we're here—and I want him to tell you. Matt?"

Matt nodded. "The simplest way is to quote the opening two sentences of the story."

Chet's teeth were like fingernails scraping a blackboard. "Chet," Rourke said, and the teeth were silent as Matt read.

"State legislators were bribed to approve a dam and resort in Nuevo, New Mexico, it was admitted today by Thaddeus Bent, Chairman of the Committee on Land Use and Recreation. Bent named the developer, Terry Ballenger, and an associate, Chester Colfax, as the men who bribed him and other committee members, and also—"

"What the devil—!" Rourke turned on Chet, his face dark. "Bribes? To state legislators? *You and Terry?* What the hell is he talking about?"

"Lies!" Chet's head swung from side to side. "He's lying!"

"I don't want interruptions," Laidlaw said. "Go on, Matt."

Again, Matt nodded. He looked directly at Rourke and Chet, but Rourke's eyes were hooded and Chet was staring fixedly at his clenched hands. Quietly, his voice level, Matt described Bent's talk with Elizabeth and Saul. Some instinct told him to leave out Tony Rourke, but he went quickly through the rest of it. When he finished, there was no sound but the scraping of Chet's teeth.

Laidlaw turned gloomy eyes on Rourke. "That's a lot of shit to hit the fan all at once. I'd be covered in it if I was running for re-election today. I'll be covered in it next year and the year after if we don't do something about it."

"You mean you believe it," Rourke said contemptuously.

"I believe it, and we're going to deal with it. God damn it, I'm worried about my campaign! I'm worried about every fucking campaign our party's going to lose if we have to drag this muck with us. It stinks to high heaven—and you know it— and I intend to take care of it! *Today*, damn it! This morning! Matt, I'm sorry, I took over your meeting."

Matt smiled at him. They liked each other and it showed;

596

Rourke's eyes narrowed even more as he saw it. "It's your plane," Matt said. "I'll be glad to listen."

"Well, then." Laidlaw became brisk; he'd never been able to turn meetings over to other people, even someone like Matt, without itching to do his own questioning. "First things first. Keegan, do you own Ballenger and Associates?"

"Of course." Rourke crossed his ankles and meticulously straightened the crease in his pants. "I own a number of corporations. It would be foolish for me to buy land openly; it would only drive prices up. Now, listen to me, Mitch." He lowered his voice, it became almost soothing. "This man has put together a clever story; he's used all the skills that attracted me to him in the first place. He's personable and talented and he takes in a good many people. I admit he took me in for a while. But he's a pathological liar and he's personally involved in Nuevo because his wife has investments there; she's been using her column to protect them. He's also had a long affair with a close friend of mine, and when she kicked him out recently he chose to believe I'd encouraged her to do it, and it's clear he's trying to ruin me. As for Terry Ballenger, I don't know much about him; this is the first time we've worked together. He offered to form a corporation to buy land in Nuevo and develop it: Rourke Enterprises would own ninety-eight percent; he would own two. Chet did a search on him and found him acceptable and so I agreed. If he's in the habit of doing business with bribes, I didn't know about it—though now I wonder if Chet discovered it in his search and knew about it all along—"

"What?" Chet's eyes bulged. "What?"

"Or if he corrupted Chet; I can't be sure. Either way, I deeply regret it; Chet's been with me a long time. It will be a serious loss to have to let him go—"

"You son of a bitch!" Chet cried.

"Chet, you don't say a word," Rourke said, his voice like a knife. "Is that clear?"

Chet's glazed eyes slid to Matt, then back to Rourke, and abruptly his face changed. They've made plans for this, Matt thought. Chet's the front man; he'll be the one to spend some

597

time in jail; and Rourke will take care of him with a job and a healthy bonus when he gets out.

"Why would you fire Chet?" the governor was asking Rourke. "If Matt is lying, why would you believe he bribed anyone?"

A small twitch appeared at the corner of Rourke's mouth. Forcibly, he stopped it. "I don't like inquisitions, Mitch. I don't have to explain my actions."

"You'll explain every goddam thing I tell you to explain. You're in trouble, damn it! We all are! When Matt publishes that story, you and your friends, *and all of us*, will be tarred with bribing legislators! That's not a practical joke; it's criminal!"

"So is faking legislative reports," Matt added quietly.

"Keep out of this!" Rourke flung at him. "Mitch and I are talking; you keep out of it!"

"Keegan, shut up." Senator Greene sighed. "I've been nice and quiet and haven't put in my two cents, which is most unusual for me, but it's time I did. I heard Matt's story yesterday and it made me feel dirty. I'm only on the edges, but still I feel soiled. Matt left something out just now, when he told you about it; he left out your little boy, Keegan, and that gets me involved."

"Little boy?" Chet asked. "Tony? What about him?"

"My, my," Greene marveled. "You didn't tell Chet."

"Tell me what?" Chet looked at Rourke. "Tell me what?"

When Rourke was silent, Matt said, "Tony has been promised Andy Greene's Senate seat for his birthday."

"The hell he has!" Chet pounded the arm of his chair. "What the hell is going on here? Since when are you buying Tony a Senate seat?" he demanded of Rourke. "You told me I could promise it to—"

"I told you to be quiet!" Rourke's fury struck Chet like a gale. "If you can't control yourself, you'll leave."

"Leave! I was already pushed! Wasn't I? Did you say you were letting me go, or not?"

"I said it would be a loss *if* I did. If you can't control yourself, you'll leave the company and you'll leave this plane—"

"When I tell him to," Laidlaw snapped.

598

"Let me clarify it," said Greene. "Chet, Keegan supported me for reelection to keep the seat warm until young Tony was ready for it. I knew that and I didn't let it bother me much because I wanted another term and how else would a lazy old man like me get it? I promised I'd endorse him, and Keegan was planning to use the PAC he set up in Arizona, and of course newspaper support—plenty there to win an election, most likely. Now I found out the other day you and Ballenger promised the same to Thaddeus Bent."

"You knew that! We told him we had your—"

"I don't want arguments! Just listen. When Bent heard about Tony, he was . . . put out, you might say. You might say he is definitely not happy with Keegan. Come to think of it, who is?"

The governor took over. "Keegan, we want some answers. You own Ballenger's company; you and Ballenger and Chet arranged to get the Nuevo funding through the committee and then the legislature. Right?"

"They may have. I only instructed them to lobby for it."

"You funded impact reports and when you didn't like what some of them said, you paid to have them altered. Right?"

"Chet and Ballenger may have. I thought they were genuine."

"The three of you bribed committee members to keep the project quiet, to schedule only one day of hearings, and to approve it no matter who testified what, and you bribed key men to get the bill through the legislature when it came to the floor. Right?"

"They may have. I knew nothing about it."

"And you promised your son you'd spend whatever it takes to get him elected when Andy retires. Right?"

"Even if it is, it doesn't concern anyone here."

"It concerns Thaddeus Bent's cooperation. You insist on denying all the rest?"

"You heard me." Rourke stood. "I've listened to a string of accusations, with not a word of proof. If you're through, I'm leaving. Don't come to me again for campaign contributions, Mitch, or introductions to my friends—"

"What about me?" Chet cried. "What the hell's going to happen to me if you leave me here?"

"He's not leaving," Greene said.

"Of course not," said the governor. "What will you do about Bent's testimony in court, Keegan?"

"Nothing. Why should I? Even if anyone believed this man's cock-and-bull story, the only people Bent has named are Chet and Ballenger. What does that have to do with me?"

"Goddammit, they work for you!" Greene bellowed.

"And may have committed crimes I knew nothing about. You fools," Rourke spat. He stood beside the door, tall, straight, his dark suit impeccably cut, his gray hair perfectly in place. Only the line of his mouth betrayed his tension. "You have nothing to tie me to anything. You have the word of that deluded hick Thaddeus Bent, *and that's all*. Ballenger is the one you should have ordered here today, and Chet, of course." He grasped the handle of the door. "Talk to them; I'm too busy to waste time on you."

"Chet," Matt said casually, "will you tell Keegan about the microphones you have in his office, or shall I?"

Rourke froze. His back to the others, he stood motionless, head tilted, as if he were listening to the echo of Matt's words.

"You fucking bastard!" cried Chet. "I had a chance! He would have taken care of me! He always said he would if somebody had to take the rap—"

"YOU DISLOYAL SON OF A BITCH!" Rourke's sleekness was gone; in one instant he lost fifty years of cultivated poise and assurance. His features contorted with fury, he leaned over Chet, his face close to Chet's wide, anguished eyes, and his voice dropped almost to a whisper. "Sneaking around at night? Hiding microphones? A clever little shit, aren't you? Spying on the only man who ever cared for you—"

"You didn't! You never did! I thought you did, once, when you treated me better than Tony—shit, did I fall for that—I thought you liked me better than your son of a bitch son! And then you got Matt! And I was nothing! *Go get Matt and the senator a drink.* You hardly knew him, but you were giving him a party and I was the servant! I'm not a servant! If I was

600

good enough to spread your money around Durango to get your ski resort built—"

"*Shut up!*"

"What difference does it make? You've fired me. You're not going to take care of me. Why should I shut up? I never made any tapes until you got Matt, but then I started thinking maybe I ought to protect myself, and see, I was right, wasn't I. I taped all that shit about bribes and blackmail—everything you wanted me to take care of. And I took care of them! I got your fucking four-lane highway through that corner of Colorado where there was another one just twenty miles away, and I spread enough money around Santa Fe to build three lousy dams, not just one, and I promised Bent, that poor ass, he could be everything but president if he was a good boy—and what good did it do me? You still treated Matt like some fucking Greek god and me like a servant. And when Matt walked out—you didn't fire him; he walked out; it's all on tape; I heard it all—when he walked out, you didn't come to me—you were too busy taking care of Tony! Who takes care of me? Tell me that! Tell me who—"

He ducked away from the blazing eyes and dead-white face just above his, and jumped from his chair, crying, "I want protection! He'll have me killed; I want protection!"

"Why do you think that?" Laidlaw asked. He had been sitting very still, listening to Rourke and Chet; now there was a different kind of alertness in his eyes. "Has anyone else been killed?"

"Not recently. Maybe never. I don't know. I just want it!"

"You're not being honest, Chet!"

"It doesn't matter! Promise me you'll take care of me!"

"All right." Laidlaw sighed deeply. "I think we all know where we stand. Keegan, sit down. We're not through. When Matt gave me all this information, he also gave me some ideas for Nuevo. I approve of them; I expect you to, as well. He's going to explain them and you're going to listen and then you're going to agree to do what we say. Chet, sit down and be quiet; once you deliver the tapes to the state's attorney, we'll all do the best we can for you. Go ahead, Matt."

"We're going to move the town," Matt said. "Money has been coming in steadily; I'm told volunteers are already arriving; Governor Laidlaw will provide emergency funding to make up the difference, if necessary, for moving the church and a few houses, building new homes and stores, and housing the people until their homes are ready. The new town will be on one hundred acres of high ground on the shore of Lake Nuevo, on the new road that's being cut into the valley and to the ski area. Keegan will donate the land and pay for the layout of the new townsite, including streets and utilities."

There was a pause. No one spoke. Rourke looked steadily at the window between the governor and Senator Greene; very slightly, he shook his head. "The townspeople are forming the Nuevo Corporation to own the town," Matt went on, talking to Rourke's averted eyes. "The corporation will also buy back from you all the land you bought for a resort, at the same price they sold it for."

"It's worth more now," Chet murmured. "The dam, the roads . . ."

"It is," Matt agreed. "However, Keegan will be paid exactly what he paid for it and the Nuevo Corporation will build the resort. To get the money, they'll sell a percentage of the corporation to a developer. The governor's staff will help them find a suitable one."

"Simple and neat," Senator Greene said. "Absolutely beautiful. Stuck in my craw to have Keegan make a profit on land that appreciated because of bribes. Of course after this I can't endorse Tony in the election, Keegan; in fact, I think you'd be wise to give up that idea. It was ill-advised, you know; he's a pleasant young man—might even make a good senator; couldn't be worse than a lot of them—but there would always be doubts about him because of your influence. Not good, you know. Empire-building causes problems."

How quickly Andy Greene has become a moralist, Matt thought.

"That's the plan, Keegan," said the governor. "You don't have to tell us you don't like it; we know. If nothing else, it'll cost you a good deal—"

602

"Twenty-five million," Rourke said through thin lips. "But I have no intention of going along with this insanity. Why should I?"

"Because you're a gambler," Laidlaw said. "You gambled on a resort bringing you a profit; this time you'll gamble on earning a few points with the state's attorney."

"You're going to make a deal with him!" Chet cried. "What about me?"

"I don't make deals. Our candidates can't run on a platform of deals; I'm going to see justice is done. But there are mitigating circumstances in every case. Helping save a town and helping poor people become part owners of a major resort are noble gestures and I believe they'd influence an attorney general to seek minimum penalties for criminal acts; they might even convince a judge to decide on probation instead of prison. One never knows what might happen."

There was a long silence. The plane was getting warm as the air conditioning struggled against the blazing sun on the unshaded tarmac. Senator Greene refilled his glass. "Keegan," said the governor.

Rourke had been gazing out the window at the tail of his own plane, parked nearby. He still had almost everything: his oil company, the Durango ski area, resorts in Arizona, television stations and newspapers—he needed a new publisher, but they were a dime a dozen—and office buildings throughout the southwest. And of course no one would send him to prison; he was too powerful. Someone, somewhere, would make a deal; someone always did.

The worst of it was that Lovell and his wife and that woman Aragon would win this one—but he could take care of them: keep the Lovells from building their own newspaper chain, defeat Aragon in the next election. It was just a question of keeping his wits about him. "All right," he said flatly. "I assume you have something you want me to sign."

Laidlaw was already pulling documents from his briefcase. "You'll want to read these. Transfer of ownership of the hundred acres for the town; bills of sale for individual plots of land—"

Rourke skimmed them, pulled a pen from his pocket, and scrawled his signature on each. He put the top back on his pen. "Am I allowed to stand up, Mitch, and leave your very warm cabin? I'm flying back to Houston."

"I thought you were going to Los Angeles," said Greene.

"I've changed my mind, Andy." He was regaining his assurance. "You know what a useful skill that is; you practice it daily."

"You'd better come to Santa Fe with us," said the governor. "To get some formalities taken care of."

"Ah." Rourke shrugged. "I suppose I can change my mind once more. Am I allowed to fly in my own plane?"

"Certainly."

"Thank you."

Matt listened to the absurd civilities. He glanced at Chet, sitting stiffly, with a fixed stare, and Andy Greene, smiling as he drank his gin and tonic in the happy knowledge that the scandal would be diluted, the party barely touched: it had cleansed itself.

Elizabeth should have been here to watch Rourke cave in, Matt thought. She should have been the one smiling with pleasure because her story on Olson had started the whole chain of events. This was all done for her; she should have been here.

But then he realized that was wrong. It hadn't been done only for her. *I owed it to her and I did it for her, but I had to get my own house in order, too. It wasn't only a political party in New Mexico that needed cleansing.*

Rourke had left, refusing to take Chet in his plane. "Matt," Laidlaw said, "Andy's going back to Washington; Chet's my only passenger. Can I offer you a scenic flight to Santa Fe?"

Matt shook his head. "Thanks, but I'm not very popular there, at least in some parts of town. I'm going to get away for a while, Mitch. I moved out of my apartment yesterday— it belongs to Keegan, as a matter of fact—and arranged to have the furniture put in storage; now I just want to get the hell out of the southwest and the newspaper business . . . everything familiar."

"The north woods?" Laidlaw hazarded.

Matt opened the door. "Palo Alto for a couple of days to see my son and daughter, and to write this story. Then Paris and Rome. Good places to recover."

"You didn't say you'd been ill."

"I was, in a way. I'll tell you about it some other time. Thanks for everything you did this morning. You were superb. They'll name a street after you in Nuevo."

They shook hands and Matt went down the steps and strode across the tarmac to the small terminal. And when he was gone, Governor Laidlaw pulled shut the door of his plane and gave instructions to the pilot to take off for Santa Fe.

C H A P T E R 19

Holly and Peter were waiting in the restaurant when Matt arrived. He hugged each of them tightly, feeling a surge of relief when they hugged him back without hesitation. "Sorry I'm late," he said. "I had to finish the story and get it to Federal Express. You look wonderful, both of you; Holly, you're so lovely, but you're pale; Peter, who's cutting your hair these days?"

"Relax, Dad," said Peter. "We love you."

After a moment, Matt put an arm around each of them. "Thanks. Is anybody hungry?"

"Always," sighed Peter. "I thought I'd outgrow it, but now I think I probably won't. Ever." They followed the hostess to a table in an alcove overlooking the bay. "I apologize for the clouds. I specifically ordered sunshine and balmy breezes."

Matt smiled. "You're forgiven. I read your story on Navaho settlements; it was very fine. But I must confess I was baffled by the boxed story on the myth of how the world began."

"It wasn't supposed to be there; it was from one of my articles they're publishing next fall. The stupid editor got them mixed up. Can I sue them?"

"Probably not. It could be worse; they could have mixed you up with someone writing on chopstick techniques."

Holly laughed with them and Matt finally did begin to relax as they talked casually together; they were good to be with, he thought: bright, warm, charming. I'd like them even if they weren't my offspring, he reflected as the waiter brought their salads. But there's that added love and pride that goes with knowing they are. As they ate, he admired the table with its white damask cloth, blue Limoges china, and slender vase with one blue iris. "Good taste," he told Peter. "Have you been here before?"

"This is Mom's favorite place when she's here."

"Well, she has good taste, too," Matt said after a moment. Then he asked about Peter's classes, and they stayed with safe subjects all through lunch.

"After my two o'clock," Peter said as they finished coffee, "I'll take you to my new apartment. I need your approval."

"Of what?" Matt asked.

"You'll see when we get there."

When they left him at the science building, Matt turned to Holly, sitting beside him in the front seat of the car. "What needs my approval?"

"Peter will tell you," she said. "It's his news; not mine. Don't worry, though; it's not anything dreadful."

"Is there something dreadful in your life?" Matt asked bluntly. Holly flushed. "No."

"It looks to me as if there is, sweetheart. I won't pressure you to tell me anything, but I'd like to help, if I can."

Holly shook her head.

"Can you tell me why you're not singing anymore?"

"How did you know that? I told Mother not to tell you!"

"She didn't. Saul told me. Can you talk about it?"

"No." When Matt did not respond, Holly's voice rose. "I'm sorry! I really am, I'd tell you if I could, but don't ask me!" Tears were running down her cheeks like shining threads. "Please! There isn't any way . . . there's *no way* I can tell you!"

"Sweetheart, it's all right," Matt said quickly. He put his arm around her. "It's all right," he repeated softly. "I know you'd tell me if you could."

Holly rested her head on his shoulder. "It's just something that happened and I can't"—Matt held out his handkerchief and she took it—"Thank you. I can't tell anybody but Mother."

He pushed aside the jealousy that flared up. "I'm glad you can tell her. It would be terrible if you couldn't talk to either one of us."

"Oh, that's nice—that you understand." Holly pressed her cheek against his shoulder. "I don't know why I'm not singing. I wish I could; I miss it; it's like a big piece of me is gone. But when I try, *nothing happens*. I'm all numb inside, where the songs begin, and I don't know what to do about it."

"Whatever happened to you must still hurt," Matt said. "Deep down. And the songs are trapped there, waiting for you to find a way to free them."

Holly looked up at him. "Mother said the same thing."

"Did she? Well, your mother and I often think alike."

Still looking at him, Holly said, "Then why don't you come home?"

He frowned. "Didn't your mother tell you . . .?"

"What?"

"That she's divorcing me?"

"Oh. Yes, but . . . oh, I don't know. That was weeks ago. We haven't talked about it since that article came out, except she told me Saul said you didn't know anything about it. I don't know whether she's even talked to her lawyer since then."

"But, Holly, as far as I know, she wants a divorce."

"Do you want one?"

He held her in silence. "I don't know," he said at last. "I don't know what I want. Everything changed so suddenly, I haven't put all the pieces together yet. One day I thought I knew what I was doing and the next it all fell apart."

"I know what that's like," Holly said. "Do you miss it? Everything that fell apart?"

"I miss parts of it a lot. I miss a job, for one thing. Do you know, I've never had a day since college when I didn't wake up in the morning knowing I had an office, work to be done, people waiting for me to make decisions . . ." He laughed ruefully. "I feel like I've come unraveled."

Holly smiled. "That's the kind of word Mother would use."

"Yes, it is, isn't it? Well, that's how I feel. And I miss being at the center of power, too. I wasn't as powerful as I thought I was, but I did have influence, I was part of an organization that made news instead of only being affected by it. It felt good to have that; it's not easy to walk away from it without missing it."

"And thinking you made a mistake by leaving it?"

"No. I'm sure I didn't make a mistake. About the job, or anything else I broke away from. It's just that I miss parts of everything I had, and I don't know what comes next. I can't even go after it until I decide what I absolutely need, and how much of it is really possible and how much is only a beautiful mirage that will disappear if I get too close." Smoothing her hair, he kissed her forehead. "Lots to think about."

"What about Mother?"

"I have to think about her, too. But your mother and I have changed, Holly. I don't know if it's ever possible to recapture what we had."

"Wasn't that what you tried to do when you bought the *Chieftain?*" Matt nodded. "Well, if it worked then, why can't it now?"

He smiled. "Damned if I know. You make it sound so simple. But we'd have to find our way through all the debris of years apart, and misunderstandings, and separate—" He stopped.

"Private affairs," Holly said.

"Yes."

She shivered. "Let's talk about something else."

"We got off the subject of your singing."

"I don't want to talk about that either. Tell me where you're going in Europe. I wish I could go."

"You will. Next time, when you're not in school. I'm going to wander around Paris and Rome and not think about newspapers or Texas or America for at least a couple of weeks. Maybe more."

"Mother was in Paris and Rome."

"I know."

"Do I really look exactly like her?"

609

"You've seen her pictures; you know you do. In every way. The arch of your eyebrows, the way your mouth curves when you smile . . . even the look in your eyes when you learn something new: like gray pearls filled with light."

Hesitantly, Holly said, "Do you know what Peter would say?"

"What?"

"That you sound like a man in love."

Matt was silent. "Would he?" he asked finally. "Well, that's something else for me to think about."

Holly sat up. "Can we drive somewhere?"

"Sure. We have half an hour before we pick up Peter." He started the car. "Holly, the hurts that we suffer fade after a while and the songs inside us come back. I know that sounds simple to the point of stupidity, but it's true. Time changes the look of almost everything. I'm not saying you forget; I'm saying you tuck things away in the crazy quilt of yesterday and the day before and last year and that way you can handle them— think about them, decide what they meant to you and what they did to you—and fit them into the whole fabric that makes up Holly Lovell. If you're lucky, you learn from the things you do. If you're not, you repeat them. I hope you're lucky." He pulled away and drove down the broad street. "Now there's a building I've always admired; what do you think of those arches? More like a Spanish church than a university building, wouldn't you say?"

Holly leaned over and kissed his cheek. "Thank you," she said. "I love you."

Peter was waiting on the steps of his class building when they drove up, and he sat on the edge of the back seat on the drive to his apartment. "You see, Dad, we talked it over," Peter said as he unlocked the front door. "And we decided that mature men and women make a commitment to each other." Inside the door, Maya waited, wearing a dress as blue as a Santa Fe sky, her eyes pleading for approval.

Without hesitation, Matt put his arms around her. "My dear," he said. "So you're the reason Peter looks so well." Over his head his eyes met Peter's. "Commitment? Are you married?"

610

"No!" said Maya against his chest.

"One commitment at a time," Peter said. "We decided that, too. But you see"—he was looking at Maya now, with a tenderness Matt had never seen in his eyes—"I need her and she says she needs me. We won't *die* if we're not together, but do you know how *incredible* it is to wake up in the morning with somebody you love and know you've got a whole day ahead of you, to be together?" He looked at Matt. "Sure you do. You did once, anyway."

After a moment, Matt held Maya away from him. "What about your parents?"

"They don't like it," she said simply. "But they like Peter. And everything is so unsettled in Nuevo, they can't spend a lot of time worrying about me, and finally I think they were relieved to turn me over to Peter."

Peter reached out his hand and Maya moved quite naturally from Matt's side to his. As they began to tell Matt about the courses Maya would take in the fall, Holly watched from the side of the room, as if she were trying to memorize the radiance on their faces. And Matt gazed at them almost reluctantly; another reminder of a time when he and Elizabeth, only a few years older than Peter and Maya, had begun living together.

Would it last for the two of them? He had no idea. They had a chance. Maybe no one could say any more than that these days: begin with love, and if you have a dream to share, grab it, hold onto it, nurture it, but don't let it consume you.

He put his arms around Peter and Maya and kissed them. *And perhaps love will endure.*

Elizabeth was in Nuevo when Saul called. Shouting so she could hear him over the construction noises outside Isabel's house, he told her about Matt's story. "He called ten minutes ago to tell me he's writing it. He was in Las Cruces yesterday and the governor will be calling Isabel any minute. I couldn't wait; I wanted to be first. This is the crucial part—are you listening?"

"Yes."

Rapidly, Saul shouted the key words. "Rourke's giving a

hundred acres . . . Nuevo Corporation . . . build and own the resort . . . Did you get that? Elizabeth? Are you still there? Hey! Is there a live person on the other end of this phone?"

"I think so," Elizabeth said. "I can't believe— He's *agreed* to all that?"

"He's already donated the land. Laidlaw's probably calling Isabel this minute and getting a busy signal. They have to get started on forming the corporation. And moving the town. And finding a developer; Laidlaw's already sounded out a few."

"Saul, I want you to be the one to tell Isabel. Would you? Hold on." She put down the telephone; her hands were trembling. The most they'd thought they would get was land for a new town; they'd never dreamed of anything like this. And Matt had thought it up! "Isabel!" she called. "Saul wants to tell you something!"

Isabel came from the bedroom where she had been packing books. "My God, you look like a kid at Christmas! What happened?"

"Here. Listen." She handed Isabel the telephone and walked outside. After the quiet winter, the valley was again shaken by Olson's construction crew. Dust, gasoline fumes, and black smoke dulled the sunlight; the river was brown and sluggish, clogged with loose soil and rocks; jackhammers, engines revving up, trucks bouncing across the valley floor, all made a deafening cacophony.

And the valley was changing. Around the town, bulldozers had stripped the land of bushes and trees, to make movement of equipment easier and also because the lake bottom had to be clear so no debris would float to the top. The town was next: Jock Olson had told Isabel he couldn't stall much longer on his orders to bulldoze the church and houses and stores, whether the people had moved out or not.

But the biggest change was the wall of earth and stone rising beside the town, wide at the base and narrowing as it grew higher each day. Begun the previous year, the Nuevo dam was two months from completion. Standing beside Isabel's house, a few hundred yards away, Elizabeth felt the earth shake beneath her. Today, for the first time, it did not make her feel sick.

"It'll be different," said Isabel, appearing beside her. "But it's ours. Ours! My God!" She threw her arms around Elizabeth. "We won! Can you believe it? We won! *You* won! Good Lord, how can we be so lucky to have you for a friend? We'll build a statue of you, pen in hand—Elizabeth the Great!"

"Stop!" Elizabeth laughed. "You'll have me believing it. Everybody helped, Isabel. I didn't win; the town did."

"Wait, I'm not through. Saul got a message while we were talking. You're back in all your newspapers! He's going to—"

"What?" Elizabeth grabbed her arm. "How does he know?"

"Paul Markham called, looking for you, and Heather talked to him and told Saul. Markham said Matt called him from Palo Alto and told him about the meeting with the governor, and said he'd send him a copy of the story when it was done."

"Matt called Paul?"

"He also called the AP," Isabel said. "And told them the same things he told Markham: the gist of the meeting and he'd be sending a copy of his story. Nice to have a wire service ready and waiting to spread your words around the country. Though Matt's almost a wire service by himself: Saul, Markham, the AP . . ." She was watching Elizabeth. "Are you divorcing him?"

"I haven't done anything about it for a while." Elizabeth's eyes were on the clouds of dust rising above the dam. "I'll have to make up my mind pretty soon."

"Good idea," Isabel said casually. "Though I don't recall that it took you so long to make up your mind to fight for Nuevo."

Elizabeth turned to look at her. "What does that have to do with it?"

"Come on, my brilliant friend, you know what I mean. How come you fought harder for all of us than you did for your marriage?"

"Harder . . . ? I don't know. You've never mentioned this before."

613

"Never thought of it before. But just now, when I heard myself saying you'd won, it came to me. Usually I'm quicker."

"Usually you're smarter. There are differences, Isabel."

"Big ones?"

"I think so. Matt wanted me to make my life fit his. I didn't want the life he had; he wouldn't make any changes in it. Why would I fight for that? It was different when I fought for Nuevo; that was something I wanted to do, and I decided how to do it and when to do it. Do you think I could have written about Jock if I'd been living with the publisher of Rourke Enterprises? I was able to help you win because I'd made a name for myself—not as somebody's wife, but as me."

"True. All true."

"Well, then?"

"I was just wondering why you never worked like hell for a compromise, which is what you and I did, finally, for Nuevo."

Silently, Elizabeth brushed away some of the dust on her jeans.

"Well, think about it," Isabel said at last. "There's no rush; after all, he's only been gone for ten months."

"He has Nicole," Elizabeth said finally.

"You had Tony."

"But he was never more than—"

"A man to be close to, when you felt alone and rejected. Maybe Matt feels the same way about his lady friend. I know you weren't the one who did the rejecting, but you didn't go with him when he asked, either. And then you never fought to get back what the two of you once had. I don't know why. Do you?"

Elizabeth gazed across the valley at the dusty mountainside. "I think I was afraid to compete for him. I think I was afraid I'd lose because he was having such a wonderful time being a success. And I resented the whole idea. Why should I have to compete with other people, other women, for my own husband? I thought contests ended when we got married."

"In an ideal world," Isabel said dryly.

"But there were other things, too. I kept wondering what would make me feel good about myself if I had to concentrate

614

on his dream instead of mine. If all I had to be proud of was famous, powerful Matt Lovell—as if I were telling everyone, Look at me! I'm important because an important man loves me!—I'd suffocate. I want to be proud because I'm me, not because I'm Matt's companion."

She paused, then shrugged. "I don't know if those were good reasons for not going after him; they seemed good at the time."

"They still sound good. But you haven't said anything about love. Or building something together. Is that all gone? Because if it isn't, and you still divorce him, wouldn't that be like letting Nuevo drown without trying to build a new town in a safer place?"

Frowning, Elizabeth picked up her sweater. "It's something to think about. I have to get home, Isabel, but I really will think about it." Her frown deepened. "I don't understand . . . I don't know why I never thought of Matt that way."

"You're too involved. It takes an observer."

Elizabeth pulled the sweater over her head. "I have to think about it. And I've got to go; I want to talk to Paul, and if I really am writing three columns a week again, I've got to start planning interviews. And you have to talk to the governor!" She put her arms around Isabel. "I'm so happy for all of you."

Isabel's arms encircled her. "Aren't we all. Mainly for having good friends. You'll help us move our town, won't you?"

"You couldn't keep me away." They heard the telephone ring. "The governor. I hope. I'll call later." With a quick kiss on Isabel's cheek, she ran to her car. It was true that she had work to do, but mainly she wanted to get away so she could think.

You fought harder for us than for your marriage. But I had reasons, she thought as she pulled onto the main road and drove away from the dirt and noise. All those reasons I gave Isabel. And Matt didn't fight for it either.

But maybe both of us were too busy going after the brass ring to think of anything else.

But I stopped. I got off that merry-go-round.

She had stopped everything but her writing. The day after she found Tony in Holly's room, Elizabeth canceled her scheduled speeches and television appearances. And she refused all the new requests that came in. She hesitated once: when her agent called with an offer from a television network to host a one-hour talk show one night a week. But she didn't hesitate long. She wanted to be home. Holly needed her—they needed each other—and Peter and Maya would be back for the summer, living wherever they decided to live, and she had her writing and her friends . . . and the hope that "Private Affairs" would be syndicated again. And that was enough.

There should be a time for all of us when we can say, This is enough for me; I know where I am; I've got what I want.

The road curved between mountainsides covered with pines and aspens bursting with the pale green leaves of spring. Elizabeth saw three pick-up trucks driving to Nuevo. A dam, a resort, a state park, wilderness areas, a new town. Because we compromised.

She drove down the sleepy main street of Pecos and made the turn toward Santa Fe. The road widened; she increased her speed and settled back. *Maybe I left something out when I said, This is enough for me. Maybe all those reasons I gave for not fighting aren't important anymore. Maybe what's really important is what I do next.*

Maybe I should go to Houston. There really are a lot of things Matt and I haven't talked about.

"He's in Europe," Holly told her. They were sitting at the kitchen counter, shelling peas. "He said he wanted to get away from everything and everybody for a while."

"Everybody? Did he go alone?"

"I'm pretty sure he did. He didn't mention . . . anybody else."

"Where will he go when he comes back?"

"I don't know. He didn't seem to, either. He said he'd call."

"How long will he be gone?"

"I don't know."

"Do you know where he's staying in Europe?"

"No. He said he'd write."

Disappointment swept over her. She hadn't realized how

much she'd looked forward to seeing him. She slipped a neat row of peas from their pod. "Well, let me know if he calls," she said, trying to keep her voice light.

"Why?" Holly asked.

Elizabeth snapped open another pod. "I was thinking I might go to Houston."

"You were? Mother! Why didn't you tell us? Why didn't you tell Daddy?"

"I've only been thinking about it for the last few days." Elizabeth studied the sudden brightness in Holly's eyes. "Do you think he would have liked it if I'd gone?"

"Yes! Well—" Holly's face clouded. "I'm not sure. I think he might have liked it, but maybe he wouldn't know that he did. That doesn't make sense, but—"

"You mean he might not have let himself admit it?"

"Maybe."

"But I gather you and Peter would like it."

"Yes," Holly said simply. She split a pea pod and opened it like a book, gazing at the row of peas, perfectly spaced, each standing straight on its tiny stalk. "Pea pods are very orderly, aren't they?"

She rested her chin on her hand and looked at her Kachina dolls lined up on the sill of the recessed window. "Sometimes, at night, when I'm in bed and everything seems bigger than in the daytime, and I get scared about not being able to sing, and I hate Tony and want him at the same time"—she did not see Elizabeth wince—"or maybe not him exactly, but just someone to love and want, the way Peter and Maya love each other and want each other, I think if at least one part of my life was back to normal, if you and Daddy were the way you used to be and all of us were *together*, then everything else wouldn't seem so . . . big. Too big for me to manage all at once."

"I've thought about it, too, Holly."

"And?"

"And I got as far as thinking I'd go to Houston. Only no one is there for me to see."

"Well, how was Daddy supposed to *know?*" Holly gathered up the empty pea pods and wiped the counter with a sponge.

"Everything seems so . . . *gray.* I just wish *somebody* would make everything seem *bright* again."

Well, don't look at me, Elizabeth thought, briefly impatient. I know it was silly to expect Matt to be sitting around waiting for me to call, but I did try. And whatever he's feeling, he isn't looking for me; he behaves like a man with his own life and his own plans. He probably thinks he did all he needed to do for me by sending his story to Paul and the AP.

It was pure luck that they had Nuevo, she thought the next afternoon. So much was happening, it was like a story, with a new chapter unfolding each time they visited. Elizabeth began picking Holly up at school every afternoon to drive out and see what had happened since the day before. "The place is jumping," Isabel would say with a grin. "Take a look."

There was activity everywhere. Dust swirled around the dam that grew higher each day; the yellow hats of construction workers moved about like small moons; trucks piled high with crushed rock made a steady procession to the dam, returning empty, leaving a trail of rocks that rolled off as they jounced along the road. One of them had knocked a porch off a house at the edge of town, another had taken a garden fence with it.

But the excitement was higher up, on the land Keegan Rourke had donated for a new town. It had begun a few days after the meeting at Las Cruces, when the governor's office sent in trailers as temporary housing for the townspeople. Overnight, a small city sprang up. And in the next week, volunteers began to appear, bringing their own trailers or tents strapped to the roofs of their cars. And another small city came to life beside the governor's trailer city.

Some of the volunteers were college students taking a break; some were men and women out of work who wanted to help and hoped to find permanent jobs at the resort or in town; some were shopkeepers, some were housewives, some were retired people who couldn't do heavy work and so brought charcoal grills and cooked for everyone, taking up a collection after each meal to buy groceries for the next.

Tables and aluminum chairs were set up beside the tents and trailers; blue smoke rose from firepits dug in the ground; the smell of roasting meat and potatoes drifted through the valley. With Isabel and Cesar supervising, the volunteers formed groups to help the townspeople move from their houses, to help Gaspar empty his general store and set up a new one in a trailer, to work with Roybal in moving the contents of his gasoline station to a trailer and connecting his hose directly to a gasoline truck.

Jock Olson, on his lunch hour, gave instructions to the largest group of volunteers, who would be moving the church and the three adobe houses, leaving only the wood houses behind. "Clear out the inside," he said at the door of the church. "Pews, altar, pulpit, the works. Then we'll take the stained glass windows out, frame and all if we can; if not, we'll have to take the glass out in sections. After that, we'll brace the building, jack it off its foundation, put supports and wheels under it, and tow it up the slope to the new foundation we'll be pouring. You can clean out the inside without me. The rest we'll do after four o'clock every day and on weekends."

Each day at four, Jock would stop working on the dam and, without taking off his construction hat, stroll a few hundred yards to take charge of what he called "my other crew." At first his construction co-workers looked on in silent disapproval; then, as the new foundation neared completion, a few began drifting over to help. By the second week, only half the crew went home at four; the other half simply moved from one part of the valley to another, bringing the construction company's equipment with them. And with more workers, and heavy-duty equipment, everything speeded up.

The crew's shouted jokes and directions to the volunteers filled the valley, along with the cries of blue jays, the noise of drills and hammers, and the shrieks and giggles of children playing in empty houses. More quietly, their parents emptied the church and moved personal possessions, and the older people turned meat on grills, cut wedges of avocados and tomatoes, stirred rice in iron pots, sliced bread or heated tortillas, set out beer and lemonade, and made pots of strong coffee. By seven o'clock the volunteers, the construction crew, and the townspeople sat down to dinner, warmed by campfires that encircled them as darkness fell.

When they were there, Holly and Elizabeth forgot everything else. They wandered everywhere, watching the building of the dam, the pouring of the new foundation, and the jacking up and moving of the church and houses. "Isn't it odd?" Holly said to Elizabeth. "We all thought the dam would destroy the town, and now they'll be built together."

"Odd and wonderful." Elizabeth's eyes brightened. "It would make a wonderful story." And she began to outline the story she would write, this time about a very public affair.

A week later, Maya suddenly appeared. "My parents called and told me what was happening and I couldn't stay away. I had to help. Peter will be here next week; he's taking a few days off so he can help, too. What can I do?"

"Everything," Isabel said. It was a Saturday morning; Holly and Elizabeth had arrived early; Luz had joined them for coffee, and Maya found the four of them sitting at a table beneath a sweet-smelling pine. Isabel had unrolled a wide sheet of paper and was sketching a layout for the new town. "The governor's sending a couple of planners next week to decide where to put power and water lines and such, and most people have ideas about where they want to live, so we're trying to draw a map of the town. All we know so far is that the church stays where they're putting it—forever, I hope. You should have seen them hauling it up the hill; I had visions of the whole thing sliding backward and collapsing in a heap of adobe bricks, after all the work of getting it ready—"

"But it didn't happen," said Luz. "It's here."

"It looks wonderful," Maya said.

"It looks like a sad old hulk with holes in the walls, perched on a rolling platform. But give Jock a few days to get it on its foundation and we'll begin putting the windows back . . . Good morning," Isabel said as Olson came up beside her. "Just in time for coffee."

He put his hand briefly on her shoulder and sat down. As he filled a mug, Holly looked from Olson to Isabel and back to Olson. "I thought you worked on the dam until four."

He nodded. "So I do. But when we work a six-day week, I

take longer coffee breaks." He glanced at the sketch in front of Isabel. "Where are you putting my house?"

"At the end of the road, next to the forest," she said. "You told me that was what you wanted."

"Just making sure. What about Elizabeth's?"

"I haven't decided," Elizabeth said.

"We're keeping a whole area undeveloped," said Isabel. "Plenty of time for people to choose later on."

"Just make sure the souvenir shops aren't near the houses," Olson said.

They all leaned over the sketch and made suggestions and Isabel wrote them down, to give to the planners. Elizabeth watched Olson reach out to point to something on the sketch, not once but again and again, and each time his hand just brushed Isabel's. How wonderful, she thought, and saw Holly and Luz watching, too.

Olson finished his coffee. "Back to work. Isabel, I've been ordered once and for all to bulldoze the town."

"When?"

"Next week."

"When next week?"

"You tell me. How much more time do you need?"

"How about Friday or Saturday?"

He laughed. "You're pushing your luck. Friday morning. Best I can do." He gave a casual wave to the others at the table and walked down the slope to rejoin his crew.

Holly and Luz had been exchanging glances. "He's extremely nice," Luz said. "I told Mother it's fine with me if she wants to be friends with him."

"I was relieved to hear it," Isabel said dryly to Elizabeth. "But Luz is right; he's a very nice man. And I like working with him. I haven't worked with a man in a long time, and you know how good it can be."

Elizabeth smiled. "I do know. Isabel, it's wonderful; I never thought of you and Jock—"

"Wait! Don't put us together like that; I'm superstitious. Anyway, there are other problems. What if I decide to run for governor?"

621

"Mother!" cried Luz.

"I said *What if*. What else will I do with myself when you're in college and the town is rebuilt and all the battles are won?"

"Your ceramics; you haven't done any for a long time."

"And?"

"You're in the legislature."

"Two months a year. Not enough. I don't know what to do with all my energy. You wouldn't deny me a respectable goal, would you? Governor Isabel Aragon. I like the sound of it."

"I do, too," said Maya. "But why couldn't a man be part of that?"

"I don't know. It's been so long since I thought about a man when I looked ahead . . . I assumed I'd never find another one and I'd leave romance to Luz and Holly; they seem to enjoy it."

Luz laughed, but Holly flushed deeply and looked away. "I'm like you, Isabel. I don't think about men when I look ahead."

"Well, I imagine that will change," Isabel said casually. "Whoever he was, the unworthy snake who made you think that, he is condemned to a life of peevish dissatisfaction under someone else's thumb. You're well rid of him."

"What makes you say that?" Elizabeth asked.

"My vast knowledge of men. A man who could make Holly unhappy and bitter is a man with no backbone, no strength of character, and no imagination. Therefore, he'll never find what he thinks he wants, so he'll be peeved and dissatisfied, and he'll be under someone's thumb because he won't be able to get anywhere on his own."

Holly was watching her with wide eyes. "You're amazing."

"Experience," said Isabel. "Do you think maybe I should aim higher than governor?"

They laughed and then Isabel said, "Well, as Jock said, back to work. If they're going to be knocking down houses next week we have to make sure everyone's out by Thursday." She looked at Elizabeth. "We have to call a meeting so everybody can vote on what to do about the town on Thursday night."

"What to do?" Maya repeated. "But everyone will be gone. The town will be empty."

"That's the idea," said Isabel. She and Elizabeth shared a smile. "We're going to burn the place down," she said.

When the wind shifted, Matt felt a light spray from the fountain and for no apparent reason thought of quick summer showers in Nuevo. He sat on the wrought-iron bench and contemplated a marble horse in a pool of water in the center of the fountain, so real he could almost hear it whinny in protest as a cherub tried to rein it in. Elizabeth had been here, too, contemplating the marble animals, gargoyles, and cherubs as he was. Holly and Peter had told Matt about her letter describing the Piazza Navona and its fountain. "She said the cherub trying to hold onto the horse reminded her of you with Mr. Rourke," Peter had said.

Seated alone in the middle of the sun-washed square, Matt smiled. I know what she meant by that. And she was right.

He wandered through the city, past museums, churches, and palaces, dodging the life-threatening Roman traffic, turning at random into private cobblestone lanes that were barely more than passages between old brick buildings shining apricot and gold in the sun, dark brown in the shade. Again he thought of Rourke, this time at their first meeting, in Aspen, when he had expressed amazement that Matt and Elizabeth had never been in Europe. He'd dangled Europe before them, just as he'd dangled a wallet before Matt, with two hundred million dollars for buying newspapers. *But in all the time I was with him, I never got to Europe. I was always too busy.*

He came out of a shadowed street into sudden brightness, and realized he had made a full circle and was back at the fountain in the Piazza Navona. It was immediately familiar— just as every place had been, all day. This is the first time I've seen any of them, he thought, struck by it, but every one has been familiar.

He sat on the bench he had occupied that morning, absently gazing at a group of American tourists clustering nearby. "The

Fountain of the Four Rivers," their guide said. "Representing the four corners of the earth . . ."

Genghis Gold had sketched portraits of tourists here, Matt thought, remembering Elizabeth's description of him. And then it came to him: he knew why the scenes of the day had been familiar. Without being aware he was doing it, he had visited every place that Elizabeth described in her "Private Affairs" stories from Rome.

"Designed by Bernini," the guide said. "And completed in 1651."

One of the tourists wandered restlessly from the group and stopped beside Matt. "Do you know how many dates I've heard on this trip?" he asked as if they were old friends. "If I never hear another one it'll be too soon for me."

Matt smiled and nodded.

"And my feet hurt," the tourist added, and sat down. After a moment he asked, "Are you an American?"

"Yes," Matt said.

"Where's your tour group?"

"I'm here alone," Matt replied.

"Seeing Europe alone? How come?"

Matt contemplated him. "Because that's what I want."

"Sorry," the man said hastily. "None of my business."

Silently Matt agreed. But he knew that even if he had wanted to reply, there was no simple answer. I'm here because I lost my balance, he thought wryly. I couldn't keep the things of my life in order. I didn't know when to say I'd had enough. I had a chance to find out what I could be, and I found out; I had a chance to see how far I could go, and I saw it. But once I'd started, I couldn't stop.

There ought to be a time when we trust ourselves enough to say, That's enough, if that's the only way we can balance the important parts of our life and not lose some of them.

The shadows were lengthening across the square. On an upper floor of one of the buildings facing him, a woman's white hand reached out to pull a shutter closed. Matt kept his eyes on the shutter long after the graceful curve of the wrist had disappeared.

I want to share it with Elizabeth, he thought. No one else. That's why I went to all the places she wrote about; it was a way of sharing my first day in Rome with her. That was why I was always too busy when Nicole suggested coming to Europe. Thousands of sights and sounds around the world waiting to be discovered. And I want to discover them with Elizabeth.

He stood and absently said goodbye to the man beside him before walking across the plaza and finding his way to his hotel. He was going back to America. *It's about time I asked my wife, for the second time, to be my traveling companion.*

CHAPTER 20

Children raced through the empty houses of Nuevo, making them echo with laughter for the last time. The townspeople followed more slowly, in each room recalling who had been born there and who had died, who had been married, who had carved or woven or painted, who had dreamed. As they left each room, they poured a thin stream of gasoline around the base of the walls, and soon the odor hovered over the whole town.

Elizabeth and Isabel stood in the empty street, listening to the excited children's voices rise above the murmuring of the adults. "Three hundred years," said Isabel, shaking her head. "There's been a town here for three hundred years. And now it's dead."

"Only the shell," Elizabeth said. "The people are still together; even the ones who moved away are coming back now that they know they can get jobs. Aren't they the real town?"

"My head says yes. My heart says I'm burning my town and whatever I build, up there, will never be the same."

"You don't want it to be the same. You want it to be better."

"True. And I want to burn this one to show it's still ours: we'll wipe it out before the bulldozers do. I know all that. But . . . look at it."

Everyone else had left; they were alone in the dusty street. Beneath heavy clouds, the rock wall of the dam loomed above the silent wooden houses. The laughter of the children drifted down from the trailers and tents above; the air was so still Elizabeth heard even the sounds of dishes and silverware being set out. "Dinner," she said, her arm around Isabel's waist. "A good way to end one story and begin another. Who's going to start the fire?"

"Padre." Isabel put her arm around Elizabeth's shoulders and they turned away from the town. "We used to walk here with our babies. And everyone called us opposite sisters. *Hermanas contrarias*. Remember?"

"Of course. We still are."

"That's probably the best of all," Isabel said. Briefly she tightened her clasp around Elizabeth's shoulders.

Elizabeth nodded; suddenly she didn't feel like talking anymore.

At the top of the slope, Holly, Luz, and Maya were helping set tables; Saul was unpacking boxes of cookies and cakes they'd brought from Santa Fe, while Heather helped Spencer and Lydia take cases of soft drinks from their car. Peter, who had arrived that morning, was taking pictures of the empty town below and the crowded clearing where dinner was being prepared; children played hide and seek in the cluster of tents and trailers; Jock Olson unreeled a long fuse that stretched from the last house below to a chair where Cesar sat, brooding.

"All ready," Jock said, and Luz banged a spoon against a pot.

Cesar stood as the crowd fell silent. "When I light this fuse, I want everybody quiet, thinking about Nuevo, because it has been good to us. And because it is good to remember what was our home, even when we leave it, even when it is gone." He waited a moment, then knelt and held a match to the fuse.

There was absolute silence until, half a minute later, the end house burst into flames, with a soft whoosh, as if a wind had come up. The children cheered. The second house caught the flames and was engulfed, and then, down the main road and the side roads, so quickly it seemed to happen all at once, the houses burned. Flames leaped to the sky.

A great sigh went through the crowd. "By God," said Cesar. "By God, that is one hell of a fire."

Everyone began to talk and mill about. Soon the cooking fires were once again being tended, the food stirred, the tables set. "And we go on," Elizabeth said to Isabel. She felt like crying, but there was something incredibly powerful about the fire below, as if its heat and light could create a world as well as destroy it.

"'I would mould a world of fire and dew,'" Peter said, beside her. "A poem I read in school. Are you all right?"

She gave a small smile. "Yes, thank you. A little melancholy."

"I'm not surprised." He put his arm around her and when Maya joined them he held her with his other arm, and the three of them stood watching the fire, already feeling its heat.

"Look!" Maya cried, looking up. The leaping flames lit the low-hanging clouds. "It's like a sunset!"

"Or sunrise," Peter said, and smiled into her eyes, looking so much like Matt that Elizabeth's throat tightened and she swallowed, to hold back the tears. "Starting again," he added. "Fire and dew."

Everyone was looking at the sky: the firelight was like a river of gold and copper spreading across the low clouds, making them shimmer as if they, too, burned, and when Matt saw it from miles away as he drove toward Nuevo he thought it was a forest fire somewhere beyond the old iron mine. But then he knew it was much closer. My God, he thought, speeding up. It's the town.

Where the road once went straight, it now bore to the right, around the new dam, turning in a wide U as it climbed to higher ground. As Matt drove around the last curve, he saw, first, the roaring cauldron below, and, then, just ahead, a festive crowd—two hundred, he thought, maybe more—sitting at long tables beneath the trees. Small fires burned in pits, with cast iron pots suspended above them; the tables were covered with large bowls and platters of food; some distance away were trailers, tents, and parked cars. It was a town.

Matt pulled off the road and stopped the car. No one seemed to have heard him; everyone was talking and the fire was as loud as a windstorm. He left the car and walked toward the group. He saw Isabel first, standing beside a chair. "To the greatest lady I've ever known," he heard her say, her strong, warm voice filling the clearing. "Who fought hard for us and never gave up."

They were all there, seated around the table: Lydia and Spencer, Heather and Saul, Peter, Maya, Holly, Luz, Cesar. A stranger sat beside Isabel, never taking his eyes off her. And then Elizabeth stood up. Matt drew in his breath as a wave of love and longing swept over him.

Her beauty was like a beacon in the crowd. She wore a long white peasant skirt and an oversize sweater, bright yellow, its sleeves pushed to her elbows. Her hair was like honey; her face was flushed in the firelight. She was a golden flame. Matt had a brief memory of a stunning woman always in black and white, starkly dramatic, her skin cool even in passion, and wondered how he could have thought that was what he wanted.

"I think we should toast the people of Nuevo," Elizabeth was saying, her voice softer than Isabel's. "And all those who came to help: Jock Olson and the men who made such good use of the construction company's equipment"—the man at Isabel's side laughed, and with him a group of men at the next table, and all the rest, laughing together, then growing quiet—"and the people who have come from all over the country, helping in every way they can. We're like a family building a house, but instead of one house we're building many houses: a whole town. And I think you're all wonderful."

Matt heard applause and someone beginning another toast, but he didn't hear the words. He was walking toward Elizabeth. He couldn't remember deciding to do that, but he was halfway to her when he realized it. Peter saw him and nudged Holly. He said something to Elizabeth. And when she whirled about, Matt saw the light in her gray eyes and that was all he saw.

She moved into his arms and held him and opened her mouth

beneath his. Their bodies met, fitting together as easily as if they had never been apart. "I love you," Matt said, his lips against hers. "Elizabeth, I love you. I don't know what happened to me, how I could have—"

"Matt," she said. "Don't talk. Not yet. I haven't kissed you enough."

He laughed, and the laughter stayed inside him as they kissed again. He held her slender body in his arms, loving her, learning again the feel of her, the long line of her back, the silk of her hair, the curve of her breast.

"My love," Elizabeth murmured. "I need to take a breath."

They smiled at each other. "I want to know what's going on with this crowd," Matt said. "But I don't want to talk; I just want to look at you and hold you."

She put her hand against his face. "It can wait a few minutes."

Matt saw Peter and Holly watching them. *Wait*, he mouthed, and they smiled, first at him and then at each other. He and Elizabeth walked among the trees; hearing voices and laughter though the clearing was no longer visible. "I guess I want to say a few things after all," he said. "You should know . . . I may not be a good risk. I failed with Rourke and I haven't decided what I want to do next—"

"You'll go to bed with your wife."

He grinned. "As soon as possible."

"And then we'll talk about tomorrow."

"No, some things I want to say now. Do you mind? I did so much thinking in Europe; I want you to know how I got here. I sat in the Piazza Navona and thought of Genghis Gold, and you, and then realized I'd spent that whole day going to every street and piazza and café you described in your stories. So I knew I wanted to share Rome with you, and Europe, and all of America . . . and the rest of my life."

She was looking at him and he stopped walking to hold her again. "I've missed you. Even when I was blind to it, I was missing you."

"I wish I'd known that," she said somberly.

Matt waited for her to say something about Tony, but she said nothing more. He'd never know about Tony, for sure, he reflected; but he also knew that Elizabeth would never ask about Nicole. They were beginning again, on equal terms, and that was enough.

"I do have some ideas about what I might do next," he said as they walked on. "I want to talk them over with you."

She smiled. "I like that. But, Matt, I don't think they should include the *Chieftain*. Saul still wants to buy it, and so does Heather, and I thought, if you don't mind—"

"We'll give it to them," he said.

She looked quickly at him, her eyes bright. "You've been thinking about it."

"That was one of my thoughts in Rome. Saul made the paper his long ago; I couldn't imagine taking it away from him. The *Sun* either. Do you remember when he predicted he'd be publisher in a few years? I like the idea of making it come true." He fell silent as they walked. "Another thought I had in Rome was that we might get some backers and start a magazine."

She stopped. "I didn't know you ever thought about magazines. What kind?"

"Regional, probably: the southwest is what I know best. Mainly people: the kind of thing you do best. Could I interest you in being half a publisher and editor-in-chief? And frequent contributor?"

"Yes."

"Can it be so simple?" he murmured. "For years everything has seemed so complicated."

"It will only get complicated if we have to start by mortgaging the house again—"

"No, we won't have any trouble. Mitch Laidlaw was the one who suggested it to me; he'll bring in others. In fact, there might be enough to go national. If we did that, as soon as enough advertising came in, we could start regional spinoffs— smaller, more involved with their communities, using local writers . . ."

Elizabeth began to laugh and after a pause Matt laughed with her. "I'm sorry. I didn't mean to go running after another brass ring before we'd even settled down from the last one."

"No, don't be sorry," she said quickly. "You made it sound

wonderful. I'd like to go after it with you. If we can do it together—"

"I promise you, that's the only way we'll do it. And whatever peaks there are, we'll conquer them together." He took her in his arms again. "Back where we started: living in Santa Fe, in love, working together . . . Or did you want something more exciting? Do you want to live somewhere else? New York? Paris? London?"

She smiled. "I want you. Anywhere."

Their lips met. After a long moment, Matt said, "Shall I take you deeper into the forest? Better yet, can we go home? Would anyone mind if we leave?" His head came up. "Elizabeth, do I hear a bell, or is it in my head?"

"You really hear it. Let's join the others, Matt. They're going to dedicate the town."

"Is this the site? The land Rourke gave them?"

"Yes. Thanks to you—"

"To you first, for your story, and then to Mitch Laidlaw—"

"I wrote you a note, thanking you for *your* story, but it came back . . . Oh, Matt, we have so much catching up to do!"

"And only a lifetime to do it in. My God, there's the church."

They were back in the clearing, on the other side of the trailers and tents. Straight ahead, on a small rise, was the shell of the church, on its new foundation. The people stood in front of it in a half circle; Cesar was in the doorway, studying his shoes. He looked up, at the silent crowd. "I asked Isabel to make this speech but she said I should do it because I am the oldest here. So. This is the first day of May, a good time for a beginning. Nuevo is gone. But we have a new home where we stand, with the church at the center. And I name it now. *Renacimiento Nuevo*. Reborn Nuevo."

"Reborn," Elizabeth murmured. "I love you, Matt."

He put his arm around her and they were holding each other close when Peter and Maya joined them. Peter rested his forehead on his father's shoulder for just an instant; then he straightened and held out his hand. "Welcome home."

"We will make this town a home," said Cesar. "We will

welcome those who are homeless because we were nearly homeless ourselves. We will make it a fine place to live, we will protect it and keep the wonderful feeling we have this minute because so many people cared about us and helped keep our town alive . . . and now it is the caring that we must keep alive." He stopped, then put out his hands. "I don't know what else to say."

Matt moved forward and began to clap. Peter followed, others took it up, and suddenly everyone was clapping and smiling and crowding up to Cesar to tell him it was a wonderful dedication. Matt and Elizabeth held back, their arms around each other again, sharing one more small moment before becoming part of the crowd. And as they looked at each other, seeing in each other's eyes the wonder of rediscovering what they had almost lost, they heard the first notes of a song.

Softly, tentatively, the song began, and then grew stronger, the silver notes rising above the voices of the crowd. Everyone fell silent, listening, as the notes rose higher, pure and clear in the mountain air. *We've come home, a thousand miles. Down the road, the winding road . . . We've come home*. The joyous song soared into the night, filled with love, and everyone in the clearing reached out to take a neighbor's hand.

And Holly sang.